PAUL AUSTER – COLLECTED NOVELS
Volume 2

Also by Paul Auster

Novels:
THE NEW YORK TRILOGY
IN THE COUNTRY OF LAST THINGS
MOON PALACE
THE MUSIC OF CHANCE
LEVIATHAN
MR VERTIGO
TIMBUKTU
THE BOOK OF ILLUSIONS
ORACLE NIGHT
THE BROOKLYN FOLLIES

Non-Fiction:
THE INVENTION OF SOLITUDE
THE ART OF HUNGER
HAND TO MOUTH
COLLECTED PROSE

Screenplays:
SMOKE & BLUE IN THE FACE
LULU ON THE BRIDGE

Poetry:
SELECTED POEMS

Editor:
TRUE TALES OF AMERICAN LIFE

Translation:
CHRONICLE OF THE GUAYAKI INDIANS
by Pierre Clastres

PAUL AUSTER

Collected Novels

VOLUME 2

The Music of Chance
Leviathan
Mr Vertigo

faber and faber

First published in 2005
by Faber and Faber Limited
3 Queen Square London WC1N 3AU

Typeset by Faber and Faber Limited
Printed and bound in Great Britain by Mackays of Chatham, plc,
Chatham, Kent

All rights reserved

The Music of Chance © Paul Auster, 1990
Leviathan © Paul Auster, 1992
Mr Vertigo © Paul Auster, 1994
This collection © Paul Auster, 2005

The right of Paul Auster to be identified as author of this
work has been asserted in accordance with Section 77 of the
Copyright, Designs and Patents Act 1988

A CIP record for this book is
available from the British Library

ISBN 0–571–22904–2

2 4 6 8 10 9 7 5 3 1

Contents

THE MUSIC OF CHANCE
1

LEVIATHAN
171

MR VERTIGO
383

THE MUSIC OF CHANCE

1

For one whole year he did nothing but drive, traveling back and forth across America as he waited for the money to run out. He hadn't expected it to go on that long, but one thing kept leading to another, and by the time Nashe understood what was happening to him, he was past the point of wanting it to end. Three days into the thirteenth month, he met up with the kid who called himself Jackpot. It was one of those random, accidental encounters that seem to materialize out of thin air – a twig that breaks off in the wind and suddenly lands at your feet. Had it occurred at any other moment, it is doubtful that Nashe would have opened his mouth. But because he had already given up, because he figured there was nothing to lose anymore, he saw the stranger as a reprieve, as a last chance to do something for himself before it was too late. And just like that, he went ahead and did it. Without the slightest tremor of fear, Nashe closed his eyes and jumped.

It all came down to a question of sequence, the order of events. If it had not taken the lawyer six months to find him, he never would have been on the road the day he met Jack Pozzi, and therefore none of the things that followed from that meeting ever would have happened. Nashe found it unsettling to think of his life in those terms, but the fact was that his father had died a full month before Thérèse walked out on him, and if he had had some inkling of the money he was about to inherit, he probably could have talked her into staying. Even if she hadn't stayed, there would have been no need to take Juliette out to Minnesota to live with his sister, and that alone would have kept him from doing what he did. But he still had his job with the fire department back then, and how was he supposed to take care of a two-year-old child when his work kept him out of the house at all hours of the day and night? If there had been some money, he would have hired a woman to live with them and look after Juliette, but if there had been any money, they wouldn't have been renting the bottom half of a dismal two-family house in Somerville, and Thérèse might never have run off in the first place. It wasn't that his salary was so bad, but his mother's stroke four years ago had emptied him out, and he was still sending monthly payments down to the rest home in Florida where she had died. Given all that, his sister's place had seemed like the only solution. At least Juliette would have a chance to live with a real family, to be surrounded by other kids and to breathe some fresh air, and that was a lot better than anything he could offer her himself. Then, out of the blue, the lawyer found him and the money fell into his lap. It was a colossal sum – close to two hundred thousand dollars, an almost unimaginable sum to Nashe – but by then it was already too late. Too many things had been set in motion during the past five months, and not even the money could stop them anymore.

He had not seen his father in over thirty years. The last time had been when he was two, and since then there had been no contact between them – not one letter, not one phone call, nothing. According to the lawyer who handled the estate, Nashe's father had spent the last twenty-six years of his life in a small California desert town not far from Palm Springs. He had owned a hardware store, had played the stock market in his spare time, and had never remarried. He had kept his past to himself, the lawyer said, and it was only when Nashe Senior walked into his office one day to make out a will that he ever mentioned having any children. 'He was dying of cancer,' the voice on the telephone continued, 'and he didn't know who else to leave his money to. He figured he might as well split it between his two kids – half for you and half for Donna.'

'A peculiar way to make amends,' Nashe said.

'Well, he was a peculiar one, your old man, no question about it. I'll never forget what he said when I asked him about you and your sister. "They probably hate my guts," he said, "but it's too late to cry about that now. I only wish I could be around after I croak – just to see the look on their faces when they get the money."'

'I'm surprised he knew where to find us.'

'He didn't,' the lawyer said. 'And believe me, I've had one hell of a time tracking you down. It's taken me six months.'

'It would have been a lot better for me if you'd made this call on the day of the funeral.'

'Sometimes you get lucky, sometimes you don't. Six months ago, I still didn't know if you were alive or dead.'

It wasn't possible to feel grief, but Nashe assumed that he would be touched in some other way – by something akin to sadness, perhaps, by a surge of last-minute angers and regrets. The man had been his father, after all, and that alone should have counted for a few somber thoughts about the mysteries of life. But it turned out that Nashe felt little else but joy. The money was so extraordinary to him, so monumental in its consequences, that it overwhelmed all the rest. Without pausing to consider the matter very carefully, he paid off his thirty-two-thousand-dollar debt to the Pleasant Acres Nursing Home, went out and bought himself a new car (a red two-door Saab 900 – the first unused car he had ever owned), and cashed in on the vacation time that he had accumulated over the past four years. The night before he left Boston, he threw a lavish party in his own honor, carried on with his friends until three o'clock in the morning, and then, without bothering to go to bed, climbed into the new car and drove to Minnesota.

That was where the roof started to cave in on him. In spite of all the celebrating and reminiscing that went on during those days, Nashe gradually understood that the situation was beyond repair. He had been away from Juliette for too long, and now that he had come back for her, it was as if she had forgotten who he was. He had thought the telephone calls would be enough, that talking to her twice a week would somehow keep him alive for her. But what do two-year-olds know about long-distance conversations? For six months, he had been nothing but a voice to her, a vaporous collection of sounds, and little by little he had turned himself into a ghost. Even after he had been in the house for two or three days, Juliette remained shy and tentative with him, shrinking back from his attempts to hold her as though she no longer fully believed in his existence. She had become a part of her new family, and he was little more than an intruder, an alien being who had dropped down from another planet. He cursed himself for having left her there, for having arranged things so well. Juliette was now the adored little princess of the household. There were three older cousins for her to play with, there was the Labrador retriever, there was the cat, there was the swing in the backyard, there was everything she could possibly want. It galled him to think that he had been usurped by his brother-in-law, and as the days wore on he had to struggle not to show his resentment. An ex-football player turned high school coach and math teacher, Ray Schweikert had always struck Nashe as something of a knucklehead, but there was no question that the guy had a way with kids. He was Mr. Good, the big-hearted American dad, and with Donna there to hold things together, the family was as solid as a rock. Nashe had some money now, but how had anything really changed? He tried to imagine how Juliette's life could be improved by going back to Boston with him, but he could not muster a single argument in his own defense. He wanted to be selfish, to stand on his rights, but his nerve kept failing him, and at last he gave in to the obvious truth. To wrench Juliette away from all this would do her more harm than good.

When he told Donna what he was thinking, she tried to talk him out of it, using many of the same arguments she had thrown at him twelve years before when he told her he was planning to quit college: Don't be rash, give it a little more time, don't burn your bridges behind you. She was wearing that worried big-sister look he had seen on her all through his childhood, and even now, three or four lifetimes later, he knew that she was the one person in the world he could trust. They wound up talking late into the night, sitting in the kitchen long after Ray and the kids had gone to bed, but for all of Donna's passion and good sense, it turned out just as it had twelve years before: Nashe wore her down until she started to cry, and then he got his way.

His one concession to her was that he would set up a trust fund for Juliette. Donna sensed that he was about to do something crazy (she told him as much that night), and before he ran through the entire inheritance, she wanted him to set aside a part of it, to put it in a place where it couldn't be touched. The following morning, Nashe spent two hours with the manager of the Northfield Bank and made the necessary arrangements. He hung around for the rest of that day and part of the next, and then he packed his bags and loaded up the trunk of his car. It was a hot afternoon in late July, and the whole family came out onto the front lawn to see him off. One after the other, he hugged and kissed the children, and when Juliette's turn came at the end, he hid his eyes from her by picking her up and crushing his face into her neck. Be a good girl, he said. Don't forget that Daddy loves you.

He had told them he was planning to go back to Massachusetts, but as it happened, he soon found himself traveling in the opposite direction. That was because he missed the ramp to the freeway – a common enough mistake – but instead of driving the extra twenty miles that would have put him back on course, he impulsively went up the next ramp, knowing full well that he had just committed himself to the wrong road. It was a sudden, unpremeditated decision, but in the brief time that elapsed between the two ramps, Nashe understood that there was no difference, that both ramps were finally the same. He had said Boston, but that was only because he had to tell them something, and

Boston was the first word that entered his head. For the fact was that no one was expecting to see him there for another two weeks, and with so much time at his disposal, why bother to go back? It was a dizzying prospect – to imagine all that freedom, to understand how little it mattered what choice he made. He could go anywhere he wanted, he could do anything he felt like doing, and not a single person in the world would care. As long as he did not turn back, he could just as well have been invisible.

He drove for seven straight hours, paused momentarily to fill up the tank with gas, and then continued for another six hours until exhaustion finally got the better of him. He was in north-central Wyoming by then, and dawn was just beginning to lift over the horizon. He checked into a motel, slept solidly for eight or nine hours, and then walked over to the diner next door and put away a meal of steak and eggs from the twenty-four-hour breakfast menu. By late afternoon, he was back in the car, and once again he drove clear through the night, not stopping until he had gone halfway through New Mexico. After that second night, Nashe realized that he was no longer in control of himself, that he had fallen into the grip of some baffling, overpowering force. He was like a crazed animal, careening blindly from one nowhere to the next, but no matter how many resolutions he made to stop, he could not bring himself to do it. Every morning he would go to sleep telling himself that he had had enough, that there would be no more of it, and every afternoon he would wake up with the same desire, the same irresistible urge to crawl back into the car. He wanted that solitude again, that nightlong rush through the emptiness, that rumbling of the road along his skin. He kept it up for the whole two weeks, and each day he pushed himself a little farther, each day he tried to go a little longer than the day before. He covered the entire western part of the country, zigzagging back and forth from Oregon to Texas, charging down the enormous, vacant highways that cut through Arizona, Montana, and Utah, but it wasn't as though he looked at anything or cared where he was, and except for the odd sentence that he was compelled to speak when buying gas or ordering food, he did not utter a single word. When Nashe finally returned to Boston, he told himself that he was on the verge of a mental breakdown, but that was only because he couldn't think of anything else to account for what he had done. As he eventually discovered, the truth was far less dramatic. He was simply ashamed of himself for having enjoyed it so much.

Nashe assumed that it would stop there, that he had managed to work out the odd little bug that had been caught in his system, and now he would slip back into his old life. At first, everything seemed to go well. On the day of his return, they teased him at the fire house for not showing up with a tan ('What did you do, Nashe, spend your vacation in a cave?'), and by midmorning he was laughing at the usual wisecracks and dirty jokes. There was a big fire in Roxbury that night, and when the alarm came for a couple of backup engines, Nashe even went so far as to tell someone that he was glad to be home, that he had missed being away from all the action. But those feelings did not continue, and by the end of the week he found that he was growing restless, that he could not close his eyes at night without remembering the car. On his day off, he drove up to Maine and back, but that only seemed to make it worse, for it left him unsatisfied, itching for more time behind the wheel. He struggled to settle down again, but his mind kept wandering back to the road, to the exhilaration he had felt for those two weeks, and little by little he began to give himself up for lost. It wasn't that he wanted to quit his job, but with no more time coming to him, what else was he supposed to do? Nashe had been with the fire department for seven years, and it struck him as perverse that he should even consider such a possibility – to throw it away on the strength of an impulse, because of some nameless agitation. It was the only job that had ever meant anything to him, and he had always felt lucky to have stumbled into it. After quitting college, he had knocked around at a number of things for the next few years – bookstore salesman, furniture mover, bartender, taxi driver – and he had only taken the fire exam on a whim, because someone he had met in his cab one night was about to do it and he talked Nashe into giving it a try. That man was turned down, but Nashe wound up receiving the highest grade given that year, and all of a sudden he was being offered a job that he had last thought about when he was four years old. Donna laughed when he called and told her the news, but he went ahead and took the training anyway. There was no question that it was a curious choice, but the work absorbed him and continued to make him happy, and he had never second-guessed himself for sticking with it. Just a few months earlier, it would have been impossible for him to imagine leaving the department, but that was before his life had turned into a soap opera, before the earth had opened around him and swallowed him up. Maybe it was time for a change. He still had over sixty thousand dollars in the bank, and maybe he should use it to get out while he still could.

He told the captain that he was moving to Minnesota. It seemed like a plausible story, and Nashe did his best to make it sound convincing, going on at some length about how he had received an offer to go into business with one of his brother-in-law's friends (a partnership in a hardware store, of all things) and why he thought it would be a decent environment for his daughter to grow up in. The captain fell for it, but that did not prevent him from calling Nashe an asshole. 'It's that bimbo wife of yours,' he said. 'Ever since she moved her pussy out of town, your brain's been fucked up, Nashe. There's nothing more pathetic than that. To see a good man go under because of pussy problems. Get a grip on yourself, fella. Forget those dimwit plans and do your job.'

'Sorry, captain,' Nashe said, 'but I've already made up my mind.'

'Mind? What mind? As far as I can tell, you don't have one anymore.'

'You're just jealous, that's all. You'd give your right arm to trade places with me.'

'And move to Minnesota? Forget it, pal. I can think of ten thousand things I'd rather do than live under a snowdrift nine months a year.'

'Well, if you're ever passing through, be sure to stop by and say hello. I'll sell you a screwdriver or something.'

'Make it a hammer, Nashe. Maybe I could use it to pound some sense into you.'

Now that he had taken the first step, it wasn't difficult for him to push on to the end. For the next five days, he took care of business, calling up his landlord and telling him to look for a new tenant, donating furniture to the Salvation Army, cutting off his gas and electric service, disconnecting his phone. There was a recklessness and violence to these gestures that deeply satisfied him, but nothing could match the pleasure of simply throwing things away. On the first night, he spent several hours gathering up Thérèse's belongings and loading them into trash bags, finally getting rid of her in a systematic purge, a mass burial of each and every object that bore the slightest trace of her presence. He swooped through her closet and dumped out her coats and sweaters and dresses; he emptied her drawers of underwear, stockings, and jewelry; he removed all her pictures from the photo album; he threw out her makeup kits and fashion magazines; he disposed of her books, her records, her alarm clock, her bathing suits, her letters. That broke the ice, so to speak, and when he began to consider his own possessions the following afternoon, Nashe acted with the same brutal thoroughness, treating his past as if it were so much junk to be carted away. The entire contents of the kitchen went to a shelter for homeless people in South Boston. His books went to the high school girl upstairs; his baseball glove went to the little boy across the street; his record collection was sold off to a secondhand music store in Cambridge. There was a certain pain involved in these transactions, but Nashe almost began to welcome that pain, to feel ennobled by it, as if the farther he took himself away from the person he had been, the better off he would be in the future. He felt like a man who had finally found the courage to put a bullet through his head – but in this case the bullet was not death, it was life, it was the explosion that triggers the birth of new worlds.

He knew that the piano would have to go as well, but he let it wait until the end, not wanting to give it up until the last possible moment. It was a Baldwin upright that his mother had bought for him on his thirteenth birthday, and he had always been grateful to her for that, knowing what a struggle it had been for her to come up with the money. Nashe had no illusions about his playing, but he generally managed to put in a few hours at the instrument every week, sitting down to muddle through some of the old pieces he had learned as a boy. It always had a calming effect on him, as if the music helped him to see the world more clearly, to understand his place in the invisible order of things. Now that the house was empty and he was ready to go, he held back for an extra day to give a long farewell recital to the bare walls. One by one, he went through several dozen of his favorite pieces, beginning with *The Mysterious Barricades* by Couperin and ending with Fats Waller's *Jitterbug Waltz*, hammering away at the keyboard until his fingers grew numb and he had to give up. Then he called his piano tuner of the past six years (a blind man named Antonelli) and arranged to sell the Baldwin to him for four hundred and fifty dollars. By the time the movers came the next morning, Nashe had already spent the money on tapes for the cassette machine in his car. It was a fitting gesture, he felt – to turn one form of music into another – and the economy of the exchange pleased him. After that, there was nothing to hold him back anymore. He stayed around long enough to watch Antonelli's men wrestle the piano out of the house, and then, without bothering to say good-bye to anyone, he was gone. He just walked out, climbed into his car, and was gone.

Nashe did not have any definite plan. At most, the idea was to let himself drift for a while, to travel around from place to place and see what happened. He figured he would grow tired of it after a couple of months, and at that point he would sit down and worry about what to do next. But two months passed, and he still was not ready to give up. Little by little, he had fallen in love with his new life of freedom and irresponsibility, and once that happened, there were no longer any reasons to stop.

Speed was of the essence, the joy of sitting in the car and hurtling himself forward through space. That became a good beyond all others, a hunger to be fed at any price. Nothing around him lasted for more than a moment, and as one moment followed another, it was as though he alone continued to exist. He was a fixed point in a whirl of changes, a body poised in utter stillness as the world rushed through him and disappeared. The car became a sanctum of invulnerability, a refuge in which nothing could hurt him anymore. As long as he was driving, he carried no burdens, was unencumbered by even the slightest particle of his former life. That is not to say that memories did not rise up in him, but they no longer seemed to bring any of the old anguish. Perhaps the music had something to do with that, the endless tapes of Bach and Mozart and Verdi that he listened to while sitting behind the wheel, as if the sounds were somehow emanating from him and drenching the landscape, turning the visible world into a reflection of his own thoughts. After three or four months, he had only to enter the car to feel that he was coming loose from his body, that once he put his foot down on the gas and started driving, the music would carry him into a realm of weightlessness.

Empty roads were always preferable to crowded roads. They demanded fewer slackenings and decelerations, and because he did not have to pay attention to other cars, he could drive with the assurance that his thoughts would not be interrupted. He therefore tended to avoid large population centers, restricting himself to open, unsettled areas: northern New York and New England, the flat farm country of the heartland, the Western deserts. Bad weather was also to be shunned, for that interfered with driving as much as traffic did, and when winter came with its storms and inclemencies, he headed south, and with few exceptions stayed there until spring. Still, even under the best of conditions, Nashe knew that no road was entirely free of danger. There were constant perils to watch out for, and anything could happen at any moment. Swerves and potholes, sudden blowouts, drunken drivers, the briefest lapse of attention – any one of those things could kill you in an instant. Nashe saw a number of fatal accidents during his months on the road, and once or twice he came within a hair's breadth of crackups himself. He welcomed these close calls, however. They added an element of risk to what he was doing, and more than anything else, that was what he was looking for: to feel that he had taken his life into his own hands.

He would check into a motel somewhere, have dinner, and then go back to his room and read for two or three hours. Before turning in, he would sit down with his road atlas and plan out the next day's itinerary, choosing a destination and carefully charting his course. He knew that it was no more than a pretext, that the places had no meaning in themselves, but he followed this system until the end – if only as a way to punctuate his movements, to give himself a reason to stop before going on again. In September, he visited his father's grave in California, traveling to the town of Riggs one blistering afternoon just to see it with his own eyes. He wanted to flesh out his feelings with an image of some kind, even if that image was no more than a few words and numbers carved into a stone slab. The lawyer who had called about the money accepted his invitation to lunch, and afterward he showed Nashe the house where his father had lived and the hardware store he had run for those twenty-six years. Nashe bought some tools for his car there (a wrench, a flashlight, an air-pressure gauge), but he could never bring himself to use them, and for the rest of the year the package lay unopened in a remote corner of the trunk. On another occasion, he suddenly found himself weary of driving, and rather than push on for no purpose, he took a room at a small hotel in Miami Beach and spent nine straight days sitting by the pool and reading books. In November, he went on a gambling jag in Las Vegas, miraculously breaking even after four days of blackjack and roulette, and not long after that, he spent half a month inching through the deep South, stopping off in a number of Louisiana Delta towns, visiting a friend who had moved to Atlanta, and taking a boat ride through the Everglades. Some of these stops were unavoidable, but once Nashe found himself somewhere, he generally tried to take advantage of it and do some poking around. The Saab had to be cared for, after all, and with the odometer ticking off several hundred miles a day, there was much to be done: oil changes, lube jobs, wheel alignments, all the fine tunings and repairs that were necessary to keep him going. He sometimes felt frustrated at having to make these stops, but with the car placed in the hands of a mechanic for twenty-four or forty-eight hours, he had no choice but to sit tight until it was ready to roll again.

Early on, he had rented a mailbox in the Northfield post office, and at the beginning of every month Nashe passed through town to collect his credit-card bills and spend a few days with his daughter. That was the only part of his life that did not change, the one commitment he adhered to. He made a special visit for Juliette's birthday in mid-October (arriving with an armful of presents), and Christmas turned out to be a boisterous, three-day affair during which Nashe dressed up as Santa Claus and entertained everyone by playing the piano and singing songs. Less than a month after that, a second door unexpectedly opened to him. That was in Berkeley, California, and like most of the things that happened to him that year, it came about purely by chance. He had gone into a bookstore one afternoon to buy books for the next leg of his journey, and just like that he ran into a woman he had once known in Boston. Her name was Fiona Wells, and she found him standing in front of the Shakespeare shelf struggling to decide which one-volume edition he should take with him. They hadn't seen each other for a couple of years, but rather than greet him in any conventional way, she sidled up next to him, tapped her finger against one of the Shakespeares, and said, 'Get this one, Jim. It has the best notes and the most readable print.'

Fiona was a journalist who had once written a feature article about him for the *Globe*, 'A Week in the Life of a Boston Fireman.' It was the usual Sunday supplement claptrap, complete with photos and comments from his friends, but Nashe had been amused by her, had in fact liked her very much, and after she had been following him around for two or three days, he had sensed that she was beginning to feel attracted to him. Certain glances were given, certain accidental brushes of the fingers took place with increasing frequency – but Nashe had been a married man back then, and what might have happened between them did not. A few months after the article was published, Fiona took a job with the AP in San Francisco, and since then he had lost track of her.

She lived in a little house not far from the bookstore, and when she invited him there to talk about the old days in Boston, Nashe understood that she was still unattached. It was not quite four o'clock when they arrived, but they settled down immediately to hard drinks, breaking open a fresh bottle of Jack Daniel's to accompany their conversation in the living room. Within an hour, Nashe had moved next to Fiona on the couch, and not long after that he was putting his hand inside her skirt. There was a strange inevitability to it, he felt, as if their fluke encounter called for an extravagant response, a spirit of anarchy and celebration. They were not creating an event so much as trying to keep up with one, and by the time Nashe wrapped his arms around Fiona's naked body, his desire for her was so powerful that it was already verging on a feeling of loss – for he knew that he was bound to disappoint her in the end, that sooner or later a moment would come when he would want to be back in the car.

He spent four nights with her, and little by little he discovered that she was much braver and smarter than he had imagined. 'Don't think I didn't want this to happen,' she said to him on the last night. 'I know you don't love me, but that doesn't mean I'm the wrong girl for you. You're a head case, Nashe, and if you've got to go away, then fine, you've got to go away. But just remember that I'm here. If you ever get the itch to crawl into someone's pants again, think about my pants first.'

He could not help feeling sorry for her, but this feeling was also tinged with admiration – perhaps even something more than that: a suspicion that she might be someone he could love, after all. For a brief moment, he was tempted to ask her to marry him, suddenly imagining a life of wisecracks and tender sex with Fiona, of Juliette growing up with brothers and sisters, but he couldn't manage to get the words out of his mouth. 'I'll just be gone for a little while,' he said at last. 'It's time for my visit to Northfield. You're welcome to come along if you want to, Fiona.'

'Sure. And what am I supposed to do about my job? Three sick days in a row is pushing it a bit far, don't you think?'

'I've got to be there for Juliette, you know that. It's important.'

'Lots of things are important. Just don't disappear forever, that's all.'

'Don't worry, I'll be back. I'm a free man now, and I can do whatever I bloody want.'

'This is America, Nashe. The home of the goddamn free, remember? We can all do what we want.'

'I didn't know you were so patriotic.'

'You bet your bottom dollar, friend. My country right or wrong. That's why I'm going to wait for you to turn up again. Because I'm free to make a fool of myself.'

'I told you I'll be back. I just made a promise.'

'I know you did. But that doesn't mean you're going to keep it.'

There had been other women before that, a series of short flings and one-night stands, but no one he had made any promises to. The divorced woman in Florida, for example, and the schoolteacher Donna had tried to set him up with in Northfield, and the young waitress in Reno – they had all vanished. Fiona was the only one who meant anything to him, and from their first chance meeting in January to the end of July, he rarely went longer than three weeks without visiting her. Sometimes he would call her from the road, and when she wasn't in, he would leave funny messages on her answering machine – just to remind her that he was thinking about her. As the months went by, Fiona's plump, rather awkward body became more and more precious to him: the large, almost unwieldy breasts; the slightly crooked front teeth; the excessive blonde hair flowing crazily in a multitude of ringlets and curls. Pre-Raphaelite hair, she called it once, and even though Nashe had not understood the reference, the phrase seemed to capture something about her, to pinpoint some inner quality that turned her ungainliness into a form of beauty. She was so different from Thérèse – the dark and languid Thérèse, the young Thérèse with her flat belly and long, exquisite limbs – but Fiona's imperfections continued to excite him, since they made him feel their lovemaking as something more than just sex, something more than just the random coupling of two bodies. It became harder for him to end his visits, and the first hours back on the road were always filled with doubts. Where was he going, after all, and what was he trying to prove? It felt absurd that he should be traveling away from her – all for the purpose of spending the night in some lumpy motel bed at the edge of nowhere.

Still, he kept going, relentlessly moving around the continent, feeling more and more at peace with himself as time rolled on. If there was any drawback, it was simply that it would have to end, that he could not go on living this life forever. At first, the money had seemed inexhaustible to him, but after he had been traveling for five or six months, more than half of it had been spent. Slowly but surely, the adventure was turning into a paradox. The money was responsible for his freedom, but each time he used it to buy another portion of that freedom, he was denying himself an equal portion of it as well. The money kept him going, but it was also an engine of loss, inexorably leading him back to the place where he had begun. By the middle of spring, Nashe finally understood that the problem could no longer be ignored. His future was precarious, and unless he made some decision about when to stop, he would barely have a future at all.

He had spent most rashly in the beginning, indulging himself with visits to any number of first-class restaurants and hotels, drinking good wines and buying elaborate toys for Juliette and her cousins, but the truth was that Nashe did not have any pronounced craving for luxuries. He had always lived too close to the bone to think much about them, and once the novelty of the inheritance had worn off, he reverted to his old modest habits: eating simple food, sleeping in budget motels, spending next to nothing in the way of clothes. Occasionally he would splurge on music cassettes or books, but that was the extent of it. The real advantage of the money was not that it had bought him things: it was the fact that it had allowed him to stop thinking about money. Now that he was being forced to think about it again, he decided to make a bargain with himself. He would keep on going until there were twenty thousand dollars left, and then he would go back to Berkeley and ask Fiona to marry him. He wouldn't hesitate; this time he would really do it.

He managed to stretch it out until late July. Just when everything had fallen into place, however, his luck began to desert him. Fiona's ex-boyfriend, who had walked out of her life a few months before Nashe entered it, had apparently returned after a change of heart, and instead of jumping at Nashe's proposal, Fiona wept steadily for over an hour as she explained why he had to stop seeing her. I can't count on you, Jim, she kept saying. I just can't count on you.

At bottom, he knew that she was right, but that did not make it any easier to absorb the blow. After he left Berkeley, he was stunned by the bitterness and anger that took hold of him. Those fires burned for many days, and even when they began to diminish, he did not recover so much as lose ground, lapsing into a second, more prolonged period of suffering. Melancholy supplanted rage, and he could no longer feel much beyond a dull, indeterminate sadness, as if everything he saw were slowly being robbed of its color. Very briefly, he toyed with the idea of moving to Minnesota and looking for work there. He even considered going to Boston and asking for his old job back, but his heart wasn't in it, and he soon abandoned those thoughts. For the rest of July he continued to wander, spending as much time in the car as ever before, on some days even daring himself to push on past the point of exhaustion: going for sixteen or seventeen straight hours, acting as though he meant to punish himself into conquering new barriers of endurance. He was gradually coming to the realization that he was stuck, that if something did not happen soon, he was going to keep on driving until the money ran out. On his visit to Northfield in early August, he went to the bank and withdrew what remained of the inheritance, converting the entire balance into cash – a neat little stack of hundred-dollar bills that he stored in the glove compartment of his car. It made him feel more in control of the crisis, as if the dwindling pile of money were an exact replica of his inner state. For the next two weeks he slept in the car, forcing the most stringent economies on himself, but the savings were finally negligible, and he wound up feeling grubby and depressed. It was no good giving in like that, he decided, it was the wrong approach. Determined to improve his spirits, Nashe drove to Saratoga and checked into a room at the Adelphi Hotel. It was the racing season, and for an entire week he spent every afternoon at the track, gambling on horses in an effort to build up his bankroll again. He felt sure that luck would be with him, but aside from a few dazzling successes with long shots, he lost more often than he won, and by the time he managed to tear himself away from the place, another chunk of his fortune was gone. He had been on the road for a year and two days, and he had just over fourteen thousand dollars left.

Nashe was not quite desperate, but he sensed that he was getting there, that another month or two would be enough to push him into a full-blown panic. He decided to go to New York, but instead of traveling down the Thruway, he opted to take his time and wander along the back-country roads. Nerves were the real problem, he told himself, and he wanted to see if going slowly might not help him to relax. He set off after an early breakfast at the Spa City Diner, and by ten o'clock he was somewhere in the middle of Dutchess County. He had been lost for much of the time until then, but since it didn't seem to matter where he was, he hadn't bothered to consult a map. Not far from the village of Millbrook, he slowed down to twenty-eight or thirty. He was on a narrow two-lane road flanked by horse farms and meadows, and he had not seen another car for more than ten minutes. Coming to the top of a slight incline, with a clear view for several hundred yards ahead, he suddenly spotted a figure moving along the side of the road. It was a jarring sight in that bucolic setting: a thin, bedraggled man lurching forward in spasms, buckling and wobbling as if he were about to fall on his face. At first, Nashe took him for a drunk, but then he realized it was too early in the morning for anyone to be in that condition. Although he generally refused to stop for hitchhikers, he could not resist slowing down to have a better look. The noise of the shifting gears alerted the stranger to his presence, and when Nashe saw him turn around, he immediately understood that the man was in trouble. He was much younger than he had appeared from the back, no more than twenty-two or twenty-three, and there was little doubt that he had been beaten. His clothes were torn, his face was covered with welts and bruises, and from the way he stood there as the car approached, he scarcely seemed to know where he was. Nashe's instincts told him to keep on driving, but he could not bring himself to ignore the young man's distress. Before he was aware of what he was doing, he had already stopped the car, had rolled down the window on the passenger side, and was leaning over to ask the stranger if he needed help. That was how Jack Pozzi stepped into Nashe's life. For better or worse, that was how the whole business started, one fine morning at the end of the summer.

2

Pozzi accepted the ride without saying a word, just nodded his head when Nashe told him he was going to New York, and scrambled in. From the way his body collapsed when it touched the seat, it was obvious that he would have gone anywhere, that the only thing that mattered to him was getting away from where he was. He had been hurt, but he also looked scared, and he behaved as though he were expecting some new catastrophe, some further attack from the people who were after him. Pozzi closed his eyes and groaned as Nashe put his foot on the accelerator, but even after they were traveling at fifty or fifty-five, he still did not say a word, had barely seemed to notice that Nashe was there. Nashe assumed he was in shock and did not press him, but it was a strange silence for all that, a disconcerting way for things to begin. Nashe wanted to know who this person was, but without some hint to go on, it was impossible to draw any conclusions. The evidence was contradictory, full of elements that did not add up. The clothes, for example, made little sense: powder blue leisure suit, Hawaiian shirt open at the collar, white loafers and thin white socks. It was garish, synthetic stuff, and even when such outfits had been in fashion (ten years ago? twenty years ago?), no one had worn them but middle-aged men. The idea was to look young and sporty, but on a young kid the effect was fairly ludicrous – as if he were trying to impersonate an older man who dressed to look younger than he was. Given the cheapness of the clothes, it seemed right that the kid should also be wearing a ring, but as far as Nashe could tell, the sapphire looked genuine, which didn't seem right at all. Somewhere along the line the kid must have had the money to pay for it. Unless he hadn't paid for it – which meant that someone had given it to him, or else that he had stolen it. Pozzi was no more than five-six or five-seven, and Nashe doubted that he weighed more than a hundred and twenty pounds. He was a wiry little runt with delicate hands and a thin, pointy face, and he could have been anything from a traveling salesman to a small-time crook. With blood dribbling out of his nose and his left temple gashed and swollen, it was hard to tell what kind of impression he normally made on the world. Nashe felt a certain intelligence emanating from him, but he couldn't be sure. For the moment, nothing was sure but the man's silence. That and the fact that he had been beaten to within several inches of his life.

After they had gone three or four miles, Nashe pulled into a Texaco station and eased the car to a halt. 'I have to get some gas,' he said. 'If you'd like to clean up in the men's room, this would be a good time to do it. It might make you feel a little better.'

There was no response. Nashe assumed that the stranger hadn't heard him, but just as he was about to repeat his suggestion, the man gave a slight, almost imperceptible nod. 'Yeah,' Pozzi said. 'I probably don't look too good, do I?'

'No,' Nashe said, 'not too good. You look like you've just crawled out of a cement mixer.'

'That's pretty much what I feel like, too.'

'If you can't make it on your own, I'll be happy to lend you a hand.'

'Naw, that's all right, buddy, I can do it. Just watch. Ain't nothing I can't do when I put my mind to it.'

Pozzi opened the door and began to extricate himself from the seat, grunting as he tried to move, clearly flabbergasted by the sharpness of the pain. Nashe came around to steady him, but the kid waved him off, shuffling toward the men's room with slow, cautious steps, as if willing himself not to fall down. In the meantime, Nashe filled the gas tank and checked the oil, and when his passenger still had not returned, he went into the garage and bought a couple of cups of coffee from the vending machine. A good five minutes elapsed, and Nashe began to wonder if the kid hadn't blacked out in the bathroom. He finished his coffee, stepped outside onto the tarmac, and was about to go knock on the door when he caught sight of him. Pozzi was moving in the direction of the car, looking somewhat more presentable after his session at the sink. At least the blood had been washed from his face, and with his hair slicked back and the torn jacket discarded, Nashe realized that he would probably mend on his own, that there would be no need to take him to a doctor.

He handed the second cup of coffee to the kid and said, 'My name is Jim. Jim Nashe. Just in case you were wondering.'

Pozzi took a sip of the now tepid drink and winced with displeasure. Then he offered his right hand to Nashe. 'I'm Jack Pozzi,' he said. 'My friends call me Jackpot.'

'I guess you hit the jackpot, all right. But maybe not the one you were counting on.'

'You've got your best of times, and you've got your worst of times. Last night was one of the worst.'

'At least you're still breathing.'

'Yeah. Maybe I got lucky, after all. Now I get a chance to see how many more dumb things can happen to me.'

Pozzi smiled at the remark, and Nashe smiled back, encouraged to know that the kid had a sense of humor. 'If you want my advice,' Nashe said, 'I'd get rid of that shirt, too. I think its best days are behind it.'

Pozzi looked down at the dirty, blood-stained material and fingered it wistfully, almost with affection. 'I would if I had another one. But I figured this was better than showing off my beautiful body to the world. Common decency, you know what I mean? People are supposed to wear clothes.'

Without saying a word, Nashe walked to the back of the car, opened the trunk, and started looking through one of his bags. A moment later, he extracted a Boston Red Sox T-shirt and tossed it to Pozzi, who caught it with his free hand. 'You can wear this,' Nashe said. 'It's way too big for you, but at least it's clean.'

Pozzi put his coffee cup on the roof of the car and examined the shirt at arm's length. 'The Boston Red Sox,' he said. 'What are you, a champion of lost causes or something?'

'That's right. I can't get interested in things unless they're hopeless. Now shut up and put it on. I don't want you smearing blood all over my goddamn car.'

Pozzi unbuttoned the torn Hawaiian shirt and let it drop to his feet. His naked torso was white, skinny, and pathetic, as if his body hadn't been out in the sun for years. Then he pulled the T-shirt over his head and opened his hands, palms up, presenting himself for inspection. 'How's that?' he asked. 'Any better?'

'Much better,' Nashe said. 'You're beginning to resemble something human now.'

The shirt was so large on Pozzi that he almost drowned in it. The cloth dangled halfway down his legs, the short sleeves hung over his elbows, and for a moment or two it looked as if he had been turned into a scrawny twelve-year-old boy. For reasons that were not quite clear to him, Nashe felt moved by that.

They headed south on the Taconic State Parkway, figuring to make it down to the city in two or two and a half hours. As Nashe soon learned, Pozzi's initial silence had been an aberration. Now that the kid was out of danger, he began to show his true colors, and it wasn't long before he was talking his head off. Nashe didn't ask for the story, but Pozzi told it to him anyway, acting as though the words were a form of repayment. You rescue a man from a difficult situation, and you've earned the right to hear how he got himself into it.

'Not one dime,' he said. 'They didn't leave us with a single fucking dime.' Pozzi let that cryptic remark hang in the air for a moment, and when Nashe said nothing, he started again, scarcely pausing to catch his breath for the next ten or fifteen minutes. 'It's four o'clock in the morning,' he continued, 'and we've been sitting at the table for seven straight hours. There's six of us in the room, and the other five are your basic chumps, chipsters of the first water. You give your right arm to get into a game with monkeys like that – the rich boys from New York who play for a little weekend excitement. Lawyers, stockbrokers, corporate hot shots. Losing doesn't bother them as long as they get their thrills. Good game, they say to you after you've won, good game, and then they shake your hand and offer you a drink. Give me a steady dose of guys like that and I could retire before I'm thirty. They're the best. Solid Republicans, with their Wall Street jokes and goddamn dry martinis. The old boys with the five-dollar cigars. True-blue American assholes.

'So there I am playing with these pillars of the community, having myself a real good time. Nice and steady, raking in my share of pots, but not trying to show off or anything – just playing it nice and steady, keeping them all in the game. You don't kill the goose that lays the golden egg. They play every month, those dumbbells, and I'd like to get invited back. It was hard enough swinging the invitation for last night. I must have worked on it for half a year, and so I was on my best behavior, all polite and deferential, talking like some faggot who goes to the country club every afternoon to play the back nine. You've got to be an actor in this business, at least if you want to move in on the real action. You want to make them feel good you're emptying their coffers, and you can't do that unless you show them you're an okay kind of guy. Always say please and thank you, smile at their dumb-ass jokes, be modest and dignified, a real gentleman. Gee, tonight must be my lucky night, George. By golly, Ralph, the cards sure are coming my way. All that kind of crap.

'Anyway, I got there with a little more than five grand in my pocket, and by four o'clock I'm almost up to nine. The game's going to break up in about an hour, and I'm getting ready to roll. I've figured those mugs out, I'm so on top of it I can tell what cards they're holding just by looking at their eyes. I figure I'll go for one more big win, walk out with twelve or fourteen thousand, and call it a good night's work.

'I'm sitting on a solid hand, jacks full, and the pot's beginning to build. The room is quiet, we're all concentrating on the bets, and then, out of nowhere, the door flies open and in burst these four huge motherfuckers. "Don't move," they shout, "don't move or you're dead" – yelling at the top of their lungs, pointing goddamn shotguns in our faces. They're all dressed in black, and they've got these stockings pulled down over their heads so you can't tell what they look like. It was the ugliest thing I ever saw – four creatures from the black lagoon. I was so scared, I thought I'd shit in my pants. Down on the floor, one of them says, lie down flat on the floor and no one will get hurt.

'People tell you about stuff like that – hijacking poker games, it's an old hustle. But you never think it's going to happen to you. And the worst part of it was, we're sitting there playing with cash. All that dough is sitting right there on the table. It's a dumb thing to do, but those rich creeps like it that way, it makes them feel important. Like desperadoes in some half-assed western movie – the big showdown at the Last Gasp Saloon. You're supposed to play with chips, everybody knows that. The whole idea is to forget about the money, to concentrate on the goddamn game. But that's how those lawyers play, and there's nothing I can do about their rinky-dink house rules.

'There's forty, maybe fifty thousand dollars' worth of legal tender sunning itself on the table. I'm spread out on the floor and can't see a thing, but I can hear them stuffing money into bags, going around the table and sweeping it off – whoosh, whoosh, making quick work of it. I figure it's going to be over soon, and maybe they won't turn their guns on us. I'm not thinking about the money anymore, I just want to get out of there with my hide intact. Fuck the money, I say to myself, just don't shoot me. It's weird how fast things can happen. One minute, I'm about to raise the guy on my left, thinking what a smart, high-class dude I am, and the next minute I'm flat on the ground, hoping I don't get my brains blown out. I'm digging my face into the goddamn shag carpet and praying like a son of a bitch those robbers are going to split before I open my eyes again.

'Believe it or not, my prayers are answered. The robbers do just what they say they're going to do, and three or four minutes later they're gone. We hear their car drive away, and we all stand up and start breathing again. My knees are knocking together, I'm shaking like a palsy victim, but it's over, and everything is all right. At least that's what I think. As it turns out, the real fun hasn't even started yet.

'George Whitney got it going. He's the guy who owns the house, one of those hot-air balloons who walks around in green plaid pants and white cashmere sweaters. Once we've had a drink and settled down a little, big George says to Gil Swanson – that's the lugger who worked out the invitation for me – "It's just like I told you, Gil," he says, "you can't bring riffraff into a game like this." "What are you talking about, George?" Gil says, and George says, "Figure it out for yourself, Gil. We play every month for seven years and nothing ever goes wrong. Then you tell me about this punk kid who's supposed to be a good player and twist my arm to bring him up, and look what happens. I had eight thousand dollars sitting on that table, and I don't take kindly to a bunch of thugs walking off with it."

'Before Gil has a chance to say anything, I walk right up to George and open my big mouth. I probably shouldn't have done that, but I'm pissed off, and it's all I can do not to punch him in the face. "What the fuck does that mean?" I say to him. "It means that you set us up, you little slimeball," he says, and then he starts poking me in the chest with his finger, pushing me back into the corner of the room. He keeps poking at me with that fat finger of his, and all the while he's still talking. "I'm not going to let you and your hoodlum friends get away with a thing like that," he says. "You're going to pay for it, Pozzi. I'll see that you get what's coming to you." On and on, jabbing with that finger of his and yammering in my face, and finally I just swat his arm away and tell him to step back. He's a big one, this George, maybe six-two or six-three. Fifty years old, but he's in good shape, and I know there'll be trouble if I try to tangle with him. "Hands off, pig," I say to him, "just keep your hands off me and step back." But the bastard is going crazy and won't stop. He grabs me by the shirt, and at that point I lose my cool and send my fist straight into his gut. I try to run away, but I don't get three feet before another one of those lawyers grabs hold of me and pins my arms behind my back. I try to break away from him, but before I can get my arms free, big George is in front of me again and letting me have it in the stomach. It was awful, man, a real Punch-and-Judy show, a bloodbath in living color. Every time I broke away, another one of them would catch me. Gil was the only one who wasn't part of it, but there wasn't much he could do against the four others. They kept working me over.

For a moment there I thought they were going to kill me, but after a while they started to run out of gas. Those turds were strong, but they didn't have much stamina, and I finally squirmed loose and made it to the door. A couple of them went after me, but there was no way I was going to let them catch me again. I tore ass out of there and headed for the woods, running for all I was worth. If you hadn't picked me up, I'd probably still be running now.'

Pozzi sighed with disgust, as if to expel the whole miserable episode from his mind. 'At least there's no permanent damage,' he continued. 'The old bones will mend, but I can't say I'm too thrilled about losing the money. It couldn't have come at a worse time. I had big plans for that little bundle, and now I'm wiped out, now I have to start all over again. Shit. You play fair and square, you win, and you wind up losing anyway. There's no justice. Day after tomorrow, I was supposed to be in one of the biggest games of my life, and now it's not going to happen. Ain't a fucking chance in hell I can raise the kind of money I need by then. The only games I know about this weekend are nickel-and-dime stuff, a total washout. Even if I got lucky, I couldn't earn more than a couple of grand. And that's probably stretching it.'

It was this last statement that finally induced Nashe to open his mouth. A small idea had flickered through him, and by the time the words came to his lips, he was already struggling to keep his voice under control. The entire process couldn't have taken longer than a second or two, but that was enough to change everything, to send him hurtling over the edge of a cliff. 'How much money do you need for this game?' he asked.

'Nothing under ten thousand,' Pozzi said. 'And that's rock bottom. I couldn't walk in with a penny less than that.'

'Sounds like an expensive proposition.'

'It was the chance of a lifetime, pal. A goddamn invitation to Fort Knox.'

'If you'd won, maybe. But the fact is you could have lost. There's always that risk, isn't there?'

'Sure there's a risk. We're talking poker here, that's the name of the game. But there's no way I could have lost. I've already played with those clowns once. It would have been a piece of cake.'

'How much were you expecting to win?'

'A ton. A whole fucking ton.'

'Give me a rough estimate. A ballpark figure.'

'I don't know. Thirty or forty thousand, it's hard to guess. Maybe fifty.'

'That's a lot of money. A lot more than your friends were playing for last night.'

'That's what I'm trying to tell you. These guys are millionaires. And they don't know the first thing about cards. I mean, they're ignoramuses, those two. You sit down with them, and it's like playing with Laurel and Hardy.'

'Laurel and Hardy?'

'That's what I call them, Laurel and Hardy. One's fat and the other's thin, just like old Stan and Ollie. They're genuine pea-brains, my friend, a pair of born chumps.'

'You sound awfully sure of yourself. How do you know they're not a couple of hustlers?'

'Because I checked them out. Six or seven years ago, they shared a ticket in the Pennsylvania state lottery and won twenty-seven million dollars. It was one of the biggest payoffs of all time. Guys with that kind of dough aren't going to bother hustling a small-time operator like me.'

'You're not making this up?'

'Why should I make it up? The fat one's name is Flower, and the skinny guy is called Stone. The weird thing is that they both have the same first name – William. But Flower goes by Bill, and Stone calls himself Willie. It's not as confusing as it sounds. Once you're with them, you don't have any trouble telling them apart.'

'Like Mutt and Jeff.'

'Yeah, that's right. They're a regular comedy team. Like those funny little buggers on TV, Ernie and Bert. Only these guys are called Willie and Bill. It has a nice ring to it, doesn't it? Willie and Bill.'

'How did you happen to meet them?'

'I ran into them in Atlantic City last month. There's a game I sometimes go to down there, and they sat in on it for a while. After twenty minutes, they were both down five thousand dollars. I never saw such stupid betting in my life. They thought they could bluff their way through anything – like they were the only ones who knew how to play, and the rest of us were just dying to fall for their Humpty-Dumpty tricks. A couple of hours later, I went over to one of the casinos to horse around, and there they were again, standing at the roulette wheel. The fat one came up to me –'

'Flower.'

'– right, Flower. He came up to me and said, I like your style, son, you play a mean hand of poker. And then he went on to say that if I ever felt like getting into a friendly little game with them, I was more than welcome to drop by their house. So that's how it happened. I told him sure, I'd love to play with them some time, and last week I called up and arranged the game for this coming Monday. That's why I'm so burned about what happened last night. It would have been a beautiful experience, an honest-to-goodness walk down Jackpot Lane.'

'You just said "their house." Does that mean they live together?'

'You're pretty sharp, aren't you? Yeah, that's what I said – "their house." It sounds a little strange, but I don't think they're a pair of fruits or anything. They're both in their fifties, and they both used to be married. Stone's wife died, and Flower and his wife are divorced. They've each got a couple of kids, and Stone's even a grandfather. He used to be an optometrist before he won the lottery, and Flower used to be an accountant. Real ordinary middle-class guys. They just happen to live in a twenty-room mansion and get one point three-five million tax-free dollars every year.'

'I guess you've been doing your homework.'

'I told you, I checked them out. I don't like to get into games when I don't know who I'm playing with.'

'Do you do anything besides play poker?'

'No, that's it. I just play poker.'

'No job? Nothing to back you up if you hit a dry spell?'

'I worked in a department store once. That was the summer after I got out of high school, and they put me in the men's shoe department. It was the pits, let me tell you, the absolute worst. Getting down on your hands and knees like some kind of dog, having to breathe in all those dirty sock smells. It used to make me want to barf. I quit after three weeks, and I haven't had a regular job since.'

'So you do all right for yourself.'

'Yeah, I do all right. I have my ups and downs, but there's never been anything I couldn't handle. The main thing is I do what I want. If I lose, it's my ass that loses. If I win, the money's mine to keep. I don't have to take shit from anyone.'

'You're your own boss.'

'Right. I'm my own boss. I call my own shots.'

'You must be a pretty good player, then.'

'I'm good, but I've still got a ways to go. I'm talking about the great ones – your Johnny Moseses, your Amarillo Slims, your Doyle Brunsons. I want to get into the same league as those guys. You ever hear about Binion's Horseshoe Club in Vegas? That's where they play the World Series of Poker. In a couple of years, I think I'll be ready for them. That's what I want to do. Build up enough cash to buy into that game and go head to head with the best.'

'That's all very nice, kid. It's good to have dreams, they help to keep a person going. But that's for later, what you might call long-range planning. What I want to know is what you're going to do today. We'll be getting to New York in about an hour, and then what's going to happen to you?'

'There's this guy I know in Brooklyn. I'll give him a buzz when we hit town and see if he's in. If he is, he'll probably put me up for a while. He's a crazy son of a bitch, but we get along okay. Crappy Manzola. It's a hell of a name, isn't it? He got it when he was a kid because he had such crappy, rotten teeth. He's got a beautiful set of false teeth now, but everyone still calls him Crappy.'

'And what happens if Crappy isn't there?'

'The fuck if I know. I'll think of something.'

'In other words, you don't have a clue. You're just going to wing it.'

'Don't worry about me, I can take care of myself. I've been in worse places than this before.'

'I'm not worried. It's just that something has occurred to me, and I have a feeling it might interest you.'

'Such as?'

'You told me you needed ten thousand dollars to play cards with Flower and Stone. What if I knew someone who would be willing to put up the money for you? What kind of arrangement would you be willing to make with him in return?'

'I'd pay him back as soon as the game was over. With interest.'

'This person isn't a moneylender. He'd probably be thinking more along the lines of a business partnership.'

'And what are you, some kind of a venture capitalist or something?'

'Forget about me. I'm just a guy who drives a car. What I want to know is what kind of offer you'd be willing to make. I'm talking about percentages.'

'Shit, I don't know. I'd pay him back the ten grand, and then I'd give him a fair share of the profits. Twenty percent, twenty-five percent, something like that.'

'That sounds a bit stingy to me. After all, this person is the one who's taking the risk. If you don't win, he's the one who loses, not you. See what I mean?'

'Yeah, I see what you mean.'

'I'm talking about an even split. Fifty percent for you, fifty percent for him. Minus the ten thousand, of course. How does that strike you? Do you think it's fair?'

'I suppose I could live with it. If that's the only way I get to play with those jokers, it's probably worth it. But where do you fit into this? As far as I can tell, it's just the two of us talking in this car. Where's this other guy supposed to be? The one with the ten thousand dollars.'

'He's around. It won't be hard to find him.'

'Yeah, that's what I figured. And if this guy just happens to be sitting next to me right now, what I'd like to know is why he wants to get involved in a thing like this. I mean, he doesn't know me from a hole in the wall.'

'No reason. He just feels like it.'

'That's not good enough. There's got to be a reason. I won't go for it unless I know.'

'Because he needs the money. That should be pretty obvious.'

'But he's already got ten thousand dollars.'

'He needs more than that. And he's running out of time. This is probably the last chance he's going to get.'

'Yeah, okay, I can buy that. It's what you would call a desperate situation.'

'But he's not stupid either, Jack. He doesn't throw his money away on grifters. So before I talk business with you, I've got to make sure you're the real thing. You might be a hell of a card player, but you also might be a bullshit artist. Before there's any deal, I've got to see what you can do with my own eyes.'

'No problem, partner. Once we get to New York, I'll show you my stuff. No problem at all. You'll be so impressed, your mouth will drop open. I guarantee it. I'll make the eyes fall out of your fucking head.'

3

Nashe understood that he was no longer behaving like himself. He could hear the words coming out of his mouth, but even as he spoke them, he felt they were expressing someone else's thoughts, as if he were no more than an actor performing on the stage of some imaginary theater, repeating lines that had been written for him in advance. He had never felt this way before, and the wonder of it was how little it disturbed him, how easily he slipped into playing his part. The money was the only thing that mattered, and if this foul-mouthed kid could get it for him, then Nashe was willing to risk everything to see that it happened. It was a crazy scheme, perhaps, but the risk was a motivation in itself, a leap of blind faith that would prove he was finally ready for anything that might happen to him.

At that point, Pozzi was simply a means to an end, the hole in the wall that would get him from one side to the other. He was an opportunity in the shape of a human being, a card-playing specter whose one purpose in the world was to help Nashe win back his freedom. Once that job was finished, they would go their separate ways. Nashe was going to use him, but that did not mean he found Pozzi entirely objectionable. In spite of his wise-ass posturing, there was something fascinating about this kid, and it was hard not to grant him a sort of grudging respect. At least he had the courage of his convictions, and that was more than could be said of most people. Pozzi had taken the plunge into himself; he was improvising his life as he went along, trusting in pure wit to keep his head above water, and even after the thrashing he had just been given, he did not seem demoralized or defeated. The kid was rough around the edges, at times even obnoxious, but he exuded a confidence that Nashe found reassuring. It was still too early to know if Pozzi could be believed, of course, but considering how little time there had been for him to invent a story, considering the farfetched plausibility of the whole situation, it seemed doubtful that he was anything other than what he claimed to be. Or so Nashe assumed. One way or the other, it wouldn't take long for him to find out.

The important thing was to appear calm, to rein in his excitement and convince Pozzi that he knew what he was doing. It wasn't exactly that he wanted to impress him, but he instinctively felt that he had to keep the upper hand, to match the kid's bravura with a quiet, unflinching confidence of his own. He would play the old man to Pozzi's upstart, using the advantage he had in size and age to give off an aura of hard-earned wisdom, a steadiness that would counterbalance the kid's nervous, impulsive manner. By the time they came to the northern reaches of the Bronx, Nashe had already settled on a plan of action. It would mean paying out a little more than he would have liked, perhaps, but in the long run he figured it would be money well spent.

The trick was not to say anything until Pozzi started asking questions, and then, when he did ask them, to be ready with good answers. That was the surest way to control the situation: to keep the kid slightly off balance, to create the illusion that he was always one step ahead of him. Without saying a word, Nashe steered the car onto the Henry Hudson Parkway, and when Pozzi finally asked him where they were going (as they drove past Ninety-sixth Street), Nashe said: 'You're all worn out, Jack. You need some food and sleep, and I could go for a little lunch myself. We'll check into the Plaza and take it from there.'

'You mean the Plaza Hotel?' Pozzi said.

'That's right, the Plaza Hotel. I always stay there when I'm in New York. Any objections?'

'No objections. I was just wondering, that's all. Sounds like a good idea to me.'

'I thought you'd like it.'

'Yeah, I like it. I like to do things in style. It's good for the soul.'

They parked the car in an underground lot on East Fifty-eighth Street, removed Nashe's bags from the trunk, and then walked around the corner to the hotel. Nashe asked for two single rooms with a connecting bath, and as he signed the register at the desk, he watched Pozzi out of the corner of his eye, noting the small, satisfied smirk on the kid's face. That look pleased him, for it seemed to indicate that Pozzi was sufficiently awed by his good fortune to appreciate what Nashe was doing for him. It all boiled down to a question of staging. Just two hours before, Pozzi's life had been in ruins, and now he was standing inside a palace, trying not to gawk at the opulence that surrounded him. Had the contrast been less striking, it would not have produced the desired effect, but as it was, Nashe had only to look at the kid's twitching mouth to know that he had made his point.

They were given rooms on the seventh floor ('Lucky seven,' as Pozzi remarked in the elevator), and once the bellboy had been tipped and they were settled in, Nashe dialed room service and ordered lunch. Two steaks, two salads, two baked potatoes, two bottles of Beck's. Meanwhile, Pozzi was marching into the bathroom to take a shower, closing the door behind him but not bothering to lock it. Nashe took that as another good sign. He listened for a moment or two as the water sizzled against the tub, then changed into a clean white shirt and dug out the money he had transferred from the glove compartment to one of his suitcases (fourteen thousand dollars wrapped in a small plastic shopping bag). Without saying anything to Pozzi, he slipped out of the room, took the elevator down to the ground floor, and deposited thirteen thousand dollars in the hotel safe. Before going back up, he made a little detour and stopped in at the newsstand to buy a deck of cards.

Pozzi was sitting in his own room when Nashe returned. The two bathroom doors were open, and Nashe could see the kid sprawled out in an armchair, his body wrapped in two or three white towels. The Saturday-afternoon kung fu movie was playing on the television, and when Nashe poked his head in to say hello, Pozzi pointed to the set and said that maybe he should start taking lessons from Bruce Lee. 'The little dude's no bigger than I am,' he said, 'but look at the way he handles those fuckers. If I knew how to do that stuff, last night never would have happened.'

'Are you feeling any better?' Nashe asked.

'My body's all sore, but I don't think anything's broken.'

'I guess you'll live, then.'

'Yeah, I guess so. I might not be able to play the violin anymore, but it looks like I'm going to live.'

'The food will be here any minute. You can put on a pair of my pants if you like. After we eat, I'll take you out to buy some new clothes.'

'That's probably a good idea. I was just thinking it might not be so hot to push this Roman senator act too far.'

Nashe tossed Pozzi a pair of blue jeans to go with the Red Sox T-shirt, and once again the kid seemed to shrink down to the size of a little boy. In order not to trip over himself, he rolled up the bottoms of the pants to his ankles. 'You've sure got a handsome wardrobe,' he said as he walked into Nashe's room, holding up the jeans by the waist. 'What are you, the Boston cowboy or something?'

'I was going to let you borrow my tux, but then I figured I'd better wait and see what your table manners are like. I wouldn't want it to get ruined just because you can't keep ketchup from dribbling out of your mouth.'

The food was wheeled in on a rattling cart, and the two of them sat down to lunch. Pozzi worked on his steak with relish, but after several minutes of steady chewing and swallowing, he put down his knife and fork as if he had suddenly lost interest. He leaned back in his chair and looked around the room. 'It's funny how you start to remember things,' he said in a subdued voice. 'I've been in this hotel before, you know, but I haven't thought about it for a long time. Not for years.'

'You must have been pretty young if it happened so long ago,' Nashe said.

'Yeah, I was just a kid. My father brought me here one weekend in the fall. I must have been eleven, maybe twelve.'

'Just the two of you? What about your mother?'

'They were divorced. They split up when I was a baby.'

'And you lived with her?'

'Yeah, we lived in Irvington, New Jersey. That's where I grew up. A sad, crummy little town.'

'Did you see much of your father?'

'I barely even knew who he was.'

'And then he showed up one day and took you to the Plaza.'

'Yeah, more or less. I saw him once before that, though. The first time was a strange business, I don't think I've ever been so spooked by anything. I was eight years old then, and one day in the middle of the summer I'm sitting on the front steps of our house. My mother was off at work, and I'm sitting there by myself sucking on this orange Popsicle and looking across the street. Don't ask me how I remember it was orange, I just do. It's like I'm still holding the damn thing in my hand now. It was a hot day, and I'm sitting there with my orange Popsicle, thinking maybe I'll get on my bike when I'm finished and go over to my friend Walt's house and get him to turn on the hose in the backyard. The Popsicle is just starting to melt on my leg, and all of a sudden this big white Cadillac comes inching down the street. It was a hell of a car. All new and spanking clean, with spiderweb hubcaps and whitewall tires. The guy behind the wheel looks like he's lost. Slowing down in front of every house, craning his neck out the window to check the addresses. So I'm watching this with the dumb Popsicle dripping all over me, and then the car stops and the guy shuts off the motor. Right in front of my house. The guy gets out and starts coming up the walk – dressed in this flashy white suit and smiling this big, friendly smile. At first I thought it was Billy Martin, he looked just like him. You know, the baseball manager. And I think to myself: why is Billy Martin coming to see me? Does he want to sign me up as his new batboy or something? Jesus, the shit that goes flying through your head when you're a kid. Well, he gets a little closer, and I see that it's not Billy Martin after all. So now I'm really confused, and to be honest with you, a little bit scared. I ditch the Popsicle in the bushes, but before I can decide what else I'm going to do, the guy's already in front of me. "Hey there, Jack," he says. "Long time no see." I don't know what he's talking about, but since he knows my name, I figure he's a friend of my mother's or something. So I tell him my mother's at work, trying to be polite, but he says yeah, he knows that, he just talked with her over at the restaurant. That's where my mother worked, she was a waitress back then. And so I say to him: "You mean you came here to see me?" And he says: "You got it, kid. I figured it was about time we caught up on each other's news. The last time I saw you, you were still in diapers." The whole conversation is making less and less sense to me now, and the only thing I can think of is that this guy must be my Uncle Vince, the one who ran off to California when my mother was still a kid. "You're Uncle Vince, aren't you?" I say to him, but he just shakes his head and smiles. "Hold onto your hat, little guy," he says, or something like that, "but believe it or not, you're looking at your father." The thing is, I don't believe it for a second. "You can't be my father," I say to him. "My father got killed in Vietnam." "Yeah, well," the guy says, "that's what everyone thought. But I wasn't really killed, see. I escaped. They had me there as a prisoner, but I dug my way out and escaped. It's taken me a long time to get here." It's starting to get a little more convincing now, but I still have my doubts. "Does that mean you're going to live with us now?" I say to him. "Not exactly," he says, "but that shouldn't stop us from getting to know each other." That seems all wrong, and now I'm pretty sure that he's trying to trick me. "You can't be my father," I say again. "Fathers don't go away. They live at home with their families." "Some fathers," the guy says, "but not all of them. Look. If you don't believe me, I'll prove it to you. Your name's Pozzi, right? John Anthony Pozzi. And your father's name has to be Pozzi, too. Right?" I just nod my head at what he's saying, and then he reaches into his pocket and pulls out his wallet. "Look at this, kid," he says, and then he takes the driver's license out of the wallet and hands it to me. "Read what it says on that piece of paper." And so I read it to him: "John Anthony Pozzi." And I'll be damned if the whole story isn't written there in black and white.'

Pozzi paused for a moment and took a sip of beer. 'I don't know,' he continued. 'When I think about it now, it's like it happened in a dream or something. I can remember parts of it, but the rest just blurs over in my mind, like maybe it never really happened. I remember that my old man took me out for a spin in his Caddy, but I don't know how long it lasted, I can't even remember what we talked about. But I remember the air conditioning in the car and the smell of the leather upholstery, I remember feeling annoyed that my hands were all sticky from the Popsicle I'd been eating. The main thing, I guess, was that I was still scared. Even though I'd seen the driver's license, I started doubting it all over again. Something funny's going on, I kept telling myself. This guy might say he's my father, but that doesn't mean he's telling the truth. It could be a trick of some kind, a hoax. All this is going through my head as we drive around town, and then all of a sudden we're back in front of my house. It's like the whole thing took about half a second. My old man doesn't even get out of the car. He just reaches into his pocket, pulls out a hundred-dollar bill, and slaps it into my hand. "Here, Jack," he says, "a little something so you'll know I'm thinking about you." Shit. It was more money than I'd ever seen in my life. I didn't even know they made things like hundred-dollar bills. So I get out of the car with this C-note in my hand, and I remember thinking to myself, Yeah, I guess this means he's my father, after all. But before I can think of anything to say, he's squeezing my shoulder and saying good-bye to me. "See you around, kid," he says, or something like that, and then he starts up the car and drives off.'

'A funny way to meet your father,' Nashe said.

'You're telling me.'

'But what about when you came here to the Plaza?'

'That didn't happen until three or four years later.'

'And you didn't see him in all that time?'

'Not once. It was like he just vanished again. I kept asking my mother about him, but she was pretty tight-lipped about it, she didn't want to say much. Later on, I found out that he'd spent a few years in the can. That's why they got divorced, she told me. He'd been up to no good.'

'What did he do?'

'Got himself involved in a boiler-room scam. You know, selling stocks in a dummy corporation. One of those high-class swindles.'

'He must have done all right after he got out. Well enough to drive a Cadillac anyway.'

'Yeah, I suppose so. I think he wound up in Florida selling real estate. Struck it rich in condo land.'

'But you're not sure.'

'I'm not sure of anything. I haven't heard from the guy in a long time. He could be dead now for all I know.'

'But he showed up again three or four years later.'

'Out of the blue, just like the first time. I'd given up on him by then. Four years is a long time to wait when you're a kid. It feels like fucking forever.'

'And what did you do with the hundred dollars?'

'It's funny you should ask that. At first I was going to spend it. You know, buy a fancy new baseball glove or something, but nothing ever seemed quite right, I could never bring myself to part with it. So I wound up saving it all those years. I kept it in a little box in my underwear drawer, and every night I would take it out and look at it – just to make sure it was really there.'

'And if it was there, that meant you had really seen your father.'

'I never thought of it that way. But yeah, that's probably it. If I held on to the money, then maybe that meant my father would be coming back.'

'A little boy's logic.'

'You're so dumb when you're a kid, it's pathetic. I can't believe I used to think like that.'

'We all did. It's part of growing up.'

'Yeah, well, it was all pretty complicated. I never showed the money to my mother, but every now and then I would take it out of the box and let my friend Walt hold it. It made me feel good, I don't know why. Like if I saw him touching it, then I knew I wasn't making it up. But the funny thing was, after about six months I got it into my head that the money was fake, that it was a counterfeit bill. It might have been something that Walt said, I can't say for sure, but I do remember thinking that if the money was fake, then the guy who gave it to me couldn't have been my father.'

'Around and around.'

'Yeah. Around and around and around. One day, Walt and I got to talking about it, and he said the only way we'd ever find out was if we took it to the bank. I didn't want to let it out of my room, but since I figured it was counterfeit anyway, it probably didn't matter. So off we go to the bank, all scared that someone's going to rob us, creeping along like we're on some goddamn dangerous mission. The teller at the bank turned out to be a nice guy. Walt says to him, "My friend here wants to know if this is a real hundred-dollar bill," and the teller takes it and looks it over real careful. He even put the thing under a magnifying glass just to make sure.'

'And what did he say?'

'"It's real, boys," he says. "A genuine U.S. Treasury note."'

'So the man who gave it to you was really your father.'

'Correct. But where does that leave me now? If this guy is really my father, then why doesn't he come back and see me? At least he could write a letter or something. But instead of getting pissed off about it, I start making up stories to explain why he's not in touch. I figure, shit, I figure he's some kind of James Bond character, one of those secret agents working for the government and he can't blow his cover by coming to see me. After all, by now I believe all that bullshit about escaping from a prison camp in Vietnam, and if he can do that, he must have been one hell of a fucking macho man, right? A stud and a half. Christ, I must have been a goddamn moron to think like that.'

'You had to invent something. It's not possible to leave it blank. The mind won't let you.'

'Maybe. But I sure spun myself a ton of crap. I was up to my neck in it.'

'What happened when he finally turned up again?'

'He called first this time and spoke to my mother. I remember that I was already in bed upstairs, and she came into my room and told me about it. "He wants to spend the weekend with you in New York," she said, and it wasn't hard to see that she was burned. "The son of a bitch has got his nerve, doesn't he?" she kept saying. "That son of a bitch has got his nerve." So Friday afternoon he pulls up in front of the house in another Cadillac. This one was black, and I remember that he was wearing one of those snappy camel-hair coats and smoking a big cigar. It had nothing to do with James Bond. He looked like some guy who'd stepped out of an Al Capone movie.'

'It was winter this time.'

'The dead of winter, and it was freezing out. We drove through the Lincoln Tunnel, checked into the Plaza, and then went out to Gallagher's on Fifty-second Street. I still remember the place. It was like walking into a slaughterhouse. Hundreds of raw steaks hanging in the window, it's enough to turn you into a vegetarian. But the dining room is okay. The walls are covered with photos of politicians and sports guys and movie stars, and I admit that I was pretty impressed. That was the whole idea of the weekend, I think. My father wanted to impress me, and he wound up doing a good job of it. After dinner, we went to the fights at the Garden. The next day, we went back there for a college basketball doubleheader, and on Sunday we drove up to the Stadium to see the Giants play the Redskins. And don't think we sat in the rafters either. Fifty-yard line, friend, the best seats in the house. Yeah, I was impressed, I was fucking bowled over by it. And everywhere we went, there's my old man peeling off bills from this fat roll he carried in his pocket. Tens, twenties, fifties – he didn't even bother to look. He gave out tips like it was nothing, you know what I mean? Ushers, headwaiters, bellboys. They all had their hands out, and he just flicked off the bucks like there was no tomorrow.'

'You were impressed. But did you have a good time?'

'Not really. I mean, if this was the way people lived, then where had I been all these years? Do you know what I'm saying?'

'I think so.'

'It was hard to talk to him, and most of the time I felt embarrassed, all tied up in knots. He kind of bragged to me the whole weekend – telling me about his business deals, trying to make me think what a great guy he was, but I really didn't know what the fuck he was talking about. He also gave me a lot of advice. "Promise me you'll finish high school" – he said that two or three times – "promise me you'll finish high school so you don't turn out to be a bum." I'm this little runt in the sixth grade, and what do I know about high school and shit like that? But he made me promise, and so I gave him my word that I would. It got to be a little creepy. But the worst thing was when I told him about the hundred dollars he'd given me the last time. I thought he'd like to hear how I hadn't spent it, but it really kind of shocked him, I could see it in his face, he acted like I'd insulted him or something. "Holding on to money is for saps," he said. "It's just a lousy piece of paper, kid, and it won't do a goddamn thing for you sitting in a box."'

'Tough guy talk.'

'Yeah, he wanted to show me what a tough guy he was. But maybe it didn't work out like he thought it would. When I got back home on

Sunday night, I remember feeling pretty shook up. He gave me another hundred-dollar bill, and the next day I went out and spent it after school – just like that. He said spend it, and so that's what I did. But the funny thing was, I didn't feel like using the money on myself. I went to this jewelry store in town and bought a pearl necklace for my mother. I still remember what it cost. A hundred and eighty-nine dollars, counting the tax.'

'And what did you do with the other eleven dollars?'

'I bought her a big box of chocolates. One of those fancy red boxes shaped like a heart.'

'She must have been happy.'

'Yeah, she broke down and cried when I gave the stuff to her. I was glad I did it. It made me feel good.'

'And what about high school? Did you stick to your promise?'

'What do you think I am, a dumbbell or something? Of course I finished high school. I did okay, too. Had a B-minus average and played on the basketball team. I was a regular Mr. Hot Shot.'

'What did you do, play on stilts?'

'I was the point guard, man, and I did all right out there, let me tell you. They called me the Mouse. I was so quick, I could pass the ball between guys' legs. One game, I set a school record with fifteen assists. I was one tough little hombre out there.'

'But you didn't get any college scholarship offers.'

'I got a few nibbles, but nothing that really interested me. Besides, I figured I could do better for myself playing poker than taking some business administration course at Bullshit Tech.'

'So you found a job in a department store.'

'Temporarily. But then my old man came through with a graduation present. He sent me a check for five thousand dollars. How do you like that? I don't see the fucker for six or seven years, and then he remembers my high school graduation. Talk about mixed reactions. I could have died I was so happy. But I also felt like kicking the son of a bitch in the balls.'

'Did you send him a thank-you note?'

'Sure I did. It's sort of required, isn't it? But the guy never answered me. I haven't heard a peep from him since.'

'Worse things have happened, I suppose.'

'Shit, I don't care anymore. It's probably all for the best.'

'And that was the beginning of your career.'

'You got it, pal. That was the beginning of my glorious career, my uninterrupted march to the heights of fame and fortune.'

After that conversation, Nashe noticed a shift in his feelings toward Pozzi. A certain softening set in, a gradual if reluctant admission that there was something inherently likable about the kid. That did not mean that Nashe was prepared to trust him, but for all his wariness, he sensed a new and growing impulse to watch out for him, to take on the role of Pozzi's guide and protector. Perhaps it had something to do with his size, the undernourished, almost stunted body – as if his smallness suggested something not yet completed – but it also might have come from the story he had told about his father. All during Pozzi's reminiscences, Nashe had inevitably thought about his own boyhood, and the curious correspondence he found between their two lives had struck a chord in him: the early abandonment, the unexpected gift of money, the abiding anger. Once a man begins to recognize himself in another, he can no longer look on that person as a stranger. Like it or not, a bond is formed. Nashe understood the potential trap of such thinking, but at that point there was little he could do to prevent himself from feeling drawn to this lost and emaciated creature. The distance between them had suddenly narrowed.

Nashe decided to put off the card test for the moment and attend to Pozzi's wardrobe. The stores would be closing in a few hours, and there was no point in making the kid walk around in his baggy clown costume for the rest of the day. Nashe realized that he probably should have been more hard-nosed about it, but Pozzi was clearly exhausted, and he did not have the heart to force him into an immediate showdown. That was a mistake, of course. If poker was a game of endurance, of quick thinking under pressure, what better moment to test someone's abilities than when his mind was clouded over with exhaustion? In all probability, Pozzi would flunk the test, and the money Nashe was about to shell out on clothes for him would be wasted. Given that impending disappointment, however, Nashe was in no rush to get down to business. He wanted to savor his anticipation a bit longer, to delude himself into believing there was still some cause for hope. Besides, he was looking forward to the little shopping excursion he had planned. A few hundred dollars wouldn't make much difference in the long run, and the thought of watching Pozzi stroll through Saks Fifth Avenue was a pleasure he didn't want to deny himself. It was a situation ripe with comic possibilities, and if nothing else, he might come out of it with the memory of a few laughs. When it came right down to it, even that was more than he had expected to accomplish when he woke up that morning in Saratoga.

Pozzi started bitching the moment they entered the store. The men's department was filled with faggot clothes, he said, and he'd rather walk around in his bath towels than be caught in any of this preppie vomit. It might be all right if your name was Dudley L. Dipshit the Third and you lived on Park Avenue, but he was Jack Pozzi from Irvington, New Jersey, and he was damned if he was going to wear one of those pink alligator shirts. Back where he came from, they'd kick your ass if you showed up in a thing like that. They'd tear you apart, and they'd flush the pieces down the toilet. As he rattled on with his abuse, Pozzi kept looking at the women who walked by, and if any of them happened to be young or attractive, he would stop talking and make a stab at eye contact, or twist his head around on his neck to watch the sway of their buttocks as they disappeared down the aisle. He winked at a couple of them, and another one who inadvertently brushed his arm he even managed to address. 'Hey, babe,' he said. 'Got any plans tonight?'

'Stay calm, Jack,' Nashe warned him once or twice. 'Just stay calm. They'll throw you out of here if you keep it up.'

'I'm calm,' Pozzi said. 'Can't a guy check out the local talent?'

At bottom, it was almost as if Pozzi were carrying on because he knew that Nashe expected it of him. It was a self-conscious performance, a whirlwind of predictable antics that he was offering up as an expression of thanks to his new friend and benefactor, and if he had sensed that Nashe wanted him to stop, he would have stopped without another word. At least that was what Nashe concluded later, for once they began studying the clothes in earnest, the kid showed a surprising lack of resistance to his arguments. The implication was that Pozzi somehow understood that he was being given the opportunity to learn something, and that in turn implied that Nashe had already won his respect.

'It's like this, Jack,' Nashe said. 'Two days from now, you're going up against a couple of millionaires. And you won't be playing in some ratty pool hall, you'll be in their house as an invited guest. They're probably planning to feed you and put you up for the night. You don't want to make a bad impression, do you? You don't want to walk in there looking like some ignorant hood. I saw the kinds of clothes you like to wear. They're a tip-off, Jack, they give you away as a cheap know-nothing. You see a man in threads like that and you say to yourself, there's a walking advertisement for Losers Anonymous. They've got no style, no class. When we were in the car, you told me you have to be an actor in your line of work. Well, an actor needs a costume. You might not like these clothes, but rich people wear them, and you want to show the world you've got some taste, that you're a man of discretion. It's time to grow up, Jack. It's time to start taking yourself seriously.'

Little by little, Nashe wore him down, and in the end they walked out of the store with five hundred dollars' worth of bourgeois sobriety and restraint, an outfit of such conventionality as to make its wearer invisible in any crowd: navy blue blazer, light gray slacks, penny loafers, and a white cotton shirt. Since the weather was still warm, Nashe said, they could dispense with a tie, and Pozzi went along with that omission, saying that enough was enough. 'I already feel like a creep,' he said. 'There's no point in trying to strangle me, too.'

It was close to five o'clock when they returned to the Plaza. After depositing the packages on the seventh floor, they went back downstairs for a drink in the Oyster Bar. After one beer, Pozzi suddenly seemed crushed with fatigue, as if he were fighting to keep his eyes open. Nashe sensed that he was also in pain, and rather than force him to hold out any longer, he called for the check.

'You're fading fast,' he said. 'It's probably time you went upstairs and took a nap.'

'I feel like shit,' Pozzi said, not bothering to protest. 'Saturday night in New York, but it doesn't look like I'm going to make it.'

'It's dreamland for you, friend. If you wake up in time, you can have a late supper, but it might be a good idea just to sleep on through till morning. There's no question you'll feel a whole lot better then.'

'Gotta stay in shape for the big fight. No fucking around with the broads. Keep your pecker in your pants and steer clear of the greasy food. Road work at five, sparring at ten. Think mean. Think mean and lean.'

'I'm glad you catch on so quickly.'

'We're talking championship bout here, Jimbo, and the Kid needs his rest. When you're in training, you've got to be ready to make every sacrifice.'

So they went upstairs again, and Pozzi crawled into bed. Before he switched off the light, Nashe made him swallow three aspirins and then left a glass of water and the aspirin bottle on the night table. 'If you happen to wake up,' he said, 'take a few more of these. They'll help dull the pain.'

'Thanks, Mom,' Pozzi said. 'I hope you don't mind if I skip my prayers tonight. Just tell God I was too sleepy, okay?'

Nashe left through the bathroom, shut both doors, and sat down on his bed. He suddenly felt at a loss, not knowing what to do with himself for the rest of the evening. He considered going out and having dinner somewhere, but in the end he decided against it. He didn't want to stray too far from Pozzi. Nothing was going to happen (he was more or less certain of that), but at the same time he felt it would be wrong to take anything for granted.

At seven o'clock, he ordered a sandwich and a beer from room service and turned on the television. The Mets were playing in Cincinnati that night, and he followed the game through to the ninth inning, shuffling and reshuffling the new cards as he sat on the bed, playing one hand of solitaire after another. At ten thirty, he switched off the television and climbed into bed with a paperback copy of Rousseau's *Confessions*, which he had started reading during his stay in Saratoga. Just before he fell asleep, he came to the passage in which the author is standing in a forest and throwing stones at trees. If I hit that tree with this stone, Rousseau says to himself, then all will go well with my life from now on. He throws the stone and misses. That one didn't count, he says, and so he picks up another stone and moves several yards closer to the tree. He misses again. That one didn't count either, he says, and then he moves still closer to the tree and finds another stone. Again he misses. That was just the final warm-up toss, he says, it's the next one that really counts. But just to make sure, he walks right up to the tree this time, positioning himself directly in front of the target. He is no more than a foot away from it by now, close enough to touch it with his hand. Then he lobs the stone squarely against the trunk. Success, he says to himself, I've done it. From this moment on, life will be better for me than ever before.

Nashe found the passage amusing, but at the same time he was too embarrassed by it to want to laugh. There was something terrible about such candor, finally, and he wondered where Rousseau had found the courage to reveal such a thing about himself, to admit to such naked self-deception. Nashe turned off the lamp, closed his eyes, and listened to the hum of the air conditioner until he couldn't hear it anymore. At some point during the night, he dreamt of a forest in which the wind passed through the trees with the sound of shuffling cards.

The next morning, Nashe continued to delay the test. It had almost become a point of honor by then, as if the real test were with himself and not with Pozzi's ability at cards. The point was to see how long he could live in a state of uncertainty: to act as though he had forgotten about it and in that way use the power of silence to force Pozzi into making the first move. If Pozzi said nothing, then that would mean the kid was nothing but talk. Nashe liked the symmetry of that conundrum. No words would mean it was all words, and all words would mean it was only air and bluff and deception. If Pozzi was serious, he would have to bring up the subject sooner or later, and as time went on, Nashe found himself more and more willing to wait. It was a bit like trying to breathe and hold your breath at the same time, he decided, but now that he had started the experiment, he knew that he was going to carry on with it to the very end.

Pozzi seemed considerably revived from his long night's sleep. Nashe heard him turn on the shower just before nine o'clock, and twenty minutes later he was standing in his room, once again wearing the outfit of white towels.

'How's the senator feeling this morning?' Nashe said.

'Better,' Pozzi said. 'The bones still ache, but Jackus Pozzius is back in business.'

'Which means that a little breakfast is probably in order.'

'Make it a big breakfast. The old pit is crying out for sustenance.'

'Sunday brunch, then.'

'Brunch, lunch, I don't care what you call it. I'm famished.'

Nashe ordered breakfast to be sent up to the room, and another hour went by with no mention of the test. Nashe began to wonder if Pozzi wasn't playing the same game that he was: refusing to be the first to talk about it, digging in for a war of nerves. But no sooner did he begin to think this than he discovered that he was wrong. After they had eaten, Pozzi went back to his room to dress. When he returned (wearing the white shirt, the gray slacks, and the loafers – which made him look quite presentable, Nashe thought) he wasted no time in getting down to it. 'I thought you wanted to see what kind of poker player I was,' he said. 'Maybe we should buy a deck of cards somewhere and get started.'

'I have the cards,' Nashe said. 'I was just waiting until you were ready.'

'I'm ready. I've been ready from the word go.'

'Good. Then it looks like we've come to the moment of truth. Sit down, Jack, and show me your stuff.'

They played seven-card stud for the next three hours, using torn-up pieces of Plaza stationery to stand in as chips. With only two of them in the game, it was difficult for Nashe to measure the full scope of Pozzi's talents, but even under those distorted circumstances (which magnified the role of luck and made full-scale betting all but impossible), the kid beat him soundly, nibbling away at Nashe's paper chips until the whole pile was gone. Nashe was no master, of course, but he was far from inept. He had played nearly every week during his two years at Bowdoin College, and after he joined the fire department in Boston, he had sat in on enough games to know that he could hold his own against most decent players. But the kid was something else, and it did not take Nashe long to understand that. He seemed to concentrate better, to analyze situations more quickly, to be more sure of himself than anyone Nashe had faced in the past. After the first wipeout, Nashe suggested that he play with two hands instead of one, but the results were essentially the same. If anything, Pozzi made faster work of it than the first time. Nashe won his share of hands, but the take from those wins was always small, significantly smaller than the sums that Pozzi's winning hands invariably produced. The kid had an unerring knack for knowing when to fold and when to stay in, and he never pushed a losing hand too far, often dropping out after only the third or fourth card had been dealt. In the beginning, Nashe stole a few hands with wild bluffs, but after twenty or thirty minutes, that strategy started to backfire on him. Pozzi had him figured out, and in the end it was almost as though he could read Nashe's mind, as though he were sitting inside his head and watching him think. This encouraged Nashe, since he wanted Pozzi to be good, but it was a disturbing sensation for all that, and the unpleasantness of it lingered for some time afterward. He began to play too conservatively, relying on caution at every turn, and from then on Pozzi took control of the game, bluffing and manipulating him almost at will. The kid did not gloat, however. He played with dead seriousness, showing no trace of his customary sarcasm and humor. It was not until Nashe called it quits that he seemed to return to himself – suddenly leaning back in his chair and breaking into a broad, satisfied smile.

'Not bad, kid,' Nashe said. 'You beat the pants off me.'

'I told you,' Pozzi said. 'I don't fuck around when it comes to poker. Nine times out of ten, I'm going to come out on top. It's like a law of nature.'

'Let's just hope that tomorrow is one of those nine times.'

'Don't worry, I'm going to kill those suckers. I guarantee it. They're not half as good as you are, and you saw what I just did to you.'

'Total destruction.'

'That's right. It was a nuclear holocaust in here. A goddamn Hiroshima.'

'Are you willing to shake on the deal we made in the car?'

'A fifty–fifty split? Yeah, I'm willing to do that.'

'Minus the initial ten thousand, of course.'

'Minus the ten grand. But there's still the other stuff to consider.'

'What other stuff?'

'The hotel. The food. The clothes you bought for me yesterday.'

'Don't worry about it. Those things are write-offs, what you might call a normal business expense.'

'Shit. You don't have to do that.'

'I don't have to do anything. But I did it, didn't I? It's my present to you, Jack, and we'll leave it at that. If you want to, you can think of it as a bonus for getting me in on the action.'

'A finder's fee.'

'Exactly. A commission for services rendered. Now all you have to do is pick up the phone and see if Laurel and Hardy are still expecting you. We wouldn't want to go there for nothing. And make sure they give you good directions. It wouldn't be nice to show up late.'

'I'd better mention that you're coming with me. Just so they know what to expect.'

'Tell them your car is in the shop for repairs and you're getting a ride with a friend.'

'I'll tell them you're my brother.'

'Let's not exaggerate.'

'Sure, I'll tell them you're my brother. That way they won't ask any questions.'

'All right, tell them whatever you want. Just don't make it too complicated. You don't want to start off with your foot in your mouth.'

'Don't worry, pal, you can trust me. I'm the Jackpot Kid, remember?

It doesn't matter what I say. As long as I'm the one who says it, everything is going to turn out right.'

They set off for the town of Ockham at one thirty the following afternoon. The game was not scheduled to begin until dark, but Flower and Stone were expecting them at four. 'It's like they can't do enough for us,' Pozzi said. 'First they're going to give us tea. Then we get a tour of the house. And before we sit down to play cards, we're all going to have dinner. How do you like that? Tea! I can't fucking believe it.'

'There's a first time for everything,' Nashe said. 'Just remember to behave yourself. No slurping. And when they ask you how many lumps of sugar you want, just say one.'

'They might be jerks, those two, but their heart seems to be in the right place. If I wasn't such a greedy son of a bitch, I'd almost begin to feel sorry for them.'

'You're the last person I'd expect to feel sorry for a couple of millionaires.'

'Well, you know what I mean. First they wine and dine us, and then we walk off with their money. You've got to feel sorry for bozos like that. Just a little bit anyway.'

'I wouldn't push it too far. No one goes into a game expecting to lose, not even millionaires with good manners. You never can tell, Jack. For all we know, they're sitting down there in Pennsylvania feeling sorry for us.'

The afternoon turned out to be warm and hazy, with thick clouds massing overhead and a threat of rain in the air. They drove through the Lincoln Tunnel and began following a series of New Jersey highways in the direction of the Delaware River. For the first forty-five minutes, neither one of them said very much. Nashe drove, and Pozzi looked out the window and studied the map. If nothing else, Nashe felt certain that he had come to a turning point, that no matter what happened in the game that night, his days on the road had come to an end. The mere fact that he was in the car with Pozzi now seemed to prove the inevitability of that end. Something was finished, and something else was about to begin, and for the moment Nashe was in between, floating in a place that was neither here nor there. He knew that Pozzi stood a good chance of winning, that the odds were in fact better than good, but the thought of winning struck him as too easy, as something that would happen too quickly and naturally to bear any permanent consequences. He therefore kept the possibility of defeat uppermost in his thoughts, telling himself it was always better to prepare for the worst than to be caught by surprise. What would he do if things went badly? How would he act if the money were lost? The strange thing was not that he was able to imagine this possibility but that he could do so with such indifference and detachment, with so little inner pain. It was as if he finally had no part in what was about to happen to him. And if he was no longer involved in his own fate, where was he, then, and what had become of him? Perhaps he had been living in limbo for too long, he thought, and now that he needed to find himself again, there was nothing to catch hold of anymore. Nashe suddenly felt dead inside, as if all his feelings had been used up. He wanted to feel afraid, but not even disaster could terrify him.

After they had been on the road for a little less than an hour, Pozzi started to talk again. They were traveling through a thunderstorm at that point (somewhere between New Brunswick and Princeton), and for the first time in the three days they had been together, he seemed to show some curiosity about the man who had rescued him. Nashe was caught with his guard down, and because he had not been prepared for Pozzi's bluntness, he found himself talking more openly than he would have expected, unburdening himself of things he normally would not have shared with anyone. As soon as he saw what he was doing, he almost cut himself short, but then he decided that it didn't matter. Pozzi would be gone from his life by the next day, and why bother to hold anything back from someone he would never see again?

'And so, Professor,' the kid said, 'what are you going to do with yourself after we strike it rich?'

'I haven't decided yet,' Nashe said. 'First thing tomorrow, I'll probably go see my daughter and spend a few days with her. Then I'll sit down and make some plans.'

'So you're a daddy, huh? I hadn't figured you for one of those family guys.'

'I'm not. But I have this little girl in Minnesota. She'll be turning four in a couple of months.'

'And no wife in the picture?'

'There used to be one, but not anymore.'

'Is she out there in Michigan with the kid?'

'Minnesota. No, the girl lives with my sister. With my sister and brother-in-law. He used to play defensive back for the Vikings.'

'No kidding? What's his name?'

'Ray Schweikert.'

'Can't say I ever heard of him.'

'He only lasted a couple of seasons. The poor lummox smashed up his knee in training camp and that was the end of him.'

'And what about the wife? Did she croak on you or something?'

'Not exactly. She's probably still alive somewhere.'

'A disappearing act, huh?'

'I guess you could call it that.'

'You mean she walked out on you and didn't take the kid? What kind of bimbo would do a thing like that?'

'I've often asked that question myself. At least she left me a note.'

'That was nice of her.'

'Yeah, it filled me with immense gratitude. The only trouble was that she put it on the kitchen counter. And since she hadn't bothered to clean up after breakfast, the counter was wet. By the time I got home that evening, the thing was soaked through. It's hard to read a letter when the ink is blurred. She even mentioned the name of the guy she ran off with, but I couldn't make it out. Gorman or Corman, I think it was, but I still don't know which.'

'I hope she was good-looking anyway. There had to be something to make you want to marry her.'

'Oh, she was good-looking all right. The first time I saw Thérèse, I thought she was about the most beautiful woman I'd ever seen. I couldn't keep my hands off her.'

'A good piece of ass.'

'That's one way of putting it. It just took me a while to realize that all her brains were down there, too.'

'It's an old story, pal. You let your dick do your thinking for you, and that's what happens. Still, if it was my wife, I would have dragged her back and pounded some sense into her.'

'There wouldn't have been any point. Besides, I had my work to do. I couldn't just take off and go looking for her.'

'Work? You mean you have a job?'

'Not anymore. I quit about a year ago.'

'What did you do?'

'I put out fires.'

'A troubleshooter, huh? Company calls you in when there's a problem, and then you go around the office looking for holes to plug. That's top-level management. You must have made some good money.'

'No, I'm talking about real fires. The kind you put out with hoses – the old hook-and-ladder routine. Axes, burning buildings, people jumping out of windows. The stuff you read about in the paper.'

'You're pulling my leg.'

'It's true. I was with the Boston fire department for close to seven years.'

'You sound pretty proud of yourself.'

'I suppose I am. I was good at what I did.'

'If you liked it so much, then why did you quit?'

'I got lucky. All of a sudden, my ship came in.'

'You win the Irish Sweepstakes or something?'

'It was more like the graduation present you told me about.'

'But bigger.'

'One would hope so.'

'And now? What are you up to now?'

'Right now I'm sitting in this car with you, little man, hoping you're going to come through for me tonight.'

'A regular soldier of fortune.'

'That's it. I'm just following my nose and waiting to see what turns up.'

'Welcome to the club.'

'Club? What club is that?'

'The International Brotherhood of Lost Dogs. What else? We're letting you in as a certified, card-carrying member. Serial number zero zero zero zero.'

'I thought that was your number.'

'It is. But it's your number, too. That's one of the beauties of the Brotherhood. Everyone who joins gets the same number.'

By the time they came to Flemington, the thunderstorm had passed. Sunlight broke through the dispersing clouds, and the wet land shimmered with a sudden, almost supernatural clarity. The trees stood out more sharply against the sky, and even the shadows seemed to cut more deeply into the ground, as if their dark, intricate outlines had been etched with the precision of scalpels. In spite of the storm, Nashe had made good time, and they were running somewhat ahead of schedule.

They decided to stop for a cup of coffee, and once they were in town, they took further advantage of the occasion to empty their bladders and buy a carton of cigarettes. Pozzi explained that he normally didn't smoke, but he liked to have cigarettes on hand whenever he played cards. Tobacco was a useful prop, and it helped to prevent his opponents from watching him too closely, as if he could literally hide his thoughts behind a cloud of smoke. The important thing was to remain inscrutable, to build a wall around yourself and not let anyone in. The game was more than just betting on your cards, it was studying your opponents for weaknesses, reading their gestures for possible tics and telltale responses. Once you were able to detect a pattern, the advantage swung heavily in your favor. By the same token, the good player always did everything in his power to deny that advantage to anyone else.

Nashe paid for the cigarettes and handed them to Pozzi, who tucked the oblong box of Marlboros under his arm. Then the two of them left the store and took a brief stroll down the main street, threading their way through the small knots of summer tourists who had reemerged with the sun. After going a couple of blocks, they came upon an old hotel with a plaque on the façade that informed them that this was where the reporters covering the Lindbergh kidnapping trial had stayed back in the 1930s. Nashe told Pozzi that Bruno Hauptmann had probably been innocent, that new evidence seemed to suggest that the wrong man had been executed for the crime. He then went on to talk about Lindbergh, the all-American hero, and how he had turned fascist during the war, but Pozzi seemed bored with his little lecture, and so they turned around and headed back to the car.

It wasn't difficult to find the bridge at Frenchtown, but once they crossed the Delaware into Pennsylvania, the route became less certain. Ockham was no more than fifteen miles from the river, but they had to make a number of complicated turns to get there, and they wound up crawling along the narrow, twisting roads for close to forty minutes. If not for the storm, it would have gone somewhat faster, but the low ground was clogged with mud, and once or twice they had to climb out of the car to remove fallen branches that were blocking their way. Pozzi kept referring to the directions he had scribbled down while talking to Flower on the phone, calling out each landmark as it came into view: a covered bridge, a blue mailbox, a gray stone with a black circle painted on it. After a while, it began to feel as if they were traveling through a maze, and when they finally approached the last turn, they both admitted that they would have been hard-pressed to find their way back to the river.

Pozzi had never seen the house before, but he had been told that it was a large and impressive place, a mansion with twenty rooms surrounded by more than three hundred acres of property. From the road, however, there was nothing to suggest the wealth that lay behind the barrier of trees. A silver mailbox with the names FLOWER and STONE written on it stood beside an unpaved road that led through a dense tangle of woods and shrubs. It looked uncared-for, as if it might have been the entrance to an old, broken-down farm. Nashe swung the Saab onto the bumpy, rut-grooved path and inched his way forward for five or six hundred yards – far enough to make him wonder if the path would ever end. Pozzi said nothing, but Nashe could feel his apprehension, a sullen, sulking sort of silence that seemed to say that he, too, was beginning to doubt the venture. At last, however, the road began to climb, and when the ground leveled off a few minutes later, they could see a tall iron gate fifty yards ahead. They drove on, and once they reached the gate, the upper portion of the house became visible through the bars: an immense brick structure looming in the near distance, with four chimneys jutting into the sky and sunlight bouncing off the pitched slate roof.

The gate was closed. Pozzi jumped out of the car to open it, but after giving two or three tugs on the handle, he turned to Nashe and shook his head, indicating that it was locked. Nashe put the car into neutral, applied the emergency brake, and climbed out to see what should be done. The air suddenly seemed cooler to him, and a strong breeze was blowing across the ridge, rustling the foliage with the first faint sign of fall. As Nashe put his feet on the ground and stood up, an overpowering sense of happiness washed through him. It lasted only an instant, then gave way to a brief, almost imperceptible feeling of dizziness, which vanished the moment he began walking toward Pozzi. After that, his head seemed curiously emptied out, and for the first time in many years, he fell into one of those trances that had sometimes afflicted him as a boy: an abrupt and radical shift of his inner bearings, as if the world around him had suddenly lost its reality. It made him feel like a shadow, like someone who had fallen asleep with his eyes open.

After examining the gate for a moment, Nashe discovered a small white button lodged in one of the stone pillars that supported the ironwork. He assumed that it was connected to a bell in the house and pushed against it with the tip of his index finger. Hearing no sound, he pushed once again for good measure, just to make sure it wasn't supposed to ring outside. Pozzi scowled, growing impatient with all the delays, but Nashe just stood there in silence, breathing in the smells of the dank earth, enjoying the stillness that surrounded them. About twenty seconds later, he caught sight of a man jogging in their direction from the house. As the figure approached, Nashe concluded that it could not have been either Flower or Stone, at least not from the way Pozzi had described them. This was a stocky man of no particular age, dressed in blue work pants and a red flannel shirt, and from his clothes Nashe guessed that he was a hireling of some sort – the gardener, or perhaps the keeper of the gate. The man spoke to them through the bars, still panting from his exertions.

'What can I do for you, boys?' he said. It was a neutral question, neither friendly nor hostile, as if it were the same question he asked every visitor who came to the house. As Nashe studied the man more closely, he was struck by the remarkable blueness of his eyes, a blue so pale that the eyes almost seemed to vanish when the light hit them.

'We're here to see Mr. Flower,' Pozzi said.

'You the two from New York?' the man said, looking past them at the Saab idling on the dirt road.

'You got it,' Pozzi said. 'Straight from the Plaza Hotel.'

'What about the car, then?' the man asked, running a set of thick, sturdy fingers through his sandy-gray hair.

'What about it?' Pozzi said.

'I was wondering,' the man said. 'You come from New York, but the tags on the car say Minnesota, "land of ten thousand lakes." Seems to me like that's somewhere in the opposite direction.'

'You got a problem or something, chief?' Pozzi said. 'What the fuck difference does it make where the car comes from?'

'You don't have to get huffy, fella,' the man replied. 'I'm just doing my job. A lot of people come prowling around here, and we can't have no uninvited guests sneaking through the gates.'

'We've got an invitation,' Pozzi said, trying to control his temper. 'We're here to play cards. If you don't believe me, go ask your boss. Flower or Stone, it doesn't matter which. They're both personal friends of mine.'

'His name is Pozzi,' Nashe added. 'Jack Pozzi. You must have been told he was expected.'

The man stuck his hand into his shirt pocket, removed a small scrap of paper, cupped it in his palm, and studied it briefly at arm's length. 'Jack Pozzi,' he repeated. 'And what about you, fella?' he said, looking at Nashe.

'I'm Nashe,' Nashe said. 'Jim Nashe.'

The man put the scrap of paper back in his pocket and sighed. 'Don't let nobody in without a name,' he said. 'That's the rule. You shoulda told me straight off. There wouldn't have been no problem then.'

'You didn't ask,' Pozzi said.

'Yeah,' the man mumbled, almost talking to himself. 'Well, maybe I forgot.'

Without saying another word, he opened both doors of the gate, then gestured to the house behind him. Nashe and Pozzi returned to the car and drove on through.

4

The doorbell chimed with the opening notes of Beethoven's Fifth Symphony. They both grinned stupidly in surprise, but before either one of them could make a remark about it, the door was opened by a black maid dressed in a starched gray uniform and she was ushering them into the house. She led them across the black-and-white checkered floor of a large entrance hall that was cluttered with several pieces of broken statuary (a naked wood nymph missing her right arm, a headless hunter, a horse with no legs that floated above a stone plinth with an iron shaft connected to its belly), took them through a high-ceilinged dining room with an immense walnut table in its center, down a dimly lit corridor whose walls were decorated with a series of small landscape paintings, and then knocked on a heavy wooden door. A voice answered from within and the maid pushed the door open, stepping aside to allow Nashe and Pozzi to enter. 'Your guests are here,' she said, barely looking into the room, and then she closed the door and made a quick, silent exit.

It was a large, almost self-consciously masculine room. Standing on the threshold during those first instants, Nashe noticed the dark wood paneling on the walls, the billiard table, the worn Persian rug, the stone fireplace, the leather chairs, the ceiling fan turning overhead. More than anything else, it made him think of a movie set, a mock-up of a British men's club in some turn-of-the-century colonial outpost. Pozzi had started it, he realized. All the talk about Laurel and Hardy had planted a suggestion of Hollywood in his mind, and now that Nashe was there, it was difficult for him not to think of the house as an illusion.

Flower and Stone were both dressed in white summer suits. One was standing by the fireplace smoking a cigar, and the other was sitting in a leather chair holding a glass that could have contained either water or gin. The white suits no doubt contributed to the colonial atmosphere, but once Flower spoke, welcoming them into the room with his rough but not unpleasant American voice, the illusion was shattered. Yes, Nashe thought, one was fat and the other was thin, but that was as far as the similarity went. Stone had a taut, emaciated look to him that recalled Fred Astaire more insistently than the long-faced, weeping Laurel, and Flower was more burly than rotund, with a jowly face that resembled some ponderous figure like Edward Arnold or Eugene Pallette rather than the corpulent yet light-footed Hardy. But for all those quibbles, Nashe understood what Pozzi had meant.

'Greetings, gentlemen,' Flower said, coming toward them with an outstretched hand. 'Delighted you could make it.'

'Hi, there, Bill,' Pozzi said. 'Good to see you again. This here's my big brother, Jim.'

'Jim Nashe, isn't it?' Flower said amiably.

'That's right,' Nashe said. 'Jack and I are half-brothers. Same mother, different fathers.'

'I don't know who's responsible for it,' Flower said, nodding in Pozzi's direction, 'but he's one hell of a little poker player.'

'I got him started when he was just a kid,' Nashe said, unable to resist the line. 'When you see talent, there's an obligation to encourage it.'

'You bet,' Pozzi said. 'Jim was my mentor. He taught me everything I know.'

'But he beats the living daylights out of me now,' Nashe said. 'I don't even dare to sit down at the same table with him anymore.'

By then, Stone had extricated himself from his chair and was walking toward them, drink still in hand. He introduced himself to Nashe, shook hands with Pozzi, and a moment later the four of them were sitting around the empty fireplace waiting for the refreshments to arrive. Since Flower did most of the talking, Nashe assumed that he was the dominant one of the pair, but for all the big man's warmth and blustery humor, Nashe found himself more attracted to the silent, bashful Stone. The small man listened attentively to what the others said, and while he made few comments of his own (stumbling inarticulately when he did, acting almost embarrassed by the sound of his voice), there was a stillness and serenity in his eyes that Nashe found deeply sympathetic. Flower was all agitation and lunging goodwill, but there was something crude about him, Nashe felt, some edge of anxiety that made him appear to be at odds with himself. Stone, on the other hand, was a simpler and gentler sort of person, a man without airs who sat comfortably inside his own skin. But those were only first impressions, Nashe realized. As he continued to watch Stone sip away at the clear liquid in his glass, it occurred to him that the man might also be drunk.

'Willie and I have always loved cards,' Flower was saying. 'Back in

Philadelphia, we used to play poker every Friday night. It was a ritual with us, and I don't think we missed more than a handful of games in ten years. Some people go to church on Sunday, but for us it was Friday-night poker. God, how we used to love our weekends back then! Let me tell you, there's no better medicine than a friendly card game for sloughing off the cares of the workaday world.'

'It's relaxing,' Stone said. 'It helps to get your mind off things.'

'Precisely,' Flower said. 'It helps to open the spirit to other possibilities, to wipe the slate clean.' He paused for a moment to pick up the thread of his story. 'Anyway,' he continued, 'for many years Willie and I had our offices in the same building on Chestnut Street. He was an optometrist, you know, and I was an accountant, and every Friday we'd close up shop promptly at five. The game was always at seven, and week in and week out we always spent those two hours in precisely the same way. First, we'd swing around to the corner newsstand and buy a lottery ticket, and then we'd go across the street to Steinberg's Deli. I would always order a pastrami on rye, and Willie would have the corned beef. We did that for a long time, didn't we, Willie? Nine or ten years, I would say.'

'At least nine or ten,' Stone said. 'Maybe eleven or twelve.'

'Maybe eleven or twelve,' Flower said with satisfaction. By now it was clear to Nashe that Flower had told this story many times in the past, but that did not prevent him from savoring the opportunity to do so again. Perhaps it was understandable. Good fortune is no less bewildering than bad, and if millions of dollars had literally tumbled down on you from the sky, perhaps you would have to go on telling the story in order to convince yourself it had really happened. 'In any case,' Flower went on, 'we stuck to this routine for a long time. Life continued, of course, but the Friday nights remained sacred, and in the end they proved stronger than anything else. Willie's wife died; my wife left me; a host of disappointments threatened to break our hearts. But through it all, those poker sessions in Andy Dugan's office on the fifth floor continued like clockwork. They never failed us, we could count on them through thick and thin.'

'And then,' Nashe interrupted, 'you suddenly struck it rich.'

'Just like that,' Stone said. 'A bolt from the blue.'

'It was almost seven years ago,' Flower said, trying not to stray from the narrative. 'October fourth, to be precise. No one had hit the winning number for several weeks, and the jackpot had grown to an all-time high. Over twenty million dollars, if you can believe it, a truly astonishing sum. Willie and I had been playing for years, and until then we hadn't won so much as a penny, not one plug nickel for all the hundreds of dollars we had spent. Nor did we ever expect to. The odds are always the same, after all, no matter how many times you play. Millions and millions to one, the longest of long shots. If anything, I think we bought those tickets just so we could talk about what we would do with the money if we ever happened to win. That was one of our favorite pastimes: sitting in Steinberg's Deli with our sandwiches and spinning out stories about how we would live if our luck suddenly turned. It was a harmless little game, and it made us happy to let our thoughts run free like that. You might even call it therapeutic. You imagine another life for yourself, and it keeps your heart pounding.'

'It's good for the circulation,' Stone said.

'Precisely,' Flower said. 'It puts some juice in the old ticker.'

At that moment, there was a knock on the door, and the maid wheeled in a tray of iced drinks and tea sandwiches. Flower paused in his telling as the snacks were distributed, but once the four of them had settled back into their chairs, he immediately started up again.

'Willie and I always went partners on a single ticket,' he said. 'It was more enjoyable that way, since it didn't put us in competition with each other. Imagine if one of us had won! It would have been unthinkable for him not to share the prize money with the other, and so rather than have to go through all that, we simply split the ticket half and half. One of us would choose the first number, the other would choose the second, and then we would go on taking turns until all the holes had been punched out. We came close a few times, missed the jackpot by only a digit or two. A loss was a loss, but I must say that we found those *almosts* rather exciting.'

'They spurred us on,' Stone said. 'They made us believe that anything was possible.'

'On the day in question,' Flower continued, 'seven years ago this October fourth, Willie and I punched out the holes a little more deliberately than usual. I can't say why that was, but for some reason we actually discussed the numbers we were going to pick. I've dealt with numbers all my life, of course, and after a while you begin to feel that each number has a personality of its own. A twelve is very different from a thirteen, for example. Twelve is upright, conscientious, intelligent, whereas thirteen is a loner, a shady character who won't think twice about breaking the law to get what he wants. Eleven is tough, an outdoorsman who likes tramping through woods and scaling mountains; ten is rather simpleminded, a bland figure who always does what he's told; nine is deep and mystical, a Buddha of contemplation. I don't want to bore you with this, but I'm sure you understand what I mean. It's all very private, but every accountant I've ever talked to has always said the same thing. Numbers have souls, and you can't help but get involved with them in a personal way.'

'So there we were,' Stone said, 'holding the lottery ticket in our hands, trying to decide which numbers to bet on.'

'And I looked at Willie,' Flower said, 'and I said "Primes." And Willie looked back at me and said "Of course." Because that was precisely what he was going to say to me. I got the word out of my mouth a split second faster than he did, but the same thought had also occurred to him. Prime numbers. It was all so neat and elegant. Numbers that refuse to cooperate, that don't change or divide, numbers that remain themselves for all eternity. And so we picked out a sequence of primes and then walked across the street and had our sandwiches.'

'Three, seven, thirteen, nineteen, twenty-three, thirty-one,' Stone said.

'I'll never forget it,' Flower said. 'It was the magic combination, the key to the gates of heaven.'

'But it shocked us just the same,' Stone said. 'For the first week or two, we didn't know what to think.'

'It was chaos,' Flower said. 'Television, newspapers, magazines. Everyone wanted to talk to us and take our pictures. It took a while for that to die down.'

'We were celebrities,' Stone said. 'Genuine folk heroes.'

'Still,' Flower said, 'we never came out with any of those ludicrous remarks you hear from other winners. The secretaries who say they're going to keep their jobs, the plumbers who swear they'll go on living in their tiny apartments. No, Willie and I were never so stupid. Money changes things, and the more money you have, the greater those changes are going to be. Besides, we already knew what we were going to do with our winnings. We had talked about it so much, it was hardly a mystery to us. Once the hubbub blew over, I sold my share of the firm, and Willie did the same with his business. At that point, we didn't have to think about it. It was a foregone conclusion.'

'But that was only the beginning,' Stone said.

'True enough,' Flower said. 'We didn't rest on our laurels. With more than a million coming in every year, we could pretty much do whatever we wanted. Even after we bought this place, there was nothing to stop us from using the money to make more money.'

'Bucks County!' Stone said, letting out a brief guffaw.

'Bingo,' Flower said, 'a perfect bull's-eye. No sooner did we become rich than we started to become very rich. And once we were very rich, we became fabulously rich. I knew my way around investments, after all. I had been handling other people's money for so many years, it was only natural that I should have learned a trick or two along the way. But to be honest with you, we never expected things to work out as well as they did. First it was silver. Then it was Eurodollars. Then it was the commodities market. Junk bonds, superconductors, real estate. You name it, and we've turned a profit on it.'

'Bill has the Midas touch,' Stone said. 'A green thumb to end all green thumbs.'

'Winning the lottery was one thing,' Flower said, 'but you'd think that would have been the end of it. A once-in-a-lifetime miracle. But good luck has continued to come our way. No matter what we do, everything seems to turn out right. So much money pours in now, we give half of it to charity – and still we have more than we know what to do with. It's as though God has singled us out from other men. He's showered us with good fortune and lifted us to the heights of happiness. I know this might sound presumptuous to you, but at times I feel that we've become immortal.'

'You might be raking it in,' Pozzi said, finally entering the conversation, 'but you didn't do so hot when you played me at poker.'

'That's true,' Flower said. 'Very true. In these past seven years, it's the one time our luck has failed us. Willie and I made many blunders that night, and you thrashed us soundly. That's why I was so eager to arrange a rematch.'

'What makes you think it's going to be any different this time?' Pozzi said.

'I'm glad you asked that question,' Flower said. 'After you beat us last month, Willie and I felt humiliated. We had always thought of ourselves as fairly respectable poker players, but you proved to us that we were wrong. So, rather than roll over and give up, we decided to get better at it. We've been practicing day and night. We even took lessons from someone.'

'Lessons?' Pozzi said.

'From a man named Sid Zeno,' Flower said. 'Have you ever heard of him?'

'Sure, I've heard of Sid Zeno,' Pozzi said. 'He lives out in Vegas. He's getting on in years now, but he used to be one of the top half dozen players in the game.'

'He still has an excellent reputation,' Flower said. 'So we had him flown out here from Nevada, and he wound up spending a week with us. I think you'll find our performance much improved this time, Jack.'

'I hope so,' Pozzi said, obviously not impressed, but still trying to remain polite. 'It would be a shame to spend all that money on lessons and not get anything out of it. I'll bet you old Sid charged a pretty penny for his services.'

'He didn't come cheap,' Flower said. 'But I think he was worth it. At one point, I asked him if he had ever heard of you, but he confessed that he didn't know your name.'

'Well, Sid's a little out of touch these days,' Pozzi said. 'Besides, I'm still at the beginning of my career. The word hasn't spread yet.'

'I suppose you could say that Willie and I are at the beginning of our careers, too,' Flower said, standing up from his seat and lighting a new cigar. 'If nothing else, the game should be exciting tonight. I'm looking forward to it immensely.'

'Me too, Bill,' Pozzi said. 'It's going to be a gas.'

They began the tour of the house on the ground floor, walking through one room after another as Flower talked to them about the furniture, the architectural improvements, and the paintings that hung on the walls. By the second room, Nashe noticed that the big man rarely neglected to mention what each thing had cost, and as the catalogue of expenses continued to grow, he found that he was developing a distinct antipathy to this boorish creature who seemed so full of himself, who exulted so shamelessly in his fussy accountant's mind. As before, Stone said almost nothing, piping in an occasional non sequitur or redundant remark, a perfect yes-man in the thrall of his larger and more aggressive friend. The whole scene was beginning to get Nashe down, and eventually he could think of little else but how absurd it was for him to be there, enumerating the odd conjunctions of chance that had put him in this particular house at this particular moment, as if for no other purpose than to listen to the bombastic prattle of a fat, overstuffed stranger.

If not for Pozzi, he might have slipped into a serious funk. But there was the kid, tripping happily from room to room, seething with sarcastic politeness as he pretended to be following what Flower said. Nashe could not help admiring him for his spirit, for his ability to make the most of the situation. When Pozzi flashed him a quick wink of amusement in the third or fourth room, he felt almost grateful to him, as if he were a morose king drawing courage from the pranks of his court jester.

Things picked up considerably once they climbed to the second floor. Rather than show them the bedrooms that stood behind the six closed doors in the main hallway, Flower took them to the end of the corridor and opened a seventh door that led to what he referred to as the 'east wing.' This door was almost invisible, and until Flower put his hand on the knob and started to open it, Nashe had not noticed it was there. Covered with the same wallpaper that ran the length of the corridor (an ugly, old-fashioned fleur-de-lys pattern in muted pinks and blues), the door was so skillfully camouflaged that it seemed to melt into the wall. The east wing, Flower explained, was where he and Willie spent most of their time. It was a new section of the house that they had built shortly after moving in (and here he gave the precise amount it had cost, a figure which Nashe promptly tried to forget), and the contrast between the dark, somewhat musty old house and this new wing was impressive, even startling. The moment they stepped across the sill, they found themselves standing under a large, many-faceted glass roof. Light poured down from above, inundating them with the brightness of the late afternoon. It took Nashe's eyes a moment to adjust, but then he saw that this was only a passageway. Directly in front of them there was another wall, a freshly painted white wall with two closed doors in it.

'One half belongs to Willie,' Flower said, 'and the other half is mine.'

'It looks like a greenhouse up here,' Pozzi said. 'Is that what you fellows do, grow plants or something?'

'Not quite,' Flower said. 'But we cultivate other things. Our interests, our passions, the garden of our minds. I don't care how much money you have. If there's no passion in your life, it's not worth living.'

'Well put,' Pozzi said, nodding his head with feigned seriousness. 'I couldn't have phrased it better myself, Bill.'

'It doesn't matter which part we visit first,' Flower said, 'but I know that Willie is especially eager to show you his city. Maybe we should start by going through the door on the left.'

Without waiting to hear Stone's opinion on the matter, Flower opened the door and gestured for Nashe and Pozzi to go in. The room was much larger than Nashe had imagined it would be, a place almost barnlike in its dimensions. With its high transparent ceiling and pale wooden floor, it seemed to be all openness and light, as if it were a room suspended in the middle of the air. Running along the wall immediately to their left was a series of benches and tables, the surfaces of which were cluttered with tools, scraps of wood, and an odd assortment of metal bric-a-brac. The only other object in the room was an enormous platform that stood in the center of the floor, covered with what seemed to be a miniature scale-model rendering of a city. It was a marvelous thing to behold, with its crazy spires and lifelike buildings, its narrow streets and microscopic human figures, and as the four of them approached the platform, Nashe began to smile, astounded by the sheer invention and elaborateness of it all.

'It's called the City of the World,' Stone said modestly, almost struggling to get the words out of his mouth. 'It's only about half-finished, but I guess you can get some idea of what it's supposed to look like.'

There was a slight pause as Stone searched for something more to say, and in that brief interval Flower jumped in and started talking again, acting like one of those proud, overbearing fathers who always pushes his son into playing the piano for the guests. 'Willie has been at it for five years now,' he said, 'and you have to admit that it's amazing, a stupendous achievement. Just look at the city hall over there. It took him four months to do that building alone.'

'I like working on it,' Stone said, smiling tentatively. 'It's the way I'd like the world to look. Everything in it happens at once.'

'Willie's city is more than just a toy,' Flower said, 'it's an artistic vision of mankind. In one way, it's an autobiography, but in another way, it's what you might call a utopia – a place where the past and future come together, where good finally triumphs over evil. If you look carefully, you'll see that many of the figures actually represent Willie himself. There, in the playground, you see him as a child. Over there, you see him grinding lenses in his shop as a grown man. There, on the corner of that street, you see the two of us buying the lottery ticket. His wife and parents are buried in the cemetery over here, but there they are again, hovering as angels over that house. If you bend down, you'll see Willie's daughter holding his hand on the front steps. That's what you might call the private backdrop, the personal material, the inner component. But all these things are put in a larger context. They're merely an example, an illustration of one man's journey through the City of the World. Look at the Hall of Justice, the Library, the Bank, and the Prison. Willie calls them the Four Realms of Togetherness, and each one plays a vital role in maintaining the harmony of the city. If you look at the Prison, you'll see that all the prisoners are working happily at various tasks, that they all have smiles on their faces. That's because they're glad they've been punished for their crimes, and now they're learning how to recover the goodness within them through hard work. That's what I find so inspiring about Willie's city. It's an imaginary place, but it's also realistic. Evil still exists, but the powers who rule over the city have figured out how to transform that evil back into good. Wisdom reigns here, but the struggle is nevertheless constant, and great vigilance is required of all the citizens – each of whom carries the entire city within himself. William Stone is a great artist, gentlemen, and I consider it a tremendous honor to count myself among his friends.'

As Stone blushed and looked down at the floor, Nashe pointed to a blank area of the platform and asked what his plans for that section were. Stone looked up, stared at the empty space for a moment, and then smiled in contemplation of the work that lay ahead of him.

'The house we're standing in now,' he said. 'The house, and then the grounds, the fields, and the woods. Over to the right' – and here he pointed in the direction of the far corner – 'I'm thinking about doing a separate model of this room. I'd have to be in it, of course, which means that I would also have to build another City of the World. A smaller one, a second city to fit inside the room within the room.'

'You mean a model of the model?' Nashe said.

'Yes, a model of the model. But I have to finish everything else first. It would be the last element, a thing to add at the very end.'

'Nobody could make anything so small,' Pozzi said, looking at Stone as though he were insane. 'You'd go blind trying to do a thing like that.'

'I have my lenses,' Stone said. 'All the small work is done under magnifying glasses.'

'But if you did a model of the model,' Nashe said, 'then theoretically you'd have to do an even smaller model of that model. A model of the model of the model. It could go on forever.'

'Yes, I suppose it could,' Stone said, smiling at Nashe's remark. 'But I think it would be very difficult to get past the second stage, don't you?

I'm not just talking about the construction, I'm also talking about time. It's taken me five years to get this far. It will probably take another five years to finish the first model. If the model of the model is as difficult as I think it's going to be, that would take another ten years, maybe even another twenty years. I'm fifty-six now. If you add it up, I'm going to be pretty old when I finish anyway. And nobody lives forever. At least that's what I think. Bill might have other ideas about that, but I wouldn't bet much money on them. Sooner or later, I'm going to leave this world like everyone else.'

'You mean,' Pozzi said, his voice rising with incredulity, 'you mean you're planning to work on this thing for the rest of your life?'

'Oh yes,' Stone said, almost shocked that anyone could have thought otherwise. 'Of course I am.'

There was a brief silence as this remark sank in, and then Flower put his arm around Stone's shoulder and said: 'I don't pretend to have any of Willie's artistic talent. But perhaps that's all for the best. Two artists in the household might be taking it a bit far. Someone has to attend to the practical side of things, eh Willie? It takes all kinds of people to make a world.'

Flower's rambling chatter continued as they left Stone's workshop, returned to the passageway, and approached the other door. 'As you will see, gentlemen,' he was saying, 'my interests lie in another direction altogether. By nature, I suppose you could call me an antiquarian. I like to track down historical objects that have some value or significance, to surround myself with tangible remnants of the past. Willie makes things; I like to collect them.'

Flower's half of the east wing was entirely different from Stone's. Instead of one large open area, his was divided into a network of smaller rooms, and if not for the glass dome perched overhead, the atmosphere might have been oppressive. Each of the five rooms was choked with furniture, overspilling bookcases, rugs, potted plants, and a multitude of knickknacks, as though the idea was to reproduce the thick, tangled feeling of a Victorian parlor. As Flower explained, however, there was a certain method to the apparent disorder. Two of the rooms were devoted to his library (first editions of English and American authors in one; his collection of history books in the other), a third room was given over to his cigars (a climate-controlled chamber with a dropped ceiling that housed his stock of hand-rolled masterpieces: cigars from Cuba and Jamaica, from the Canary Islands and the

Philippines, from Sumatra and the Dominican Republic), and a fourth room served as the office in which he conducted his financial affairs (an old-fashioned room like the others, but with several pieces of modern equipment in it as well: telephone, typewriter, computer, fax machine, stock ticker, file cabinets, and so on). The last room was twice the size of any of the others, and as it was also significantly less cluttered, Nashe found it almost pleasant by contrast. This was the place where Flower kept his historical memorabilia. Long rows of glassed-in display cabinets occupied the center of the room, and the walls were fitted with mahogany shelves and cupboards with protective glass doors. Nashe felt as if he had walked into a museum. When he looked over at Pozzi, the kid gave him a goofy grin and rolled his eyes, making it perfectly clear that he was already bored to death.

Nashe did not think the collection dull so much as curious. Neatly mounted and labeled, each object sat under the glass as though proclaiming its own importance, but in fact there was little to get excited about. The room was a monument to trivia, packed with articles of such marginal value that Nashe wondered if it were not some kind of joke. But Flower seemed too proud of himself to understand how ridiculous it was. He kept referring to the pieces as 'gems' and 'treasures,' oblivious to the possibility that there might be people in the world who did not share his enthusiasm, and as the tour continued over the next half hour, Nashe had to fight back an impulse to feel sorry for him.

In the long run, however, the impression that lingered of that room was quite different from what Nashe had imagined it would be. In the weeks and months that followed, he often found himself thinking back to what he had seen there, and it stunned him to realize how many of the objects he could remember. They began to take on a luminous, almost transcendent quality for him, and whenever he stumbled across one of them in his mind, he would unearth an image so distinct that it seemed to glow like an apparition from another world. The telephone that had once sat on Woodrow Wilson's desk. A pearl earring worn by Sir Walter Raleigh. A pencil that had fallen from Enrico Fermi's pocket in 1942. General McClellan's field glasses. A half-smoked cigar filched from an ashtray in Winston Churchill's office. A sweatshirt worn by Babe Ruth in 1927. William Seward's Bible. The cane used by Nathaniel Hawthorne after he broke his leg as a boy. A pair of spectacles worn by Voltaire. It was all so random, so misconstrued, so utterly beside the point. Flower's museum was a graveyard of shadows, a demented shrine to the spirit of nothingness. If those objects continued to call out to him, Nashe decided, it was because they were impenetrable, because they refused to divulge anything about themselves. It had nothing to do with history, nothing to do with the men who had once owned them. The fascination was simply for the objects as material things, and the way they had been wrenched out of any possible context, condemned by Flower to go on existing for no reason at all: defunct, devoid of purpose, alone in themselves now for the rest of time. It was the isolation that haunted Nashe, the image of irreducible separateness that burned down into his memory, and no matter how hard he struggled, he never managed to break free of it.

'I've begun to branch out into new areas,' Flower said. 'The things you see here are what you might call snippets, dwarf mementoes, motes of dust that have slipped through the cracks. I've started a new project now, and in the end it will make all this look like child's play.' The fat man paused for a moment, put a match to his dead cigar, and then puffed until his face was surrounded by smoke. 'Last year Willie and I went on a trip to England and Ireland,' he said. 'We haven't done much traveling, I'm afraid to say, and this glimpse of life abroad gave us enormous pleasure. The best thing about it was discovering how many old things there are in that part of the world. We Americans are always tearing down what we build, destroying the past in order to start over again, rushing headlong into the future. But our cousins on the other side of the pond are more attached to their history, it comforts them to know that they belong to a tradition, to age-old habits and customs. I won't bore you by going into my love of the past. You have only to look around you to know how much it means to me. While I was over there with Willie, visiting the ancient sites and monuments, it occurred to me that I had the opportunity to do something grand. We were in the west of Ireland then, and one day as we were motoring around the countryside, we came upon a fifteenth-century castle. It was no more than a heap of stones, really, sitting forlornly in a little valley or glen, and it was so sad and neglected that my heart went out to it. To make a long story short, I decided to buy it and have it shipped back to America. That took some time, of course. The owner was an old codger by the name of Muldoon, Patrick Lord Muldoon, and he was naturally quite reluctant to sell. Some persuasion was required on my part, but money talks, as they say, and in the end I got what I wanted. The stones of the castle were loaded onto trucks – lorries, as they call them over there –

and transported to a ship in Cork. Then they were sent across the ocean, once again loaded onto lorries – trucks, as we call them over here, ha! – and brought to our little spot in the Pennsylvania woods. Amazing, isn't it? The whole thing cost a bundle, I can assure you, but what do you expect? There were over ten thousand stones, and you can imagine what that kind of cargo must have weighed. But why worry when money is no object? The castle arrived less than a month ago, and even as we speak, it's sitting on this property – over there in a meadow at the northern edge of our land. Just think, gentlemen. A fifteenth-century Irish castle destroyed by Oliver Cromwell. An historical ruin of major significance, and Willie and I own it.'

'You're not planning to rebuild the thing, are you?' Nashe asked. For some reason, the idea struck him as grotesque. Instead of the castle, he kept seeing the bent old figure of Lord Muldoon, wearily submitting to the blunderbuss of Flower's fortune.

'We thought about it, Willie and I,' Flower said, 'but we finally dismissed it as impractical. Too many pieces are missing.'

'A hodgepodge,' Stone said. 'In order to rebuild it, we'd have to mix in new materials with the old. And that would defeat the purpose.'

'So you have ten thousand stones sitting in a meadow,' Nashe said, 'and you don't know what to do with them.'

'Not anymore,' Flower said. 'We know exactly what we're going to do with them. Don't we, Willie?'

'Absolutely,' Stone said, suddenly beaming with pleasure. 'We're going to build a wall.'

'A monument, to be more precise,' Flower said. 'A monument in the shape of a wall.'

'How fascinating,' Pozzi said, his voice oozing with unctuous contempt. 'I can't wait to see it.'

'Yes,' Flower said, failing to catch the kid's mocking tone, 'it's an ingenious solution, if I do say so myself. Rather than try to reconstruct the castle, we're going to turn it into a work of art. To my mind, there's nothing more mysterious or beautiful than a wall. I can already see it: standing out there in the meadow, rising up like some enormous barrier against time. It will be a memorial to itself, gentlemen, a symphony of resurrected stones, and every day it will sing a dirge for the past we carry within us.'

'A Wailing Wall,' Nashe said.

'Yes,' Flower said, 'a Wailing Wall. A Wall of Ten Thousand Stones.'

'Who's going to put it together for you, Bill?' Pozzi asked. 'If you need a good contractor, I might be able to help you out. Or are you and Willie planning to do it yourselves?'

'I think we're a bit too old for that now,' Flower said. 'Our handyman will hire the workers and oversee the day-to-day operations. I think you've already met him. His name is Calvin Murks. He's the man who let you through the gate.'

'And when do things get started?' Pozzi asked.

'Tomorrow,' Flower said. 'We have a little job of poker to take care of first. Once that's out of the way, the wall is our next project. To tell you the truth, we've been too busy preparing for tonight to give it much attention. But tonight is nearly upon us now, and then it's on to the next thing.'

'From cards to castles,' Stone said.

'Precisely,' Flower answered. 'And from talk to food. Believe it or not, my friends, I think it's time for dinner.'

Nashe no longer knew what to think. At first he had taken Flower and Stone for a pair of amiable eccentrics – a trifle daft, perhaps, but essentially harmless – but the more he saw of them and listened to what they said, the more uncertain his feelings had become. Sweet little Stone, for example, whose manner was so humble and benign, turned out to spend his days constructing a model of some bizarre, totalitarian world. Of course it was charming, of course it was deft and brilliant and admirable, but there was a kind of warped, voodoo logic to the thing, as if under all the cuteness and intricacy one was supposed to feel a hint of violence, an atmosphere of cruelty and revenge. With Flower, too, everything was ambiguous, difficult to pin down. One moment, he seemed perfectly sensible; the next moment, he sounded like a lunatic, rambling on like an out-and-out madman. There was no question that he was gracious, but even his joviality seemed forced, suggesting that if he did not bombard them with all that pedantic, overly articulate talk, the mask of fellowship might somehow slip from his face. To show what? Nashe had not formed any definite opinion, but he knew that he was feeling more and more unsettled. If nothing else, he told himself, he would have to watch carefully, he would have to stay on his guard.

The dinner turned out to be a ridiculous affair, a low-level farce that seemed to nullify Nashe's doubts and prove that Pozzi had been right all along: Flower and Stone were no more than grown-up children, a pair of half-wit clowns who did not deserve to be taken seriously. By the time they came downstairs from the east wing, the huge walnut table in the dining room had been set for four. Flower and Stone took their usual seats at the two ends, and Nashe and Pozzi sat across from each other in the middle. The initial surprise occurred when Nashe glanced down at his placemat. It was a plastic novelty item that appeared to date from the 1950s, and its vinyl surface was emblazoned with a full-color photograph of Hopalong Cassidy, the old cowboy star from the Saturday matinees. Nashe's first thought was to interpret it as a piece of self-conscious kitsch, a little stab at humor on the part of his hosts, but then the food was brought in, and the meal turned out to be no more than a kiddie banquet, a dinner fit for six-year-olds: hamburger patties on white, untoasted buns, bottles of Coke with plastic straws sticking out of them, potato chips, corn on the cob, and a ketchup dispenser in the shape of a tomato. Except for the absence of paper hats and noisemakers, it reminded Nashe of the birthday parties he had attended as a small boy. He kept looking at Louise, the black maid who served the food, searching her expression for something that would give away the joke, but she never cracked a smile, going about her business with all the solemnity of a waitress in a four-star restaurant. To make matters worse, Flower ate with his paper napkin tucked under his chin (presumably to avoid splattering his white suit), and when he saw that Stone had eaten only half his hamburger, he actually leaned forward with a gluttonous light in his eye and asked his friend if he could finish it for him. Stone was only too happy to comply, but rather than pass his entire plate, he simply picked up the half-eaten hamburger, handed it to Pozzi, and asked him to give it to Flower. From the look on Pozzi's face at that moment, Nashe thought he was about to throw it at the fat man, yelling something like *Catch!* or *Think fast!* as the food sailed through the air. For dessert, Louise brought out four dishes of raspberry Jell-O, each one topped with a little mound of whipped cream and a maraschino cherry.

The strangest thing about the dinner was that no one said anything about it. Flower and Stone acted as though it were perfectly normal for adults to eat this way, and neither one of them offered any apologies or explanations. At one point, Flower mentioned that they always had hamburgers on Monday night, but that was the extent of it. Otherwise, the conversation flowed along as it had before (which is to say, Flower discoursed at length and the others listened to him), and by the time they were crunching on the last of the potato chips, the talk had come around to poker. Flower enumerated all the reasons why the game was so attractive to him – the sense of risk, the mental combat, the absolute purity of it – and for once Pozzi seemed to be paying more than half-hearted attention to him. Nashe himself said nothing, knowing that he had little to add to the subject. Then the meal was over, and the four of them were finally standing up from the table. Flower asked if anyone would care for a drink, and when both Nashe and Pozzi declined, Stone rubbed his hands together and said, 'Then maybe we should go into the other room and break out the cards.' And just like that, the game began.

5

They played in the same room where the tea had been served. A large folding table had been set up in an open area between the sofa and the windows, and when he saw that blank wooden surface and the empty chairs poised around it, Nashe suddenly understood how much was at stake for him. This was the first time he had seriously confronted what he was doing, and the force of that awareness came very abruptly – with a surging of his pulse and a frantic pounding in his head. He was about to gamble his life on that table, he realized, and the insanity of that risk filled him with a kind of awe.

Flower and Stone went about their preparations with a dogged, almost grim sense of purpose, and as Nashe watched them count out the chips and examine the sealed packages of cards, he understood that nothing was going to be simple, that Pozzi's triumph was by no means certain. The kid had stepped outside to fetch his cigarettes from the car, and when he entered the room he was already smoking, puffing away at his Marlboro with short, nervous drags. The festive atmosphere of just a short while ago seemed to vanish in that smoke, and the whole room was suddenly tense with anticipation. Nashe wished that he were going to be playing a more active role in what happened, but that was the bargain he had struck with Pozzi: once the first card was dealt, he would be shunted off to the sidelines, and from then on there would be nothing for him to do but watch and wait.

Flower walked to the far end of the room, opened a safe in the wall beside the billiard table, and asked Nashe and Pozzi to come over and look inside it. 'As you can see for yourselves,' he said, 'it's perfectly empty. I thought we could use it as our bank. Cash for chips, and the cash goes here. Once we've finished playing, we'll open the safe again and distribute the money according to what happens. Does either of you object to that?' Neither one of them did, and Flower continued. 'In the interests of fairness,' he said, 'it seems to me that we should all go in for the same amount. The verdict will be more decisive that way, and since Willie and I aren't just playing for money, we'll be happy to go along with any amount you choose. What do you say, Mr. Nashe?

How much were you planning to spend on backing your brother?'

'Ten thousand dollars,' Nashe said. 'If it's no problem for you, I think I'd like to turn the whole amount into chips before we start.'

'Excellent,' Flower said. 'Ten thousand dollars, a good round sum.'

Nashe hesitated for a moment, and then he said: 'A dollar for every stone in your wall.'

'Indeed,' Flower answered, with a touch of condescension in his voice. 'And if Jack does his job, maybe you'll have enough to build a castle when you're finished.'

'A castle in Spain, perhaps,' Stone suddenly chimed in. Then, grinning at his own witticism, he unexpectedly lowered himself to the floor, reached under the billiard table, and pulled out a small satchel. Still crouching on the rug, he opened the bag and started removing thousand-dollar bundles of cash, smacking each one onto the felt surface above him. When he had counted out twenty of these bundles, he zipped up the bag, shoved it back under the table, and climbed to his feet. 'Here you are,' he said to Flower. 'Ten thousand for you and ten thousand for me.'

Flower asked Nashe and Pozzi if they would like to count the money themselves, and Nashe was surprised when the kid said yes. As Pozzi meticulously thumbed through each bundle, Nashe slipped ten one-thousand-dollar bills out of his wallet and laid them gently on the billiard table. He had gone to a bank early that morning in New York and converted his horde of hundreds into these monstrous notes. It was not for the convenience so much as to spare himself embarrassment when the time came to purchase the chips – realizing that he did not want to be placed in the position of having to dump wads of rumpled cash onto a stranger's floor. There was something clean and abstract about doing it this way, he found, a sense of mathematical wonder in seeing his world reduced to ten small pieces of paper. He still had a bit left over, of course, but twenty-three hundred dollars didn't amount to much. He had kept this reserve in more modest denominations, stuffing the money into two envelopes and then placing each envelope in an inside breast pocket of his sport jacket. For the time being, that was all he had: twenty-three hundred dollars and a pile of plastic poker chips. If the chips were lost, he wouldn't be able to get very far. Three or four weeks, maybe, and then he'd barely have a pot to piss in.

After a short discussion, Flower, Stone, and Pozzi settled on the ground rules of the game. They would play seven-card stud from start to finish, with no wild cards or jokers – straight hardball all the way, as Pozzi put it. If Pozzi pulled ahead early, the other two would be allowed to replenish their stakes to a maximum of thirty thousand dollars. There would be a five-hundred-dollar limit on bets, and the game would keep going until one player was wiped out. If all three of them managed to stay in, they would call a stop to it after twenty-four hours, no questions asked. Then, like diplomats who had just concluded a peace treaty, they shook hands and walked over to the billiard table to collect their chips.

Nashe took a seat behind Pozzi's right shoulder. Neither Flower nor Stone mentioned it, but he knew that it would be bad form to wander around the room while they were playing. He was an interested party, after all, and he had to avoid doing anything that might look suspicious. If he happened to be in a place where he could glimpse their hands, they might think that he and Pozzi were cheats, communicating through a code of private signals: coughs, for example, or eye blinks, or scratches of the head. The possibilities for deception were infinite. They all knew that, and therefore no one bothered to say a word.

The first few hands were undramatic. The three of them played cautiously, circling like boxers in the early rounds of a fight, testing each other with jabs and head-feints, gradually settling into the feel of the ring. Flower lit up a fresh cigar, Stone chewed on a stick of Doublemint gum, and Pozzi kept a cigarette burning between the fingers of his left hand. Each was pensive and withdrawn, and Nashe began to be a little surprised by the lack of talk. He had always associated poker with a kind of freewheeling roughhouse chatter, an exchange of foul-mouthed jokes and friendly insults, but these three were all business, and it wasn't long before Nashe felt an atmosphere of genuine antagonism insinuate itself into the room. The sounds of the game took over for him, as if everything else had been erased: the clinking of the chips, the noise of the stiff cards being shuffled before each hand, the dry announcements of bets and raises, the plunges into total silence. Eventually, Nashe started taking cigarettes from Pozzi's pack on the table – lighting up unconsciously, not realizing that he was smoking for the first time in over five years.

He was hoping for an early blowout, a massacre, but in the first two hours Pozzi merely held his own, winning about a third of the pots and making little if any headway. The cards weren't coming to him, and any number of times he was forced to fold after betting on the initial three or four cards of a hand, occasionally using his bad luck to bluff out a victory, but clearly not wanting to push that tactic too far. Fortunately, the bets were rather low in the beginning, with no one daring to go in for more than one fifty or two hundred on any given round, and that helped to keep the damage to a minimum. Nor did Pozzi show any signs of panic. Nashe was reassured by that, and as time went on, he sensed that the kid's patience was going to pull them through. Still, it meant giving up on his dream of rapid annihilation, and that was something of a disappointment. It was going to be an intense, grueling affair, he realized, which proved that Flower and Stone were no longer the same players they had been when Pozzi saw them in Atlantic City. Perhaps the lessons with Sid Zeno were responsible for the change. Or perhaps they had always been good and had used that other game to lure Pozzi into this one. Of the two possibilities, Nashe found the second far more disturbing than the first.

Then things took a turn for the better. Just before eleven o'clock, the kid hauled in a three-thousand-dollar pot with aces and queens, and for the next hour he went on a tear, winning three out of every four hands, playing with such assurance and cunning that Nashe could see the other two begin to sag, as if their wills were buckling, visibly giving way to the attack. Flower bought another ten thousand dollars' worth of chips at midnight, and fifteen minutes later Stone sprang for another five. The room was filled with smoke by then, and when Flower finally inched open one of the windows, Nashe was startled by the din of crickets singing in the grass outside. Pozzi was sitting on twenty-seven thousand dollars at that point, and for the first time all evening, Nashe allowed his mind to wander away from the game, feeling that his concentration was somehow no longer required. Everything was under control now, and there could be no harm in drifting off a little, in indulging himself with an occasional reverie about the future. Incongruous as it seemed to him later, he even started to think about settling down somewhere, of moving out to Minnesota and buying a house with the money he was going to win. Costs were low in that part of the country, and he didn't see why there wouldn't be enough for a down payment. After that, he'd talk to Donna about having Juliette live with him again, and then maybe he'd pull some strings in Boston to work out a job with the local fire department. The fire engines in Northfield were pale green, he remembered, and it amused him to think about that, wondering how many other things would be different in the Midwest and how many would be the same.

They opened a new deck of cards at one o'clock, and Nashe took advantage of the interruption to excuse himself to go to the bathroom. He fully intended to come right back, but once he flushed the toilet and stepped back into the darkened hallway, he could not help noticing how pleasurable it felt to be stretching his legs. He was tired from sitting in a cramped position for so many hours, and since he was already on his feet, he decided to take a little stroll through the house to get a second wind. In spite of his exhaustion, he was filled with happiness and excitement, and he did not feel ready to return yet. For the next three or four minutes, he groped his way through the unlit rooms that Flower had shown them before dinner, bumping blindly into doorframes and pieces of furniture until he found himself in the front hall. A lamp was on at the top of the stairs, and as he lifted his eyes to look at it, he suddenly remembered Stone's workshop in the east wing. Nashe hesitated to go up there without permission, but the urge to see the model again was too strong to resist. Brushing aside his qualms, he grabbed hold of the bannister and started up the stairs two at a time.

He spent close to an hour looking at the City of the World, examining it in a way that had not been possible before – without the distraction of pretending to be polite, without Flower's commentaries buzzing in his ears. This time he was able to sink himself into the details, moving slowly from one area of the model to another, studying the minute architectural flourishes, the painstaking application of colors, the vivid, sometimes startling expressions on the faces of the tiny, one-inch figures. He saw things that had entirely escaped him during the first visit, and many of these discoveries turned out to be marked by wicked flashes of humor: a dog pissing against a fireplug in front of the Hall of Justice; a group of twenty men and women marching down the street, all of them wearing glasses; a masked robber slipping on a banana peel in a back alley. But these funny bits only made the other elements seem more ominous, and after a while Nashe found himself concentrating almost exclusively on the prison. In one corner of the exercise yard, the inmates were talking in small groups, playing basketball, reading books; but then, with a kind of horror, he saw a blindfolded prisoner standing against the wall just behind them, about to be executed by a firing squad. What did this mean? What crime had this man committed, and why was he being punished in this terrible way? For all the warmth and sentimentality depicted in the model, the overriding mood was one of terror, of dark dreams sauntering down the avenues in broad daylight. A threat of punishment seemed to hang in the air – as if this were a city at war with itself, struggling to mend its ways before the prophets came to announce the arrival of a murderous, avenging God.

Just as he was about to switch off the light and leave the room, Nashe turned around and walked back to the model. Fully conscious of what he was about to do, and yet with no sense of guilt, feeling no compunctions whatsoever, he found the spot where Flower and Stone were standing in front of the candy store (arms flung around each other's shoulders, looking at the lottery ticket with their heads bowed in concentration), lowered his thumb and middle finger to the place where their feet joined the floor, and gave a little tug. The figures were glued fast, and so he tried again, this time with a swift, impulsive jerk. There was a dull snap, and a moment later he was holding the two wooden men in the palm of his hand. Scarcely bothering to look at them, he shoved the souvenir into his pocket. It was the first time that Nashe had stolen anything since he was a small boy. He was not sure why he had done it, but the last thing he was looking for just then was a reason. Even if he could not articulate it to himself, he knew that it had been absolutely necessary. He knew that in the same way he knew his own name.

When Nashe took his seat behind Pozzi again, Stone was shuffling the cards, getting ready to deal the next hand. It was past two o'clock by then, and one look at the table was enough to tell Nashe that everything had changed, that tremendous battles had been fought in his absence. The kid's mountain of chips had dwindled to one-third its former size, and if Nashe's calculations were correct, that meant they were back where they had been at the start, perhaps even a thousand or two in the hole. It didn't seem possible. Pozzi had been flying high, on the brink of sewing up the whole business, and now they seemed to have him on the run, pushing hard to break his confidence, to crush him once and for all. Nashe could barely imagine what had happened.

'Where the fuck have you been?' Pozzi said, whispering with pent-up fury.

'I took a nap on the sofa in the living room,' Nashe lied. 'I couldn't help it. I was exhausted.'

'Shit. Don't you know better than to walk out on me like that? You're my lucky charm, asshole. As soon as you left, the goddamn roof started to collapse.'

Flower interrupted at that point, too pleased with himself not to jump in and offer his own version of what had taken place. 'We've had some big hands,' he said, trying not to gloat. 'Your brother went for broke on a full house, but Willie came through on the last card and beat him out with four sixes. Then, just a few hands later, there was a dramatic showdown, a duel to the death. In the end, my three kings prevailed over your brother's three jacks. You've missed some excitement, young man, I can tell you that. This is poker as it was meant to be played.'

Curiously enough, Nashe did not feel alarmed by these drastic reversals. If anything, Pozzi's slump had a galvanizing effect on him, and the more frustrated and confused the kid became, the more Nashe's confidence seemed to grow, as if it were precisely this sort of crisis that he had been searching for all along.

'Maybe it's time to inject a few vitamins into my brother's stake,' he said, smiling at the pun. He reached into his jacket pockets and pulled out the two envelopes of money. 'Here's twenty-three hundred dollars,' he said. 'Why don't we buy some more chips, Jack? It's not much, but at least it will give you a little more room to work with.'

Pozzi knew that it was the last money Nashe had in the world, and he hesitated to accept it. 'I'm still hanging in there,' he said. 'Let's give it a few more hands and see what happens.'

'Don't worry about it, Jack,' Nashe said. 'Take the money now. It'll change the mood, help to get you going again. You've just hit a lull, that's all, but you'll come roaring back. It happens all the time.'

But Pozzi didn't come roaring back. Even with the new chips, things continued to go against him. He won the occasional hand, but those victories were never large enough to shore up his eroding funds, and every time his cards seemed to offer some promise, he would bet too much and wind up losing, squandering his resources on luckless, desperation efforts. By the time dawn came, he was down to eighteen hundred dollars. His nerves were shot, and if Nashe still had any hopes of winning, he had only to study Pozzi's trembling hands to know that the hour of miracles had passed. The birds were waking up outside, and as the first glimmers of light entered the room, Pozzi's bruised and pale face seemed ghastly in its whiteness. He was turning into a corpse before Nashe's eyes.

Still, the show wasn't over yet. On the next hand, Pozzi was dealt two kings in the hole and the ace of hearts up, and when the fourth card was another king – the king of hearts – Nashe sensed that the tide was about to turn again. The betting was heavy, however, and before the fifth card was even dealt, the kid had just three hundred dollars left. Flower and Stone were running him out of the game: he wasn't going to have enough to see him to the end of the hand. Without even thinking, Nashe stood up and said to Flower, 'I want to make a proposition.'

'A proposition?' Flower said. 'What are you talking about?'

'We're almost out of chips.'

'Fine. Then go ahead and buy some more.'

'We would, but we've also run out of cash.'

'Then I suppose that means the game is over. If Jack can't stay in for the rest of the hand, then we'll have to put an end to it. Those were the rules we agreed on before.'

'I know that. But I want to propose something else, something other than cash.'

'Please, Mr. Nashe, no IOUs. I don't know you well enough to offer credit.'

'I'm not asking for credit. I want to put up my car as collateral.'

'Your car? And what kind of car is that? A second-hand Chevy?'

'No, it's a good car. A year-old Saab in perfect condition.'

'And what am I supposed to do with it? Willie and I already have three cars in the garage. We're not in the market for another one.'

'Sell it, then. Give it away. What difference does it make? It's the only thing I have to offer. Otherwise, the game has to stop. And why put an end to it when we don't have to?'

'And how much do you think this car of yours is worth?'

'I don't know. I paid sixteen thousand dollars for it. It's probably worth at least half that now, maybe even ten.'

'Ten thousand dollars for a used car? I'll give you three.'

'That's absurd. Why don't you go outside and have a look at it before you make an offer?'

'Because I'm in the middle of a hand now. I don't want to break my concentration.'

'Then give me eight, and we'll call it a deal.'

'Five. That's my final offer. Five thousand dollars.'

'Seven.'

'No, five. Take it or leave it, Mr. Nashe.'

'All right, I'll take it. Five thousand for the car. But don't worry. We'll deduct it from our winnings at the end. I wouldn't want you to be stuck with something you don't want.'

'We'll see about that. In the meantime, let's count out the chips and get on with it. I can't stand these interruptions. They destroy all the pleasure.'

Pozzi had been given an emergency transfusion, but that did not mean he was going to live. He would pull through the present crisis, perhaps, but the long-term prospects were still cloudy, touch-and-go at best. Nashe had done everything he could, however, and that in itself was a consolation, even a point of pride. But he also knew that the blood bank was exhausted. He had gone much farther than he thought he would, as far as it was possible for him to go, but still it might not be far enough.

Pozzi had the two kings in the hole, with the king and ace of hearts showing. Flower's two up cards were a six of diamonds and a seven of clubs – a possible straight, perhaps, but still weak when compared to the three kings the kid was already holding. Stone's hand was a potential threat, however. Two eights were showing, and from the way he had led off the betting on the fourth card (coming on strong, with consecutive raises of three hundred and four hundred dollars), Nashe suspected that good things were hidden in his hole cards. Another pair, perhaps, or even the third and fourth eights. Nashe pinned his hopes on Pozzi drawing the fourth king, but he wanted it to come at the end, face-down on the seventh deal. In the meantime, he thought, give him two more hearts. Even better, give him the queen and jack of hearts. Make it look as though he's risking everything on a possible straight flush – and then stun them with the four kings at the end.

Stone dealt the fifth cards. Flower received a five of spades; Pozzi got his heart. It wasn't the queen or jack, but it was almost as good: the eight of hearts. The flush was still intact, and Stone no longer had a chance of drawing the fourth eight. As Stone dealt himself the three of clubs, Pozzi turned to Nashe and smiled for the first time in several hours. All of a sudden, things were looking hopeful.

In spite of the three, Stone opened by betting the limit, the full five hundred. This puzzled Nashe somewhat, but then he decided it had to be a bluff. They were trying to squeeze out the kid, and with so much money in reserve, they could afford to take a few wild punches. Flower stayed in with his possible straight, and then Pozzi saw the five hundred and raised another five hundred, which Stone and Flower both matched.

Flower's sixth card turned out to be the jack of diamonds, and the moment he saw it skidding across the table, he let out a sigh of disappointment. Nashe assumed that he was dead. Then, as if by magic, Pozzi came up with the three of hearts. When Stone drew the nine of spades, however, Nashe suddenly began to worry that Pozzi's cards were too strong. But Stone bet high again, and even after Flower dropped out, the hand was alive and well, still growing as they moved into the home stretch.

Stone and Pozzi went head to head on their sixth cards, going back and forth in a flurry of raises and counterraises. By the time they were done, Pozzi had just fifteen hundred dollars left to use on the last deal. Nashe had figured that ransoming the car would buy them at least another hour or two, but the betting had become so furious that everything had suddenly boiled down to the one hand. The pot was enormous. If Pozzi won, he would be off and running again, and this time Nashe sensed that there would be no stopping him. But he had to win. If he lost, that would be the end of it.

Nashe knew that it would be too much to hope for the fourth king. The odds against it were simply too great. But no matter what happened, Stone would have to assume that Pozzi was holding a flush. The four exposed hearts had seen to that, and since the kid was playing with his back to the wall, his big bets would seem to eliminate the possibility of a bluff. Even if the seventh card was a dud, the three kings would probably do the trick anyway. It was a good hand, Nashe thought, a solid hand, and from the looks of things on the table, the chances of Stone beating it were slim.

Pozzi drew the four of clubs. In spite of everything, Nashe could not help feeling a bit let down. Not so much for the king, perhaps, but at least for the absence of another heart. *Heart failure*, he said to himself, not sure if it was meant entirely in jest, and then Stone dealt himself the last card and they were ready to square off and finish the hand.

It all happened very quickly. Stone, still leading with his two eights, went in for five hundred. Pozzi saw the five hundred, then raised another five hundred. Stone saw Pozzi's raise, hesitated for a second or two with the chips in his hand, and clinked down another five hundred. Then, with only five hundred left at that point, the kid pushed his remaining chips into the center of the table. 'All right, Willie,' he said. 'Let's see what you've got.'

Stone's face gave away nothing. One by one, he turned over his hole cards, but even after all three of them were showing, it would have been difficult to tell whether he had won or lost. 'I have these two eights,' he said. 'And then I have this ten' (turning it over), 'and then I have this other ten' (turning it over), 'and then I have this third eight' (turning over the seventh and last card).

'A full house!' Flower roared, pounding his fist on the table. 'What can you do to answer that, Jack?'

'Not a thing,' Pozzi said, not bothering to turn over his cards. 'He's got me beat.' The kid stared down at the table for several moments, as if trying to absorb what had happened. Then, mustering his courage, he wheeled around and grinned at Nashe. 'Well, old buddy,' he said. 'It looks like we have to walk home.'

As he spoke those words, Pozzi's face was filled with such embarrassment that Nashe could only feel sorry for him. It was odd, but the fact was that he felt worse for the kid than he felt for himself. Everything was lost, and yet the only feeling inside him was one of pity.

Nashe clapped Pozzi on the shoulder, as if to reassure him, and then he heard Flower burst out laughing. 'I hope you boys have comfortable shoes,' the fat man said. 'It's a good eighty or ninety miles back to New York, you know.'

'Cool your jets, Tubby,' Pozzi said, finally forgetting his manners. 'We owe you five thousand bucks. We'll give you a marker, you give us the car, and we'll pay you back within a week.'

Flower, unruffled by the insult, burst out laughing again. 'Oh no,' he said. 'That's not the deal I made with Mr. Nashe. The car belongs to me now. If you don't have any other way of getting home, then you'll just have to walk. That's the way it goes.'

'What kind of bullshit poker player are you, Hippo-Face?' Pozzi said. 'Of course you'll take our marker. That's the way it works.'

'I said it before,' Flower answered calmly, 'and I'll say it again. No credit. I'd be a fool to trust a pair like you. The minute you drove away from here, my money would be gone.'

'All right, all right,' Nashe said, hastily trying to improvise a solution. 'We'll cut for it. If I win, you give us back the car. Just like that. One cut, and it's finished.'

'No problem,' Flower said. 'But what happens if you don't win?'

'Then I owe you ten thousand dollars,' Nashe said.

'You should think carefully, my friend,' Flower said. 'This hasn't been your lucky night. Why make things worse for yourself?'

'Because we need the car to get out of here, asshole,' Pozzi said.

'No problem,' Flower repeated. 'But just remember that I warned you.'

'Shuffle the cards, Jack,' Nashe said, 'and then hand them to Mr. Flower. We'll give him the first try.'

Pozzi opened a new deck, discarded the jokers, and shuffled as Nashe had asked him to. With exaggerated ceremony, he leaned forward and slapped the cards down in front of Flower. The fat man didn't hesitate. He had nothing to lose, after all, and so he promptly reached for the cards, lifting half the deck between his thumb and middle finger. A moment later he was holding up the seven of hearts. Stone shrugged when he saw it, and Pozzi clapped his hands – just once, very fiercely, celebrating the mediocre draw.

Then Nashe was holding the deck in his hands. He felt utterly blank inside, and for a brief moment he marveled at how ridiculous this little drama was. Just before he cut, he thought to himself: This is the most ridiculous moment of my life. Then he winked at Pozzi, lifted the cards, and came up with the four of diamonds.

'A four!' Flower yelled, slapping his hand against his forehead in disbelief. 'A four! You couldn't even beat my seven!'

Everything went silent after that. A long moment passed, and then, in a voice that sounded more weary than triumphant, Stone finally said: 'Ten thousand dollars. It looks like we've hit the magic number again.'

Flower leaned back in his chair, puffed on his cigar for several moments, and studied Nashe and Pozzi as though he were seeing them for the first time. His expression made Nashe think of a high school principal sitting in his office with a couple of delinquent kids. His face did not reflect anger so much as puzzlement, as if he had just been presented with a philosophical problem that had no apparent answer. A punishment would have to be meted out, that was certain, but for the moment he seemed to have no idea what to suggest. He didn't want to be harsh, but neither did he want to be too lenient. He needed something to fit the crime, a fair punishment that would have some educational value to it – not punishment for its own sake, but something creative, something that would teach the culprits a lesson.

'I think we have a dilemma here,' he said at last.

'Yes,' Stone said. 'A real dilemma. What you might call a situation.'

'These two fellows owe us money,' Flower continued, acting as though Nashe and Pozzi were no longer there. 'If we let them leave, they'll never pay us back. But if we don't let them leave, they won't have a chance to come up with the money they owe us.'

'I guess you'll just have to trust us, then,' Pozzi said. 'Isn't that right, Mr. Butterball?'

Flower ignored Pozzi's remark and turned to Stone. 'What do you think, Willie?' he said. 'It's something of a quandary, isn't it?'

As he listened to this conversation, Nashe suddenly remembered Juliette's trust fund. It probably wouldn't be difficult to withdraw ten thousand dollars from it, he thought. A call to the bank in Minnesota could get things started, and by the end of the day the money would be sitting in Flower and Stone's account. It was a practical solution, but once he worked out the sequence in his head, he rejected it, appalled at himself for even considering such a thing. The equation was too terrible: to pay off his gambling debts by stealing from his daughter's future. No matter what happened, it was out of the question. He had brought this problem down on himself, and now he would have to take his medicine. Like a man, he thought. He would have to take it like a man.

'Yes,' Stone said, mulling over Flower's last comment, 'it's a difficult one, all right. But that doesn't mean we won't think of something.' He lapsed into thought for ten or twenty seconds, and then his face gradually began to brighten. 'Of course,' he said, 'there's always the wall.'

'The wall?' Flower said. 'What do you mean by that?'

'The wall,' Stone repeated. 'Someone has to build it.'

'Ah . . .,' Flower said, catching on at last. 'The wall! A brilliant idea, Willie. By God, I think you've really surpassed yourself this time.'

'Honest work for an honest wage,' Stone said.

'Exactly,' Flower said. 'And little by little the debt will be paid off.'

But Pozzi was not having any of it. The instant he realized what they were proposing, his mouth literally dropped open in astonishment. 'You've got to be kidding,' he said. 'If you think I'm going to do that, you're out of your minds. There's no way. There's absolutely no fucking way.' Then, starting to lift himself out of his chair, he turned to Nashe and said, 'Come on, Jim, let's get out of here. These two guys are full of shit.'

'Take it easy, kid,' Nashe said. 'There's no harm in listening. We've got to work out something, after all.'

'No harm!' Pozzi shouted. 'They belong in the nuthouse, can't you see that? They're one-hundred-percent bonkers.'

Pozzi's agitation had a curiously calming effect on Nashe, as if the more vehemently the kid acted, the more clearheaded Nashe found it necessary to become. There was no doubt that things had taken a strange turn, but Nashe realized that he had somehow been expecting it, and now that it was happening, there was no panic inside him. He felt lucid, utterly in control of himself.

'Don't worry about it, Jack,' he said. 'Just because they make us an offer, that doesn't mean we have to accept. It's a question of manners, that's all. If they have something to tell us, then we owe them the courtesy of hearing them out.'

'It's a waste of time,' Pozzi muttered, sinking back into his chair. 'You don't negotiate with madmen. Once you start to do that, your brain gets all fucked up.'

'I'm glad you brought your brother along with you,' Flower said, letting out a sigh of disgust. 'At least there's one reasonable man we can talk to.'

'Shit,' Pozzi said. 'He's not my brother. He's just some guy I met on Saturday. I barely even know him.'

'Well, whether you're related to him or not,' Flower said, 'you're lucky to have him here. For the fact is, young man, you're staring at a heap of trouble. You and Nashe owe us ten thousand dollars, and if you try to walk out without paying, we'll call the police. It's as simple as that.'

'I already said we'd listen to you,' Nashe interrupted. 'You don't have to make threats.'

'I'm not making threats,' Flower said. 'I'm just presenting you with the facts. Either you show some cooperation and we work out an amicable arrangement, or we take more drastic measures. There are no other alternatives. Willie has come up with a solution, a perfectly ingenious solution in my opinion, and unless you have something better to offer, I think we should get down to brass tacks.'

'The specifics,' Stone said. 'Hourly wage, living quarters, food. The practical details. It's probably best to get those things settled before we start.'

'You can live right out there in the meadow,' Flower said. 'There's a trailer on the premises already – what they call a mobile home. It hasn't been used for some time, but it's in perfectly good condition. Calvin lived there a few years ago while we were building his cottage for him. So there's no problem about putting you up. All you have to do is move in.'

'It has a kitchen,' Stone added. 'A fully equipped kitchen. A refrigerator, a stove, a sink, all the modern conveniences. A well for water, electrical hookup, baseboard heating. You can do your cooking there and eat whatever you want. Calvin will keep you stocked with supplies, whatever you ask him for he'll bring. Just give him a shopping list every day, and he'll go into town and get what you need.'

'We'll provide you with work clothes, of course,' Flower said, 'and if there's anything else you want, all you have to do is ask. Books, newspapers, magazines. A radio. Extra blankets and towels. Games. Whatever you decide. We don't want you to be uncomfortable, after all. In the final analysis, you might even enjoy yourselves. The work won't be too strenuous, and you'll be outdoors in this beautiful weather. It will be a working holiday, so to speak, a short, therapeutic respite from your normal lives. And every day you'll see another section of the wall go up. That will be immensely satisfying, I think: to see the tangible fruits of your labor, to be able to step back and see the progress you've made. Little by little, the debt will be paid off, and when the time comes for you to go, not only will you walk out of here free men, but you'll have left something important behind you.'

'How long do you think it will take?' Nashe said.

'That depends,' Stone answered. 'You'll get so much per hour. Once your total earnings come to ten thousand dollars, you'll be free to go.'

'What if we finish the wall before we've earned ten thousand dollars?'

'In that case,' Flower said, 'we'll consider the debt paid in full.'

'And if we don't finish, what are you planning to pay us?'

'Something commensurate with the task. A normal wage for workers on this kind of job.'

'Such as?'

'Five, six dollars an hour.'

'That's too low. We won't even consider it for less than twelve.'

'This isn't brain surgery, Mr. Nashe. It's unskilled labor. Piling one stone on top of another. It doesn't require much study to do that.'

'Still, we're not going to do it for six dollars an hour. If you can't do any better than that, you might as well call the police.'

'Eight, then. My final offer.'

'It's still not good enough.'

'Stubborn, aren't you? And what if I went up to ten? What would you say to that?'

'Let's figure it out, and then we'll see.'

'Fine. It won't take but a second. Ten dollars apiece comes to twenty dollars an hour for the two of you. If you put in an average of ten hours of work – just to keep the figures simple – then you'll be earning two hundred dollars a day. Two hundred into ten thousand is fifty. Which means it will take you approximately fifty days. If it's late August now, that comes out to some time in the middle of October. Not so long. You'll be finished just as the leaves are beginning to turn.'

Bit by bit, Nashe found himself giving in to the idea, gradually accepting the wall as the only solution to his predicament. Exhaustion might have played a part in it – the lack of sleep, the inability to think anymore – but somehow he thought not. Where was he going to go, anyway? His money was gone, his car was gone, his life was in a shambles. If nothing else, perhaps those fifty days would give him a chance to take stock, to sit still for the first time in over a year and ponder his next move. It was almost a relief to have the decision taken out of his hands, to know that he had finally stopped running. The wall would not be a punishment so much as a cure, a one-way journey back to earth.

The kid was beside himself, however, and all during the conversation he kept emitting disgruntled, petulant noises, aghast at Nashe's acquiescence and the insane haggling over money. Before Nashe had a chance to shake hands on a deal with Flower, Pozzi grabbed hold of his arm and announced that he had to talk to him in private. Then, not bothering to wait for a response, he yanked Nashe out of his chair and dragged him into the hall, slamming the door shut with his foot.

'Come on,' he said, still pulling on Nashe's arm. 'Let's go. It's time to leave.'

But Nashe shrugged off Pozzi's hand and stood his ground. 'We can't leave,' he said. 'We owe them money, and I'm not in the mood to get hauled off to jail.'

'They're just bluffing. There's no way they'd get the fuzz involved in this.'

'You're wrong, Jack. Guys with money like that can do anything they want. The minute those two called, the cops would jump. We'd be picked up before we were half a mile from here.'

'You sound scared, Jimbo. Not a good sign. It makes you look ugly.'

'I'm not scared. I'm just being smart.'

'Crazy, you mean. Keep it up, pal, and pretty soon you'll be as crazy as they are.'

'It's less than two months, Jack, no big deal. They'll feed us, give us a place to live, and before you know it, we'll be gone. Why worry about it? We might even have some fun.'

'Fun? You call lifting stones fun? It sounds like a goddamn chain gang to me.'

'It can't kill us. Not fifty days of it. Besides, the exercise will probably do us some good. Like lifting weights. People pay good money to do that in health clubs. We've already paid our membership fee, so we might as well take advantage of it.'

'How do you know it will be only fifty days?'

'Because that's the agreement.'

'And what if they don't stick to the agreement?'

'Look, Jack, don't worry so much. If we run into any problems, we'll take care of them.'

'It's a mistake to trust those fuckers, I'm telling you.'

'Then maybe you're right, maybe you should go now. I'm the one who got us into this mess, so the debt is my responsibility.'

'I'm the one who lost.'

'You lost the money, but I'm the one who cut for the car.'

'You mean you'd stay here and do it alone?'

'That's what I'm saying.'

'Then you really are crazy, aren't you?'

'What difference does it make what I am? You're a free man, Jack. You can walk out now, and I won't hold it against you. That's a promise. No hard feelings.'

Pozzi looked at Nashe for a long moment, wrestling with the choice he had just been given, searching Nashe's eyes to see if he had meant what he had said. Then, very slowly, a smile began to form on the kid's face, as if he had just understood the punch line to an obscure joke. 'Shit,' he said. 'Do you really think I'd leave you alone, old man? If you did that work yourself, you'd probably drop dead of a heart attack.'

Nashe had not been expecting it. He had assumed that Pozzi would jump at his offer, and during those moments of certainty, he had already begun to imagine what it would be like to live out in the meadow alone, trying to resign himself to that solitude, coming to a point of such resolve that he was almost beginning to welcome it. But now that the kid was in, he felt glad. As they walked back into the room to announce their decision, it fairly stunned him to realize how glad he was.

They spent the next hour putting it all in writing, drawing up a document that stated the terms of their agreement in the clearest possible language, with clauses that covered the amount of the debt, the conditions of repayment, the hourly wage, and so on. Stone typed it out twice, and then all four of them signed at the bottom of both copies. After that, Flower announced that he was going off to look for Murks and make the necessary arrangements concerning the trailer, the work site, and the purchase of supplies. It would take several hours, he said, and in the meantime they were welcome to have breakfast in the kitchen if they were hungry. Nashe asked a question about the design of the wall, but Flower told him not to trouble himself about that. He and Stone had already finished the blueprints, and Murks knew exactly what had to be done. As long as they followed Calvin's instructions, nothing could go wrong. On that confident note, the fat man left the room, and Stone led Nashe and Pozzi to the kitchen, where he asked Louise to cook up some breakfast for them. Then, mumbling a brief, awkward good-bye, the thin man vanished as well.

The maid clearly resented having to prepare the meal, and as she went about the business of beating eggs and frying bacon, she took out her displeasure by refusing to address a word to either one of them – muttering a string of invective under her breath, acting as if the task were an insult to her dignity. Nashe realized how thoroughly things had changed for them. He and Pozzi had been stripped of their status, and henceforth they would no longer be treated as invited guests. They had been reduced to the level of hired hands, tramps who come begging for leftovers at the back door. It was impossible not to notice the difference, and as he sat there waiting for his food, he wondered how Louise had caught on so quickly to their demotion. The day before, she had been perfectly polite and respectful; now, just sixteen hours later, she could barely hide her contempt for them. And yet neither Flower nor Stone had said a word to her. It was as if some secret communiqué had been broadcast silently through the house, informing her that he and Pozzi no longer counted, that they had been relegated to the category of nonpersons.

But the food was excellent, and they both ate with considerable appetite, wolfing down extra helpings of toast along with numerous cups of coffee. Once their stomachs were full, however, they lapsed into a state of drowsiness, and for the next half hour they struggled to keep their eyes open by smoking more of Pozzi's cigarettes. The long night had finally caught up with them, and neither one seemed capable of talking anymore. Eventually, the kid dozed off in his chair, and for a long time after that Nashe just stared into space, seeing nothing as his body gave in to a deep and languorous exhaustion.

Murks arrived a few minutes past ten, bursting into the kitchen with a clatter of work boots and jangling keys. The noise immediately brought Nashe back to life, and he was out of his chair before Murks reached the table. Pozzi slept on, however, oblivious to the commotion around him.

'What's the matter with him?' Murks said, gesturing with his thumb at Pozzi.

'He had a rough night,' Nashe said.

'Yeah, well, from what I heard, things didn't go too good for you either.'

'I don't need as much sleep as he does.'

Murks pondered the remark for a moment, and then he said, 'Jack and Jim, huh? And which one are you, fella?'

'Jim.'

'I guess that makes your friend Jack.'

'Good thinking. After that, the rest is easy. I'm Jim Nashe, and he's Jack Pozzi. It shouldn't take long for you to get the hang of it.'

'Yeah, I remember. Pozzi. What's he, some kind of Spaniard or something?'

'More or less. He's a direct descendant of Christopher Columbus.'

'No kidding?'

'Would I make up something like that?'

Again, Murks fell silent, as if trying to absorb this curious bit of information. Then, looking at Nashe with his pale blue eyes, he abruptly changed the subject. 'I took your stuff out of the car and put it in the jeep,' he said. 'The bags and all those tapes. I figured you might as well have it with you. They said you're going to be here for a while.'

'And what about the car?'

'I drove it over to my place. If you want, you can sign the registration papers tomorrow. There's no rush.'

'You mean they gave the car to you?'

'Who else? They didn't want it, and Louise just bought a new car last month. It seems like a good one to me. Handles real nice.'

Murks's statement hit him like a fist in the stomach, and for a moment or two Nashe actually felt himself fighting back tears. It had not occurred to him to think about the Saab, and now, all of a sudden, the sense of loss was absolute, as if he had just been told his closest friend was dead. 'Sure,' he said, making a great effort not to show his feelings. 'Just bring the papers around to me tomorrow.'

'Good. We'll be plenty busy today anyway. There's lots to do. Got to get you boys settled in first, and then I'll show you the plans and walk you around the place. You wouldn't believe how many stones there are. It's about like a mountain is what it is, an honest-to-goodness mountain. I ain't never seen so many stones in all my life.'

6

There was no road from the house to the meadow, so Murks drove the jeep straight through the woods. He was apparently an old hand at it, and he charged along at a frenetic pace – maneuvering around the trees with abrupt, hairpin turns, bouncing recklessly over stones and exposed roots, yelling at Nashe and Pozzi to duck clear of hanging branches. The jeep made a tremendous racket, and birds and squirrels scattered as they approached, bolting helter-skelter through the leaf-covered darkness. After Murks had roared along in this way for fifteen minutes or so, the sky suddenly brightened, and they found themselves on a grassy verge studded with low-lying bushes and thin shoots. The meadow was just ahead of them. The first thing Nashe noticed was the trailer – a pale green structure propped up on several rows of cinder blocks – and then, all the way at the other end of the field, he saw the remains of Lord Muldoon's castle. Contrary to what Murks had told them, the stones did not form a mountain so much as a series of mountains – a dozen haphazard piles jutting up from the ground at different angles and elevations, a chaos of towering rubble strewn about like a set of children's blocks. The meadow itself was much larger than Nashe had expected. Surrounded by woods on all four sides, it seemed to cover an area roughly equivalent to three or four football fields: it was an immense territory of short, stubbled grass, as flat and silent as the bottom of a lake. Nashe turned around and looked for the house, but it was no longer visible. He had imagined that Flower and Stone would be standing at a window watching them through a telescope or a pair of binoculars, but the woods were mercifully in the way. Just knowing that he would be hidden from them was something to be thankful for, and in those first moments after climbing from the jeep, he began to sense that he had already won back a measure of his freedom. Yes, the meadow was a desolate place; but there was also a certain forlorn beauty to it, an air of remoteness and calm that could almost be called soothing. Not knowing what else to think, Nashe tried to take heart from that.

The trailer turned out to be not half bad. It was hot and dusty inside, but the dimensions were spacious enough for two people to live there in reasonable comfort: a kitchen, a bathroom, a living room, and two small bedrooms. The electricity worked, the toilet flushed, and water ran into the sink when Murks turned the faucet. The furnishings were sparse, and what there was had a dull and impersonal look to it, but it was no worse than what you found in your average cheap motel. There were towels in the bathroom, the kitchen was stocked with cookware and eating utensils, there was bedding on the beds. Nashe felt relieved, but Pozzi didn't say much of anything, walking through the tour as though his mind were somewhere else. Still brooding about poker, Nashe thought. He decided to leave the kid alone, but it was hard not to wonder how long it would take him to get over it.

They aired out the place by opening the windows and turning on the fan, and then they sat down to study the blueprints in the kitchen. 'We're not talking about anything fancy here,' Murks said, 'but that's probably just as well. This thing's going to be a monster, and there's no point in trying to make it pretty.' He carefully removed the plans from a cardboard cylinder and spread them out on the table, weighting down each corner with a coffee cup. 'What you got here is your basic wall,' he continued. 'Two thousand feet long and twenty feet high – ten rows of a thousand stones each. No twists or turns, no arches or columns, no frills of any sort. Just your basic, no-nonsense wall.'

'Two thousand feet,' Nashe said. 'That's more than a third of a mile long.'

'That's what I'm trying to tell you. This baby is a giant.'

'We'll never finish,' Pozzi said. 'There's no way two men can build that sucker in fifty days.'

'The way I understand it,' Murks said, 'you don't have to. You just put in your time, do as much as you can, and that's it.'

'You got it, gramps,' Pozzi said. 'That's it.'

'We'll see how far you get,' Murks said. 'They say faith can move mountains. Well, maybe muscles can do it, too.'

The plans showed the wall cutting a diagonal line between the northeast and southwest corners of the meadow. As Nashe discovered after studying the diagram, this was the only way a two-thousand-foot wall could fit within the boundaries of the rectangular field (which was roughly twelve hundred feet wide and eighteen hundred feet long). But just because the diagonal was a mathematical necessity, that did not make it a bad choice. To the extent that he bothered to think about it, even Nashe admitted that a slant was preferable to a square. The wall would have a greater visual impact that way – splitting the meadow into triangles rather than boxes – and for whatever it was worth, it pleased him that no other solution was possible.

'Twenty feet high,' Nashe said. 'We're going to need a scaffold, won't we?'

'When the time comes,' Murks said.

'And who's supposed to build it? Not us, I hope.'

'Don't worry about things that might never happen,' Murks said. 'We don't have to think about a scaffold until you get to the third row. That's two thousand stones. If you get that far in fifty days, I can build you something real fast. Won't take me longer than a few hours.'

'And then there's the cement,' Nashe continued. 'Are you going to bring in a machine, or do we have to mix it ourselves?'

'I'll get you bags from the hardware store in town. There's a bunch of wheelbarrows out in the tool shed, and you can use one of those to mix it in. You won't need much – just a dab or two in the right places. Those stones are solid. Once they're up, there ain't nothing that's going to knock them down.'

Murks rolled up the plans and slipped them back into the tube. Nashe and Pozzi then followed him outside, and the three of them climbed into the jeep and drove to the other end of the meadow. Murks explained that the grass was short because he had mowed it just a few days before, and the fact was that it smelled good, adding a hint of sweetness to the air that reminded Nashe of things from long ago. It put him in a pleasant mood, and by the time the little drive was over, he was no longer fretting about the details of the work. The day was too beautiful for that, and with the warmth of the sun pouring down on his face, it seemed ridiculous to worry about anything. Just take it as it comes, he told himself. Just be glad you're alive.

It had been one thing to look at the stones from a distance, but now that he was there, he found it impossible not to want to touch them, to run his hands along their surfaces and discover what they felt like. Pozzi seemed to respond in the same way, and for the first few minutes the two of them just wandered around the clusters of granite, timidly patting the smooth gray blocks. There was something awesome about them, a stillness that was almost frightening. The stones were so massive, so cool against the skin, it was hard to believe they had once belonged to a castle. They felt too old for that – as if they had been dug out from the deepest layers of the earth, as if they were relics from a time before man had ever been dreamt of.

Nashe saw a stray stone at the edge of one of the piles and bent down to lift it, curious to know how heavy it was. The first tug sent a knot of pressure into his lower back, and by the time he had the thing off the ground, he was grunting from the strain of it, feeling as though the muscles in his legs were about to cramp. He took three or four steps and then put it down. 'Jesus,' he said. 'Not very cooperative, is it?'

'They weigh somewhere between sixty and seventy pounds,' Murks said. 'Just enough to make you feel each one.'

'I felt it,' Nashe said. 'There's no doubt about that.'

'So what's the scoop, old-timer?' Pozzi said, turning to Murks. 'Do we move these pebbles with the jeep, or are you going to give us something else? I'm looking around for a truck, but I don't see one in the vicinity.'

Murks smiled and slowly shook his head. 'You don't think they're stupid, do you?'

'What's that supposed to mean?' Nashe said.

'If we give you a truck, you'll just use it to sneak out of here. That's pretty obvious, isn't it? No sense in giving you an opportunity to escape.'

'I didn't know we were in prison,' Nashe said. 'I thought we'd been hired to do some work.'

'That's it,' Murks said. 'But they don't want you welshing on the deal.'

'So how do we move them?' Pozzi said. 'They're not sugar cubes, you know. We can't just stuff them in our pockets.'

'No need to get worked up about it,' Murks said. 'We've got a wagon in the shed, and it'll do the job just fine.'

'It will take forever that way,' Nashe said.

'So what? As long as you put in your hours, you boys are home free. Why should you care how long it takes?'

'God dang it,' Pozzi said, snapping his fingers and talking in a dumb hick's voice. 'Thanks for setting me straight, Calvin. I mean, hell, what's to complain about? We've got our wagon now, and when you consider how much help it'll be with the work – and the Lord's work it is, too, Brother Calvin – I guess we should be feeling pretty happy. I just wasn't looking at it in the right way. Why Jim and me here, we've got to be about the luckiest fellas that ever walked the earth.'

They drove back to the trailer after that and unloaded Nashe's things from the jeep, depositing the suitcases and the bags of books and tapes on the living room floor. Then they sat down at the kitchen table again and drew up a shopping list. Murks did the writing, and he formed his letters so slowly and painstakingly that it took them close to an hour to cover everything: the various foods and drinks and condiments, the work clothes, the boots and gloves, the extra clothes for Pozzi, the sunglasses, the soaps and garbage bags, the flyswatters. Once they had taken care of the essentials, Nashe added a portable radio-tape-player to the list, and Pozzi asked for a number of small items: a deck of cards, a newspaper, a copy of *Penthouse* magazine. Murks told them he would be back by midafternoon, and then, suppressing a yawn, he stood up from the table and began to leave. Just as he was on his way out, however, Nashe remembered a question he had meant to ask before.

'I wonder if I could make a phone call,' he said.

'There's no phone here,' Murks said. 'You can see that for yourself.'

'Maybe you could drive me back to the house, then.'

'What do you want to make a phone call for?'

'I doubt that's any of your business, Calvin.'

'No, I don't suppose it is. But I can't just take you to the house without knowing why.'

'I want to call my sister. She's expecting me in a few days, and I don't want her to worry when I don't show up.'

Murks thought about it for a moment and then shook his head. 'Sorry. I'm not allowed to take you there. They gave me special instructions.'

'How about a telegram? If I wrote down the message, you could call it in yourself.'

'No, I couldn't do that. The bosses wouldn't like it. But you can send a postcard if you want to. I'd be happy to mail it for you.'

'Make it a letter. You can buy me some paper and envelopes in town. If I send it tomorrow, I suppose it will reach her in time.'

'Okay, paper and envelopes. You got it.'

After Murks had driven off in the jeep, Pozzi turned to Nashe and said, 'Do you think he'll mail it?'

'I have no idea. If I had to bet on it, I'd say there's a good chance. But it's hard to be sure.'

'One way or another, you'll never know. He'll tell you he sent it, but that doesn't mean you can trust him.'

'I'll ask my sister to write back. If she doesn't, then we'll know our friend Murks was lying.'

Pozzi lit a cigarette and then pushed the pack of Marlboros across the table to Nashe, who debated for a moment before accepting. Smoking the cigarette made him realize how tired he was, how utterly drained of energy. He snubbed it out after three or four puffs and said, 'I think I'm going to take a nap. There's nothing to do now anyway, so I might as well try out my new bed. Which room do you want, Jack? I'll take the other one.'

'I don't care,' Pozzi answered. 'Take your pick.'

As Nashe stood up, he moved in such a way that the wooden figures in his pocket were disturbed. They pressed uncomfortably against his leg, and for the first time since stealing them, he remembered they were there. 'Look at this,' he said, pulling out Flower and Stone and standing them on the table. 'Our two little friends.'

Pozzi scowled, then slowly broke into a smile as he examined the minuscule, lifelike men. 'Where the hell did they come from?'

'Where do you think?'

Pozzi looked up at Nashe with an odd, disbelieving expression on his face. 'You didn't steal them, did you?'

'Of course I did. How else do you think they wound up in my pocket?'

'You're nuts, you know that? You're even nuttier than I thought you were.'

'It didn't seem right to walk off without taking a souvenir,' Nashe said, smiling as though he had just received a compliment.

Pozzi smiled back, clearly impressed by Nashe's audacity. 'They're not going to be too happy when they find out,' he said.

'Too bad for them.'

'Yeah,' Pozzi said, picking up the two tiny men from the table and studying them more closely, 'too bad for them.'

Nashe shut the blinds in his room, stretched out on the bed, and fell asleep as the sounds of the meadow washed over him. Birds sang in the distance, the wind passed through the trees, a cicada clicked in the grass below his window. His last thought before losing consciousness was of Juliette and her birthday. October twelfth was forty-six days away, he told himself. If he had to spend the next fifty nights sleeping in this bed, he wasn't going to make it. In spite of what he had promised her, he would still be in Pennsylvania on the day of her party.

*

The next morning, Nashe and Pozzi learned that building a wall was not as simple as they had imagined. Before the actual construction could get underway, all sorts of preparations had to be attended to. Lines had to be drawn, a trench had to be dug, a flat surface had to be created. 'You can't just plop down stones and hope for the best,' Murks said. 'You've got to do things right.'

Their first job was to roll out two parallel lengths of string and stretch them between the corners of the meadow, marking off the space to be occupied by the wall. Once those lines had been established, Nashe and Pozzi fastened the string to small wooden stakes and then drove the stakes into the ground at five-foot intervals. It was a laborious process that entailed constant measuring and remeasuring, but Nashe and Pozzi were in no particular rush, since they knew that each hour spent with the string would mean one less hour they would have to spend lifting stones. Considering that there were eight hundred stakes to be planted, the three days it took them to finish this task did not seem excessive. Under different circumstances, they might have dragged it out a bit longer, but Murks was never very far away, and his pale blue eyes did not miss a trick.

The next morning they were handed shovels and told to dig a shallow trench between the two lines of string. The fate of the wall hinged on making the bottom of that trench as level as possible, and they therefore proceeded with caution, advancing by only the smallest of increments. Since the meadow was not perfectly flat, they were obliged to eliminate the various bumps and hillocks they encountered along the way, uprooting grass and weeds with their shovels, then turning to picks and crowbars to extract any stones that were lodged beneath the surface. Some of these stones turned out to be fiercely resistant. They refused to unlock themselves from the earth, and Nashe and Pozzi spent the better part of six days doing battle with them, struggling to wrench each one of these impediments from the stubborn soil. The larger stones left behind holes, of course, which subsequently had to be filled in with dirt; then all the excess matter disgorged by the excavation had to be carted off in wheelbarrows and dumped in the woods that surrounded the meadow. The work was slow going, but neither one of them found it especially difficult. By the time they came to the finishing touches, in fact, they were almost beginning to enjoy it. For an entire afternoon they did nothing but smooth out the bottom of the trench, then pound it flat with hoes. For the space of those few hours, the job felt no more strenuous than working in a garden.

It did not take them long to settle into their new life. After three or four days in the meadow, the routine was already familiar to them, and by the end of the first week they no longer had to think about it. Every morning, Nashe's alarm clock would wake them at six. Then, after taking turns in the bathroom, they would go into the kitchen and cook breakfast (Pozzi handling the orange juice, toast, and coffee, Nashe preparing the scrambled eggs and sausages). Murks would show up promptly at seven, give a little knock at the trailer door, and then they would step out into the meadow to begin the day's work. After doing a five-hour shift in the morning, they would return to the trailer for lunch (an hour off without pay), and then put in another five hours in the afternoon. Quitting time came at six o'clock, and that was always a good moment for both of them, a prelude to the comforts of a warm shower and a quiet beer in the living room. Nashe would then withdraw to the kitchen and prepare dinner (simple concoctions for the most part, the old American standbys: steaks and chops, chicken casseroles, mounds of potatoes and vegetables, puddings and ice cream for dessert), and once they had filled their stomachs, Pozzi would do his bit by cleaning up the mess. After that, Nashe would stretch out on the living room sofa, listening to music and reading books, and Pozzi would sit down at the kitchen table and play solitaire. Sometimes they talked, sometimes they said nothing. Sometimes they went outside and played a form of basketball that Pozzi had invented: throwing pebbles into a garbage can from a distance of ten feet. And once or twice, when the evening air was especially beautiful, they sat on the steps of the trailer and watched the sun go down behind the woods.

Nashe was not nearly as restless as he had thought he would be. Once he accepted the fact that the car was gone, he felt little or no desire to be back on the road, and the ease with which he adjusted to his new circumstances left him somewhat bewildered. It made no sense that he should be able to abandon it all so quickly. But Nashe discovered that he liked working out in the open air, and after a while the stillness of the meadow seemed to have a tranquilizing effect on him, as if the grass and the trees had brought about a change in his metabolism. That did not mean he felt entirely at home there, however. An atmosphere of suspicion and mistrust continued to hover around the place, and Nashe resented the implication that he and the kid were not going to keep their end of the bargain. They had given their word, they had even put their signatures on a contract, and yet the whole setup was built on the assumption that they would try to escape. Not only were they not allowed to work with machines, but Murks now came to the meadow every morning on foot, proving that even the jeep was considered too dangerous a temptation, as if its presence would make it impossible to resist stealing it. These precautions were bad enough, but even more sinister was the chain-link fence that Nashe and Pozzi discovered on the evening that followed their first full day of work. After dinner, they had decided to explore some of the wooded areas that surrounded the meadow. They went to the far end first, entering the woods along a dirt path that appeared to have been cut quite recently. Felled trees lay on either side of it, and from the tire tracks embedded in the soft, loamy earth, they gathered that this was where the trucks had driven in to deliver their cargo of stones. Nashe and Pozzi kept on walking, but before they reached the highway that marked the northern edge of the property, they were stopped by the fence. It was eight or nine feet tall, crowned by a menacing tangle of barbed wire. One section looked newer than the rest, which seemed to indicate that a piece of it had been removed to allow the trucks in, but other than that, all traces of entry had been eliminated. They continued walking alongside the fence, wondering if they would find any break in it, and by the time darkness fell an hour and a half later, they had returned to the same spot where they had begun. At one point, they passed the stone gate they had driven through on the day of their arrival, but that was the only interruption. The fence went everywhere, encompassing the entire extent of Flower and Stone's domain.

They did their best to laugh it off, saying that rich people always lived behind fences, but that did not erase the memory of what they had seen. The barrier had been erected to keep things out, but now that it was there, what was to prevent it from keeping things in as well? All sorts of threatening possibilities were buried in that question. Nashe tried not to let his imagination run away from him, but it was not until a letter from Donna arrived on the eighth day that he was able to put his fears to rest. Pozzi found it reassuring that someone knew where they were now, but as far as Nashe was concerned, the important thing was that Murks had kept his promise. The letter was a demonstration of good faith, tangible proof that no one had been out to deceive them.

All during those early days in the meadow, Pozzi's conduct was exemplary. He seemed to have made up his mind to stick by Nashe, and no matter what was asked of him, he did not complain. He went about his work with stolid goodwill, he pitched in with the household chores, he even pretended to enjoy the classical music that Nashe played every night after dinner. Nashe had not expected the kid to be so obliging, and he was grateful to him for making the effort. But the truth was that he was merely getting back what he had already earned. He had gone the full distance for Pozzi on the night of the poker match, pushing on past any reasonable limit, and even though he had been wiped out in the process, he had won himself a friend. That friend now seemed prepared to do anything for him, even if it meant living in a godforsaken meadow for the next fifty days, busting his chops like some convict sentenced to a term at hard labor.

Still, loyalty was not the same thing as belief. From Pozzi's point of view, the whole situation was absurd, and just because he had chosen to support his friend, that did not mean he felt that Nashe was in his right mind. The kid was indulging him, and once Nashe understood that, he did everything in his power to keep his thoughts to himself. The days passed, and even though there was rarely a moment when they were not together, he continued to say nothing about what truly concerned him – nothing about the struggle to put his life together again, nothing about how he saw the wall as a chance to redeem himself in his own eyes, nothing about how he welcomed the hardships of the meadow as a way to atone for his recklessness and self-pity – for once he got started, he knew that all the wrong words would come tumbling from his mouth, and he didn't want to make Pozzi any more nervous than he already was. The point was to keep him in good spirits, to get him through the fifty days as painlessly as possible. Much better to speak of things only in the most superficial terms – the debt, the contract, the hours they put in – and to bluster along with funny remarks and ironic shrugs of the shoulders. It was sometimes a lonely business for Nashe, but he didn't see what else he could do. If he ever bared his soul to the kid, all hell would break loose. It would be like opening a can of worms, like asking for the worst kind of trouble.

Pozzi continued on his best behavior with Nashe, but with Murks it was another story, and not a day went by when he didn't tease him and insult him and verbally attack him. In the beginning, Nashe interpreted it as a good sign, thinking that if the kid could return to his old rambunctious self, then perhaps that meant he was coping with the situation fairly well. The abuse was delivered with such sarcasm, with such an assortment of smiles and sympathetic nods of the head, that Murks barely seemed to know he was being made fun of. Nashe, who had no particular liking for Murks himself, did not blame Pozzi for letting off a little steam at the foreman's expense. But as time went on, he began to feel that the kid was carrying it too far – not just acting out of innate subversiveness, but responding to panic, to pent-up fears and confusion. The kid made Nashe think of a cornered animal, waiting to strike at the first thing that approached it. As it happened, that thing was always Murks, but no matter how obnoxious Pozzi became, no matter how provocative he tried to be, old Calvin never flinched. There was something so deeply imperturbable about the man, so fundamentally oblique and humorless, that Nashe could never decide if he was inwardly laughing at them or just plain dumb. He simply went about his job, plodding along at the same slow and thorough pace, never offering a word about himself, never asking any questions of Nashe or Pozzi, never showing the slightest hint of anger or curiosity or pleasure. He came punctually every morning at seven, delivering whatever groceries and provisions had been ordered the day before, and then he was all business for the next eleven hours. It was difficult to know what he thought about the wall, but he supervised the work with meticulous attention to detail, leading Nashe and Pozzi through each step of the construction as though he knew what he was talking about. He kept his distance from them, however, and never lent a hand or involved himself in any of the physical aspects of the work. His job was to oversee the building of the wall, and he adhered to that role with strict and absolute superiority over the men in his charge. Murks had the smugness of someone content with his place in the hierarchy, and as with most of the sergeants and crew chiefs of this world, his loyalties were firmly on the side of the people who told him what to do. He never ate lunch with Nashe and Pozzi, for example, and when the workday was done, he never lingered to chat. Work stopped precisely at six, and that was always the end of it. 'See you tomorrow, boys,' he would say, and then he would shuffle off into the woods, disappearing from sight within a matter of seconds.

It took them nine days to finish the preliminaries. Then they started in on the wall itself, and the world suddenly changed again. As Nashe and

Pozzi discovered, it was one thing to lift a sixty-pound stone, but once that stone had been lifted, it was quite another thing to lift a second sixty-pound stone, and still another thing to take on a third stone after lifting the second. No matter how strong they felt while lifting the first, much of that strength would be gone by the time they came to the second, and once they had lifted the second, there would be still less of that strength to call upon for the third. So it went. Every time they worked on the wall, Nashe and Pozzi came up against the same bewitching conundrum: all the stones were identical, and yet each stone was heavier than the one before it.

They spent the mornings hauling stones across the meadow in a little red wagon, depositing each one along the side of the trench and then going back for another. In the afternoons, they worked with trowels and cement, carefully putting the stones into place. Of the two jobs, it was difficult to know which one was worse: the endless lifting and lowering that went on in the mornings, or the pushing and shoving that started in after lunch. The first took more out of them, perhaps, but there was a hidden reward in having to move the stones over such great distances. Murks had instructed them to begin at the far end of the trench, and each time they dropped off another stone, they had to go back empty-handed for the next one – which gave them a small interval in which to catch their breath. The second job was less taxing, but it was also more relentless. There were the brief pauses to slap on the cement, but they were not nearly as long as the return walks across the meadow, and when it came right down to it, it was probably harder to move a stone several inches than to raise it off the ground and put it in a wagon. When all the other variables were taken into consideration – the fact that they usually felt stronger in the morning, the fact that the weather was usually hotter in the afternoon, the fact that their disgust inevitably mounted as the day wore on – it was probably a wash. Six of one, half a dozen of another.

They carted the stones in a Fast Flyer, the same kind of children's wagon that Nashe had bought for Juliette on her third birthday. It seemed like a joke at first, and both he and Pozzi had laughed when Murks wheeled it out and presented it to them. 'You're not serious, are you?' Nashe said. But Murks was very serious, and in the long run the toy wagon proved more than adequate for the job: its metal body could support the loads, and its rubber tires were sturdy enough to withstand any bumps and divots in the terrain. Still, there was something ridiculous about having to use such a thing, and Nashe resented the weird, infantilizing effect it had on him. The wagon did not belong in the hands of a grown man. It was an object fit for the nursery, for the trivial, make-believe worlds of children, and every time he pulled it across the meadow, he felt ashamed of himself, afflicted by a sense of his own helplessness.

The work advanced slowly, by almost imperceptible degrees. On a good morning, they could move twenty-five or thirty stones over to the trench, but never more than that. If Pozzi had been a little stronger, they could have doubled their progress, but the kid wasn't up to lifting the stones by himself. He was too small and frail, too unaccustomed to manual work. He could get the stones off the ground, but once he had them there, he was incapable of carrying them for any distance. As soon as he tried to walk, the weight would throw him off balance, and by the time he had taken two or three steps, the thing would start to slip out of his hands. Nashe, who had eight inches and seventy pounds on the kid, did not experience any of these difficulties. It wouldn't have been fair for him to do all the work, however, and so they wound up lifting the stones in tandem. Even then, it still would have been possible to load the wagon with two stones (which would have upped their progress by roughly a third), but Pozzi did not have it in him to pull over a hundred pounds. He could handle sixty or seventy without much strain, and since they had agreed to split the work down the middle – which meant that they took turns pulling the wagon – they kept each load to a single stone. In the end, that was probably for the best. The work was grueling enough anyway, and there was no point in letting it crush them.

Little by little, Nashe settled into it. The first few days were the hardest, and there was rarely a moment when he was not dragged down by an almost intolerable exhaustion. His muscles ached, his mind was clouded over, his body called out constantly for sleep. He had been softened by all those months of sitting in the car, and the relatively light work of the first nine days had done nothing to prepare him for the shock of real exertion. But Nashe was still young, still strong enough to recover from his long bout of inactivity, and as time went on, he began to notice that he was becoming tired a bit later in the day, that whereas previously a morning's work had been enough to bring him to the limit of his endurance, he was now able to get through a large part of the afternoon before that happened. Eventually, he found that it was no longer necessary to crawl into bed straight after dinner. He started reading books again, and by the middle of the second week, he understood that the worst of it was behind him.

Pozzi, on the other hand, did not adjust so well. The kid had been reasonably happy during the early days of digging the trench, but once they moved on to the next stage of the work, he grew more and more miserable. There was no question that the stones took more out of him than they took out of Nashe, but his irritability and moroseness seemed to have less to do with physical suffering than with a sense of moral outrage. The work was appalling to him, and the longer it went on, the more obvious it became to him that he was the victim of a terrible injustice, that his rights had been abused in some monstrous, unspeakable way. He kept going over the poker game with Flower and Stone, again and again replaying the hands out loud to Nashe, unable to accept the fact that he had lost. By the time he had been working on the wall for ten days, he was convinced that he had been cheated, that Flower and Stone had stolen the money by using marked cards or some other illegal trick. Nashe did his best to steer clear of the subject, but the truth was that he was not entirely convinced Pozzi was wrong. The same thought had already occurred to him, but without any evidence to support the accusation, he saw no point in encouraging the kid. Even if he was right, there wasn't a damned thing they could do about it.

Pozzi kept waiting for a chance to have it out with Flower and Stone, but the millionaires never showed up. Their absence was inexplicable, and as time went on, Nashe became more and more perplexed by it. He had assumed that they would come poking around the meadow every day. The wall was their idea, after all, and it seemed only natural that they should want to know how the work was coming along. But the weeks passed, and still there was no sign of them. Whenever Nashe asked Murks where they were, Calvin would shrug his shoulders, look down at the ground, and say that they were busy. It didn't make any sense. Nashe tried talking to Pozzi about it, but the kid was off in another orbit by then, and he always had a ready answer for him. 'It means they're guilty,' he would say. 'The fuckers know I'm on to them, and they're too scared to show their faces.'

One night, Pozzi drank five or six beers after dinner and got himself good and drunk. He was in a foul mood, and after a while he began to stagger around the trailer, spouting all kinds of gibberish about the raw deal he was getting. 'I'm going to fix those shitbirds,' he told Nashe. 'I'm going to make that gumbo-gut confess.' Without stopping to explain what he had in mind, he grabbed a flashlight off the kitchen counter, opened the door of the trailer, and plunged out into the darkness. Nashe scrambled to his feet and went after him, shouting at the kid to come back. 'Get off my case, fireman,' Pozzi said, waving the flashlight wildly around the grass. 'If those turds won't come out here to talk to us, then we'll just have to go to them.'

Short of punching him in the face, Nashe realized, there wasn't any way he could stop him. The kid was juiced, utterly beyond the pull of words, and trying to talk him out of it wasn't going to help. But Nashe had no desire to hit Pozzi. The thought of beating up a desperate, drunken kid was hardly his idea of a solution, and so he made up his mind to do nothing – to play along and see that Pozzi kept himself out of trouble.

They walked through the woods together, guiding themselves by the beam of the flashlight. It was close to eleven o'clock, and the sky was overcast, obscuring the moon and whatever stars there might have been. Nashe kept expecting to see a light from the house, but all was dark over in that direction, and after a while he wasn't sure if they would ever find it. It seemed to be taking a long time, and what with Pozzi tripping over stones and knocking into thorny bushes, the whole expedition began to feel rather pointless. But then they were there, stepping onto the edge of the lawn and approaching the house. It seemed too early for Flower and Stone to be in bed, but not a single window was lit. Pozzi walked around to the front door and pushed the bell, which again played the opening bars of Beethoven's Fifth Symphony. The kid muttered something under his breath, not half as amused as he had been the first time, and waited for someone to open the door. But nothing happened, and after fifteen or twenty seconds he rang again.

'It looks like they're out for the night,' Nashe said.

'No, they're in there,' Pozzi said. 'They're just too chicken to answer.'

But no lights went on after the second ring, and the door remained closed.

'I think it's time to give it up,' Nashe said. 'If you want to, we'll come back tomorrow.'

'What about the maid?' Pozzi said. 'You figure she's got to be in. We could leave a message with her.'

'Maybe she's a heavy sleeper. Or maybe they gave her the night off. It looks pretty dead in there to me.'

Pozzi kicked the door in frustration, then suddenly began to curse at the top of his voice. Instead of ringing a third time, he stepped back into the driveway and continued shouting at one of the upstairs windows, venting his rage at the empty house. 'Hey, Flower!' he boomed. 'That's right, fat man, I'm talking to you! You're a creep, mister, you know that? You and your little friend, you're both creeps, and you're going to pay for what you did to me!' It went on like that for a good three or four minutes, a belligerent outpouring of wild and useless threats, and even as it grew in intensity, it became progressively more pathetic, more dismal in the shrillness of its despair. Nashe's heart filled with pity for the kid, but there wasn't much he could do until Pozzi's anger burned itself out. He stood in the darkness, watching the bugs swarm in the beam of the flashlight. Off in the distance an owl hooted once, twice, and then stopped.

'Come on, Jack,' Nashe said. 'Let's head back to the trailer and get some sleep.'

But Pozzi wasn't quite finished. Before leaving, he bent down in the driveway, scooped up a handful of pebbles, and threw them at the house. It was a stupid gesture, the petty wrath of a twelve-year-old. The gravel splattered like buckshot off the hard surface, and then, almost as an echo, Nashe heard the faint treble sound of breaking glass.

'Let's call it a night,' he said. 'I think we've had enough.'

Pozzi turned and started walking toward the woods. 'Assholes,' he said to himself. 'The whole world is run by assholes.'

After that night, Nashe understood that he would have to keep a closer watch over the kid. Pozzi's inner resources were being used up, and they hadn't even come to the halfway point of their term. Without making an issue of it, Nashe began doing more than his share of the work, lifting and carting stones by himself while Pozzi rested, figuring that a little more sweat on his part might help to keep things under control. He didn't want any more outbursts or drunken binges, he didn't want to be constantly worrying that the kid was about to crack up. He could take the extra work, and in the long run it seemed simpler than trying to lecture Pozzi on the virtues of patience. It would all be over in thirty days, he told himself, and if he couldn't manage to see it through until then, what kind of a man was he?

He gave up reading books after dinner and spent those hours with Pozzi instead. The evening was a dangerous time, and it didn't help matters to let the kid sit there brooding alone in the kitchen, working himself into a frenzy of murderous thoughts. Nashe tried to be subtle about it, but from then on he put himself at Pozzi's disposal. If the kid felt like playing cards, he would play cards with him; if the kid felt like having a few drinks, he would open a bottle and match him glass for glass. As long as they were talking to each other, it didn't matter how they filled the time. Every now and then, Nashe would tell stories about the year he had spent on the road, or else he would talk about some of the big fires he had fought in Boston, dwelling on the most ghastly details for Pozzi's benefit, thinking it might get the kid's mind off his own troubles if he heard about what other people had gone through. For a short time at least, Nashe's strategy seemed to work. The kid became noticeably calmer, and the vicious talk about confronting Flower and Stone suddenly stopped, but it wasn't long before new obsessions rose up to replace the old ones. Nashe could handle most of them without much difficulty – girls, for example, and Pozzi's growing preoccupation with getting laid – but others were not so easy to dismiss. It wasn't as though the kid were threatening anyone, but every once in a while, right in the middle of a conversation, he would come out with such schizy, crackpot stuff, it would scare Nashe just to hear it.

'It was going along just the way I'd planned it,' Pozzi said to him one night. 'You remember that, Jim, don't you? Real smooth it was, as good as you could possibly want it. I'd just about tripled our stake, and there I was, getting ready to zero in for the kill. Those shits were finished. It was just a matter of time before they went belly-up, I could feel it in my bones. That's the feeling I always wait for. It's like a switch turns on inside me, and my whole body starts to hum. Whenever I get that feeling, it means I'm home free, I can coast all the way to the end. Do you follow what I'm saying, Jim? Until that night, I'd never been wrong about it, not once.'

'There's a first time for everything,' Nashe said, still not sure what the kid was driving at.

'Maybe. But it's hard to believe that's what happened to us. Once your luck starts to roll, there's not a damn thing that can stop it. It's like the whole world suddenly falls into place. You're kind of outside your body, and for the rest of the night you sit there watching yourself perform miracles. It doesn't really have anything to do with you anymore. It's out of your control, and as long as you don't think about it too much, you can't make a mistake.'

'It looked good for a while, Jack, I'll admit that. But then it started to turn around. Those are the breaks, and there's nothing to be done about it. It's like a batter who goes four for four, and then the game goes into the bottom of the ninth, and the next time up he strikes out with the bases loaded. His team loses, and maybe you can say he's responsible for the loss. But that doesn't mean he had a bad night.'

'No, you're not listening to me. I'm telling you there's no way I can strike out in that situation. The ball looks as big as a fucking watermelon to me by then. I just step into the batter's box, wait for my pitch, and then swat it up the gap for the game-winning hit.'

'All right, you hit a line drive into the gap. But the center fielder is after it like a shot, and just when the ball is about to go past him, he leaps up and snags it in the webbing of his glove. It's an impossible catch, one of the great catches of all time. But it's still an out, isn't it, and there's no way you can fault the batter for not doing his best. That's all I'm trying to tell you, Jack. You did your best, and we lost. Worse things have happened in the history of the world. It's not something to worry about anymore.'

'Yeah, but you still don't understand what I'm talking about. I'm just not getting through to you.'

'It sounds fairly simple to me. For most of the night, it looked like we were going to win. But then something went wrong, and we didn't.'

'Exactly. Something went wrong. And what do you think it was?'

'I don't know, kid. You tell me.'

'It was you. You broke the rhythm, and after that everything went haywire.'

'As I remember it, you were the one playing cards. The only thing I did was sit there and watch.'

'But you were a part of it. Hour after hour, you sat there right behind me, breathing down my neck. At first it was a little distracting to have you so close, but then I got used to it, and after a while I knew you were there for a reason. You were breathing life into me, pal, and every time I felt your breath, good luck came pouring into my bones. It was all so perfect. We had everything balanced, all the wheels were turning, and it was beautiful, man, really beautiful. And then you had to get up and leave.'

'A call of nature. You didn't expect me to piss in my pants, did you?'

'Sure, fine, go to the bathroom. I don't have any problem with that. But how long does it take? Three minutes? Five minutes? Sure, go ahead and take a leak. But Christ, Jim, you were gone for a whole fucking hour!'

'I was worn out. I had to lie down and take a nap.'

'Yeah, but you didn't take any nap, did you? You went upstairs and started prowling around that dumb-ass City of the World. Why the hell did you have to do a crazy thing like that? I'm sitting downstairs waiting for you to come back, and little by little I start to lose my concentration. Where is he? I keep saying to myself, what the hell happened to him? It's getting worse now, and I'm not winning as many hands as I was before. And then, just at the moment when things get really bad, it pops into your head to steal a chunk of the model. I can't believe what a mistake that was. No class, Jim, an amateurish stunt. It's like committing a sin to do a thing like that, it's like violating a fundamental law. We had everything in harmony. We'd come to the point where everything was turning into music for us, and then you have to go upstairs and smash all the instruments. You tampered with the universe, my friend, and once a man does that, he's got to pay the price. I'm just sorry I have to pay it with you.'

'You're starting to sound like Flower, Jack. The guy wins the lottery, and all of a sudden he thinks he was chosen by God.'

'I'm not talking about God. God has nothing to do with it.'

'It's just another word for the same thing. You want to believe in some hidden purpose. You're trying to persuade yourself there's a reason for what happens in the world. I don't care what you call it – God or luck or harmony – it all comes down to the same bullshit. It's a way of avoiding the facts, of refusing to look at how things really work.'

'You think you're smart, Nashe, but you don't know a goddamn thing.'

'That's right, I don't. And neither do you, Jack. We're just a pair of know-nothings, you and I, a couple of dunces who got in over our heads. Now we're trying to square the account. If we don't mess up, we'll be out of here in twenty-seven days. I'm not saying it's fun, but maybe we'll learn something before it's over.'

'You shouldn't have done it, Jim. That's all I'm trying to tell you. Once you stole those little men, things went out of whack.'

Nashe let out a sigh of exasperation, stood up from his chair, and pulled the model of Flower and Stone from his pocket. Then he walked over to where Pozzi was sitting and held the figures in front of his eyes. 'Take a good look,' he said, 'and tell me what you see.'

'Christ,' Pozzi said. 'What do you want to be playing games for?'

'Just look,' Nashe said sharply. 'Come on, Jack, tell me what I'm holding in my hand.'

Pozzi stared up at Nashe with a wounded expression in his eyes, then reluctantly obeyed him. 'Flower and Stone,' he said.

'Flower and Stone? I thought Flower and Stone were bigger than this. I mean, look at them, Jack, these two guys aren't more than an inch and a half tall.'

'Okay, so they're not really Flower and Stone. It's what you call a replica.'

'It's a piece of wood, isn't it? A stupid little piece of wood. Isn't that right, Jack?'

'If you say so.'

'And yet you believe this little scrap of wood is stronger than we are, don't you? You think it's so strong, in fact, that it made us lose all our money.'

'That's not what I said. I just meant you shouldn't have pinched it. Some other time, maybe, but not when we were playing poker.'

'But here it is. And every time you look at it, you get a little scared, don't you? It's like they're casting an evil spell over you.'

'Sort of.'

'What do you want me to do with them? Should I give them back? Would that make you feel better?'

'It's too late now. The damage has already been done.'

'There's a remedy for everything, kid. A good Catholic boy like you should know that. With the proper medicine, any illness can be cured.'

'You've lost me now. I don't know what the fuck you're talking about.'

'Just watch. In a few minutes, all your troubles will be over.'

Without saying another word, Nashe went into the kitchen and retrieved a baking tin, a book of matches, and a newspaper. When he returned to the living room, he put the baking tin on the floor, positioning it just a few inches in front of Pozzi's feet. Then he crouched down and placed the figures of Flower and Stone in the center of the tin. He tore out a sheet of newspaper, tore that sheet into several strips, and wadded each strip into a little ball. Then, very delicately, he put the balls around the wooden statue in the tin. He paused for a moment at that point to look into Pozzi's eyes, and when the kid didn't say anything, he went ahead and lit a match. One by one, he touched the flame to the paper wads, and by the time they were fully ignited, the fire had caught hold of the wooden figures, producing a bright surge of crackling heat as the colors burned and melted away. The wood below was soft and porous, and it could not resist the onslaught. Flower and Stone turned black, shrinking as the fire ate into their bodies, and less than a minute later, the two little men were gone.

Nashe pointed to the ashes at the bottom of the tin and said, 'You see? There's nothing to it. Once you know the magic formula, no obstacle is too great.'

The kid finally pulled his eyes away from the floor and looked at Nashe. 'You're out of your mind,' he said. 'I hope you realize that.'

'If I am, then that makes two of us, my friend. At least you won't have to suffer alone anymore. That's something to be thankful for, isn't it? I'm with you every step of the way, Jack. Every damned step, right to the end of the road.'

By the middle of the fourth week, the weather started to turn. The warm, humid skies gave way to the chill of early fall, and on most mornings now they went off to work wearing sweaters. The bugs had disappeared, the battalions of gnats and mosquitoes that had plagued them for so long, and with the leaves beginning to change color in the woods, dying into a profusion of yellows and oranges and reds, it was hard not to feel a little better about things. The rain could be nasty at times, it was true, but even rain seemed preferable to the rigors of the heat, and they did not let it stop them from going on with their work. They were provided with rubber ponchos and baseball caps, and those served reasonably well to protect them from the downpours. The essential thing was to push on, to put in their ten hours every day and wrap up their business on schedule. Since the beginning, they had not taken any time off, and they weren't about to let a little rain intimidate them now. On this point, curiously enough, Pozzi was the more determined of the two. But that was because he was more eager than Nashe to finish, and even on the stormiest, most gloomy days, he trudged off to work without protesting. In some sense, the more violent the weather, the happier he was – for Murks had to be out there with them, and nothing pleased Pozzi more than the sight of the grim, bowlegged foreman decked out in his yellow raingear, standing under a black umbrella for all those hours as his boots sank deeper and deeper into the mud. He loved to see the old guy suffer like that. It was a form of consolation, somehow, a small payback for all the suffering he had gone through himself.

The rain caused problems, however. One day in the last week of September it came down so hard that nearly a third of the trench was destroyed. They had put in approximately seven hundred stones by then, and they were figuring to complete the bottom row in another ten or twelve days. But a huge storm blew up overnight, pummeling the meadow with ferocious, windswept rain, and when they went out the next morning to begin work, they discovered that the exposed portion of the trench had filled up with several inches of water. Not only would it be impossible to put in any more stones until the dirt dried, but all the exacting, meticulous labor of leveling the bottom of the trench had been ruined. The foundation for the wall had turned into an oozing mess of rivulets and mud. They spent the next three days carting stones in the afternoon as well as the morning, filling in the time as best they could, and then, when the water finally evaporated, they abandoned the stones for a couple of days and set about rebuilding the bottom of the trench. It was at this juncture that things finally exploded between Pozzi and Murks. Calvin was suddenly involved in the work again, and instead of standing off to the side and watching them from a safe distance (as he was wont to do), he now spent his days hovering around them, fussing and nagging with constant little comments and instructions to make sure the repairs were done correctly. Pozzi bore up to it on the first morning, but when the interference continued through the afternoon, Nashe could see that it was starting to get under his skin. Another three or four hours went by, and then the kid finally lost his temper.

'All right, big mouth,' he said, throwing down his shovel and glaring at Murks in disgust, 'if you're such an expert at all this, then why the fuck don't you do it yourself!'

Murks paused for a moment, apparently caught off guard. 'Because it's not my job,' he finally said, speaking in a very low voice. 'You boys are supposed to do the work. I'm just here to see you don't screw up.'

'Yeah?' the kid came back at him. 'And what makes you so high and mighty, Mr. Potato Head? How come you get to stand there with your goddamn hands in your pockets while we're busting our dicks in this dungheap? Huh? Come on, Mr. Bumpkin, out with it. Give me one good reason.'

'That's simple,' Murks said, unable to suppress the smile that was forming on his lips. 'Because you play cards and I don't.'

It was the smile that did it, Nashe felt. A look of deep and genuine contempt flashed across Murks's face, and a moment later Pozzi was charging toward him with clenched fists. At least one blow landed cleanly, for by the time Nashe managed to pull the kid away, blood was dribbling from a corner of Calvin's mouth. Pozzi, still seething with unspent rage, bucked wildly in Nashe's arms for close to a minute after that, but Nashe held on for all he was worth, and eventually the kid settled down. Meanwhile, Murks had backed off a few feet and was dabbing the cut with a handkerchief. 'It don't matter,' he finally said. 'The little squirt can't handle the pressure, that's all. Some guys got what it takes, others don't. The only thing I'm going to say is this: Just don't let it happen again. Next time I won't be so nice about it.' He looked down at the watch on his wrist and said, 'I think we'll knock off early today. It's getting on close to five now, and there's no sense in starting up again with tempers so hot.' Then, giving them his customary little wave, he walked off across the meadow and vanished into the woods.

Nashe could not help admiring Murks for his composure. Most men would have struck back after an assault like that, but Calvin hadn't even raised his hands to defend himself. There was a certain arrogance to it, perhaps – as if he were telling Pozzi that he couldn't hurt him, no matter how hard he tried – but the fact was that the incident had been defused with astonishing quickness. Considering what could have happened, it was a miracle that no greater damage had been done. Even Pozzi seemed aware of that, and while he scrupulously avoided talking about the subject that night, Nashe could tell that he was embarrassed, glad that he had been stopped before it was too late.

There was no reason to think there would be any repercussions. But the next morning at seven o'clock, Murks showed up at the trailer carrying a gun. It was a thirty-eight policeman's revolver, and it was strapped into a leather holster that hung from a cartridge belt around Murks's waist. Nashe noticed that six bullets were missing from the belt – almost certain proof that the weapon was loaded. It was bad enough that things had come to such a pass, he thought, but what made it even worse was that Calvin acted as though nothing had happened. He did not mention the gun, and that silence was finally more troubling to Nashe than the gun itself. It meant that Murks felt he had a right to carry it – and that he had felt that right from the very beginning. Freedom, therefore, had never been an issue. Contracts, handshakes, goodwill – none of that had meant a thing. All along, Nashe and Pozzi had been working under the threat of violence, and it was only because they had chosen to cooperate with Murks that he had left them alone. Bitching and grumbling were apparently allowed, but once their discontent moved beyond the realm of words, he was more than ready to take drastic, intimidating measures against them. And given the way things had been set up, there was no question that he was acting on orders from Flower and Stone.

Still, it didn't seem likely that Murks was planning to use the gun. Its function was symbolic, and just having it there in front of them was enough to make the point. As long as they didn't provoke him, Calvin wouldn't do much more than strut around with the weapon on his hip, doing some half-assed impersonation of a town marshal. When it came right down to it, Nashe felt, the only real danger was Pozzi. The kid's behavior had become so erratic, it was hard to know if he would do something foolish or not. As it turned out, he never did, and eventually Nashe was forced to admit that he had underestimated him. Pozzi had been expecting trouble all along, and when he saw the gun that morning, it did not surprise him so much as confirm his deepest suspicions. Nashe was the one who was surprised, Nashe was the one who had tricked himself into a false reading of the facts, but Pozzi had always known what they were up against. He had known it since the first day in the meadow, and the implications of that knowledge had scared him half to death. Now that everything was finally out in the open, he almost looked relieved. The gun did not change the situation for him, after all. It merely proved that he had been right.

'Well, old buddy,' he said to Murks as the three of them walked across the grass, 'it looks like you've finally put your cards on the table.'

'Cards?' Murks said, confused by the reference. 'I told you yesterday I don't play cards.'

'Just a figure of speech,' Pozzi said, smiling pleasantly. 'I'm talking about that funny lollypop you've got there. That dingdong hanging from your waist.'

'Oh, that,' Murks said, patting the gun in its holster. 'Yeah, well, I figured I shouldn't take no more chances. You're a crazy son of a bitch, little guy. No telling what you might do.'

'It kind of narrows the possibilities, though, doesn't it?' Pozzi said. 'I mean, a thing like that can seriously hamper a man's ability to express himself. Curtail his First Amendment rights, if you know what I'm talking about.'

'You don't have to be cute, mister,' Murks said. 'I know what the First Amendment is.'

'Of course you do. That's why I like you so much, Calvin. You're a sharp customer, a real whiz and a half. No one can put anything over on you.'

'Like I said yesterday, I'm always willing to give a man a break. But only one. After that, you've got to take appropriate action.'

'Like laying your cards out on the table, huh?'

'If that's how you want to put it.'

'It's just good to keep things straight, that's all. In fact, I'm kind of glad you put on your dress-up belt today. It gives my friend Jim here a better picture of things.'

'That's the idea,' Murks said, patting the gun once again. 'It does have a way of adjusting the focus, don't it?'

They finished repairing the trench by the end of the morning, and after that work returned to normal. Except for the gun (which Murks continued to wear every day), the outward circumstances of their life did not seem to change much. If anything, Nashe sensed that they were actually beginning to improve. The rain had stopped, for one thing, and instead of the wet, clammy days that had bogged them down for more than a week, they entered a period of superb fall weather: crisp, shimmering skies; firm ground underfoot; the crackle of leaves scudding past them in the wind. But Pozzi seemed to have improved as well, and it was no longer such a strain for Nashe to be with him. The gun had been a turning point, somehow, and since then he had managed to recover much of his bounce and spirit. The crazy talk had stopped; he kept his anger under control; the world was beginning to amuse him again. That was real progress, but there was also the progress of the calendar, and perhaps that meant more than anything else. They had made it into October now, and all of a sudden the end was in sight. Just knowing that was enough to awaken some hope in them, some flicker of optimism that had not been there before. There were sixteen days to go, and not even the gun could take that away from them. As long as they kept on working, the work was going to make them free.

They put in the thousandth stone on October eighth, polishing off the bottom row with more than a week to spare. In spite of everything, Nashe could not help feeling a sense of accomplishment. They had made a mark somehow, they had done something that would remain after they were gone, and no matter where they happened to be, a part of this wall would always belong to them. Even Pozzi looked happy about it, and when the last stone was finally cemented into place, he stepped back for a moment and said to Nashe, 'Well, my man, get a load of what we just did.' Uncharacteristically, the kid then hopped up onto the stones and started prancing down the length of the row, holding out his arms like a tightrope walker. Nashe was glad to see the kid respond in that way, and as he watched the small figure tiptoe off into the distance, following the pantomime of the high-wire stunt (as though he were in danger, as though he were about to fall from a great height), something suddenly choked up inside him, and he felt himself on the verge of tears. A moment later, Murks came up beside him and said, 'It looks like the little bugger is feeling pretty proud of himself, don't it?'

'He deserves to,' Nashe said. 'He's worked hard.'

'Well, it hasn't been easy, I'll grant you that. But it looks like we're coming along now. It looks like this thing is finally going up.'

'Little by little, one stone at a time.'

'That's the way it's done. One stone at a time.'

'I guess you'll have to start looking for some new workers. The way Jack and I figure it, we're due to leave here on the sixteenth.'

'I know that. It's kind of a shame, though. I mean, just when you boys are getting the hang of it and all.'

'Those are the breaks, Calvin.'

'Yeah, I guess so. But if nothing better comes along, you might consider coming back. I know that sounds crazy to you right now, but give it a little thought anyway.'

'Thought?' Nashe said, not knowing if he was about to laugh or cry.

'It's really not such bad work,' Murks continued. 'At least it's all there in front of you. You put down a stone, and something happens. You put down another stone, and something more happens. There's no big mystery to it. You can see the wall going up, and after a while it starts to give you a good feeling. It's not like mowing the grass or chopping wood. That's work, too, but it don't ever amount to much. When you work on a wall like this, you've always got something to show for it.'

'I suppose it has its points,' Nashe said, a little dumbfounded by Murks's venture into philosophy, 'but I can think of other things I'd rather be doing.'

'Suit yourself. But just remember we've got nine rows left. You could earn yourself some good money if you stuck with it.'

'I'll bear that in mind. But if I were you, Calvin, I wouldn't hold my breath.'

7

There was a problem, however. It had been there all along, a small thing in the back of their minds, but now that the sixteenth was only a week away, it suddenly grew larger, attaining such proportions as to dwarf everything else. The debt would be paid off on the sixteenth, but at that point they would only be back to zero. They would be free, perhaps, but they would also be broke, and how far would that freedom take them if they had no money? They wouldn't even be able to afford the price of a bus ticket. The moment they walked out of there, they would be turned into bums, a pair of penniless drifters trying to make their way in the dark.

For a few minutes, it looked as though Nashe's credit card might rescue them, but when he pulled it out of his wallet and showed it to Pozzi, the kid discovered that it had expired at the end of September. They talked about writing to someone to ask for a loan, but the only people they could think of were Pozzi's mother and Nashe's sister, and that didn't sit too well with either of them. It wasn't worth the embarrassment, they said, and besides, it was probably too late anyway. By the time they sent off their letter and received an answer, it would already be past the sixteenth.

Then Nashe told Pozzi about the conversation he had had with Murks that afternoon. It was a terrible prospect (at one point, it even looked as though the kid was about to start crying), but little by little they came around to the idea that they would have to stay with the wall a bit longer. There just wasn't any choice. Unless they built up some cash for themselves, there would only be more trouble after they left, and neither one of them felt equal to it. They were too worn out, too shaken to run that risk now. One or two extra days ought to do it, they said, just a couple of hundred dollars apiece to get them going. In the long run, maybe it wouldn't be as bad as all that. At least they would be working for themselves, and that was bound to make a difference. Or so they said – but what else could they say to each other at that moment? They had drunk close to a fifth of bourbon by then, and dwelling on the truth only would have made things worse than they already were.

They talked to Calvin about it the next morning, just to make sure he had been serious about his offer. He didn't see why not, he said. In fact, he'd already talked to Flower and Stone about it last night, and they hadn't raised any objections. If Nashe and Pozzi wanted to go on working after the debt had been squared, they were free to do so. They could earn the same ten dollars an hour they had been earning all along, and the offer would stand until the wall was finished.

'We're just talking about two or three extra days,' Nashe said.

'Sure, I understand,' Murks said. 'You want to set aside a little nest egg before you leave. I figured you'd get around to my way of thinking sooner or later.'

'It has nothing to do with that,' Nashe said. 'We're staying because we have to, not because we want to.'

'One way or the other,' Murks said, 'it comes down to the same thing, don't it? You need money, and this here job is the way to get it.'

Before Nashe could answer, Pozzi broke in and said, 'We're not going to stay unless we have it in writing. The exact terms, everything spelled out.'

'What you call a rider to the contract,' Murks said. 'Is that what you mean?'

'Yeah, that's it,' Pozzi said. 'A rider. If we don't get that, then we walk out of here on the sixteenth.'

'Fair enough,' Murks said, looking more and more pleased with himself. 'But you don't have to worry. It's already been taken care of.' The foreman then popped open the snaps of his blue down jacket, reached into the inner pocket with his right hand, and pulled out two sheets of folded paper. 'Read these over and tell me what you think,' he said.

It was the original and a duplicate of the new clause: a brief, simply stated paragraph setting out the conditions for 'labor subsequent to the discharge of the debt.' Both copies had already been signed by Flower and Stone, and as far as Nashe and Pozzi could tell, everything was in order. That was what was so strange about it. They hadn't even come to a decision until last night, and yet here were the results of that decision already waiting for them, boiled down into the precise language of contracts. How was that possible? It was as if Flower and Stone had been able to read their thoughts, as if they had known what they would do before they knew it themselves. For one short paranoid moment, Nashe wondered if the trailer had been bugged. It was a gruesome thought, but nothing else seemed to explain it. What if there were listening devices in the walls? Flower and Stone could easily have picked up their conversations then – they could have been following every word he and the kid had spoken to each other for the past six weeks. Maybe that was their nighttime entertainment, Nashe thought. Turn on the radio and listen to Jim and Jack's Comedy Hour. Fun for the whole family, a guaranteed laugh riot.

'You're awfully sure of yourself, Calvin, aren't you?' he said.

'Just common sense,' Murks replied. 'I mean, it was only a matter of time before you asked me about it. Ain't no other way it could have gone. So I figured I'd get ready for you and have the bosses draw up the papers. It didn't take but a minute.'

So they put their signatures on both copies of the rider, and the business was settled. Another day went by. When they sat down to dinner that evening, Pozzi said that he thought they should plan a celebration for the night of the sixteenth. Even if they weren't going to leave then, it seemed wrong to let the day slip by without doing something special. They should whoop it up a little, he said, throw a shindig of some kind to welcome in the new era. Nashe assumed he was talking about a cake or a bottle of champagne, but Pozzi had bigger plans than that. 'No,' he said, 'I mean let's really do it right. Lobsters, caviar, the whole works. And we'll bring in some girls, too. You can't have a party without girls.'

Nashe couldn't help smiling at the kid's enthusiasm. 'And what girls would those be, Jack?' he said. 'The only girl I've ever seen around here is Louise, and somehow she doesn't strike me as your type. Even if we invited her, I doubt she'd want to come.'

'No, no, I'm talking about real broads. Hookers. You know, juicy babes. Girls we can fuck.'

'And where do we find these juicy babes? Out there in the woods?'

'We bring them in. Atlantic City's not far from here, you know. That burg is crawling with female flesh. There's pussy for sale on every corner down there.'

'Fine. And what makes you think Flower and Stone will agree to it?'

'They said we could have anything we want, didn't they?'

'Food is one thing, Jack. A book, a magazine, even a bottle of bourbon or two. But don't you think this is pushing it a bit far?'

'Anything means anything. There's no harm in asking, anyway.'

'Sure, you can ask all you want. Just don't be surprised when Calvin laughs at you.'

'I'll bring it up with him first thing tomorrow morning.'

'You do that. But just ask for one girl, all right? Old grandpa here doesn't know if he's up for that kind of celebrating.'

'Well, this little boy is up for it, I can tell you that. It's been so long now, my pecker's about ready to explode.'

Contrary to what Nashe had predicted, Murks didn't laugh at Pozzi the next morning. But the look of confusion and embarrassment that swept across his face was almost as good as a laugh, perhaps even better. He had been prepared for their questions the day before, but this time he was stumped, could scarcely even take in what the kid was talking about. After the second or third go-through, he finally caught on, but that only seemed to add to his embarrassment. 'You mean a hoor?' he said. 'Is that what you're trying to tell me? You want us to get you a hoor?'

Murks did not have the authority to handle such an unorthodox request, but he promised to take it up with the bosses that night. Unbelievably, when he came back with the answer the next morning, he told Pozzi it would be taken care of, he would have his girl on the sixteenth. 'That was the deal,' he said. 'Whatever you want, you can get. I can't say they looked too happy about it, but a deal's a deal, they said, and there you have it. If you ask me, it was kind of big of them. They're nice fellas, those two, and once they give their word about something, they'll bend over backwards to make it good.'

It felt all wrong to Nashe. Flower and Stone weren't the kind of men who threw away their money on parties for other people, and the fact that they had gone along with Pozzi's request immediately put him on his guard. For their own sakes, he thought, it would have been better to push on with the work and then creep out of there as quickly and quietly as possible. The second row was proving less difficult than the first, and the work was advancing steadily, perhaps more steadily than ever before. The wall was higher now, and they no longer had to put their backs through the multiple contortions of bending and squatting to push the stones into place. A single, economical gesture was all that was required, and once they had mastered the finer points of this new rhythm, they were able to increase their output to as many as forty stones a day. How simple it would have been to go on like that to the end. But the kid had his heart set on a party, and now that the girl was coming, Nashe realized there was nothing he could do to prevent it. If he spoke up, it would only sound as if he were trying to spoil Pozzi's fun, and that was the last thing he wanted. The kid deserved to have his little romp, and even if it led to more trouble than it was worth, Nashe felt a moral obligation to play along with him.

Over the next few nights, he assumed the role of caterer, sitting in the living room with a pencil and jotting down notes as he helped Pozzi work out the details of the celebration. There were endless decisions to be made, and Nashe was determined that the kid be satisfied on every point. Should the meal begin with shrimp cocktail or French onion soup? Should the main course consist of steak or lobster or both? How many bottles of champagne should they order? Should the girl be there for dinner, or should they eat alone and have her join them for dessert? Were decorations necessary, and if so, what color balloons did they want? They handed the completed list to Murks on the morning of the fifteenth, and that same night the foreman made a special trip to the meadow to deliver the packages. For once he came in the jeep, and Nashe wondered if that wasn't an encouraging sign, a token of their impending freedom. Then again, it could have meant nothing. There were many packages, after all, and he could have driven there simply because the load was too big to carry in his arms. For if they were about to become free men, why would Murks bother to go on wearing the gun?

They put in forty-seven stones on the last day, surpassing their previous record by five. It took an enormous effort to pull it off, but they both wanted to end with a flourish, and they worked as if they were out to prove something, never once slackening their pace, wielding the stones with an assurance that bordered on contempt, as if the only thing that mattered now was to show they had not been defeated, that they had triumphed over the whole rotten business. Murks called them to a halt at six sharp, and they put down their tools with the cold autumn air still burning in their lungs. Darkness came earlier now, and when Nashe looked up at the sky, he saw that evening was already upon them.

For several moments he was too stunned to know what to think. Pozzi came over to him and pounded him on the back, chattering with excitement, but Nashe's mind remained curiously empty, as if he were unable to absorb the magnitude of what he had done. I'm back to zero, he finally said to himself. And all of a sudden he knew that an entire period of his life had just ended. It wasn't just the wall and the meadow, it was everything that had put him there in the first place, the whole crazy saga of the past two years: Thérèse and the money and the car, all of it. He was back to zero again, and now those things were gone. For even the smallest zero was a great hole of nothingness, a circle large enough to contain the world.

The girl was supposed to be chauffeured up by limousine from Atlantic City. Murks had told them to expect her at around eight o'clock, but it was closer to nine when she finally walked through the door of the trailer. Nashe and Pozzi had polished off a bottle of champagne by then, and Nashe was fussing over the lobster pot in the kitchen, watching the water as it approached the boiling point for the third or fourth time that evening. The three lobsters in the bathtub were barely alive, but Pozzi had chosen to include the girl for dinner ('It makes a better impression that way'), and so there was nothing to do but hang around until she showed up. Neither one of them was used to drinking champagne, and the bubbles had quickly gone to their heads, leaving them both a bit punchy by the time the celebration finally got started.

The girl called herself Tiffany, and she couldn't have been more than eighteen or nineteen years old. She was one of those pale, skinny blondes with sloped shoulders and a sunken chest, and she tottered around on her three-inch heels as if she were trying to walk on ice skates. Nashe noted the small, yellowing bruise on her left thigh, the overdone makeup, the dismal miniskirt that exposed her thin, shapeless legs. Her face was almost pretty, he felt, but in spite of her pouting, childlike expression, there was a worn-out quality to her, a sullenness that glowed through the smiles and apparent gaiety of her manner. It didn't matter how young she was. Her eyes were too hard, too cynical, and they bore the look of someone who had already seen too much.

The kid popped open another bottle of champagne, and the three of them sat down for a pre-dinner drink – Pozzi and the girl on the couch, Nashe in a chair several feet away.

'So what's the story, fellas?' she said, sipping daintily from her glass. 'Is this going to be a threesome, or do I take you on one at a time?'

'I'm just the cook,' Nashe said, a little thrown by the girl's bluntness. 'Once dinner is over, I'm finished for the night.'

'Old Jeeves here is a wizard in the kitchen,' Pozzi said, 'but he's scared of the ladies. It's just one of those things. They make him nervous.'

'Yeah, sure,' the girl said, studying Nashe with a cold, appraising look. 'What's the matter, big guy, not in the mood tonight?'

'It's not that,' Nashe said. 'It's just that I have a lot of reading to catch up on. I've been trying to learn a new recipe, and some of the ingredients are pretty complicated.'

'Well, you can always change your mind,' the girl said. 'That fat guy shelled out plenty for this, and I came here thinking I was going to fuck you both. It's no skin off my back. For that kind of money, I'd fuck a dog if I had to.'

'I understand,' Nashe said. 'But I'm sure you'll have your hands full with Jack anyway. Once he gets started, he can be a real savage.'

'That's right, babe,' Pozzi said, squeezing the girl's thigh and pulling her toward him for a kiss. 'My appetite's insatiable.'

It promised to be a sad and lugubrious dinner, but Pozzi's high spirits turned it into something else – something buoyant and memorable, a free-for-all of slithering lobster shells and drunken laughter. The kid was a whirlwind that night, and neither Nashe nor the girl could resist his happiness, the manic energy that kept pouring out from him and flooding the room. It seemed that he knew exactly what to say to the girl at every moment, how to flatter her and to tease her and to make her laugh, and Nashe was astonished to see how she slowly gave in to the assault of his charms, how her face softened and her eyes grew steadily brighter. Nashe had never had this talent with girls, and he watched Pozzi's performance with a mounting sense of wonder and envy. It was all a matter of treating everyone the same, he realized, of giving as much care and attention to a sad, unattractive prostitute as you would to the girl of your dreams. Nashe had always been too fussy for that, too self-contained and serious, and he admired the kid for making the girl laugh so hard, for loving life so much at that moment that he was able to draw out what was still alive in her.

The best bit of improvisation came halfway through the meal, when Pozzi suddenly began to talk about their work. He and Nashe were architects, he explained, and they had come to Pennsylvania a couple of weeks ago to oversee the construction of a castle they had designed. They were specialists in the art of 'historical reverberation,' and because so few people could afford to hire them, they invariably wound up working for eccentric millionaires. 'I don't know what the fat man in the house told you about us,' he said, 'but you can forget it right now. He's a great kidder, that one, and he'd just as soon wet his pants in public as give you a straight answer about anything.' A crew of thirty-six masons and carpenters came to the meadow every day, but he and Jim were living on the construction site because they always did that. Atmosphere meant everything, and the job always turned out better if they lived the life they'd been hired to create. This job was a 'medieval reverberation,' so for the time being they had to live like monks. Their next job would be taking them to Texas, where an oil baron had asked them to build a replica of Buckingham Palace in his backyard. That might sound easy, but once you realized that every stone had to be numbered in advance, you could begin to understand how complicated it was. If the stones weren't put together in the right order, the whole thing would come tumbling down. Imagine building the Brooklyn Bridge in San Jose, California. Well, they had done that for someone just last year. Think about designing a life-size Eiffel Tower to fit over a ranch house in the New Jersey suburbs. That was on their résumé as well. Sure, there were times when they felt like packing it in and moving to a condo in West Palm Beach, but the work was finally too damned interesting to stop, and what with all the American millionaires who wanted to live in European castles, they didn't have the heart to turn everyone down.

All this nonsense was accompanied by the noise of cracking lobster shells and the slurping of champagne. When Nashe stood up to clear the table, he stumbled against a leg of his chair and dropped two or three dishes to the floor. They broke with a great clattering din, and because one of them happened to be a bowl containing the remnants of the melted butter, the mess on the linoleum ran riot. Tiffany made a move to help Nashe clean it up, but walking had never been her strong point, and now that the champagne bubbles were percolating in her bloodstream, she could manage no more than two or three steps before she fell into Pozzi's lap, overcome by a fit of laughter. Or perhaps it was Pozzi who grabbed hold of her before she could get away from him (by then, Nashe could no longer keep track of such nuances), but however it may have happened, by the time Nashe stood up with the shards of broken crockery in his hand, the two young people were sitting on the chair together, locked in a passionate kiss. Pozzi started to rub one of the girl's breasts, and a moment later Tiffany was reaching out for the bulge in his crotch, but before things could go any further, Nashe (not knowing what else to do) cleared his throat and announced that it was time for dessert.

They had ordered one of those chocolate layer cakes you find in the frozen-food department of the A&P, but Nashe carried it out with all the pomp and ceremony of a lord high chamberlain about to place a crown on the head of a queen. In keeping with the solemnity of the occasion, he suddenly and unexpectedly found himself singing a hymn from his boyhood. It was 'Jerusalem,' with words by William Blake, and although he hadn't sung it in over twenty years, all the verses came back to him, rolling off his tongue as though he had spent the past two months rehearsing for this moment. Hearing the words as he sang them, the *burning gold* and the *mental fight* and the *dark satanic mills*, he understood how beautiful and painful they were, and he sang them as though to express his own longing, all the sadness and joy that had welled up in him since the first day in the meadow. It was a difficult melody, but except for a few false notes in the opening stanza, his voice did not betray him. He sang as he had always dreamed of singing, and he knew that he was not deluding himself from the way Pozzi and the girl looked at him, from the stunned expressions on their faces when they realized that the sounds were coming from his mouth. They listened in silence to the end, and then, when Nashe sat down and forced an embarrassed smile in their direction, they both began to clap, and they did not stop until he finally agreed to stand up again and take a bow.

They drank the last bottle of champagne with the cake, telling stories about their childhoods, and then Nashe realized it was time to back off. He didn't want to be in the kid's way anymore, and now that the food was gone, he had run out of excuses for being there. This time, the girl didn't ask him to reconsider, but she gave him a big hug anyway and said she hoped they would run into each other again. He thought that was nice of her and said he hoped so too, and then he winked at the kid and stumbled off to bed.

Still, it wasn't easy lying there in the dark, listening to their laughter and thumping out in the other room. He tried not to imagine what was going on, but the only way he could do that was by thinking about Fiona, and that only seemed to make matters worse. Luckily, he was too drunk to keep his eyes open for very long. Before he could begin to feel truly sorry for himself, he was already dead to the world.

They planned to take the next day off. It seemed only appropriate after working for seven straight weeks, and what with the hangovers that were bound to follow their night of carousing, they had arranged this respite with Murks several days in advance. Nashe awoke shortly past ten, head cracking in both temples, and started off toward the shower.

On the way, he glanced into Pozzi's room and saw that the kid was still asleep, alone in his bed with his arms flung out on both sides. Nashe stood under the water for a good six or seven minutes, then stepped out into the living room with a towel around his waist. A lacy black bra sat tangled on a cushion of the sofa, but the girl herself was gone. The room looked as though a marauding army had camped there for the night, and the floor was a chaos of empty bottles and overturned ashtrays, of fallen streamers and shriveled balloons. Picking his way through the debris, Nashe went into the kitchen and made himself a pot of coffee.

He drank three cups, sitting at the table and smoking cigarettes from a pack the girl had left behind. When he felt sufficiently awake to start moving again, he stood up and began cleaning the trailer, working as quietly as possible so as not to wake the kid. He took care of the living room first, systematically attacking each category of refuse (ashes, balloons, broken glasses), and then headed into the kitchen, where he scraped plates, discarded lobster shells, and washed the dishes and silverware. It took him two hours to put the little house in order, and Pozzi slept through it, never once stirring from his room. Once the cleanup was finished, Nashe made himself a ham and cheese sandwich and a fresh pot of coffee, and then he tiptoed back into his own room to retrieve one of his unread books – *Our Mutual Friend*, by Charles Dickens. He ate the sandwich, drank another cup of coffee, and then carried one of the kitchen chairs outside, positioning it so as to prop up his legs on the steps of the trailer. It was an unusually warm and sunny day for mid-October, and as Nashe sat there with the book in his lap, lighting up one of the cigars they had ordered for the party, he suddenly felt so tranquil, so profoundly at peace with himself, that he decided not to open the book until he had smoked the cigar to the end.

He had been at it for nearly twenty minutes when he heard a sound of thrashing leaves off in the woods. He rose from his chair, turned in the direction of the sound, and saw Murks walking toward him, emerging from the foliage with the holster cinched around his blue jacket. Nashe was so accustomed to the gun by then that he failed to notice it, but he was surprised to see Murks, and since there was no question of doing any work that day, he wondered what this unexpected visit could mean. They made small talk for the first three or four minutes, referring vaguely to the party and the mild weather. Murks told him that the chauffeur had driven off with the girl at five thirty, and from the way the kid was sleeping in there, he said, it looked like he'd had a busy night. Yes, Nashe said, he hadn't been disappointed, the whole thing had worked out well.

There was a long pause after that, and for the next fifteen or twenty seconds, Murks looked at the ground, poking the dirt with the tip of his shoe. 'I'm afraid I've got some bad news for you,' he said at last, still not daring to look Nashe in the eye.

'I know that,' Nashe said. 'You wouldn't have come out here today unless you did.'

'Well, I'm awful sorry,' Murks said, taking a sealed envelope from his pocket and handing it to Nashe. 'It kind of confused me when they told me about it, but I suppose they're within their rights. It all depends on how you look at it, I guess.'

Seeing the envelope, Nashe automatically assumed it was a letter from Donna. No one else would bother to write to him, he thought, and the moment this thought entered his consciousness, he was overwhelmed by a sudden attack of nausea and shame. He had forgotten Juliette's birthday. The twelfth had come and gone five days ago, and he hadn't even noticed.

Then he looked at the envelope and saw that it was blank. It couldn't have come from Donna without stamps, he told himself, and when he finally tore it open, he found a single sheet of typed paper inside – words and numbers arranged in perfect columns with a heading that read, NASHE AND POZZI: EXPENSES.

'What's this supposed to be?' he asked.

'The bosses' figures,' Murks said. 'Credits and debits, the balance sheet of money spent and money earned.'

When Nashe examined the page more closely, he saw that it was precisely that. It was an accountant's statement, the meticulous work of a bookkeeper, and if nothing else it proved that Flower had not forgotten his old profession since striking it rich seven years ago. The pluses were itemized in the left-hand column, all duly noted according to Nashe and Pozzi's calculations, with no quibbles or discrepancies: 1000 hours of work at $10 per hour = $10,000. But then there were the minuses in the right-hand column, a list of sums that amounted to an inventory of everything that had happened to them in the past fifty days:

Food	$1628.41
Beer, liquor	217.36
Books, newspapers, magazines	72.15

Tobacco	87.48
Radio	59.86
Broken window	66.50
Entertainment (10/16)	900.00
– hostess $400	
– car $500	
Miscellaneous	41.14

($3072.90)

'What's this,' Nashe said, 'some kind of prank?'

'I'm afraid not,' Murks said.

'But all these things were supposed to be included.'

'I thought so, too. But I guess we were wrong.'

'What do you mean, wrong? We all shook hands on it. You know that as well as I do.'

'Maybe so. But if you look at the contract, you'll see there's no mention of food. Lodging, yes. Work clothes, yes. But there's not a word in there about food.'

'This is a dark and dirty thing, Calvin. I hope you understand that.'

'It's not for me to say. The bosses have always treated me fair, and I've never had any reason to complain. The way they figure it, a job means earning money for the work you do, but how you spend that money is your own business. That's how it is with me. They give me my salary and a house to live in, but I buy my own food. It's a nice arrangement as far as I'm concerned. Nine-tenths of the folks that work ain't half so lucky. They got to pay for everything. Not just food, but lodging as well. That's the way it is the world over.'

'But these are special circumstances.'

'Well, maybe they're not so special, after all. When you come right down to it, you should be glad they didn't charge you for rent and utilities.'

Nashe saw that the cigar he was smoking had gone out. He studied it for a moment without really seeing it, then tossed it to the ground and crushed it underfoot. 'I think it's time I went over to the main house and had a talk with your bosses,' he said.

'Can't do that now,' Murks said. 'They're gone.'

'Gone? What are you talking about?'

'That's right, they're gone. They left for Paris, France, about three hours ago, and they won't be back until after Christmas.'

'It's hard to believe they'd just take off like that – without bothering to look at the wall. It doesn't make any sense.'

'Oh, they saw it all right. I took them out here early this morning when you and the kid were still asleep. They thought it was coming along real nice. Good job, they said, keep up the good work. They couldn't have been happier.'

'Shit,' Nashe said. 'Shit on them and their goddamned wall.'

'No sense in getting angry, friend. It's only another two or three weeks. If you cut out the parties and such, you'll be out of here before you know it.'

'Three weeks from now, it will be November.'

'That's all right. You're a tough one, Nashe, you can handle it.'

'Sure, I can handle it. But what about Jack? Once he sees this paper, it's going to kill him.'

Ten minutes after Nashe went back into the trailer, Pozzi woke up. The kid looked so touseled and swollen-eyed that Nashe didn't have the heart to spring the news on him, and for the next half hour he allowed the conversation to drift along with aimless, inconsequential remarks, listening to Pozzi's blow-by-blow description of what he and the girl had done to each other after Nashe had gone to bed. It seemed wrong to interrupt such a story and spoil the kid's pleasure in telling it, but once a decent interval had elapsed, Nashe finally changed the subject and pulled out the envelope that Murks had given him.

'It's like this, Jack,' he said, barely giving the kid a chance to look at the paper. 'They've pulled a fast one on us, and now we're sunk. We thought we were even, but the way they've worked it out, we're still three thousand dollars in the hole. Food, magazines, even the goddamned broken window – they've charged us for all of it. Not to speak of Miss Hot Pants and her chauffeur, which probably goes without saying. We just took it for granted that those things were covered by the contract, but the contract doesn't say anything about them. Fine. So we made a mistake. The point is: What do we do now? As far as I'm concerned, you're not in it anymore. You've done enough, and from now on this thing is my problem. So I'm going to get you out of here. We'll dig a hole under the fence, and once it gets dark, you'll crawl through that hole and be on your way.'

'And what about you?' Pozzi said.

'I'm going to stay and finish the job.'

'Not a chance. You're crawling through that hole with me.'

'Not this time, Jack. I can't.'

'And why the hell not? You afraid of holes or something? You've already been living in one for the past two months – or haven't you noticed?'

'I promised myself I'd see it through to the end. I'm not asking you to understand it, but I'm just not going to run away. I've done too much of that already, and I don't want to live like that anymore. If I sneak out of here before the debt is paid off, I won't be worth a goddamned thing to myself.'

'Custer's last stand.'

'That's it. The old put-up-or-shut-up routine.'

'It's the wrong battle, Jim. You'll just be wasting your time, fucking yourself over for nothing. If the three grand is so important to you, why don't you send them a check? They don't care how they get their money, and they'll have it a whole lot sooner if you leave with me tonight. Shit, I'll even go half-and-half with you. I know a guy in Philly who can get us into a game tomorrow night. All we have to do is hitch a ride, and we'll have the dough in less than forty-eight hours. Simple. We'll send it to them special delivery, and that will be that.'

'Flower and Stone aren't here. They left for Paris this morning.'

'Jesus, you're a stubborn son of a bitch, aren't you? Who the fuck cares where they are?'

'Sorry, kid. No dice. You can talk yourself blue in the face, but I'm not going.'

'It will take you twice as long working by yourself, asshole. Did you ever think of that? Ten dollars an hour, not twenty. You'll be lugging around those stones until Christmas.'

'I know that. Just don't forget to send me a card, Jack, that's all I ask. I usually get kind of sentimental around that time of year.'

They kept it up for another forty-five minutes, arguing back and forth until Pozzi finally slammed down his fist on the kitchen table and left the room. He was so angry at Nashe that he wouldn't talk to him for the next three hours, hiding behind the closed door of his bedroom and refusing to come out. At four o'clock, Nashe went to the door and announced that he was going outside to start digging the hole. Pozzi didn't respond, but not long after Nashe put on his jacket and left the trailer, he heard the door slam again, and a moment later the kid was trotting across the meadow to catch up with him. Nashe waited, and then they walked to the tool shed together in silence, neither one of them daring to reopen the argument.

'I've been thinking it over,' Pozzi said, as they stood before the locked door of the shed. 'What's the point of going through all this escape business? Wouldn't it be simpler if we just went to Calvin and told him I'm leaving? As long as you're still here to honor the contract, what difference could it make?'

'I'll tell you why,' Nashe said, picking up a small stone from the ground and smashing it against the door to break the lock. 'Because I don't trust him. Calvin isn't as stupid as he looks, and he knows your name is on that contract. With Flower and Stone gone, he'll say he doesn't have the authority to make any changes, that we can't do anything until they get back. That's his line, isn't it? I just work here, boys, and I do what the bosses tell me. But he knows what's going on, he's been part of it from the beginning. Otherwise, Flower and Stone wouldn't have taken off and left him in charge. He pretends to be on our side, but he belongs to them, he doesn't give a rat's ass about us. As soon as we told him you wanted to leave, he'd figure out you were going to escape. That's the next step, isn't it? And I don't want to give him any advance warning. Who knows what kind of trick he'd pull on us then?'

So they broke open the door of the shed, took out two shovels, and carried them down the dirt path that led through the woods. It was a longer walk to the fence than they had remembered, and by the time they started digging, the light had already begun to fade. The ground was hard and the bottom of the fence ran deep, and they both grunted each time they struck their shovels into the dirt. They could see the road right before them, but only one car passed in the half hour they spent there, a battered station wagon with a man, a woman, and a small boy inside it. The boy waved to them with a startled expression on his face as the car drove by, but neither Nashe nor Pozzi waved back. They dug on in silence, and when they had finally carved out a hole large enough for Pozzi's body to fit through, their arms were aching with exhaustion. They flung down their shovels at that point and headed back to the trailer, crossing into the meadow as the sky grew purple around them, glowing thinly in the mid-October dusk.

They ate their last meal together as if they were strangers. They didn't know what to say to each other anymore, and their attempts at conversation were awkward, at times even embarrassing. Pozzi's departure was too near to allow them to think of anything else, and yet neither one of them was willing to talk about it, so for long stretches they sat there locked in silence, each one imagining what would become of him without the other. There was no point in reminiscing about the past, in looking back over the good times they had spent together, for there hadn't been any good times, and the future was too uncertain to be anything but a shadow, a formless, unarticulated presence that neither one of them wished to examine very closely. It was only after they stood up from the table and began clearing their plates that the tension spilled over into words again. Night had come, and suddenly they had reached the moment of last-minute preparations and farewells. They exchanged addresses and telephone numbers, promising to stay in touch with each other, but Nashe knew that it would never happen, that this was the last time he would ever see Pozzi. They packed a small bag of provisions – food, cigarettes, road maps of Pennsylvania and New Jersey – and then Nashe handed Pozzi a twenty-dollar bill, which he had found at the bottom of his suitcase earlier that afternoon.

'It's not much,' he said, 'but I suppose it's better than nothing.'

The air was cold that night, and they bundled up in sweatshirts and jackets before leaving the trailer. They walked across the meadow carrying flashlights, moving along the length of the unfinished wall as a way to guide them in the darkness. When they came to the end and saw the immense piles of stones standing at the edge of the woods, they played their beams along the surfaces for a moment as they passed by. It produced a ghostly effect of weird shapes and darting shadows, and Nashe could not help thinking that the stones were alive, that the night had turned them into a colony of sleeping animals. He wanted to make a joke about it, but he couldn't come up with anything fast enough, and a moment later they were walking down the dirt path in the woods. When they reached the fence, he saw the two shovels they had left on the ground and realized that it wouldn't look right if Murks found both of them. One shovel would mean that Pozzi had planned his escape alone, but two shovels would mean that Nashe had been a part of it as well. As soon as Pozzi was gone, he would have to pick one up and carry it back to the shed.

Pozzi struck a match, and as he lifted the flame to his cigarette, Nashe noticed that his hand was trembling. 'Well, Mr. Fireman,' he said, 'it looks like we've come to a parting of the ways.'

'You'll be fine, Jack,' Nashe said. 'Just remember to brush your teeth after every meal, and nothing bad can happen to you.'

They grasped each other by the elbows, squeezing hard for a moment or two, and then Pozzi asked Nashe to hold the cigarette while he crawled through the hole. A moment later he was standing on the other side of the fence, and Nashe handed the cigarette back to him.

'Come with me,' Pozzi said. 'Don't be a jerk, Jim. Come with me now.'

He said it with such earnestness that Nashe almost gave in, but then he waited too long before giving an answer, and in that interval the temptation passed. 'I'll catch up with you in a couple of months,' he said. 'You'd better get moving.'

Pozzi backed off from the fence, dragged once on the cigarette, and then flicked it away from him, causing a small shower of sparks to flare up briefly on the road. 'I'll call your sister tomorrow and tell her you're okay,' he said.

'Just beat it,' Nashe said, rattling the fence with an abrupt, impatient gesture. 'Go as fast as you can.'

'I'm already out of here,' Pozzi said. 'By the time you count to a hundred, you won't even remember who I am.'

Then, without saying good-bye, he turned on his heels and started running down the road.

Lying in bed that night, Nashe rehearsed the story he was planning to tell Murks in the morning, going over it several times until it began to sound like the truth: how he and Pozzi had gone to sleep at around ten o'clock, how he hadn't heard a sound for the next eight hours ('I always sleep like a log'), and how he had come out of his room at six to prepare breakfast, had knocked on the kid's door to wake him up, and had discovered that he was gone. No, Jack hadn't talked about running away, and he hadn't left a note or any clue as to where he might be. Who knows what happened to him? Maybe he got up early and decided to take a walk. Sure, I'll help you look for him. He's probably wandering around in the woods somewhere, trying to catch a glimpse of the migrating geese.

But Nashe never had a chance to tell any of those lies. When his alarm rang at six o'clock the next morning, he went into the kitchen to boil a pot of water for coffee, and then, curious to know what the temperature was, he opened the door of the trailer and stuck his head outside to test the air.

That was when he saw Pozzi – although it took several moments before he realized who it was. At first he saw no more than an indistinguishable heap, a bundle of blood-spattered clothing sprawled out on the ground, and even after he saw that a man was in those clothes, he did not see Pozzi so much as he saw a hallucination, a thing that could not have been there. He noticed that the clothes were remarkably similar to the ones that Pozzi had been wearing the night before, that the man was dressed in the same windbreaker and hooded sweatshirt, the same blue jeans and mustard-colored boots, but even then Nashe could not put those facts together and say to himself: *I am looking at Pozzi*. For the man's limbs were oddly tangled and inert, and from the way his head was cocked to one side (twisted at an almost impossible angle, as if the head were about to separate itself from the body), Nashe felt certain that he was dead.

He started down the steps a moment later, and at that point he finally understood what he was seeing. As he walked across the grass toward the kid's body, Nashe felt a series of small gagging sounds escape from his throat. He fell to his knees, took Pozzi's battered face in his hands, and discovered that a pulse was still fluttering weakly in the veins of the kid's neck. 'My God,' he said, only half-aware that he was talking out loud. 'What have they done to you, Jack?' Both the kid's eyes were swollen shut, ugly gashes had been opened on his forehead, temples, and mouth, and several teeth were gone: it was a pulverized face, a face beaten beyond recognition. Nashe heard the gagging sounds escape from his throat again, and then, almost whimpering, he gathered Pozzi into his arms and carried him up the steps of the trailer.

It was impossible to know how serious the injuries were. The kid was unconscious, perhaps even in a coma, but lying out there in the frigid autumn weather for God knows how many hours had only made matters worse. In the end, that had probably done as much damage as the beating itself. Nashe laid the kid out on the sofa and then rushed into both bedrooms and stripped the blankets off the beds. He had seen several people die of shock after being rescued from fires, and Pozzi had all the symptoms of a bad case: the dreadful pallor, the blueness of the lips, the icy, corpselike hands. Nashe did everything he could to keep him warm, rubbing his body under the blankets and tilting his legs to get the blood flowing again, but even after the kid's temperature began to rise a little, he showed no signs of waking up.

Things happened quickly after that. Murks arrived at seven, tramping up the steps of the trailer and giving his customary knock on the door, and when Nashe called for him to come in, his first response on seeing Pozzi was to laugh. 'What's the matter with him?' he said, gesturing at the sofa with his thumb. 'Did he tie one on again last night?' But once he stepped into the room and was close enough to see Pozzi's face, his amusement turned to alarm. 'Christ almighty,' he said. 'This boy's in trouble.'

'You're damn right he's in trouble,' Nashe said. 'If we don't get him to a hospital in the next hour, he's not going to make it.'

So Murks ran back to the house to fetch the jeep, and in the meantime Nashe dragged out the mattress from Pozzi's bed and leaned it against the wall of the trailer, keeping it there to be used for their makeshift ambulance. The ride was going to be hard enough anyway, but perhaps the cushion would prevent the kid from being jolted around too much. When Murks finally returned, there was another man sitting with him in the front of the jeep. 'This here is Floyd,' he said. 'He can help us carry the kid.' Floyd was Murks's son-in-law, and he looked to be somewhere in his mid to late twenties – a large, solidly built young man who stood at least six four or six five, with a smooth reddish face and a woolen hunting cap on his head. He seemed no more than moderately intelligent, however, and when Murks introduced him to Nashe he extended his hand with a clumsy, earnest cheerfulness that was entirely inappropriate for the situation. Nashe was so disgusted that he refused to offer his hand in return, merely staring at Floyd until the big man dropped his arm to his side.

Nashe maneuvered the mattress into the back of the jeep, and then the three of them went into the trailer and lifted Pozzi off the sofa, carrying him outside with the blankets still wrapped around his body. Nashe tucked him in, trying to make him as comfortable as possible, but every time he looked down at the kid's face, he knew there was no hope. Pozzi didn't have a chance anymore. By the time they got him to the hospital, he would already be dead.

But worse was still to come. Murks clapped his hand on Nashe's shoulder at that point and said, 'We'll be back as soon as we can,' and when it finally dawned on Nashe that they weren't planning to take him along, something in him snapped, and he turned on Murks in a sudden fit of rage. 'Sorry,' Murks said. 'I can't let you do that. There's been enough commotion around here for one day, and I don't want things getting out of hand. You don't have to worry, Nashe. Floyd and me can manage on our own.'

But Nashe was beside himself, and instead of backing off, he lunged at Murks and grabbed hold of his jacket, calling him a liar and a goddamn son of a bitch. Before he could bring his fist into Calvin's face, however, Floyd was all over him, wrapping his arms around him from behind and yanking him off the ground. Murks took two or three steps back, pulled his gun out of the holster, and pointed it at Nashe. But not even that was enough to put an end to it, and Nashe went on yelling and kicking in Floyd's arms. 'Shoot me, you son of a bitch!' he said to Murks. 'Come on, go ahead and shoot me!'

'He don't know what he's saying anymore,' Murks said calmly, glancing over at his son-in-law. 'The poor bugger's lost it.'

Without warning, Floyd threw Nashe violently to the ground, and before Nashe could get up to resume the assault, a foot came crashing into his stomach. It knocked the wind out of him, and as he lay there gasping for breath, the two men broke for the jeep and climbed in. Nashe heard the engine kick over, and by the time he was able to stand up again, they were already driving off, disappearing with Pozzi into the woods.

He did not hesitate after that. He went inside, put on his jacket, stuffed the pockets with as much food as they would hold, and immediately left the trailer again. His only thought was to get out of there. He would never have a better chance to escape, and he wasn't going to squander the opportunity. He would crawl through the hole he had dug with Pozzi the night before, and that would be the end of it.

He walked across the meadow at a quick pace, not even bothering to look at the wall, and when he reached the woods on the other side, he suddenly started to run, charging down the dirt path as if his life depended on it. He came to the fence a few minutes later, breathing hard from the exertion, staring out at the road before him with his arms pressed against the barrier for support. For a moment or two, it didn't even occur to him that the hole had vanished. But once he began to recover his breath, he looked down at his feet and saw that he was standing on level ground. The hole had been filled in, the shovel was gone, and what with the leaves and twigs scattered around him, it was almost impossible to know that a hole had ever been there.

Nashe gripped the fence with all ten fingers and squeezed as hard as he could. He held on like that for close to a minute, and then, opening his hands again, he brought them to his face and began to sob.

8

For several nights after that, he had the same recurring dream. He would imagine that he was waking up in the darkness of his own room, and once he understood that he was no longer asleep, he would put on his clothes, leave the trailer, and start walking across the meadow. When he came to the tool shed at the other end, he would kick down the door, grab a shovel, and continue on into the woods, running down the dirt path that led to the fence. The dream was always vivid and exact, less a distortion of the real than a simulacrum, an illusion so rich in the details of waking life that Nashe never suspected that he was dreaming. He would hear the faint crackling of the earth underfoot, he would feel the chill of the night air against his skin, he would smell the pungent autumn decay wafting through the woods. But every time he came to the fence with the shovel in his hand, the dream would suddenly stop, and he would wake up to discover that he was still lying in his own bed.

The question was: Why didn't he get up at that point and do what he had just done in the dream? There was nothing to prevent him from trying to escape, and yet he continued to balk at it, refused even to consider it as a possibility. At first, he attributed this reluctance to fear. He was convinced that Murks was responsible for what had happened to Pozzi (with a helping hand from Floyd, no doubt), and there was every reason to believe that something similar would be in store for him if he tried to run out on the contract. It was true that Murks had looked upset when he saw Pozzi that morning in the trailer, but who was to say he hadn't been putting on an act? Nashe had seen Pozzi running down the road, and how could he have wound up in the meadow again if Murks hadn't put him there? If the kid had been beaten by someone else, his attacker would have left him on the road and run away. And even if Pozzi had still been conscious then, he wouldn't have had the strength to crawl back through the hole, let alone cross the entire meadow by himself. No, Murks had put him there as a warning, to show Nashe what happened to people who tried to escape. His story was that he had driven Pozzi to the Sisters of Mercy Hospital in Doylestown, but why couldn't he have been lying about that as well? They could just as easily have dumped the kid in the woods somewhere and buried him. What difference would it make if he had still been alive? Cover a man's face with dirt, and he'll smother to death before you can count to a hundred. Murks was a master at filling in holes, after all. Once he got through with one of them, you couldn't even tell if it had been there or not.

Little by little, however, Nashe understood that fear had nothing to do with it. Every time he imagined himself running away from the meadow, he saw Murks pointing a gun at his back and slowly pulling the trigger – but the thought of the bullet ripping through his flesh and rupturing his heart did not frighten him so much as make him angry. He deserved to die, perhaps, but he did not want to give Murks the satisfaction of killing him. That would be too easy, too predictable a way for things to end. He had already caused Pozzi's death by forcing him to escape, but even if he let himself die as well (and there were times when this thought became almost irresistible to him), it wasn't going to undo the wrong he had done. That was why he continued working on the wall – not because he was afraid, not because he felt obliged to pay off the debt anymore, but because he wanted revenge. He would finish out his time there, and once he was free to go, he would call in the cops and have Murks arrested. That was the least he could do for the kid now, he felt. He had to keep himself alive long enough to see that the son of a bitch got what was coming to him.

He sat down and wrote a letter to Donna, explaining that his construction job was taking longer than expected. He had thought they would be finished by now, but it looked like the work was going to last another six to eight weeks. He felt certain that Murks would open the letter and read it before sending it off, and so he made sure not to mention anything about what had happened to Pozzi. He tried to keep the tone light and cheerful, adding a separate page for Juliette with a drawing of a castle and several riddles he thought would amuse her, and when Donna wrote back a week later, she said that she was happy to hear him sounding so well. It didn't matter what kind of work he was doing, she added. As long as he was enjoying it, that was reward enough in itself. But she did hope he would think about settling down after the job was over. They all missed him terribly, and Juliette couldn't wait to see him again.

It pained Nashe to read this letter, and for many days afterward he cringed whenever he thought of how thoroughly he had deceived his sister. He was more cut off from the world now than ever before, and there were times when he could feel something collapsing inside him, as if the ground he stood on were gradually giving way, crumbling under the pressure of his loneliness. The work continued, but that was a solitary business as well, and he avoided Murks as much as possible, refusing to speak to him except when it was absolutely necessary. Murks maintained the same placid demeanor as before, but Nashe would not be lulled by it, and he resisted the foreman's apparent friendliness with barely hidden contempt. At least once a day he went through an elaborate scene in which he imagined himself turning on Murks in a sudden outburst of violence – jumping on top of him and wrestling him to the ground, then freeing the gun from its holster and pointing it straight between his eyes. Work was the only escape from this tumult, the mindless labor of lifting and carting stones, and he threw himself into it with a grim and relentless passion, doing more on his own each day than he and Pozzi had ever managed together. He finished the second row of the wall in less than a week, loading up the wagon with three or four stones at once, and every time he made another journey across the meadow, he would inexplicably find himself thinking about Stone's miniature world in the main house, as if the act of touching a real stone had called forth a memory of the man who bore that name. Sooner or later, Nashe thought, there would be a new section to represent where he was now, a scale model of the wall and the meadow and the trailer, and once those things were finished, two tiny figures would be set down in the middle of the field: one for Pozzi and one for himself. The idea of such extravagant smallness began to exert an almost unbearable fascination over Nashe. Sometimes, powerless to stop himself, he even went so far as to imagine that he was already living inside the model. Flower and Stone would look down on him then, and he would suddenly be able to see himself through their eyes – as if he were no larger than a thumb, a little gray mouse darting back and forth in his cage.

It was worst at night, however, after the work had ended and he went back to the trailer alone. That was when he missed Pozzi the most, and in the beginning there were times when his sorrow and nostalgia were so acute that he could barely muster the strength to cook a proper meal for himself. Once or twice, he did not eat anything at all, but sat down in the living room with a bottle of bourbon and spent the hours until bedtime listening to requiem masses by Mozart and Verdi with the volume at full blast, literally weeping as he sat there amid the uproar of the music, remembering the kid through the onrushing wind of human voices as though he were no more than a piece of earth, a brittle clot of earth scattering into the dust he was made of. It soothed him to indulge in these histrionics of grief, to sink to the depths of a lurid, imponderable sadness, but even after he caught hold of himself and began to adjust to his solitude, he never fully recovered from Pozzi's absence, and he went on mourning the kid as though a part of himself had been lost forever. His domestic routines became dry and meaningless, a mechanical drudgery of preparing food and shoveling it into his mouth, of making things dirty and cleaning them up, the clockwork of animal functions. He tried to fill the emptiness by reading books, remembering how much pleasure they had given him on the road, but he found it difficult to concentrate now, and no sooner would he begin to read the words on the page than his head would swarm with images from his past: an afternoon he had spent in Minnesota five months ago, blowing bubbles with Juliette in the backyard; watching his friend Bobby Turnbull fall through a burning floor in Boston; the precise words he had spoken to Thérèse when he asked her to marry him; his mother's face when he walked into the hospital room in Florida for the first time after her stroke; Donna jumping up and down as a cheerleader in high school. He didn't want to remember any of these things, but without the stories in the books to take him away from himself, the memories kept pouring through him whether he liked it or not. He endured these assaults every night for close to a week, and then, not knowing what else to do, he broke down one morning and asked Murks if he could have a piano. No, it didn't have to be a real piano, he said, he just needed something to keep himself busy, a distraction to steady his nerves.

'I can understand that,' Murks said, trying to sound sympathetic. 'It must get lonely out here all by yourself. I mean, the kid had some peculiar ways about him, but at least he was company. It'll cost you, though. Not that you don't know that already.'

'I don't care,' Nashe said. 'I'm not asking for a real piano. It can't come to that much.'

'First time I ever heard of a piano that's not a piano. What kind of instrument are we talking about?'

'An electronic keyboard. You know, one of those portable things you plug into a socket in the wall. It comes with speakers and funny little plastic keys. You've probably seen them around in the stores.'

'I can't say that I have. But that don't mean nothing. You just tell me what you want, Nashe, and I'll see that you get it.'

Fortunately, he still had his books of music, and there was no shortage of material for him to play. Once he had sold his piano, there had seemed little reason to hold onto them, but he hadn't been able to throw them out, and so they had spent the whole year traveling around in the trunk of his car. There were about a dozen books in all: selections from a variety of composers (Bach, Couperin, Mozart, Beethoven, Schubert, Bartok, Satie), a couple of Czerny exercise books, and a fat volume of popular jazz and blues numbers transcribed for piano. Murks showed up with the instrument the next evening, and although it was a bizarre and ridiculous piece of technology – scarcely better than a toy, in fact – Nashe happily removed the thing from its box and set it up on the kitchen table. For a couple of nights he spent the hours between dinner and bedtime teaching himself how to play again, going through countless finger exercises to limber up his rusty joints as he learned the possibilities and limitations of the curious machine: the oddness of the touch, the amplified sounds, the lack of percussive force. In that respect, the keyboard functioned more like a harpsichord than a piano, and when he finally started to play real pieces on the third night, he discovered that older works – pieces written before the invention of the piano – tended to sound better than the new ones. This led him to concentrate on works by pre-nineteenth-century composers: *The Notebook of Anna Magdalena Bach*, *The Well-Tempered Clavier*, 'The Mysterious Barricades.' It was impossible for him to play this last piece without thinking about the wall, and he found himself returning to it more often than any of the others. It took just over two minutes to perform, and at no point in its slow, stately progress, with all its pauses, suspensions, and repetitions, did it require him to touch more than one note at a time. The music started and stopped, then started again, then stopped again, and yet through it all the piece continued to advance, pushing on toward a resolution that never came. Were those the mysterious barricades? Nashe remembered reading somewhere that no one was certain what Couperin had meant by that title. Some scholars interpreted it as a comical reference to women's underclothing – the impenetrability of corsets – while others saw it as an allusion to the unresolved harmonies in the piece. Nashe had no way of knowing. As far as he was concerned, the barricades stood for the wall he was building in the meadow, but that was quite another thing from knowing what they meant.

He no longer looked upon the hours after work as a blank and leaden time. Music brought oblivion, the sweetness of no longer having to think about himself, and once he had finished practicing for the night, Nashe usually felt so languorous and empty of emotion that he was able to fall asleep without much trouble. Still, he despised himself for allowing his feelings to soften toward Murks, for remembering the foreman's kindness to him with such gratitude. It wasn't just that Murks had gone out of his way to buy the keyboard – he had positively jumped at the chance, acting as though his single desire in life were to restore Nashe's good opinion of him. Nashe wanted to hate Murks totally, to turn him into something less than human by the sheer force of that hatred, but how was that possible when the man refused to act like a monster? Murks began showing up at the trailer with little presents (pies baked by his wife, woolen scarves, extra blankets), and at work he was never less than indulgent, always telling Nashe to slow down and not to push so hard. Most troubling of all, he even seemed to be worried about Pozzi, and several times a week he would give Nashe a progress report on the kid's condition, talking as though he were in constant touch with the hospital. What was Nashe to make of this solicitude? He sensed it was a trick, a smoke screen to cover up the true danger that Murks posed to him – and yet how could he be sure? Little by little, he felt himself weakening, gradually giving in to the foreman's quiet persistence. Every time he accepted another gift, every time he paused to chat about the weather or smiled at one of Calvin's remarks, he felt that he was betraying himself. And yet he kept on doing it. After a while, the only thing that prevented him from capitulating was the continued presence of the gun. That was the ultimate sign of how things stood between them, and he had only to look at the weapon on Murks's waist to remind himself of their fundamental inequality. Then one day, just to see what would happen, he turned to Murks and said, 'What's with the gun, Calvin? Are you still expecting trouble?' And Murks glanced down at the holster with a puzzled look on his face and said, 'I don't know. I just got into the habit of wearing it, I guess.' And when he came out to the meadow the next morning to begin work, the gun was gone.

Nashe didn't know what to think anymore. Was Murks telling him that he was free now, or was this simply another twist in an elaborate strategy of deception? Before Nashe could begin to decide, yet another element was thrown into the maelstrom of his uncertainty. It came in the form of a small boy, and for several days after that, Nashe felt that he was standing on the edge of a precipice, staring into the bowels of a private hell that he had never even known was there: a fiery underworld of clamoring beasts and dark, unimaginable impulses. On October thirtieth, just two days after Murks stopped wearing the gun, he came to the meadow holding the hand of a four-year-old boy whom he introduced as his grandson, Floyd Junior.

'Floyd Senior lost his job in Texas this summer,' he said, 'and now him and my daughter Sally are back here trying to make a fresh start. They're both out looking for work and a place to live, and since Addie's feeling a bit under the weather this morning, she thought it might be a good idea if little Floyd tagged along with me. I hope you don't mind. I'll keep an eye on him and make sure he doesn't get in your way.'

He was a scrawny child with a long, narrow face and a runny nose, and he stood there beside his grandfather bundled up in a thick red parka, gazing at Nashe with both curiosity and detachment, as if he had been plunked down in front of an odd-looking bird or shrub. No, Nashe didn't mind, but even if he had, how could he have dared to say it? For the better part of the morning, the boy scrambled among the piles of stones in the corner of the meadow, cavorting like some strange and silent monkey, but every time Nashe returned to that area to load up the wagon again, the boy would stop what he was doing, squat down on his perch, and study Nashe with those same rapt and expressionless eyes. It began to make Nashe feel uncomfortable, and after it had happened five or six times, he was so unnerved by it that he forced himself to look up at the boy and smile – simply as a way to break the spell. Unexpectedly, the boy smiled back at him and waved, and just then, as if remembering something from another century, Nashe understood that this was the same boy who had waved to him and Pozzi that night from the back of the station wagon. Was that how they had been found out? he wondered. Had the boy told his mother and father that he had seen two men digging a hole under the fence? Had the father then gone to Murks and reported what the boy had said? Nashe could never quite grasp how it happened, but an instant after this thought occurred to him, he looked up at Murks's grandson again and realized that he hated him more than he had ever hated anyone in his life. He hated him so much, he felt he wanted to kill him.

That was when the horror began. A tiny seed had been planted in Nashe's head, and before he even knew it was there, it was already sprouting inside him, proliferating like some wild, mutant flower, an ecstatic burgeoning that threatened to overrun the entire field of his consciousness. All he had to do was snatch the boy, he thought, and everything would change for him: he would suddenly know what he had to know. The boy for the truth, he would say to Murks, and at that point Calvin would have to talk, he would have to tell him what he had done with Pozzi. There wouldn't be any choice. If he didn't talk, his grandson would be dead. Nashe would make sure of that. He would strangle the kid right in front of his eyes.

Once Nashe allowed that thought to enter his head, it was succeeded by others, each one more violent and repulsive than the last. He slit the boy's throat with a razor. He kicked him to death with his boots. He took his head and smashed it against a stone, beating in his little skull until his brains turned to pulp. By the end of the morning, Nashe was in a frenzy, a delirium of homicidal lust. No matter how desperately he tried to erase those images, he would begin to hunger for them the moment they disappeared. That was the true horror: not that he could imagine killing the boy, but that even after he had imagined it, he wanted to imagine it again.

The worst part of it was that the boy kept coming back to the meadow – not just the next day, but the day after that as well. The first hours had been bad enough, but then the boy took it into his head to become infatuated with Nashe, responding to their exchange of smiles as if they had sworn an oath to each other and were now friends for life. Even before lunch, Floyd Junior had crawled down from his mountain of stones and was trotting after Nashe as his new hero pulled the wagon back and forth across the meadow. Murks made a move to stop him, but Nashe, already dreaming of how he was going to kill the child, waved him off and said it was all right. 'I don't mind,' he said. 'I like kids.' By then, Nashe had already begun to sense that something was wrong with the boy – some dullness or simplemindedness that made him appear subnormal. He was barely able to talk, and the only thing he said as he ran along behind him through the grass was *Jim! Jim! Jim!* pronouncing the name over and over again in a kind of moronic incantation. Except for his age, he seemed to have nothing in common with Juliette, and when Nashe compared the sad pallor of this little boy with the brightness and sparkle of his curly-headed daughter, his darling dervish with her crystal laugh and chubby knees, he felt nothing but contempt for him. With every hour that passed, his urge to attack him became stronger and more uncontrollable, and when six o'clock finally rolled around, it seemed almost a miracle to Nashe that the boy was still alive. He put away his tools in the shed, and just as he was about to shut the door, Murks came up to him and patted him on the shoulder. 'I have to hand it to you, Nashe,' he said. 'You've got the magic touch. The little fella ain't never taken to anyone like he did to you today. If I hadn't seen it with my own eyes, I wouldn't have believed it.'

The next morning, the boy came to the meadow dressed in his Halloween costume: a black-and-white skeleton outfit with a mask that looked like a skull. It was one of those crude, flimsy things you buy in a box at Woolworth's, and because the weather was cold that day, he wore it over his outer garments, which gave him an oddly bloated appearance, as if he had doubled his weight overnight. According to Murks, the boy had insisted on wearing the costume so that Nashe could see how he looked in it, and in his demented state at that moment, Nashe immediately began to wonder if the boy wasn't trying to tell him something. The costume stood for death, after all, death in its purest and most symbolic form, and perhaps that meant the boy knew what Nashe was planning, that he had come to the meadow dressed as death because he knew he was going to die. Nashe could not help seeing it as a message written in code. The boy was telling him that it was all right, that as long as Nashe was the one who killed him, everything was going to be all right.

He warred against himself for the whole of that day, devising any number of ruses to keep the skeleton boy at a safe distance from his murderous hands. In the morning, he told him to watch a particular stone at the back of one of the piles, instructing him to guard it so that it would not disappear, and in the afternoon Nashe let him play with the wagon while he went off and busied himself with masonry work at the other end of the meadow. But inevitably there were lapses, moments when the boy's concentration broke down and he came running toward Nashe, or else, even from a distance, those times when Nashe had to endure the litany of his name, the endless *Jim, Jim, Jim*, resounding like an alarm from the depths of his own fear. Again and again, he wanted to tell Murks not to bring him around anymore, but the struggle to keep his feelings under control took so much out of him, brought him so close to the point of mental collapse, that he could no longer trust himself with the words he wanted to say. He drank himself into a stupor that night, and the next morning, as if waking into the fullness of a nightmare, he opened the door of the trailer and saw that the boy was back – clutching a bag of Halloween candies against his chest, and then, without saying a word, solemnly handing it over to Nashe like a young brave delivering the spoils of his first hunt to the tribal chief.

'What's this for?' Nashe said to Murks.

'Jim,' the boy said, answering the question himself. 'Sweeties for Jim.'

'That's right,' Murks said. 'He wanted to share his candy with you.'

Nashe opened the bag a crack and peered down at the jumble of candy bars, apples, and raisins inside. 'This is taking it a bit far, don't you think, Calvin? What's the kid trying to do, poison me?'

'He don't mean nothing by it,' Murks said. 'He just felt sorry for you – missing out on the trick-or-treating and all. It's not like you have to eat it.'

'Sure,' Nashe said, staring at the boy and wondering how he was going to live through another day of this. 'It's the thought that counts, right?'

But he couldn't stand it anymore. The moment he stepped out into the meadow, he knew that he had reached his limit, that the boy would be dead within the next hour if he did not find a way to stop himself. He put one stone into the wagon, started to lift another, and then let it fall from his hands, listening to the thud as it crashed against the ground.

'There's something wrong with me today,' he said to Murks. 'I don't feel like myself.'

'Maybe it's that flu bug that's been going around,' Murks said.

'Yeah, that must be it. I'm probably coming down with the flu.'

'You work too hard, Nashe, that's the problem. You're all worn out.'

'If I lie down for an hour or two, maybe I'll feel better this afternoon.'

'Forget this afternoon. Take the whole day off. There's no sense in pushing too hard, no sense at all. You need to get your strength back.'

'All right, then. I'll take a couple of aspirins and crawl into bed. I hate to lose the day, though. But I guess it can't be helped.'

'Don't worry about the money. I'll give you credit for the ten hours anyway. We'll call it a baby-sitting bonus.'

'There's no need for that.'

'No, I don't suppose there is, but that don't mean I can't do it. It's probably just as well, anyway. The weather's too cold out here for little Floyd. He'd catch his death standing around in this meadow all day.'

'Yeah, I think you're right.'

'Of course I'm right. The kid would catch his death on a day like this.'

Nashe's head buzzed with these strangely omniscient words as he walked back to the trailer with Murks and the boy, and by the time he opened the door, he discovered that he was actually feeling ill. His body ached, and his muscles had become inexpressibly weak with exhaustion, as if he were suddenly burning up with a high fever. It was odd how quickly it had come over him: no sooner had Murks mentioned the word *flu* than he seemed to have caught it. Perhaps he had used himself up, he thought, and there was nothing left inside him. Perhaps he was so empty now that even a word could make him sick.

'Oh my gosh,' Murks said, slapping himself against the forehead just as he was about to leave. 'I almost forgot to tell you.'

'Tell me?' Nashe said. 'Tell me what?'

'About Pozzi. I called the hospital last night to see how he was, and the nurse said he was gone.'

'Gone. Gone in what sense?'

'Gone. As in gone good-bye. He just got himself up out of bed, put on his clothes, and walked out of the hospital.'

'You don't have to make up stories, Calvin. Jack's dead. He died two weeks ago.'

'No, sir, he ain't dead. It looked pretty bad there for a while, I'll grant you that, but then he pulled through. The little runt was tougher than we thought. And now he's got himself all better. At least better enough to stand up and walk out of the hospital. I thought you'd want to know.'

'I only want to know the truth. Nothing else interests me.'

'Well, that's the truth. Jack Pozzi's gone, and you don't have to worry about him no more.'

'Then let me call the hospital myself.'

'I can't do that, son, you know that. No calls allowed until you finish paying off the debt. At the rate you're going, it won't be long now. Then you can make all the calls you want. As far as I'm concerned, you can go on calling till kingdom come.'

It was three days before Nashe was able to work again. For the first two days he slept, rousing himself only when Murks entered the trailer to deliver aspirin and tea and canned soup, and when he was sufficiently conscious to realize that those two days had been lost to him, he understood that sleep had not only been a physical necessity, it had been a moral imperative as well. The drama with the little boy had changed him, and if not for the hibernation that followed, those forty-eight hours in which he had temporarily vanished from himself, he might never have woken up into the man he had become. Sleep was a passage from one life into another, a small death in which the demons inside him had caught fire again, melting back into the flames they were born of. It wasn't that they were gone, but they had no shape anymore, and in their formless ubiquity they had spread themselves through his entire body – invisible yet present, a part of him now in the same way that his blood and chromosomes were, a fire awash in the very fluids that kept him alive. He did not feel that he was any better or worse than he had been before, but he was no longer frightened. That was the crucial difference. He had rushed into the burning house and pulled himself out of the flames, and now that he had done it, the thought of doing it again no longer frightened him.

On the third morning he woke up hungry, instinctively climbing out of bed and heading for the kitchen, and although he was remarkably unsteady on his feet, he knew that hunger was a good sign, that it meant he was getting well. Rummaging around in one of the drawers for a clean spoon, he came upon a slip of paper with a telephone number written on it, and as he studied the childish, unfamiliar penmanship, he suddenly found himself thinking of the girl. She had written down her number for him at some point during the party on the sixteenth, he remembered, but several minutes passed before he could bring back her name. He ran through an inventory of near misses (Tammy, Kitty, Tippi, Kimberly), went blank for thirty or forty seconds after that, and then, just when he was about to give up, he found it: Tiffany. She was the only person who could help him, he realized. It would cost him a fortune to get that help, but what did it matter if his questions were finally answered? The girl had liked Pozzi, she seemed to have been crazy about him in fact, and once she heard the story of what had happened to him after the party, chances were that she would be willing to call the hospital. That was all it would take – one telephone call. She would ask them if Jack Pozzi had ever been a patient there, and then she would write to Nashe – a short letter telling him what she had found out. There might be a problem with the letter, of course, but that was a risk he'd have to take. He didn't think the letters from Donna had been opened. At least the envelopes hadn't looked tampered with, and why shouldn't Tiffany's letter get through to him as well? It was worth a try in any case. The more Nashe thought about this plan, the more promising it felt to him. What did he have to lose except money? He sat down at the kitchen table and began to drink his tea, trying to imagine what would happen when the girl came to visit him in the trailer. Before he could think of any of the words he would say to her, he discovered that he had an erection.

It took some doing to get Murks to go along with it, however. When Nashe explained that he wanted to see the girl, Calvin reacted with surprise, and then, almost immediately afterward, a look of profound disappointment. It was as though Nashe had let him down, as though he had reneged on some tacit understanding between them, and he wasn't about to let it happen without putting up a fight.

'It don't make sense,' Murks said. 'Nine hundred dollars for a roll in the hay. That's nine days' work, Nashe, ninety hours of sweat and toil for nothing. It just don't add up. A little taste of girlie flesh against all that. Anybody can see it don't add up. You're a smart fella, Nashe, it's not like you don't know what I'm talking about.'

'I don't ask you how you spend your money,' Nashe said. 'And it's none of your business how I spend mine.'

'I just hate to see a man make a fool of himself, that's all. Especially when there's no need for it.'

'Your needs are not my needs, Calvin. As long as I do the work, I'm entitled to any damned thing I want. It's written in the contract, and it's not your place to say a word about it.'

So Nashe won the argument, and even though Murks continued to grumble about it, he went ahead and arranged for the girl's visit. She was due to come on the tenth, less than a week after Nashe had found her telephone number in the drawer, and it was a good thing he didn't have to wait any longer than that, for once he had convinced Murks to call her, he found it impossible to think about anything else. Long before the girl showed up, therefore, he knew that his reasons for inviting her were only partly connected to Pozzi. The erection had proved that (along with the others that followed), and he spent the next few days alternating between fits of dread and excitement, skulking around the meadow like some hormone-crazed adolescent. But he had not been with a woman since the middle of the summer – not since that day in Berkeley when he had held the sobbing Fiona in his arms – and it was probably inevitable that the girl's impending visit should fill his head with thoughts about sex. That was her business, after all. She fucked men for money, and since he was already paying for it, what was the harm in fulfilling his end of the exchange? It wouldn't prevent him from asking for her help, but that was only going to take twenty or thirty minutes, and in order to get her there to spend that time with him, he had to buy her services for the whole evening. There would be no point in wasting those hours. They belonged to him, and just because he wanted the girl for one thing, that didn't mean it was wrong to want her for another thing as well.

The tenth turned out to be a cold night, more like winter than fall, with strong winds gusting across the meadow and a sky full of stars. The girl arrived in a fur coat, cheeks red and eyes tearing from the chill, and Nashe felt that she was prettier than he had remembered, although it could have been the color in her face that made him think that. Her clothes were less provocative than the last time – white turtleneck sweater, blue jeans with woolen leg warmers, the ever-present spike heels – and all in all it was an improvement over the gaudy costume she had worn in October. She seemed more her age now, and for whatever it was worth, Nashe decided that he preferred her this way, that it made him feel less uncomfortable to look at her.

It helped that she smiled at him when she entered the trailer, and even though he found it a somewhat florid and theatrical smile, there was enough warmth in it to persuade him that she was not unhappy to be seeing him again. He realized that she had expected Pozzi to be there as well, and when she glanced around the room and did not find him, it was only natural that she should ask Nashe where he was. But Nashe couldn't quite bring himself to tell the truth – at least not yet. 'Jack was called away on another job,' he said. 'Remember the Texas project he told you about last time? Well, our oilman had some questions about the drawings, and so he flew Jack down to Houston last night on his private jet. It was one of those spur-of-the-moment things. Jack was real sorry about it, but that's how it is with our work. We have to keep our clients happy.'

'Geez,' the girl said, making no attempt to hide her disappointment. 'I liked that little guy a whole lot. I was looking forward to seeing him again.'

'He's one in a million,' Nashe said. 'They don't make them any better than Jack.'

'Yeah, he's a terrific guy. You get a john like that, and it doesn't feel like work anymore.'

Nashe smiled at the girl, and then he reached out tentatively and touched her shoulder. 'I'm afraid you'll have to settle for me tonight,' he said.

'Well, worse things have happened,' she replied, recovering quickly with a playful, down-from-under look. To emphasize the point, she moaned softly and began running her tongue over her lips. 'I might be wrong,' she said, 'but I seem to remember that we had some unfinished business to take care of anyway.'

Nashe had half a mind to tell her to take off her clothes right then, but he suddenly felt self-conscious, tongue-tied by his own arousal, and instead of taking her in his arms, he just stood where he was, wondering what to do next. He wished that Pozzi could have left behind a couple of jokes for him to use then, a few wisecracks to lighten up the atmosphere.

'How about a little music?' he suggested, seizing on the first thing that popped into his head. Before the girl could answer, he was already down on the floor, digging through the piles of cassettes he kept under the coffee table. After clattering among the operas and classical pieces for close to a minute, he finally pulled out his tape of Billie Holiday songs, *Billie's Greatest Hits*.

The girl frowned at what she called the 'old-fashioned' music, but when Nashe asked her to dance, she seemed touched by the quaintness of the proposal, as if he had just asked her to partake of some prehistoric rite – a taffy pull, for example, or bobbing for apples in a wooden bucket. But the fact was that Nashe liked to dance, and he thought the movement might help to steady his nerves. He took hold of her with a firm grip, guiding her in small circles around the living room, and after a few minutes she seemed to settle into it, following him more gracefully than he would have expected. In spite of the high heels, she was impressively light on her feet.

'I've never known anyone named Tiffany before,' he said. 'I think it's very nice. It makes me think of beautiful and expensive things.'

'That's the idea,' she said. 'It's supposed to make you see diamonds.'

'Your parents must have known you'd turn out to be a beautiful girl.'

'My parents had nothing to do with it. I picked the name myself.'

'Oh. Well, that makes it even better. There's no point in being stuck with a name you don't like, is there?'

'I couldn't stand mine. As soon as I got away from home, I changed it.'

'Was it really that bad?'

'How would you like to be called Dolores? It's about the worst name I can think of.'

'That's funny. My mother's name was Dolores, and she never liked it either.'

'No shit? Your old lady was a Dolores?'

'Honest. She was Dolores from the day she was born until the day she died.'

'If she didn't like being Dolores, why didn't she change it?'

'She did. Not in a big way like you, but she used to go by a nickname. In fact, I never knew her real name was Dolores until I was about ten years old.'

'What did she call herself?'

'Dolly.'

'Yeah, I tried that for a while, too, but it wasn't much better. It only works if you're fat. Dolly. It's a name for a fat woman.'

'Well, my mother was pretty fat, now that you mention it. Not always, but in the last few years of her life, she put on a lot of weight. Too much booze. It does that to some people. It has something to do with how the alcohol metabolizes in your blood.'

'My old man drank like a fish for years, but he was always a skinny bastard. The only way you could tell was by looking at the veins around his nose.'

The conversation went back and forth like that for a while, and when the tape ran out, they sat down on the sofa and opened a bottle of Scotch. Almost predictably, Nashe imagined that he was falling for her, and now that the ice had been broken, he began to ask her all sorts of questions about herself, trying to create an intimacy that would somehow mask the nature of their transaction and turn her into someone real. But the talk was part of the transaction, too, and even though she went on at great length about herself, at bottom he understood that she was only doing her job, talking because he was one of those customers who liked to talk. Everything she said seemed plausible, but at the same time he felt that she had been through it all before, that her words were not false so much as untrue, a delusion that she had little by little convinced herself to believe in, much as Pozzi had deluded himself with his dreams about the World Series of Poker. At one point, she even told him that hooking was only a temporary solution for her. 'Once I get enough cash together,' she said, 'I'm going to quit the life and go into show business.' It was impossible not to feel sorry for her, impossible not to feel saddened by her childish banality, but Nashe was too far gone by then to let that stand in his way.

'I think you'll make a wonderful actress,' he said. 'The minute I started dancing with you, I could tell you were the real thing. You move like an angel.'

'Fucking keeps you in shape,' she said seriously, announcing it as though it were a medical fact. 'It's good for the pelvis. And if there's one thing I've done a lot of in the past couple of years, it's fuck. I must be as limber as a goddamn contortionist by now.'

'It so happens that I know a few agents in New York,' Nashe said, unable to stop himself anymore. 'One of them has a big operation, and I'm sure he'd be interested in taking a look at you. A fellow by the name of Sid Zeno. If you like, I can call him tomorrow and set up an appointment.'

'We're not talking about skin flicks, are we?'

'No, no, nothing like that. Zeno's strictly on the up-and-up. He handles some of the best young talent in the movies today.'

'It's not that I wouldn't do it, you understand. But once you get into that biz, it's hard to get out. They typecast you, and then you never get a chance to play any parts with your clothes on. I mean, my bod's okay, but it's nothing to get worked up about. I'd rather do something where I can really act. You know, land a part in one of the daytime soaps, or maybe even try out for a sitcom. It might not be obvious to you, but once I get going, I can be pretty funny.'

'No problem. Sid has good contacts with television, too. That's how he got started in fact. Back in the fifties, he was one of the first agents to work exclusively in television.'

Nashe hardly knew what he was saying anymore. Filled with desire, and yet half dreading what would come of that desire, he blathered on as if he thought the girl might actually believe the nonsense he was telling her. But once they adjourned to the bedroom, she did not disappoint him. She began by letting him kiss her on the mouth, and because Nashe hadn't dared to hope for such a thing, he instantly imagined that he was falling in love with her. It was true that her naked body was less than beautiful, but now that he understood that she wasn't going to rush him through it or humiliate him by acting bored, he didn't care what she looked like. It had been so long, after all, and once they moved onto the bed, she demonstrated the talents of her overworked pelvis with such pride and abandon, it never occurred to him that the pleasure he seemed to be giving her could be anything but authentic. After a while, his brains became so scrambled that he lost his head, and he wound up saying a number of idiotic things to her, things so stupid and inappropriate, in fact, that if he hadn't been the one who was saying them, he would have thought he was insane.

What he proposed was that she stay there and live with him while he worked on the wall. He would take care of her, he said, and once the work was finished, they would go to New York together and he would manage her career. Forget Sid Zeno. He would do a better job because he believed in her, because he was crazy about her. They wouldn't be in the trailer more than a month or two, and she wouldn't have to do anything but rest and take it easy. He would do all the cooking, all the household chores, and it would be like a vacation for her, a way of getting the past two years out of her system. It wasn't a bad life in the meadow. It was calm and simple and good for the soul. He just needed to share it with someone now. He had been alone for too long, and he didn't think he could go on by himself anymore. It was too much to ask of anyone, he said, and the loneliness was beginning to drive him crazy. Just last week, he had almost killed someone, an innocent little boy, and he was afraid that worse things would happen to him if he didn't make some changes in his life very soon. If she agreed to stay there with him, he would do anything for her. He would give her anything she wanted. He would love her until she exploded with happiness.

Fortunately, he delivered this speech with such passion and sincerity that he left her with no alternative but to think it was a joke. No one could say such things with a straight face and expect to be believed, and the very foolishness of Nashe's confession was what saved him from total embarrassment. The girl took him for a prankster, an oddball with a gift for making up wild stories, and instead of telling him to drop dead (which she might have done if she had taken him seriously), she smiled at the trembling supplication in his voice and played along as if it were the funniest thing he had said all night. 'I'll be happy to live here with you, honey,' she said. 'All you have to do is take care of Regis, and I'll move in with you first thing tomorrow morning.'

'Regis?' he said.

'You know, the guy who handles my appointments. My pimp.'

Hearing that response, Nashe understood how ridiculous he must have sounded. But her sarcasm had given him a second chance, an escape from impending disaster, and rather than let his feelings show (the hurt, the wretchedness, the misery her words had caused), he bounced up naked from the bed and clapped his hands together in mock exuberance. 'Great!' he said. 'I'll kill the bastard tonight, and then you'll be mine forever.'

She started laughing then, as though a part of her actually enjoyed hearing him say those things, and the moment he became conscious of what that laughter meant, he felt a strange and powerful bitterness surge up inside him. He started laughing himself, joining in with her to keep the taste of that bitterness in his mouth, to revel in the comedy of his own abjection. Then, out of nowhere, he suddenly remembered Pozzi. It came like an electric shock, and the jolt of it nearly threw him to the floor. He hadn't given Jack a single thought in the past two hours, and the selfishness of that neglect mortified him. He stopped laughing with almost terrifying abruptness, and then he started climbing into his clothes, yanking on his pants as if a bell had just sounded in his head.

'There's only one problem,' the girl said through her subsiding laughter, still bent on prolonging the game. 'What happens when Jack comes back from his trip? I mean, it could get a little crowded around here, don't you think? He's a cute guy, too, you know, and maybe there'll be nights when I feel like sleeping with him. What would you do then? Would you be jealous or what?'

'That's just it,' Nashe said, his voice suddenly grim and hard. 'Jack's not coming back. He disappeared almost a month ago.'

'What do you mean? I thought you said he was in Texas.'

'I was just making that up. There's no job in Texas, there's no oilman, there's no nothing. The day after you came here for the party, Jack tried to escape. I found him lying outside the trailer the next morning. His skull was bashed in, and he was unconscious – just lying there in a pool of his own blood. Chances are he's dead by now, but I'm not sure. That's what I want you to find out for me.'

He told her everything then, going through the whole story about Pozzi and the card game and the wall, but he had already told her so many lies that night, it was hard to make her believe a word he said. She just looked at him as though he were mad, a lunatic foaming at the mouth with tales of little purple men in flying saucers. But Nashe kept hammering away, and after a while his vehemence began to frighten her. If she hadn't been sitting naked on the bed, she probably would have made a run for it, but as it was she was trapped, and eventually Nashe managed to wear her down, describing the results of Pozzi's beating in such ugly and elaborate detail that the full horror of it finally sank in, and by the time that happened, she was sobbing there on the bed, her face buried in her hands and her thin back shaking in fierce, uncontrollable spasms.

Yes, she said. She would call the hospital. She promised she would.

Poor Jack. Of course she would call the hospital. Jesus Christ poor Jack. Jesus Christ poor Jack sweet mother of God. She would call the hospital, and then she would write him a letter. Goddamn them. Of course she would do it. Poor Jack. Goddamn them to hell. Sweet Jack oh Jesus poor Jesus poor mother of God. Yes, she would do it. She promised she would. The moment she got home, she would pick up the phone and do it. Yes, he could count on her. God God God God God. She promised. She promised she would do it.

9

Crazy with loneliness. Every time Nashe thought of the girl, those were the first words that entered his head: *crazy with loneliness*. Eventually, he repeated that phrase so often to himself, it began to lose its meaning.

He never held it against her that the letter did not come. He knew that she had kept her promise, and because he continued to believe that, he did not despair. If anything, he began to feel encouraged. He was at a loss to explain this change of heart, but the fact was that he was growing optimistic, perhaps more optimistic than at any time since the first day in the meadow.

There was no point in asking Murks what he had done with the girl's letter. He only would have lied to him, and Nashe didn't want to expose his suspicions if nothing could be gained by it. Eventually, he was going to learn the truth. He knew that now, and the certainty of that knowledge comforted him, kept him going from one day to the next. 'Things happen in their own sweet time,' he told himself. Before you could learn the truth, you had to learn patience.

Meanwhile, work on the wall advanced. After the third row was completed, Murks built a wooden platform for him, and Nashe now had to mount the steps of this little structure each time he put another stone in place. It slowed his progress somewhat, but that meant nothing compared to the pleasure he felt in being able to work off the ground. Once he started on the fourth row, the wall began to change for him. It was taller than a man now, taller even than a big man like himself, and the fact that he could no longer see past it, that it blocked his view to the other side, made him feel as though something important had begun to happen. All of a sudden, the stones were turning into a wall, and in spite of the pain it had cost him, he could not help admiring it. Whenever he stopped and looked at it now, he felt awed by what he had done.

For several weeks he read almost nothing. Then one night in late November he picked up a book by William Faulkner (*The Sound and the Fury*), opened it at random, and came across these words in the middle of a sentence: '. . . until someday in very disgust he risks everything on the single blind turn of a card . . .'

Sparrows, cardinals, chickadees, blue jays. Those were the only birds left in the woods now. And crows. Those best of all, Nashe felt. Every now and then, they would come swooping down over the meadow, letting out their strange, throttled cries, and he would interrupt what he was doing to watch them pass overhead. He loved the suddenness of their comings and goings, the way they would appear and disappear, as if for no reason at all.

Standing out by his trailer in the early morning, he could look through the bare trees and see the outlines of Flower and Stone's house. On some mornings, however, the fog was too thick for him to see that far. Even the wall could vanish then, and he would have to scan the meadow a long time before he could tell the difference between the gray stones and the gray air around them.

He had never thought of himself as a man destined for great things. All his life, he had assumed that he was just like everyone else. Now, little by little, he was beginning to suspect that he had been wrong.

Those were the days when he thought most about Flower's collection of objects: the handkerchiefs, the spectacles, the rings, the mountains of absurd memorabilia. Every couple of hours, it seemed, another one of them would appear in his head. He was not disturbed by this, however, merely astonished.

Every night before going to bed, he would write down the number of stones he had added to the wall that day. The figures themselves were unimportant to him, but once the list had grown to ten or twelve entries, he began to take pleasure in the simple accumulation, studying the results in the same way he had once read the box scores in the morning paper. At first, he imagined it was a purely statistical pleasure, but after a while he sensed that it was fulfilling some inner need, some compulsion to keep track of himself and not lose sight of where he was. By early December, he began to think of it as a journal, a logbook in which the numbers stood for his most intimate thoughts.

Listening to *The Marriage of Figaro* in the trailer at night. Sometimes, when a particularly beautiful aria came on, he would imagine that Juliette was singing to him, that it was her voice he was hearing.

The cold weather bothered him less than he thought it would. Even on the bitterest days, he would shed his jacket within an hour of starting work, and by midafternoon he would often be down to his shirtsleeves.

Murks would stand there in his heavy coat, shivering against the wind, and yet Nashe would feel almost nothing. It made so little sense to him, he wondered if his body hadn't caught fire.

One day, Murks suggested that they begin using the jeep to cart the stones. They could increase the loads that way, he said, and the wall could go up more quickly. But Nashe turned him down. The noise of the engine would distract him, he said. And besides, he was used to the old way of doing things. He liked the slowness of the wagon, the long walks across the meadow, the odd little rumbling sound of the wheels. 'If it ain't broke,' he said, 'why fix it?'

Some time in the third week of November, Nashe realized that it would be possible to bring himself back to zero on his birthday, which fell on December thirteenth. It would mean making several small adjustments in his habits (spending a bit less on food, for example, cutting out newspapers and cigars), but the symmetry of the plan appealed to him, and he decided it would be worth the effort. If all went well, he would win back his freedom on the day he turned thirty-four. It was an arbitrary ambition, but once he put his mind to it, he found that it helped him to organize his thoughts, to concentrate on what had to be done.

He went over his calculations with Murks every morning, toting up the pluses and minuses to make sure there were no discrepancies, checking and rechecking until their figures matched. On the night of the twelfth, therefore, he knew for certain that the debt would be paid off by three o'clock the next day. He wasn't planning to stop then, however. He had already told Murks that he wanted to make use of the contract rider to earn some traveling money, and since he knew exactly how much he was going to need (enough to pay for cabs, a plane ticket to Minnesota, and Christmas presents for Juliette and her cousins), he had resigned himself to staying on for another week. That would take him up to the twentieth. The first thing he would do after that was get a cab to drive him to the hospital in Doylestown, and once he found out that Pozzi had never been there, he would call another cab and go to the police. He would probably have to hang around for a while to help with the investigation, but no more than a few days, he thought, perhaps only one or two. If he was lucky, he might even get back to Minnesota in time for Christmas Eve.

He didn't tell Murks it was his birthday. He felt oddly out of sorts that morning, and even as the day wore on and three o'clock approached, an overwhelming sadness continued to drag down his spirits. Until then, Nashe had assumed that he would want to celebrate – to light up an imaginary cigar, perhaps, or merely to shake Murks's hand – but the memory of Pozzi weighed too heavily on him, and he couldn't rouse himself into the proper mood. Each time he picked up another stone, he felt as if he were carrying Pozzi in his arms again, lifting him off the ground and looking into his poor, annihilated face, and when two o'clock came round and the time had dwindled to a matter of minutes, he suddenly found himself thinking back to that day in October when he and the kid had reached this point together, working their heads off in a manic burst of happiness. He missed him so much, he realized. He missed him so much, it ached just to think about him.

The best way to handle it was to do nothing, he decided, just go on working and ignore the whole business, but at three o'clock he was jolted by a strange piercing noise – a whoop or a shriek or a cry of distress – and when Nashe looked up to see what the trouble was, he saw Murks waving his hat at him from across the meadow. *You did it!* Nashe heard him say. *You're a free man now!* Nashe stopped for a moment and waved back with a casual flip of his hand, and then he immediately bent down over his work again, fixing his attention on the wheelbarrow in which he was stirring cement. Very briefly, he fought off an impulse to start crying, but it didn't last more than a couple of seconds, and by the time Murks had walked over to congratulate him, he was fully in control of himself again.

'I figured maybe you'd like to go out for a drink with me and Floyd tonight,' Calvin said.

'What for?' Nashe answered, barely looking up from his work.

'I don't know. Just to get out and see what the world looks like again. You've been cooped up here a long time, son. It might not be a bad idea to do a little celebrating.'

'I thought you were against celebrations.'

'Depends on what kind of celebrating you mean. I'm not talking about anything fancy here. Just a few drinks over at Ollie's in town. A workingman's night out.'

'You forget that I don't have any money.'

'That's all right. The drinks are on me.'

'Thanks, but I think I'll pass. I was planning on writing a few letters tonight.'

'You can always write them tomorrow.'

'That's true. But then again, I could be dead tomorrow. You never know what's going to happen.'

'All the more reason not to worry about it.'

'Maybe some other time. It's nice of you to offer, but I'm just not in the mood tonight.'

'I'm just trying to be friendly, Nashe.'

'I know you are, and I appreciate it. But you don't have to worry about me. I can take care of myself.'

Cooking dinner alone in the trailer that night, however, Nashe regretted his stubbornness. There was no question that he had done the right thing, but the truth was that he was desperate for a chance to leave the meadow, and the moral correctness he had shown in refusing Murks's invitation felt like a paltry triumph to him now. He spent ten hours a day in the man's company, after all, and just because they sat down together and had a drink, it wasn't going to stop him from turning the son of a bitch over to the police. As it happened, Nashe got precisely what he wanted anyway. Just after he finished dinner, Murks and his son-in-law came around to the trailer to ask him if he had changed his mind. They were going out now, they said, and it didn't seem fair that he should miss out on the fun.

'It's not like you're the only one who's been set free today,' Murks said, blowing his nose into a large white handkerchief. 'I've been out there in that field same as you, freezing my butt off seven days a week. It's about the worst damned job I've ever had. I've got nothing personal against you, Nashe, but it's been no picnic. No, sir, no picnic at all. Maybe it's about time we sat down and buried the hatchet.'

'You know,' Floyd said, smiling at Nashe as if to encourage him, 'let bygones be bygones.'

'You guys don't give up, do you?' Nashe said, still trying to sound reluctant.

'We're not twisting your arm or anything,' Murks said. 'Just trying to enter into the Christmas spirit.'

'Like Santa's helpers,' Floyd said. 'Spreading good cheer wherever we go.'

'All right,' Nashe said, studying their expectant faces. 'I'll go out for a drink with you. Why the hell not?'

Before they could drive to town, they had to stop off at the main house to get Murks's car. Murks's car meant his car, of course, but in the excitement of the moment Nashe had forgotten all about that. He sat in the back of the jeep as they bounced along through the dark and icy woods, and it wasn't until this first little journey was over that he realized his mistake. He saw the red Saab parked in the driveway, and the moment he understood what he was looking at, he felt himself go numb with grief. The thought of riding in it again made him sick, but there was no way he could back out of it now. They were set to go, and he had already caused enough fuss for one night.

He didn't say a word. He took his place in the backseat and closed his eyes, trying to make his mind go blank, listening to the familiar sound of the engine as the car moved along the road. He could hear that Murks and Floyd were talking in the front, but he didn't pay attention to what they said, and after a while their voices blurred with the sound of the engine, producing a low, continuous hum that vibrated in his ears, a lulling music that sang along his skin and dug down into the depths of his body. He didn't open his eyes again until the car stopped, and then he found himself standing in a parking lot at the edge of a small, deserted town, listening to a traffic sign rattle in the wind. Christmas decorations blinked in the distance down the street, and the cold air was red with the pulsing reflections, the throbs of light that bounced off the shop windows and glowed on the frozen sidewalks. Nashe had no idea where he was. They could still be in Pennsylvania, he thought, but then again, they could have crossed the river and gone into New Jersey. For a brief moment, he considered asking Murks which state they were in, but then he decided that he didn't care.

Ollie's was a dark and noisy place, and he took an immediate dislike to it. Country-and-western songs thundered out of a jukebox in one corner, and the bar was thronged with a crush of beer-drinkers – men in flannel shirts, for the most part, decked out in fancy baseball caps and wearing belts with large, elaborate buckles. They were farmers and mechanics and truck drivers, Nashe supposed, and the few women scattered among them looked like regulars – puffy, dough-faced alcoholics who sat on the barstools and laughed as loudly as the men. Nashe had been in a hundred places like this before, and it didn't take thirty seconds for him to realize that he wasn't up to it tonight, that he had been away from crowds for too long. Everyone was talking at once, it seemed, and the ruckus of loud voices and blaring music was already hurting his head.

They drank several rounds at a table in the far corner of the room, and after the first couple of bourbons Nashe began to feel somewhat revived. Floyd did most of the talking, addressing nearly all his remarks to Nashe, and after a while it became hard not to notice how little Murks was contributing to the conversation. He looked more under the weather than usual, Nashe thought, and every so often he would turn away and cough violently into his handkerchief, hawking up nasty gobs of phlegm. These fits seemed to take a lot out of him, and afterward he would sit there in silence, pale and shaken from the effort to still his lungs.

'Granddad hasn't been feeling too well lately,' Floyd said to Nashe (he always referred to Murks as Granddad). 'I've been trying to talk him into taking a couple of weeks off.'

'It's nothing,' Murks said. 'Just a touch of the ague, that's all.'

'The ague?' Nashe said. 'Where the hell did you learn to talk, Calvin?'

'What's wrong with the way I talk?' Murks said.

'No one uses words like that anymore,' Nashe said. 'They went out about a hundred years ago.'

'I learned it from my mother,' Murks said. 'And she only died six years back. She'd be eighty-eight if she was alive today – which proves that word ain't as old as you think it is.'

Nashe found it strange to hear Murks talking about his mother. It was difficult to imagine that he had once been a child, let alone that twenty or twenty-five years ago he had once been Nashe's age – a young man with a life to look forward to, a person with a future. For the first time since they had been thrown together, Nashe realized that he knew next to nothing about Murks. He didn't know where he had been born; he didn't know how he had met his wife or how many children he had; he didn't even know how long he had been working for Flower and Stone. Murks was a creature who existed wholly in the present for him, and beyond that present he was nothing, a being as insubstantial as a shadow or a thought. When all was said and done, however, that was precisely how Nashe wanted it. Even if Murks had turned to him at that moment and offered to tell the story of his life, he would have refused to listen.

Meanwhile, Floyd was telling him about his new job. Since Nashe seemed to have played some part in his finding it, he had to sit through an exhaustive, rambling account of how Floyd had struck up a conversation with the chauffeur who had driven the girl from Atlantic City on the night of her visit last month. The limousine company had apparently been looking for new drivers, and Floyd had gone down the very next day to apply for a job. He was only working on a part-time basis now, just two or three days a week, but he was hoping they'd have more work for him after the first of the year. Just for something to say, Nashe asked him how he liked wearing the uniform. Floyd said it didn't bother him. It was nice to have something special to wear, he said, it made him feel like someone important.

'The main thing is that I love to drive,' he continued. 'I don't care what kind of car it is. As long as I'm sitting behind the wheel and moving down the road, I'm a happy man. I can't think of a better way to make a living. Imagine getting paid for something you love to do. It almost doesn't feel right.'

'Yes,' Nashe said, 'driving is a good thing. I agree with you about that.'

'Well, you ought to know,' Floyd said. 'I mean, look at Granddad's car. That's a beautiful machine. Isn't that so, Granddad?' he said to Murks. 'It's a stunner, isn't it?'

'A fine piece of work,' Calvin said. 'Handles real good. Takes the curves and hills like nobody's business.'

'You must have enjoyed driving around in that thing,' Floyd said to Nashe.

'I did,' Nashe said. 'It was the best car I ever owned.'

'There's one thing that puzzles me, though,' Floyd said. 'How did you ever manage to put so many miles on it? I mean, it's a pretty new model, and the odometer's already showing close to eighty thousand miles. That's an awful lot of driving to do in one year.'

'I suppose it is,' Nashe said.

'Were you some kind of traveling salesman or something?'

'Yeah, that's it, I was a traveling salesman. They gave me a large territory, and so I had to be on the road a lot. You know, lugging around the samples in the trunk, living out of a suitcase, staying in a different city every night. I moved around so much, I sometimes forgot where I lived.'

'I think I'd like that,' Floyd said. 'It sounds like a good job to me.'

'It's not bad. You have to like being alone, but once you've taken care of that, the rest is easy.'

Floyd was beginning to get on his nerves. The man was an oaf, Nashe thought, a full-fledged imbecile, and the longer he went on talking, the more he reminded Nashe of his son. They both had that same desperate desire to please, that same fawning timidity, that same lostness in the eyes. To look at him, you would never think he would harm a soul – but he had harmed Jack that night, Nashe was sure of it, and it was precisely that emptiness inside him that had made it possible, that immense chasm of want. It wasn't that Floyd was a cruel or violent person, but he was big and strong and ever so willing, and he loved Granddad more than anyone else in the world. It was written all over his face, and every time he turned his eyes in Murks's direction, it was as though he were looking at a god. Granddad had told him what to do, and he had gone ahead and done it.

After the third or fourth round of drinks, Floyd asked Nashe if he would care to play some pool. There were several tables in the back room, he said, and one of them was bound to be free. Nashe was feeling a little woozy by then, but he accepted anyway, welcoming it as a chance to get up from his seat and end the conversation. It was close to eleven o'clock, and the crowd at Ollie's had become thinner and less boisterous. Floyd asked Murks if he wanted to join them, but Calvin said he'd rather stay where he was and finish his drink.

It was a large, dimly lit room with four pool tables in the center and a number of pinball machines and computer games along the side walls. They stopped by the rack near the door to choose their sticks, and as they walked over to one of the free tables, Floyd asked if it might not be more interesting if they made a friendly little bet on the action. Nashe had never been much of a pool player, but he didn't think twice about saying yes. He wanted to beat Floyd in the worst way, he realized, and there was no question that putting some money on it would help him to concentrate.

'I don't have any cash,' he said. 'But I'll be good for it as soon as I get paid next week.'

'I know that,' Floyd said. 'If I didn't think you'd be good for it, I wouldn't have asked.'

'How much do you want to make it for?'

'I don't know. Depends on what you've got in mind.'

'How about ten dollars a game?'

'Ten dollars? All right, sounds good to me.'

They played eight-ball on one of those bumpy, quarter-a-rack tables, and Nashe scarcely said a word the whole time they were there. Floyd wasn't bad, but in spite of his drunkenness, Nashe was better, and he wound up playing his heart out, zeroing in on his shots with a skill and precision that surpassed anything he had done before. He felt utterly happy and loose, and once he fell into the rhythm of the clicking, tumbling balls, the stick began to glide through his fingers as if it were moving on its own. He won the first four games by steadily increasing margins (by one ball, by two balls, by four balls, by six balls), and then he won the fifth game before Floyd could even take a turn, sinking two striped balls on the break and going on from there to clear the table, ending with a flourish as he sank the eight-ball on a three-way combination shot in the corner pocket.

'That's enough for me,' Floyd said after the fifth game. 'I figured you might be good, but this is ridiculous.'

'Just luck,' Nashe said, struggling to keep a smile off his face. 'I'm generally pretty feeble. Things kept falling my way tonight.'

'Feeble or not, it looks like I owe you fifty bucks.'

'Forget the money, Floyd. It doesn't make any difference to me.'

'What do you mean, forget it? You just won yourself fifty bucks. It's yours.'

'No, no, I'm telling you to keep it. I don't want your money.'

Floyd kept trying to press the fifty dollars into Nashe's hand, but Nashe was just as adamant about refusing it, and after a few moments it finally dawned on Floyd that Nashe meant what he was saying, that he wasn't just putting on an act.

'Buy your little boy a present,' Nashe said. 'If you want to make me happy, use it on him.'

'It's awfully good of you,' Floyd said. 'Most guys wouldn't let fifty bucks slip through their fingers like that.'

'I'm not most guys,' Nashe said.

'I guess I owe you one,' Floyd said, patting Nashe's back in an awkward show of gratitude. 'Any time you need a favor, all you have to do is ask.'

It was one of those empty, obliging remarks that people often make at such moments, and under any other circumstances Nashe probably would have let it pass. But he suddenly found himself glowing with the warmth of an idea, and rather than lose the opportunity he had just been given, he looked straight back at Floyd and said, 'Well, now that you mention it, maybe there is one thing you can do for me. It's a very small thing really, but your help would mean a lot.'

'Sure, Jim,' Floyd said. 'Just name it.'

'Let me drive the car back home tonight.'

'You mean Granddad's car?'

'That's right, Granddad's car. The car I used to own.'

'I don't think it's for me to say whether you can or not, Jim. It's Granddad's car, and he's the one you'll have to ask. But I'll certainly put in a word for you.'

As it turned out, Murks didn't mind. He was feeling pretty tuckered, he said, and he was planning to ask Floyd to drive the car anyway. If Floyd wanted to let Nashe do it, that was all right with him. As long as they got to where they were going, what difference did it make?

When they stepped outside, they discovered that it was snowing. It was the first snow of the year, and it fell in thick, moist flakes, most of it melting the instant it touched the ground. The Christmas decorations had been turned off down the street, and the wind had stopped blowing. The air was still now, so still that the weather felt almost warm. Nashe took a deep breath, glanced up at the sky, and stood there for a moment as the snow fell against his face. He was happy, he realized, happier than he had been in a long time.

When they came to the parking lot, Murks handed him the keys to the car. Nashe unlocked the front door, but just as he was about to open it and climb in, he pulled back his hand and started to laugh. 'Hey, Calvin,' he said. 'Where the hell are we?'

'What do you mean where are we?' Murks said.

'What town?'

'Billings.'

'Billings? I thought that was in Montana.'

'Billings, New Jersey.'

'So we're not in Pennsylvania anymore?'

'No, you have to cross the bridge to get back there. Don't you remember?'

'I don't remember anything.'

'Just take Route Sixteen. It carries you right on through.'

He hadn't thought it would be so important to him, but once he positioned himself behind the wheel, he noticed that his hands were trembling. He started the engine, flicked on the headlights and windshield wipers, and then backed out slowly from the parking space. It hadn't been so long, he thought. Just three and a half months, and yet it took a while before he felt any of the old pleasure again. He was distracted by Murks coughing beside him in the front seat, by Floyd rattling on about how he had lost at pool in the back, and it was only when Nashe turned on the radio that he was able to forget they were there with him, that he was not alone as he had been for all those months when he had driven back and forth across America. He never wanted to do that again, he realized, but once he left the town behind him and could accelerate on the empty road, it was hard not to pretend for a little while, to imagine that he was back in those days before the real story of his life had begun. This was the only chance he would have, and he wanted to savor what had been given to him, to push the memory of who he had once been as far as it would go. The snow whirled down onto the windshield before him, and in his mind he saw the crows swooping down over the meadow, calling out with their mysterious cries as he watched them pass overhead. The meadow would look beautiful under the snow, he thought, and he hoped it would go on falling through the night so he could wake up to see it that way in the morning. He imagined the immensity of the white field, and the snow continuing to fall until even the mountains of stones were covered, until everything disappeared under an avalanche of whiteness.

He had turned the radio to a classical station, and he recognized the music as something familiar, a piece he had listened to many times before. It was the andante from an eighteenth-century string quartet, but even though Nashe knew every passage by heart, the name of the composer kept eluding him. He quickly narrowed it down to Mozart or Haydn, but after that he felt stuck. For several moments it would sound like the work of one, and then, almost immediately, it would begin to sound like something by the other. It might have been one of the quartets that Mozart dedicated to Haydn, Nashe thought, but it might have been the other way around. At a certain point, the music of both men seemed to touch, and it was no longer possible to tell them apart. And yet Haydn had lived to a ripe old age, honored with commissions and court appointments and every advantage the world of that time could offer. And Mozart had died young and poor, and his body had been thrown into a common grave.

Nashe had the car up to sixty by then, feeling in absolute control as he whipped along the narrow, twisting country road. The music had pushed Murks and Floyd far into the background, and he could no longer hear anything but the four stringed instruments pouring out their sounds into the dark, enclosed space. Then he was doing seventy, and immediately after that he heard Murks shouting at him through another fit of coughing. 'You damned fool,' Nashe heard him say.

'You're driving too fast!' By way of response, Nashe pressed down on the accelerator and pushed the car up to eighty, taking the curve with a light and steady grip on the wheel. What did Murks know about driving? he thought. What did Murks know about anything?

At the precise moment the car hit eighty-five, Murks leaned forward and snapped off the radio. The sudden silence came as a jolt to Nashe, and he automatically turned to the old man and told him to mind his own business. When he looked at the road again a moment later, he could already see the headlight looming up at him. It seemed to come out of nowhere, a cyclops star hurtling straight for his eyes, and in the sudden panic that engulfed him, his only thought was that this was the last thought he would ever have. There was no time to stop, no time to prevent what was going to happen, and so instead of slamming his foot on the brakes, he pressed down even harder on the gas. He could hear Murks and his son-in-law howling in the distance, but their voices were muffled, drowned out by the roar of blood in his head. And then the light was upon him, and Nashe shut his eyes, unable to look at it anymore.

(1988–1989)

LEVIATHAN

For Don DeLillo

Every actual State is corrupt.
Ralph Waldo Emerson

1

Six days ago, a man blew himself up by the side of a road in northern Wisconsin. There were no witnesses, but it appears that he was sitting on the grass next to his parked car when the bomb he was building accidentally went off. According to the forensic reports that have just been published, the man was killed instantly. His body burst into dozens of small pieces, and fragments of his corpse were found as far as fifty feet away from the site of the explosion. As of today (July 4, 1990), no one seems to have any idea who the dead man was. The FBI, working along with the local police and agents from the Bureau of Alcohol, Tobacco and Firearms, began their investigation by looking into the car, a seven-year-old blue Dodge with Illinois license plates, but they quickly learned that it had been stolen – filched in broad daylight from a Joliet parking lot on June 12. The same thing happened when they examined the contents of the man's wallet, which by some miracle had come through the explosion more or less unscathed. They thought they had stumbled onto a wealth of clues – driver's license, Social Security number, credit cards – but once they fed these documents into the computer, each one turned out to have been either forged or stolen. Fingerprints would have been the next step, but in this case there were no fingerprints, since the man's hands had been obliterated by the bomb. Nor was the car of any help to them. The Dodge had been turned into a mass of charred steel and melted plastic, and in spite of their efforts, not a single print could be found on it. Perhaps they'll have more luck with his teeth, assuming there are enough teeth to work with, but that's bound to take some time, perhaps as long as several months. In the end, there's no doubt they'll think of something, but until they can establish the identity of their mangled victim, their case has little chance of getting off the ground.

As far as I'm concerned, the longer it takes them the better. The story I have to tell is rather complicated, and unless I finish it before they come up with their answer, the words I'm about to write will mean nothing. Once the secret is out, all sorts of lies are going to be told, ugly distortions will circulate in the newspapers and magazines, and within a matter of days a man's reputation will be destroyed. It's not that I want to defend what he did, but since he's no longer in a position to defend himself, the least I can do is explain who he was and give the true story of how he happened to be on that road in northern Wisconsin. That's why I have to work fast: to be ready for them when the moment comes. If by some chance the mystery remains unsolved, I'll simply hold on to what I have written, and no one will need to know a thing about it. That would be the best possible outcome: a perfect standstill, not one word spoken by either side. But I mustn't count on that. In order to do what I have to do, I have to assume they're already closing in on him, that sooner or later they're going to find out who he was. And not just when I've had enough time to finish this – but at any moment, at any moment beginning now.

The day after the explosion, the wire services ran a brief article about the case. It was one of those cryptic, two-paragraph stories they bury in the middle of the paper, but I happened to catch it in *The New York Times* while I was eating lunch that afternoon. Almost inevitably, I began to think about Benjamin Sachs. There was nothing in the article that pointed to him in any definite way, and yet at the same time everything seemed to fit. We hadn't talked in close to a year, but he had said enough during our last conversation to convince me that he was in deep trouble, rushing headlong toward some dark, unnameable disaster. If that's too vague, I should add that he mentioned bombs as well, that he talked about them endlessly during his visit, and for the next eleven months I had walked around with just such a fear inside me – that he was going to kill himself, that one day I would open the newspaper and read that my friend had blown himself up. It was no more than a wild intuition at that point, one of those insane leaps into the void, and yet once the thought entered my head, I couldn't get rid of it. Then, two days after I ran across the article, a pair of FBI agents came knocking at my door. The moment they announced who they were, I understood that I was right. Sachs was the man who had blown himself up. There couldn't be any question about it. Sachs was dead, and the only way I could help him now was to keep his death to myself.

It was probably fortunate that I read the article when I did, although I remember wishing at the time that I hadn't even seen it. If nothing else, it gave me a couple of days to absorb the shock. When the FBI men showed up here to ask their questions, I was already prepared for them, and that helped me to keep myself under control. It also didn't hurt that an extra forty-eight hours had gone by before they managed to track me down. Among the objects recovered from Sachs's wallet, it seems there was a slip of paper bearing my initials and telephone number. That was how they came to be looking for me, but as luck would have it, the number was for my telephone back home in New York, and for the past ten days I've been in Vermont, living with my family in a rented house where we plan to spend the rest of the summer. God knows how many people they had to talk to before they discovered I was here. If I mention in passing that this house is owned by Sachs's ex-wife, it is only to give one example of how tangled and complicated this story finally is.

I did my best to play dumb for them, to give away as little as I could. No, I said, I hadn't read the article in the paper. I didn't know anything about the bombs or stolen cars or back-country roads in Wisconsin. I was a writer, I said, a man who wrote novels for a living, and if they wanted to check into who I was, they could go right ahead – but it wasn't going to help them with their case, they'd only be wasting their time. Probably so, they said, but what about the slip of paper in the dead man's wallet? They weren't trying to accuse me of anything, but the fact that he'd been carrying around my telephone number seemed to prove there was a connection between us. I had to admit that, didn't I? Yes, I said, of course I did, but just because it looked like that didn't mean it was true. There were a thousand ways that man could have gotten hold of my number. I had friends scattered all over the world, and any one of them could have passed it on to a stranger. Perhaps that stranger had passed it on to another stranger, who in turn had passed it on to yet another stranger. Perhaps, they said, but why would anyone carry around the telephone number of a person he didn't know? Because I'm a writer, I said. Oh? they said, and what difference does that make? Because my books are published, I said. People read them, and I don't have any idea who they are. Without even knowing it, I enter the lives of strangers, and for as long as they have my book in their hands, my words are the only reality that exists for them. That's normal, they said, that's the way it is with books. Yes, I said, that's the way it is, but sometimes these people turn out to be crazy. They read your book, and something about it strikes a chord deep in their soul. All of a sudden, they imagine that you belong to them, that you're the only friend they have in the world. To illustrate my point, I gave them several examples – all of them true, all of them taken directly from my own experience. The unbalanced letters, the telephone calls at three o'clock in the morning, the anonymous threats. Just last year, I continued, I discovered that someone had been impersonating me – answering letters in my name, walking into bookstores and autographing my books, hovering like some malignant shadow around the edges of my life. A book is a mysterious object, I said, and once it floats out into the world, anything can happen. All kinds of mischief can be caused, and there's not a damned thing you can do about it. For better or worse, it's completely out of your control.

I don't know if they found my denials convincing or not. I tend to think not, but even if they didn't believe a word I said, it's possible that my strategy bought me some time. Considering that I had never spoken to an FBI agent before, I don't feel too bad about the way I handled myself during the interview. I was calm, I was polite, I managed to project the proper combination of helpfulness and bafflement. That alone was something of a triumph for me. Generally speaking, I don't have much talent for deception, and in spite of my efforts over the years, I've rarely fooled anyone about anything. If I managed to turn in a creditable performance the day before yesterday, the FBI men were at least partially responsible for it. It wasn't anything they said so much as how they looked, the way they dressed for their roles with such perfection, confirming in every detail the way I had always imagined FBI men should look: the lightweight summer suits, the sturdy brogans, the wash-and-wear shirts, the aviator sunglasses. These were the obligatory sunglasses, so to speak, and they lent an artificial quality to the scene, as if the men who wore them were merely actors, walk-ons hired to play a bit part in some low-budget movie. All this was oddly comforting to me, and when I look back on it now, I understand how this sense of unreality worked to my advantage. It allowed me to think of myself as an actor as well, and because I had become someone else, I suddenly had the right to deceive them, to lie without the slightest twinge of conscience.

They weren't stupid, however. One was in his early forties, and the other was a good deal younger, perhaps as young as twenty-five or twenty-six, but they both had a certain look in their eyes that kept me on my guard the whole time they were here. It's difficult to pinpoint exactly what was so menacing about that look, but I think it had something to do with its blankness, its refusal to commit itself, as if it were watching everything and nothing at the same time. So little was divulged by that look, I could never be sure what either of those men was thinking. Their eyes were too patient, somehow, too skilled at suggesting indifference, but for all that they were alert, relentlessly alert in fact, as if they had been trained to make you feel uncomfortable, to make you conscious of your flaws and transgressions, to make you squirm in your skin. Their names were Worthy and Harris, but I forget which one was which. As physical specimens, they were disturbingly alike, almost as if they were younger and older versions of the same person: tall, but not too tall; well built, but not too well built; sandy hair, blue eyes, thick hands with impeccably clean fingernails. It's true that their conversational styles were different, but I don't want to make too much of first impressions. For all I know they take turns, switching roles back and forth whenever they feel like it. For my visit two days ago, the young one played the heavy. His questions were very blunt, and he seemed to take his job too much to heart, rarely cracking a smile, for example, and treating me with a formality that sometimes verged on sarcasm and irritation. The old one was more relaxed and amiable, readier to let the conversation take its natural course. He's no doubt more dangerous because of that, but I have to admit that talking to him wasn't entirely unpleasant. When I began to tell him about some of the crackpot responses to my books, I could see that the subject interested him, and he let me go on with my digression longer than I would have expected. I suppose he was feeling me out, encouraging me to ramble on so he could get some sense of who I was and how my mind worked, but when I came to the business about the impostor, he actually offered to start an investigation into the problem for me. That might have been a trick, of course, but I somehow doubt it. I don't need to add that I turned him down, but if the circumstances had been any different, I probably would have thought twice about accepting his help. It's something that has plagued me for a long time now, and I would dearly love to get to the bottom of it.

'I don't read many novels,' the agent said. 'I never seem to have time for them.'

'No, not many people do,' I said.

'But yours must be pretty good. If they weren't, I doubt you'd be bothered so much.'

'Maybe I get bothered because they're bad. Everyone is a literary critic these days. If you don't like a book, threaten the author. There's a certain logic to that approach. Make the bastard pay for what he's done to you.'

'I suppose I should sit down and read one of them myself,' he said. 'To see what all the fuss is about. You wouldn't mind, would you?'

'Of course I wouldn't mind. That's why they're in the bookstores. So people can read them.'

It was a curious way for the visit to end – writing down the titles of my books for an FBI agent. Even now, I'm hard-pressed to know what he was after. Perhaps he thinks he'll find some clues in them, or perhaps it was just a subtle way of telling me that he'll be back, that he hasn't finished with me yet. I'm still their only lead, after all, and if they go on the assumption that I lied to them, then they're not about to forget me. Beyond that, I haven't the vaguest notion of what they're thinking. It seems unlikely that they consider me a terrorist, but I say that only because I know I'm not. They know nothing, and therefore they could be working on that premise, furiously searching for something that would link me to the bomb that went off in Wisconsin last week. And even if they aren't, I have to accept the fact that they'll be on my case for a long time to come. They'll ask questions, they'll dig into my life, they'll find out who my friends are, and sooner or later Sachs's name will come up. In other words, the whole time I'm here in Vermont writing this story, they'll be busy writing their own story. It will be my story, and once they've finished it, they'll know as much about me as I do myself.

My wife and daughter returned home about two hours after the FBI men left. They had gone off early that morning to spend the day with friends, and I was glad they hadn't been around for Harris's and Worthy's visit. My wife and I share almost everything with each other, but in this case I don't think I should tell her what happened. Iris has always been very fond of Sachs, but I come first for her, and if she discovered that I was about to get into trouble with the FBI because of him, she would do everything in her power to make me stop. I can't run that risk now. Even if I managed to convince her that I was doing the right thing, it would take a long time to wear her down, and I don't have that luxury, I have to spend every minute on the job I've set for myself. Besides, even if she gave in, she would only worry herself sick about it, and I don't see how any good could come of that. Eventually, she's going to learn the truth anyway; when the time comes, everything will be dragged out into the open. It's not that I want to deceive her, I simply want to spare her for as long as possible. As it happens, I don't think that will be terribly difficult. I'm here to write, after all, and if Iris thinks I'm up to my old tricks out in my little shack every day, what harm can come of that? She'll assume I'm scribbling away on my new novel, and when she sees how much time I'm devoting to it, how much progress is being made from my long hours of work, she'll feel happy. Iris is a part of the equation, too, and without her happiness I don't think I would have the courage to begin.

This is the second summer we've spent in this place. Back in the old days, when Sachs and his wife used to come here every July and August, they would sometimes invite me up to visit, but those were always brief excursions, and I rarely stayed for more than three or four nights. After Iris and I were married nine years ago, we made the trip together several times, and once we even helped Fanny and Ben paint the outside of the house. Fanny's parents bought the property during the Depression, at a time when farms like this one could be had for next to nothing. It came with more than a hundred acres and its own private pond, and although the house was run down, it was spacious and airy inside, and only minor improvements were needed to make it habitable. The Goodmans were New York City school teachers, and they could never afford to do much with the place after they bought it, so for all these years the house has kept its primitive, bare-bones look: the iron bedsteads, the potbellied stove in the kitchen, the cracked ceilings and walls, the gray painted floors. Still, there's something solid in this dilapidation, and it would be difficult for anyone not to feel at home here. For me, the great lure of the house is its remoteness. It sits on top of a small mountain, four miles from the nearest village by way of a narrow dirt road. The winters must be ferocious on this mountain, but during the summer everything is green, with birds singing all around you, and the meadows are filled with countless wildflowers: orange hawkweed, red clover, maiden pink, buttercup. About a hundred feet from the main house, there's a simple outbuilding that Sachs used as his work studio whenever he was here. It's hardly more than a cabin, with three small rooms, a kitchenette, and a bathroom, and ever since it was vandalized twelve or thirteen winters ago, it has fallen into disrepair. The pipes have cracked, the electricity has been turned off, the linoleum is peeling up from the floor. I mention these things because that is where I am now – sitting at a green table in the middle of the largest room, holding a pen in my hand. For as long as I knew him, Sachs spent every summer writing at this same table, and this is the room where I saw him for the last time, where he poured out his heart to me and let me in on his terrible secret. If I concentrate hard enough on the memory of that night, I can almost delude myself into thinking that he's still here. It's as if his words were still hanging in the air around me, as if I could still reach out my hand and touch him. It was a long and grueling conversation, and when we finally came to the end of it (at five or six in the morning), he made me promise not to let his secret go beyond the walls of this room. Those were his exact words: that nothing he said should escape this room. For the time being, I'll be able to keep my promise. Until the moment comes for me to show what I've written here, I can comfort myself with the thought that I won't be breaking my word.

The first time we met, it was snowing. More than fifteen years have gone by since that day, but I can still bring it back whenever I wish. So many other things have been lost for me, but I remember that meeting with Sachs as clearly as any event in my life.

It was a Saturday afternoon in February or March, and the two of us had been invited to give a joint reading of our work at a bar in the West Village. I had never heard of Sachs, but the person who called me was too rushed to answer my questions over the phone. 'He's a novelist,' she said. 'His first book was published a couple of years ago.' Her call came on a Wednesday night, just three days before the reading was supposed to take place, and there was something close to panic in her voice. Michael Palmer, the poet who was supposed to appear on Saturday, had just canceled his trip to New York, and she wondered if I would be willing to stand in for him. It was a somewhat backhanded request, but I told her I would do it anyway. I hadn't published much work at that point in my life – six or seven stories in little magazines, a handful of articles and book reviews – and it wasn't as though people were clamoring for the privilege of hearing me read out loud to them. So I accepted the frazzled woman's offer, and for the next two days I fell into a panic of my own, frantically searching through the midget world of my collected stories for something that wouldn't embarrass me, for one scrap of writing that would be good enough to expose to a roomful of strangers. On Friday afternoon, I stopped in at several bookstores and asked for Sachs's novel. It seemed only right that I should know something about his work before I met him, but the book was already two years old, and no one had it in stock.

As chance would have it, an immense storm blew in from the Midwest on Friday night, and by Saturday morning a foot and a half of snow had fallen on the city. The reasonable thing would have been to get in touch with the woman who had called me, but I had stupidly forgotten to ask for her number, and when I still hadn't heard from her by one o'clock, I figured I should get myself downtown as quickly as possible. I bundled up in my overcoat and galoshes, stuck the manuscript of my most recent story into one of the coat pockets, and then tramped out onto Riverside Drive, heading toward the subway station at 116th Street and Broadway. The sky was beginning to clear by then, but the streets and sidewalks were still clogged with snow, and there was scarcely any traffic. A few cars and trucks had been abandoned in tall drifts by the curb, and every now and then a lone vehicle would come inching down the street, skidding out of control whenever the driver tried to stop for a red light. I normally would have enjoyed this mayhem, but the weather was too fierce that day for me to lift my nose out of my scarf. The temperature had been falling steadily since sunrise, and by now the air was bitter, with wild surges of wind blowing off the Hudson, enormous gusts that literally pushed my body up the street. I was half-numb by the time I reached the subway station, but in spite of everything, it appeared that the trains were still running. This surprised me, and as I walked down the stairs and bought my token, I assumed that meant the reading was on after all.

I made it to Nashe's Tavern at ten past two. The place was open, but once my eyes adjusted to the darkness inside, I saw that no one was there. A bartender in a white apron stood behind the bar, methodically drying shot-glasses with a red towel. He was a hefty man of about forty, and he studied me carefully as I approached, almost as if he regretted this interruption of his solitude.

'Isn't there supposed to be a reading here in about twenty minutes?' I asked. The moment the words left my mouth, I felt like a fool for saying them.

'It was canceled,' the bartender said. 'With all that slop out there today, there wouldn't have been much point to it. Poetry's a beautiful thing, but it's hardly worth freezing your ass off for.'

I sat down on one of the barstools and ordered a bourbon. I was still shivering from my walk in the snow, and I wanted to warm my innards before I ventured outside again. I polished off the drink in two swallows, then ordered a refill because the first one had tasted so good. Midway through that second bourbon, another customer walked into the bar. He was a tall, exceedingly thin young man with a narrow face and a full brown beard. I watched him as he stamped his boots on the floor a couple of times, smacked his gloved hands together, and exhaled loudly from the effects of the cold. There was no question that he cut an odd figure – towering there in his moth-eaten coat with a New York Knicks baseball cap perched on his head and a navy blue scarf wrapped around the cap to protect his ears. He looked like someone with a bad toothache, I thought, or else like some half-starved Russian soldier stranded on the outskirts of Stalingrad. These two images came to me in rapid succession, the first one comic, the second one forlorn. In spite of his ridiculous get-up, there was something fierce in his eyes, an intensity that quelled any desire to laugh at him. He resembled Ichabod Crane, perhaps, but he was also John Brown, and once you got past his costume and his gangly basketball forward's body, you began to see an entirely different sort of person: a man who missed nothing, a man with a thousand wheels turning in his head.

He stood in the doorway for a few moments scanning the empty room, then walked up to the bartender and asked more or less the same question that I had asked ten minutes earlier. The bartender gave more or less the same answer he had given me, but in this case he also gestured with a thumb in my direction, pointing to where I was sitting at the end of the bar. 'That one came for the reading, too,' he said. 'You're probably the only two guys in New York who were crazy enough to leave the house today.'

'Not quite,' said the man with the scarf wrapped around his head. 'You forgot to count yourself.'

'I didn't forget,' the bartender said. 'It's just that I don't count. I've got to be here, you see, and you don't. That's what I'm talking about. If I don't show up, I lose my job.'

'But I came here to do a job, too,' the other one said. 'They told me I was going to earn fifty dollars. Now they've called off the reading, and I've lost the subway fare to boot.'

'Well, that's different, then,' the bartender said. 'If you were supposed to read, then I guess you don't count either.'

'That leaves just one person in the whole city who went out when he didn't have to.'

'If you're talking about me,' I said, finally entering the conversation, 'then your list is down to zero.'

The man with the scarf wrapped around his head turned to me and smiled. 'Ah, then that means you're Peter Aaron, doesn't it?'

'I suppose it does,' I said. 'But if I'm Peter Aaron, then you must be Benjamin Sachs.'

'The one and only,' Sachs answered, letting out a short, self-deprecatory laugh. He walked over to where I was sitting and extended his right hand. 'I'm very happy you're here,' he said. 'I've been reading some of your stuff lately and was looking forward to meeting you.'

That was how our friendship began – sitting in that deserted bar fifteen years ago, each one buying drinks for the other until we both ran out of money. It must have lasted three or four hours, for I distinctly remember that when we finally staggered out into the cold again, night had already fallen. Now that Sachs is dead, I find it unbearable to think back to what he was like then, to remember all the generosity and humor and intelligence that poured out of him that first time we met. In spite of the facts, it's difficult for me to imagine that the person who sat with me in the bar that day was the same person who wound up destroying himself last week. The journey must have been so long for him, so horrible, so fraught with suffering, I can scarcely think about it without wanting to cry. In fifteen years, Sachs traveled from one end of himself to the other, and by the time he came to that last place, I doubt he even knew who he was anymore. So much distance had been covered by then, it wouldn't have been possible for him to remember where he had begun.

'I generally manage to keep up with what's going on,' he said, untying the scarf from under his chin and removing it along with the baseball cap and his long brown overcoat. He flung the whole pile onto the barstool next to him and sat down. 'Until two weeks ago, I'd never even heard of you. Now, all of a sudden, you seem to be popping up everywhere. To begin with, I ran across your piece on Hugo Ball's diaries. An excellent little article, I thought, deft and nicely argued, an admirable response to the issues at stake. I didn't agree with all your points, but you made your case well, and I respected the seriousness of your position. This guy believes in art too much, I said to myself, but at least he knows where he stands and has the wit to recognize that other views are possible. Then, three or four days after that, a magazine arrived in the mail, and the first thing I opened to was a story with your name on it. *The Secret Alphabet*, the one about the student who keeps finding messages written on the walls of buildings. I loved it. I loved it so much that I read it three times. Who is this Peter Aaron? I wondered, and where has he been hiding himself? When Kathy what's-her-name called to tell me that Palmer had bagged out of the reading, I suggested that she get in touch with you.'

'So you're the one responsible for dragging me down here,' I said, too stunned by his lavish compliments to think of anything but that feeble reply.

'Well, admittedly it didn't work out the way we thought it would.'

'Maybe that's not such a bad thing,' I said. 'At least I won't have to stand up in the dark and listen to my knees knock together. There's something to be said for that.'

'Mother Nature to the rescue.'

'Exactly. Lady Luck saves my skin.'

'I'm glad you were spared the torment. I wouldn't want to be walking around with that on my conscience.'

'But thank you for getting me invited. It meant a lot to me, and the truth is I'm very grateful to you.'

'I didn't do it because I wanted your gratitude. I was curious, and sooner or later I would have been in touch with you myself. But then the opportunity came along, and I figured this would be a more elegant way of going about it.'

'And here I am, sitting at the North Pole with Admiral Peary himself. The least I can do is buy you a drink.'

'I accept your offer, but only on one condition. You have to answer my question first.'

'I'll be glad to, as long as you tell me what the question is. I don't seem to remember that you asked me one.'

'Of course I did. I asked you where you've been hiding yourself. I could be mistaken, but my guess is that you haven't been in New York very long.'

'I used to be here, but then I went away. I just got back five or six months ago.'

'And where were you?'

'France. I lived there for close to five years.'

'That explains it, then. But why on earth would you want to live in France?'

'No particular reason. I just wanted to be somewhere that wasn't here.'

'You didn't go to study? You weren't working for UNESCO or some hot-shot international law firm?'

'No, nothing like that. I was pretty much living hand to mouth.'

'The old expatriate adventure, was that it? Young American writer goes off to Paris to discover culture and beautiful women, to experience the pleasures of sitting in cafés and smoking strong cigarettes.'

'I don't think it was that either. I felt I needed some breathing room, that's all. I picked France because I was able to speak French. If I spoke Serbo-Croat, I probably would have gone to Yugoslavia.'

'So you went away. For no particular reason, as you put it. Was there any particular reason why you came back?'

'I woke up one morning last summer and told myself it was time to come home. Just like that. I suddenly felt I'd been there long enough. Too many years without baseball, I suppose. If you don't get your ration of double plays and home runs, it can begin to dry up your spirit.'

'And you're not planning to leave again?'

'No, I don't think so. Whatever I was trying to prove by going there doesn't feel important to me anymore.'

'Maybe you've proved it already.'

'That's possible. Or maybe the question has to be stated in different terms. Maybe I was using the wrong terms all along.'

'All right,' Sachs said, suddenly slapping his hand on the bar. 'I'll take that drink now. I'm beginning to feel satisfied, and that always makes me thirsty.'

'What will you have?'

'The same thing you're having,' he said, not bothering to ask me what it was. 'And since the bartender has to come over here anyway, tell him to pour you another. A toast is in order. It's your homecoming, after all, and we have to welcome you back to America in style.'

I don't think anyone has ever disarmed me as thoroughly as Sachs did that afternoon. He came on like gangbusters from the first moment, storming through my most secret dungeons and hiding places, opening one locked door after another. As I later learned, it was a typical performance for him, an almost classic example of how he steered himself through the world. No beating about the bush, no standing on ceremony – just roll up your sleeves and start talking. It was nothing for him to strike up conversations with absolute strangers, to plunge in and ask questions no one else would have dared to ask, and more often than not to get away with it. You felt that he had never learned the rules, that because he was so utterly lacking in self-consciousness, he expected everyone else to be as open-hearted as he was. And yet there was always something impersonal about his probing, as if he weren't trying to make a human connection with you so much as to solve some intellectual problem for himself. It gave his remarks a certain abstract coloration, and this inspired trust, made you willing to tell him things that in some cases you hadn't even told yourself. He never judged anyone he met, never treated anyone as an inferior, never made distinctions between people because of their social rank. A bartender interested him just as much as a writer, and if I hadn't shown up that day, he probably would have spent two hours talking to that same man I hadn't bothered to exchange ten words with. Sachs automatically assumed great intelligence on the part of the person he was talking to, thereby investing that person with a sense of his own dignity and importance. I think it was that quality I admired most about him, that innate skill at drawing out the best in others. He often came across as an oddball, a gawky stick of a man with his head in the clouds, permanently distracted by obscure thoughts and preoccupations, and yet again and again he would surprise you with a hundred little signs of his attentiveness. Like everyone else in the world, but only more so perhaps, he managed to combine a multitude of contradictions into a single, unbroken presence. No matter where he was, he always seemed to be at home in his surroundings, and yet I've rarely met anyone who was so clumsy, so physically inept, so helpless at negotiating the simplest operations. All during our conversation that afternoon, he kept knocking his coat off the barstool onto the floor. It must have happened six or seven times, and once, when he bent down to pick it up, he even managed to bang his head against the bar. As I later discovered, however, Sachs was an excellent athlete. He had been the leading scorer on his high school basketball team, and in all the games of one-on-one we played against each other over the years, I don't think I beat him more than once or twice. He was garrulous and often sloppy in the way he spoke, and yet his writing was marked by great precision and economy, a genuine gift for the apt phrase. That he wrote at all, for that matter, often struck me as something of a puzzle. He was too out there, too fascinated by other people, too happy mixing with crowds for such a lonely occupation, I thought. But solitude scarcely disturbed him, and he always worked with tremendous discipline and fervor, sometimes holing up for weeks at a stretch in order to complete a project. Given who he was, and the singular way in which he kept these various sides of himself in motion, Sachs was not someone you would have expected to be married. He seemed too ungrounded for domestic life, too democratic in his affections to be capable of sustaining intimate relations with any one person. But Sachs married young, much younger than anyone else I knew, and he kept that marriage alive for close to twenty years. Nor was Fanny the kind of wife who seemed particularly well suited to him. In a pinch, I could have imagined him with a docile, mothering sort of woman, one of those wives who stands contentedly in her husband's shadow, devoted to protecting her boy-man from the harsh practicalities of the everyday world. But Fanny was nothing like that. Sachs's partner was every bit his equal, a complex and highly intelligent woman who led her own independent life, and if he managed to hold onto her for all those years, it was only because he worked hard at it, because he had an enormous talent for understanding her and keeping her in balance with herself. His sweet temper no doubt helped the marriage, but I wouldn't want to overemphasize that aspect of his character. In spite of his gentleness, Sachs could be rigidly dogmatic in his thinking, and there were times when he let loose in savage fits of anger, truly terrifying outbursts of rage. These were not directed at the people he cared about so much as at the world at large. The stupidities of the world appalled him, and underneath his jauntiness and good humor, you sometimes felt a deep reservoir of intolerance and scorn. Nearly everything he wrote had a peevish, embattled edge to it, and over the years he developed a reputation as a troublemaker. I suppose he deserved it, but in the end that was only one small part of who he was. The difficulty comes from trying to pin him down in any conclusive way. Sachs was too unpredictable for that, too large-spirited and cunning, too full of new ideas to stand in one place for very long. I sometimes found it exhausting to be with him, but I can't say it was ever dull. Sachs kept me on my toes for fifteen years, constantly challenging and provoking me, and as I sit here now trying to make sense of who he was, I can hardly imagine my life without him.

'You've put me at a disadvantage,' I said, taking a sip of bourbon from my replenished glass. 'You've read nearly every word I've written, and I haven't seen a single line of yours. Living in France had its benefits, but keeping up with new American books wasn't one of them.'

'You haven't missed much,' Sachs said. 'I promise you.'

'Still, I find it a little embarrassing. Other than the title, I don't know a thing about your book.'

'I'll give you a copy. Then you won't have any more excuses for not reading it.'

'I looked for it in a few stores yesterday . . .'

'That's all right, save your money. I have about a hundred copies, and I'm happy to get rid of them.'

'If I'm not too drunk, I'll start reading it tonight.'

'There's no rush. It's only a novel, after all, and you shouldn't take it too seriously.'

'I always take novels seriously. Especially when they're given to me by the author.'

'Well, this author was very young when he wrote his book. Maybe too young, in fact. Sometimes he feels sorry it was ever published.'

'But you were planning to read from it this afternoon. You can't think it's that bad, then.'

'I'm not saying it's bad. It's just young, that's all. Too literary, too full of its own cleverness. I wouldn't even dream of writing something like that today. If I have any interest in it now, it's only because of where it was written. The book itself doesn't mean much, but I suppose I'm still attached to the place where it was born.'

'And what place was that?'

'Prison. I started writing the book in prison.'

'You mean an actual prison? With locked cells and bars? With numbers stenciled on the front of your shirt?'

'Yes, a real prison. The federal penitentiary in Danbury, Connecticut. I was a guest in that hotel for seventeen months.'

'Good lord. And how did you happen to wind up there?'

'It was very simple, really. I refused to go into the army when they called me up.'

'Were you a conscientious objector?'

'I wanted to be, but they turned down my application. I'm sure you know the story. If you belong to a religion that preaches pacifism and is opposed to all wars, then there's a chance they'll consider your case. But I'm not a Quaker or a Seventh-Day Adventist, and the fact is I'm not opposed to all wars. Only to that war. Unfortunately, that was the one they were asking me to fight in.'

'But why go to jail? There were other choices. Canada, Sweden, even France. Thousands of people took off to those places.'

'Because I'm a stubborn son of a bitch, that's why. I didn't want to run away. I felt I had a responsibility to stand up and tell them what I thought. And I couldn't do that unless I was willing to put myself on the line.'

'So they listened to your noble statement, and then they locked you up anyway.'

'Of course. But it was worth it.'

'I suppose. But those seventeen months must have been awful.'

'They weren't as bad as you'd think. You don't have to worry about anything in there. You're given three meals a day, you don't have to do your laundry, your whole life is mapped out for you in advance. You'd be surprised how much freedom that gives you.'

'I'm glad you're able to joke about it.'

'I'm not joking. Well, maybe just a little. But I didn't suffer in any of the ways you're probably imagining. Danbury isn't some nightmare prison like Attica or San Quentin. Most of the inmates are there for white-collar crimes – embezzlement, tax fraud, writing bad checks, that kind of thing. I was lucky to be sent there, but the main advantage was that I was prepared. My case dragged on for months, and since I always knew that I was going to lose, I had time to adjust myself to the idea of prison. I wasn't one of those sad-sacks who moped around counting the days, crossing out another box on the calendar every time I went to bed. When I went in there, I told myself this is it, this is where you live now, old man. The boundaries of my world had shrunk, but I was still alive, and as long as I could go on breathing and farting and thinking my thoughts, what difference did it make where I was?'

'Strange.'

'No, not strange. It's like the old Henny Youngman joke. The husband comes home, walks into the living room, and sees a cigar burning in an ashtray. He asks his wife what's going on, but she pretends not to know. Still suspicious, the husband starts looking through the house. When he gets to the bedroom, he opens the closet and finds a stranger in there. "What are you doing in my closet?" the husband asks. "I don't know," the man stutters, shaking and sweating all over. "Everybody has to be somewhere."'

'All right, I get the point. But still, there must have been some rough characters in that closet with you. It couldn't always have been very pleasant.'

'There were a few dicey moments, I'll admit that. But I learned how to handle myself pretty well. It was the one time in my life when my funny looks proved to be helpful. No one knew what to make of me, and after a while I managed to convince most of the other inmates that I was crazy. You'd be astounded at how thoroughly people leave you alone when they think you're nuts. Once you get that look in your eye, it inoculates you against trouble.'

'And all because you wanted to stand up for your principles.'

'It wasn't so hard. At least I always knew why I was there. I didn't have to torture myself with regrets.'

'I was lucky compared to you. I flunked the physical because of asthma, and I never had to think about it again.'

'So you went to France, and I went to jail. We both went somewhere, and we both came back. As far as I can tell, we're both sitting in the same place now.'

'That's one way of looking at it.'

'It's the only way of looking at it. Our methods were different, but the results were exactly the same.'

We ordered another round of drinks. That led to another round, and then another, and then another one after that. In between, the bartender stood us to a couple of glasses on the house, an act of kindness that we promptly repaid by encouraging him to pour one for himself. Then the tavern began to fill up with customers, and we went off to sit at a table in the far corner of the room. I can't remember everything we talked about, but the beginning of that conversation is a lot clearer to me than the end. By the time we came to the last half hour or forty-five minutes, there was so much bourbon in my system that I was actually seeing double. This had never happened to me before, and I had no idea how to bring the world back into focus. Whenever I looked at Sachs, there were two of him. Blinking my eyes didn't help, and shaking my head only made me dizzy. Sachs had turned into a man with two heads and two mouths, and when I finally stood up to leave, I can remember how he caught me in his four arms just as I was about to fall. It was probably a good thing that there were so many of him that afternoon. I was nearly a dead weight by then, and I doubt that one man could have carried me.

I can only speak about the things I know, the things I have seen with my own eyes and heard with my own ears. Except for Fanny, it's possible that I was closer to Sachs than anyone else, but that doesn't make me an expert on the details of his life. He was already pushing thirty when I met him, and neither one of us spent much time talking about our pasts. His childhood is largely a mystery to me, and beyond a few casual remarks he made about his parents and sisters over the years, I know next to nothing about his family. If the circumstances were different, I would try to talk to some of these people now, I would make an effort to fill in as many blanks as I could. But I'm not in a position to start hunting for Sachs's grade school teachers and high school friends, to set up interviews with his cousins and college classmates and the men he was in prison with. There isn't enough time for that, and because I'm forced to work quickly, I have nothing to rely on but my own memories. I'm not saying that these memories should be doubted, that there is anything false or tainted about the things I do know about Sachs, but I don't want to present this book as something it's not. There is nothing definitive about it. It's not a biography or an exhaustive psychological portrait, and even though Sachs confided a great deal to me over the years of our friendship, I don't claim to have more than a partial understanding of who he was. I want to tell the truth about him, to set down these memories as honestly as I can, but I can't dismiss the possibility that I'm wrong, that the truth is quite different from what I imagine it to be.

He was born on August 6, 1945. I remember the date because he always made a point of mentioning it, referring to himself in various conversations as 'America's first Hiroshima baby,' 'the original bomb child,' 'the first white man to draw breath in the nuclear age.' He used to claim that the doctor had delivered him at the precise moment Fat Man was released from the bowels of the *Enola Gay*, but that always struck me as an exaggeration. The one time I met Sachs's mother, she wasn't able to recall when the birth had taken place (she'd had four children, she said, and their births were all mixed up in her mind), but at least she confirmed the date, adding that she distinctly remembered that she was told about Hiroshima *after* her son was born. If Sachs invented the rest, it was no more than a bit of innocent mythologizing on his part. He was a great one for turning facts into metaphors, and since he always had an abundance of facts at his disposal, he could bombard you with a never-ending supply of strange historical connections, yoking together the most far-flung people and events. Once, for example, he told me that during Peter Kropotkin's first visit to the United States in the 1890s, Mrs Jefferson Davis, the widow of the Confederate president, requested a meeting with the famous anarchist prince. That was bizarre enough, Sachs said, but then, just minutes after Kropotkin arrived at Mrs Davis's house, who else should turn up but Booker T. Washington? Washington announced that he was looking for the man who had accompanied Kropotkin (a mutual friend), and when Mrs Davis learned that he was standing in the entrance hall, she sent word that he should come in and join them. So for the next hour this unlikely trio sat around drinking tea together and making polite conversation:

the Russian nobleman who sought to bring down all organized government, the ex-slave turned writer and educator, and the wife of the man who led America into its bloodiest war in defense of the institution of slavery. Only Sachs could have known something like that. Only Sachs could have informed you that when the film actress Louise Brooks was growing up in a small town in Kansas at the beginning of the century, her next-door playmate was Vivian Vance, the same woman who later starred in the *I Love Lucy* show. It thrilled him to have discovered this: that the two sides of American womanhood, the vamp and the frump, the libidinous sex-devil and the dowdy housewife, should have started in the same place, on the same dusty street in the middle of America. Sachs loved these ironies, the vast follies and contradictions of history, the way in which facts were constantly turning themselves on their head. By gorging himself on those facts, he was able to read the world as though it were a work of the imagination, turning documented events into literary symbols, tropes that pointed to some dark, complex pattern embedded in the real. I could never be quite sure how seriously he took this game, but he played it often, and at times it was almost as if he were unable to stop himself. The business about his birth was part of this same compulsion. On the one hand, it was a form of gallows humor, but it was also an attempt to define who he was, a way of implicating himself in the horrors of his own time. Sachs often talked about 'the bomb.' It was a central fact of the world for him, an ultimate demarcation of the spirit, and in his view it separated us from all other generations in history. Once we acquired the power to destroy ourselves, the very notion of human life had been altered; even the air we breathed was contaminated with the stench of death. Sachs was hardly the first person to come up with this idea, but considering what happened to him nine days ago, there's a certain eeriness to the obsession, as if it were a kind of deadly pun, a mixed-up word that took root inside him and proliferated beyond his control.

His father was an Eastern European Jew, his mother was an Irish Catholic. As with most American families, disaster had brought them here (the potato famine of the 1840s, the pogroms of the 1880s), but beyond these rudimentary details, I have no information about Sachs's ancestors. He was fond of saying that a poet was responsible for bringing his mother's family to Boston, but that was only a reference to Sir Walter Ralegh, the man who introduced the potato to Ireland and hence had caused the blight that occurred three hundred years later. As for his father's family, he once told me that they had come to New York because of the death of God. This was another one of Sachs's enigmatic allusions, and until you penetrated the nursery-rhyme logic behind it, it seemed devoid of sense. What he meant was that the pogroms began after the assassination of Czar Alexander II; that Alexander had been killed by Russian Nihilists; that the Nihilists were nihilists because they believed there was no God. It was a simple equation, finally, but incomprehensible until the middle terms were restored to the sequence. Sachs's remark was like someone telling you that the kingdom had been lost for want of a nail. If you knew the poem, you got it. If you didn't know it, you didn't.

When and where his parents met, who they had been in early life, how their respective families reacted to the prospect of a mixed marriage, at what point they moved to Connecticut – all this falls outside the realm of what I am able to discuss. As far as I know, Sachs had a secular upbringing. He was both a Jew and a Catholic, which meant that he was neither one nor the other. I don't recall that he ever talked about going to religious school, and to the best of my knowledge he was neither confirmed nor bar-mitzvahed. The fact that he was circumcised was no more than a medical detail. On several occasions, however, he alluded to a religious crisis that took place in his middle teens, but evidently it burned itself out rather quickly. I was always impressed by his familiarity with the Bible (both Old and New Testaments), and perhaps he started reading it back then, during that period of inner struggle. Sachs was more interested in politics and history than in spiritual questions, but his politics were nevertheless tinged with something I would call a religious quality, as if political engagement were more than a way of confronting problems in the here and now, but a means to personal salvation as well. I believe this is an important point. Sachs's political ideas never fell into any of the conventional categories. He was wary of systems and ideologies, and though he could talk about them with considerable understanding and sophistication, political action for him boiled down to a matter of conscience. That was what made him decide to go to prison in 1968. It wasn't because he thought he could accomplish anything there, but because he knew he wouldn't be able to live with himself if he didn't go. If I had to sum up his attitude toward his own beliefs, I would begin by mentioning the Transcendentalists of the nineteenth century. Thoreau was his model, and without the example of *Civil Disobedience*, I doubt that Sachs would have turned out as he did. I'm not just talking about prison now, but a whole approach to life, an attitude of remorseless inner vigilance. Once, when *Walden* came up in conversation, Sachs confessed to me that he wore a beard 'because Henry David had worn one' – which gave me a sudden insight into how deep his admiration was. As I write these words now, it occurs to me that they both lived the same number of years. Thoreau died at forty-four, and Sachs wouldn't have passed him until next month. I don't suppose there's anything to be made of this coincidence, but it's the kind of thing that Sachs always liked, a small detail to be noted for the record.

His father worked as a hospital administrator in Norwalk, and from all I can gather the family was neither well-to-do nor particularly strapped. Two daughters were born first, then Sachs came along, and then there was a third daughter, all four of them arriving within a span of six or seven years. Sachs seems to have been closer to his mother than his father (she is still alive, he is not), but I never sensed that there were any great conflicts between father and son. As an example of his stupidity as a little boy, Sachs once mentioned to me how upset he had been when he learned that his father hadn't fought in World War II. In light of Sachs's later position, that response becomes almost comical, but who knows how severely his disappointment affected him back then? All his friends used to brag about their fathers' exploits as soldiers, and he envied them for the battle trophies they would trot out for the war games they played in their suburban backyards: the helmets and cartridge belts, the holsters and canteens, the dog tags, hats, and medals. But why his father hadn't served in the army was never explained to me. On the other hand, Sachs always spoke proudly of his father's socialist politics in the thirties, which apparently involved union organizing or some other job connected with the labor movement. If Sachs gravitated more toward his mother than his father, I think it was because their personalities were so alike: both of them garrulous and blunt, both of them endowed with an uncanny talent for getting others to talk about themselves. According to Fanny (who told me as much about these things as Ben ever did), Sachs's father was quieter and more evasive than his mother, more closed in on himself, less inclined to let you know what he was thinking. Still, there must have been a strong bond between them. The most certain proof I can think of comes from a story that Fanny once told me. Not long after Ben's arrest, a local reporter came to the house to interview her father-in-law about the trial. The journalist was clearly looking to write a story about generational conflict (a big subject back in those days), but once Mr Sachs caught wind of his intentions, this normally subdued and taciturn man pounded his fist on the arm of the chair, looked the journalist straight in the eye, and said: 'Ben is a terrific kid. We always taught him to stand up for what he believes in, and I'd be crazy not to be proud of what he's doing now. If there were more young men like my son in this country, it would be a hell of a lot better place.'

I never met his father, but I remember a Thanksgiving that I spent at his mother's house extremely well. The visit came a few weeks after Ronald Reagan was elected president, which means it was November 1980 – going on ten years now. It was a bad time in my life. My first marriage had broken up two years before, and I wasn't destined to meet Iris until the end of February, a good three months down the road. My son David was just over three then, and his mother and I had arranged for him to spend the holiday with me, but the plans I made for us had fallen through at the last minute. The alternatives seemed rather grim: either go out to a restaurant somewhere or eat frozen turkey dinners at my small apartment in Brooklyn. Just when I was beginning to feel sorry for myself (it could have been as late as Monday or Tuesday), Fanny rescued the situation by asking us up to Ben's mother's house in Connecticut. All the nieces and nephews would be there, she said, and it was bound to be fun for David.

Mrs Sachs has since moved to a retirement home, but at the time she was still living in the house in New Canaan where Ben and his sisters had grown up. It was a big place just outside town that looked to have been built in the second half of the nineteenth century, one of those gabled Victorian labyrinths with pantry closets, back staircases, and odd little passageways on the second floor. The interiors were dark, and the living room was cluttered with piles of books, newspapers, and magazines. Mrs Sachs must have been in her mid to late sixties then, but there was nothing old or grandmotherly about her. She had been a social worker for many years in the poor neighborhoods of Bridgeport, and it wasn't hard to see that she had been good at her job: an outspoken woman, full of opinions, with a brash, cockeyed sense of humor. She seemed to be amused by many things, a person given neither to sentimentality nor to bad temper, but whenever the subject turned to politics (as it did quite often that day), she proved to have a wickedly sharp tongue. Some of her remarks were downright raunchy, and at one point, when she called Nixon's convicted associates 'the sort of men who fold up their underpants before they go to bed at night,' one of her daughters glanced at me with an embarrassed look on her face, as if to apologize for her mother's unladylike behavior. She needn't have worried. I took an immense liking to Mrs Sachs that day. She was a subversive matriarch who still enjoyed throwing punches at the world, and she seemed as ready to laugh at herself as at everyone else – her children and grandchildren included. Not long after I got there, she confessed to me that she was a terrible cook, which was why she had delegated the responsibility of preparing the dinner to her daughters. But, she added (and here she drew close to me and whispered in my ear), those three girls were none too swift in the kitchen either. After all, she said, she had taught them everything they knew, and if the teacher was an absentminded clod, what could you expect of the disciples?

It's true that the meal was dreadful, but we scarcely had time to notice. What with so many people in the house that day, and the constant racket of five children under the age of ten, our mouths were kept busier with talk than with food. Sachs's family was a noisy bunch. His sisters and their husbands had flown in from various parts of the country, and since most of them hadn't seen each other in a long while, the dinner conversation quickly became a free-for-all, with everyone talking at once. At any given moment, four or five separate dialogues were going on across the table, but because people weren't necessarily talking to the person next to them, these dialogues kept intersecting with one another, causing abrupt shifts in the pairings of the speakers, so that everyone seemed to be taking part in all the conversations at the same time, simultaneously chattering away about his or her own life and eavesdropping on everyone else as well. Add to this the frequent interruptions from the children, the comings and goings of the different courses, the pouring of wine, the dropped plates, overturned glasses, and spilled condiments, the dinner began to resemble an elaborate, hastily improvised vaudeville routine.

It was a sturdy family, I thought, a teasing, fractious group of individuals who cared for one another but didn't cling to the life they had shared in the past. It was refreshing for me to see how little animosity there was among them, how few old rivalries and resentments came to the surface, but at the same time there wasn't much intimacy, they didn't seem as connected to one another as the members of most successful families are. I know that Sachs was fond of his sisters, but only in an automatic and somewhat distant sort of way, and I don't think he was particularly involved with any of them during his adult life. It might have had something to do with his being the only boy, but whenever I happened to catch a glimpse of him during the course of that long afternoon and evening, he seemed to be talking either to his mother or to Fanny, and he probably showed more interest in my son David than in any of his own nephews or nieces. I doubt that I'm trying to make a specific point about this. These kinds of partial observations are subject to any number of errors and misreadings, but the fact is that Sachs behaved like something of a loner in his own family, a figure who stood slightly apart from the rest. That isn't to say that he shunned anyone, but there were moments when I sensed that he was ill at ease, almost bored by having to be there.

Based on the little I know about it, his childhood seems to have been unremarkable. He didn't do especially well in school, and if he won honors for himself in any way, it was only to the extent that he excelled at pranks. He was apparently fearless in confronting authority, and to listen to him tell it, he spent the years from about six to twelve in a continuous ferment of creative sabotage. He was the one who designed the booby traps, who fastened the Kick Me signs on the teacher's back, who set off the fire crackers in the cafeteria garbage cans. He spent hundreds of hours sitting in the principal's office during those years, but punishment was a small price to pay for the satisfaction these triumphs gave him. The other boys respected him for his boldness and invention, which was probably what inspired him to take such risks in the first place. I've seen some of Sachs's early photographs, and there's no question that he was an ugly duckling, a genuine sore thumb: one of those beanstalk assemblages with big ears, buck teeth, and a goofy, lopsided grin. The potential for ridicule must have been enormous; he must have been a walking target for all sorts of jokes and savage stings. If he managed to avoid that fate, it was because he forced himself to be a little wilder than everyone else. It couldn't have been the most pleasant role to play, but he worked hard at mastering it, and after a while he held undisputed dominion over the territory.

Braces aligned his crooked teeth; his body filled out; his limbs gradually learned to obey him. By the time he reached adolescence, Sachs began to resemble the person he would later become. His height worked to his advantage in sports, and when he started to play basketball at thirteen or fourteen, he quickly developed into a promising player. The practical jokes and renegade antics died out then, and while his academic performance in high school was hardly outstanding (he always described himself as a lazy student, with only minimal interest in getting good grades), he read books constantly and was already beginning to think of himself as a future writer. By his own admission, his first works were awful – 'romantico-absurdist soul-searchings,' he once called them, wretched little stories and poems that he kept an absolute secret from everyone. But he stuck with it, and as a sign of his growing seriousness, he went out and bought himself a pipe at the age of seventeen. This was the badge of every true writer, he thought, and during his last year of high school he spent every evening sitting at his desk, pen in one hand, pipe in the other, filling his room with smoke.

These stories came straight from Sachs himself. They helped to define my sense of what he had been like before I met him, but as I repeat his comments now, I realize that they could have been entirely false. Self-deprecation was an important element of his personality, and he often used himself as the butt of his own jokes. Especially when talking about the past, he liked to portray himself in the most unflattering terms. He was always the ignorant kid, the pompous fool, the mischief-maker, the bungling oaf. Perhaps that was how he wanted me to see him, or perhaps he found some perverse pleasure in pulling my leg. For the fact is that it takes a great deal of self-confidence for a person to poke fun at himself, and a person with that kind of self-confidence is rarely a fool or a bungler.

There is only one story from that early period that I feel at all confident about. I heard it toward the end of my visit to Connecticut in 1980, and since it came as much from his mother as it did from him, it falls into a different category from the rest. In itself, this anecdote is less dramatic than some of the others Sachs told me, but looking at it now from the perspective of his whole life, it stands out in special relief – as though it were the announcement of a theme, the initial statement of a musical phrase that would go on haunting him until his last moments on earth.

Once the table was cleared, the people who hadn't helped with the dinner were assigned to wash-up duty in the kitchen. There were just four of us: Sachs and his mother, Fanny and myself. It was a big job, with mess and crockery jammed onto every counter, and as we took turns scraping and sudsing and rinsing and drying, we chatted about this and that, drifting aimlessly from one topic to another. After a while, we found ourselves talking about Thanksgiving, which led to a discussion of other American holidays, which in turn led to some glancing remarks about national symbols. The Statue of Liberty was mentioned, and then, almost as if the memory had returned to both of them at the same time, Sachs and his mother started reminiscing about a trip they had made to Bedloes Island back in the early fifties. Fanny had never heard the story before, so she and I became the audience, standing there with dish towels in our hands as the two of them performed their little act.

'Do you remember that day, Benjy?' Mrs Sachs began.

'Of course I remember,' Sachs said. 'It was one of the turning points of my childhood.'

'You were just a wee little man back then. No more than six or seven.'

'It was the summer I turned six. Nineteen fifty-one.'

'I was a few years older than that, but I'd never been to the Statue of Liberty. I figured it was about time, so one day I hustled you into the car, and off we went to New York. I don't remember where the girls were that morning, but I'm pretty sure it was just the two of us.'

'Just the two of us. And Mrs Something-stein and her two sons. We met them when we got down there.'

'Doris Saperstein, my old friend from the Bronx. She had two boys about your age. Regular little ragamuffins they were, a couple of wild Indians.'

'Just normal kids. They were the ones who caused the whole dispute.'

'What dispute?'

'You don't remember that part, do you?'

'No, I only remember what happened later. That wiped out everything else.'

'You made me wear those terrible short pants with the white knee socks. You always dressed me up when we went out, and I hated it. I felt like a sissy in those clothes, a Fauntleroy in full regalia. It was bad enough on family outings, but the thought of turning up like that in front of Mrs Saperstein's sons was intolerable to me. I knew they'd be wearing T-shirts, dungarees, and sneakers, and I didn't know how I was going to face them.'

'But you looked like an angel in that outfit,' his mother said.

'Maybe so, but I didn't want to look like an angel. I wanted to look like a regular American boy. I begged to wear something else, but you refused to budge. Visiting the Statue of Liberty isn't like playing in the backyard, you said. It's the symbol of our country, and we have to show it the proper respect. Even then, the irony of the situation didn't escape me. There we were, about to pay homage to the concept of freedom, and I myself was in chains. I lived in an absolute dictatorship, and for as long as I could remember my rights had been trampled underfoot. I tried to explain about the other boys, but you wouldn't listen to me. Nonsense, you said, they'll be wearing their dress-up clothes, too. You were so damned sure of yourself, I finally plucked up my courage and offered to make a bargain with you. All right, I said, I'll wear the clothes today. But if the other boys are wearing dungarees and sneakers, then it's the last time I ever have to do it. From then on, you'll give me permission to wear whatever I want.'

'And I agreed to that? I allowed myself to bargain with a six-year-old?'

'You were just humoring me. The possibility of losing the bet didn't even occur to you. But lo and behold, when Mrs Saperstein arrived at the Statue of Liberty with her two sons, the boys were dressed exactly as I had predicted. And just like that, I became the master of my own wardrobe. It was the first major victory of my life. I felt as if I'd struck a blow for democracy, as if I'd risen up in the name of oppressed peoples all over the world.'

'Now I know why you're so partial to blue jeans,' Fanny said. 'You discovered the principle of self-determination, and at that point you determined to be a bad dresser for the rest of your life.'

'Precisely,' Sachs said. 'I won the right to be a slob, and I've been carrying the banner proudly ever since.'

'And then,' Mrs Sachs continued, impatient to get on with the story, 'we started to climb.'

'The spiral staircase,' her son added. 'We found the steps and started to go up.'

'It wasn't so bad at first,' Mrs Sachs said. 'Doris and I let the boys go on ahead, and we took the stairs nice and easy, holding onto the rail. We got as far as the crown, looked out at the harbor for a couple of minutes, and everything was more or less okay. I thought that was it, that we'd start back down then and go for an ice cream somewhere. But they still let you into the torch in those days, which meant climbing up another staircase – right through Miss Battle-Axe's arm. The boys were crazy to go up there. They kept hollering and whining about how they wanted to see everything, and so Doris and I gave in to them. As it turned out, this staircase didn't have a railing like the other one. It was the narrowest, twistingest little set of iron rungs you ever saw, a fire pole with bumps on it, and when you looked down through the arm, you felt like you were three hundred miles up in the air. It was pure nothingness all around, the great void of heaven. The boys scampered up into the torch by themselves, but by the time I was two-thirds of the way up, I realized I wasn't going to make it. I'd always thought of myself as a pretty tough cookie. I wasn't one of those hysterical women who screamed when she saw a mouse. I was a hefty, down-to-earth broad who'd been around the block a few times, but standing on those stairs that day, I got all weak inside, I had the cold sweats, I thought I was going to throw up. By then, Doris wasn't in such good shape herself, and so we each sat down on one of the steps, hoping that might steady our nerves. It helped a little, but not much, and even with my backside planted on something solid, I still felt I was about to fall, that any second I'd find myself hurtling head-first to the bottom. It was the worst panic I ever felt in my life. I was completely rearranged. My heart was in my throat, my head was in my hands, my stomach was in my feet. I got so scared thinking about Benjamin that I started screaming for him to come down. It was hideous. My voice echoing through the Statue of Liberty like the howls of some tormented spirit. The boys finally left the torch, and then we all went down the stairs sitting, one step at a time. Doris and I tried to make a game out of it for the boys, pretending that this was the fun way to travel. But nothing was going to make me stand up on those stairs again. I'd have sooner jumped off than allow myself to do that. It must have taken us half an hour to get to the bottom again, and by then I was a wreck, a blob of flesh and bone. Benjy and I stayed with the Sapersteins on the Grand Concourse that night, and since then I've had a mortal fear of high places. I'd rather be dead than set foot in an airplane, and once I get above the third or fourth story of a building, I turn to jello inside. How do you like that? And it all started that day when Benjamin was a little boy, climbing into the torch of the Statue of Liberty.'

'It was my first lesson in political theory,' Sachs said, turning his eyes away from his mother to look at Fanny and me. 'I learned that freedom can be dangerous. If you don't watch out, it can kill you.'

I don't want to make too much of this story, but at the same time I don't think it should be entirely neglected. In itself, it was no more than a trivial episode, a bit of family folklore, and Mrs Sachs told it with enough humor and self-mockery to sweep aside its rather terrifying implications. We all laughed when she was finished, and then the conversation moved on to something else. If not for Sachs's novel (the same book he carried through the snow to our aborted reading in 1975), I might have forgotten all about it. But since that book is filled with references to the Statue of Liberty, it's hard to ignore the possibility of a connection – as if the childhood experience of witnessing his mother's panic somehow lay at the heart of what he wrote as a grown man twenty years later. I asked him about it as we were driving back to the city that night, but Sachs only laughed at my question. He hadn't even remembered that part of the story, he said. Then, dismissing the subject once and for all, he launched into a comic diatribe against the pitfalls of psychoanalysis. In the end, none of that matters. Just because Sachs denied the connection doesn't mean that it didn't exist. No one can say where a book comes from, least of all the person who writes it. Books are born out of ignorance, and if they go on living after they are written, it's only to the degree that they cannot be understood.

The New Colossus was the one novel Sachs ever published. It was also the first piece of writing I read by him, and there's no doubt that it played a significant role in getting our friendship off the ground. It was one thing to have liked Sachs in person, but when I learned that I could admire his work as well, I became that much more eager to know him, that much more willing to see him and talk to him again. That instantly set him apart from all the other people I had met since moving back to America. He was more than just a potential drinking companion, I discovered, more than just another acquaintance. An hour after cracking open Sachs's book fifteen years ago, I understood that it would be possible for us to become friends.

I have just spent the morning scanning through it again (there are several copies here in the cabin) and am astonished by how little my feelings for it have changed. I don't think I have to say much more than that. The book continues to exist, it's available in bookstores and libraries, and anyone who cares to read it can do so without difficulty. It was issued in paperback a couple of months after Sachs and I first met, and since then it has stayed mostly in print, living a quiet but healthy life in the margins of recent literature, a crazy hodgepodge of a book that has kept its own small spot on the shelf. The first time I read it, however, I walked into it cold. After listening to Sachs in the bar, I assumed that he had written a conventional first novel, one of those thinly veiled attempts to fictionalize the story of his own life. I wasn't planning to hold that against him, but he had talked so disparagingly about the book that I felt I had to brace myself for some kind of letdown. He autographed a copy for me that day in the bar, but the only thing I noticed at the time was that it was big, a book that ran to more than four hundred pages. I started reading it the next afternoon, sprawled out in bed after drinking six cups of coffee to kill the hangover from Saturday's binge. As Sachs had warned me, it was a young man's book – but not in any of the ways I was expecting it to be. *The New Colossus* had nothing to do with the sixties, nothing to do with Vietnam or the antiwar movement, nothing to do with the seventeen months he had served in prison. That I had been looking for all that stemmed from a failure of imagination on my part. The idea of prison was so terrible to me, I couldn't imagine how anyone who had been there could not write about it.

As every reader knows, *The New Colossus* is a historical novel, a meticulously researched book set in America between 1876 and 1890 and based on documented, verifiable facts. Most of the characters are people who actually lived at the time, and even when the characters are imaginary, they are not inventions so much as borrowings, figures stolen from the pages of other novels. Otherwise, all the events are true – true in the sense that they follow the historical record – and in those places where the record is unclear, there is no tampering with the laws of probability. Everything is made to seem plausible, matter-of-fact, even banal in the accuracy of its depiction. And yet Sachs continually throws the reader off guard, mixing so many genres and styles to tell his story that the book begins to resemble a pinball machine, a fabulous contraption with blinking lights and ninety-eight different sound effects. From chapter to chapter, he jumps from traditional third-person narratives to first-person diary entries and letters, from chronological charts to small anecdotes, from newspaper articles to essays to dramatic dialogues. It's a whirlwind performance, a marathon sprint from the first line to the last, and whatever you might think of the book as a whole, it's impossible not to respect the author's energy, the sheer gutsiness of his ambitions.

Among the characters who appear in the novel are Emma Lazarus, Sitting Bull, Ralph Waldo Emerson, Joseph Pulitzer, Buffalo Bill Cody, Auguste Bartholdi, Catherine Weldon, Rose Hawthorne (Nathaniel's daughter), Ellery Channing, Walt Whitman, and William Tecumseh Sherman. But Raskalnikov is also there (straight from the epilogue of *Crime and Punishment* – released from prison and newly arrived as an immigrant in the United States, where his name is anglicized to Ruskin), as is Huckleberry Finn (a middle-aged drifter who befriends Ruskin), and Ishmael from *Moby Dick* (who has a brief walk-on role as a bartender in New York). *The New Colossus* begins in the year of America's centennial and works its way through the major events of the next decade and a half: Custer's defeat at the Little Big Horn, the building of the Statue of Liberty, the general strike of 1877, the exodus of Russian Jews to America in 1881, the invention of the telephone, the Haymarket riots in Chicago, the spread of the Ghost Dance religion among the Sioux, the massacre at Wounded Knee. But small events are also recorded, and these are finally what give the book its texture, what turn it into something more than a jigsaw puzzle of historical facts. The opening chapter is a good case in point. Emma Lazarus goes to Concord, Massachusetts to stay as a guest in Emerson's house. While there, she is introduced to Ellery Channing, who accompanies her on a visit to Walden Pond and talks about his friendship with Thoreau (dead now for fourteen years). The two are drawn to each other and become friends, another of those odd juxtapositions that Sachs was so fond of: the white-haired New Englander and the young Jewish poet from Millionaire's Row in New York. At their last meeting, Channing hands her a gift, which he tells her not to open until she is on the train heading back home. When she unwraps the parcel, she finds a copy of Channing's book on Thoreau, along with one of the relics the old man has been hoarding since his friend's death: Thoreau's pocket compass. It's a beautiful moment, very sensitively handled by Sachs, and it plants an important image in the reader's head that will recur in any number of guises throughout the book. Although it isn't said in so many words, the message couldn't be clearer. America has lost its way. Thoreau was the one man who could read the compass for us, and now that he is gone, we have no hope of finding ourselves again.

There is the strange story of Catherine Weldon, the middle-class woman from Brooklyn who goes out west to become one of Sitting Bull's wives. There is a farcical account of the Russian Grand Duke Alexei's tour of the United States – hunting buffalo with Bill Cody, traveling down the Mississippi with General and Mrs George Armstrong Custer. There is General Sherman, whose middle name gives homage to an Indian warrior, receiving an appointment in 1876 (just one month after Custer's last stand) 'to assume military control of all reservations in the Sioux country and to treat the Indians there as prisoners of war,' and then, one year later, receiving another appointment from the

American Committee on the Statue of Liberty 'to decide whether the statue should be located on Governor's or Bedloe's Island.' There is Emma Lazarus dying from cancer at age thirty-seven, attended by her friend Rose Hawthorne – who is so transformed by the experience that she converts to Catholicism, enters the order of St Dominic as Sister Alphonsa, and devotes the last thirty years of her life to caring for the terminally ill. There are dozens of such episodes in the book. All of them are true, each is grounded in the real, and yet Sachs fits them together in such a way that they become steadily more fantastic, almost as if he were delineating a nightmare or a hallucination. As the book progresses, it takes on a more and more unstable character – filled with unpredictable associations and departures, marked by increasingly rapid shifts in tone – until you reach a point when you feel the whole thing begin to levitate, to rise ponderously off the ground like some gigantic weather balloon. By the last chapter, you've traveled so high up into the air, you realize that you can't come down again without falling, without being crushed.

There are definite flaws, however. Although Sachs works hard to mask them, there are times when the novel feels too constructed, too mechanical in its orchestration of events, and only rarely do any of the characters come fully to life. Midway through my first reading of it, I remember telling myself that Sachs was more of a thinker than an artist, and his heavy-handedness often disturbed me – the way he kept hammering home his points, manipulating his characters to underscore his ideas rather than letting them create the action themselves. Still, in spite of the fact that he wasn't writing about himself, I understood how deeply personal the book must have been for him. The dominant emotion was anger, a full-blown, lacerating anger that surged up on nearly every page: anger against America, anger against political hypocrisy, anger as a weapon to destroy national myths. But given that the war in Vietnam was still being fought then, and given that Sachs had gone to jail because of that war, it wasn't hard to understand where his anger had come from. It gave the book a strident, polemical tone, but I also believe it was the secret of its power, the engine that pushed the book forward and made you want to go on reading it. Sachs was only twenty-three when he started *The New Colossus*, and he stuck with the project for five years, writing seven or eight drafts in the process. The published version came to four hundred and thirty-six pages, and I had read them all by the time I went to sleep on Tuesday night. Whatever reservations

I might have had were dwarfed by my admiration for what he had accomplished. When I came home from work on Wednesday afternoon, I immediately sat down and wrote him a letter. I told him that he had written a great novel. Any time he wanted to share another bottle of bourbon with me, I would be honored to match him glass for glass.

We started seeing each other regularly after that. Sachs had no job, and that made him more available than most of the people I knew, more flexible in his routines. Social life in New York tends to be quite rigid. A simple dinner can take weeks of advance planning, and the best of friends can sometimes go months without any contact at all. With Sachs, however, impromptu meetings were the norm. He worked when the spirit moved him (most often late at night), and the rest of the time he roamed free, prowling the streets of the city like some nineteenth-century *flâneur*, following his nose wherever it happened to take him. He walked, he went to museums and art galleries, he saw movies in the middle of the day, he read books on park benches. He wasn't beholden to the clock in the way other people are, and as a consequence he never felt as if he were wasting his time. That doesn't mean he wasn't productive, but the wall between work and idleness had crumbled to such a degree for him that he scarcely noticed it was there. This helped him as a writer, I think, since his best ideas always seemed to come to him when he was away from his desk. In that sense, then, everything fell into the category of work for him. Eating was work, watching basketball games was work, sitting with a friend in a bar at midnight was work. In spite of appearances, there was hardly a moment when he wasn't on the job.

My days weren't nearly as open as his were. I had returned from Paris the previous summer with nine dollars in my pocket, and rather than ask my father for a loan (which he probably wouldn't have given me anyway), I had snatched at the first job I was offered. By the time I met Sachs, I was working for a rare-book dealer on the Upper East Side, mostly sitting in the back room of the shop writing catalogues and answering letters. I went in every morning at nine and left at one. In the afternoons, I translated at home, working on a history of modern China by a French journalist who had once been stationed in Peking – a slapdash, poorly written book that demanded more effort than it deserved. My hope was to quit the job with the book dealer and start earning my living as a translator, but it still wasn't clear that my plan would work.

In the meantime, I was also writing stories and doing occasional book reviews, and what with one thing and another, I wasn't getting a lot of sleep. Still, I saw Sachs more often than seems possible now, considering the circumstances. One advantage was that we had turned out to live in the same neighborhood, and our apartments were within easy walking distance of each other. This led to quite a few late-night meetings in bars along Broadway, and then, after we discovered a mutual passion for sports, weekend afternoons as well, since the ball-games were always on in those places and neither one of us owned a television set. Almost at once, I began seeing Sachs on the average of twice a week, far more than I saw anyone else.

Not long after these get-togethers began, he introduced me to his wife. Fanny was a graduate student in the art history department at Columbia then, teaching courses at General Studies and finishing up her dissertation on nineteenth-century American landscape painting. She and Sachs had met at the University of Wisconsin ten years before, literally bumping into each other at a peace rally that had been organized on campus. By the time Sachs was arrested in the spring of 1967, they had already been married for close to a year. They lived at Ben's parents' house in New Canaan during the period of the trial, and once the sentence was handed down and Ben went off to prison (early in 1968), Fanny moved back to her own parents' apartment in Brooklyn. At some point during all this, she applied to the graduate program at Columbia and was accepted with a faculty fellowship – which included free tuition, a living stipend of several thousand dollars, and responsibility for teaching a couple of courses. She spent the rest of that summer working as an office temp in Manhattan, found a small apartment on West 112th Street in late August, and then started classes in September, all the while commuting up to Danbury every Sunday on the train to visit Ben. I mention these things now because I happened to see her a number of times during that year – without having the slightest idea who she was. I was still an undergraduate at Columbia then, and my apartment was only five blocks away from hers, on West 107th Street. As chance would have it, two of my closest friends lived in her building, and on several of my visits I actually ran into her in the elevator or the downstairs lobby. Beyond that, there were the times when I saw her walking along Broadway, the times when I found her standing ahead of me at the counter of the discount cigarette store, the times when I caught a glimpse of her entering a building on campus. In the spring, we were even in a class together, a large lecture course on the history of aesthetics given by a professor in the philosophy department. I noticed her in all these places because I found her attractive, but I could never quite muster the courage to talk to her. There was something intimidating about her elegance, a walled-off quality that seemed to discourage strangers from approaching her. The wedding ring on her left hand was partly responsible, I suppose, but even if she hadn't been married, I'm not sure it would have made any difference. Still, I made a conscious effort to sit behind her in that philosophy class, just so I could spend an hour every week watching her out of the corner of my eye. We smiled at each other once or twice as we were leaving the lecture hall, but I was too timid to push it any farther than that. When Sachs finally introduced me to her in 1975, we recognized each other immediately. It was an unsettling experience, and it took me several minutes to regain my composure. A mystery from the past had suddenly been solved. Sachs was the missing husband of the woman I had watched so attentively six or seven years before. If I had stayed in the neighborhood, it's almost certain that I would have seen him after he was released from prison. But I graduated from college in June, and Sachs didn't come to New York until August. By then, I had already moved out of my apartment and was on my way to Europe.

There's no question that it was a strange match. In almost every way that I can think of, Ben and Fanny seemed to exist in mutually exclusive realms. Ben was all arms and legs, an erector set of sharp angles and bony protrusions, whereas Fanny was short and round, with a smooth face and olive skin. Ben was ruddy by comparison, with frizzy, unkempt hair, and skin that burned easily in the sun. He took up a lot of room, seemed to be constantly in motion, changed facial expressions every five or six seconds, whereas Fanny was poised, sedentary, catlike in the way she inhabited her body. She wasn't beautiful to me so much as exotic, although that might be too strong a word for what I'm trying to express. An ability to fascinate is probably closer to what I'm looking for, a certain air of self-sufficiency that made you want to watch her, even when she just sat there and did nothing. She wasn't funny in the way Ben could be, she wasn't quick, she never ran off at the mouth. And yet I always felt that she was the more articulate of the two, the more intelligent, the one with greater analytical powers. Ben's mind was all intuition. It was bold but not especially subtle, a mind that loved to take risks, to leap into the dark, to make improbable connections. Fanny, on the other hand, was thorough and dispassionate, unremitting in her patience, not prone to quick judgments or ungrounded remarks. She was a scholar, and he was a wise guy; she was a sphinx, and he was an open wound; she was an aristocrat, and he was the people. To be with them was like watching a marriage between a panther and a kangaroo. Fanny, always superbly dressed, stylish, walking alongside a man nearly a foot taller than she was, an oversize kid in black Converse All-Stars, blue jeans, and a gray hooded sweatshirt. On the surface, it seemed to make no sense. You saw them together, and your first response was to think they were strangers.

But that was only on the surface. Underneath his apparent clumsiness, Sachs had a remarkable understanding of women. Not just of Fanny, but of nearly all the women he met, and again and again I was surprised by how naturally they were drawn to him. Growing up with three sisters might have had something to do with it, as if the intimacies learned in childhood had impregnated him with some occult knowledge, a way into feminine secrets that other men spend their whole lives trying to discover. Fanny had her difficult moments, and I don't imagine she was ever an easy person to live with. Her outward calm was often a mask for inner turbulence, and on several occasions I saw for myself how quickly she could fall into dark, depressive moods, overcome by some indefinable anguish that would suddenly push her to the point of tears. Sachs protected her at those times, handling her with a tenderness and discretion that could be very moving, and I think Fanny learned to depend on him for that, to realize that no one was capable of understanding her as deeply as he did. More often than not, this compassion was expressed indirectly, in a language that outsiders couldn't penetrate. The first time I went to their apartment, for example, the dinner conversation came around to the subject of children – whether or not to have them, when was the best time if you did, how many changes they caused, and so on. I remember talking strongly in favor of having them. Sachs, on the other hand, went into a long song and dance about why he disagreed. The arguments he used were fairly conventional (the world is too terrible a place, the population is too big, too much freedom would be lost), but he delivered them with such vehemence and conviction that I assumed he was speaking for Fanny as well and that both of them were dead-set against becoming parents. Years later, I discovered that just the opposite was true. They had desperately wanted to have children, but Fanny was unable to conceive. After numerous attempts to get her pregnant, they had consulted doctors, had tried fertility drugs, had gone through any number of herbal remedies, but nothing had helped. Just days before that dinner in 1975, they had been given definitive word that nothing they did would ever help. It was a crushing blow to Fanny. As she later confessed to me, it was her worst sorrow, a loss she would go on mourning for the rest of her life. Rather than make her talk about it in front of me that evening, Sachs had boiled up a concoction of spontaneous lies, a kettle of steam and hot air to obscure the issue on the table. I heard only a fragment of what he actually said, but that was because I thought he was addressing his remarks to me. As I later understood, he had been talking to Fanny all along. He was telling his wife that he loved her. He was telling her that she didn't have to give him a child to make him go on loving her.

I saw Ben more often than I saw Fanny, and the times when I did see her Ben was always there, but little by little we managed to form a friendship on our own. In some ways, my old infatuation made this closeness seem inevitable, but it also stood as a barrier between us, and several months went by before I was able to look at her without feeling embarrassed. Fanny was an ancient daydream, a phantom of secret desire buried in my past, and now that she had unexpectedly materialized in a new role – as flesh-and-blood woman, as wife of my friend – I admit that I was thrown off balance. It led me to say some stupid things when I first met her, and these blunders only compounded my sense of guilt and confusion. During one of the early evenings I spent at their apartment, I even told her that I hadn't listened to a single word in the class we had taken together. 'Every week, I would spend the whole hour staring at you,' I said. 'Practice is more important than theory, after all, and I figured why waste my time listening to lectures on aesthetics when the beautiful was sitting there right in front of me.'

It was an attempt to apologize for my past behavior, I think, but it came out sounding awful. Such things should never be said under any circumstances, least of all in a flippant tone of voice. They put a terrible burden on the person they're addressed to, and no good can possibly come of them. The moment I spoke those words, I could see that Fanny was startled by my bluntness. 'Yes,' she said, forcing a little smile, 'I remember that class. It was pretty dry stuff.'

'Men are monsters,' I said, unable to stop myself. 'They have ants in their pants, and their heads are crammed with filth. Especially when they're young.'

'Not filth,' Fanny said. 'Just hormones.'

'Those too. But sometimes it's hard to tell the difference.'

'You always wore an earnest look on your face,' she said. 'I remember thinking that you must have been a very serious person. One of those young men who was either going to kill himself or change the world.'

'So far, I haven't done either. I guess that means I've given up my old ambitions.'

'And a good thing, too. You don't want to get stuck in the past. Life is too interesting for that.'

In her own cryptic way, Fanny was letting me off the hook – and also giving me a warning. As long as I behaved myself, she wouldn't hold my past sins against me. It made me feel as though I were on trial, but the fact was that she had every reason to be wary of her husband's new friend, and I don't blame her for keeping me at a distance. As we got to know each other better, the awkwardness began to fade. Among other things, we discovered that we had the same birthday, and though neither one of us had any use for astrology, the coincidence helped to form a link between us. That Fanny was a year older than I was allowed me to treat her with mock deference whenever the subject came up, a standing gag that never failed to get a laugh out of her. Since she was not someone who laughed readily, I took it as a sign of progress on my part. More importantly, there was her work, and my discussions with her about early American painting led to an abiding passion for such artists as Ryder, Church, Blakelock, and Cole – who were scarcely even known to me before I met Fanny. She defended her dissertation at Columbia in the fall of 1975 (one of the first monographs to be published on Albert Pinkham Ryder) and was then hired as an assistant curator of American art at the Brooklyn Museum, where she has continued to work ever since. As I write these words now (July 11), she still has no idea what happened to Ben. She went off on a trip to Europe last month and isn't scheduled to return until after Labour Day. I suppose it would be possible for me to contact her, but I don't see what purpose that would serve. There isn't a damned thing she can do for him at this point, and unless the FBI comes up with an answer before she returns, it's probably best that I keep it to myself. At first, I thought it might be my duty to call her, but now that I've had time to mull it over, I've decided not to ruin her vacation. She's been through enough as it is, and the telephone is hardly an appropriate way to break this kind of news. I'll hold off until she comes back, and then I'll sit her down and tell her what I know in person.

Remembering the early days of the friendship now, I am struck most of all by how much I admired the two of them, both separately and as a couple. Sachs's book had made a deep impression on me, and beyond simply liking him for who he was, I was flattered by the interest he took in my work. He was only two years older than I was, and yet compared to what he had accomplished so far, I felt like a rank beginner. I had missed the reviews of *The New Colossus*, but by all accounts the book had generated a good deal of excitement. Some critics slammed it – largely on political grounds, condemning Sachs for what they saw as his blatant 'anti-Americanism' – but there were others who raved, calling him one of the most promising young novelists to have come along in years. Not much happened on the commercial front (sales were modest, it took two years before a paperback was published), but Sachs's name had been put on the literary map. One would think he would have been gratified by all this, but as I quickly learned about him, Sachs could be maddeningly oblivious when it came to such things. He rarely talked about himself in the way other writers do, and my sense was that he had little or no interest in pursuing what people refer to as a 'literary career.' He wasn't competitive, he wasn't worried about his reputation, he wasn't puffed-up about his talent. That was one of the things that most appealed to me about him: the purity of his ambitions, the absolute simplicity of the way he approached his work. It sometimes made him stubborn and cantankerous, but it also gave him the courage to do exactly what he wanted to do. After the success of his first novel, he immediately started to write another, but once he was a hundred pages into it, he tore up the manuscript and burned it. Inventing stories was a sham, he said, and just like that he decided to give up fiction writing. This was some time in late 1973 or early 1974, about a year before I met him. He began writing essays after that, all kinds of essays and articles on a countless variety of subjects: politics, literature, sports, history, popular culture, food, whatever he felt like thinking about that week or that day. His work was in demand, so he never had trouble finding magazines to publish his pieces, but there was something indiscriminate in the way he went about it. He wrote with equal fervor for national magazines and obscure literary journals, hardly noticing that some publications paid large sums of money for articles and others paid nothing at all. He refused to work with an agent, feeling that would corrupt the process, and therefore he earned considerably less than he should have. I argued with him on this point for many years, but it wasn't until the early eighties that he finally broke down and hired someone to do his negotiating for him.

    I was always astonished by how quickly he worked, by his ability to crank out articles under the pressure of deadlines, to produce so much without seeming to exhaust himself. It was nothing for Sachs to write ten or twelve pages at a single sitting, to start and finish an entire piece without once standing up from his typewriter. Work was like an athletic contest for him, an endurance race between his body and his mind, but since he was able to bear down on his thoughts with such concentration, to think with such unanimity of purpose, the words always seemed to be there for him, as if he had found a secret passageway that ran straight from his head to the tips of his fingers. 'Typing for Dollars,' he sometimes called it, but that was only because he couldn't resist making fun of himself. His work was never less than good, I thought, and more often than not it was brilliant. The better I got to know him, the more his productivity awed me. I have always been a plodder, a person who anguishes and struggles over each sentence, and even on my best days I do no more than inch along, crawling on my belly like a man lost in the desert. The smallest word is surrounded by acres of silence for me, and even after I manage to get that word down on the page, it seems to sit there like a mirage, a speck of doubt glimmering in the sand. Language has never been accessible to me in the way that it was for Sachs. I'm shut off from my own thoughts, trapped in a no-man's-land between feeling and articulation, and no matter how hard I try to express myself, I can rarely come up with more than a confused stammer. Sachs never had any of these difficulties. Words and things matched up for him, whereas for me they are constantly breaking apart, flying off in a hundred different directions. I spend most of my time picking up the pieces and gluing them back together, but Sachs never had to stumble around like that, hunting through garbage dumps and trash bins, wondering if he hadn't fit the wrong pieces next to each other. His uncertainties were of a different order, but no matter how hard life became for him in other ways, words were never his problem. The act of writing was remarkably free of pain for him, and when he was working well, he could put words down on the page as fast as he could speak them. It was a curious talent, and because Sachs himself was hardly even aware of it, he seemed to live in a state of perfect innocence. Almost like a child, I sometimes thought, like a prodigious child playing with his toys.

2

The initial phase of our friendship lasted for approximately a year and a half. Then, within several months of each other, we both left the Upper West Side, and another chapter began. Fanny and Ben went first, moving to an apartment in the Park Slope section of Brooklyn. It was a roomier, more comfortable place than Fanny's old student digs near Columbia, and it put her within walking distance of her job at the museum. That was the fall of 1976. In the time that elapsed between their finding the apartment and moving into it, my wife Delia discovered that she was pregnant. Almost at once, we began making plans to move as well. Our place on Riverside Drive was too cramped to accommodate a child, and with things already growing rocky between us, we figured we might have a better chance if we left the city altogether. I was translating books full-time by then, and as far as work was concerned, it made no difference where we lived.

I can't say that I have any desire to talk about my first marriage now. To the extent that it touches on Sachs's story, however, I don't see how I can entirely avoid the subject. One thing leads to another, and whether I like it or not, I'm as much a part of what happened as anyone else. If not for the breakup of my marriage to Delia Bond, I never would have met Maria Turner, and if I hadn't met Maria Turner, I never would have known about Lillian Stern, and if I hadn't known about Lillian Stern, I wouldn't be sitting here writing this book. Each one of us is connected to Sachs's death in some way, and it won't be possible for me to tell his story without telling each of our stories at the same time. Everything is connected to everything else, every story overlaps with every other story. Horrible as it is for me to say it, I understand now that I'm the one who brought all of us together. As much as Sachs himself, I'm the place where everything begins.

The sequence breaks down like this: I pursued Delia off and on for seven years (1967–74), I convinced her to marry me (1975), we moved to the country (March 1977), our son David was born (June 1977), we separated (November 1978). During the eighteen months I was out of New York, I stayed in close touch with Sachs, but we saw each other less often than before. Postcards and letters took the place of late-night talks in bars, and our contacts were necessarily more circumscribed and formal. Fanny and Ben occasionally drove up to spend weekends with us in the country, and Delia and I visited their house in Vermont for a short stretch one summer, but these get-togethers lacked the anarchic and improvisational quality of our meetings in the past. Still, it wasn't as if the friendship suffered. Every now and then I would have to go down to New York on business: delivering manuscripts, signing contracts, picking up new work, discussing projects with editors. This happened two or three times a month, and whenever I was there I would spend the night at Fanny's and Ben's place in Brooklyn. The stability of their marriage had a calming effect on me, and if I was able to keep some semblance of sanity during that period, I think they were at least partly responsible for it. Going back to Delia the next morning could be difficult, however. The spectacle of domestic happiness I had just witnessed made me understand how seriously I had botched things for myself. I began to dread plunging back into my own turmoil, the deep thickets of disorder that had grown up all around me.

I'm not about to speculate on what did us in. Money was in short supply during our last couple of years together, but I wouldn't want to cite that as a direct cause. A good marriage can withstand any amount of external pressure, a bad marriage cracks apart. In our case, the nightmare began no more than hours after we left the city, and whatever fragile thing that had been holding us together came permanently undone.

Given our lack of money, our original plan had been quite cautious: to rent a house somewhere and see if living in the country suited us or not. If it did, we would stay; if it didn't, we would go back to New York after the lease ran out. But then Delia's father stepped in and offered to advance us ten thousand dollars for a down payment on a place of our own. With country houses selling for as little as thirty or forty thousand at the time, this sum represented much more than it would now. It was a generous thing for Mr Bond to do, but in the end it worked against us, locking us into a situation neither one of us was prepared to handle. After searching for a couple of months, we found an inexpensive place in Dutchess County, an old and somewhat sagging house with plenty of room inside and a splendid set of lilac bushes in the yard. The day after we moved in, a ferocious thunderstorm swept through the town. Lightning struck the branch of a tree next to the house, the branch caught fire, the fire spread to an electric line that ran through the tree, and we lost our electricity. The moment that happened, the sump pump shut off, and in less than an hour the cellar was flooded. I spent the better part of the night knee-deep in cold rain, working by flashlight as I bailed out the water with buckets. When the electrician arrived the next afternoon to assess the damage, we learned that the entire electrical system had to be replaced. That cost several hundred dollars, and when the septic tank gave out the following month, it cost us more than a thousand dollars to remove the smell of shit from our backyard. We couldn't afford any of these repairs, and the assault on our budget left us dizzy with apprehension. I stepped up the pace of my translation work, taking any assignments that came along, and by mid-spring I had all but abandoned the novel I had been writing for the past three years. Delia was hugely pregnant by then, but she continued to plug away at her own job (freelance copyediting), and in the last week before she went into labor, she sat at her desk from morning to night correcting a manuscript of over nine hundred pages.

After David was born, the situation only grew worse. Money became my single, overriding obsession, and for the next year I lived in a state of continual panic. With Delia no longer able to contribute much in the way of work, our income fell at the precise moment our expenses began to go up. I took the responsibilities of fatherhood seriously, and the thought of not being able to provide for my wife and son filled me with shame. Once, when a publisher was slow in paying me for work I had handed in, I drove down to New York and stormed into his office, threatening him with physical violence unless he wrote out a check to me on the spot. At one point, I actually grabbed him by the collar and pushed him against the wall. This was utterly implausible behavior for me, a betrayal of everything I believed in. I hadn't fought with anyone since I was a child, and if I let my feelings run away from me in that man's office, it only proves how unhinged I had become. I wrote as many articles as I could, I took on every translation job I was offered, but still it wasn't enough. Assuming that my novel was dead, that my dreams of becoming a writer were finished, I went out and started hunting for a permanent job. But times were bad just then, and opportunities in the country were sparse. Even the local community college, which had advertised for someone to teach a full load of freshman composition courses at the paltry wage of eight thousand dollars a year, received more than three hundred applications for the post. Without any prior teaching experience, I was rejected without an interview. After that, I tried to join the staffs of several of the magazines I had written for, figuring I could commute down to the city if I had to, but the editors only laughed at me and treated my letters as a joke. This is no job for a writer, they answered back, you'd just be wasting your time. But I wasn't a writer anymore, I was a drowning man. I was a man at the end of his rope.

Delia and I were both exhausted, and as time went on our quarreling became automatic, a reflex that neither one of us could control. She nagged and I sulked; she harangued and I brooded; we went days without having the courage to talk to each other. David was the only thing that seemed to bring us pleasure anymore, and we talked about him as if no other subject existed, wary of overstepping the boundaries of that neutral zone. As soon as we did, the snipers would jump back into their trenches, shots would be exchanged, and the war of attrition would begin all over again. It seemed to drag on interminably, a subtle conflict with no definable objective, fought with silences, misunderstandings, and hurt, bewildered looks. For all that, I don't think that either one of us was willing to surrender. We had both dug in for the long haul, and the idea of giving up had never even occurred to us.

All that changed very suddenly in the fall of 1978. One evening, while we were sitting in the living room with David, Delia asked me to fetch her glasses from a shelf in her upstairs study, and when I entered the room I saw her journal lying open on the desk. Delia had been keeping a journal since the age of thirteen or fourteen, and by now it ran to dozens of volumes, notebook after notebook filled with the ongoing saga of her inner life. She had often read passages from it to me, but until that evening I had never so much as dared to look at it without her permission. Standing there at that moment, however, I found myself gripped by a tremendous urge to read those pages. In retrospect, I understand that this meant our life together was already finished, that my willingness to break this trust proved that I had given up any hope for our marriage, but I wasn't aware of it then. At the time, the only thing I felt was curiosity. The pages were open on the desk, and Delia had just asked me to go into the room for her. She must have understood that I would notice them. Assuming that was true, it was almost as if she were inviting me to read what she had written. In all events, that was the excuse I gave myself that night, and even now I'm not so sure I was wrong. It would have been just like her to act indirectly, to provoke a crisis she would never have to claim responsibility for. That was her special talent: taking matters into her own hands, even as she convinced herself that her hands were clean.

So I looked down at the open journal, and once I crossed that threshold, I wasn't able to turn back. I saw that I was the subject of that day's entry, and what I found there was an exhaustive catalogue of complaints and grievances, a grim little document set forth in the language of a laboratory report. Delia had covered everything, from the way I dressed to the foods I ate to my incorrigible lack of human understanding. I was morbid and self-centered, frivolous and domineering, vengeful and lazy and distracted. Even if every one of those things had been true, her portrait of me was so ungenerous, so mean-spirited in its tone, that I couldn't even bring myself to feel angry. I felt sad, hollowed out, dazed. By the time I reached the last paragraph, her conclusion was already self-evident, a thing that no longer needed to be expressed. 'I have never loved Peter,' she wrote. 'It was a mistake to think I ever could. Our life together is a fraud, and the longer we go on like this, the closer we come to destroying each other. We never should have gotten married. I let Peter talk me into it, and I've been paying for it ever since. I didn't love him then, and I don't love him now. No matter how long I stay with Peter, I will never love him.'

It was all so abrupt, so final, that I almost felt relieved. To understand that you are despised in this way eliminates any excuse for self-pity. I couldn't doubt where things stood anymore, and however shaken I might have been in those first moments, I knew that I had brought this disaster down on myself. I had thrown away eleven years of my life in search of a figment. My whole youth had been sacrificed to a delusion, and yet rather than crumple up and mourn what I had just lost, I felt strangely invigorated, set free by the bluntness and brutality of Delia's words. All this strikes me as inexplicable now. But the fact was that I didn't hesitate. I went downstairs with Delia's glasses, told her that I had read her journal, and the next morning I moved out. She was stunned by my decisiveness, I think, but given how thoroughly we had always misread each other, that was probably to be expected. As far as I was concerned, there was nothing to talk about anymore. The deed had already been done, and there wasn't any room for second thoughts.

Fanny helped me find a sublet in lower Manhattan, and by Christmas I was living in New York again. A painter friend of hers was about to go off to Italy for a year, and she had talked him into renting me his spare room for only fifty dollars a month – which was the absolute limit of what I could afford. It was located directly across the hall from his loft (which was occupied by other tenants), and until I moved in, it had served as a kind of enormous storage closet. All manner of junk and debris was stashed away in there: broken bicycles, abandoned paintings, an old washing machine, empty cans of turpentine, newspapers, magazines, and innumerable fragments of copper wire. I shoved these things to one side of the room, which left me half the space to live in, but after a short period of adjustment, that proved to be large enough. My only household possessions that year were a mattress, a small table, two chairs, a hotplate, a smattering of kitchen utensils, and a single carton of books. It was basic, no-nonsense survival, but the truth is that I was happy in that room. As Sachs put it the first time he came to visit me, it was a sanctuary of inwardness, a room in which the only possible activity was thought. There was a sink and a toilet, but no bath, and the wooden floor was in such poor condition that it gave me splinters whenever I walked on it with bare feet. But I started working on my novel again in that room, and little by little my luck changed. A month after I moved in, I won a grant of ten thousand dollars. The application had been sent in so long before, I had completely forgotten that I was a candidate. Then, just two weeks after that, I won a second grant of seven thousand dollars, which had been applied for in the same flurry of desperation as the first. All of a sudden, miracles had become a common occurrence in my life. I handed over half the money to Delia, and still there was enough to keep me going in a state of relative splendor. Every week, I would shuttle up to the country to spend a day or two with David, sleeping at a neighbor's house down the road. This arrangement lasted for roughly nine months, and when Delia and I finally sold our house the following September, she moved to an apartment in South Brooklyn, and I was able to see David for longer stretches at a time. We both had lawyers by then, and our divorce was already in the works.

Fanny and Ben took an active interest in my new career as a single man. To the degree that I talked to anyone about what I was up to, they were my confidants, the ones I kept abreast of my comings and goings. They had both been upset by the breakup with Delia, but less so Fanny than Ben, I think, although she was the one who worried more about David, zeroing in on that aspect of the problem once she understood that Delia and I had no chance of getting back together. Sachs, on the other hand, did everything he could to talk me into giving it another try. That went on for several weeks, but once I moved back to the city and settled into my new life, he stopped belaboring the point. Delia and I had never let our differences show in public, and our separation came as a shock to most of the people we knew, particularly to close friends like Sachs. Fanny, however, seemed to have had her suspicions all along. When I announced the news in their apartment on the first night I spent away from Delia, she paused for a moment at the end of my story and then said, 'It's a hard thing to swallow, Peter, but in some ways it's probably for the best. As time goes on, I think you're going to be much happier.'

They gave a lot of dinner parties that year, and I was invited to nearly all of them. Fanny and Ben knew an astounding number of people, and at one time or another it seemed that half of New York wound up sitting at the large oval table in their dining room. Artists, writers, professors, critics, editors, gallery owners – they all tramped out to Brooklyn and gorged themselves on Fanny's food, drinking and talking well into the night. Sachs was always the master of ceremonies, an effusive maniac who kept conversations humming along with well-timed jokes and provocative remarks, and I grew to depend on these dinners as my chief source of entertainment. My friends were watching out for me, doing everything in their power to show the world that I was back in circulation. They never talked about matchmaking in so many words, but enough unmarried women turned up at their house on those evenings for me to understand that they had my best interests at heart.

Early in 1979, about three or four months after I returned to New York, I met someone there who played a central role in Sachs's death. Maria Turner was twenty-seven or twenty-eight at the time, a tall, self-possessed young woman with closely cropped blonde hair and a bony, angular face. She was far from beautiful, but there was an intensity in her gray eyes that attracted me, and I liked the way she carried herself in her clothes, with a kind of prim, sensual grace, a reserve that would unmask itself in little flashes of erotic forgetfulness – letting her skirt drift up along her thighs as she crossed and uncrossed her legs, for example, or the way she touched my hand whenever I lit a cigarette for her. It wasn't that she was a tease or explicitly tried to arouse. She struck me as a good bourgeois girl who had mastered the rules of social behavior, but at the same time it was as if she no longer believed in them, as if she were walking around with a secret she might or might not be willing to share with you, depending on how she felt at that moment.

She lived in a loft on Duane Street, not far from my place on Varick, and after the party broke up that night, we shared a ride with a Brooklyn car service back to Manhattan. That was the beginning of what turned out to be a sexual alliance that lasted for close to two years. I use that phrase as a precise, clinical description, but that doesn't mean our relations were only physical, that we had no interest in each other beyond the pleasures we found in bed. Still, what went on between us was devoid of romantic trappings or sentimental illusions, and the nature of our understanding did not change significantly after that first night. Maria wasn't hungry for the sorts of attachments that most people seem to want, and love in the traditional sense was something alien to her, a passion that lay outside the sphere of what she was capable of. Given my own inner state at the time, I was perfectly willing to accept the conditions she imposed on me. We made no claims on each other, saw each other only intermittently, pursued strictly independent lives. And yet there was a solid affection between us, an intimacy that I had never quite managed to achieve with anyone else. It took me a while to catch on, however. In the beginning, I found her a little scary, perhaps even perverse (which lent a certain excitement to our initial contacts), but as time went on I understood that she was merely eccentric, an unorthodox person who lived her life according to an elaborate set of bizarre, private rituals. Every experience was systematized for her, a self-contained adventure that generated its own risks and limitations, and each one of her projects fell into a different category, separate from all the others. In my case, I belonged to the category of sex. She appointed me as her bed partner on that first night, and that was the function I continued to serve until the end. In the universe of Maria's compulsions, I was just one ritual among many, but I was fond of the role she had picked for me, and I never found any reason to complain.

Maria was an artist, but the work she did had nothing to do with creating objects commonly defined as art. Some people called her a photographer, others referred to her as a conceptualist, still others considered her a writer, but none of these descriptions was accurate, and in the end I don't think she can be pigeonholed in any way. Her work was too nutty for that, too idiosyncratic, too personal to be thought of as belonging to any particular medium or discipline. Ideas would take hold of her, she would work on projects, there would be concrete results that could be shown in galleries, but this activity didn't stem from a desire to make art so much as from a need to indulge her obsessions, to live her life precisely as she wanted to live it. Living always came first, and a number of her most time-consuming projects were done strictly for herself and never shown to anyone.

Since the age of fourteen, she had saved all the birthday presents that had ever been given to her – still wrapped, neatly arranged on shelves according to the year. As an adult, she held an annual birthday dinner in her own honor, always inviting the same number of guests as her age. Some weeks, she would indulge in what she called 'the chromatic diet,' restricting herself to foods of a single color on any given day. Monday orange: carrots, cantaloupe, boiled shrimp. Tuesday red: tomatoes, persimmons, steak tartare. Wednesday white: flounder, potatoes, cottage cheese. Thursday green: cucumbers, broccoli, spinach – and so on, all the way through the last meal on Sunday. At other times, she would make similar divisions based on the letters of the alphabet. Whole days would be spent under the spell of *b*, *c*, or *w*, and then, just as suddenly as she had started it, she would abandon the game and go on to something else. These were no more than whims, I suppose, tiny experiments with the idea of classification and habit, but similar games were just as likely to go on for many years. There was the long-term project of dressing Mr L., for example, a stranger she had once met at a party. Maria found him to be one of the handsomest men she had ever seen, but his clothes were a disgrace, she thought, and so without announcing her intentions to anyone, she took it upon herself to improve his wardrobe. Every year at Christmas she would send him an anonymous gift – a tie, a sweater, an elegant shirt – and because Mr L. moved in roughly the same social circles that she did, she would run into him every now and again, noting with pleasure the dramatic changes in his sartorial appearance. For the fact was that Mr L. always wore the clothes that Maria sent him. She would even go up to him at these gatherings and compliment him on what he was wearing, but that was as far as it went, and he never caught on that she was the one responsible for those Christmas packages.

She had grown up in Holyoke, Massachusetts, the only child of parents who divorced when she was six. After graduating from high school in 1970, she had gone down to New York with the idea of attending art school and becoming a painter, but she lost interest after one term and dropped out. She bought herself a secondhand Dodge van and took off on a tour of the American continent, staying for exactly two weeks in each state, finding temporary work along the way whenever possible – waitressing jobs, migrant farm jobs, factory jobs, earning just enough to keep her going from one place to the next. It was the first of her mad, compulsive projects, and in some sense it stands as the most extraordinary thing she ever did: a totally meaningless and arbitrary act to which she devoted almost two years of her life. Her only ambition was to spend fourteen days in every state, and beyond that she was free to do whatever she wanted. Doggedly and dispassionately, never questioning the absurdity of her task, Maria stuck it out to the end. She was just nineteen when she started, a young girl entirely on her own, and yet she managed to fend for herself and avoid major catastrophes, living the sort of adventure that boys her age only dream of. At one point in her travels, a co-worker gave her an old thirty-five millimeter camera, and without any prior training or experience, she began taking photographs. When she saw her father in Chicago a few months after that, she told him that she had finally found something she liked doing. She showed him some of her photographs, and on the strength of those early attempts, he offered to make a bargain with her. If she went on taking photographs, he said, he would cover her expenses until she was in a position to support herself. It didn't matter how long it took, but she wasn't allowed to quit. That was the story she told me in any case, and I never had grounds to disbelieve it. All during the years of our affair, a deposit of one thousand dollars showed up in Maria's account on the first of every month, wired directly from a bank in Chicago.

She returned to New York, sold her van, and moved into the loft on Duane Street, a large empty room located on the floor above a wholesale egg and butter business. The first months were lonely and disorienting for her. She had no friends, no life to speak of, and the city seemed menacing and unfamiliar, as if she had never been there before. Without any conscious motives, she began following strangers around the streets, choosing someone at random when she left her house in the morning and allowing that choice to determine where she went for the rest of the day. It became a method of acquiring new thoughts, of filling up the emptiness that seemed to have engulfed her. Eventually, she began going out with her camera and taking pictures of the people she followed. When she returned home in the evening, she would sit down and write about where she had been and what she had done, using the strangers' itineraries to speculate about their lives and, in some cases, to compose brief, imaginary biographies. That was more or less how

Maria stumbled into her career as an artist. Other works followed, all of them driven by the same spirit of investigation, the same passion for taking risks. Her subject was the eye, the drama of watching and being watched, and her pieces exhibited the same qualities one found in Maria herself: meticulous attention to detail, a reliance on arbitrary structures, patience bordering on the unendurable. In one work, she hired a private detective to follow her around the city. For several days, this man took pictures of her as she went about her rounds, recording her movements in a small notebook, omitting nothing from the account, not even the most banal and transitory events: crossing the street, buying a newspaper, stopping for a cup of coffee. It was a completely artificial exercise, and yet Maria found it thrilling that anyone should take such an active interest in her. Microscopic actions became fraught with new meaning, the driest routines were charged with uncommon emotion. After several hours, she grew so attached to the detective that she almost forgot she was paying him. When he handed in his report at the end of the week and she studied the photographs of herself and read the exhaustive chronologies of her movements, she felt as if she had become a stranger, as if she had been turned into an imaginary being.

For her next project, Maria took a temporary job as a chambermaid in a large midtown hotel. The point was to gather information about the guests, but not in any intrusive or compromising way. She intentionally avoided them in fact, restricting herself to what could be learned from the objects scattered about their rooms. Again she took photographs; again she invented life stories for them based on the evidence that was available to her. It was an archeology of the present, so to speak, an attempt to reconstitute the essence of something from only the barest fragments: a ticket stub, a torn stocking, a blood stain on the collar of a shirt. Some time after that, a man tried to pick up Maria on the street. She found him distinctly unattractive and rebuffed him. That same evening, by pure coincidence, she ran into him at a gallery opening in SoHo. They talked once again, and this time she learned from the man that he was leaving the next morning on a trip to New Orleans with his girlfriend. Maria would go there as well, she decided, and follow him around with her camera for the entire length of his visit. She had absolutely no interest in him, and the last thing she was looking for was an amorous adventure. Her intention was to keep herself hidden, to resist all contact with him, to explore his outward behavior and make no effort to interpret what she saw. The next morning, she caught a flight from LaGuardia to New Orleans, checked into a hotel, and bought herself a black wig. For three days she made inquiries at dozens of hotels, trying to track down the man's whereabouts. She discovered him at last, and for the rest of the week she walked behind him like a shadow, taking hundreds of photographs, documenting every place he went to. She kept a written diary as well, and when the time came for him to go back to New York, she returned on an earlier flight – in order to be waiting at the airport for a last sequence of pictures as he stepped off the plane. It was a complex and disturbing experience for her, and it left her feeling that she had abandoned her life for a kind of nothingness, as though she had been taking pictures of things that weren't there. The camera was no longer an instrument that recorded presences, it was a way of making the world disappear, a technique for encountering the invisible. Desperate to undo the process she had set in motion, Maria launched into a new project just days after returning to New York. Walking through Times Square with her camera one afternoon, she got into a conversation with the doorman of a topless go-go bar. The weather was warm, and Maria was dressed in shorts and a T-shirt, an unusually skimpy outfit for her. But she had gone out that day in order to be noticed. She wanted to affirm the reality of her body, to make heads turn, to prove to herself that she still existed in the eyes of others. Maria was well put together, with long legs and attractive breasts, and the whistles and lewd remarks she received that day helped to revive her spirits. The doorman told her that she was a pretty girl, just as pretty as the girls inside, and as their conversation continued, she suddenly found herself being offered a job. One of the dancers had called in sick, he said, and if she wanted to fill in for her, he'd introduce her to the boss and see if something couldn't be worked out. Scarcely pausing to think about it, Maria accepted. That was how her next work came into being, a piece that eventually came to be known as *The Naked Lady*. Maria asked a friend to come along that night and take pictures of her as she performed – not to show anyone, but for herself, in order to satisfy her own curiosity about what she looked like. She was consciously turning herself into an object, a nameless figure of desire, and it was crucial to her that she understand precisely what that object was. She only did it that once, working in twenty-minute shifts from eight o'clock in the evening until two in the morning, but she didn't hold back, and the whole time she was on stage, perched behind the bar with colored strobe lights bouncing off her bare skin, she danced her heart out.

Dressed in a rhinestone G-string and a pair of two-inch heels, she shook her body to loud rock and roll and watched the men stare at her. She wiggled her ass at them, she ran her tongue over her lips, she winked seductively as they slipped her dollar bills and urged her on. As with everything else she tried, Maria was good at it. Once she got herself going, there was hardly any stopping her.

As far as I know, she went too far only once. That was in the spring of 1976, and the ultimate effects of her miscalculation proved to be catastrophic. At least two lives were lost, and even though it took years for that to happen, the connection between the past and the present is inescapable. Maria was the link between Sachs and Lillian Stern, and if not for Maria's habit of courting trouble in whatever form she could find it, Lillian Stern never would have entered the picture. After Maria turned up at Sachs's apartment in 1979, a meeting between Sachs and Lillian Stern became possible. It took several more unlikely twists before that possibility was realized, but each of them can be traced directly back to Maria. Long before any of us knew her, she went out one morning to buy film for her camera, saw a little black address book lying on the ground, and picked it up. That was the event that started the whole miserable story. Maria opened the book, and out flew the devil, out flew a scourge of violence, mayhem, and death.

It was one of those standard little address books manufactured by the Schaeffer Eaton Company, about six inches tall and four inches across, with a flexible imitation leather cover, spiral binding, and thumb tabs for each letter of the alphabet. It was a well-worn object, filled with over two hundred names, addresses, and telephone numbers. The fact that many of the entries had been crossed out and rewritten, that a variety of writing instruments had been used on almost every page (blue ballpoints, black felt tips, green pencils) suggested that it had belonged to the owner for a long time. Maria's first thought was to return it, but as is often the case with personal property, the owner had neglected to write his name in the book. She searched in all the logical places – the inside front cover, the first page, the back – but no name was to be found. Not knowing what to do with it after that, she dropped the book into her bag and carried it home.

Most people would have forgotten about it, I think, but Maria wasn't one to shy away from unexpected opportunities, to ignore the promptings of chance. By the time she went to bed that night, she had already come up with a plan for her next project. It would be an elaborate piece, much more difficult and complicated than anything she had attempted before, but the sheer scope of it threw her into a state of intense excitement. She was almost certain that the owner of the address book was a man. The handwriting had a masculine look to it; there were more listings for men than for women; the book was in ragged condition, as if it had been treated roughly. In one of those sudden, ridiculous flashes that everyone is prey to, she imagined that she was destined to fall in love with the owner of the book. It lasted only a second or two, but in that time she saw him as the man of her dreams: beautiful, intelligent, warm; a better man than she had ever loved before. The vision dispersed, but by then it was already too late. The book had been transformed into a magical object for her, a storehouse of obscure passions and unarticulated desires. Chance had led her to it, but now that it was hers, she saw it as an instrument of fate.

She studied the entries that first evening and found no names that were familiar to her. That was the perfect starting point, she felt. She would set out in the dark, knowing absolutely nothing, and one by one she would talk to all the people listed in the book. By finding out who they were, she would begin to learn something about the man who had lost it. It would be a portrait *in absentia*, an outline drawn around an empty space, and little by little a figure would emerge from the background, pieced together from everything he was not. She hoped that she would eventually track him down that way, but even if she didn't, the effort would be its own reward. She wanted to encourage people to open up to her when she saw them, to tell her stories about enchantment and lust and falling in love, to confide their deepest secrets in her. She fully expected to work on these interviews for months, perhaps even for years. There would be thousands of photographs to take, hundreds of statements to transcribe, an entire universe to explore. Or so she thought. As it happened, the project was derailed after just one day.

With only one exception, every person in the book was listed under his or her last name. In among the Ls, however, there was an entry for someone named Lilli. Maria assumed it was a woman's first name. If that were so, then this unique departure from the directory style could have been significant, a sign of some special intimacy. What if Lilli was the girlfriend of the man who had lost the address book? Or his sister, or even his mother? Rather than go through the names in alphabetical order as she had originally planned, Maria decided to jump ahead to L and pay a call on the mysterious Lilli first. If her hunch was correct, she might suddenly find herself in a position to learn who the man was.

She couldn't approach Lilli directly. Too much hinged on the meeting, and she was afraid of destroying her chances by blundering into it unprepared. She had to get a sense of who this woman was before she talked to her, to see what she looked like, to follow her around for a while and discover what her habits were. On the first morning, she traveled uptown to the East eighties to stake out Lilli's apartment. She entered the vestibule of the small building to check the buzzers and mailboxes, and just then, as she began to study the list of names on the wall, a woman stepped out of the elevator and opened the inner door. Maria turned to look at her, but before the face had registered, she heard the woman speak her name. 'Maria?' she said. The word was uttered as a question, and an instant later Maria understood that she was looking at Lillian Stern, her old friend from Massachusetts. 'I can't believe it,' Lillian said. 'It's really you, isn't it?'

They hadn't seen each other in more than five years. After Maria set off on her strange journey around America, they had lost contact, but until then they had been close, and their friendship went all the way back to childhood. In high school, they had been nearly inseparable, two offbeat girls struggling through adolescence together, plotting their escape from small-town life. Maria had been the serious one, the quiet intellectual, the one who had trouble making friends, whereas Lillian had been the girl with a reputation, the wild one who slept around and took drugs and played hooky from school. For all that, they were unshakeable allies, and in spite of their differences there was much more that drew them together than pulled them apart. Maria once confessed to me that Lillian had been a great example to her, and it was only by knowing her that she had ever learned how to be herself. But the influence seemed to work both ways. Maria was the one who talked Lillian into moving down to New York after high school, and for the next several months they had shared a cramped, roach-filled apartment on the Lower East Side. While Maria went to art classes, Lillian studied acting and worked as a waitress. She also took up with a rock-and-roll drummer named Tom, and by the time Maria left New York in her van, he had become a permanent fixture in the apartment. She wrote Lillian a number of postcards during her two years on the road, but without an address there was no way that Lillian could write back. When Maria returned to the city, she did everything she could to find her friend, but someone else was living in the old apartment, and there was no listing for her in the phone book. She tried calling Lillian's parents in Holyoke, but they had apparently moved to another town, and suddenly she was out of options. When she ran into Lillian in the vestibule that day, she had given up hope of ever seeing her again.

    It was an extraordinary encounter for both of them. Maria told me that they both screamed, then fell into each other's arms, then broke down and wept. Once they were able to talk again, they took the elevator upstairs and spent the rest of the day in Lillian's apartment. There was so much catching up to do, Maria said, the stories just poured out of them. They ate lunch together, and then dinner, and by the time she went home and crawled into bed, it was close to three o'clock in the morning.

    Curious things had happened to Lillian in those years, things that Maria never would have thought possible. My knowledge of them is only secondhand, but after talking to Sachs last summer, I believe that the story Maria told me was essentially accurate. She could have been wrong about some of the minor details (as Sachs could have been), but in the long run that's unimportant. Even if Lillian is not always to be trusted, even if her penchant for exaggeration is as pronounced as I'm told it is, the basic facts are not in question. At the time of her accidental meeting with Maria in 1976, Lillian had spent the past three years supporting herself as a prostitute. She entertained her clients in her apartment on East Eighty-seventh Street, and she worked entirely on her own – a part-time hustler with a thriving, independent business. All that is certain. What remains in doubt is exactly how it began. Her boyfriend Tom seems to have been involved in some way, but the full extent of his responsibility is unclear. In both versions of the story, Lillian described him as having a serious drug habit, an addiction to heroin that eventually got him thrown out of his band. According to the story Maria heard, Lillian remained desperately in love with him. She was the one who cooked up the idea herself, volunteering to sleep with other men in order to provide Tom with money. It was fast and painless, she discovered, and as long as she kept his connection happy, she knew that Tom would never leave her. At that point in her life, she said, she was willing to do anything to hold onto him, even if it meant going down the tubes herself. Eleven years later, she told Sachs something altogether different. Tom was the one who talked her into it, she said, and because she was scared of him, because he had threatened to kill her if she didn't go along with it, she'd had no choice but to give in. In this second version, Tom was the one who arranged the appointments for her, literally pimping for his own girlfriend as a way to cover the costs of his addiction. In the end, I don't suppose it matters which version was true. They were equally sordid, and they both led to the same result. After six or seven months, Tom vanished. In Maria's story, he ran off with someone else; in Sachs's story, he died of an overdose. One way or another, Lillian was alone again. One way or another, she continued sleeping with men to pay her bills. What astonished Maria was how matter-of-factly Lillian talked to her about it – with no shame or embarrassment. It was just a job like any other, she said, and when push came to shove, it was a damn sight better than serving drinks or waiting on tables. Men were going to drool wherever you went, and there was nothing you could do to stop them. It made a lot more sense to get paid for it than to fight them off – and besides, a little extra fucking never harmed anyone. If anything, Lillian was proud of how well she had done for herself. She met with clients only three days a week, she had money in the bank, she lived in a comfortable apartment in a good neighborhood. Two years earlier, she had enrolled in acting school again. She felt that she was making progress now, and in the past few weeks she had begun to audition for some parts, mostly in small downtown theaters. It wouldn't be long before something came her way, she said. Once she managed to build up another ten or fifteen thousand dollars, she was planning to close down her business and pursue acting full-time. She was just twenty-four years old, after all, and everything was still in front of her.

Maria had brought along her camera that day, and she took a number of photographs of Lillian during the time they spent together. When she told me the story three years later, she spread out these pictures in front of me as we talked. There must have been thirty or forty of them, full-size black-and-white photographs that caught Lillian from a variety of angles and distances – some of them posed, some of them not. These portraits were my one and only encounter with Lillian Stern. More than ten years have gone by since that day, but I have never forgotten the experience of looking at those pictures. The impression they made on me was that strong, that lasting.

'She's beautiful, isn't she?' Maria said.

'Yes, extremely beautiful,' I said.

'She was on her way out to buy groceries when we bumped into each other. You see what she's wearing. A sweatshirt, blue jeans, old sneakers.

She was dressed for one of those five-minute dashes to the corner store and then back again. No makeup, no jewelry, no props. And still she's beautiful. Enough to take your breath away.'

'It's her darkness,' I said, searching for an explanation. 'Women with dark features don't need a lot of makeup. You see how round her eyes are. The long lashes set them off. And her bones are good, too, we mustn't forget that. Bones make all the difference.'

'It's more than that, Peter. There's a certain inner quality that's always coming to the surface with Lillian. I don't know what to call it. Happiness, grace, animal spirits. It makes her seem more alive than other people. Once she catches your attention, it's hard to stop looking at her.'

'You get the feeling that she's comfortable in front of the camera.'

'Lillian's always comfortable. She's completely relaxed in her own skin.'

I flipped through some more of the photographs and came to a sequence that showed Lillian standing in front of an open closet, in various stages of undress. In one picture, she was taking off her blue jeans; in another, she was removing her sweatshirt; in the next one, she was down to a pair of minuscule white panties and a white sleeveless undershirt; in the next, the panties were gone; in the next one after that, the undershirt was gone as well. Several nude shots followed. In the first, she was facing the camera, head thrown back, laughing, her small breasts almost flattened against her chest, taut nipples protruding over the horizon; her pelvis was thrust forward, and she was clutching the meat of her inner thighs with her two hands, her thatch of dark pubic hair framed by the whiteness of her curled fingers. In the next one she was turned the other way, ass front, jutting her hip to one side and looking over her other shoulder at the camera, still laughing, striking the classic pinup pose. She was clearly enjoying herself, clearly delighted by the opportunity to show herself off.

'This is pretty racy stuff,' I said. 'I didn't know you took girlie pictures.'

'We were getting ready to go out for dinner, and Lillian wanted to change her clothes. I followed her into the bedroom so we could continue talking. I still had my camera with me, and when she started to undress, I took some more pictures. It just happened. I wasn't planning to do it until I saw her peeling off her clothes.'

'And she didn't mind?'

'It doesn't look like she minded, does it?'

'Did it turn you on?'

'Of course it did. I'm not made of wood, you know.'

'What happened next? You didn't sleep together, did you?'

'Oh no, I'm too much of a prude for that.'

'I'm not trying to force a confession out of you. Your friend looks pretty irresistible to me. As much to women as to men, I would think.'

'I admit that I was aroused. If Lillian had made some kind of move then, maybe something would have happened. I've never slept with another woman, but that day with her, I might have done it. It crossed my mind, in any case, and that's the only time I ever felt like that. But Lillian was just fooling around for the camera, and it never got any farther than the striptease. It was all in fun, and both of us were laughing the whole time.'

'Did you ever get around to showing her the address book?'

'Eventually. I think it was after we came back from the restaurant. Lillian spent a long time looking through it, but she couldn't really say who it belonged to. It had to be a client, of course. Lilli was the name she used for her work, but beyond that she wasn't sure.'

'It narrowed down the list of possibilities, though.'

'True, but it might not have been someone she'd met. A potential client, for example. Maybe one of Lillian's satisfied customers had passed on her name to someone else. A friend, a business associate, who knows. That's how Lillian got her new clients, by word of mouth. The man wrote down her name in his book, but that doesn't mean he'd gotten around to calling her yet. Maybe the man who'd given him the name hadn't called either. Hookers circulate like that – their names ripple out in concentric circles, weird networks of information. For some men, it's enough to carry around a name or two in their little black book. For future reference, as it were. In case their wife leaves them, or for sudden fits of horniness or frustration.'

'Or when they happen to be passing through town.'

'Exactly.'

'Still, you had your first clues. Until Lillian turned up, the owner of the book could have been anyone. At least you had a fighting chance now.'

'I suppose. But things didn't work out that way. Once I started talking to Lillian, the whole project changed.'

'You mean she wouldn't give you the list of her clients?'

'No, nothing like that. She would have done it if I'd asked her.'

'What was it, then?'

'I'm not quite sure how it happened, but the more we talked, the more definite our plan became. It didn't come from either one of us. It was just floating in the air, a thing that already seemed to exist. Running into each other had a lot to do with it, I think. It was all so wonderful and unexpected, we were sort of beside ourselves. You have to understand how close we'd been. Bosom buddies, sisters, pals for life. We really cared about each other, and I thought I knew Lillian as well as I knew myself. And then what happens? After five years, I discover that my best friend has turned into a whore. It knocked me off balance. I felt awful about it, almost as if I'd been betrayed. But at the same time – and this is where it starts to get murky – I realized that I envied her, too. Lillian hadn't changed. She was the same terrific kid I'd always known. Crazy, full of mischief, exciting to be with. She didn't think of herself as a slut or fallen woman, her conscience was clear. That was what impressed me so much: her absolute inner freedom, the way she lived by her own rules and didn't give a damn what anybody thought. I had already done some fairly excessive things myself by then. The New Orleans project, the 'Naked Lady' project, I was pushing myself a little farther along each time, testing the limits of what I was capable of. But next to Lillian I felt like some spinster librarian, a pathetic virgin who hadn't done much of anything. I thought to myself: If she can do it, why can't I?'

'You're kidding.'

'Wait, let me finish. It was more complicated than that. When I told Lillian about the address book and the people I was going to talk to, she thought it was fantastic, the greatest thing she'd ever heard. She wanted to help me. She wanted to go around and talk to the people in the book, just like I was going to do. She was an actress, remember, and the idea of pretending to be me got her all worked up. She was positively inspired.'

'So you switched. Is that what you're trying to tell me? Lillian talked you into trading places with her.'

'No one talked anyone into anything. We decided on it together.'

'Still . . .'

'Still nothing. We were equal partners from beginning to end. And the fact was, Lillian's life changed because of it. She fell in love with one of the people in the book and wound up marrying him.'

'It gets stranger and stranger.'

'It was strange, all right. Lillian went out with one of my cameras and the address book, and the fifth or sixth person she saw was the man who became her husband. I knew there was a story hidden in that book – but it was Lillian's story, not mine.'

'And you actually met this man? She wasn't making it up?'

'I was their witness at the wedding in City Hall. As far as I know, Lillian never told him how she'd been earning her living, but why should he have to know? They live in Berkeley, California, now. He's a college teacher, a terrifically nice guy.'

'And how did things turn out for you?'

'Not so well. Not so well at all. The same day that Lillian went off with my spare camera, she had an afternoon appointment with one of her regular clients. When he called that morning to confirm, she explained that her mother was sick and she had to leave town. She'd asked a friend to fill in for her, and if he didn't mind seeing someone else this once, she guaranteed he wouldn't regret it. I can't remember her exact words, but that was the general drift. She gave me a big buildup, and after some gentle persuasion the man went along with it. So there I was, sitting alone in Lillian's apartment that afternoon, waiting for the doorbell to ring, getting ready to fuck a man I'd never seen before. His name was Jerome, a squat little man in his forties with hair on his knuckles and yellow teeth. He was a salesman of some sort. Wholesale liquor, I think it was, but it might have been pencils or computers. It doesn't make any difference. He rang the doorbell on the dot of three, and the moment he walked into the apartment, I realized I couldn't go through with it. If he'd been halfway attractive, I might have been able to pluck up my courage, but with a charmer like Jerome it just wasn't possible. He was in a hurry and kept looking at his watch, eager to get started, to get it over with and get out. I played along, not knowing what else to do, trying to think of something as we went into the bedroom and took off our clothes. Dancing naked in a topless bar had been one thing, but standing there with that fat, furry salesman was so intimate, I couldn't even look him in the eyes. I'd hidden my camera in the bathroom, and I figured if I was going to get any pictures out of this fiasco, I'd have to act now. So I excused myself and trotted off to the potty, leaving the door open just a crack. I turned on both faucets in the sink, took out my loaded camera, and started snapping shots of the bedroom. I had a perfect angle. I could see Jerome sprawled out on the bed.

He was looking up at the ceiling and wiggling his dick in his hand, trying to get a hard on. It was disgusting, but also comical in some way, and I was glad to be getting it on film. I guessed there'd be time for ten or twelve pictures, but after I'd taken six or seven of them, Jerome suddenly bounced up from the bed, walked over to the bathroom, and yanked open the door before I had a chance to shut it. When he saw me standing there with the camera in my hands, he went crazy. I mean really crazy, out of his mind. He started yelling, accusing me of taking pictures so I could blackmail him and ruin his marriage, and before I knew it he'd snatched the camera from me and was smashing it against the bathtub. I tried to run away, but he grabbed hold of my arm before I could get out, and then he started pounding me with his fists. It was a nightmare. Two naked strangers, slugging it out in a pink tiled bathroom. He kept grunting and shouting as he hit me, yelling at the top of his lungs, and then he landed one that knocked me out. It broke my jaw, if you can believe it. But that was only part of the damage. I also had a broken wrist, a couple of cracked ribs, and bruises all over my body. I spent ten days in the hospital, and afterward my jaw was wired shut for six weeks. Little Jerome beat me to a pulp. He kicked the living shit out of me.'

When I met Maria at Sachs's apartment in 1979, she hadn't slept with a man in close to three years. It took her that long to recover from the shock of the beating, and abstinence was not a choice so much as a necessity, the only possible cure. As much as the physical humiliation she had suffered, the incident with Jerome had been a spiritual defeat. For the first time in her life, Maria had been chastened. She had stepped over the boundaries of herself, and the brutality of that experience had altered her sense of who she was. Until then, she had imagined herself capable of anything: any adventure, any transgression, any dare. She had felt stronger than other people, immunized against the ravages and failures that afflict the rest of humanity. After the switch with Lillian, she learned how badly she had deceived herself. She was weak, she discovered, a person hemmed in by her own fears and inner constraints, as mortal and confused as anyone else.

It took three years to repair the damage (to the extent that it was ever repaired), and when we crossed paths at Sachs's apartment that night, she was more or less ready to emerge from her shell. If I was the one she offered her body to, it was only because I happened to come along at the right moment. Maria always scoffed at that interpretation, insisting that I was the only man she could have gone for, but I would be crazy to think it was because I possessed any supernatural charms. I was just one man among many possible men, damaged goods in my own right, and if I corresponded to what she was looking for just then, so much the better for me. She was the one who set the rules of our friendship, and I stuck to them as best I could, a willing accomplice to her whims and urgent demands. At Maria's request, I agreed that we would never sleep together two nights in a row. I agreed that I would never talk to her about any other woman. I agreed that I would never ask her to introduce me to any of her friends. I agreed to act as though our affair were a secret, a clandestine drama to be hidden from the rest of the world. None of these restraints bothered me. I dressed in the clothes that Maria wanted me to wear, I indulged her appetite for odd meeting places (subway token booths, Off-Track Betting parlors, restaurant bathrooms), I ate the same color-coordinated meals that she did. Everything was play for Maria, a call to constant invention, and no idea was too outlandish not to be tried at least once. We made love with our clothes off and our clothes on, with lights and without lights, indoors and outdoors, on her bed and under it. We put on togas, caveman suits, and rented tuxedos. We pretended to be strangers, we pretended to be married. We acted out doctor-and-nurse routines, waitress-and-customer routines, teacher-and-student routines. It was all fairly childish, I suppose, but Maria took these escapades seriously – not as diversions but as experiments, studies in the shifting nature of the self. If she hadn't been so earnest, I doubt that I could have carried on with her in the way I did. I saw other women during that time, but Maria was the only one who meant anything to me, the only one who is still part of my life today.

In September of that year (1979), someone finally bought the house in Dutchess County, and Delia and David moved back to New York, settling into a brownstone apartment in the Cobble Hill section of Brooklyn. This made things both better and worse for me. I was able to see my son more often, but it also meant more frequent contacts with my soon-to-be ex-wife. Our divorce was well underway by then, but Delia was starting to have misgivings, and in those last months before the papers went through, she made an obscure, halfhearted attempt to win me back. If there had been no David in the picture, I would have been able to resist this campaign without any trouble. But the little boy was clearly suffering from my absence, and I held myself responsible for his bad dreams, his bouts with asthma, his tears. Guilt is a powerful persuader, and Delia instinctively pushed all the right buttons whenever I was around. Once, for example, after a man she was acquainted with had come to her house for dinner, she reported to me that David had crawled into his lap and asked him if he was going to be his new father. Delia wasn't throwing this incident in my face, she was simply sharing her concern with me, but each time I heard another one of these stories, I sank a little deeper into the quicksand of my remorse. It wasn't that I wanted to live with Delia again, but I wondered if I shouldn't resign myself to it, if I wasn't destined to be married to her after all. I considered David's welfare more important than my own, and yet for close to a year I had been cavorting like an idiot with Maria Turner and the others, ignoring every thought that touched on the future. It was difficult to justify this life to myself. Happiness wasn't the only thing that counted, I argued. Once you became a parent, there were duties that couldn't be shirked, obligations that had to be fulfilled, no matter what the cost.

Fanny was the one who saved me from what would have been a terrible decision. I can say that now in the light of what happened later, but back then nothing was clear to me. When the lease on my Varick Street sublet ran out, I rented an apartment just six or seven blocks from Delia's place in Brooklyn. I hadn't been intending to move so close to her, but the prices in Manhattan were too steep for me, and once I started looking on the other side of the river, every apartment I was shown seemed to be in her neighborhood. I wound up with a shabby floor-through in Carroll Gardens, but the rent was affordable, and the bedroom was large enough for two beds – one for me and one for David. He started spending two or three nights a week with me, which was a good change in itself, but one that pushed me into a precarious position with Delia. I had allowed myself to slip back into her orbit, and I could feel my resolve beginning to waver. By an unfortunate coincidence, Maria had left town for a couple of months at the time of my move, and Sachs was gone as well – off to California to work on a screenplay of *The New Colossus*. An independent producer had bought the film rights to his novel, and Sachs had been hired to write the script in collaboration with a professional screenwriter who lived in Hollywood. I will return to that story later, but for now the point is that I was alone, stranded in New York without my usual companions. My whole future was being thrown into question again, and I needed someone to talk to, to hear myself think out loud.

One night, Fanny called me at my new apartment and invited me to dinner. I assumed it would be one of her standard parties, with five or six other guests, but when I showed up at her house the following evening, I discovered that I was the only person she had asked. This came as a surprise to me. In all the years we had known each other, Fanny and I had never spent any time by ourselves. Ben had always been around, and except for the odd moments when he left the room or was called away to the telephone, we had scarcely even spoken to each other without someone else listening to what we said. I had become so accustomed to this arrangement, I didn't bother to question it anymore. Fanny had always been a remote and idealized figure for me, and it seemed fitting that our relations should be indirect, perpetually mediated by others. In spite of the affection that had grown up between us, it still made me a little nervous to be with her. My self-consciousness tended to make me rather whimsical, and I often went out of my way to make her laugh, cracking bad jokes and delivering atrocious puns, translating my awkwardness into a blithe and puerile banter. All this disturbed me, since I never acted that way with anyone else. I am not a jocular person, and I knew that I was giving her a false impression of who I was, but it wasn't until that night that I understood why I had always hidden myself from her. Some thoughts are too dangerous, and you mustn't allow yourself to get near them.

I remember the white silk blouse she wore that evening and the white pearls around her brown neck. I think she noticed how puzzled I was by her invitation, but she didn't let on about it, acting as though it were perfectly normal for friends to have dinner in this way. It probably was, but not from my point of view, not with the history of evasions that existed between us. I asked her if there was anything special she wanted to talk about. No, she said, she just felt like seeing me. She had been working hard ever since Ben left town, and when she woke up yesterday morning, it suddenly occurred to her that she missed me. That was all. She missed me and wanted to know how I was.

We started with drinks in the living room, mostly talking about Ben for the first few minutes. I mentioned a letter he had written to me the week before, and then Fanny described a phone conversation she'd had with him earlier that day. She didn't believe the movie would ever get made, she said, but Ben was earning good money for the script, and that was bound to help. The house in Vermont needed a new roof, and maybe they'd be able to go ahead with it before the old one caved in. We might have talked about Vermont after that, or else her work at the museum, I forget. By the time we sat down for dinner, we had somehow moved on to my book. I told Fanny that I was still making progress, but less than before, since several days a week were now given over entirely to David. We lived like a couple of old bachelors, I said, shuffling around the apartment in our slippers, smoking pipes in the evening, talking philosophy over a glass of brandy as we studied the embers in the fireplace.

'A little like Holmes and Watson,' Fanny said.

'We're getting there. Defecation remains a lively topic these days, but once my colleague is out of diapers, I'm sure we'll be tackling other subjects.'

'It could be worse.'

'Of course it could. You don't hear me complaining, do you?'

'Have you introduced him to any of your lady friends?'

'Maria, for example?'

'For example.'

'I've thought about it, but there never seems to be a good time. It's probably because I don't want to. I'm afraid he'll get confused.'

'And what about Delia? Has she been seeing other men?'

'I think so, but she isn't very forthcoming about her private business.'

'Just as well, I suppose.'

'I can't really say. From the looks of things now, she seems fairly happy that I've moved into her neighborhood.'

'Good God. You're not encouraging this, are you?'

'I'm not sure. It's not as though I'm thinking about marrying anyone else.'

'David's not a good enough reason, Peter. If you went back to Delia now, you'd begin to hate yourself for it. You'd turn into a bitter old man.'

'Maybe that's what I am already.'

'Nonsense.'

'I try not to be, but it gets harder and harder to look at the mess I've made without feeling pretty stupid.'

'You feel responsible, that's all. It's tugging you in opposite directions.'

'Whenever I leave, I tell myself I should have stayed. Whenever I stay, I tell myself I should have left.'

'It's called ambivalence.'

'Among other things. If that's the term you want to use, I'll let it stand.'

'Or, as my grandmother once put it to my mother: "Your father would be a wonderful man, if only he were different."'

'Ha.'

'Yes, ha. A whole epic of pain and suffering reduced to a single sentence.'

'Matrimony as a swamp, as a lifelong exercise in self-delusion.'

'You just haven't met the right person yet, Peter. You've got to give yourself more time.'

'You're saying I don't know what real love is. And once I do, my feelings will change. It's nice of you to think that, but what if it never happens? What if it's not in the cards for me?'

'It is, I guarantee it.'

'And what makes you so sure?'

Fanny paused for a moment, put down her knife and fork, and then reached across the table and took hold of my hand. 'You love me, don't you?'

'Of course I love you,' I said.

'You've always loved me, haven't you? From the first moment you laid eyes on me. It's true, isn't it? You've loved me for all these years, and you still love me now.'

I pulled my hand away and looked down at the table, overcome by embarrassment. 'What is this?' I said. 'A forced confession?'

'No, I'm just trying to prove that you married the wrong woman.'

'You're married to someone else, remember? I always thought that kept you off the list of candidates.'

'I'm not saying you should have married me. But you shouldn't have married the person you did.'

'You're talking in circles, Fanny.'

'It's perfectly clear. You just don't want to understand what I'm saying.'

'No, there's a flaw in your argument. I grant you that marrying Delia was a mistake. But loving you doesn't prove that I can love someone else. What if you're the only woman I could ever love? I pose this question hypothetically, of course, but it's a crucial point. If it's true, then your argument makes no sense.'

'Things don't work that way, Peter.'

'That's the way they work for you and Ben. Why make an exception for yourself?'

'I'm not.'

'And what's that supposed to mean?'

'I don't have to spell everything out for you, do I?'

'You'll have to forgive me, but I'm beginning to feel a little confused. If I didn't know I was talking to you, I'd swear you were coming on to me.'

'Are you saying you'd object?'

'Jesus, Fanny, you're married to my best friend.'

'Ben has nothing to do with it. This is strictly between us.'

'No it's not. It has everything to do with him.'

'And what do you think Ben is doing out in California?'

'He's writing a movie script.'

'Yes, he's writing a movie script. And he's also fucking a girl named Cynthia.'

'I don't believe you.'

'Why don't you call him and find out for yourself? Just ask him. He'll tell you the truth. Just say: Fanny tells me you're fucking a girl named Cynthia; what about it, old man? He'll give you a straight answer, I know he will.'

'I don't think we should be having this conversation.'

'And then ask him about the other ones before Cynthia. Grace, for example. And Nora, and Martine, and Val. Those are the first names that spring to mind, but if you give me a minute, I'll think of some more. Your friend is a cunt-hound, Peter. You never knew that about him, did you?'

'Don't talk that way. It's disgusting.'

'I'm only giving you the facts. It's not as though Ben hides it from me. He has my permission, you see. He can do anything he wants. And I can do anything I want.'

'Why bother to stay married, then? If all this is true, there's no reason for you to be together.'

'We love each other, that's why.'

'It certainly doesn't sound like it.'

'But we do. This is the way we've arranged things. If I didn't give Ben his freedom, I'd never be able to hold onto him.'

'So he runs around while you stay put, waiting for your prodigal husband to come home again. It doesn't sound like a fair arrangement to me.'

'It's fair. It's fair because I accept it, because I'm happy with it. Even if I've used my own freedom only sparingly, it's still mine, it still belongs to me. It's a right I can exercise whenever I choose.'

'Such as now.'

'This is it, Peter. You're finally going to get what you've always wanted. And you don't have to feel that you're betraying Ben. What happens tonight is strictly between you and me.'

'You said that before.'

'Maybe you understand it a little better now. You don't have to tie yourself up in knots. If you want me, you can have me.'

'Just like that.'

'Yes, just like that.'

I found her assertiveness daunting, incomprehensible. If I hadn't been so thrown by it, I probably would have stood up from the table and left, but as it was, I just sat in my chair and said nothing. Of course I wanted to sleep with her. She had understood that all along, and now that I had been exposed, now that she had turned my secret into a blunt and vulgar proposition, I scarcely knew who she was anymore. Fanny had become someone else. Ben had become someone else. In the space of one brief conversation, all my certainties about the world had collapsed.

Fanny took hold of my hand again, and instead of trying to talk her out of it, I responded with a weak, embarrassed smile. She must have interpreted that as capitulation, for a moment later she stood up from her chair and walked around the table to where I was sitting. I opened my arms to her, and without saying a word she crawled into my lap, planted her haunches firmly against my thighs, and took hold of my face with her hands. We started kissing. Mouths open, tongues thrashing, slobbering onto each other's chins, we started kissing like a couple of teenagers in the backseat of a car.

We carried on like that for the next three weeks. Almost at once, Fanny became recognizable to me again, a familiar and enigmatic point of stillness. She was no longer the same, of course, but not in any of the ways that had stunned me that first night, and the aggressiveness she had shown then was never repeated. I began to forget all about it, accustoming myself to our altered relations, to the ongoing rush of desire. Ben was still out of town, and except for the nights David was with me, I spent every night at his house, sleeping in his bed and making love to his wife. I took it for granted that I was going to marry Fanny. Even if it meant destroying my friendship with Sachs, I was fully prepared to go ahead with it. For the time being, however, I kept this knowledge to myself. I was still too awed by the strength of my feelings, and I didn't want to overwhelm her by speaking too soon. That was how I justified my silence, in any case, but the truth was that Fanny showed little inclination to talk about anything but the day-to-day, the logistics of the next meeting. Our lovemaking was wordless and intense, a swoon to the depths of immobility. Fanny was all languor and compliance, and I fell in love with the smoothness of her skin, with the way she would close her eyes whenever I stole up behind her and kissed the back of her neck. For the first couple of weeks, I didn't want anything more than that. Touching her was enough, and I lived for the barely audible purrings that came from her throat, for the feel of her back slowly arching against my palms.

I imagined Fanny as David's stepmother. I imagined the two of us setting up house in a different neighborhood and living there for the rest of our lives. I imagined storms, dramatic scenes, immense shouting matches with Sachs before any of this could happen. Perhaps it would finally come to blows, I thought. I found myself ready for anything, and even the idea of squaring off against my friend failed to shock me. I pressed Fanny to talk about him, hungry to listen to her grievances in order to vindicate myself in my own eyes. If I could establish that he had been a bad husband, then my plan to steal her away from him would be given the weight and sanctity of a moral purpose. I wouldn't be stealing her, I would be rescuing her, and my conscience would remain clear. What I was too naïve to grasp was that enmity can also be a dimension of love. Fanny suffered from Ben's sexual conduct; his strayings and pecadillos were a source of constant pain for her, but once she began to confide in me about these things, the bitterness I was expecting to hear from her never advanced beyond a sort of mild rebuke. Opening up to me seemed to relieve some pressure inside her, and now that she had committed a sin of her own, perhaps she was able to pardon him for the sins he had committed against her. This was the economy of justice, so to speak, the quid pro quo that turns the victim into the one who victimizes, the act that puts the scales in balance. In the end, I learned a great deal about Sachs from Fanny, but it never provided me with the ammunition I was looking for. If anything, her disclosures had just the opposite effect. One night, for example, when we started talking about the time he had spent in prison, I found out that those seventeen months had been far more terrible for him than he had ever allowed me to know. I don't think that Fanny was specifically trying to defend him, but when I heard about the things he had lived through (random beatings, continual harassment and threats, a possible incident of homosexual rape), I found it difficult to muster any resentment against him. Sachs as seen through Fanny's eyes was a more complicated and troubled person than the one I thought I knew. He wasn't just the ebullient and gifted extrovert who had become my friend, he was also a man who hid himself from others, a man burdened with secrets he had never shared with anyone. I wanted an excuse to turn against him, but all through those weeks I spent with Fanny, I felt as close to him as ever before. Strangely enough, none of that interfered with my feelings for her. Loving her was simple, even if everything that surrounded that love was fraught with ambiguity. She was the one who had thrown herself at me, after all, and yet the more tightly I held her, the less sure I became of what I was holding.

The affair coincided exactly with Ben's absence. A couple of days before he was scheduled to return, I finally brought up the subject of what we were going to do once he was back in New York. Fanny proposed that we go on in the same way, seeing each other whenever we wished. I told her that wasn't possible, that she would have to make a break with Ben and move in with me if we were going to continue. There wasn't any room for duplicity, I said. We should tell him what had happened, resolve things as quickly as we could, and then plan on getting married. It never occurred to me that this wasn't what Fanny wanted, but that only proves how ignorant I was, how badly I had misread her intentions from the start. She wouldn't leave Ben, she said. She had never even considered it. No matter how much she loved me, it wasn't something she was prepared to do.

It turned into an agonizing conversation that lasted for several hours, a vortex of circular arguments that never took us anywhere. We both did a lot of crying, each one imploring the other to be reasonable, to give in, to look at the situation from a new perspective, but it didn't work. Perhaps it never could have worked, but as it was happening, I felt it was the worst conversation of my life, a moment of absolute ruin. Fanny wouldn't leave Ben, and I wouldn't stay with her unless she did. It's got to be all or nothing, I kept telling her. I loved her too much to settle for just a part of her. As far as I was concerned, anything less than all would be nothing, a misery I could never bring myself to live with. So I got my misery and my nothing, and the affair ended with our conversation that night. Over the months that followed, there was scarcely a moment when I didn't regret it, when I didn't grieve over my stubbornness, but there was never any chance to undo the finality of my words.

Even now, I'm at a loss to understand Fanny's behavior. One could dismiss the whole thing, I suppose, and say that she was simply amusing herself with a brief romp while her husband was out of town. But if sex was all she'd been after, it made no sense to have chosen me as the person to have it with. Given my friendship with Ben, I was the last person she would have turned to. She might have been acting out of revenge, of course, seizing on me as a way to square her accounts with Ben, but in the long run I don't think that explanation goes deep enough. It presupposes a kind of cynicism that Fanny never really possessed, and too many questions are left unanswered. It's also possible that she thought she knew what she was doing and then began to lose her nerve. A classic case of cold feet, as it were, but then what to make of the fact that she never hesitated, that she never showed the slightest glimmer of regret or indecision? Right up to the last moment, it never even crossed my mind that she had any doubts about me. If the affair ended as abruptly as it did, it had to be because she was expecting it to, because she had known it would happen that way all along. This seems perfectly plausible. The only problem is that it contradicts everything she said and did during the three weeks we spent together. What looks like a clarifying thought is finally no more than another snag. The moment you accept it, the conundrum starts all over again.

It wasn't all bad for me, however. In spite of how it ended, the episode had a number of positive results, and I look back on it now as a critical juncture in my own private story. For one thing, I gave up the idea of returning to my marriage. Loving Fanny had shown me how futile that would have been, and I laid those thoughts to rest once and for all. There's no question that Fanny was directly responsible for this change of heart. If not for her, I never would have been in a position to meet Iris, and from then on my life would have developed in an altogether different way. A worse way, I'm convinced; a way that would have turned me toward the bitterness that Fanny had warned me against the first night we spent together. By falling in love with Iris, I fulfilled the prophecy she made about me that same night – but before I could believe that prophecy, I first had to fall in love with Fanny. Was that what she was trying to prove to me? Was that the hidden motive behind our whole crazy affair? It seems preposterous even to suggest it, and yet it tallies with the facts more closely than any other explanation. What I'm saying is that Fanny threw herself at me in order to save me from myself, that she did what she did to prevent me from going back to Delia. Is such a thing possible? Can a person actually go that far for the sake of someone else? If so, then Fanny's actions become nothing less than extraordinary, a pure and luminous gesture of self-sacrifice. Of all the interpretations I've considered over the years, this is the one I like best. That doesn't mean it's true, but as long as it could be true, it pleases me to think it is. After eleven years, it's the only answer that still makes any sense.

Once Sachs returned to New York, I planned to avoid seeing him. I had no idea if Fanny was going to tell him what we'd done, but even if she kept it a secret, the prospect of having to hide it from him myself struck me as intolerable. Our relations had always been too honest and straightforward for that, and I was in no mood to start telling him stories now. I figured he would see through me anyway, and if Fanny happened to tell him what we'd been up to, I would be laying myself open to all kinds of disasters. One way or the other, I wasn't prepared to see him. If he knew, then acting as if he didn't know would be an insult. And if he didn't know, then every minute I spent with him would be a torture.

I worked on my novel, I took care of David, I waited for Maria to return to the city. Under normal circumstances, Sachs would have called me within two or three days. We rarely went longer than that without being in touch, and now that he was back from his Hollywood adventure, I fully expected to hear from him. But three days went by, and then another three days, and little by little I understood that Fanny had let him in on the secret. No other explanation was possible. I assumed that meant our friendship was over and that I would never see him again. Just when I was beginning to come to grips with this idea (on the seventh or eighth day), the telephone rang, and there was Sachs on the other end of the line, sounding in top form, cracking jokes with the same enthusiasm as ever. I tried to match his cheerfulness, but I was too taken aback to do a very good job of it. My voice shook, and I said all the wrong things. When he asked me to come to dinner that night, I made up an excuse and said I would call back tomorrow to work out something else. I didn't call. Another day or two went by, and then Sachs rang up again, still sounding chipper, as though nothing had changed between us. I did my best to fend him off, but this time he wouldn't take no for an answer. He offered to buy me lunch that same afternoon, and before I could think of a way to wriggle out of it, I heard myself accept his invitation. In less than two hours, we were supposed to meet at Costello's Restaurant, a little diner on Court Street just a few blocks from my house. If I didn't show up, he would simply walk over to my place and knock on the door. I hadn't been quick enough, and now I was going to have to face the music.

He was already there when I arrived, sitting in a booth at the back of the restaurant. *The New York Times* was spread out on the Formica table in front of him, and he seemed engrossed in what he was reading, smoking a cigarette and absentmindedly flicking ashes onto the floor after each puff. This was early 1980, the days of the hostage crisis in Iran, the Khmer Rouge atrocities in Cambodia, the war in Afghanistan. Sachs's hair had grown lighter in the California sun, and his bronzed face was smattered with freckles. He looked good, I thought, more rested than the last time I'd seen him. As I walked toward the table, I wondered how close I would have to get before he noticed I was there. The sooner it happened, the worse our conversation was going to be, I said to myself. If he looked up, that would mean he was anxious – which would prove that Fanny had already talked to him. On the other hand, if he kept his nose buried in his paper, that would show he was calm, which might mean that Fanny hadn't talked to him. Each step I took through the crowded restaurant would be a sign in my favor, I felt, a small piece of evidence that he was still in the dark, that he still didn't know I had betrayed him. As it happened, I got all the way to the booth without receiving a single glance.

'That's a nice suntan you've got there, Mr Hollywood,' I said.

As I slid onto the bench across from him, Sachs jerked up his head, stared blankly at me for a moment or two, and then smiled. It was as though he hadn't been expecting to see me, as though I had suddenly appeared in the booth by accident. That was taking it too far, I thought, and in the small silence that preceded his answer, it occurred to me that he had only been pretending to be distracted. In that case, the newspaper was no more than a prop. The whole time he'd been sitting there waiting for me to come, he'd merely been turning pages, blindly scanning the words without bothering to read them.

'You don't look too bad yourself,' he said. 'The cold weather must agree with you.'

'I don't mind it. After spending last winter in the country, this feels like the tropics.'

'And what have you been up to since I went out there to massacre my book?'

'Massacring my own book,' I said. 'Every day, I add another few paragraphs to the catastrophe.'

'You must have quite a bit by now.'

'Eleven chapters out of thirteen. I suppose that means the end is in sight.'

'Any idea when you'll be finished?'

'Not really. Three or four months, maybe. But it could be twelve. And then again, it could be two. It gets harder and harder to make any predictions.'

'I hope you'll let me read it when you're done.'

'Of course you can read it. You'll be the first person I give it to.'

At that point, the waitress arrived to take our orders. That's how I remember it in any case: an early interruption, a brief pause in the flow of our talk. Since moving into the neighborhood, I had been going to Costello's for lunch about twice a week, and the waitress knew who I was. She was an immensely fat and friendly woman who waddled among the tables in a pale green uniform and kept a yellow pencil stuck in her frizzy gray hair at all times. She never wrote with that pencil, using one she stored in her apron pocket instead, but she liked to have it on hand in case there was an emergency. I've forgotten this woman's name now, but she used to call me 'hon' and to stand around and chat with me whenever I came in – never about anything in particular, but always in a way that made me feel welcome. Even with Sachs there that afternoon, we went through one of our typically long-winded exchanges. It doesn't matter what we talked about, but I mention it in order to show what kind of mood Sachs was in that day. Not only did he not talk to the waitress (which was highly unusual for him), but the moment she walked off with our orders, he picked up the conversation exactly where we had stopped, as if we had never been interrupted. It was only then that I began to understand how agitated he must have been. Later on, when the food was served, I don't think he ate more than two or three bites of it. He smoked and drank coffee, dousing his cigarettes in the flooded saucers.

'The work is what counts,' he said, closing up the newspaper and tossing it onto the bench beside him. 'I just want you to know that.'

'I don't think I follow you,' I said, realizing that I followed him all too well.

'I'm telling you not to worry, that's all.'

'Worry? Why should I worry?'

'You shouldn't,' Sachs said, breaking into a warm, astonishingly radiant smile. For a moment or two, he looked almost beatific. 'But I've known you long enough to feel pretty certain that you will.'

'Am I missing something, or have we decided to talk in circles today?'

'It's all right, Peter. That's the only point I'm trying to make. Fanny told me, and you don't have to walk around feeling bad about it.'

'Told you what?' It was a ridiculous question, but I was too stunned by his composure to say anything else.

'What happened while I was gone. The bolt of lightning. The fucking and sucking. The whole bloody thing.'

'I see. Not much left to the imagination.'

'No, not a hell of a lot.'

'So what happens now? Is this the moment when you hand me your card and tell me to contact my seconds? We'll have to meet at dawn, of course. Somewhere good, somewhere with the appropriate scenic value. The walkway of the Brooklyn Bridge, for example, or maybe the Civil War monument at Grand Army Plaza. Something majestic. A place where the sky can dwarf us, where the sunlight can glint off our raised pistols. What do you say, Ben? Is that how you want to do it? Or would you rather get it over with now? American-style. You reach across the table, you punch me in the nose, and then you walk out. Either way is fine with me. I leave it up to you.'

'There's also a third possibility.'

'Ah, the third path,' I said, all anger and facetiousness. 'I hadn't realized there were so many options available to us.'

'Of course there are. More than we can count. The one I'm thinking of is quite simple. We wait for our food to arrive, we eat it, then I pay the check and we leave.'

'That's not good enough. There's no drama in it, no confrontation. We have to force things out into the open. If we back down now, I won't feel satisfied.'

'There's nothing to quarrel about, Peter.'

'Yes there is. There's everything to quarrel about. I asked your wife to marry me. If that isn't sufficient grounds for a quarrel, then neither one of us deserves to live with her.'

'If you want to get it off your chest, go ahead. I'm perfectly willing to listen. But you don't have to talk about it if you don't want to.'

'No one can care so little about his own life. It's almost criminal to be so indifferent.'

'I'm not indifferent. It's just that it was bound to happen sooner or later. I'm not dumb, after all. I know how you feel about Fanny. You've always felt that way. It's written all over you every time you come near her.'

'Fanny was the one who made the first move. If she hadn't wanted it, nothing would have happened.'

'I'm not blaming you. If I were in your position, I would have done the same thing.'

'That doesn't make it right, though.'

'It's not a question of right and wrong. That's the way the world works. Every man is the prisoner of his pecker, and there's not a damned thing we can do about it. We try to fight it sometimes, but it's always a losing battle.'

'Is this a confession of guilt, or are you trying to tell me you're innocent?'

'Innocent of what?'

'Of what Fanny told me. Your carryings-on. Your extra-curricular activities.'

'She told you that?'

'At great length. She wound up giving me quite an earful. Names, dates, descriptions of the victims, the whole works. It's had an impact. Since then, my idea of who you are has been completely altered.'

'I'm not sure you want to believe everything you hear.'

'Are you calling Fanny a liar?'

'Of course not. It's just that she doesn't always have a firm grasp of the truth.'

'That sounds like the same thing to me. You're saying it differently, that's all.'

'No, I'm telling you that Fanny can't help what she thinks. She's convinced herself that I'm unfaithful, and no amount of talk is ever going to dissuade her.'

'And you're saying that you're not?'

'I've had my lapses, but never to the extent she imagines. Considering how long we've been together, it's not a bad record. Fanny and I have had our ups and downs, but there's never been a moment when I haven't wanted to be married to her.'

'So where does she get the names of all these other women?'

'I tell her stories. It's part of a game we play. I make up stories about my imaginary conquests, and Fanny listens. It excites her. Words have power, after all. For some women, there's no stronger aphrodisiac. You must have learned that about Fanny by now. She loves dirty talk. And the more graphic you make it, the more turned on she gets.'

'That wasn't what it sounded like to me. Every time Fanny talked about you, she was dead serious. Not a word about "imaginary conquests." They were all very real to her.'

'Because she's jealous, and a part of her insists on believing the worst. It's happened many times now. At any given moment, Fanny has me conducting a passionate affair with someone or other. It's been going on for years, and the list of women I've slept with keeps getting longer. After a while, I learned it didn't do any good to deny it. That only made her more suspicious of me, and so rather than tell her the truth, I tell her what she wants to hear. I lie in order to keep her happy.'

'Happiness is hardly the word I'd use for it.'

'To keep us together, then. To keep us in some kind of balance. The stories help. Don't ask me why, but once I start telling them to her, things clear up between us again. You thought I'd stopped writing fiction, but I'm still at it. My audience is down to just one person now, but she's the only one who really counts.'

'And you expect me to believe this?'

'Don't think I'm enjoying myself. It's not easy to talk about it. But I figure you have a right to know, and I'm doing the best I can.'

'And Valerie Maas? You're telling me that nothing ever went on with her?'

'That's a name that used to come up often. She's an editor at one of the magazines I've written for. A year or two ago, we had a number of lunches together. Strictly business. We'd discuss my pieces, talk about future projects, that kind of thing. Eventually, Fanny got it into her head that Val and I were having an affair. I can't say that I wasn't attracted to her. If the circumstances had been different, I might have done something stupid. Fanny sensed all that, I think. I probably mentioned Val's name once too often around the house or made too many flattering remarks about what a good editor she was. But the truth is that Val isn't interested in men. She's been living with another woman for the past five or six years, and I couldn't have gotten anywhere with her even if I'd tried.'

'Didn't you tell that to Fanny?'

'There wouldn't have been any point. Once she's made up her mind, there's never any talking her out of it.'

'You make her sound so unstable. But Fanny isn't like that. She's a solid person, one of the least deluded people I've ever met.'

'She is. In many ways, she's as strong as they come. But she's also suffered a lot, and the last few years have been hard on her. She wasn't always like this, you understand. Until four or five years ago, there wasn't a jealous bone in her body.'

'Five years ago is when I met her. Officially, that is.'

'It's also when the doctor told her she'd never have any children. Things changed for her after that. She's been seeing a therapist for the past couple of years, but I don't think it's done much good. She feels undesirable. She feels that no man can possibly love her. That's why she imagines I'm carrying on with other women. Because she thinks she's failed me. Because she thinks I must be punishing her for having let me down. Once you turn against yourself, it's hard not to believe that everyone else is against you, too.'

'None of this ever shows.'

'That's part of the problem. Fanny doesn't talk enough. She bottles up things inside her, and when they do come out, it's always in oblique ways. That only makes the situation worse. Half the time, she suffers without being aware of it.'

'Until last month, I always thought you had a perfect marriage.'

'We never know anything about anyone. I used to think the same thing about your marriage, and look what happened to you and Delia. It's hard enough keeping track of ourselves. Once it comes to other people, we don't have a clue.'

'But Fanny knows I love her. I must have said it a thousand times, and I'm sure she believes me. I can't imagine that she doesn't.'

'She does. And that's why I think what happened is a good thing. You've helped her, Peter. You've done more for her than anyone else.'

'So now you're thanking me for going to bed with your wife?'

'Why not? Because of you, there's a chance that Fanny will start believing in herself again.'

'Just call Doctor Fixit, huh? He repairs broken marriages, mends wounded souls, saves couples in distress. No appointment necessary, house calls twenty-four hours a day. Dial our toll-free number now. That's Doctor Fixit. He gives you his heart and asks for nothing in return.'

'I don't blame you for feeling resentful. It can't be a very good time for you now, but for whatever it's worth, Fanny thinks you're the greatest man who ever lived. She loves you. She's never going to stop loving you.'

'Which doesn't change the fact that she wants to go on being married to you.'

'It goes too far back, Peter. We've been through too much together. Our whole lives are bound up in it.'

'And where does that leave me?'

'Where you've always been. As my friend. As Fanny's friend. As the person we care most about in the world.'

'So it starts up all over again.'

'If you want it to, yes. As long as you can stand it, it's as if nothing has changed.'

I was suddenly on the verge of tears. 'Just don't blow it,' I said. 'That's all I've got to say to you. Just don't blow it. Make sure you take good care of her. You've got to promise me that. If you don't keep your word, I think I'll kill you. I'll hunt you down and strangle you with my own two hands.'

I stared down at my plate, struggling to keep myself under control. When I finally looked up again, I saw that Sachs was staring at me. His eyes were somber, his expression fixed in an attitude of pain. Before I could get up from the table to leave, he stretched out his right hand and held it in midair, unwilling to drop it until I took it in my own. 'I promise,' he said, squeezing hard, steadily tightening his grip. 'I give you my word.'

After that lunch, I no longer knew what to believe. Fanny had told me one thing, Sachs had told me another, and as soon as I accepted one story, I would have to reject the other. There wasn't any alternative. They had presented me with two versions of the truth, two separate and distinct realities, and no amount of pushing and shoving could ever bring them together. I understood that, and yet at the same time I realized that both stories had convinced me. In the morass of sorrow and confusion that bogged me down over the next several months, I hesitated to choose between them. I don't think it was a question of divided loyalties (although that might have been part of it), but rather a certainty that both Fanny and Ben had been telling me the truth. The truth as they saw it, perhaps, but nevertheless the truth. Neither one of them had been out to deceive me; neither one had intentionally lied. In other words, there was no universal truth. Not for them, not for anyone else. There was no one to blame or to defend, and the only justifiable response was compassion. I had looked up to them both for too many years not to feel disappointed by what I had learned, but I wasn't disappointed only in them. I was disappointed in myself. I was disappointed in the world. Even the strongest were weak, I told myself; even the bravest lacked courage; even the wisest were ignorant.

I found it impossible to rebuff Sachs anymore. He had been so forthright during our conversation over lunch, so clear about wanting our friendship to continue, that I couldn't bring myself to turn my back on him. But he had been wrong to assume that nothing would change between us. Everything had changed, and like it or not, our friendship had lost its innocence. Because of Fanny, we had each crossed over into the other's life, had each made a mark on the other's internal history, and what had once been pure and simple between us was now infinitely muddy and complex. Little by little, we began to adjust to these new conditions, but with Fanny it was another story. I kept my distance from her, always seeing Sachs alone, always begging off when he invited me to their house. I accepted the fact that she belonged with Ben, but that didn't mean I was ready to see her. She understood my reluctance, I think, and though she continued to send me her love through Sachs, she never pressed me to do anything I didn't want to do. It wasn't until November that she finally called, a good six or seven months later. That was when she invited me to Thanksgiving dinner at Ben's mother's house in Connecticut. In the intervening half year, I had talked myself into thinking there had never been any hope for us, that even if she had left Ben to live with me, it wouldn't have worked. That was a fiction, of course, and I have no way of knowing what would have happened, no way of knowing anything. But it helped to get me through those months without losing my mind, and when I suddenly heard Fanny's voice again on the telephone, I figured the moment had come to test myself in a real situation. So David and I drove up to Connecticut and back, and I spent an entire day in her company. It wasn't the happiest day I've ever spent, but I managed to survive it. Old wounds opened, I bled a little bit, but when I returned home that night with the sleeping David in my arms, I discovered that I was still more or less in one piece.

I don't want to suggest that I accomplished this cure on my own.

Once Maria returned to New York, she played a large part in holding me together, and I immersed myself in our private escapades with the same passion as before. Nor was she the only one. When Maria wasn't available, I found still others to distract me from my broken heart. A dancer named Dawn, a writer named Laura, a medical student named Dorothy. At one time or another, each of them held a singular place in my affections. Whenever I stopped and examined my own behavior, I concluded that I wasn't cut out for marriage, that my dreams of settling down with Fanny had been misguided from the start. I wasn't a monogamous person, I told myself. I was too drawn by the mystery of first encounters, too infatuated with the theater of seduction, too hungry for the excitement of new bodies, and I couldn't be counted on over the long haul. That was the logic I used on myself in any case, and it functioned as an effective smokescreen between my head and my heart, between my groin and my intelligence. For the truth was that I had no idea what I was doing. I was out of control, and I fucked for the same reason that other men drink: to drown my sorrows, to dull my senses, to forget myself. I became *homo erectus*, a heathen phallus gone amok. Before long I was entangled in several affairs at once, juggling girlfriends like a demented acrobat, hopping in and out of different beds as often as the moon changes shape. In that this frenzy kept me occupied, I suppose it was successful medicine. But it was the life of a crazy person, and it probably would have killed me if it had lasted much longer than it did.

But there was more to it than just sex. I was working well, and my book was finally coming to the end. No matter how many disasters I created for myself, I managed to work through them, to push on without slackening my pace. My desk had become a sanctuary, and as long as I continued to sit there, struggling to find the next word, nothing could touch me anymore: not Fanny, not Sachs, not even myself. For the first time in all the years I had been writing, I felt as though I had caught fire. I couldn't tell if the book was good or bad, but that no longer seemed important. I had stopped questioning myself. I was doing what I had to do, and I was doing it in the only way that was possible for me. Everything else followed from that. It wasn't that I began to believe in myself so much as that I was inhabited by a sublime indifference. I had become interchangeable with my work, and I accepted that work on its own terms now, understanding that nothing could relieve me of the desire to do it. This was the bedrock epiphany, the illumination in which doubt gradually dissolved. Even if my life fell apart, there would still be something to live for.

I finished *Luna* in mid-April, two months after my talk with Sachs in the restaurant. I kept my word and gave him the manuscript, and four days later he called to tell me that he'd finished it. To be more exact, he started shouting into the telephone, heaping me with such outlandish praise that I felt myself blush on the other end. I hadn't dared to dream of a response like that. It so buoyed up my spirits that I was able to shrug off the disappointments that followed, and even as the book made the rounds of the New York publishing houses, collecting one rejection after another, I didn't let it interfere with my work. Sachs's encouragement made all the difference. He kept assuring me that I had nothing to worry about, that everything would work out in the end, and in spite of the evidence, I continued to believe him. I began writing a second novel. When *Luna* was finally taken (seven months and sixteen rejections later), I was already well into my new project. That happened in late November, just two days before Fanny invited me to Thanksgiving dinner in Connecticut. No doubt that contributed to my decision to go. I said yes to her because I'd just heard the news about my book. Success made me feel invulnerable, and I knew there would never be a better moment to face her.

Then came my meeting with Iris, and the madness of those two years abruptly ended. That was on February 23, 1981: three months after Thanksgiving, one year after Fanny and I cut off our affair, six years after my friendship with Sachs had begun. It strikes me as both strange and fitting that Maria Turner should have been the person who made that meeting possible. Again, it had nothing to do with intentionality, nothing to do with a conscious desire to make things happen. But things did happen, and if not for the fact that February twenty-third was the night that Maria's second exhibition opened in a small gallery on Wooster Street, I'm certain that Iris and I never would have met. Decades would have passed before we found ourselves standing in the same room again, and by then the opportunity would have been lost. It's not that Maria actually brought us together, but our meeting took place under her influence, so to speak, and I feel indebted to her because of that. Not to Maria as flesh-and-blood woman, perhaps, but to Maria as the reigning spirit of chance, as goddess of the unpredictable.

Because our affair continued to be a secret, there was no question of my serving as her escort that night. I showed up at the gallery just like any other guest, gave Maria a quick kiss of congratulations, and then stood among the crowd with a plastic cup in my hand, sipping cheap white wine as I scanned the room for familiar faces. I didn't see anyone I knew. At one point, Maria looked over in my direction and winked, but other than the brief smile I threw her in return, I kept my end of the bargain and avoided contact with her. Less than five minutes after that wink, someone came up from behind and tapped me on the shoulder. It was a man named John Johnston, a passing acquaintance whom I hadn't seen in a number of years. Iris was standing next to him, and after he and I exchanged greetings, he introduced us to each other. Based on her appearance, I gathered that she was a fashion model – an error that most people still make when seeing her for the first time. Iris was just twenty-four back then, a dazzling blonde presence, six feet tall with an exquisite Scandinavian face and the deepest, merriest blue eyes to be found between heaven and hell. How could I have guessed that she was a graduate student in English literature at Columbia University? How could I have known that she had read more books than I had and was about to begin a six-hundred-page dissertation on the works of Charles Dickens?

Since I assumed that she and Johnston were intimate friends, I shook her hand politely and did my best not to stare at her. Johnston had been married to someone else the last time I'd seen him, but I figured he was divorced now, and I didn't question him about it. As it happened, he and Iris scarcely knew each other. The three of us talked for several minutes, and then Johnston suddenly turned around and started talking to someone else, leaving me alone with Iris. It was only then that I began to suspect how casual their relations were. Unaccountably, I pulled out my wallet and showed her some snapshots of David, bragging about my little son as though he were a well-known public figure. To listen to Iris recall that evening now, it was at that moment that she decided she was in love with me, that she understood I was the person she was going to marry. It took me a little longer to understand how I felt about her, but only by a few hours. We continued talking over dinner in a nearby restaurant and then on through drinks at yet another place. It must have been past eleven o'clock by the time we finished. I waved down a cab for her on the street, but before I opened the door to let her in, I reached out and grabbed her, drawing her close to me and kissing her deep inside the mouth. It was one of the most impetuous things I have ever done, a moment of insane, unbridled passion. The cab drove off, and Iris and I continued standing in the middle of the street, wrapped in each other's arms. It was as though we were the first people who had ever kissed, as though we invented the art of kissing together that night. By the next morning, Iris had become my happy ending, the miracle that had fallen down on me when I was least expecting it. We took each other by storm, and nothing has ever been the same for me since.

Sachs was my best man at the wedding in June. There was a dinner after the ceremony, and about halfway through the meal he stood up from the table to make a toast. It turned out to be very short, and because he said so little, I can bring back every word of it. 'I'm taking this out of the mouth of William Tecumseh Sherman,' he said. 'I hope the general doesn't mind, but he got there before I did and I can't think of a better way to express it.' Then, turning in my direction, Sachs lifted his glass and said: 'Grant stood by me when I was crazy. I stood by him when he was drunk, and now we stand by each other always.'

3

The era of Ronald Reagan began. Sachs went on doing what he had always done, but in the new American order of the 1980s, his position became increasingly marginalized. It wasn't that he had no audience, but it grew steadily smaller, and the magazines that published his work became steadily more obscure. Almost imperceptibly, Sachs came to be seen as a throwback, as someone out of step with the spirit of the time. The world had changed around him, and in the present climate of selfishness and intolerance, of moronic, chest-pounding Americanism, his opinions sounded curiously harsh and moralistic. It was bad enough that the Right was everywhere in the ascendant, but even more disturbing to him was the collapse of any effective opposition to it. The Democratic Party had caved in; the Left had all but disappeared; the press was mute. All the arguments had suddenly been appropriated by the other side, and to raise one's voice against it was considered bad manners. Sachs continued to make a nuisance of himself, to speak out for what he had always believed in, but fewer and fewer people bothered to listen. He pretended not to care, but I could see that the battle was wearing him down, that even as he tried to take comfort from the fact that he was right, he was gradually losing faith in himself.

If the movie had been made, it might have turned things around for him. But Fanny's prediction proved to be correct, and after six or eight months of revisions, renegotiations, and ditherings back and forth, the producer finally let the project drop. It's difficult to gauge the full extent of Sachs's disappointment. On the surface, he affected a jocular attitude about the whole business, cracking jokes, telling Hollywood stories, laughing about the large sums of money he had earned. This might or might not have been a bluff, but I'm convinced that a part of him had set great store in the possibility of seeing his book turned into a film. Unlike some writers, Sachs bore no grudge against popular culture, and he had never felt any conflict about the project. It wasn't a question of compromising himself, it was an opportunity to reach large numbers of people, and he didn't hesitate when the offer came. Although he never said it in so many words, I sensed that the call from Hollywood had flattered his vanity, stunning him with a brief, intoxicating whiff of power. It was a perfectly normal response, but Sachs was never easy on himself, and chances are that he later regretted these overblown dreams of glory and success. That would have made it more difficult for him to talk about his true feelings once the project failed. He had looked to Hollywood as a way to escape the impending crisis growing inside him, and once it became clear that there was no escape, I believe he suffered a lot more than he ever let on.

All this is speculation. As far as I could tell, there were no abrupt or radical shifts in Sachs's behavior. His work schedule was the same mad scramble of overcommitments and deadlines, and once the Hollywood episode was behind him, he went on producing as much as ever, if not more. Articles, essays, and reviews continued to pour out of him at a staggering rate, and I suppose it could be argued that far from having lost his direction, he was in fact barreling ahead at full tilt. If I question this optimistic portrait of Sachs during those years, it's only because I know what happened later. Immense changes occurred inside him, and while it's simple enough to pinpoint the moment when these changes began, to zero in on the night of his accident and blame everything on that freakish occurrence, I no longer believe that explanation is adequate. Is it possible for someone to change overnight? Can a man fall asleep as one person and then wake up as another? Perhaps, but I wouldn't be willing to bet on it. It's not that the accident wasn't serious, but there are a thousand different ways in which a person can respond to a brush with death. That Sachs responded in the way he did doesn't mean I think he had any choice in the matter. On the contrary, I look on it as a reflection of his state of mind before the accident ever took place. In other words, even if Sachs seemed to be doing more or less well just then, even if he was only dimly aware of his own distress during the months and years that preceded that night, I am convinced that he was in a very bad way. I have no proof to offer in support of this statement – except the proof of hindsight. Most men would have considered themselves lucky to have lived through what happened to Sachs that evening and then shrugged it off. But Sachs didn't, and the fact that he didn't – or, more precisely, the fact that he couldn't – suggests that the accident did not change him so much as make visible what had previously been hidden. If I'm wrong about this, then everything I've written so far is rubbish, a heap of irrelevant musings. Perhaps Ben's life did break in two that night, dividing into a distinct before and after – in which case everything from before can be struck from the record. But if that's true, it would mean that human behavior makes no sense. It would mean that nothing can ever be understood about anything.

I didn't witness the accident, but I was there the night it happened. There must have been forty or fifty of us at the party, a mass of people crowded into the confines of a cramped Brooklyn Heights apartment, sweating, drinking, raising a ruckus in the hot summer air. The accident took place at around eleven o'clock, but by then most of us had gone up to the roof to watch the fireworks. Only two people actually saw Sachs fall: Maria Turner, who was standing next to him on the fire escape, and a woman named Agnes Darwin, who inadvertently caused him to lose his balance by tripping into Maria from behind. There is no question that Sachs could have been killed. Given that he was four stories off the ground, it seems almost a miracle that he wasn't. If not for the clothesline that broke his fall about five feet from the bottom, there's no way he could have escaped without some permanent injury: a broken back, a fractured skull, any one of countless misfortunes. As it was, the rope snapped under the weight of his falling body, and instead of tumbling head-first onto the bare cement, he landed in a cushioning tangle of bathmats, blankets, and towels. The impact was still tremendous, but nothing close to what it could have been. Not only did Sachs survive, but he emerged from the accident relatively unharmed: a few cracked ribs, a mild concussion, a broken shoulder, some nasty bumps and bruises. One can take comfort from that, I suppose, but in the end the real damage had little to do with Sachs's body. This is the thing I'm still struggling to come to terms with, the mystery I'm still trying to solve. His body mended, but he was never the same after that. In those few seconds before he hit the ground, it was as if Sachs lost everything. His entire life flew apart in midair, and from that moment until his death four years later, he never put it back together again.

It was July 4, 1986, the one hundredth anniversary of the Statue of Liberty. Iris was off on a six-week tour of China with her three sisters (one of whom lived in Taipei), David was spending two weeks at a summer camp in Bucks County, and I was holed up in the apartment, working on a new book and seeing no one. Ordinarily, Sachs would have been in Vermont by then, but he had been commissioned by the *Village Voice* to write an article about the festivities, and he wasn't planning to leave the city until he handed in the article. Three years earlier, he had finally succumbed to my advice and entered into an agreement with a literary agent (Patricia Clegg, who also happened to be my agent), and it was Patricia who threw the party that night. Since Brooklyn was ideally situated for watching the fireworks, Ben and Fanny had accepted Patricia's invitation. I had been invited as well, but I wasn't planning to go. I was too inside my work to want to leave the house, but when Fanny called that afternoon and told me that she and Ben would be there, I changed my mind. I hadn't seen either of them for close to a month, and with everyone about to disperse for the summer, I figured it would be my last chance to talk to them until the fall.

As it happened, I scarcely talked to Ben. The party was in full swing by the time I got there, and within three minutes of saying hello to him we had been pushed to opposite corners of the room. By pure chance, I was jostled up against Fanny, and before long we were so engrossed in conversation that we lost track of where Ben was. Maria Turner was also there, but I didn't see her in the crowd. It was only after the accident that I learned she had come to the party – had in fact been standing with Sachs on the fire escape before he fell – but by then there was so much confusion (shrieking guests, sirens, ambulances, scurrying paramedics) that the full impact of her presence failed to register with me. In the hours that preceded that moment, I enjoyed myself a good deal more than I had been expecting to. It wasn't the party so much as being with Fanny, the pleasure of talking to her again, of knowing that we were still friends in spite of all the years and all the disasters that stood behind us. To tell the truth, I was feeling rather mawkish that night, in the grip of oddly sentimental thoughts, and I remember looking into Fanny's face and realizing – very suddenly, as if for the first time – that we were no longer young, that our lives were slipping away from us. It could have been the alcohol I had drunk, but this thought struck me with all the force of a revelation. We were all growing old, and the only thing we could count on anymore was each other. Fanny and Ben, Iris and David: this was my family. They were the people I loved, and it was their souls I carried around inside me.

We went up to the roof with the others, and in spite of my initial reluctance, I was glad not to have missed the fireworks. The explosions had turned New York into a spectral city, a metropolis under siege, and I savored the sheer mayhem of it all: the incessant noise, the corollas of bursting light, the colors wafting through immense dirigibles of smoke.

The Statue of Liberty stood off to our left in the harbor, incandescent in its floodlit glory, and every so often I felt as if the buildings of Manhattan were about to uproot themselves, just take off from the ground and never come back again. Fanny and I sat a little behind the others, heels dug in to balance ourselves against the pitch of the roof, shoulders touching, talking about nothing in particular. Reminiscences, Iris's letters from China, David, Ben's article, the museum. I don't want to make too much of it, but just moments before Ben fell, we drifted onto the story that he and his mother had told about their visit to the Statue of Liberty in 1951. Under the circumstances, it was natural that the story should have come up, but it was gruesome just the same, for no sooner did we both laugh at the idea of falling through the Statue of Liberty than Ben fell from the fire escape. An instant later, Maria and Agnes started screaming below us. It was as if uttering the word *fall* had precipitated a real fall, and even if there was no connection between the two events, I still gag every time I think of what happened. I still hear those screams coming from the two women, and I still see the look on Fanny's face when Ben's name was called out, the look of fear that invaded her eyes as the colored lights of the explosions continued to ricochet against her skin.

He was taken to Long Island College Hospital, still unconscious. Even though he woke up within an hour, they kept him there for the better part of two weeks, conducting a series of brain tests to measure the precise extent of the damage. They would have discharged him sooner, I think, but Sachs said nothing for the first ten days, uttering not a single syllable to anyone – not to Fanny, not to me, not to Maria Turner (who came to visit every afternoon), not to the doctors or nurses. The garrulous, irrepressible Sachs had fallen silent, and it seemed logical to assume that he had lost the power of speech, that the jolt to his head had caused grave internal damage.

It was a hellish period for Fanny. She took off from work and spent every day sitting in the room with Ben, but he was unresponsive to her, often closing his eyes and pretending to be asleep when she came in, returning her smiles with blank stares, seeming to take no comfort from her presence. It made an already difficult situation nearly intolerable for her, and I don't think I've ever seen her so worried, so distraught, so close to full-scale unhappiness as she was then. Nor did it help that Maria kept turning up as well. Fanny imputed all kinds of motives to these visits, but the fact was that they were unfounded. Maria scarcely knew Ben, and many years had gone by since their last encounter. Seven years, to be exact – the last time having been at the dinner in Brooklyn where Maria and I first met. Maria's invitation to the Statue of Liberty party had nothing to do with her knowing Ben or Fanny or myself. Agnes Darwin, an editor who was preparing a book about Maria's work, happened to be a friend of Patricia Clegg's, and she was the one responsible for bringing her to the gathering that night. Watching Ben fall had been a terrifying experience for Maria, and she came to the hospital out of alarm, out of concern, because it wouldn't have felt right to her not to come. I knew that, but Fanny didn't, and as I watched her distress whenever she and Maria crossed paths (understanding that she suspected the worst, that she had convinced herself that Maria and Ben were carrying on a secret liaison), I invited the two of them to lunch in the hospital cafeteria one afternoon in order to clear the air.

According to Maria, she and Ben had talked for a while in the kitchen. He had been animated and charming, regaling her with arcane anecdotes about the Statue of Liberty. When the fireworks began, he suggested that they climb through the kitchen window and watch from the fire escape instead of going to the roof. She hadn't thought he'd been drinking excessively, but at a certain point, completely out of the blue, he jumped up, swung himself over the railing, and sat down on the edge of the iron banister, legs dangling below him in the darkness. This frightened her, she said, and she rushed over and put her arms around him from behind, grabbing hold of his torso to prevent him from falling. She tried to talk him into coming down, but he only laughed and told her not to worry. Just then, Agnes Darwin walked into the kitchen and saw Maria and Ben through the open window. Their backs were turned, and with all the noise and commotion outside, they didn't have the slightest clue that she was there. A chubby, high-spirited woman who had already drunk more than was good for her, Agnes got it into her head to go out and join them on the fire escape. Carrying a glass of wine in one hand, she maneuvered her ample body through the window, landed on the platform with the heel of her left shoe caught between two iron slats, tried to right her balance, and suddenly lurched forward. There wasn't much room out there, and half a step later she had stumbled into Maria from behind, crashing squarely into her friend's back with the full force of her weight. The shock of the blow caused Maria's arms to fly open, and once she lost her grip on Sachs, he went hurtling over the edge of the railing. Just like that, she said, without any warning at all. Agnes bumped into her, she bumped into Sachs, and an instant later he was falling head-first into the night.

It relieved Fanny to learn that her suspicions were groundless, but at the same time nothing had really been explained. Why had Sachs climbed onto the banister in the first place? He had always been scared of heights, and it seemed like the last thing he would have done under the circumstances. And if all had been well between him and Fanny before the accident, why had he turned against her now, why did he recoil from her every time she entered the room? Something had happened, something more than the physical injuries caused by the accident, and until Sachs was able to speak, or until he decided he wanted to speak, Fanny would never know what it was.

It took nearly a month before Sachs told me his side of the story. He was home then, still recuperating but no longer forced to lie in bed, and I went over to his apartment one afternoon while Fanny was at work. It was a sweltering day in early August. We drank beer in the living room, I remember, watching a baseball game on television with the sound off, and whenever I think of that conversation now, I see the silent ballplayers on the small, flickering screen, prancing about in a procession of dimly observed movements, an absurd counterpoint to the painful confidences that my friend poured out to me.

At first, he said, he was only vaguely aware of who Maria Turner was. He recognized her when he saw her at the party, but he couldn't recall the context of their previous meeting. I never forget a face, he told her, but I'm having trouble attaching a name to yours. Elusive as ever, Maria just smiled, saying that it would probably come to him after a while. I was at your house once, she added, by way of a hint, but she wouldn't divulge more than that. Sachs understood that she was playing with him, but he rather enjoyed the way she went about it. He was intrigued by her amused and ironic smile, and he had no objection to being led into a little game of cat and mouse. She clearly had the wit for it, and that was already interesting, already something worth taking the trouble to pursue.

If she had told him her name, Sachs said, he probably wouldn't have acted in the way he did. He knew that Maria Turner and I had been involved with each other before I met Iris, and he knew that Fanny still had some contact with her, since every now and then she would talk to him about Maria's work. But there had been a mixup the night of the dinner party seven years earlier, and Sachs had never properly understood who Maria Turner was. Three or four young women artists had been sitting at the table that evening, and since Sachs was meeting all of them for the first time, he had made the common enough error of jumbling up their names and faces, assigning the wrong name to each face. In his mind, Maria Turner was a short woman with long brown hair, and whenever I had mentioned her to him, that was the image he saw.

They carried their drinks into the kitchen, which was somewhat less crowded than the living room, and sat down on a radiator by the open window, thankful for the slight breeze blowing against their backs. Contrary to Maria's statement about his sober condition, Sachs told me that he was already quite drunk. His head was spinning, and even though he kept warning himself to stop, he belted back at least three bourbons in the next hour. Their conversation developed into one of those mad, elliptical exchanges that come to life when people are flirting with each other at parties, a series of riddles, *non sequiturs*, and clever jabs of one-upmanship. The trick is to say nothing about oneself in as elegant and circuitous a manner as possible, to make the other person laugh, to be deft. Both Sachs and Maria were good at that kind of thing, and they managed to keep it up through the three bourbons and a couple of glasses of wine.

Because the weather was hot, and because Maria had been hesitant about going to the party (thinking it would be dull), she had put on the skimpiest outfit in her wardrobe: a sleeveless, skin-tight, crimson leotard with a plunging neckline on top, a tiny black miniskirt below, bare legs, spike heels, a ring on each finger and a bracelet on each wrist. It was an outrageous, provocative costume, but Maria was in one of those moods, and if nothing else it guaranteed that she wouldn't be lost in the crowd. As Sachs told it to me that afternoon in front of the silent television, he had been on his best behavior for the past five years. He hadn't looked at another woman in all that time, and Fanny had learned how to trust him again. Saving his marriage had been hard work; it had called for an immense effort from both of them over a long and difficult period, and he had vowed never to put his life with Fanny in jeopardy again. Now here he was, sitting on the radiator next to Maria at the party, pressed up against a half-naked woman with splendid, inviting legs – already half out of control, with too much drink circulating in his bloodstream. Little by little, Sachs was engulfed by an almost uncontrollable urge to touch those legs, to run his hand up and down the smoothness of that skin. To make matters worse, Maria was wearing an expensive and dangerous perfume (Sachs had always had a weakness for perfume), and as their teasing, bantering conversation continued, it was all he could do to fight against committing a serious, humiliating blunder. Fortunately, his inhibitions won out over his desires, but that did not prevent him from imagining what would have happened if they had lost. He saw his fingertips falling gently on a spot just above her left knee; he saw his hand as it traveled up into the silky regions of her inner thigh (those small areas of flesh still hidden by the skirt), and then, after allowing his fingers to roam there for several seconds, felt them slip past the rim of her undies into an Eden of buttocks and dense, tingling pubes. It was a lurid mental performance, but once the projector started rolling in his head, Sachs was powerless to turn it off. Nor did it help that Maria seemed to know precisely what he was thinking. If she had looked offended, the spell might have been broken, but Maria evidently liked being the object of such lascivious thoughts, and from the way she looked at him whenever he looked at her, Sachs began to suspect that she was silently egging him on, daring him to go ahead and do what he wanted to do. Knowing Maria, I said, I could think of any number of obscure motives to account for her behavior. It could have been connected to a project she was working on, for example, or else she was enjoying herself because she knew something that Sachs didn't know, or else, somewhat more perversely, she had decided to punish him for not remembering her name. (Later on, when I had a chance to talk to her about it in private, she confessed that this last reason was in fact true.) But Sachs wasn't aware of any of this at the time. He could only be certain of what he felt, and that was very simple: he was lusting after a strange, attractive woman, and he despised himself for it.

'I don't see that you have anything to be ashamed of,' I said. 'You're human, after all, and Maria can be pretty fetching when she puts her mind to it. As long as nothing happened, it's hardly worth reproaching yourself for.'

'It's not that I was tempted,' Sachs said slowly, carefully choosing his words. 'It's that I was tempting her. I wasn't going to do that kind of thing anymore, you see. I'd promised myself that it was over, and here I was doing it again.'

'You're confusing thoughts with deeds,' I said. 'There's a world of difference between doing something and just thinking about it. If we didn't make that distinction, life would be impossible.'

'I'm not talking about that. The point was that I wanted to do something that just a moment before I hadn't been aware of wanting to do. It wasn't a question of being unfaithful to Fanny, it was a question of self-knowledge. I found it appalling to discover that I was capable of tricking myself like that. If I'd put a stop to it right then and there, it wouldn't have been so bad, but even after I understood what I was up to, I went on flirting with her anyway.'

'But you didn't touch her. In the end, that's the only thing that counts.'

'No, I didn't touch her. But I worked things out so she would have to touch me. As far as I'm concerned, that's even worse. I was dishonest with myself. I stuck to the letter of the law like a good little Boy Scout, but I utterly betrayed its spirit. That's why I fell off the fire escape. It wasn't really an accident, Peter. I caused it myself. I acted like a coward, and then I had to pay for it.'

'Are you telling me you jumped?'

'No, nothing as simple as that. I ran a stupid risk, that's all. I did something unforgivable because I was too ashamed to admit to myself that I wanted to touch Maria Turner's leg. In my opinion, a man who goes to such lengths of self-deception deserves whatever he gets.'

That was why he took her out onto the fire escape. It was an exit from the awkward scene that had developed in the kitchen, but it was also the first step of an elaborate plan, a ruse that would allow him to rub up against Maria Turner's body and still keep his honor intact. This was what so galled him in retrospect: not the fact of his desire, but the denial of that desire as a duplicitous means of fulfilling it. Everything was chaos out there, he said. Cheering crowds, exploding fireworks, a frenetic, pulsing din in his ears. They stood on the platform for several moments watching a volley of rockets illuminate the sky, and then he put the first part of his plan into effect. Given a lifetime of fear in such situations, it was remarkable that he did not hesitate. Moving forward to the edge of the platform, he swung his right leg over the railing, briefly steadied himself by taking hold of the bar with his two hands, and then swung his left leg over as well. Rocking slightly back and forth as he corrected his balance, he heard Maria gasp behind him. She thought he was about to jump, Sachs realized, and so he quickly reassured her, insisting that he was only trying to get a better view. Fortunately, Maria wasn't satisfied with his answer. She pleaded with him to climb down, and when he wouldn't do that, she did the very thing he was hoping she would do, the very thing his reckless stratagems had been calculated to make happen. She rushed up from behind him and wrapped her arms around his chest. That was all: a tiny act of concern that disguised itself as a passionate, full-fledged embrace. If it didn't quite produce the ecstatic response he had been looking forward to (he was too scared to give it his full attention), neither did it wholly disappoint him. He could feel the warmth of her breath fluttering against the back of his neck, he could feel her breasts pushing into his spine, he could smell her perfume. It was the briefest of moments, the smallest of small, ephemeral pleasures, but as her bare, slender arms tightened around him, he experienced something that resembled happiness – a microscopic shudder, a surge of transitory bliss. His gamble seemed to have paid off. He had only to get himself down from there, and the whole masquerade would have been worth it. His plan was to lean back against Maria and use her body for support as he lowered himself to the platform (which would prolong the contact between them until the last possible second), but just as Sachs started shifting his weight to carry out this operation, Agnes Darwin was catching the heel of her shoe and stumbling into Maria from behind. Sachs had loosened his grip from the bar of the railing, and when Maria suddenly crashed into him with a violent forward thrust, his fingers opened and his hands lost contact with the bar. His center of gravity heaved upward, he felt himself pitching out from the building, and an instant later he was surrounded by nothing but air.

'It couldn't have taken me long to reach the ground,' he said. 'Maybe a second or two, three at most. But I distinctly remember having more than one thought during that time. First came the horror, the moment of recognition, the instant when I understood that I was falling. You'd think that would have been all, that I wouldn't have had time to think of anything else. But the horror didn't last. No, that's wrong, the horror continued, but there was another thought that grew up inside it, something stronger than just horror alone. It's hard to give it a name. A feeling of absolute certainty, perhaps. An immense, overpowering rush of conviction, a taste of some ultimate truth. I've never been so certain of anything in my life. First I realized that I was falling, and then I realized that I was dead. I don't mean that I sensed I was going to die, I mean that I was already dead. I was a dead man falling through the air, and even though I was technically still alive, I was dead, as dead as a man who's been buried in his grave. I don't know how else to put it. Even as I fell, I was already past the moment of hitting the ground, past the moment of impact, past the moment of shattering into pieces. I had turned into a corpse, and by the time I hit the clothesline and landed in those towels and blankets, I wasn't there anymore. I had left my body, and for a split second I actually saw myself disappear.'

There were questions I wanted to ask him then, but I didn't interrupt. Sachs was having trouble getting the story out, talking in a trance of hesitations and awkward silences, and I was afraid that a sudden word from me would throw him off course. To be honest, I didn't quite understand what he was trying to say. There was no question that the fall had been a ghastly experience, but I was confused by how much effort he put into describing the small events that had preceded it. The business with Maria struck me as trivial, of no genuine importance, a trite comedy of manners not worth talking about. In Sachs's mind, however, there was a direct connection. The one thing had caused the other, which meant that he didn't see the fall as an accident or a piece of bad luck so much as some grotesque form of punishment. I wanted to tell him that he was wrong, that he was being overly hard on himself – but I didn't. I just sat there and listened to him as he went on analyzing his own behavior. He was trying to present me with an absolutely precise account, splitting hairs with the patience of a medieval theologian, straining to articulate every nuance of his harmless dalliance with Maria out on the fire escape. It was infinitely subtle, infinitely labored and complex, and after a while I began to understand that this lilliputian drama had taken on the same magnitude for him as the fall itself. There was no difference anymore. A quick, ludicrous embrace had become the moral equivalent of death. If Sachs hadn't been so earnest about it, I would have found it comical. Unfortunately, it didn't occur to me to laugh. I was trying to be sympathetic, to hear him out and accept what he had to say on its own terms. Looking back on it now, I believe I would have served him better if I had told him what I thought. I should have laughed in his face. I should have told him he was crazy and made him stop. If there was ever a moment when I failed Sachs as a friend, it was that afternoon four years ago. I had my chance to help him, and I let the opportunity slip through my fingers.

He never made a conscious decision not to speak, he said. It just happened that way, and even as his silence continued, he felt ashamed of himself for causing so many people to worry. There was never any question of brain damage or shock, never any sign of physical impairment. He understood everything that was said to him, and in his heart he knew that he was capable of expressing himself on any subject. The pivotal moment had come at the beginning, when he opened his eyes and saw an unfamiliar woman staring directly into his face – a nurse, as he later discovered. He heard her announce to someone that Rip Van Winkle had finally woken up – or perhaps those words were addressed to him, he couldn't be sure. He wanted to say something back to her, but his mind was already in a tumult, wheeling in all directions at once, and with the pain in his bones suddenly making itself felt, he decided that he was too weak to answer her just then and let the opportunity pass. Sachs had never done anything like that before, and as the nurse continued to chatter away at him, eventually joined by a doctor and a second nurse, the three of them crowding around his bed, encouraging him to tell them how he felt, Sachs went on thinking his own thoughts as if they weren't there, glad to have released himself from the burden of answering them. He assumed it would happen just that once, but the same thing happened the next time, and then the next time, and the time after that as well. Whenever someone spoke to him, Sachs was seized by the same odd compulsion to hold his tongue. As the days went on, he became ever more steadfast in his silence, acting as though it were a point of honor, a secret challenge to keep faith with himself. He would listen to the words that people directed at him, carefully weighing each sentence as it entered his ears, but then, instead of offering a remark of his own, he would turn away, or close his eyes, or stare back at his interlocutor as though he could see straight through him. Sachs knew how childish and petulant this behavior was, but that didn't make it any less difficult for him to stop. The doctors and nurses meant nothing to him, and he felt no great responsibility toward Maria, or myself, or any of his other friends. Fanny was different, however, and there were several instances when he came close to backing down for her sake. At the very least, a flicker of regret would pass through him whenever she came to visit. He understood how cruel he was being to her, and it filled him with a sense of worthlessness, a loathsome aftertaste of guilt. Sometimes, as he lay there in bed warring with his conscience, he would make a feeble attempt to smile at her, and once or twice he actually went so far as to move his lips, producing some faint gurgling sounds in the back of his throat to convince her that he was doing his best, that sooner or later real words would start coming out of him. He hated himself for these shams, but too many things were happening inside his silence now, and he couldn't summon the will to break it.

Contrary to what the doctors supposed, Sachs remembered every detail of the accident. He had only to think about any one moment of that night for the whole night to return in all its sickening immediacy: the party, Maria Turner, the fire escape, the first moments of his fall, the certainty of death, the clothesline, the cement. None of it was dim, no piece of it was less vivid than any other piece. The entire event stood in a surfeit of clarity, an avalanche of overpowering recall. Something extraordinary had taken place, and before it lost its force within him, he needed to devote his unstinting attention to it. Hence his silence. It was not a refusal so much as a method, a way of holding onto the horror of that night long enough to make sense of it. To be silent was to enclose himself in contemplation, to relive the moments of his fall again and again, as if he could suspend himself in midair for the rest of time – forever just two inches off the ground, forever waiting for the apocalypse of the last moment.

He had no intention of forgiving himself, he told me. His guilt was a foregone conclusion, and the less time he wasted on it the better. 'At any other moment in my life,' he said, 'I probably would have looked for excuses. Accidents happen, after all. Every hour of every day, people are dying when they least expect it. They burn up in fires, they drown in lakes, they drive their cars into other cars, they fall out of windows. You read about it in the paper every morning, and you'd have to be a fool not to know that your life could end just as abruptly and pointlessly as any one of those poor bastards'. But the fact was that my accident wasn't caused by bad luck. I wasn't just a victim, I was an accomplice, an active partner in everything that happened to me, and I can't ignore that, I have to take some responsibility for the role I played. Does this make sense to you, or am I talking gibberish? I'm not saying that flirting with Maria Turner was a crime. It was a shabby business, a despicable little stunt, but not a hell of a lot more than that. I might have felt like a shit for lusting after her, but if that tweak in my gonads was the whole story, I would have forgotten all about it by now. What I'm saying is that I don't think sex had much to do with what happened that night. That's one of the things I figured out in the hospital, lying in bed for all those days without talking. If I'd really been serious about chasing after Maria Turner, why did I go to such ridiculous lengths to trick her into touching me? God knows there were less dangerous ways of going about it, a hundred more effective strategies for achieving the same result. But I turned myself into a daredevil out there on the fire escape, I actually risked my life. For what? For a tiny squeeze in the dark, for nothing at all. Looking back on that scene from my hospital bed, I finally understood that everything was different from how I had imagined it. I had gotten it backwards, I had been looking at it upsidedown. The point of my crazy antics wasn't to get Maria Turner to put her arms around me, it was to risk my life. She was only a pretext, an instrument for getting me onto the railing, a hand to guide me to the edge of disaster. The question was: Why did I do it? Why was I so eager to court that risk? I must have asked myself that question six hundred times a day, and each time I asked it, a tremendous chasm would open up inside me, and immediately after that I would be falling again, plunging headlong into the darkness. I don't want to be overly dramatic about it, but those days in the hospital were the worst days of my life. I had put myself in a position to fall, I realized, and I had done it on purpose. That was my discovery, the unassailable conclusion that rose up out of my silence. I learned that I didn't want to live. For reasons that are still impenetrable to me, I climbed onto the railing that night in order to kill myself.'

'You were drunk,' I said. 'You didn't know what you were doing.'

'I was drunk, and I knew exactly what I was doing. It's just that I didn't know I knew it.'

'That's double-talk. Pure sophistry.'

'I didn't know that I knew, and the drinks gave me the courage to act. They helped me do the thing I didn't know I wanted to do.'

'You told me you fell because you were too afraid to touch Maria's leg. Now you change your story and tell me that you fell on purpose. You can't have it both ways. It's got to be one or the other.'

'It's both. The one thing led to the other, and they can't be separated. I'm not saying I understand it, I'm just telling you how it was, what I know to be true. I was ready to do away with myself that night. I can still feel it in my gut, and it scares the hell out of me to walk around with that feeling.'

'There's a part in everyone that wants to die,' I said, 'a little caldron of self-destructiveness that's always boiling under the surface. For some reason, the fires were stoked too high for you that night, and something crazy happened. But just because it happened once, it doesn't mean it's going to happen again.'

'Maybe so. But that doesn't wash away the fact that it happened, and it happened for a reason. If I could be caught by surprise like that, it must mean there's something fundamentally wrong with me. It must mean that I don't believe in my life anymore.'

'If you didn't believe in it, you wouldn't have started talking again. You must have come to some kind of decision. You must have settled things for yourself by then.'

'Not really. You walked into the room with David, and he came up to my bed and smiled at me. I suddenly found myself saying hello to him. It was as simple as that. He looked so nice. All tanned and healthy from his weeks at camp, a perfect nine-year-old boy. When he walked up to my bed and smiled at me, it never occurred to me not to talk to him.'

'There were tears in your eyes. I thought that meant you had resolved something for yourself, that you were on your way back.'

'It meant that I knew I'd hit bottom. It meant that I understood I had to change my life.'

'Changing your life isn't the same thing as wanting to end it.'

'I want to end the life I've been living up to now. I want everything to change. If I don't manage to do that, I'm going to be in deep trouble. My whole life has been a waste, a stupid little joke, a dismal string of petty failures. I'm going to be forty-one years old next week, and if I don't take hold of things now, I'm going to drown. I'm going to sink like a stone to the bottom of the world.'

'You just need to get back to work. The minute you start writing again, you'll begin to remember who you are.'

'The idea of writing disgusts me. It doesn't mean a goddamned thing to me anymore.'

'This isn't the first time you've talked like this.'

'Maybe not. But this time I mean it. I don't want to spend the rest of my life rolling pieces of blank paper into a typewriter. I want to stand up from my desk and do something. The days of being a shadow are over. I've got to step into the real world now and do something.'

'Like what?'

'Who the hell knows?' Sachs said. His words hung in the air for several seconds, and then, without warning, his face broke into a smile. It was the first smile I had seen on him in weeks, and for that one transitory moment, he almost began to look like his old self again. 'When I figure it out,' he said, 'I'll write you a letter.'

*

I left Sachs's apartment thinking he would pull through the crisis. Not right away, perhaps, but over the long term I found it difficult to imagine that things wouldn't return to normal for him. He had too much resiliency, I told myself, too much intelligence and stamina to let the accident crush him. It's possible that I was underestimating the degree to which his confidence had been shaken, but I tend to think not. I saw how tormented he was, I saw the anguish of his doubts and self-recriminations, but in spite of the hateful things he said about himself that afternoon, he had also flashed me a smile, and I read that fugitive burst of irony as a signal of hope, as proof that Sachs had it in him to make a full recovery.

Weeks passed, however, and then months, and the situation remained exactly what it had been. It's true that he regained much of his social poise, and as time went on his suffering became less obvious (he no longer brooded in company, he no longer seemed quite so absent), but that was only because he talked less about himself. It wasn't the same silence as the one in the hospital, but its effect was similar. He talked now, he opened his mouth and used words at the appropriate moments, but he never said anything about what really concerned him, never anything about the accident or its aftermath, and little by little I sensed that he had pushed his suffering underground, burying it in a place where no one could see it. If all else had been equal, this might not have troubled me so much. I could have learned to live with this quieter and more subdued Sachs, but the outward signs were too discouraging, and I couldn't shake the feeling that they were symptoms of some larger distress. He turned down assignments from magazines, made no effort to renew his professional contacts, seemed to have lost all interest in ever sitting behind his typewriter again. He had told me as much after he came home from the hospital, but I hadn't believed him. Now that he was keeping his word, I began to grow frightened. For as long as I had known him, Sachs's life had revolved around his work, and to see him suddenly without that work made him seem like a man who had no life. He was adrift, floating in a sea of undifferentiated days, and as far as I could tell, it was all one to him whether he made it back to land or not.

Some time between Christmas and the start of the new year, Sachs shaved off his beard and cut his hair down to normal length. It was a drastic change, and it made him look like an altogether different person. He seemed to have shrunk somehow, to have grown both younger and older at the same time, and a good month went by before I began to get used to it, before I stopped being startled every time he walked into a room. It's not that I preferred him to look one way or the other, but I regretted the simple fact of change, of any change in and of itself. When I asked him why he had done it, his first response was a noncommittal shrug. Then, after a short pause, realizing that I expected a fuller answer than that, he muttered something about not wanting to take the trouble anymore. He was into low maintenance, he said, the no-fuss approach to personal hygiene. Besides, he wanted to do his bit for capitalism. By shaving three or four times a week, he would be helping to keep the razor blade companies in business, which meant that he would be contributing to the good of the American economy, to the health and prosperity of all.

This was pretty lame stuff, but after we talked about it that one time, the subject never came up again. Sachs clearly didn't want to dwell on it, and I didn't press him for further explanations. That doesn't mean it was unimportant to him, however. A man is free to choose how he looks, but in Sachs's case I felt it was a particularly violent and aggressive act, almost a form of self-mutilation. The left side of his face and scalp had been badly cut from his fall, and the doctors had stitched up several areas around his temple and lower jaw. With a beard and long hair, the scars from these wounds had been hidden from sight. Once the hair was gone, the scars had become visible, the dents and gashes stood out nakedly for everyone to see. Unless I've seriously misunderstood him, I think that's why Sachs changed his appearance. He wanted to display his wounds, to announce to the world that these scars were what defined him now, to be able to look at himself in the mirror every morning and remember what had happened to him. The scars were an amulet against forgetting, a sign that none of it would ever be lost.

One day in mid-February, I went out to lunch with my editor in Manhattan. The restaurant was somewhere in the West Twenties, and after the meal was over I started walking up Eighth Avenue toward Thirty-fourth Street, where I planned to catch a subway back to Brooklyn. Five or six blocks from my destination, I happened to see Sachs on the other side of the street. I can't say that I'm proud of what I did after that, but it seemed to make sense at the time. I was curious to know what he did on these rambles of his, desperate for some kind of information about how he occupied his days, and so instead of calling out to him I hung back and kept myself hidden. It was a cold afternoon, with a raw gray sky and a threat of snow in the air. For the next couple of hours, I followed Sachs around the streets, shadowing my friend through the canyons of New York. As I write about this now, it sounds a lot worse than it actually was, at least in terms of what I imagined I was doing. I had no intention of spying on him, no wish to penetrate any secrets. I was looking for something hopeful, some glimmer of optimism to assuage my worry. I said to myself: He's going to surprise me; he's going to do something or go somewhere that will prove he's all right. But two hours went by, and nothing happened. Sachs wandered around the streets like a lost soul, roaming haphazardly between Times Square and Greenwich Village at the same slow and contemplative pace, never rushing, never seeming to care where he was. He gave coins to beggars. He stopped to light a fresh cigarette every ten or twelve blocks. He browsed in a bookstore for several minutes, at one point removing one of my books from the shelf and studying it with some attentiveness. He entered a porno shop and looked at magazines of naked women. He paused in front of an electronics store window. Eventually, he bought a newspaper, walked into a coffee house on the corner of Bleecker and MacDougal Streets, and settled down at a table. That was where I left him, just as the waitress came over to take his order. I found it all so bleak, so depressing, so tragic, that I couldn't even bring myself to talk to Iris about it when I got home.

Knowing what I know now, I can see how little I really understood. I was drawing conclusions from what amounted to partial evidence, basing my response on a cluster of random, observable facts that told only a small piece of the story. If more information had been available to me, I might have had a different picture of what was going on, which might have made me a bit slower to despair. Among other things, I was completely in the dark about the special role Maria Turner had assumed for Ben. Ever since October, they had been seeing each other on a regular basis, spending every Thursday together from ten in the morning until five in the afternoon. I only learned about this two years after the fact. As they each told me (in separate conversations at least two months apart), there was never any sex involved. Given what I know about Maria's habits, and given that Sachs's story tallied with hers, I see no point in doubting what they told me.

As I look back on the situation today, it makes perfect sense that Sachs should have reached out to her. Maria was the embodiment of his catastrophe, the central figure in the drama that had precipitated his fall, and therefore no one could have been as important to him. I have already talked about his determination to hold onto the events of that night. What better method to accomplish this than by staying in touch with Maria? By turning her into a friend, he would be able to keep the symbol of his transformation constantly before his eyes. His wounds would remain open, and every time he saw her he could reenact the same sequence of torments and emotions that had come so close to killing him. He would be able to repeat the experience again and again, and with enough practice and hard work, perhaps he would learn to master it. That was how it must have begun. The challenge wasn't to seduce Maria or to take her to bed, it was to expose himself to temptation and see if he had the strength to resist it. Sachs was searching for a cure, for a way to win back his self-respect, and only the most drastic measures would suffice. In order to find out what he was worth, he had to risk everything all over again.

But there was more to it than that. It wasn't just a symbolic exercise for him, it was a step forward into a real friendship. Sachs had been moved by Maria's visits to the hospital, and even then, as early as the first weeks of his recovery, I think he understood how deeply the accident had affected her. That was the initial bond between them. They had both lived through something terrible, and neither one of them was inclined to dismiss it as a simple piece of bad luck. More importantly, Maria was aware of the part she had played in what happened. She knew that she had encouraged Sachs on the night of the party, and she was honest enough with herself to admit what she had done, to realize that it would have been morally wrong to look for excuses. In her own way, she was just as troubled by the event as Sachs was, and when he finally called in October to thank her for coming to the hospital so often, she saw it as a chance to make amends, to undo some of the damage she had caused. I'm not just guessing when I say this. Maria held nothing back from me when we talked last year, and the whole story comes straight from her mouth.

'The first time Ben came to my place,' she said, 'he asked me a lot of questions about my work. He was probably just being polite. You know how it is: you're feeling awkward, and you don't know what to talk about, so you start asking questions. After a while, though, I could see that he was getting interested. I brought out some old projects for him to look at, and his comments struck me as very intelligent, a lot more perceptive than most of the things I hear. What he especially seemed to like was the combination of documentary and play, the objectification of inner states. He understood that all my pieces were stories, and even if they were true stories, they were also invented. Or even if they were invented, they were also true. So we talked about that for a while, and then we got onto various other things, and by the time he left I was already beginning to cook up one of my weird ideas. The guy was so lost and miserable, I thought maybe it would be a good thing if we started working on a piece together. I didn't have anything specific in mind at that point – just that the piece would be about him. He called again a few days later, and when I told him what I was thinking, he seemed to catch on right away. That surprised me a little. I didn't have to argue my case or talk him into it. He just said yes, that sounds like a promising idea, and we went ahead and did it. From then on, we spent every Thursday together. For the next four or five months, we spent every Thursday working on the piece.'

As far as I am able to judge, it never really amounted to anything. Unlike Maria's other projects, this one had no organizing principle or clearly defined purpose, and rather than start with a fixed idea as she always had in the past (to follow a stranger, for example, or to look up names in an address book), 'Thursdays with Ben' was essentially formless: a series of improvisations, a picture album of the days they spent in each other's company. They had agreed beforehand that they wouldn't follow any rules. The only condition was that Sachs arrive at Maria's house promptly at ten o'clock, and from then on they would play it by ear. For the most part, Maria took pictures of him, maybe two or three rolls' worth, and then they would spend the rest of the day talking. A few times, she asked him to dress up in costumes. At other times, she recorded their conversations and took no pictures at all. When Sachs cut off his beard and shortened his hair, it turned out that he was acting on Maria's advice, and the operation took place in her loft. She recorded the whole thing with her camera: the before, the after, and all the steps in between. It begins with Sachs in front of a mirror, clutching a pair of scissors in his right hand. With each successive shot, a little more of his hair is gone. Then we see him lathering up his stubbled cheeks, and after that he gives himself a shave. Maria stopped shooting at that point (to put the finishing touches on his haircut), and then there's one last picture of Sachs: short-haired and beardless, grinning into the camera like one of those slick hairdo boys you see on barbershop walls. I found it a nice touch. Not only was it funny in itself, but it proved that Sachs was able to enjoy the fun. After I saw that picture, I realized there were no simple solutions. I had underestimated him, and the story of those months was finally much more complicated than I had allowed myself to believe. Then came the shots of Sachs outside. In January and February, Maria had apparently followed him around the streets with her camera. Sachs had told her that he wanted to know what it felt like to be watched, and Maria had obliged him by resurrecting one of her old pieces: only this time it was done in reverse. Sachs took on the role she had played, and she turned herself into the private detective. That was the scene I had stumbled across in Manhattan when I saw Sachs walking along the other side of the street. Maria had been there as well, and what I had taken as conclusive evidence of my friend's misery was in fact no more than a charade, a little bit of play-acting, a silly re-enactment of Spy versus Spy. God knows how I managed to miss seeing Maria that day. I must have been concentrating so hard on Sachs that I was blind to everything else. But she saw me, and when she finally told me about it when we talked last fall, I felt crushed with shame. Luckily, she didn't manage to take any pictures of me and Sachs together. Everything would have been out in the open then, but I had been following him from too far away for her to catch us in the same shot.

She took several thousand pictures of him in all, most of which were still on contact sheets when I saw them last September. Even if the Thursday sessions never developed into a coherent, ongoing work, they had a therapeutic value for Sachs – which was all Maria had hoped to accomplish with them in the first place. When Sachs came to visit her in October, he had withdrawn so far into his pain that he was no longer able to see himself. I mean that in a phenomenological sense, in the same way that one talks about self-awareness or the way one forms an image of oneself. Sachs had lost the power to step out from his thoughts and take stock of where he was, to measure the precise dimensions of the space around him. What Maria achieved over the course of those months was to lure him out of his own skin. Sexual tension was a part of it, but there was also her camera, the constant assault of her cyclops machine. Every time Sachs posed for a picture, he was forced to impersonate himself, to play the game of pretending to be who he was. After a while, it must have had an effect on him. By repeating the process so often, he must have come to a point where he started seeing himself through Maria's eyes, where the whole thing doubled back on him and he was able to encounter himself again. They say that a camera can rob a person of his soul. In this case, I believe it was just the opposite. With this camera, I believe that Sachs's soul was gradually given back to him.

He was getting better, but that didn't mean he was well, that he would ever be the person he had been. Deep down, he knew that he could never return to the life he had led before the accident. He had tried to explain that to me during our conversation in August, but I hadn't understood. I had thought he was talking about work – to write or not to write, to abandon his career or not – but it turned out that he had been talking about everything: not just himself, but his life with Fanny as well. Within a month of coming home from the hospital, I think he was already looking for a way to break free of his marriage. It was a unilateral decision, a product of his need to wipe the slate clean and start over again, and Fanny was no more than an innocent victim of the purge. Months passed, however, and he couldn't bring himself to tell her. This probably accounts for many of the puzzling contradictions in his behavior during that time. He didn't want to hurt Fanny, and yet he knew he was going to hurt her, and this knowledge only increased his despair, only made him hate himself more than he already did. Thus the long period of waffling and inaction, of simultaneous recovery and decline. If nothing else, I believe it points to the essential goodness of Sachs's heart. He had convinced himself that his survival hinged on committing an act of cruelty, and for several months he chose not to commit it, wallowing in the depths of a private torment in order to spare his wife from the brutality of his decision. He came close to destroying himself out of kindness. His bags were already packed, and yet he stayed on because her feelings meant as much to him as his own.

When the truth finally emerged, it was scarcely recognizable anymore. Sachs never managed to come out and tell Fanny that he wanted to leave her. His nerve had failed him too badly for that; his shame was too profound for him to be capable of expressing such a thought. Rather, in a much more oblique and circuitous manner, he began to make it known to Fanny that he was no longer worthy of her, that he no longer deserved to be married to her. He was ruining her life, he said, and before he dragged her down with him into hopeless misery, she should cut her losses and run. I don't think there's any question that Sachs believed this. Whether on purpose or not, he had manufactured a situation in which these words could be spoken in good faith. After months of conflict and indecision, he had hit upon a way to spare Fanny's feelings. He wouldn't have to hurt her by announcing his intention to walk out. Rather, by inverting the terms of the dilemma, he would convince her to walk out on him. She would initiate her own rescue; he would help her to stand up for herself and save her own life.

Even if Sachs's motives were hidden from him, he was at last maneuvering himself into a position to get what he wanted. I don't mean to sound cynical about it, but it strikes me that he subjected Fanny to many of the same elaborate self-deceptions and tricky reversals he had used with Maria Turner out on the fire escape the previous summer. An overly refined conscience, a predisposition toward guilt in the face of his own desires, led a good man to act in curiously underhanded ways, in ways that compromised his own goodness. This is the nub of the catastrophe, I think. He accepted everyone else's frailties, but when it came to himself he demanded perfection, an almost superhuman rigor in even the smallest acts. The result was disappointment, a dumbfounding awareness of his own flawed humanity, which drove him to place ever more stringent demands on his conduct, which in turn led to ever more suffocating disappointments. If he had learned how to love himself a little more, he wouldn't have had the power to cause so much unhappiness around him. But Sachs was driven to do penance, to take on his guilt as the guilt of the world and to bear its marks in his own flesh. I don't blame him for what he did. I don't blame him for telling Fanny to leave him or for wanting to change his life. I just feel sorry for him, inexpressibly sorry for the terrible things he brought down on himself.

It took some time before his strategy had any effect. But what is a woman supposed to think when her husband tells her to fall in love with someone else, to get rid of him, to run away from him and never come back? In Fanny's case, she dismissed this talk as nonsense, as further evidence of Ben's growing instability. She had no intention of doing any of these things, and unless he told her straight out that he was finished, that he no longer wanted to be married to her, she was determined to stay put. The standoff lasted for four or five months. This feels like an unendurable length of time to me, but Fanny refused to back down. He was putting her to a test, she felt, trying to push her out of his life in order to see how tenaciously she would hold on, and if she let go now, his worst fears about himself would come true. Such was the circular logic of her struggle to save their marriage. Every time Ben spoke to her, she interpreted it to mean the opposite of what he said. Leave meant don't leave; love someone else meant love me; give up meant don't give up. In the light of what happened later, I'm not so sure that she was wrong. Sachs thought he knew what he wanted, but once he got it, it no longer had any value to him. But by then it was too late. What he had lost, he had lost forever.

According to what Fanny told me, there was never any decisive break between them. Sachs wore her down instead, exhausting her with his persistence, slowly debilitating her until she no longer had the strength to fight back. There had been a few hysterical scenes in the beginning, she said, a few outbursts of tears and shouting, but all that eventually stopped. Little by little, she had run out of counterarguments, and when Sachs finally spoke the magic words, telling her one day in early March that a trial separation might be a good idea, she just nodded her head and went along with him. At the time, I knew nothing about any of this. Neither one of them had opened up to me about their troubles, and since my own life was particularly frantic just then, I wasn't able to see them as often as I would have wished. Iris was pregnant; we were searching for a new place to live; I was commuting to a teaching job in Princeton twice a week and working hard on my next book. Still, it seems that I played an unwitting part in their marital negotiations. What I did was to provide Sachs with an excuse, a way to walk out on her without appearing to have slammed the door shut. It all goes back to that day in February when I followed him around the streets. I had just spent two and a half hours with my editor, Nan Howard, and during the course of our conversation Sachs's name had been mentioned more than once. Nan knew how close we were. She had been at the Fourth of July party herself, and since she knew about the accident and the tough times he had been going through since then, it was normal that she should ask me how he was. I told her that I was still worried – not so much by his mood anymore, but by the fact that he hadn't done a stitch of work. 'It's been seven months now,' I said, 'and that's too long a holiday, especially for someone like Ben.' So we talked about work for a few minutes, wondering what it would take for him to get going again, and just as we started in on dessert, Nan came up with what struck me as a terrific idea. 'He should put his old pieces together and publish them as a book,' she said. 'It wouldn't be very difficult. All he'd have to do is pick out the best ones, maybe touch up a couple of sentences here and there. But once he sits down with his old work, who knows what might happen? It could make him want to start writing again.'

'Are you saying you'd be interested in publishing this book?' I said.

'I don't know,' she said, 'is that what I'm saying?' Nan paused for a moment and laughed. 'I suppose I just said it, didn't I?' Then she paused again, as if to catch herself before she went too far. 'But still, why the hell not? It's not as though I don't know Ben's stuff. I've been reading it since high school, for Christ's sake. Maybe it's about time someone twisted his arm and got him to do it.'

Half an hour later, when I caught sight of Sachs on Eighth Avenue, I was still thinking about this conversation with Nan. The idea of the book had settled comfortably inside me by then, and for once I was feeling encouraged, more hopeful than I had been in a long time. Perhaps that explains why I became so depressed afterward. I found a man living in what looked like a state of utter abjection, and I couldn't bring myself to accept what I had seen: my once brilliant friend, wandering around for hours in a quasi-trance, scarcely distinguishable from the ruined men and women who begged coins from him in the street. I got home that evening feeling sick at heart. The situation was out of control, I told myself, and unless I acted fast, there wouldn't be a prayer of saving him.

I invited him out to lunch the following week. The moment he sat down in his chair, I plunged in and started talking about the book. This notion had been bandied about a few times in the past, but Sachs had always been reluctant to commit himself. He felt his magazine pieces were things of the moment, written for specific reasons at specific times, and a book would be too permanent a place for them. They should be allowed to die a natural death, he'd once told me. Let people read them once and forget them – there was no need to erect a tomb. I was already familiar with this defense, so I didn't present the idea in literary terms. I talked about it strictly as a money proposition, a cold cash deal. He had been sponging off Fanny for the past seven months, I said, and maybe it was time for him to start pulling his own weight. If he wasn't willing to go out and find a job, the least he could do was publish this book. Forget about yourself for once, I told him. Do it for her.

I don't think I'd ever spoken to him so emphatically. I was so wound up, so filled with passionate good sense, that Sachs started smiling before I was halfway into my harangue. I suppose there was something comical about my behavior that afternoon, but that was only because I hadn't expected to win so easily. As it turned out, Sachs needed little convincing. He made up his mind to do the book as soon as he heard about my conversation with Nan, and everything I said to him after that was unnecessary. He tried to get me to stop, but since I thought that meant he didn't want to talk about it, I kept on arguing with him, which was a bit like telling someone to eat a meal that was already inside his stomach. I'm sure he found me laughable, but none of that makes any difference now. What matters is that Sachs agreed to do the book, and at the time I felt it was a major victory, a gigantic step in the right direction. I knew nothing about Fanny, of course, and therefore I had no idea that the project was simply a ploy, a strategic move to help him bring his marriage to an end. That doesn't mean Sachs wasn't planning to publish the book, but his motives were quite different from the ones I imagined. I saw the book as a way back into the world, whereas he saw it as an escape, as a last gesture of goodwill before he slipped off into the darkness and disappeared.

That was how he found the courage to talk to Fanny about a trial separation. He would go to Vermont to work on the book, she would stay in the city, and meanwhile they would both have a chance to think about what they wanted to do. The book made it possible for him to leave with her blessing, for both of them to ignore the true purpose of his departure. Over the next two weeks, Fanny organized Ben's trip to Vermont as if it were still one of her wifely duties, actively dismantling their marriage as if she believed they would go on being married forever. The habit of caring for him was so automatic by then, so deeply ingrained in who she was, that it probably never occurred to her to stop and consider what she was doing. That was the paradox of the end. I had lived through something similar with Delia: that strange postscript when a couple is neither together nor not together, when the last thing holding you together is the fact that you are apart. Fanny and Ben acted no differently. She helped him move out of her life, and he accepted that help as the most natural thing in the world. She went down to the cellar and lugged up sheafs of old articles for him; she made photocopies of yellowed, crumbling originals; she visited the library and searched through spools of microfilm for errant pieces; she put the whole mass of clippings and tear sheets and jagged pages into chronological order. On the last day, she even went out and bought cardboard file boxes to store the papers in, and the next morning, when it came time for Sachs to leave, she helped him carry these boxes downstairs and load them into the trunk of the car. So much for making a clean break. So much for giving off unambiguous signals. At that point, I don't think either one of them would have been capable of it.

That was some time in late March. Innocently accepting what Sachs had told me, I assumed that he was going to Vermont in order to work. He had gone there alone before, and the fact that Fanny was staying behind in New York didn't strike me as unusual. She had her job, after all, and since no one had mentioned how long Sachs would be gone, I figured it would be a relatively short trip. A month maybe, six weeks at the most. Putting together the book would not be a difficult task, and I didn't see how it could take him longer than that. And even if it did, there was nothing to prevent Fanny from visiting him in the meantime. So I didn't question any of their arrangements. They all made sense to me, and when Sachs called to say good-bye on the last night, I told him how glad I was that he was going. Good luck, I said, I'll see you soon. And that was it. Whatever he might have been planning then, he didn't say a word to make me think he wouldn't be back.

After Sachs left for Vermont, my thoughts turned elsewhere. I was busy with work, with Iris's pregnancy, with David's troubles in school, with deaths of relatives on both sides of the family, and the spring passed very quickly. Perhaps I felt relieved that he was gone, I don't know, but there's no doubt that country life had improved his spirits. We talked on the phone about once a week, and I gathered from these conversations that things were going well for him. He had started work on something new, he told me, and I took this as such a momentous event, such a turnaround from his previous state, that I suddenly allowed myself to stop worrying about him. Even when he kept putting off his return to New York, prolonging his absence through April, then May, and then June, I didn't feel any alarm. Sachs was writing again, I told myself, Sachs was healthy again, and as far as I was concerned, that meant all was right with the world.

Iris and I saw Fanny on several occasions that spring. I remember at least one dinner, a Sunday brunch, and a couple of outings to the movies. To be perfectly honest, I didn't detect any signs of distress or unease in her. It's true that she talked about Sachs very little (which should have alerted me to something), but whenever she did talk about him, she sounded pleased, even excited by what was happening in Vermont. Not only was he writing again, she told us, but he was writing a novel. This was so much better than anything she could have imagined, it made no difference that the essay book had been shunted to the side. He was working up a storm, she said, scarcely even pausing to eat or sleep, and whether these reports were exaggerated or not (either by

Sachs or by her), they put an end to all further questions. Iris and I never asked her why she didn't go up to visit Ben. We didn't ask because the answer was already obvious. He was on a roll with his work, and after waiting so long for this to happen, she wasn't about to interfere.

She was holding back on us, of course, but more to the point was that Sachs had been cut out of the picture as well. I only learned about this later, but all during the time he spent in Vermont, it seems that he knew as little about what Fanny was thinking as I did. She hardly could have expected it to work out that way. Theoretically, there was still some hope for them, but once Ben packed the car with his belongings and drove off to the country, she realized that they were finished. It didn't take more than a week or two for this to happen. She still cared about him and wished him well, but she had no desire to see him, no desire to talk to him, no desire to make any more efforts. They had talked about keeping the door open, but now it seemed as if the door had vanished. It wasn't that it had closed, it simply wasn't there anymore. Fanny found herself looking at a blank wall, and after that she turned away. They were no longer married, and what she did with her life from then on was her own business.

In June, she met a man named Charles Spector. I don't feel I have a right to talk about this, but to the degree that it affected Sachs, it's impossible to avoid mentioning it. The crucial thing here is not that Fanny wound up marrying Charles (the wedding took place four months ago) but that once she started falling in love with him that summer, she didn't come forward and let Ben know what was happening. Again, it's not a matter of affixing blame. There were reasons for her silence, and under the circumstances I think she acted properly, with no hint of selfishness or deceit. The affair with Charles caught her by surprise, and in those early stages she was still too confused to know what her feelings were. Rather than rush into telling Ben about something that might not last, she decided to hold off for a while, to spare him from further dramas until she was certain of what she wanted to do. Through no fault of her own, this waiting period lasted too long. Ben found out about Charles purely by accident – returning home to Brooklyn one night and seeing him in bed with Fanny – and the timing of that discovery couldn't have been worse. Considering that Sachs was the one who had pushed for the separation in the first place, this probably shouldn't have mattered. But it did. Other factors were involved as well, but this one counted as much as any of those others. It kept the music playing, so to speak, and what might have ended at that point did not. The waltz of disasters went on, and after that there was no stopping it.

But that was later, and I don't want to run ahead of myself. On the surface, things purred along as they had for the past several months. Sachs worked on his novel in Vermont, Fanny went to her job at the museum, and Iris and I waited for our baby to be born. After Sonia arrived (on June twenty-seventh), I lost touch with everyone for the next six or eight weeks. Iris and I were in Babyland, a country where sleep is forbidden and day is indistinguishable from night, a walled-off kingdom governed by the whims of a tiny, absolute monarch. We asked Fanny and Ben to be Sonia's godparents, and they both accepted with elaborate declarations of pride and gratitude. Gifts poured in after that, Fanny delivering hers in person (clothes, blankets, rattles) and Ben's turning up by mail (books, bears, rubber ducks). I was particularly moved by Fanny's response, by the way she would stop in after work just to hold Sonia for fifteen or twenty minutes, cooing at her with all kinds of affectionate nonsense. She seemed to glow with the baby in her arms, and it always saddened me to think how none of this had been possible for her. 'My little beauty,' she would call Sonia, 'my angel girl,' 'my dark passion flower,' 'my heart.' In his own way, Sachs was no less enthusiastic than she was, and I took the small packages that kept appearing in the mail as a sign of real progress, decisive proof that he was well again. In early August, he began urging us to come up to Vermont to see him. He was ready to show me the first part of his book, he said, and he wanted us to introduce him to his goddaughter. 'You've kept her from me long enough,' he said. 'How can you expect me to take care of her if I don't know what she looks like?'

So Iris and I rented a car and a baby seat and drove up north to spend a few days with him. I remember asking Fanny if she wanted to join us, but it seemed that the timing was bad. She had just started her catalogue essay for the Blakelock exhibition she was curating at the museum that winter (her most important show to date), and she was anxious about meeting the deadline. She planned to visit Ben as soon as it was done, she explained, and because this seemed like a legitimate excuse, I didn't press her to go. Again, I had been confronted with a significant piece of evidence, and again I had ignored it. Fanny and Ben hadn't seen each other in five months, and it still hadn't dawned on me that they were in any trouble. If I had bothered to open my eyes for a few minutes, I might have noticed something. But I was too wrapped up in my own happiness, too absorbed in my own little world to pay any attention.

Still, the trip was a success. After spending four days and three nights in his company, I concluded that Sachs was on firm ground again, and I went away feeling as close to him as I had ever felt in the past. I'm tempted to say that it was just like old times, but that wouldn't be quite accurate. Too much had happened to him since his fall, there had been too many changes in both of us for our friendship to be exactly what it had been. But that doesn't mean these new times were less good than the old. In many ways, they were better. In that they represented something I felt I had lost, something I had despaired of ever finding again, they were much better.

Sachs had never been a well-organized person, and it startled me to see how thoroughly he had prepared for our visit. There were flowers in the room where Iris and I slept, guest towels were neatly folded on the bureau, and he had made the bed with all the precision of a veteran innkeeper. Downstairs, the kitchen had been stocked with food, there was an ample supply of wine and beer, and, as we discovered each night, the dinner menus had been worked out in advance. These small gestures were significant, I felt, and they helped set the tone of our stay. Daily life was easier for him than it had been in New York, and little by little he had managed to regain control of himself. As he put it to me in one of our late-night conversations, it was a bit like being in prison again. There weren't any extraneous preoccupations to bog him down. Life had been reduced to its bare-bones essentials, and he no longer had to question how he spent his time. Every day was more or less a repetition of the day before. Today resembled yesterday, tomorrow would resemble today, and what happened next week would blur into what had happened this week. There was comfort for him in that. The element of surprise had been eliminated, and it made him feel sharper, better able to concentrate on his work. 'It's odd,' he continued, 'but the two times I've sat down and written a novel, I've been cut off from the rest of the world. First in jail when I was a kid, and now up here in Vermont, living like a hermit in the woods. I wonder what the hell it means.'

'It means that you can't live without other people,' I said. 'When they're there for you in the flesh, the real world is sufficient. When you're alone, you have to invent imaginary characters. You need them for the companionship.'

All through the visit, the three of us kept ourselves busy doing nothing. We ate and drank, we swam in the pond, we talked. Sachs had installed an all-weather basketball court behind the house, and for an hour or so each morning we shot hoops and played one-on-one (he whipped me soundly every time). While Iris napped in the afternoons, he and I would take turns carrying Sonia around the yard, rocking her to sleep as we talked. The first night, I stayed up late and read the typescript of his book-in-progress. The other two nights, we stayed up late together, discussing what he had written so far and what was still to come. The sun shone on three of the four days; the temperatures were warm for that time of year. All in all, it was just about perfect.

Sachs's book was only a third written at that point, and the piece I read was still a long way from being finished. Sachs understood that, and when he gave me the manuscript the first night I was there, he wasn't looking for detailed criticisms or suggestions on how to improve this or that passage. He just wanted to know if I thought he should continue. 'I've reached a stage where I don't know what I'm doing anymore,' he said. 'I can't tell if it's good or bad. I can't tell if it's the best thing I've ever done or a pile of garbage.'

It wasn't garbage. That much was clear to me from the first page, but as I worked my way through the rest of the draft, I also realized that Sachs was onto something remarkable. This was the book I had always imagined he could write, and if it had taken a disaster to get him started, then perhaps it hadn't been a disaster at all. Or so I persuaded myself at the time. Whatever problems I found in the manuscript, whatever cuts and changes would ultimately have to be made, the essential thing was that Sachs had begun, and I wasn't going to let him stop. 'Just keep writing and don't look back,' I told him over breakfast the next morning. 'If you can push on to the end, it's going to be a great book. Mark my words: a great and memorable book.'

It's impossible for me to know if he could have pulled it off. At the time, I felt certain that he would, and when Iris and I said good-bye to him on the last day, it never even crossed my mind to doubt it. The pages I had read were one thing, but Sachs and I had also talked, and based on what he said about the book over the next two nights, I was convinced that he had the situation well in hand, that he understood what lay ahead of him. If that's true, then I can't imagine anything more sickening or terrible. Of all the tragedies my poor friend created for himself, leaving this book unfinished becomes the hardest one to bear. I don't mean to say that books are more important than life, but the fact is that everyone dies, everyone disappears in the end, and if Sachs had managed to finish his book, there's a chance it might have outlived him. That's what I've chosen to believe, in any case. As it stands now, the book is no more than the promise of a book, a potential book buried in a box of messy manuscript pages and a smattering of notes. That's all that's left of it, along with our two late-night conversations out in the open air, sitting under a moonless sky crammed full of stars. I thought his life was beginning all over again, that he had come to the brink of an extraordinary future, but it turned out that he was almost at the end. Less than a month after I saw him in Vermont, Sachs stopped working on his book. He went out for a walk one afternoon in the middle of September, and the earth suddenly swallowed him up. That was the long and the short of it, and from that day on he never wrote another word.

To mark what will never exist, I have given my book the same title that Sachs was planning to use for his: *Leviathan*.

4

I didn't see him again for close to two years. Maria was the only person who knew where he was, and Sachs had made her promise not to tell. Most people would have broken that promise, I think, but Maria had given her word, and no matter how dangerous it was for her to keep it, she refused to open her mouth. I must have run into her half a dozen times in those two years, but even when we talked about Sachs, she never let on that she knew more about his disappearance than I did. Last summer, when I finally learned how much she had been holding back from me, I got so angry that I wanted to kill her. But that was my problem, not Maria's, and I had no right to vent my frustration on her. A promise is a promise, after all, and even though her silence wound up causing a lot of damage, I don't think she was wrong to do what she did. If anyone should have spoken up, it was Sachs. He was the one responsible for what happened, and it was his secret that Maria was protecting. But Sachs said nothing. For two whole years, he kept himself hidden and never said a word.

We knew that he was alive, but as the months passed and no message came from him, not even that was certain anymore. Only bits and pieces remained, a few ghostlike facts. We knew that he had left Vermont, that he had not driven his own car, and that for one horrible minute Fanny had seen him in Brooklyn. Beyond that, everything was conjecture. Since he hadn't called to announce he was coming, we assumed that he had something urgent to tell her, but whatever that thing was, they never got around to talking about it. He just showed up one night out of the blue ('all distraught and crazy in the eyes,' as Fanny put it) and burst into the bedroom of their apartment. That led to the awful scene I mentioned earlier. If the room had been dark, it might have been less embarrassing for all of them, but several lights happened to be on, Fanny and Charles were naked on top of the covers, and Ben saw everything. It was clearly the last thing he expected to find. Before Fanny could say a word to him, he had already backed out of the room, stammering that he was sorry, that he hadn't known, that he hadn't meant to disturb her. She scrambled out of bed, but by the time she reached the front hall, the apartment door had banged shut and Sachs was racing down the stairs. She couldn't go outside with nothing on, so she rushed into the living room, opened the window, and called down to him in the street. Sachs stopped for a moment and waved up to her. 'My blessings on you both!' he shouted. Then he blew her a kiss, turned in the other direction, and ran off into the night.

Fanny telephoned us immediately after that. She figured he might be on his way to our place next, but her hunch proved wrong. Iris and I sat up half the night waiting for him, but Sachs never appeared. From then on, there were no more signs of his whereabouts. Fanny called the house in Vermont repeatedly, but no one ever answered. That was our last hope, and as the days went by, it seemed less and less likely that Sachs would return there. Panic set in; a contagion of morbid thoughts spread among us. Not knowing what else to do, Fanny rented a car that first weekend and drove up to the house herself. As she reported to me on the phone after she arrived, the evidence was puzzling. The front door had been left unlocked, the car was sitting in its usual place in the yard, and Ben's work was laid out on the desk in the studio: finished manuscript pages stacked in one pile, pens scattered beside it, a half-written page still in the typewriter. In other words, it looked as though he were about to come back any minute. If he had been planning to leave for any length of time, she said, the house would have been closed. The pipes would have been drained, the electricity would have been turned off, the refrigerator would have been emptied. 'And he would have taken his manuscript,' I added. 'Even if he had forgotten everything else, there's no way he would have left without that.'

The situation refused to add up. No matter how thoroughly we analyzed it, we were always left with the same conundrum. On the one hand, Sachs's departure had been unexpected. On the other hand, he had left of his own free will. If not for that fleeting encounter with Fanny in New York, we might have suspected foul play, but Sachs had made it down to the city unharmed. A bit frazzled, perhaps, but essentially unharmed. And yet, if nothing had happened to him, why hadn't he returned to Vermont? Why had he left behind his car, his clothes, his work? Iris and I talked it out with Fanny again and again, going over one possibility after another, but we never reached a satisfactory conclusion. There were too many blanks, too many variables, too many things we didn't know. After a month of beating it into the ground, I suggested that Fanny go to the police and report Ben as missing. She resisted the idea, however. She had no claims on him anymore, she said, which meant that she had no right to interfere. After what had happened in the apartment, he was free to do what he liked, and it wasn't up to her to drag him back. Charles (whom we had met by then and who turned out to be quite well off) was willing to hire a private detective at his own expense. 'Just so we know that Ben's all right,' he said. 'It's not a question of dragging him back, it's a question of knowing that he disappeared because he wanted to disappear.' Iris and I both thought that Charles's plan was sensible, but Fanny wouldn't allow him to go ahead with it. 'He gave us his blessings,' she said. 'That was the same thing as saying good-bye. I lived with him for twenty years, and I know how he thinks. He doesn't want us to look for him. I've already betrayed him once, and I'm not about to do it again. We have to leave him alone. He'll come back when he's ready to come back, and until then we have to wait. Believe me, it's the only thing to be done. We just have to sit tight and learn to live with it.'

Months passed. Then it was a year, and then it was two years, and the enigma remained unsolved. By the time Sachs showed up in Vermont last August, I was long past thinking we would ever find an answer. Iris and Charles both believed that he was dead, but my hopelessness didn't stem from anything as specific as that. I never had a strong feeling about whether Sachs was alive or dead – no sudden intuitions, no bursts of extrasensory knowledge, no mystical experiences – but I was more or less convinced that I would never see him again. I say 'more or less' because I wasn't sure of anything. In the first months after he disappeared, I went through a number of violent and contradictory responses, but these emotions gradually burned themselves out, and in the end terms such as *sadness* or *anger* or *grief* no longer seemed to apply. I had lost contact with him, and his absence felt less and less like a personal matter. Every time I tried to think about him, my imagination failed me. It was as if Sachs had become a hole in the universe. He was no longer just my missing friend, he was a symptom of my ignorance about all things, an emblem of the unknowable itself. This probably sounds vague, but I can't do any better than that. Iris told me that I was turning into a Buddhist, and I suppose that describes my position as accurately as anything else. Fanny was a Christian, Iris said, because she never abandoned her faith in Sachs's eventual return; she and Charles were atheists; and I was a Zen acolyte, a believer in the power of nothing. In all the years she had known me, she said, it was the first time I hadn't expressed an opinion.

Life changed, life went on. We learned, as Fanny had begged us, to live with it. She and Charles were together now, and in spite of ourselves, Iris and I were forced to admit that he was a decent fellow. Mid to late forties, an architect, formerly married, the father of two boys, intelligent, desperately in love with Fanny, beyond reproach. Little by little, we managed to form a friendship with him, and a new reality took hold for all of us. Last spring, when Fanny mentioned that she wasn't planning to go to Vermont for the summer (she just couldn't, she said, and probably never would again), it occurred to her that perhaps Iris and I would like to use the house. She wanted to give it to us for nothing, but we insisted on paying some kind of rent, and so we worked out an arrangement that would at least cover her costs – a pro-rated share of the taxes, the maintenance, and so on. That was how I happened to be present when Sachs turned up last summer. He arrived without warning, chugging into the yard one night in a battered blue Chevvy, spent the next couple of days here, and then vanished again. In between, he talked his head off. He talked so much, it almost scared me. But that was when I heard his story, and given how determined he was to tell it, I don't think he left anything out.

He went on working, he said. After Iris and I left with Sonia, he went on working for another three or four weeks. Our conversations about *Leviathan* had apparently been helpful, and he threw himself back into the manuscript that same morning, determined not to leave Vermont until he had finished a draft of the whole book. Everything seemed to go well. He made progress every day, and he felt happy with his monk's life, as happy as he had been in years. Then, early one evening in the middle of September, he decided to go out for a walk. The weather had turned by then, and the air was crisp, infused with the smells of fall. He put on his woolen hunting jacket and tramped up the hill beyond the house, heading north. He figured there was an hour of daylight left, which meant that he could walk for half an hour before he had to turn around and start back. Ordinarily, he would have spent that hour shooting baskets, but the change of seasons was in full swing now, and he wanted to have a look at what was happening in the woods: to see the red and yellow leaves, to watch the slant of the setting sun among the birches and maples, to wander in the glow of the pendant colors. So he set off on his little jaunt, with no more on his mind than what he was going to cook for dinner when he got home.

Once he entered the woods, however, he became distracted. Instead of looking at the leaves and migrating birds, he started thinking about his book. Passages he had written earlier that day came rushing back to him, and before he was conscious of what he was doing, he was already composing new sentences in his head, mapping out the work he wanted to do the next morning. He kept on walking, thrashing through the dead leaves and thorny underbrush, talking out loud to himself, chanting the words of his book, paying no attention to where he was. He could have gone on like that for hours, he said, but at a certain point he noticed that he was having trouble seeing. The sun had already set, and because of the thickness of the woods, night was fast coming on. He looked around him, hoping to get his bearings, but nothing was familiar, and he realized that he had never been in this place before. Feeling like an idiot, he turned around and started running in the direction he had come from. He had just a few minutes before everything disappeared, and he knew he would never make it. He had no flashlight, no matches, no food in his pockets. Sleeping outdoors promised to be an unpleasant experience, but he couldn't think of any alternative. He sat down on a tree stump and started to laugh. He found himself ridiculous, he said, a comic figure of the first rank. Then night fell in earnest, and he couldn't see a thing. He waited for a moon to appear, but the sky clouded over instead. He laughed again. He wasn't going to give the matter another thought, he decided. He was safe where he was, and freezing his ass off for one night wasn't going to kill him. So he did what he could to make himself comfortable. He stretched out on the ground, he covered himself haphazardly with some leaves and twigs, and tried to think about his book. Before long, he even managed to fall asleep.

He woke up at dawn, bone-cold and shivering, his clothes wet with dew. The situation didn't seem so funny anymore. He was in a foul temper, and his muscles ached. He was hungry and disheveled, and the only thing he wanted was to get out of there and find his way home. He took what he thought was the same path he had taken the previous evening, but after he had walked for close to an hour, he began to suspect that he was on the wrong path. He considered turning around and heading back to the place where he had started, but he wasn't sure he would be able to find it again – and even if he did, it was doubtful he would recognize it. The sky was gloomy that morning, with dense swarms of clouds blocking the sun. Sachs had never been much of a woodsman, and without a compass to orient his position, he couldn't tell if he was traveling east or west or north or south. On the other hand, it wasn't as though he were trapped in a primeval forest. The woods were bound to end sooner or later, and it hardly mattered which direction he followed, just as long as he walked in a straight line. Once he made it to an open road, he would knock on the door of the first house he saw. With any luck, the people inside would be able to tell him where he was.

It took a long time before any of that happened. Since he had no watch, he never knew exactly how long, but he guessed somewhere between three and four hours. He was thoroughly disgusted by then, and he cursed his stupidity over the last miles with a growing sense of rage. Once he came to the end of the woods, however, his dark mood lifted, and he stopped feeling sorry for himself. He was on a narrow dirt road, and even if he didn't know where he was, even if there wasn't a single house in sight, he could comfort himself with the thought that the worst of it was over. He walked for ten or fifteen more minutes, making bets with himself about how far he had strayed from home. If it was under five miles, he would spend fifty dollars on a present for Sonia. If it was over five but under ten, he would spend a hundred dollars. Over ten would be two hundred. Over fifteen would be three hundred, over twenty would be four hundred, and so on. As he was showering these imaginary gifts on his goddaughter (stuffed panda bears, dollhouses, ponies), he heard a car rumbling in the distance behind him. He stopped and waited for it to approach. It turned out to be a red pick-up truck, speeding along at a good clip. Figuring he had nothing to lose, Sachs stuck up his hand to get the driver's attention. The truck barreled past him, but before Sachs could turn around again, it slammed to a halt. He heard a clamor of flying pebbles, dust rose everywhere, and then a voice was calling out to him, asking if he needed a lift.

The driver was a young man in his early twenties. Sachs sized him up as a local kid, a road mender or plumber's assistant, maybe, and though he didn't feel much inclined to talk at first, the boy turned out to be so friendly and ingratiating that he soon fell into a conversation with him. There was a metal softball bat lying on the floor in front of Sachs's seat, and when the kid put his foot on the accelerator to get the truck going again, the bat lurched up and hit Sachs in the ankle. That was the opener, so to speak, and once the kid had apologized for the inconvenience, he introduced himself as Dwight (Dwight McMartin, as Sachs later learned) and they started in on a discussion about softball. Dwight told him that he played on a team sponsored by the volunteer fire department in Newfane. The regular season had ended last week, and the first game of the playoffs was scheduled to be played that evening – 'if the weather holds,' he added several times, 'if the weather holds and the rain don't fall.' Dwight was the first baseman, the cleanup hitter, and number two in the league in homeruns, a bulky gulumph in the mold of Moose Skowron. Sachs said he'd try to make it down to the field to watch, and Dwight answered in all seriousness that it was bound to be worth it, that it was sure to be a terrific game. Sachs couldn't help smiling. He was rumpled and unshaven, there were brambles and leaf particles stuck to his clothes, and his nose was running like a spigot. He probably looked like a hobo, he thought, and yet Dwight didn't press him with personal questions. He didn't ask him why he had been walking on that deserted road, he didn't ask him where he lived, he didn't even bother to ask his name. He could have been a simpleton, Sachs realized, or maybe he was just a nice guy, but one way or the other, it was hard not to appreciate that discretion. All of a sudden, Sachs wished that he hadn't kept so much to himself over the past months. He should have gone out and mingled with his neighbors a bit more; he should have made an effort to learn something about the people around him. Almost as an ethical point, he told himself that he mustn't forget the softball game that night. It would do him some good, he thought, give him something to think about other than his book. If he had some people to talk to, maybe he wouldn't be so apt to get lost the next time he went walking in the woods.

When Dwight told him where they were, Sachs was appalled by how far he had drifted off course. He had evidently walked over the hill and down the other side, landing two towns to the east of where he lived. He had covered only ten miles on foot, but the return distance by car was well over thirty. For no particular reason, he decided to spill the whole business to Dwight. Out of gratitude, perhaps, or simply because he found it amusing now. Maybe the kid would tell it to his buddies on the softball team, and they'd all have a good laugh at his expense. Sachs didn't care. It was an exemplary tale, a classic moron joke, and he didn't mind being the butt of his own folly. The city slicker plays Daniel Boone in the Vermont woods, and look what happens to him, fellas. But once he began to talk about his misadventures, Dwight responded with unexpected compassion. The same thing had happened to him once, he told Sachs, and it hadn't been a bit of fun. He'd only been eleven or twelve at the time, and he'd been scared shitless, crouching behind a tree the whole night waiting for a bear to attack him. Sachs couldn't be sure, but he suspected that Dwight was inventing this story to make him feel a little less miserable. In any case, the kid didn't laugh at him. In fact, once he'd heard what Sachs had to say, he even offered to drive him home. He was running late as it was, he said, but a few more minutes wouldn't make any difference, and Christ, if he were in Sachs's shoes, he'd expect someone to do the same for him.

They were traveling along a paved road at that point, but Dwight said he knew a shortcut to Sachs's house. It meant turning around and backtracking for a couple of miles, but once he worked out the arithmetic in his head, he decided it made sense to change course. So he slammed on the brakes, did a U-turn in the middle of the road, and headed back in the other direction. The shortcut turned out to be the narrowest of dirt trails, a bumpy, one-lane sliver of ground that cut through a dark, tree-clogged patch of woods. Not many people knew about it, Dwight said, but if he wasn't mistaken it would lead them to a somewhat wider dirt road and that second road would spit them out on the county highway about four miles from Sachs's house. Dwight probably knew what he was talking about, but he never got a chance to demonstrate the correctness of his theory. Less than a mile after they started down the first dirt road, they ran into something unexpected. And before they could move around it, their journey came to an end.

It all happened very quickly. Sachs experienced it as a churning in the gut, a spinning in the head, a rush of fear in the veins. He was so exhausted, he told me, and so little time elapsed from beginning to end, that he could never quite absorb it as real – not even in retrospect, not even when he sat down to tell me about it two years later. One moment, they were tooling along through the woods, he said, and the next moment they had stopped. A man was standing up ahead of them on the road, leaning against the trunk of a white Toyota and smoking a cigarette. He looked to be in his late thirties, a tallish, slender man dressed in a flannel work shirt and loose Khaki pants. The only other thing Sachs noticed was that he had a beard – not unlike the one he used to wear himself, but darker. Thinking the man must be having car trouble, Dwight climbed out of the truck and walked toward him, asking if he needed help. Sachs couldn't hear the man's response, but the tone sounded angry, unnecessarily hostile somehow, and as he continued to watch them through the windshield, he was surprised when the man answered Dwight's next question with something even more vicious: fuck off, or get the fuck away from me, words to that effect. That was when the adrenaline started pumping through him, Sachs said, and he instinctively reached for the metal bat on the floor. Dwight was too good-natured to take the hint, however. He kept on walking toward the man, shrugging off the insult as if it didn't matter, repeating that he only wanted to help. The man backed away in agitation, and then he ran around to the front of the car, opened the door on the passenger's side, and reached for something in the glove compartment. When he straightened up and turned toward Dwight again, there was a gun in his hand. He fired it once. The big kid howled and clutched his stomach, and then the man fired again. The kid howled a second time and started staggering up the road, moaning and weeping in pain. The man turned to follow him with his eyes, and Sachs jumped out of the truck, holding the bat in his right hand. He didn't even think, he told me. He rushed up behind the man just as the third shot went off, got a good grip on the handle of the bat, and swung for all he was worth. He aimed for the man's head – hoping to split his skull in two, hoping to kill him, hoping to empty his brains all over the ground. The bat landed with horrific force, smashing into a spot just behind the man's right ear. Sachs heard the thud of impact, the cracking of cartilage and bone, and then the man dropped. He just fell down dead in the middle of the road, and everything went quiet.

Sachs ran over to Dwight, but when he bent down to examine the kid's body, he saw that the third shot had killed him. The bullet had gone straight into the back of his head, and his cranium was shattered. Sachs had lost his chance. It was all a matter of timing, and he had been too slow. If he had managed to get to the man a split-second earlier, that last shot would have missed, and instead of looking down at a corpse, he would have been bandaging Dwight's wounds, doing everything he could to save his life. A moment after he thought this thought, Sachs felt his own body start to tremble. He sat down on the road, put his head between his knees, and struggled not to throw up. Time passed. He felt the air blowing through his clothes; he heard a blue jay squawking in the woods; he shut his eyes. When he opened them again, he picked up a handful of loose dirt from the road and crushed it against his face. He put the dirt in his mouth and chewed it, letting the grit scrape against his teeth, feeling the pebbles against his tongue. He chewed until he couldn't stand it anymore, and then he bent over and spat the mess out, groaning like a sick, demented animal.

If Dwight had lived, he said, the whole story would have been different. The idea of running away never would have occurred to him, and once that first step had been eliminated, none of the things that followed from it would have happened. But standing out there alone in the woods, Sachs suddenly fell into a deep, unbridled panic. Two men were dead, and the idea of going to the state troopers seemed unimaginable to him. He had already served time in prison. He was a convicted felon, and without any witnesses to corroborate his story, no one was going to believe a word he said. It was all too bizarre, too implausible. He wasn't thinking too clearly, of course, but whatever thoughts he had were centered entirely on himself. He couldn't do anything for Dwight, but at least he could save his own skin, and in his panic the only solution that came to him was to get the hell away from there.

He knew the police would figure out that a third man had been present. It would be obvious that Dwight and the stranger hadn't killed each other, since a man with three bullets in his body would scarcely have the strength to bludgeon someone to death, and even if he did, he wouldn't be able to walk twenty feet down the road after he had done it, least of all with one of those bullets lodged in his skull. Sachs also knew that he was bound to leave some traces behind him. No matter how assiduously he cleaned up after himself, a competent forensic team would have no trouble unearthing something to work with: a footprint, a strand of hair, a microscopic fragment. But none of that would make any difference. As long as he managed to remove his fingerprints from the truck, as long as he remembered to take the bat with him, there wouldn't be anything to identify him as the missing man. That was the crucial point. He had to make sure that the missing man could have been anyone. Once he did that, he would be home free.

He spent several minutes wiping down the surfaces of the truck: the dashboard, the seat, the windows, the inside and outside door handles, everything he could think of. As soon as he was finished, he did it again, and then he did it once more for good measure. After collecting the bat from the ground, he opened the door of the stranger's car, saw that the key was still in the ignition, and climbed in behind the wheel. The engine kicked over on the first try. There were going to be tread marks, of course, and those marks would remove any doubt that a third man had been there, but Sachs was too frightened to leave on foot. That's what would have made the most sense: to walk away, to go home, to forget the whole nasty business. But his heart was pounding too fast for that, his thoughts were charging out of control, and deliberate actions of that sort were no longer possible. He craved speed. He craved the speed and noise of the car, and now that he was ready, all he wanted was to be gone, to be sitting in the car and driving as fast as he could. Only that would be able to match the tumult inside him. Only that would allow him to silence the roar of terror in his head.

He drove north on the Interstate for two and a half hours, following the Connecticut River until he reached the latitude of Barre. That was where hunger finally got the better of him. He was afraid he'd have trouble holding the food down, but he hadn't eaten in over twenty-four hours, and he knew he had to give it a try. He pulled off the Interstate at the next exit, drove along a two-lane road for fifteen or twenty minutes, and then stopped for lunch in a small town whose name he couldn't remember. Taking no chances, he ordered soft-boiled eggs and toast. After he was done, he went into the men's room and cleaned himself up, soaking his head in a sinkful of warm water and removing the twigs and dirt stains from his clothes. It made him feel much better. By the time he paid his bill and walked out of the restaurant, he understood that the next step was to turn around and go to New York. It wasn't going to be possible to keep the story to himself. That much was clear now, and once he realized he had to talk to someone, he knew that person had to be Fanny. In spite of everything that had happened in the past year, he suddenly ached to see her again.

As he walked toward the dead man's car, Sachs noticed that it had California license plates. He wasn't sure what to make of this discovery, but it surprised him just the same. How many other details had he missed? he wondered. Before returning to the Interstate and heading south, he turned off the main road and parked at the edge of what appeared to be a large forest preserve. It was a secluded spot, with no signs of anyone for miles around. Sachs opened all four doors of the car, got down on his hands and knees, and systematically combed the interior. Thorough as he was, the results of this search were disappointing. He found a few coins wedged under the front seat, some wadded-up balls of paper strewn about the floor (fast food wrappers, ticket stubs, crumpled cigarette packs), but nothing with a name on it, nothing that told him a single fact about the man he had killed. The glove compartment was similarly blank, containing nothing but the Toyota owner's manual, a box of thirty-eight caliber bullets, and an unopened carton of Camel Filters. That left the trunk, and when Sachs finally got around to opening it, the trunk proved to be a different matter.

There were three bags inside it. The largest one was filled with clothes, shaving equipment, and maps. At the very bottom, tucked away in a small white envelope, there was a passport. When he looked at the photograph on the first page, Sachs recognized the man from that morning – the same man minus the beard. The name given was Reed Dimaggio, middle initial N. Date of birth: November 12, 1950. Place of birth: Newark, New Jersey. The passport had been issued in San Francisco the previous July, and the back pages were empty, with no visa stamps or customs markings. Sachs wondered if it hadn't been forged. Given what had taken place in the woods that morning, it seemed almost certain that Dwight wasn't the first person Dimaggio had killed. And if he was a professional thug, there was a chance that he had been traveling with false documents. Still, the name was somehow too singular, too odd not to have been real. It must have belonged to someone, and for want of any other clues concerning the man's identity, Sachs decided to accept that someone as the man he had killed. Reed Dimaggio. Until something better came along, that was the name he would give him.

The next article was a steel suitcase, one of those shiny silver boxes that photographers sometimes carry their equipment in. The first bag had opened without a key, but this one was locked, and Sachs spent half an hour struggling to pry the hinges loose from their bolts. He hammered away at them with the jack and tire iron, and every time the box moved, he heard metallic objects rattling around inside it. He assumed they were weapons: knives, guns, and bullets, the tools of Dimaggio's trade. When the box finally relented, however, it yielded up a baffling collection of bric-a-brac, not at all what Sachs had been expecting. He found spools of electric wire, alarm clocks, screwdrivers, microchips, string, putty, and several rolls of black duct tape. One by one, he picked up each item and studied it, groping to fathom its purpose, but even after he had sifted through the entire contents of the box, he still couldn't guess what these things signified. It was only later that it hit him – long after he was back on the road. Driving down to New York that night, he suddenly understood that these were the materials for constructing a bomb.

The third piece of luggage was a bowling bag. There was nothing remarkable about it (a small leather pouch with red, white, and blue panels, a zipper, and a white plastic handle), but it frightened Sachs more than the other two, and he had instinctively saved it for last. Anything could have been hidden in there, he realized. Considering that it belonged to a madman, to a homicidal maniac, that *anything* became more and more monstrous for him to contemplate. By the time he had finished with the other two bags, Sachs had nearly lost the courage to open it. Rather than confront what his imagination had put in there, he had nearly talked himself into throwing it away. But he didn't. Just when he was on the point of lifting it out of the trunk and tossing it into the woods, he closed his eyes, hesitated, and then, with a single frantic tug, undid the zipper.

There was no head in the bag. There were no severed ears, no lopped-off fingers, no private parts. What there was was money. And not just a little money, but lots of it, more money than Sachs had ever seen in one place before. The bag was packed solid with it: thick bundles of one-hundred-dollar bills fastened with rubber bands, each bundle representing three, four, or five thousand dollars. When Sachs had finished counting them, he was reasonably sure that the total fell somewhere between one hundred sixty and one hundred sixty-five thousand. His first response on discovering the cash was relief, gratitude that his fears had come to naught. Then, as he added it up for the first time, a sense of shock and giddiness. The next time he counted the bills, however, he found himself getting used to them. That was the strangest part of it, he told me: how quickly he digested the whole improbable occurrence. By the time he counted the money again, he had already begun to think of it as his own.

He kept the cigarettes, the softball bat, the passport, and the money. Everything else he threw away, scattering the contents of the suitcase and the metal strong-box deep inside the woods. A few minutes after that, he deposited the empty luggage in a dumpster at the edge of town. It was past four o'clock by then, and he had a long drive ahead of him. He stopped for another meal in Springfield, Massachusetts, smoking Dimaggio's Camels as he filled himself with extra coffee, and then made it down to Brooklyn a little after one in the morning. That was where he abandoned the car, leaving it on one of the cobbled streets near the Gowanus Canal, a no-man's-land of empty warehouses and packs of thin, roving dogs. He was careful to scrub the surfaces clean of fingerprints, but that was just an added precaution. The doors were unlocked, the key was in the ignition, and the car was sure to be stolen before the night was out.

He traveled the rest of the way on foot, carrying the bowling bag in one hand and the softball bat and cigarettes in the other. At the corner of Fifth Avenue and President Street, he slid the bat into a crowded trash receptacle, angling it in among the heaped-up newspapers and cracked melon rinds. That was the last piece of business he had to think about. There was still another mile to go, but in spite of his exhaustion, he trudged on toward his apartment with a growing sense of calm. Fanny would be there for him, he thought, and once he saw her, the worst of it would be finished.

That explains the confusion that followed. Not only was Sachs caught off balance when he entered the apartment, but he was in no condition to absorb the least new fact about anything. His brain was already overcharged, and he had gone home to Fanny precisely because he assumed there would be no surprises there, because it was the one place where he could count on being taken care of. Hence his bewilderment, his stunned reaction when he saw her rolling around naked on the bed with Charles. His certainty had dissolved into humiliation, and it was all he could do to mutter a few words of apology before rushing out of the apartment. Everything had happened at once, and while he managed to regain enough composure to shout his blessings from the street, that was no more than a bluff, a feeble, last-minute effort to save face. In point of fact, he felt as if the sky had fallen on his head. He felt as if his heart had been ripped out of him.

He ran down the block, running only to be gone, with no thought of what to do next. At the corner of Third Street and Seventh Avenue, he spotted a pay phone, and that gave him the idea to call me and ask for a place to spend the night. When he dialed my number, however, the line was busy. I must have been talking to Fanny at that moment (she called immediately after Sachs dashed away), but Sachs interpreted the busy signal to mean that Iris and I had taken our phone off the hook. That was a sensible conclusion, since it wasn't likely that either one of us would be talking to someone at two o'clock in the morning. Therefore, he didn't bother to try us again. When his quarter came back to him, he used it to call Maria instead. The ringing pulled her out of a deep sleep, but once she heard the desperation in his voice, she told him to come right over. Subways were scarce at that hour, and by the time he caught the train at Grand Army Plaza and traveled to her loft in Manhattan, she was already dressed and wide awake, sitting at the kitchen table and drinking her third cup of coffee.

It was the logical place for him to go. Even after his removal to the country, Sachs had stayed in touch with Maria, and when I finally talked to her about these things last fall, she showed me more than a dozen letters and postcards he had sent her from Vermont. There had been a number of phone conversations as well, she said, and in the six months he was out of town, she didn't think more than ten days had gone by without news from him of one sort or another. The point was that Sachs trusted her, and with Fanny suddenly gone from his life (and with my phone ostensibly off the hook), it was a natural step for him to turn to Maria. Since his accident the previous July, she was the only person he had unburdened himself to, the only person he had allowed into the inner sanctum of his thoughts. When all was said and done, she was probably closer to him at that moment than anyone else.

Still, it turned out to be a terrible mistake. Not because Maria wasn't willing to help him, not because she wasn't prepared to drop everything to see him through the crisis, but because she was in possession of the one fact powerful enough to turn an ugly misfortune into a full-scale tragedy. If Sachs hadn't gone to her, I'm certain that things would have been resolved rather quickly. He would have calmed down after a night's rest, and after that he would have contacted the police and told them the truth. With the help of a good lawyer, he would have walked away a free man. But a new element was added to the already unstable mixture of the past twenty-four hours, and it wound up producing a deadly compound, a beakerful of acid that hissed forth its dangers in a billowing profusion of smoke.

Even now, it's difficult for me to accept any of it. And I speak as someone who should know better, as someone who has thought long and hard about the issues at stake here. My whole adulthood has been spent writing stories, putting imaginary people into unexpected and often unlikely situations, but none of my characters has ever experienced anything as improbable as Sachs did that night at Maria Turner's house. If it still shocks me to report what happened, that is because the real is always ahead of what we can imagine. No matter how wild we think our inventions might be, they can never match the unpredictability of what the real world continually spews forth. This lesson seems inescapable to me now. *Anything can happen.* And one way or another, it always does.

The first hours they spent together were painful enough, and they both remembered them as a kind of tempest, an inward pummeling, a maelstrom of tears, silences, and choked-off words. Little by little, Sachs managed to get the story out. Maria held him in her arms through most of it, listening in rapt disbelief as he told her as much as he was able to tell. That was when she made her promise, when she gave him her word and swore to keep the killings to herself. Later on, she planned to talk him into going to the police, but for now her only concern was to protect him, to prove her loyalty. Sachs was falling apart, and once the words started coming out of his mouth, once he started listening to himself describe the things he had done, he was seized by revulsion. Maria tried to make him understand that he had acted in self-defense – that he wasn't responsible for the stranger's death – but Sachs refused to accept her argument. Like it or not, he had killed a man, and no amount of talk would ever obliterate that fact. But if he hadn't killed the stranger, Maria said, he would have been killed himself. Maybe so, Sachs answered, but in the long run that would have been preferable to the position he was in now. It would have been better to die, he said, better to have been shot and killed that morning than to have this memory with him for the rest of his life.

They kept on talking, weaving in and out of these tortured arguments, weighing the act and its consequences, reliving the hours Sachs had spent in the car, the scene with Fanny in Brooklyn, his night in the woods, going over the same ground three or four times, neither one of them able to sleep, and then, right in the middle of this conversation, everything stopped. Sachs opened the bowling bag to show Maria what he had found in the trunk of the car, and there was the passport lying on top of the money. He pulled it out and handed it to her, insisting that she take a look at it, intent on proving that the stranger had been a real person – a man with a name, an age, a place of birth. It made it all so concrete, he said. If the man had been anonymous, it might have been possible to think of him as a monster, to imagine that he had deserved to die, but the passport demythologized him, showed him to be a man like any other man. Here were his vital statistics, the delineation of an actual life. And here was his picture. Unbelievably, the man *was smiling* in the photograph. As Sachs told Maria when he put the document in her hand, he was convinced that smile would destroy him. No matter how far he traveled from the events of that morning, he would never manage to escape it.

So Maria opened the passport, already thinking of what she would say to Sachs, already casting about for some words that would reassure him, and glanced down at the picture inside. Then she took a second look, moving her eyes back and forth between the name and the photograph, and all of a sudden (as she put it to me last year) she felt as if her head were about to explode. Those were the precise words she used to describe what happened: 'I felt as if my head were about to explode.'

Sachs asked her if something was wrong. He had seen the change of expression in her face, and he didn't understand it.

'Jesus God,' she said.

'Are you okay?'

'This is a joke, right? It's all some kind of stupid gag, isn't it?'

'You're not making sense.'

'Reed Dimaggio. This is a picture of Reed Dimaggio.'

'That's what it says. I have no idea if that's his real name.'

'I know him.'

'You what?'

'I know him. He was married to my best friend. I was at their wedding. They named their little girl after me.'

'Reed Dimaggio.'

'There's only one Reed Dimaggio. And this is his picture. I'm looking at it right now.'

'That's not possible.'

'Do you think I'd make it up?'

'The man was a killer. He shot down a boy in cold blood.'

'I don't care. I knew him. He was married to my friend Lillian Stern. If it hadn't been for me, they never would have met.'

It was almost dawn then, but they went on talking for several more hours, staying up until nine or ten o'clock as Maria recounted the history of her friendship with Lillian Stern. Sachs, whose body had been crumbling with exhaustion, caught his second wind and refused to go to bed until she had finished. He heard about Maria and Lillian's early days in Massachusetts, about their move to New York after high school, about the long period when they lost contact with each other, about their unexpected reunion in the entryway of Lillian's apartment house.

Maria went through the saga of the address book, she dug up the photographs she had taken of Lillian and spread them out on the floor for him, she told about their experiment in switching identities. This had led directly to Lillian's meeting with Dimaggio, she explained, and to the whirlwind romance that followed. Maria herself never got to know him very well, and except for the fact that she liked him, she couldn't say much about who he was. Only a few random details had stuck in her mind. She remembered that he had fought in Vietnam, but whether he had been drafted into the Army or had enlisted wasn't clear anymore. He must have been discharged some time in the early seventies, however, since she knew for a fact that he had gone to college on the GI bill, and when Lillian met him in 1976, he had already finished his BA and was about to go off to Berkeley as a graduate student in American history. All in all, she had met him only five or six times, and several of those encounters had taken place right at the beginning, just when he and Lillian were falling in love. Lillian went out to California with him the following month, and after that Maria saw him on only two other occasions: at the wedding in 1977, and after their daughter was born in 1981. The marriage ended in 1984. Lillian talked to Maria several times during the period of the breakup, but since then their contacts had been fitful, with wider and wider intervals between each call.

She had never seen any cruelty in Dimaggio, she said, nothing to suggest that he would have been capable of hurting anyone – let alone shooting down a stranger in cold blood. The man wasn't a criminal. He was a student, an intellectual, a teacher, and he and Lillian had lived a rather dull life in Berkeley. He taught classes as a graduate assistant at the university and worked on his doctorate; she studied acting, held different part-time jobs, and performed in local theater productions and student films. Lillian's savings helped get them through the first couple of years, but after that money was tight, and more often than not it was a struggle to make ends meet. Hardly the life of a criminal, Maria said.

Nor was it the life she imagined her friend would choose for herself. After those wild years in New York, it seemed strange that Lillian would have settled down with someone like Dimaggio. But she had already been thinking about leaving New York, and the circumstances of their meeting were so extraordinary (so 'rapturous' as Maria put it), that the idea of running off with him must have been irresistible – not so much a choice as a matter of destiny. It's true that Berkeley wasn't Hollywood, but neither was Dimaggio some cringing little bookworm with wire-rimmed spectacles and a caved-in chest. He was a strong, good-looking young man, and physical attraction couldn't have been a problem. Just as important, he was smarter than anyone she had ever met: he talked better and knew more than anyone else, and he had all kinds of impressive opinions about everything. Lillian, who hadn't read more than two or three books in her life, must have been overpowered by him. As Maria saw it, she probably imagined that Dimaggio would transform her, that just knowing him would lift her out of her mediocrity and help her to make something of herself. Becoming a movie star was only a childish dream anyway. She might have had the looks for it, she might even have had enough talent – but, as Maria explained to Sachs, Lillian was far too lazy to pull it off, too impulsive to bear down and concentrate, too lacking in ambition. When she asked Maria for advice, Maria told her flat out to forget the movies and stick with Dimaggio. If he was willing to marry her, then she should jump at the chance. And that's exactly what Lillian did.

As far as Maria could tell, it seemed to be a successful marriage. Lillian never complained about it in any case, and though Maria began to have some doubts after she visited California in 1981 (finding Dimaggio morose and overbearing, devoid of any sense of humor), she attributed it to the early flutters of parenthood and kept her thoughts to herself. Two and a half years later, when Lillian called to announce their impending separation, Maria was caught by surprise. Lillian claimed that Dimaggio was seeing another woman, but then in the next breath she mentioned something about her past 'catching up with her.' Maria had always assumed that Lillian had told Dimaggio about her life in New York, but it seems that she had never gotten around to it, and once they moved to California, she decided it would be better for both of them if he didn't know. One evening, while she and Dimaggio were eating dinner in a San Francisco restaurant, a former client of hers happened to sit down at the next table. The man was drunk, and after Lillian refused to acknowledge his stares and smiles and obnoxious winks, he stood up and made some loud, insulting remarks, spilling her secret right there in front of her husband. According to what she told Maria, Dimaggio went into a rage when they returned home. He pushed her to the ground, he kicked her, he threw pots and pans against the wall, he yelled 'whore' at the top of his voice. If the baby hadn't woken up, she said, there was a chance he would have killed her. The next day, however, when she talked to Maria again, Lillian never even referred to this incident. This time, her story was that Dimaggio 'had gone weird on her,' that he was hanging out with 'a bunch of idiot radicals' and had turned into a 'creep.' So she had finally gotten fed up and kicked him out of the house. That made three different stories, Maria said, a typical example of how Lillian confronted the truth. One of the stories might have been real. It was even possible that all of them were real – but then again, it was just as possible that all of them were false. You could never tell with Lillian, she explained to Sachs. For all she knew, Lillian might have been unfaithful to Dimaggio, and he had walked out on her. It might have been that simple. And then again, it might not.

They were never officially divorced. Dimaggio, who finished his degree in 1982, had been teaching at a small private college in Oakland for the past couple of years. After the final rupture with Lillian (fall 1984), he moved to a one-room efficiency flat in the center of Berkeley. For the next nine months, he came to the house every Saturday to pick up little Maria and spend the day with her. He always arrived punctually at ten in the morning, and he always brought her back by eight at night. Then, after close to a year of this routine, he failed to show up. There was never any excuse, never any word of explanation. Lillian called his apartment several times over the next two days, but no one answered. On Monday, she tried to reach him at work, and when no one picked up the phone in his office, she redialed and asked for the secretary of the history department. It was only then that she learned that Dimaggio had quit his position at the college. Just last week, the secretary said, on the day he handed in his final grades for the semester. He had told the chairman that he'd been hired for a tenure-track job at Cornell, but when Lillian called the history department at Cornell, no one there had heard of him. After that, she never saw Dimaggio again. For the next two years, it was as if he had vanished from the face of the earth. He didn't write, he didn't call, he didn't make a single attempt to contact his daughter. Until he materialized in the Vermont woods on the day of his death, the story of those two years was a complete blank.

In the meantime, Lillian and Maria continued to talk on the phone. After Dimaggio had been missing for a month, Maria suggested that Lillian pack a suitcase and come with little Maria to New York. She even offered to pay the fare, but considering how broke Lillian was just then, they both decided the money would be better spent on paying bills. So Maria wired Lillian a loan of three thousand dollars (every penny she could afford), and the trip was shelved for some future date. Two years later, it still hadn't happened. Maria kept imagining that she would go out to California to spend a couple of weeks with Lillian, but there never seemed to be a good time, and it was all she could do to keep up with her work. After the first year, they began calling each other less. At one point, Maria sent another fifteen hundred dollars, but it had been four months since their last conversation, and she suspected that Lillian was in rather poor shape. It was a terrible way to treat a friend, she said, suddenly giving in to a fresh round of tears. She didn't even know what Lillian was doing anymore, and now that this wretched thing had happened, she saw how selfish she had been, she realized how badly she had let her down.

Fifteen minutes later, Sachs was stretched out on the sofa in Maria's studio, drifting off to sleep. He could give in to his exhaustion because he had already worked out a plan, because he was no longer in doubt about what to do next. Once Maria had told him about Dimaggio and Lillian Stern, he understood that the nightmare coincidence was in fact a solution, an opportunity in the shape of a miracle. The essential thing was to accept the uncanniness of the event – not to deny it, but to embrace it, to breathe it into himself as a sustaining force. Where all had been dark for him, he now saw a beautiful, awesome clarity. He would go to California and give Lillian Stern the money he had found in Dimaggio's car. Not just the money – but the money as a token of everything he had to give, his entire soul. The alchemy of retribution demanded it, and once he had performed this act, perhaps there would be some peace for him, perhaps he would have some excuse to go on living. Dimaggio had taken a life; he had taken Dimaggio's life. Now it was his turn, now his life had to be taken from him. That was the inner law, and unless he found the courage to obliterate himself, the circle of damnation would never be closed. No matter how long he lived, his life would never belong to him again. By handing the money over to Lillian Stern, he would be putting himself in her hands. That would be his penance: to use his life in order to give life to someone else; to confess; to risk everything on an insane dream of mercy and forgiveness.

He never talked about any of these things to Maria. He was afraid that she wouldn't understand him, and he dreaded the thought of confusing her, of causing her any further alarm. Still, he put off leaving as long as he could. His body required rest, and since Maria was in no hurry to get rid of him, he wound up staying with her for three more days. In all that time, he never set foot outside her loft. Maria bought new clothes for him; she shopped for groceries and cooked him meals; she supplied him with newspapers every morning and afternoon. Beyond reading the papers and watching the television news, he did almost nothing. He slept. He stared out the window. He thought about the immensity of fear.

On the second day, there was a small article in *The New York Times* that reported the discovery of the two bodies in Vermont. That was how Sachs learned that Dwight's last name had been McMartin, but the piece was too sketchy to offer any details about the investigation that was apparently underway. In the *New York Post* that afternoon, there was a second story that emphasized how baffled the local authorities were by the case. But nothing about a third man, nothing about a white Toyota abandoned in Brooklyn, nothing about any evidence that would establish a link between Dimaggio and McMartin. The headline announced: *Mystery in the Northern Woods*. That night on the national news, one of the networks picked up the story, but other than a short, tasteless interview with McMartin's parents (the mother weeping in front of the camera, the father stone-faced and rigid) and a shot of Lillian Stern's house ('Mrs Dimaggio refused to talk to reporters') there were no significant developments. A police spokesman came on and said that paraffin tests proved that Dimaggio had fired the gun that killed McMartin, but Dimaggio's own death was still unexplained. A third man had clearly been involved, he added, but they still had no idea who he was or where he had gone. For all intents and purposes, the case was an enigma.

The whole time Sachs spent with Maria, she kept calling Lillian's number in Berkeley. At first, there was no answer. Then, when she tried again an hour later, she was greeted by a busy signal. After several more attempts, she called the operator and asked if there was trouble on the line. No, she was informed, the phone had been taken off the hook. Once the report was shown on television the next evening, the busy signal became understandable. Lillian was protecting herself from reporters, and for the rest of Sachs's stay in New York, Maria was unable to get through to her. In the long run, perhaps that was just as well. No matter how urgently she wanted to talk to her friend, Maria would have been hard-pressed to tell her what she knew: that Dimaggio's killer was a friend of hers, that he was standing next to her at that very moment. Things were awful enough without having to grope for the words to explain all that. On the other hand, it might have been useful to Sachs if Maria had managed to talk to Lillian before he left. The way would have been smoothed for him, so to speak, and his first hours in California would have been considerably less difficult. But how could Maria have known that? Sachs said nothing to her about his plan, and beyond the brief note of thanks he put on the kitchen table when she was out shopping for dinner on the third day, he didn't even say good-bye to her. It embarrassed him to behave like that, but he knew she wouldn't let him go without some explanation, and the last thing he wanted was to tell her lies. So once she had gone out to do the shopping, he gathered his belongings together and went downstairs to the street. His luggage consisted of the bowling bag and a plastic sack (into which he had dumped his shaving equipment, his toothbrush, and the few articles of clothing that Maria had found for him). From there he walked over to West Broadway, waved down a cab, and asked the driver to take him to Kennedy Airport. Two hours later, he boarded a plane for San Francisco.

She lived in a small, pink stucco house in the Berkeley flats, a poor neighborhood of cluttered lawns and peeling façades and sidewalks sprouting with weeds. Sachs pulled up in his rented Plymouth a little past ten in the morning, but no one answered the door when he rang. This was the first time he had been in Berkeley, but rather than go off to explore the town and come back later, he parked himself on the front steps and waited for Lillian Stern to appear. The air throbbed with an uncommon sweetness. As he paged through his copy of the *San Francisco Chronicle*, he smelled the jacaranda bushes, the honeysuckle, the eucalyptus trees, the shock of California in its eternal bloom. It didn't matter to him how long he had to sit there. Talking to this woman had become the sole task of his life now, and until that happened, it was as though time had stopped for him, as though nothing could exist but the suspense of waiting. Ten minutes or ten hours, he told himself: as long as she turned up, it wasn't going to make any difference.

There was a piece in that morning's *Chronicle* about Dimaggio, and it proved to be longer and fuller than anything Sachs had read in New York. According to local sources, Dimaggio had been involved with a left-wing ecology group, a small band of men and women committed to shutting down the operations of nuclear power plants, logging companies, and other 'despoilers of the earth.' The article speculated that

Dimaggio might have been on a mission for this group at the time of his death, an accusation strenuously denied by the chairman of the Berkeley chapter of Children of the Planet, who stated that his organization was ideologically opposed to all forms of violent protest. The reporter then went on to suggest that Dimaggio could have been acting on his own initiative, a renegade member of the Children who had disagreed with the group on questions of tactics. None of this was substantiated, but it hit Sachs hard to learn that Dimaggio had been no ordinary criminal. He had been something altogether different: a crazed idealist, a believer in a cause, a person who had dreamed of changing the world. That didn't eliminate the fact that he had killed an innocent boy, but it somehow made it worse. He and Sachs had stood for the same things. In another time and another place, they might even have been friends.

Sachs spent an hour with the paper, then tossed it aside and stared out at the street. Dozens of cars drove past the house, but the only pedestrians were the very old or the very young: little children with their mothers, an ancient black man inching along with a cane, a white-haired Asian woman with an aluminum walker. At one o'clock, Sachs temporarily abandoned his post to look for something to eat, but he returned within twenty minutes and consumed his fast food lunch on the steps. He was counting on her to come by five thirty or six o'clock, hoping that she was off at work somewhere, doing her job as she always did, continuing to go through the paces of her normal routine. But that was only a guess. He didn't know that she had a job, and even if she did have one, it was by no means certain that she was still in town. If the woman had disappeared, his plan would be worthless, and yet the only way to find out was to go on sitting where he was. He suffered through the early evening hours in a tumult of anticipation, watching the clouds darken overhead as dusk turned into night. Five o'clock became six o'clock, six o'clock became seven o'clock, and from then on it was all he could do not to feel singed by disappointment. He went out for more food at seven thirty, but again he returned to the house, and again he went on waiting. She could have been at a restaurant, he told himself, or visiting friends, or doing any number of other things that would explain her absence. And if and when she did return, it was essential that he be there. Unless he talked to her before she entered the house, he might lose his chance forever.

Even so, when she finally did turn up, Sachs was caught by surprise. It was a few minutes past midnight, and because he was no longer expecting her by then, he had allowed his vigilance to slacken. He had leaned his shoulder against the cast-iron railing, his eyes had shut, and he was just on the point of dozing off when the sound of an idling car engine roused him back to alertness. He opened his eyes and saw the car standing in a parking space directly across the street. An instant later, the engine was silent and the headlights were turned off. Still unsure whether it was Lillian Stern, Sachs climbed to his feet and watched from his position on the steps – heart pounding, the blood singing in his brain.

She came toward him with a sleeping child in her arms, scarcely bothering to glance at the house as she crossed the street. Sachs heard her whisper something into her daughter's ear, but he couldn't make out what it was. He realized that he was no more than a shadow, an invisible figure hidden in the darkness, and the moment he opened his mouth to speak, the woman would be frightened half to death. He hesitated for several seconds. Then, still unable to see her face, he plunged in at last, breaking the silence when she was halfway up the front walk.

'Lillian Stern?' he said. The moment he heard his own words, he knew his voice had betrayed him. He had wanted the question to carry a certain warmth and friendliness, but it came out awkwardly, sounding tense and belligerent, as if he were planning to do her harm.

He heard a quick, shuddering gasp escape from the woman's throat. She stopped short, adjusted the child in her arms, and then answered in a low voice that seethed with anger and frustration: 'Get the fuck away from my house, mister. I'm not talking to anyone.'

'I just want a word with you,' Sachs said, beginning to descend the stairs. He waved his open hands back and forth in a gesture of negation, as if to prove he had come in peace. 'I've been waiting here since ten o'clock this morning. I've got to talk to you. It's very important.'

'No reporters. I'm not talking to any reporters.'

'I'm not a reporter. I'm a friend. You don't have to say a word to me if you don't want to. I'm only asking you to listen.'

'I don't believe you. You're just another one of those filthy pricks.'

'No, you're wrong. I'm a friend. I'm a friend of Maria Turner's. She's the one who gave me your address.'

'Maria?' the woman said. There was a sudden, unmistakable softening in her voice. 'You know Maria?'

'I know her very well. If you don't believe me, you can go inside and call her. I'll wait out here until you're finished.'

He had reached the bottom of the stairs, and once again the woman was walking toward him, as if freed to move now that Maria's name had been mentioned. They were standing on the flagstone path within two feet of each other, and for the first time since her arrival, Sachs was able to make out her features. He saw the same extraordinary face he had seen in the photographs at Maria's house, the same dark eyes, the same neck, the same short hair, the same full lips. He was nearly a foot taller than she was, and as he looked down at her with the little girl's head resting against her shoulder, he realized that in spite of the pictures, he hadn't expected her to be so beautiful.

'Who the hell are you?' she said.

'My name is Benjamin Sachs.'

'And what do you want from me, Benjamin Sachs? What are you doing here in front of my house in the middle of the night?'

'Maria's tried to get in touch. She called you for days, and when she couldn't get through, I decided to come out here instead.'

'All the way from New York?'

'There wasn't any other choice.'

'And why would you want to do that?'

'Because I have something important to tell you.'

'I don't like the way that sounds. The last thing I need is more bad news.'

'This isn't bad news. Strange news, maybe, even incredible news, but it's definitely not bad. As far as you're concerned, it's very good. Astounding, in fact. Your whole life's about to take a turn for the better.'

'You're awfully sure of yourself, aren't you?'

'Only because I know what I'm talking about.'

'And this can't wait until morning?'

'No. I've got to talk to you now. Just give me half an hour, and then I'll leave you alone. I promise.'

Without saying another word, Lillian Stern removed a set of keys from her coat pocket, walked up the steps, and opened the door to the house. Sachs followed her across the threshold and entered the darkened hallway. Nothing was taking place as he had imagined it would, and even after the light went on, even after he watched her carry her daughter upstairs to bed, he wondered how he was going to find the courage to talk to her, to tell her what he had come three thousand miles to tell.

He heard her close the door of her daughter's bedroom, but instead of coming downstairs, she went into another room and used the phone. He distinctly heard her dial a number, but then, just as she spoke Maria's name, the door slammed shut and the ensuing conversation was lost to him. Lillian's voice filtered down through the ceiling as a wordless rumble, an erratic hum of sighs and pauses and muffled bursts. Desperate as he was to know what she was saying, his ears weren't sharp enough, and he abandoned the effort after one or two minutes. The longer the conversation continued, the more nervous he became. Not knowing what else to do, he left his spot at the bottom of the stairs and began wandering in and out of the ground-floor rooms. There were just three of them, and each one was in woeful disarray. Dirty dishes were piled high in the kitchen sink; the living room was a chaos of scattered pillows, overturned chairs, and brimming ashtrays; the dining room table had collapsed. One by one, Sachs switched on the lights and then switched them off. It was a mean place, he discovered, a house of unhappiness and troubled thoughts, and it stunned him just to look at it.

The phone conversation lasted another fifteen or twenty minutes. By the time he heard Lillian hang up, Sachs was in the hall again, waiting for her at the bottom of the stairs. She came down looking grim-faced and sullen, and from the faint trembling he detected in her lower lip, he gathered that she had been crying. The coat she had been wearing earlier was gone, and her dress had been replaced by a pair of black jeans and a white T-shirt. Her feet were bare, he noted, and her toenails were painted a vivid red. Even though he was looking straight at her the whole time, she refused to return his glance as she descended the stairs. When she reached the bottom, he moved aside to let her pass, and it was only then, when she was halfway to the kitchen, that she stopped and turned to him, addressing him from over her left shoulder.

'Maria says hello,' she said. 'She also says that she doesn't understand what you're doing here.'

Without waiting for a response, she continued on into the kitchen. Sachs couldn't tell if she wanted him to follow her or stay where he was, but he decided to go in anyway. She flicked on the overhead light, groaned softly to herself when she saw the state of the room, and then turned her back on him and opened a cupboard. She took out a bottle of Johnnie Walker, found an empty glass in another cupboard, and poured herself a drink. It would have been impossible not to see the hostility buried in that gesture. She neither offered him a drink nor asked him to sit down, and all of a sudden Sachs realized that he was in danger of losing control of the situation. It had been his show, after all, and now here he was with her, inexplicably reeling and tongue-tied, unsure of how to begin.

She took a sip of her drink and eyed him from across the room. 'Maria says she doesn't understand what you're doing here,' she repeated. Her voice was husky and without expression, and yet the very flatness of it conveyed scorn, a scorn verging on contempt.

'No,' Sachs said, 'I don't imagine she does.'

'If you have something to tell me, you'd better tell it to me now. And then I want you on your way. Do you understand that? On your way and out of here.'

'I'm not going to cause any trouble.'

'There's nothing to stop me from calling the police, you know. All I have to do is pick up the phone, and your life goes straight down the toilet. I mean, what fucking planet were you born on anyway? You shoot my husband, and then you come out here and expect me to be nice to you?'

'I didn't shoot him. I've never held a gun in my life.'

'I don't care what you did. It's got nothing to do with me.'

'Of course it does. It has everything to do with you. It has everything to do with both of us.'

'You want me to forgive you, don't you? That's why you came. To fall on your knees and beg my forgiveness. Well, I'm not interested. It's not my job to forgive people. That's not my line of work.'

'Your little girl's father is dead, and you're telling me you don't care?'

'I'm telling you it's none of your business.'

'Didn't Maria mention the money?'

'The money?'

'She told you, didn't she?'

'I don't know what you're talking about.'

'I have money for you. That's why I'm here. To give you the money.'

'I don't want your money. I don't want a goddamned thing from you. I just want you to get out.'

'You're turning me down before you've heard what I have to say.'

'Because I don't trust you. You're after something, and I don't know what it is. No one gives away money for nothing.'

'You don't know me, Lillian. You don't have the slightest idea of what I'm about.'

'I've learned enough. I've learned enough to know that I don't like you.'

'I didn't come here to be liked. I came here to help you, that's all, and what you think of me is unimportant.'

'You're crazy, do you know that? You talk just like a crazy man.'

'The only crazy thing would be for you to deny what's happened. I've taken something from you, and now I'm here to give you something back. It's that simple. I didn't choose you. Circumstances gave you to me, and now I've got to make good on my end of the bargain.'

'You're beginning to sound like Reed. A fast-talking son of a bitch, all puffed up with your stupid arguments and theories. But it won't wash, professor. There is no bargain. It's all in your head, and I don't owe you a thing.'

'That's just it. You don't. I'm the one who owes you.'

'Bullshit.'

'If my reasons don't interest you, then don't think about my reasons. But take the money. If not for yourself, then at least for your little girl. I'm not asking you for anything. I just want you to have it.'

'And then what?'

'Then nothing.'

'I'll be in your debt, won't I? That's what you'll want me to think. Once I take your money, you'll feel that you own me.'

'Own you?' Sachs said, suddenly giving in to his exasperation. 'Own you? I don't even *like* you. From the way you've acted with me tonight, the less I have to do with you the better.'

At that moment, without the least hint of what was coming, Lillian started to smile. It was a spontaneous interruption, a wholly involuntary response to the war of nerves that had been building between them. Even though it lasted no more than a second or two, Sachs was encouraged. Something had been communicated, he felt, some little connection had been established, and even though he couldn't say what that thing was, he sensed that the mood had shifted.

He didn't waste any time after that. Seizing on the opportunity that had just presented itself, he told her to stay where she was, left the room, and then walked outside to fetch the money from the car. There was no point in trying to explain himself to her. The moment had come to offer proof, to eliminate the abstractions and let the money talk for itself. That was the only way to make her believe him: to let her touch it, to let her see it with her own eyes.

But nothing was simple anymore. Now that he had unlocked the trunk of the car and was looking at the bag again, he hesitated to follow his impulse. All along, he had seen himself giving the money to her in one go: walking into her house, handing over the bag, and then walking out. It was supposed to have been a quick, dream-like gesture, an action that would take no time at all. He would swoop down like an angel of mercy and shower her with wealth, and before she realized that he was there, he would vanish. Now that he had talked to her, however, now that he had stood face to face with her in the kitchen, he saw how absurd that fairy tale was. Her animosity had frightened him and demoralized him, and he had no way to predict what would happen next. If he gave her the money all at once, he would lose whatever advantage he still had over her. Anything would be possible then, any number of grotesque reversals could follow from that error. She might humiliate him by refusing to accept it, for example. Or, even worse, she might take the money and then turn around and call the police. She had already threatened to do that, and given the depth of her anger and suspicion, he wouldn't have put it past her to betray him.

Instead of carrying the bag into the house, he counted out fifty one-hundred-dollar bills, shoved the money into his two jacket pockets, then zipped up the bag again and slammed the trunk shut. He had no idea what he was doing anymore. It was an act of pure improvisation, a blind leap into the unknown. When he turned toward the house again, he saw Lillian standing in the doorway, a small, illuminated figure with her hands on her hips, watching intently as he went about his business in the quiet street. He crossed the lawn knowing that her eyes were on him, suddenly exhilarated by his own uncertainty, by the madness of whatever terrible thing was about to happen.

When he reached the top of the steps, she moved aside to let him in and then closed the door behind him. He didn't wait for an invitation this time. Entering the kitchen before she did, he walked over to the table, pulled out one of the rickety wooden chairs, and sat down. A moment later, Lillian sat down opposite him. There were no more smiles, no more flashes of curiosity in her eyes. She had turned her face into a mask, and as he looked across at her, searching for a signal, for some clue that would help him to begin, he felt as though he were studying a wall. There was no way to get through to her, no way to penetrate what she was thinking. Neither one of them spoke. Each was waiting for the other to start, and the longer her silence went on, the more obstinately she seemed to resist him. At a certain point, understanding that he was about to choke, that a scream was beginning to gather in his lungs, Sachs lifted his right arm and calmly swept everything in front of him onto the floor. Dirty dishes, coffee cups, ashtrays, and silverware landed with a ferocious clatter, breaking and skidding across the green linoleum. He looked straight into her eyes, but she refused to respond, continuing to sit there as though nothing had happened. It was a sublime moment, he felt, a moment for the ages, and as they went on looking at each other, he almost began to tremble with happiness, with a wild happiness that came surging up from his fear. Then, not missing a beat, he pulled the two bundles of cash from his pockets, slapped them onto the table, and pushed them toward her.

'This is for you,' he said. 'It's yours if you want it.'

She glanced down at the money for a split second but made no move to touch it. 'Hundred-dollar bills,' she said. 'Or are those just the ones on top?'

'It's hundreds all the way through. Five thousand dollars' worth.'

'Five thousand dollars isn't nothing. Even rich people wouldn't sneeze at five thousand dollars. But it's not exactly the kind of money that changes anyone's life.'

'This is only the beginning. What you might call a down payment.'

'I see. And what kind of balance are you talking about?'

'A thousand dollars a day. A thousand dollars a day for as long as it lasts.'

'And how long is that?'

'A long time. Long enough for you to pay off your debts and quit your job. Long enough to move away from here. Long enough to buy yourself a new car and a new wardrobe. And once you've done all that, you'll still have more than you know what to do with.'

'And what are you supposed to be, my fairy godmother?'

'Just a man paying off a debt, that's all.'

'And what if I told you I didn't like the arrangement? What if I said I'd rather have the money all at once?'

'That was the original plan, but things changed after I got here. We're on to Plan B now.'

'I thought you were trying to be nice to me.'

'I am. But I want you to be nice to me, too. If we do it this way, there's a better chance of keeping things in balance.'

'You're saying you don't trust me, is that it?'

'Your attitude makes me a little nervous. I'm sure you can understand that.'

'And what happens while you're giving me these daily installments? Do you show up every morning at an appointed hour, hand over the money, and then split, or are you thinking about staying for breakfast, too?'

'I told you before: I don't want anything from you. You get the money free and clear, and you don't owe me a thing.'

'Yeah, well, just so we've got it straight, wiseguy. I don't know what Maria told you about me, but my pussy's not for sale. Not for any amount of money. Do you understand that? Nobody forces me into bed. I fuck who I want to fuck, and fairy godmother keeps her wand to herself. Am I making myself clear?'

'You're telling me I'm not in your plans. And I've just finished telling you you're not in mine. I don't see how it could be any clearer than that.'

'Good. Now give me some time to think about all this. I'm dead tired, and I've got to go to sleep.'

'You don't have to think. You know the answer already.'

'Maybe I do, maybe I don't. But I'm not going to talk about it anymore tonight. It's been a rough day, and I'm about to fall over. But just to show you how nice I can be, I'm going to let you sleep on the couch in the living room. For Maria's sake – just this once. It's the middle of the night, and you'll never find a motel if you start looking now.'

'You don't have to do that.'

'I don't have to do anything, but that doesn't mean I can't do it. If you want to stay, then stay. If you don't, then don't. But you'd better decide now, because I'm going up to bed.'

'Thank you, I appreciate it.'

'Don't thank me, thank Maria. The living room's a mess. If something's in your way, just shove it onto the floor. You've already shown me you know how to do that.'

'I don't usually go in for such primitive forms of communication.'

'As long as you don't do any more communicating with me tonight, I don't care what happens down here. But upstairs is off limits. Capeesh? There's a gun in my bedside table, and if anyone comes prowling around, I know how to use it.'

'That would be like killing the goose who laid the golden egg.'

'No it wouldn't. You might be the goose, but the eggs are somewhere else. All snug in the trunk of your car, remember? Even if the goose got killed, I'd still have all the eggs I needed.'

'So we're back to making threats, are we?'

'I don't believe in threats. I'm just asking you to be nice to me, that's all. To be very nice. And not to get any funny ideas into your head about who I am. If you don't, then we might be able to do business together. I'm not making any promises, but if you don't screw up, I might even learn to stop hating you.'

He was woken the next morning by a warm breath fluttering against his cheek. When he opened his eyes, he found himself looking into the face of a child, a little girl frozen in concentration, exhaling tremulously through her mouth. She was on her knees beside the sofa, and her head was so close to his that their lips were almost touching. From the dimness of the light filtering through her hair, Sachs gathered that it was only six thirty or seven o'clock. He had been asleep for less than four hours, and in those first moments after he opened his eyes, he felt too groggy to move, too leaden to stir a muscle. He wanted to close his eyes again, but the little girl was watching him too intently, and so he went on staring into her face, gradually coming to the realization that this was Lillian Stern's daughter.

'Good morning,' she said at last, responding to his smile as an invitation to talk. 'I thought you'd never wake up.'

'Have you been sitting here long?'

'About a hundred years, I think. I came downstairs to look for my doll, and then I saw you sleeping on the couch. You're a very long man, did you know that?'

'Yes, I know that. I'm what you call a beanpole.'

'Mr Beanpole,' the girl said thoughtfully. 'That's a good name.'

'And I'll bet that your name is Maria, isn't it?'

'To some people it is, but I like to call myself Rapunzel. It's much prettier, don't you think?'

'Much prettier. And how old are you, Miss Rapunzel?'

'Five and three-quarters.'

'Ah, five and three-quarters. An excellent age.'

'I'll be six in December. My birthday is the day after Christmas.'

'That means you get presents two days in a row. You must be a clever girl to have worked out a system like that.'

'Some people have all the luck. That's what Mommy says.'

'If you're five and three-quarters, then you've probably started school, haven't you?'

'Kindergarten. I'm in Mrs Weir's class. Room one-oh-four. The kids call her Mrs Weird.'

'Does she look like a witch?'

'Not really. I don't think she's old enough to be a witch. But she does have an awfully long nose.'

'And shouldn't you be getting ready to go to kindergarten now? You don't want to be late.'

'Not today, silly. There's no school on Saturday.'

'Of course. I'm such a dingbat sometimes, I don't even know what day it is.'

He was awake by then, awake enough to feel the urge to stand up. He asked the girl if she was interested in eating breakfast, and when she answered that she was starving, he promptly rolled off the couch and put on his shoes, pleased to have this little job in front of him. They took turns using the downstairs bathroom, and once Sachs had emptied his bladder and splashed some water on his face, he moved on into the kitchen to begin. The first thing he saw there was the five thousand dollars – still sitting on the table, in the same spot where he had put it the night before. It puzzled him that Lillian hadn't taken it upstairs with her. Was there a hidden meaning to this, he wondered, or was it simply the result of negligence on her part? Fortunately, Maria was still in the bathroom then, and by the time she joined him in the kitchen, he had already removed the cash from the table and stored it on a shelf in one of the cupboards.

The breakfast got off to a shaky start. The milk in the refrigerator had turned sour (which eliminated the possibility of cereal), and since the stock of eggs seemed to have been exhausted as well, he was unable to make French toast or an omelet (her second and third choices). He managed to find a package of sliced whole wheat bread, however, and once he had discarded the top four pieces (which were covered with a fuzzy, bluish mold), they settled on a meal of toast and strawberry jam. While the bread was warming in the toaster, Sachs unearthed a snow-encrusted can of frozen orange juice from the back of the freezer, mixed it up in a plastic pitcher (which first had to be washed), and served it along with the food. No true coffee was on hand, but after a thorough search of the cupboards, he finally discovered a jar of decaffeinated instant. As he drank down the bitter concoction, he made funny faces and clutched at his throat. Maria laughed at the performance, which inspired him to stagger around the room and emit a series of dreadful gagging noises. 'Poison,' he whispered, as he sank slowly to the floor, 'the scoundrels have poisoned me.' This made her laugh even harder, but once the stunt was over and he sat down in his chair again, her amusement quickly faded, and he noticed a troubled look in her eyes.

'I was only pretending,' he said.

'I know,' she said. 'It's just that I don't like people to die.'

He understood his mistake then, but it was too late to undo the damage. 'I'm not going to die,' he said.

'Yes you will. Everybody has to die.'

'I mean not today. And not tomorrow either. I'm going to be around for a long time to come.'

'Is that why you slept on the sofa? Because you're going to live with us now?'

'I don't think so. But I'm here to be your friend. And your mother's friend, too.'

'Are you Mommy's new man?'

'No, I'm just her friend. If she lets me, I'm going to help her out.'

'That's good. She needs somebody to help her out. They're putting Daddy in the ground today, and she's very sad.'

'Is that what she told you?'

'No, but I saw her crying. That's how I know she's sad.'

'Is that where you're going today? To watch them put your daddy in the ground?'

'No, they won't let us. Grandma and Grandpa said we couldn't.'

'And where do your Grandma and Grandpa live? Here in California?'

'I don't think so. It's somewhere far away. You have to take a plane to get there.'

'Somewhere back East, maybe.'

'It's called Maplewood. I don't know where it is.'

'Maplewood, New Jersey?'

'I don't know. It's very far away. Whenever Daddy talked about it, he said it was the end of the world.'

'It makes you sad when you think about your father, doesn't it?'

'I can't help it. Mommy said he didn't love us anymore, but I don't care. I wish he would come back.'

'I'm sure he wanted to.'

'That's what I think. But he wasn't able to, that's all. He had an accident, and instead of coming back to us, he had to go to heaven.'

She was so small, Sachs thought, and yet she handled herself with almost frightening composure, her fierce little eyes boring steadily into him as she spoke – unflinching, without the slightest tremor of confusion. It astonished him that she could mimic the ways of adults so well, that she could appear so self-possessed when in fact she knew nothing, knew absolutely nothing at all. He pitied her for her courage, for the sham heroism of her bright and earnest face, and he wished he could take back everything he had said and turn her into a child again, something other than this pathetic, miniaturized grown-up with her missing teeth and the yellow-ribboned barrette dangling from her curly hair.

As they polished off the last fragments of their toast, Sachs saw by the kitchen clock that it was only a few minutes past seven thirty. He asked Maria how long she thought her mother would go on sleeping, and when she said it could be another two or three hours, an idea suddenly occurred to him. Let's plan a surprise for her, he said. If we get busy now, we might be able to clean the whole downstairs before she wakes up. Wouldn't that be nice? She'll come down here and find everything all neat and sparkling. That's bound to make her feel better, don't you think? The little girl thought so. More than that, she seemed excited by the prospect, as if she were relieved that someone had finally stepped in to take charge of the situation. But we must be quiet, Sachs said, putting his finger to his lips. As quiet as elves.

So the two of them set to work, moving about the kitchen in brisk and silent harmony as the table was cleared, the broken crockery was swept up from the floor, and the sink was filled with warm suds. In order to keep the clamor to a minimum, they scraped the dishes with their bare fingers, smearing their hands with garbage as they dumped uneaten food and crushed cigarettes into a paper bag. It was foul work, and they registered their disgust by sticking out their tongues and pretending to vomit. Still, Maria more than kept up her end, and once the kitchen was in passable shape, she marched out to the living room with undiminished enthusiasm, eager to push on with the next task. It was getting close to nine o'clock by then, and sunlight was pouring in through the front windows, illuminating slender trails of dust in the air. As they surveyed the mess before them, discussing how they should best attack it, a look of apprehension swept across Maria's face. Without saying a word, she lifted her arm and pointed to one of the windows. Sachs turned, and an instant later he saw it too: a man standing on the lawn and looking up at the house. He was wearing a checkered tie and a brown corduroy jacket, a youngish man with prematurely thinning hair who looked as though he were debating whether to walk up the steps and ring the bell. Sachs patted Maria on the head and told her to go back to the kitchen and pour herself another glass of juice. She seemed as if she were about to balk, but then, not wanting to disappoint him, she nodded her head and reluctantly did as she was told. Sachs then picked his way through the living room to the front door, pulled it open as softly as he could, and stepped outside.

'Is there something I can do for you?' he said.

'Tom Mueller,' the man said. '*San Francisco Chronicle*. I wonder if I could have a word with Mrs Dimaggio.'

'Sorry. She's not giving any interviews.'

'I don't want an interview, I just want to talk to her. My paper is interested in hearing her side of the story. We're willing to pay for an exclusive article.'

'Sorry, no dice. Mrs Dimaggio isn't talking to anyone.'

'Don't you think the lady should have a chance to turn me down herself?'

'No, I don't think so.'

'And who are you, Mrs Dimaggio's press agent?'

'A friend of the family.'

'I see. And you're the one who does her talking for her.'

'That's right. I'm here to protect her from guys like you. Now that we've settled that question, I think it's time for you to leave.'

'And how would you suggest that I get in touch with her?'

'You could write her a letter. That's how it's generally done.'

'A good idea. I'll write her a letter, and then you can throw it away before she reads it.'

'Life is filled with disappointments, Mr Mueller. And now if you don't mind, I think it's time for you to be on your way. I'm sure you don't want me to call the police. But you are standing on Mrs Dimaggio's property, you know.'

'Yeah, I know. Thanks a lot, pal. You've been a tremendous help.'

'Don't feel too bad. This too shall pass. In another week's time, there won't be a person in San Francisco who can remember what this story was about. If someone mentions Dimaggio to them, the only person they'll think of is Joe.'

That ended the conversation, but even after Mueller had left the yard, Sachs went on standing in front of the door, determined not to move until he had seen the man drive away. The reporter crossed the street, climbed into his car, and started the engine. As a farewell gesture, he raised the middle finger of his right hand as he drove by the house, but Sachs shrugged off the obscenity, understanding that it was unimportant, that it merely proved how well he had handled the confrontation. As he turned to go back inside, he couldn't help smiling at the man's anger. He didn't feel like a press agent so much as a town marshal, and when all was said and done, it wasn't an entirely unpleasant feeling.

The moment he entered the house again, he looked up and saw Lillian standing at the top of the stairs. She was dressed in a white terry-cloth robe, looking puffy-eyed and tousled, struggling to shake the sleep out of her system.

'I suppose I should thank you for that,' she said, running a hand through her short hair.

'Thank me for what?' Sachs said, feigning ignorance.

'For getting rid of that guy. You were very smooth about it. I was impressed.'

'That? Aw shucks. T'weren't nothin', ma'am. Just doin' my job, that's all. Just doin' my job.'

She smiled briefly at his dumb hick's twang. 'If that's the job you want, then you can have it. You're a lot better at it than I am.'

'I told you I'm not all bad,' he said, speaking in his normal voice again. 'If you give me a chance, I might even turn out to be useful.'

Before Lillian could answer this last remark, Maria came running into the hallway. Lillian shifted her eyes away from Sachs and said, 'Hi, baby. You were up early, weren't you?'

'You'll never guess what we've been doing,' the little girl said. 'You won't believe your eyes, Mommy.'

'I'll be down in a few minutes. I have to take a shower first and then put on some clothes. Remember, we're going to Billie and Dot's house today, and we don't want to be late.'

She disappeared upstairs again, and in the thirty or forty minutes it took her to get ready, Sachs and Maria resumed their assault on the living room. They rescued pillows and cushions from the floor, tossed out newspapers and coffee-soaked magazines, vacuumed up cigarette ashes from the interstices of the woolen rug. The more areas they were able to clear (progressively giving themselves more space to move in), the faster they were able to work, until, at the very end, they began to resemble two speeded-up characters in an old film.

It would have been hard for Lillian not to notice the difference, but once she came downstairs, she responded with less enthusiasm than Sachs had thought she would – if only for Maria's sake. 'Nice,' she said, pausing briefly on the threshold and nodding her head, 'very nice. I should remember to sleep late more often.' She smiled, she made her small show of gratitude, and then, scarcely bothering to glance around her, she strode on into the kitchen to look for something to eat.

Sachs felt minimally assuaged by the kiss she planted on her daughter's forehead, but once Maria had been shooed upstairs to change her clothes, he didn't know what to do with himself anymore. Lillian paid only the scantest attention to him, moving about the kitchen in her own private world, and so he clung to his spot in the doorway, standing there in silence as she dug out a bag of real coffee from the freezer (which he had managed to overlook) and placed a kettle of water on the stove to boil. She was dressed in casual clothes – dark slacks, white turtleneck, flat shoes – but she had put on lipstick and eye-shadow, and there was an unmistakable smell of perfume in the air. Again, Sachs had no idea how to interpret what was going on. Her behavior was unfathomable to him – one moment friendly, one moment closed off, one moment alert, one moment distracted – and the more he tried to make sense of it, the less he understood.

Eventually, she invited him in for a cup of coffee, but even then she barely spoke, continuing to act as if she wasn't sure whether she wanted him to be there or to vanish. For want of anything else to say, he started talking about the five thousand dollars he'd found on the table that morning, opening up the cupboard and pointing to where he had stored the cash. It didn't seem to make much of an impression on her. 'Oh,' she said, nodding at the sight of the money, and then she turned and gazed out the window into the backyard, drinking her coffee in silence. Undaunted, Sachs put down his cup and announced that he was going to give her that day's installment. Without waiting for an answer, he went outside to his car and collected the money from the bowling bag in the trunk. When he returned to the kitchen three or four minutes later, she was still standing in the same position, staring out the window with one hand on her hip, following some secret train of thought. He walked right up to her, flapped the thousand dollars in her face, and asked her where he should put it. Wherever you like, she said. Her passivity was beginning to unnerve him, and so rather than place the money on the counter, Sachs went over to the refrigerator, opened the top door, and tossed the bills into the freezer. This produced the desired result. She turned on him with a puzzled look on her face and asked him why he had done that. Instead of answering her, he walked back to the cupboard, removed the original five thousand dollars from the shelf, and put that bundle in the freezer as well. Then, patting the freezer door, he turned to her and said: 'Frozen assets. Since you won't tell me if you want the money or not, we'll just put your future on ice. Not bad, huh? We'll bury your nest egg in the snow, and when spring comes and the ground starts to thaw, you'll look in here and discover that you're rich.'

A vague smile began to form at the corners of her mouth, signaling that she had weakened, that he had managed to draw her into the game. She took another sip of coffee, buying herself a little time as she prepared her comeback. 'It doesn't sound like such a good investment to me,' she finally said. 'If the money just sits there, it won't collect any interest, will it?'

'I'm afraid not. There's no interest until you start to get interested. After that, the sky's the limit.'

'I haven't said I'm not interested.'

'True. But you haven't said you are, either.'

'As long as I don't say no, it could be I'm saying yes.'

'Or it could be you aren't saying anything. That's why we shouldn't talk about it anymore. Until you know what you want to do, we'll keep our mouths shut, okay? We'll just pretend it isn't happening.'

'That's fine with me.'

'Good. In other words, the less said the better.'

'We won't say a word. And one day I'll open my eyes, and you won't be there anymore.'

'Exactly. The genie will crawl back into his bottle, and you'll never have to think about him again.'

His strategy seemed to have worked, but other than causing a general change in the mood, it was difficult to know what this conversation had accomplished. When Maria came bouncing into the kitchen a few moments later, decked out in a pink-and-white jumper and patent-leather shoes, he discovered that it had accomplished a great deal. Breathless and excited, she asked her mother if Sachs was going with them to Billie and Dot's house. Lillian said no, he wasn't, and Sachs was about to take that as his cue to drive off and look for a motel when Lillian added that he was nevertheless welcome to stay, that since she and Maria would be gone until late that night, there was no rush for him to leave the house. He could shower and shave if he wanted to, she said, and as long as he shut the door firmly behind him and made sure it was locked, it didn't matter when he left. Sachs hardly knew how to respond to this offer. Before he could think of anything to say, Lillian had coaxed Maria into the downstairs bathroom to brush her hair, and by the time they came out again, it was somehow a foregone conclusion that they would be going before he did. All this struck Sachs as remarkable, a turnaround that defied understanding. But there it was, and the last thing he wanted to do was object. Less than five minutes later, Lillian and Maria were walking out the front door, and less than a minute after that, they were gone, driving down the street in their dusty blue Honda and vanishing into the bright, midmorning sun.

He spent close to an hour in the upstairs bathroom – first soaking in the tub, then shaving in front of the mirror. It was altogether odd to be there, he found, lying naked in the water as he stared up at Lillian's things: the endless jars of creams and lotions, the lipstick containers and eye-liner bottles, the soaps and nail polishes and perfumes. There was a forced intimacy to it that both excited him and repulsed him. He had been allowed into her secret realm, the place where she enacted her most private rituals, and yet even here, sitting in the heart of her kingdom, he was no closer to her than he had been before. He could sniff and delve and touch all he liked. He could wash his hair with her shampoo, he could shave his beard with her razor, he could brush his teeth with her toothbrush – and yet the fact that she had let him do those things only proved how little they meant to her.

Still, the bath relaxed him, made him feel almost drowsy, and for several minutes he wandered in and out of the upstairs rooms, absent-mindedly drying his hair with a towel. There were three small bedrooms on the second floor. One of them was Maria's, another belonged to Lillian, and the third, scarcely bigger than a large closet, had once evidently served as Dimaggio's study or office. It was furnished with a desk and bookcase, but so much junk had been squeezed into its narrow confines (cardboard boxes, piles of old clothes and toys, a black-and-white television set) that Sachs did no more than poke his head in there before shutting the door again. He went into Maria's room next, browsing among her dolls and books, the nursery school photos on the wall, the board games and stuffed animals. Disordered as the room was, it turned out to be in better shape than Lillian's. That was the capital of mess, the headquarters of catastrophe. He took note of the unmade bed, the clumps of discarded clothes and underwear, the portable television crowned with two lipstick-stained coffee cups, the books and magazines scattered on the floor. Sachs scanned a few of the titles at his feet (an illustrated guide to Oriental massage, a study of reincarnation, a couple of paperback detective novels, a biography of Louise Brooks) and wondered if any conclusions could be drawn from this assortment. Then, almost in a trance, he began to pull open the drawers of the bureau and look through Lillian's clothes, examining her panties and bras, her stockings and slips, holding each article in his hand for a moment before moving on to the next one. After doing the same with the things in the closet, he turned his attention to the bedside tables, suddenly remembering the threat she had made the night before. After looking on both sides of the bed, however, he concluded that she had been lying. There was no gun anywhere to be found.

Lillian had disconnected the phone, and the instant he plugged it back into the wall, it started to ring. The sound made him jump, but rather than lift the receiver off the hook, he sat down on the bed and waited for the caller to give up. The phone rang another eighteen or twenty times. As soon as it stopped, Sachs grabbed the receiver and dialed Maria Turner's number in New York. Now that she had talked to Lillian, he couldn't put it off any longer. It wasn't just a matter of clearing the air between them, it was a matter of clearing his own conscience. If nothing else, he owed her an explanation, an apology for having run out on her in the way he did.

He knew that she would be angry, but he wasn't prepared for the barrage of insults that followed. The moment she heard his voice, she started calling him names: idiot, bastard, double-crosser. He had never heard her talk like that before – not to anyone, not under any circumstances – and her fury became so large, so monumental, that several minutes passed before she allowed him to speak. Sachs was mortified. As he sat there listening to her, he finally understood what he had been too stupid to recognize in New York. Maria had fallen for him, and beyond all the obvious reasons for her attack (the suddenness of his departure, the affront of his ingratitude), she was talking to him like a jilted lover, like a woman who had been spurned for someone else. To make matters worse, she imagined that that someone else had once been her closest friend. Sachs struggled to disabuse her of this notion. He had gone to California for his own private reasons, he said, Lillian meant nothing to him, this wasn't what she thought it was, and so on – but he made a clumsy job of it, and Maria accused him of lying. The conversation was in danger of turning ugly, but Sachs somehow managed to resist answering her, and in the end Maria's pride won out over her anger, which meant that she no longer had the will to keep insulting him. She started to laugh at him instead, or perhaps laugh at herself, and then, without any perceptible transition, the laughter changed to tears, a fit of awful sobbing that made him feel every bit as wretched as she did. It took some time before the storm passed, but after that they were able to talk. Not that the talk led them anywhere, but at least the rancor was gone. Maria wanted him to call Fanny – just to let her know that he was alive – but Sachs wouldn't do it. Contacting her would be risky, he said. Once they started to talk, he was bound to tell her about Dimaggio, and he didn't want to implicate her in any of his troubles. The less she knew, the safer she would be, and why drag her into it when it wasn't necessary? Because it was the right thing to do, Maria said. Sachs went through his argument all over again, and for the next half hour they continued to talk in circles, with neither one of them able to convince the other. There was no right and wrong anymore, only opinions and theories and interpretations, a swamp of conflicting words. For all the difference it made, they could just as well have kept those words to themselves.

'It's no use,' Maria finally said. 'I'm not getting through to you, am I?'

'I hear you,' Sachs answered. 'It's just that I don't agree with what you're saying.'

'You're only going to make things worse for yourself, Ben. The longer you keep it to yourself, the harder it's going to be when you have to talk.'

'I'm never going to have to talk.'

'You can't know that. They might find you, and then you won't have any choice.'

'They're never going to find me. The only way that could happen is if someone tips them off, and you wouldn't do that to me. At least I don't think you would. I can trust you that far, can't I?'

'You can trust me. But I'm not the only person who knows. Lillian's in on it now, too, and I'm not sure she's as good at keeping promises as I am.'

'She wouldn't talk. It wouldn't make sense for her to talk. She'd stand to lose too much.'

'Don't count on sense when you're dealing with Lillian. She doesn't think the way you do. She doesn't play by your rules. If you haven't figured that out yet, you're only asking for trouble.'

'Trouble's all I've got anyway. A little more won't hurt me.'

'Clear out now, Ben. I don't care where you go or what you do, but get into your car and drive away from that house. Right now, before Lillian comes back.'

'I can't do that. I've already started this thing, and I have to see it through to the end. There's no other way. This is my chance, and I can't blow it by being scared.'

'You'll be in over your head.'

'That's where I am now. The whole point of this is to get out from under.'

'There are simpler ways.'

'Not for me there aren't.'

There was a long pause on the other end, an intake of breath, another pause. When Maria spoke again, her voice was trembling. 'I'm trying to decide if I should pity you or just open my mouth and scream.'

'You don't have to do either one.'

'No, I don't suppose I do. I can forget all about you, can't I? There's always that option.'

'You can do whatever you want, Maria.'

'Right. And if you want to go off the deep end, that's your business. But just remember that I told you so. Okay? Just remember that I tried to talk to you like a friend.'

He was badly shaken after they hung up. Maria's last words had been a kind of farewell, a declaration that she was no longer with him. It didn't matter what had led to the disagreement: whether it had been provoked by jealousy or honest concern or a combination of the two. The result was that he wouldn't be able to turn to her anymore. Even if she hadn't meant for him to think that, even if she would welcome hearing from him again, the conversation had left behind too many clouds, too many uncertainties. How could he look to her for support when the very act of talking to him would cause her pain? He hadn't intended to go that far, but now that the words had been spoken, he understood that he had lost his best ally, the one person he could have counted on for help. He had been in California for just over a day, and already his bridges were burning behind him.

He could have repaired the damage by calling her back, but he didn't do it. Instead, he returned to the bathroom and put on his clothes, brushed his hair with Lillian's brush, and spent the next eight and a half hours cleaning the house. Every now and then he would pause for a snack, scavenging the refrigerator and kitchen cupboards for something edible (canned soup, liverwurst, cocktail nuts), but other than that he stuck with it, working without interruption until past nine o'clock. His goal was to make the house spotless, to turn it into a model of domestic order and tranquility. There was nothing he could do about the tattered furniture, of course, or the cracked ceilings in the bedrooms, or the rusted enamel in the sinks, but at least he could make the place clean. Tackling one room at a time, he scrubbed and dusted and scoured and rearranged, progressing methodically from the back to the front, from the first floor to the second, from large messes to small. He washed out toilets, he reorganized the silverware, he folded and put away clothes, he collected Lego pieces, miniature tea-set utensils, the amputated limbs of plastic dolls. Last of all, he repaired the legs of the dining-room table, fastening them back into position with an assortment of nails and screws he found at the bottom of a kitchen drawer. The only room he didn't touch was Dimaggio's study. He was reluctant to open the door again, but even if he had wanted to go in there, he wouldn't have known what to do with all the debris. Time was running short by then, and he wouldn't have been able to finish the job.

He knew that he should be going. Lillian had made it clear that she wanted him out of the house before she returned, but instead of driving off to look for a motel, he went back to the living room, slid out of his shoes, and lay down on the sofa. He only wanted to rest for a few minutes. He was tired from the work he had done, and there didn't seem to be any harm in lingering. By ten o'clock, however, he still hadn't made a move for the front door. He knew that crossing Lillian could be dangerous, but the thought of going out into the night filled him with dread. The house felt safe to him, safer than anywhere else, and even if he had no right to take this liberty, he suspected that it might not be such a bad thing for her to walk in and find him there. She would be shocked, perhaps, but at the same time an important point would be established, the one point that needed to be made above all others. She would see that he meant for there to be no getting rid of him, that he was already an inescapable fact of her life. Depending on how she responded, he would be able to judge whether she understood that or not.

His plan was to pretend to be asleep when she arrived. But Lillian came home late, long past the hour she had mentioned that morning, and by then Sachs's eyes had closed on him and he was sleeping in earnest. It was an unpardonable lapse – sprawled out on the sofa with the lights burning all around him – but in the end it didn't seem to matter. The noise of a slamming door jolted him awake at one thirty, and the first thing he saw was Lillian standing in the entranceway with Maria in her arms. Their eyes met, and for the briefest moment a smile flashed across her lips. Then, without saying a word to him, she marched up the stairs with her daughter. He assumed she would come down again after she put Maria to bed, but as with so many other assumptions he made in that house, he was wrong. He heard Lillian go into the upstairs bathroom and brush her teeth, and then, after a time, he followed the sound of her footsteps as she went into her bedroom and turned on the television. The volume was low, and the only thing he could make out was a blur of mumbling voices, a thump of music vibrating in the walls. He sat on the sofa, fully conscious now, expecting her to come down any minute and talk to him. He waited ten minutes, then twenty minutes, then half an hour, and at last the television went off. He waited another twenty minutes after that, and when she still hadn't come down by then, he understood that she had no intention of talking to him, that she had already gone to sleep for the night. It was a triumph of sorts, he felt, but now that it was over, he wasn't quite sure what to make of his victory. He turned off the lamps in the living room, stretched out on the sofa again, and then lay in the darkness with his eyes open, listening to the silence of the house.

After that, there was no more talk of moving to a motel. The living room sofa became Sachs's bed, and he started sleeping there every night. They all took this for granted, and the fact that he now belonged to the household was never so much as even mentioned. It was a natural development, a phenomenon as little worth discussing as a tree or a stone or a particle of dust in the air. That was precisely what Sachs had hoped for, and yet his role among them was never clearly defined. Everything had been set up according to some secret, unspoken understanding, and he instinctively knew that it would be a mistake to confront Lillian with questions about what she wanted of him. He had to figure it out on his own, to find a spot for himself on the strength of the smallest hints and gestures, the most inscrutable remarks and evasions. It wasn't that he was afraid of what might happen if he did the wrong thing (although he never doubted that the situation could turn on him, that she could back up her threat and call the police), but rather that he wanted his conduct to be exemplary. That was the reason he had come to California in the first place: to reinvent his life, to embody an ideal of goodness that would put him in an altogether different relation with himself. But Lillian was the instrument he had chosen, and it was only through her that this transformation could be achieved. He had thought of it as a journey, as a long voyage into the darkness of his soul, but now that he was on his way, he couldn't be sure if he was traveling in the right direction or not.

It might not have been so hard on him if Lillian had been someone else, but the strain of sleeping under the same roof with her every night kept him permanently off balance. After just two days, it appalled him to discover how desperately he wanted to touch her. The problem wasn't her beauty, he realized, but the fact that her beauty was the only part of herself she allowed him to know. If she had been less intransigent, less unwilling to engage him in a directly personal way, he would have had something else to think about, and the spell of desire might have been broken. As it was, she refused to reveal herself to him, which meant that she never became more than an object, never more than the sum of her physical self. And that physical self carried a tremendous power within it: it dazzled and assaulted, it quickened the pulse, it demolished every lofty resolve. This wasn't the kind of struggle Sachs had prepared himself for. It didn't fit into the scheme he had worked out so carefully in his head. His body had been added to the equation now, and what had once seemed simple was turned into a morass of feverish strategies and clandestine motives.

He kept all this hidden from her. Under the circumstances, his only recourse was to match her indifference with an unflappable calm, to pretend that he was perfectly happy with the way things stood between them. He affected a lighthearted manner when he was with her; he was nonchalant, friendly, accommodating; he smiled often; he never complained. Since he knew that she was already on her guard, that she already suspected him of the feelings he was now guilty of, it was particularly important that she never see him looking at her in the way he wanted to look at her. A single glance could ruin him, especially with a woman as experienced as Lillian. She had spent her whole life being stared at by men, and she would be highly sensitive to his looks, to the smallest hint of meaning in his eyes. This produced an almost unbearable tension in him whenever she was around, but he hung on bravely and never abandoned hope. He asked nothing from her, expected nothing from her, and prayed that he would eventually wear her down. That was the only weapon at his disposal, and he brought it out at every opportunity, humiliating himself before her with such purpose, such passionate self-denial, that his very weakness became a form of strength.

For the first twelve or fifteen days, she scarcely said a word to him. He had no idea what she did during her long and frequent absences from the house, and though he would have given almost anything to find out, he never dared to ask. Discretion was more important than knowledge, he felt, and rather than run the risk of offending her, he kept his curiosity to himself and waited to see what would happen. On most mornings, she would leave the house by nine or ten o'clock. Sometimes, she would return in the evening, and at other times she would stay out late, not returning until well past midnight. Sometimes, she would go out in the morning, return to the house in the evening to change her clothes, and then vanish for the rest of the night. On two or three occasions, she did not return until the following morning, at which point she would walk into the house, change her clothes, and then promptly leave again. Sachs assumed that she spent those late nights in the company of men – perhaps one man, perhaps different men – but it was impossible to know where she went during the day. It seemed likely that she had a job of some kind, but that was only a guess. For all he knew, she could have spent her time driving around in her car, or going to the movies, or standing by the water and looking at the waves.

In spite of these mysterious comings and goings, Lillian never failed to tell him when he could expect her to turn up again. This was more for Maria's sake than for his, and even if the hours she gave were only approximate ('I won't be back until late,' 'See you tomorrow morning'), it helped him to structure his own time and keep the household from falling into confusion. With Lillian gone so often, the job of looking after Maria fell almost entirely to Sachs. That was the strangest twist of all, he found, for however curt and standoffish she might have been when they were together, the fact that Lillian showed no hesitation in letting him care for her daughter proved that she already trusted him, perhaps more than she even realized herself. Sachs tried to take heart from this anomaly. He never doubted that on one level she was taking advantage of him – palming off her responsibilities on a willing dupe – but on another level the message seemed quite clear: she felt safe with him, she knew that he wasn't there to hurt her.

Maria became his companion, his consolation prize, his indelible reward. He cooked breakfast for her every morning, he walked her to school, he picked her up in the afternoon, he brushed her hair, he gave her baths, he tucked her in at night. These were pleasures he couldn't have anticipated, and as his place in her routine became more firmly entrenched, the affection between them only deepened. In the past, Lillian had relied on a woman who lived down the block to look after Maria, but amiable as Mrs Santiago was, she had a large family of her own and rarely paid much attention to Maria except when one of her children was picking on her. Two days after Sachs moved in, Maria solemnly announced that she was never going to Mrs Santiago's house again. She preferred the way he took care of her, she said, and if it didn't bother him too much, she would just as soon spend her time with him. Sachs told her he would enjoy that. They were walking down the street just then, on their way home from school, and a moment after he gave that answer, he felt her tiny hand grab hold of his thumb. They walked on in silence for half a minute, and then Maria stopped and said: 'Besides, Mrs Santiago has her own children, and you don't have any little girls or boys, do you?' Sachs had already told her that he didn't, but he shook his head to show her that her reasoning was correct. 'It's not fair that someone has too many and another person is all alone, is it?' she continued. Again, Sachs shook his head and didn't interrupt. 'I think this is good,' she said. 'You'll have me now, and Mrs Santiago will have her own children, and everyone will be happy.'

On the first Monday, he rented a mailbox at the Berkeley post office to give himself an address, returned the Plymouth to the local branch of the car agency, and bought a nine-year-old Buick Skylark for less than a thousand dollars. On Tuesday and Wednesday, he opened eleven different savings accounts at various banks around town. He was wary of depositing all the money in one place, and starting multiple accounts seemed more prudent than walking in somewhere with a bundle of over a hundred and fifty thousand dollars in cash. Besides, he would call less attention to himself when he made his daily withdrawals for Lillian. His business would be kept in permanent rotation, and that would prevent any of the tellers or bank managers from getting to know him too well. At first, he figured he would visit each bank every eleven days, but when he discovered that withdrawals of one thousand dollars required a special signature from the manager, he started going to two different banks every morning and using the automatic cash machines, which disbursed a maximum of five hundred dollars per transaction. That amounted to weekly withdrawals of just five hundred dollars from each bank, a piddling sum by any standard. It was an efficient arrangement, and in the end he much preferred slipping his plastic card into the slot and pushing buttons than having to talk to a living person.

The first few days were hard on him, however. He suspected that the money he had found in Dimaggio's car was stolen – which could have meant that the serial numbers on the bills had been circulated by computer to banks around the country. But faced with a choice between running that risk or keeping the money in the house, he had decided to run the risk. It was too early to know if Lillian could be trusted, and leaving the money under her nose would hardly be an intelligent way to find out. At each bank he went to, he kept expecting the manager to glance down at the money, excuse himself from the conversation, and return to the office with a policeman in tow. But nothing like that ever happened. The men and women who opened his accounts were exceedingly courteous. They counted his money with swift, robotlike skill; they smiled, shook his hand, and told him how happy they were to have him as a customer. As a bonus for coming in with initial deposits of over ten thousand dollars, he received five toaster-ovens, four clock radios, a portable television set, and an American flag.

By the beginning of the second week, his days had fallen into a regular pattern. After taking Maria to school, he would walk back to the house, clean up the breakfast dishes, and then drive off to the two banks on his list. Once he had completed his withdrawals (with an occasional visit to a third bank to take out money for himself), he would go to one of the espresso bars along Telegraph Avenue, settle into a quiet corner, and spend an hour drinking cappuccinos as he read through the *San Francisco Chronicle* and *The New York Times*. As it turned out, surprisingly little was reported about the case in either paper. The *Times* had stopped talking about Dimaggio's death even before Sachs's departure from New York, and except for a short follow-up interview with a captain from the Vermont State Police, nothing further was published. As for the *Chronicle*, they seemed to be tiring of the business as well. After a flurry of articles about the ecology movement and the Children of the

Planet (all of them written by Tom Mueller), Dimaggio's name was no longer mentioned. Sachs was comforted by this, but in spite of the diminishing pressure, he never went so far as to suppose it couldn't tighten again. All during his stay in California, he continued to study the papers every morning. It became his private religion, his form of daily prayer. Scan the newspapers and hold your breath. Make sure they weren't after you. Make sure you could go on living another twenty-four hours.

The rest of the morning and early afternoon were devoted to practical tasks. Like any other American housewife, he shopped for food, he cleaned, he took dirty clothes to the laundromat, he worried about buying the right brand of peanut butter for school lunches. On days when he had some time to spare, he would stop in at the local toy store before picking up Maria. He showed up at school with dolls and hair ribbons, with storybooks and crayons, with yoyos, bubble gum, and stick-on earrings. He didn't do this to bribe her. It was a simple outpouring of affection, and the better he got to know her, the more seriously he took the job of making her happy. Sachs had never spent much time with children, and it startled him to discover how much effort was involved in taking care of them. It required an enormous inner adjustment, but once he settled into the rhythm of Maria's demands, he began to welcome them, to relish the effort for its own sake. Even when she was gone, she kept him occupied. It was a remedy against loneliness, he found, a way to relieve the burden of always having to think about himself.

Every day, he put another thousand dollars in the freezer. The bills were stored in a plastic bag to protect them from moisture, and each time Sachs added a new allotment, he would check to see if any of the money had been removed. As it happened, not a single bill was ever touched. Two weeks passed, and the sum kept growing by increments of a thousand dollars a day. Sachs had no idea what to make of this detachment, this strange disregard for what he had given her. Did it mean that she wanted no part of it, that she was refusing to accept his terms? Or was she telling him that the money was unimportant, that it had nothing to do with her decision to allow him to live in her house? Both interpretations made sense, and therefore they cancelled each other out, leaving him with no way to understand what was happening in Lillian's mind, no way to decipher the facts that confronted him.

Not even his growing closeness to Maria seemed to affect her. It provoked no fits of jealousy, no smiles of encouragement, no response that he could measure. She would walk into the house while he and the little girl were curled up on the sofa reading a book, or crouched on the floor drawing pictures, or arranging a tea party for a roomful of dolls, and all Lillian would do was say hello, give her daughter a perfunctory kiss on the cheek, and then go off to her bedroom, where she would change her clothes and get ready to leave again. She was nothing more than a specter, a beautiful apparition who floated in and out of the house at irregular intervals and left no traces behind her. Sachs felt that she must have known what she was doing, that there must have been a reason for this enigmatic behavior, but none of the reasons he could think of ever satisfied him. At most, he concluded that she was putting him to a test, titillating him with this game of peekaboo to see how long he could stand it. She wanted to know if he would crack, she wanted to know if his will was as strong as hers.

Then, with no apparent cause, everything suddenly changed. Late one afternoon in the middle of the third week, Lillian walked into the house carrying a bag of groceries and announced that she was taking charge of dinner that night. She was in high spirits, full of jokes and fast, amusing patter, and the difference in her was so great, so bewildering, that the only explanation Sachs could think of was that she was on drugs. Until then, the three of them had never sat down to a meal together, but Lillian seemed not to notice what an extraordinary breakthrough this dinner represented. She pushed Sachs out of the kitchen and worked steadily for the next two hours, preparing what turned out to be a delicious concoction of vegetables and lamb. Sachs was impressed, but given everything that had preceded this performance, he wasn't quite prepared to accept it at face value. It could have been a trap, he felt, a ruse to trick him into letting down his guard, and while he wanted nothing more than to go along with her, to join in with the flow of Lillian's gaiety, he couldn't bring himself to do it. He was stiff and awkward, at a loss for words, and the blithe manner he had worked so hard to affect with her suddenly abandoned him. Lillian and Maria did most of the talking, and after a while he was scarcely more than an observer, a dour presence lurking around the edges of the party. He hated himself for acting like that, and when he refused a second glass of wine that Lillian was about to pour for him, he began to think of himself with disgust, as an out-and-out dunce. 'Don't worry,' she said as she poured the wine into his glass anyway. 'I'm not going to bite you.' 'I know that,' Sachs answered. 'It's just that I thought –' Before he could complete the sentence, Lillian interrupted him. 'Don't think so much,' she said. 'Just take the wine and enjoy it. It's good for you.'

The next day, however, it was as though none of this had happened. Lillian left the house early, did not return until the following morning, and for the rest of that week continued to make herself as scarce as possible. Sachs grew numb with confusion. Even his doubts were now subject to doubt, and little by little he could feel himself buckling under the weight of the whole terrible adventure. Perhaps he should have listened to Maria Turner, he thought. Perhaps he had no business being there and should pack his bags and get out. For several hours one night, he even toyed with the idea of turning himself in to the police. At least the agony would be over then. Instead of throwing away the money on a person who didn't want it, perhaps he should use it to hire a lawyer, perhaps he should start thinking about how to keep himself out of jail.

Then, less than an hour after thinking these thoughts, everything turned upside-down again. It was somewhere between twelve and one o'clock in the morning, and Sachs was drifting off to sleep on the living room sofa. Footsteps began to stir on the second floor. He figured that Maria was on her way to the toilet, but just as he started to drift off again, he heard the sound of someone coming down the stairs. Before he could throw off the blanket and stand up, the living room lamp was turned on, and his makeshift bed was inundated with light. He automatically covered his eyes, and when he forced them open a second later, he saw Lillian sitting in the armchair directly opposite the sofa, dressed in her terrycloth robe. 'We have to talk,' she said. He studied her face in silence as she pulled out a cigarette from the pocket of her robe and lit it with a match. The bright confidence and flagrant posing of the past weeks were gone, and even her voice sounded hesitant to him now, more vulnerable than it had ever been before. She put the matches down on the coffee table between them. Sachs followed the movement of her hand, then glanced down at the writing on the matchbook cover, momentarily distracted by the lurid green letters emblazoned against the pink background. It turned out to be an advertisement for telephone sex, and just then, in one of those unbidden flashes of insight, it occurred to him that nothing was meaningless, that everything in the world was connected to everything else.

'I've decided that I don't want you to think of me as a monster anymore,' Lillian said. Those were the words that started it, and in the next two hours she told him more about herself than in all the previous weeks combined, talking to him in a way that gradually eroded the resentments he had been harboring against her. It wasn't that she came out and apologized for anything, nor was it that he jumped to believe what she said, but little by little, in spite of his wariness and suspicion, he understood that she was no better off than he was, that he had made her just as miserable as she had made him.

It took a while, however. At first, he assumed it was all an act, yet another ploy to keep his nerves on edge. In the whirl of nonsense that stormed through him, he even managed to convince himself that she knew he was planning to run away – as if she could read his mind, as if she had entered his brain and heard him thinking those thoughts. She hadn't come downstairs to make peace with him. She had done it to soften him up, to make sure he wouldn't decamp before he had given her all the money. He was on the point of delirium by then, and if Lillian hadn't mentioned the money herself, he never would have known how badly he had misjudged her. That was the moment when the conversation turned. She started talking about the money, and what she said bore so little resemblance to what he had imagined she would say, he suddenly felt ashamed of himself, ashamed enough to start listening to her in earnest.

'You've given me close to thirty thousand dollars,' she said. 'It keeps coming in, more and more of it every day, and the more money there is, the more scared of it I feel. I don't know how long you're planning to keep this up, but thirty thousand dollars is enough. It's more than enough, and I think we should stop before things get out of hand.'

'We can't stop,' Sachs found himself saying to her. 'We've only just started.'

'I'm not sure I can take it anymore.'

'You can take it. You're the toughest person I've ever seen, Lillian. As long as you don't worry, you can take it just fine.'

'I'm not tough. I'm not tough, and I'm not good, and once you get to know me, you'll wish you'd never set foot in this house.'

'The money isn't about goodness. It's about justice, and if justice means anything, it has to be the same for everyone, whether they're good or not.'

She began to cry then, staring straight ahead at him and letting the tears run down her cheeks – without touching them, as if she didn't want to acknowledge that they were there. It was a proud sort of crying, Sachs felt, at once a baring of distress and a refusal to submit to it, and he respected her for holding onto herself as tightly as she did. As long as she ignored them, as long as she didn't wipe them away, those tears would never humiliate her.

Lillian did most of the talking after that, chain-smoking her way through a long monologue of regrets and self-recriminations. Much of it was difficult for Sachs to follow, but he didn't dare to interrupt, fearing that a wrong word or badly timed question might bring her to a halt. She rambled on for a while about a man named Frank, then talked about another man named Terry, and then, a moment later, she was going over the last years of her marriage to Dimaggio. That led to something about the police (who had apparently questioned her after Dimaggio's body was discovered), but before she had finished with that, she was telling him about her plan to move, to leave California and start over again somewhere else. She had pretty much decided to do it, she said, but then he turned up on her doorstep, and the whole thing fell apart. She couldn't think straight anymore, she didn't know if she was coming or going. He expected her to continue with that a bit longer, but then she digressed onto the topic of work, talking almost boastfully about how she had managed to fend for herself without Dimaggio. She had a license as a trained masseuse, she told him, she did some modeling for department-store catalogues, and all in all she'd kept her head above water. But then, very abruptly, she waved off the subject as if it were of no importance and started crying again.

'Everything will work out,' Sachs said. 'You'll see. All the bad things are behind you now. You just haven't realized it yet.'

It was the correct thing to say, and it ended the conversation on a positive note. Nothing had been resolved, but Lillian seemed comforted by his remark, touched by his encouragement. When she gave him a quick hug of thanks before going up to bed, he resisted the temptation to squeeze any harder than he should have. Nevertheless, it was an exquisite moment for him, a moment of true and undeniable contact. He felt her naked body under the robe, he kissed her gently on the cheek, and understood that they were back at the beginning now, that everything that had come before this moment had been erased.

The next morning, Lillian left the house when she always did, disappearing while Sachs and Maria were on their way to school. But this time there was a note in the kitchen when he returned, a brief message that seemed to support his wildest, most improbable hopes. 'Thanks for last night,' it said. 'XXX.' He liked it that she had used kiss marks instead of signing her name. Even if they had been put there with the most innocent intentions – as a reflex, as a variant on the standard salutation – the triple-X hinted at other things as well. It was the same code for sex he had seen on the matchbook cover the night before, and it excited him to imagine that she had done it on purpose, that she had substituted those marks for her name in order to plant that association in his mind.

On the strength of this note, he went ahead and did something he knew he shouldn't have done. Even as he was doing it, he understood that it was wrong, that he was beginning to lose his head, but he no longer had it in him to stop. After he finished his morning rounds, he looked up the address of the massage studio where Lillian told him she worked. It was somewhere out on Shattuck Avenue in North Berkeley, and without even bothering to call for an appointment, he climbed into his car and drove over. He wanted to surprise her, to walk in unannounced and say hello – very casually, as if they were old friends. If she happened to be free at that moment, he would ask for a massage. That would give him a legitimate excuse to be touched by her again, and even as he savored the feel of her hands along his skin, he could still his conscience with the thought that he was helping her to earn her living. I've never been massaged by a professional, he would say to her, and I just wanted to know what it felt like. He found the place without difficulty, but when he walked inside and asked the woman at the front desk for Lillian Stern, he was given a curt, glacial response. 'Lillian Stern quit on me last spring,' the woman said, 'and she hasn't shown her face in here since.'

It was the last thing he had expected, and he walked out of there feeling betrayed, scorched by the lie she had told him. Lillian didn't come home that night, and he was almost glad to be left to himself, to be spared the awkwardness of having to see her. There was nothing he could say, after all. If he mentioned where he had been that afternoon, his secret would be exposed, and that would destroy whatever chance he still had with her. In the long run, perhaps he was lucky to have been through this now rather than later. He would have to be more careful with his feelings, he told himself. No more impulsive gestures. No more flights of enthusiasm. It was a lesson he had needed to learn, and he hoped he wouldn't forget it.

But he did. And not just in due course, but the very next day. Again, it was after dark. Again, he had already put Maria to bed, and again he was camped out on the living room sofa – still awake this time, reading one of Lillian's books about reincarnation. It appalled him that she could be interested in such claptrap, and he read on with a kind of vindictive sarcasm, studying each page as though it were a testament to her stupidity, to the breathtaking shallowness of her mind. She was ignorant, he told himself, a brainless muddle of fads and half-baked notions, and how could he expect a person like that to understand him, to absorb the tenth part of what he was doing? But then, just as he was about to put down the book and turn out the light, Lillian walked through the front door, her face flushed with drink, wearing the tightest, smallest black dress he had ever seen, and he couldn't help but smile when he saw her. She was that ravishing. She was that beautiful to look at, and now that she was standing in the room with him, he couldn't turn his eyes away from her.

'Hi, kiddo,' she said. 'Did you miss me?'

'Nonstop,' he said. 'From the minute I last saw you until now.' He delivered the line with enough bravura to make it sound like a joke, a bit of facetious banter, but the truth was that he meant it.

'Good. Because I missed you, too.'

She stopped in front of the coffee table, let out a short laugh, and then spun around in a full circle, arms spread like a fashion model, pivoting deftly on her toes. 'How do you like my dress?' she asked. 'Six hundred dollars on sale. A hell of a bargain, don't you think?'

'It was worth every penny. And just the right size, too. If it was any smaller, the imagination would be out of business. You'd hardly be wearing it when you put it on.'

'That's the look. Simple and seductive.'

'I'm not so sure about simple. The other thing, yes, but definitely not simple.'

'But not vulgar.'

'No, not at all. It's too well-made for that.'

'Good. Someone told me it was vulgar, and I wanted to get your opinion before I took it off.'

'You mean the fashion show is over?'

'All over. It's getting late, and you can't expect an old broad like me to stand on her feet all night.'

'Too bad. Just when I was beginning to enjoy it.'

'You're kind of thick sometimes, aren't you?'

'Probably. I'm often good at complicated things. But simple things tend to confuse me.'

'Like taking off a dress, I suppose. If you drag it out much longer, I'm going to have to take it off myself. And that wouldn't be so good, would it?'

'No, not so good. Especially since it doesn't look very hard. No buttons or snaps to fiddle with, no zippers to snag. Just pull from the bottom and slide it off.'

'Or start from the top and work your way down. The choice is yours, Mr Sachs.'

A moment later, she was sitting beside him on the sofa, and a few moments after that the dress was on the floor. Lillian went at him with a mixture of fury and playfulness, attacking his body in short, breathless surges, and at no point did he do anything to stop her. Sachs knew that she was drunk, but even if it was all an accident, even if it was only booze and boredom that had pushed her into his arms, he was willing to settle for it. There might never be another chance, he told himself, and after four weeks of waiting for precisely this one thing to happen, it would have been unimaginable to turn her down.

They made love on the sofa, and then they made love in Lillian's bed upstairs, and even after the effects of the alcohol had worn off, she remained as ardent as she had been in the first few moments, offering herself to him with an abandon and a concentration that nullified any lingering doubts he might have had. She swept him away, she emptied him out, she dismantled him. And the remarkable thing was that early the next morning, when they woke up and found each other in bed, they went at it again, and this time, with the pale light spreading into the corners of the small room, she said that she loved him, and Sachs, who was looking straight into her eyes at that moment, saw nothing in those eyes to make him disbelieve her.

It was impossible to know what had happened, and he never found the courage to ask. He simply went with it, floating along on a wave of inexplicable happiness, wanting nothing else but to be exactly where he was. Overnight, he and Lillian had become a couple. She stayed home with him during the day now, sharing the chores of the household, taking on her responsibilities as Maria's mother again, and every time she looked at him, it was as though she were repeating what she had told him that first morning in bed. A week passed, and the less likely it seemed that she would recant, the more he came to accept what was happening. For several days in a row, he took Lillian out on buying sprees – showering her with dresses and shoes, with silk underwear, with ruby earrings and a strand of pearls. They binged on good restaurants and expensive wines, they talked, they made plans, they fucked until the cows came home. It was too good to be true, perhaps, but by then he was no longer able to think about what was good or what was true. When it came right down to it, he was no longer able to think about anything.

There's no telling how long it could have gone on. If it had just been the two of them, they might have made something of this sexual explosion, this bizarre and wholly implausible romance. In spite of its demonic implications, it's possible that Sachs and Lillian could have settled down somewhere and had a real life together. But other realities impinged on them, and less than two weeks after this new life began, it was already being called into question. They had fallen in love, perhaps, but they had also upset the balance of the household, and little Maria wasn't the least bit happy with the change. Her mother had been given back to her, but she had lost something as well, and from her point of view this loss must have felt like the crumbling of a world. For nearly a month, she and Sachs had lived together in a kind of paradise. She had been the sole object of his affections, and he had coddled her and doted on her in ways that no one else had ever done. Now, without a single word of warning, he had abandoned her. He had moved into her mother's bed, and rather than stay at home and keep her company, he left her with babysitters and went out every night. She resented all this. She resented her mother for coming between them, and she resented Sachs for letting her down, and by the time she had put up with it for three or four days, the normally obliging and affectionate Maria had turned into a horror, a tiny engine of sulks and tantrums and angry tears.

On the second Sunday, Sachs proposed a family outing to the Rose Garden in the Berkeley Hills. For once, Maria seemed to be in good spirits, and after Lillian fetched an old quilt from the upstairs closet, the three of them climbed into the Buick and drove to the other end of town. Everything went well for the first hour. Sachs and Lillian lay on the quilt, Maria played on the swings, and the sun burned off the last of the morning fog. Even when Maria banged her head on the jungle gym a little while later, there didn't seem to be any cause for alarm. She came running to them in tears, just as any other child would have done, and Lillian hugged her and soothed her, kissing the red mark on her temple with particular care and tenderness. It was good medicine, Sachs felt, the time-honored treatment, but in this case it had little or no effect. Maria went on crying, refusing to be consoled by her mother, and even though the injury was no more than a scratch, she complained about it vehemently, sobbing so hard that she nearly began to choke. Undaunted, Lillian hugged her again, but this time Maria recoiled from her, accusing her mother of squeezing her too hard. Sachs could see the hurt in Lillian's eyes when this happened, and then, when Maria pushed Lillian away from her, a flash of anger as well. Out of nowhere, they seemed to be on the verge of a full-blown crisis. An ice cream vendor had set up a stand about fifty feet from their quilt, and Sachs, thinking it might be a useful diversion, offered to buy Maria a cone. It will make you feel better, he said, smiling as sympathetically as he could, and then he ran off to the multicolored umbrella parked on the footpath just below them. It turned out that there were sixteen different flavors to choose from. Not knowing which one to pick, he settled on a combination of pistachio and tutti frutti. If nothing else, he thought, the sounds of the words might amuse her. But they didn't. Even though her tears had slackened by the time he returned, Maria eyed the scoops of green ice cream suspiciously, and when he handed the cone to her and she took her first tentative bite, all hell broke loose again. She made a terrible face, spat out the ice cream as though it were poison, and pronounced it 'disgusting.' This led to another fit of sobbing, and then, as her fury mounted, she took the cone in her right hand and hurled it at Sachs. It hit him squarely in the stomach, splattering all over his shirt. As he glanced down at the damage, Lillian rushed over to where Maria was standing and slapped her across the face.

'You brat!' she screamed at the little girl. 'You miserable, ungrateful brat! I'll kill you, do you understand! I'll kill you right here in front of all these people!' And then, before Maria had time to put up her hands and protect her face, Lillian slapped her again.

'Stop it,' Sachs said. His voice was hard, aghast with anger, and for a moment he was tempted to push Lillian to the ground. 'Don't you dare lay a hand on that child, do you hear me?'

'Butt out, mister,' she said, every bit as angry as he was. 'She's my kid, and I'll do what I damn please with her.'

'No hitting. I won't allow it.'

'If she deserves to be hit, I'll hit her. And no one interferes. Not even you, smartass.'

It got worse before it got better. Sachs and Lillian ranted at each other for the next ten minutes, and if they hadn't been in a public place, arguing in front of several dozen onlookers, God knows how far it might have gone. As it was, they eventually got a grip on themselves and reined in their tempers. Each one apologized to the other, they kissed and made up, and no more was said about it for the rest of the afternoon. The three of them went to the movies, then out to a Chinese restaurant for dinner, and by the time they returned home and Maria was put to bed, the incident had been all but forgotten. Or so they thought. In point of fact, that was the first sign of doom, and from the moment Lillian slapped Maria across the face until the moment Sachs left Berkeley five weeks later, nothing was ever the same for them again.

5

On January 16, 1988, a bomb went off in front of the court house in Turnbull, Ohio, blowing up a small, scale-model replica of the Statue of Liberty. Most people assumed it was a teenage prank, an act of petty vandalism without political motives, but because a national symbol had been destroyed, the incident was reported briefly by the wire services the next day. Six days after that, another Statue of Liberty was blown up in Danburg, Pennsylvania. The circumstances were almost identical: a small explosion in the middle of the night, no injuries, nothing damaged except the statue itself. Still, it was impossible to know if the same person was involved in both bombings or if the second blast was an imitation of the first – a so-called copy-cat crime. No one seemed to care much at that point, but one prominent conservative senator issued a statement condemning 'these deplorable acts' and urged the culprits to stop their shenanigans at once. 'It's not funny,' he said. 'Not only have you destroyed property, but you've desecrated a national icon. Americans love their statue, and they don't take kindly to this brand of horseplay.'

All in all, there are some one hundred and thirty scale-model replicas of the Statue of Liberty standing in public places across America. They can be found in city parks, in front of town halls, on the tops of buildings. Unlike the flag, which tends to divide people as much as it brings them together, the statue is a symbol that causes no controversy. If many Americans are proud of their flag, there are many others who feel ashamed of it, and for every person who regards it as a holy object, there is another who would like to spit on it, or burn it, or drag it through the mud. The Statue of Liberty is immune from these conflicts. For the past hundred years, it has transcended politics and ideology, standing at the threshold of our country as an emblem of all that is good within us. It represents hope rather than reality, faith rather than facts, and one would be hard-pressed to find a single person willing to denounce the things it stands for: democracy, freedom, equality under the law. It is the best of what America has to offer the world, and however pained one might be by America's failure to live up to those ideals, the ideals themselves are not in question. They have given comfort to millions. They have instilled the hope in all of us that we might one day live in a better world.

Eleven days after the Pennsylvania incident, another statue was destroyed on a village green in central Massachusetts. This time there was a message, a prepared statement phoned into the offices of the *Springfield Republican* the next morning. 'Wake up, America,' the caller said. 'It's time to start practicing what you preach. If you don't want any more statues blown up, prove to me that you're not a hypocrite. Do something for your people besides building them bombs. Otherwise, my bombs will keep going off. Signed: The Phantom of Liberty.'

Over the next eighteen months, nine more statues were destroyed in various parts of the country. Everyone will remember this, and there's no need for me to give an exhaustive account of the Phantom's activities. In some towns, twenty-four-hour guards were posted around the statues, manned by volunteer groups from the American Legion, the Elks Club, the high school football team, and other local organizations. But not every community was so vigilant, and the Phantom continued to elude detection. Each time he struck, there would be a pause before the next explosion, a long enough period to make people wonder if that was the end of it. Then, out of the blue, he would turn up somewhere a thousand miles away, and another bomb would go off. Many people were outraged, of course, but there were others who found themselves in sympathy with the Phantom's objectives. They were in the minority, but America is a large place, and their numbers were by no means small. To them, the Phantom eventually became a kind of underground folk hero. The messages had a lot to do with it, I think, the statements he phoned into newspapers and radio stations the morning after each explosion. They were necessarily short, but they seemed to get better as time went on: more concise, more poetic, more original in the way they expressed his disappointment in the country. 'Each person is alone,' one of them began, 'and therefore we have nowhere to turn but to each other.' Or: 'Democracy is not given. It must be fought for every day, or else we run the risk of losing it. The only weapon at our disposal is the Law.' Or: 'Neglect the children, and we destroy ourselves. We exist in the present only to the degree that we put our faith in the future.' Unlike the typical terrorist pronouncement with its inflated rhetoric and belligerent demands, the Phantom's statements did not ask for the impossible. He simply wanted America to look after itself and mend its ways.

In that sense, there was something almost Biblical about his exhortations, and after a while he began to sound less like a political revolutionary than some anguished, soft-spoken prophet. At bottom, he was merely articulating what many people already felt, and in some circles at least, there were those who actually spoke out in support of what he was doing. His bombs hadn't hurt anyone, they argued, and if these two-bit explosions forced people to rethink their positions about life, then maybe it wasn't such a bad idea after all.

To be perfectly honest, I didn't follow this story very closely. There were more important things happening in the world just then, and whenever the Phantom of Liberty caught my attention, I shrugged him off as a crank, as one more transient figure in the annals of American madness. Even if I had been more interested, however, I don't think I ever could have guessed that he and Sachs were the same person. It was too far removed from what I was capable of imagining, too alien to anything that seemed possible, and I don't see how it ever would have occurred to me to make the connection. On the other hand (and I know this will sound odd), if the Phantom made me think about anyone, it was Sachs. Ben had been missing for four months when the first bombings were reported, and mention of the Statue of Liberty immediately brought him to mind. That was natural enough, I suppose – considering the novel he had written, considering the circumstances of his fall two years earlier – and from then on the association stuck. Every time I read about the Phantom, I would think about Ben. Memories of our friendship would come rushing back to me, and all of a sudden I would begin to ache, trembling at the thought of how much I missed him.

But that was as far as it went. The Phantom was a sign of my friend's absence, a catalyst for personal pain, but more than a year went by before I took notice of the Phantom himself. That was in the spring of 1989, and it happened when I switched on my television set and saw the students of the Chinese democracy movement unveil their clumsy imitation of the Statue of Liberty in Tienanmen Square. I realized then that I had underestimated the power of the symbol. It stood for an idea that belonged to everyone, to everyone in the world, and the Phantom had played a crucial part in resurrecting its meaning. I had been wrong to dismiss him. He had caused a disturbance somewhere deep inside the earth, and the waves were now beginning to rise to the surface, touching every part of the ground at once. Something had happened, something new was in the air, and there were days that spring when I walked through the city and almost imagined that I could feel the sidewalks vibrating under my feet.

I had started a new novel at the beginning of the year, and by the time Iris and I left New York for Vermont last summer, I was buried in my story, scarcely able to think about anything else. I settled into Sachs's old studio on June twenty-fifth, and not even that potentially eerie situation could disrupt my rhythm. There is a point at which a book begins to take over your life, when the world you have imagined becomes more important to you than the real world, and it barely crossed my mind that I was sitting in the same chair that Sachs used to sit in, that I was writing at the same table he used to write at, that I was breathing the same air he had once breathed. If anything, it was a source of pleasure to me. I enjoyed having my friend close to me again, and I sensed that if he had known I was occupying his old space, he would have been glad. Sachs was a welcoming ghost, and he'd left behind no threats or evil spirits in his shack. He wanted me to be there, I felt, and even though I had gradually come around to Iris's opinion (that he was dead, that he would never come back), it was as if we still understood each other, as if nothing between us had changed.

In early August, Iris left for Minnesota to take part in the wedding of a childhood friend. Sonia went with her, and with David still off at summer camp until the end of the month, I hunkered down here alone and pushed on with my book. After a couple of days, I found myself slipping into the same patterns that set in whenever Iris and I are apart: too much work; too little food; restless, insomniac nights. With Iris in bed with me I always sleep, but the instant she goes away I dread just closing my eyes. Each night becomes a little harder than the night before, and in no time at all I'm up with the lamp on until one, two, or three o'clock in the morning. None of this is important, but because I was having these same troubles during Iris's absence last summer, I happened to be awake when Sachs made his sudden, unexpected appearance in Vermont. It was nearly two o'clock, and I was lying in bed upstairs reading a trashy thriller, a murder mystery that some guest had left behind years before, when I heard the sound of a car chugging up the dirt road. I lifted my eyes from the book, waiting for the car to move on past the house, but then, unmistakably, the engine slowed, the headlights swept their beams across my window, and the car turned, scraping against the hawthorn bushes as it came to a halt in the yard. I pulled on a pair of pants and rushed downstairs, arriving in the kitchen just seconds after the engine was turned off. There was no time to think. I went straight for the utensils on the counter, grabbed the longest knife I could find, and then stood there in the darkness, waiting for whoever it was to walk in. I figured it was a burglar or a maniac, and for the space of the next ten or twenty seconds, I was as scared as I've ever been in my life.

The light went on before I could attack him. It was an automatic gesture – stepping into the kitchen and turning on the light – and the instant after my ambush was foiled, I realized that Sachs was the person who had done it. There was the smallest interval between these two perceptions, however, and in that time I gave myself up for dead. He took three or four steps into the room and then froze. That was when he saw me standing in the corner – the knife still poised in the air, my body still ready to pounce.

'Jesus God,' he said. 'It's you.'

I tried to say something, but no words came out of my mouth.

'I saw the light,' Sachs said, still staring at me in disbelief. 'I thought it was probably Fanny.'

'No,' I said. 'It's not Fanny.'

'No, it doesn't look that way.'

'But it's not you either. It can't be you, can it? You're dead. Everyone knows that now. You're lying in a ditch somewhere at the edge of a road, rotting under a mound of leaves.'

It took some time to recover from the shock, but not long, not as long as I would have thought. He was looking well, I found, as clear-eyed and fit as I had ever seen him, and except for the gray that had spread through his hair now, he was essentially the same person he had always been. That must have reassured me. This was no specter who had returned – it was the old Sachs, as vibrant and full of words as ever. Fifteen minutes after he walked into the house, I was already used to him again, I was already willing to accept that he was alive.

He hadn't expected to run into me, he said, and before we sat down and began to talk, he apologized several times for having looked so stunned. Under the circumstances, I doubted that any apologies were necessary. 'It was the knife,' I said. 'If I'd walked in here and found someone about to stab me, I think I would have looked stunned, too.'

'It's not that I'm unhappy to see you. I just wasn't counting on it, that's all.'

'You don't have to be happy. After all this time, there's no reason why you should be.'

'I don't blame you for feeling burned.'

'I don't. At least I didn't until now. I admit that I was pretty angry at first, but that went away after a few months.'

'And then?'

'Then I began to feel scared for you. I suppose I've been scared ever since.'

'And what about Fanny? Has she been scared, too?'

'Fanny's braver than I am. She's never stopped thinking you were alive.'

Sachs smiled, visibly pleased by what I had said. Until that moment, I hadn't been sure if he was planning to stay or go, but now, suddenly, he pulled out a chair from the kitchen table and sat down, acting as though he had just come to an important decision. 'What are you smoking these days?' he said, looking up at me with the smile still on his face.

'Schimmelpennincks. The same thing I've always smoked.'

'Good. Let's have a couple of your little cigars, and then maybe a bottle of something to drink.'

'You must be tired.'

'Of course I'm tired. I've just driven four hundred miles, and it's two o'clock in the morning. But you want me to talk to you, don't you?'

'It can wait until tomorrow.'

'There's a chance I'll lose my nerve by tomorrow.'

'And you're ready to talk now?'

'Yes, I'm ready to talk. Until I came in here and saw you holding that knife, I wasn't going to say a word. That was always the plan: to say nothing, to keep it all to myself. But I think I've changed my mind now. It's not that I can't live with it, but it suddenly occurs to me that someone should know. Just in case something happens to me.'

'Why should anything happen to you?'

'Because I'm in a dangerous spot, that's why, and my luck could run out.'

'But why tell me?'

'Because you're my best friend, and I know you can keep a secret.' He paused for a moment and looked straight into my eyes. 'You can keep a secret, can't you?'

'I think so. To tell you the truth, I'm not sure I've ever heard one. I'm not sure I've ever had one to keep.'

That was how it started: with these enigmatic remarks and hints of impending disaster. I found a bottle of bourbon in the pantry, collected two clean glasses from the drainboard, and then led Sachs across the yard to the studio. That was where I kept my cigars, and for the next five hours he smoked and drank, struggling against exhaustion as he spilled out his story to me. We were both sitting in armchairs, facing each other across my cluttered work table, and in all that time neither one of us moved. Candles burned all around us, flickering and sputtering as the room filled with his voice. He talked and I listened, and bit by bit I learned everything I have told so far.

Even before he began, I knew that something extraordinary must have happened to him. Otherwise, he wouldn't have kept himself hidden for so long, he wouldn't have gone to so much trouble to make us believe he was dead. That much was clear, and now that Sachs had returned, I was ready to accept the most far-flung and outrageous disclosures, to listen to a story I never could have dreamed of myself. It wasn't that I was expecting him to tell *this particular story*, but I knew that it would be something like it, and when Sachs finally began (leaning back in his chair and saying, 'You've heard of the Phantom of Liberty, I suppose?') I scarcely even blinked. 'So that's what you've been up to,' I said, interrupting him before he could go any further. 'You're the funny little man who's been blowing up all those statues. A nice line of work if you can get it, but who on earth picked you as the conscience of the world? The last time I saw you, you were writing a novel.'

It took him the rest of the night to answer that question. Even then there were gaps, holes in the account I haven't been able to fill in. Roughly speaking, the idea seems to have come to him in stages, beginning with the slap he witnessed that Sunday afternoon in Berkeley and ending with the disintegration of his affair with Lillian. In between, there was a gradual surrender to Dimaggio, a growing obsession with the life of the man he had killed.

'I finally found the courage to go into his room,' Sachs said. 'That's what started it, I think, that was the first step toward some kind of legitimate action. Until then, I hadn't even opened the door. Too scared, I suppose, too afraid of what I might find if I started looking. But Lillian was gone again, and Maria was off at school, and there I was sitting alone in the house, slowly beginning to lose my mind. Predictably enough, most of Dimaggio's belongings had been cleared out of the room. Nothing personal was left – no letters or documents, no diaries or telephone numbers, no clues about his life with Lillian. But I did stumble across some books. Three or four volumes of Marx, a biography of Bakunin, a pamphlet by Trotsky on race relations in America, that sort of thing. And then, sitting in a black binder in the bottom drawer of his desk, I found a copy of his dissertation. That was the key. If I hadn't found that, I don't think any of the other things would have happened.

'It was a study of Alexander Berkman – a reappraisal of his life and works in four hundred fifty-odd pages. I'm sure you've run across the name. Berkman was the anarchist who shot Henry Clay Frick – the man whose house is now a museum on Fifth Avenue. That was during the Homestead Steel Strike in 1892, when Frick called in an army of Pinkertons and had them open fire on the workers. Berkman was twenty at the time, a young Jewish radical who'd emigrated from Russia just a few years before, and he traveled down to Pennsylvania and went after Frick with a gun, hoping to eliminate this symbol of capitalist oppression. Frick survived the attack, and Berkman was thrown into the state penitentiary for fourteen years. After his release, he wrote *Prison Memoirs of an Anarchist* and continued to involve himself in political work, mostly with Emma Goldman. He was the editor of *Mother Earth*, helped found a libertarian school, gave speeches, agitated for causes like the Lawrence textile strike, and so on. When America entered the First World War, he was put in jail again, this time for speaking out against conscription. Two years later, not long after he was released, he and Emma Goldman were deported to Russia. At the farewell dinner before they left, news came that Frick had died that same evening. Berkman's only comment was: "Deported by God." An exquisite statement, no? In Russia, it didn't take long for him to become disillusioned. The Bolsheviks had betrayed the Revolution, he felt; one kind of despotism had replaced another, and after the Kronstadt rebellion was crushed in 1921, he decided to emigrate from Russia for the second time. He eventually settled in the South of France, where he lived out the last ten years of his life. He wrote the *ABC of Communist Anarchism*, kept body and soul together by doing translations, editing, and ghost-writing, but still needed help from friends in order to survive. By 1936, he was too sick to go on, and rather than continue to ask for handouts, he picked up a gun and shot himself through the head.

'It was a good dissertation. A bit clumsy and didactic at times, but well-researched and passionate, a thorough and intelligent job. It was hard not to respect Dimaggio for it, to see that he'd been a man with a real mind. Considering what I knew about his later activities, the dissertation was obviously something more than just an academic exercise. It was a step in his inner development, a way of coming to grips with his own ideas about political change. He didn't come right out and say it, but I could tell that he supported Berkman, that he believed there was a moral justification for certain forms of political violence. Terrorism had its place in the struggle, so to speak. If used correctly, it could be an effective tool for dramatizing the issues at stake, for enlightening the public about the nature of institutional power.

'I couldn't help myself after that. I started to think about Dimaggio all the time, to compare myself to him, to question how we'd come to be together on that road in Vermont. I sensed a kind of cosmic attraction, the pull of some inexorable force. Lillian wouldn't tell me much about him, but I knew he'd been a soldier in Vietnam and that the war had turned him inside-out, that he'd left the army with a new understanding of America, of politics, of his own life. It fascinated me to think that I'd gone to prison because of that war – and that fighting in it had brought him around to more or less the same position as mine. We'd both become writers, we both knew that fundamental changes were needed – but whereas I started to lose my way, to dither around with half-assed articles and literary pretensions, Dimaggio kept developing, kept moving forward, and in the end he was brave enough to put his ideas to the test. It's not that I think blowing up logging camps is a good idea, but I envied him for having the balls to act. I'd never lifted a finger for anything. I'd sat around grumbling and complaining for the past fifteen years, but for all my self-righteous opinions and embattled stances, I'd never put myself on the line. I was a hypocrite and Dimaggio wasn't, and when I thought about myself in comparison to him, I began to feel ashamed.

'My first thought was to write something about him. Something similar to what he had written about Berkman – only better, deeper, a genuine examination of his soul. I planned it as an elegy, a memorial in the shape of a book. If I could do this for him, I thought, then maybe I could start to redeem myself, then maybe something good could start to come out of his death. I would have to talk to a lot of people, of course, go around the country gathering information, setting up interviews with as many people as I could find: his parents and relatives, his army buddies, the people he went to school with, professional colleagues, old girlfriends, members of Children of the Planet, hundreds of different people. It would be an enormous project, a book that would take me years to finish. But that was the point somehow. As long as I was devoting myself to Dimaggio, I would be keeping him alive. I would give him my life, so to speak, and in exchange he would give my life back to me. I'm not asking you to understand this. I barely understood it myself. But I was groping, you see, thrashing out blindly for something to cling to, and for a little while this felt solid, a better solution than anything else.

'I never got anywhere with it. I sat down a few times to take notes, but I couldn't concentrate, I couldn't organize my thoughts. I don't know what the problem was. Maybe I still had too much hope that things would work out with Lillian. Maybe I didn't believe it would be possible for me to write again. God knows what was stopping me, but every time I picked up a pen and tried to start, I would break out in a cold sweat, my head would spin, and I'd feel as though I was about to fall. Just like the time I fell off the fire escape. It was the same panic, the same feeling of helplessness, the same rush toward oblivion.

'Then something strange happened. I was walking down Telegraph Avenue one morning to get my car when I spotted someone I knew from New York. Cal Stewart, a magazine editor I'd written a couple of articles for back in the early eighties. It was the first time since coming to California that I'd seen anyone I knew, and the thought that he might recognize me stopped me dead in my tracks. If one person knew where I was, I'd be finished, I'd be absolutely destroyed. I ducked into the first doorway I came to, just to get myself off the street. It turned out to be a used bookstore, a big place with high ceilings and six or seven rooms. I went all the way to the back and hid out behind a row of tall shelves, my heart thumping, trying to pull myself together. There was a mountain of books in front of me, millions of words piled on top of each other, a whole universe of discarded literature – books that people no longer wanted, that had been sold, that had outlived their usefulness. I didn't realize it at first, but I happened to be standing in the American fiction section, and right there at eye level, the first thing I saw when I started to look at the titles, was a copy of *The New Colossus*, my own little contribution to this graveyard. It was an astonishing coincidence, a thing that hit me so hard I felt it had to be an omen.

'Don't ask me why I bought it. I had no intention of reading the book, but once I saw it there on the shelf, I knew I had to have it. The physical object, the thing itself. It cost only five dollars for the original hardcover edition, complete with dust jacket and purple end papers. And there was my picture on the back flap: the portrait of the artist as a young moron. Fanny took that photo, I remember. I was twenty-six or twenty-seven at the time, with my beard and long hair, and I'm staring into the lens with an unbelievably earnest, soulful expression in my eyes. You've seen that picture, you know the one I'm talking about. When I opened up the book and saw it in the store that day, I almost burst out laughing.

'Once the coast was clear, I left the store and drove back to Lillian's house. I knew I couldn't stay in Berkeley anymore. Seeing Cal Stewart had scared the hell out of me, and I suddenly understood how precarious my position was, how vulnerable I had made myself. When I got home with the book, I put it on the coffee table in the living room and sat down on the sofa. I had no ideas anymore. I had to leave, but at the same time I couldn't leave, I couldn't bring myself to walk out on Lillian. I had just about lost her, but I wasn't willing to let go, I couldn't face the thought of never seeing her again. So I sat there on the sofa, staring at the cover of my novel, feeling like someone who's just run into a brick wall. I hadn't done anything with the book about Dimaggio; I'd thrown away more than a third of the money; I'd botched every hope for myself. Out of pure wretchedness, I kept my eyes fixed on the cover of the book. For a long time I don't think I even saw it, but then, little by little, something began to happen. It must have taken close to an hour, but once the idea took hold of me, I couldn't stop thinking about it. The Statue of Liberty, remember? That strange, distorted drawing of the Statue of Liberty. That was where it started, and once I realized where I was going, the rest followed, the whole cockeyed plan fell into place.

'I closed out a few of my bank accounts that afternoon and then took care of the others the next morning. I needed cash to do what I had to do, which meant reversing all the commitments I had made – taking the rest of the money for myself instead of giving it to Lillian. It bothered me to have broken my word, but not as much as I would have thought. I had already given her sixty-five thousand dollars, and even if it wasn't all there was, it was a lot of money, a lot more than she had been expecting me to give her. The ninety-one thousand I still had would take me a long way, but it wasn't as if I was going to blow it on myself. The purpose I had contrived for that money was just as meaningful as my original plan. More meaningful, in fact. Not only would I be using it to carry out Dimaggio's work, but I would be using it to express my own convictions, to take a stand for what I believed in, to make the kind of difference I had never been able to make before. All of a sudden, my life seemed to make sense to me. Not just the past few months, but my whole life, all the way back to the beginning. It was a miraculous confluence, a startling conjunction of motives and ambitions. I had found the unifying principle, and this one idea would bring all the broken pieces of myself together. For the first time in my life, I would be whole.

'I can't begin to convey the power of my happiness to you. I felt free again, utterly liberated by my decision. It wasn't that I wanted to leave Lillian and Maria, but there were more important things to take care of now, and once I understood that, all the bitterness and suffering of the past month just melted out of my heart. I was no longer bewitched. I felt inspired, invigorated, cleansed. Almost like a man who had found religion. Like a man who had heard the call. The unfinished business of my life suddenly ceased to matter. I was ready to march out into the wilderness and spread the word, ready to begin all over again.

'Looking back on it now, I see how pointless it was to have pinned my hopes on Lillian. Going out there was a crazy thing to do, an act of desperation. It might have worked if I hadn't fallen in love with her, but once that happened, the venture was doomed to fail. I had put her in an impossible bind, and she didn't know how to cope with it. She wanted the money, and she didn't want it. It made her greedy, and her greed humiliated her. She wanted me to love her, and she hated herself for loving me back. I don't blame her for putting me through hell anymore. She's a wild person, Lillian. Not just beautiful, you understand, but incandescent. Fearless, out of control, ready for anything – and she never had a chance to be who she was with me.

'In the end, the remarkable thing wasn't that I left, but that I managed to stay as long as I did. The circumstances were so peculiar, so dangerous and unsettling, that I think they began to excite her. That's what sucked her in: not me, but the excitement of my being there, the darkness I represented. The situation was fraught with all sorts of romantic possibilities, and after a while she couldn't resist them anymore, she let herself go a lot farther than she ever intended to. Not unlike the weird and implausible way she had met Dimaggio. That had led to marriage. In my case, it led to a honeymoon, those two dazzling weeks when nothing could go wrong for us. It doesn't matter what happened after that. We couldn't have sustained it, and sooner or later she would have started running around again, she would have slipped back into her old life. But while it lasted, I don't think there's any question that she was in love with me. Whenever I begin to doubt it, I have only to remember the proof. She could have turned me in to the police, and she didn't. Even after I told her the money had run out. Even after I was gone. If nothing else, that proves that I meant something to her. It proves that everything that happened to me in Berkeley really happened.

'But no regrets. Not anymore at least. It's all behind me – over and done with, ancient history. The hard part was having to leave the little girl. I didn't think it would affect me, but I missed her for a long time, much more than I ever missed Lillian. Whenever I happened to be driving west, I'd start to think about going all the way to California – just to look her up and pay her a visit. But I never did. I was afraid of what might happen if I saw Lillian again, so I kept myself clear of California, and I haven't set foot in the state since the morning I left. Eighteen, nineteen months ago. By now, Maria's probably forgotten who I am. At one time, before things fell apart with Lillian, I used to think I'd wind up adopting her, that she would actually become my daughter. It would have been good for her, I think, good for both of us, but it's too late to dream about that now. I don't suppose I was ever meant to be a father. It didn't work with Fanny, and it didn't work with Lillian. Little seeds. Little eggs and seeds. You get just so many chances, and then life takes hold of you, and then you're off on your own forever. I've become who I am now, and there's no going back. This is it, Peter. For as long as I make it last, this is it.'

He was beginning to ramble. The sun was already up by then, and a thousand birds were singing in the trees: larks, finches, warblers, the morning chorus at full strength. Sachs had been talking for so many hours, he scarcely knew what he was saying anymore. As the light streamed through the windows, I could see that his eyes were about to close on him. We can go on talking later, I said. If you don't lie down and get some sleep, you're probably going to black out, and I'm not sure I'm strong enough to carry you over to the house.

I put him in one of the empty bedrooms on the second floor, pulled down the shades, and then tiptoed back to my own room. I doubted that I would be able to sleep. There were too many things to digest, too many images churning in my mind, but the moment my head touched the pillow, I began to lose consciousness. I felt as if I'd been clubbed, as if my skull had been crushed by a stone. Some stories are too terrible, perhaps, and the only way to let them into you is to escape, to turn your back on them and steal off into the darkness.

I woke up at three in the afternoon. Sachs slept on for another two or two and a half hours, and in the interval I puttered around the yard, staying out of the house so as not to disturb him. Sleep had done nothing for me. I was still too numb to think, and if I managed to keep myself busy during those hours, it was only by planning out the menu for dinner that night. I struggled over every decision, weighing each pro and con as if the fate of the world depended on it: whether to cook the chicken in the oven or on the grill, whether to serve rice or potatoes, whether there was enough wine left in the cupboard. It's odd how vividly all this comes back to me now. Sachs had just told me how he had killed a man, how he had spent the past two years roaming the country as a fugitive, and all I could think about was what to prepare for dinner. It was as if I needed to pretend that life still consisted of such mundane particulars. But that was only because I knew it didn't.

We stayed up late again that night, talking through dinner and on into the early hours of the morning. We were outside this time, sitting in the same Adirondack chairs we had sat in on so many other nights over the years: two disembodied voices in the dark, invisible to each other, seeing nothing except when one of us struck a match and our faces flared up briefly from the shadows. I remember the glowing ends of cigars, the fireflies pulsing in the bushes, an enormous sky of stars overhead – the same things I remember from so many other nights in the past. That helped to keep me calm, I think, but even more than the setting there was Sachs himself. The long sleep had refreshed him, and right from the start he was in full command of the conversation. There was no uncertainty in his voice, nothing to make me feel I couldn't trust him. That was the night he told me about the Phantom of Liberty, and at no point did he sound like a man confessing to a crime. He was proud of what he had done, unshakeably at peace with himself, and he talked with the assurance of an artist who knows he has just created his most important work.

It was a long, incredible tale, a saga of journeys and disguises, of lulls and frenzies and last-minute escapes. Until I heard it from Sachs, I never would have guessed how much work went into each explosion: the weeks of planning and preparation, the elaborate, roundabout methods for amassing the materials to construct the bombs, the meticulous alibis and deceptions, the distances that had to be covered. Once he had selected the town, he had to find a way to spend some time there without arousing suspicion. The first step was to concoct an identity and a cover story, and since he was never the same person twice, his powers of invention were constantly put to the test. He always had a different name, as bland and nondescript as he could make it (Ed Smith, Al Goodwin, Jack White, Bill Foster), and from one operation to the next, he did what he could to produce minor alterations in his physical appearance (beardless one time, bearded another, dark-haired in one place, light-haired in the next, wearing glasses or not wearing glasses, dressed in a suit or dressed in work clothes – a set number of variables that he would mix into different combinations for each town). The fundamental challenge, however, was to come up with a reason for being there, a plausible excuse to spend several days in a community where no one knew him. Once he posed as a college professor, a sociologist doing research for a book on small-town American life and values. Another time, he pretended to be on a sentimental journey, an adopted child looking for information about his biological parents. Another time he was a businessman hoping to invest in local commercial property. Another time he was a widower, a man who had lost his wife and children in an auto accident and was thinking about settling in a new town. Then, almost perversely, once the Phantom had made a name for himself, he showed up in a small Nebraska city as a newspaper reporter, at work on a feature article about the attitudes and opinions of people who lived in places with their own replicas of the Statue of Liberty. What did they think about the bombings? he asked them. And what did the statue mean to them? It was a nerve-shattering experience, he said, but worth every minute.

Early on, he decided that openness was the most useful strategy, the best way to avoid creating the wrong impression. Rather than skulk around and keep himself hidden, he chatted people up, he charmed them, he got them to think of him as an okay kind of guy. This friendliness came naturally to Sachs, and it gave him the breathing room he needed. Once people knew why he was there, they wouldn't be alarmed to see him strolling through town, and if he happened to pass the site of the statue several times during the course of his walks, no one would pay any attention. Likewise with the tours he made after dark, driving through the shut-up town at two in the morning to familiarize himself with the traffic patterns, to calculate the odds of anyone being in the vicinity when he planted the bomb. He was thinking of moving there, after all, and who could blame him if he wanted to get a feel for the place after the sun went down? He realized that it was a flimsy excuse, but these nocturnal outings were unavoidable, a necessary precaution, for not only did he have to save his own skin, he had to make sure that no one was ever hurt. A bum sleeping at the base of the pedestal, two teenagers necking on the grass, a man out walking his dog in the middle of the night – it would only take a single fragment of flying stone or metal to kill someone, and then the entire cause would be ruined. That was Sachs's greatest fear, and he went to enormous lengths to guard against accidents. The bombs he built were small, much smaller than he would have liked, and even though it increased the risks, he never set the timer to go off more than twenty minutes after he had taped the explosives to the crown of the statue. There was nothing to say that someone couldn't pass by in those twenty minutes, but given the hour, and given the nature of those towns, the chances were slim.

Along with everything else, Sachs gave vast amounts of technical information that night, a crash course in the mechanics of bomb-building. I confess that most of it went straight through me. I have no knack for mechanical things, and my ignorance made it difficult for me to follow what he said. I understood the occasional word, terms like *alarm clock, gunpowder, fuse,* but the rest was incomprehensible to me, a foreign language I couldn't penetrate. Still, judging from the way he talked, I gathered that a great deal of ingenuity was involved. He didn't rely on any pre-established formulas, and with the added burden of having to cover his tracks, he took great pains to use only the most homespun materials, to put together his explosives from odds and ends that could be found in any hardware store. It must have been an arduous process, traveling somewhere just to buy a clock, then driving fifty miles down the road to buy a spool of wire, then going somewhere else to buy a package of tape. No purchase was ever larger than twenty dollars, and he was careful to avoid using anything but cash – in every store, in every restaurant, in every broken-down motel. In and out; hello and good-bye. Then he would be gone, as if his body had melted into thin air. It was hard work, but after a year and a half, he hadn't left a single trace behind him.

He had a cheap apartment on the South Side of Chicago, which he rented under the name of Alexander Berkman, but that was a refuge more than a home, a place to pause between travels, and he spent no more than a third of his time there. Just thinking about this life made me uncomfortable. The constant movement, the pressure of always pretending to be someone else, the loneliness – but Sachs shrugged off my qualms as if they were of no importance. He was too preoccupied, he said, too absorbed by what he was doing to think about such things. If he had created any problem for himself, it was only how to cope with success. With the Phantom's reputation steadily increasing, it had become more and more difficult to find any statues to attack. Most of them were guarded now, and whereas in the beginning it had taken him anywhere from one to three weeks to accomplish his missions, the average time had grown to nearly two and a half months. Earlier that summer, he had been forced to abandon a project at the last minute, and several others had been postponed – put off until winter, when the cold temperatures would no doubt slacken the determination of the all-night guards. But still, for every obstacle that arose, there was a compensating benefit, another sign that proved how far his influence had spread. In the past few months, the Phantom of Liberty had been the subject of editorials and sermons. He had been discussed on call-in radio shows, caricatured in political cartoons, excoriated as a menace to society, extolled as a man of the people. Phantom of Liberty T-shirts and buttons were on sale in novelty shops, jokes had begun to circulate, and just last month two strippers in Chicago had presented an act in which the Statue of Liberty was gradually disrobed and then seduced by the Phantom. He was making a mark, he said, a much greater mark than he had ever thought possible. As long as he could keep it up, he was willing to face any inconvenience, to gut his way through any hardship. It was the kind of thing a fanatic would say, I later realized, an admission that he didn't need a life of his own anymore, but he spoke with such happiness, such enthusiasm and lack of doubt, that I scarcely understood the implication of those words at the time.

There was more to be said. All sorts of questions had accumulated in my mind, but dawn had come by then, and I was too exhausted to go on. I wanted to ask him about the money (how much was left, what he was going to do when it ran out); I wanted to know more about his breakup with Lillian Stern; I wanted to ask him about Maria Turner, about Fanny, about the manuscript of *Leviathan* (which he hadn't even bothered to look at). There were a hundred loose threads, and I figured I had a right to know everything, that he had an obligation to answer all my questions. But I didn't push him to continue. We would talk about those things over breakfast, I told myself, but now it was time for bed.

When I woke up later that morning, Sachs's car was gone. I assumed he had driven to the store and would be coming back any minute, but after waiting over an hour for him to return, I began to lose hope. I didn't want to believe that he had left without saying good-bye, and yet I knew that anything was possible. He had run out on others before, and why should I think he would act any differently with me? First Fanny, then Maria Turner, then Lillian Stern. Perhaps I was only the latest in a long line of silent departures, another person he had crossed off his list.

At twelve thirty, I went over to the studio to sit down with my book. I didn't know what else to do, and rather than go on waiting outside, feeling more and more ridiculous as I stood there listening for the sound of Sachs's car, I thought it might help to distract myself with some work. That was when I found his letter. He had placed it on top of my manuscript, and I saw it the moment I sat down at my desk.

'I'm sorry to sneak out on you like this,' it began, 'but I think we've covered almost everything. If I stayed around any longer, it would only cause trouble. You'd try to talk me out of what I'm doing (because you're my friend, because you'd see that as your responsibility to me as a friend), and I don't want to fight with you, I don't have the stomach for arguments now. Whatever you might think of me, I'm grateful to you for listening. The story needed to be told, and better to you than to anyone else. If and when the time comes, you'll know how to tell it to others, you'll make them understand what this business is all about. Your books prove that, and when everything is said and done, you're the only person I can count on. You've gone so much farther than I ever did, Peter. I admire you for your innocence, for the way you've stuck to this one thing for your whole life. My problem was that I could never believe in it. I always wanted something else, but I never knew what it was. Now I know. After all the horrible things that happened, I've finally found something to believe in. That's all that matters to me anymore. Sticking with this one thing. Please don't blame me for it – and above all, don't feel sorry for me. I'm fine. I've never been better. I'm going to keep on giving them hell for as long as I can. The next time you read about the Phantom of Liberty, I hope it gives you a good laugh. Onward and upward, old man. I'll see you in the funny papers. Ben.'

I must have read through this note twenty or thirty times. There was nothing else to do, and it took me at least that long to absorb the shock of his departure. The first few readings left me feeling hurt, angry at him for absconding when my back was turned. But then, very slowly, as I went through the letter again, I grudgingly began to admit to myself that Sachs had been right. The next conversation would have been more difficult than the others. It was true that I had been planning to confront him, that I had made up my mind to do what I could to talk him out of continuing. He had sensed that, I suppose, and rather than allow any bitterness to develop between us, he had left. I couldn't really blame him for it. He had wanted our friendship to survive, and since he knew this visit could be the last time we ever saw each other, he hadn't wanted it to end badly. That was the purpose of the note. It had brought things to an end without ending them. It had been his way of telling me that he couldn't say good-bye.

He lived for another ten months, but I never heard from him again. The Phantom of Liberty struck twice during that period – once in Virginia and once in Utah – but I didn't laugh. Now that I knew the story, I couldn't feel anything but sadness, an immeasurable grief. The world went through extraordinary changes in those ten months. The Berlin Wall was torn down, Havel became president of Czechoslovakia, the Cold War suddenly stopped. But Sachs was still out there, a solitary speck in the American night, hurtling toward his destruction in a stolen car. Wherever he was, I was with him now. I had given him my word to say nothing, and the longer I kept his secret, the less I belonged to myself. God knows where my stubbornness came from, but I never breathed a hint to anyone. Not to Iris, not to Fanny and Charles, not to a living soul. I had taken on the burden of that silence for him, and in the end it nearly crushed me.

I saw Maria Turner in early September, a few days after Iris and I returned to New York. It was a relief to be able to talk to someone about Sachs, but even with her I held back as much as I could. I didn't even mention that I had seen him – only that he had called and that we had talked on the phone for an hour. It was a grim little dance I danced with Maria that day. I accused her of misguided loyalty, of betraying Sachs by keeping her promise to him, while all along that was precisely what I was doing myself. We had both been let in on the secret, but I knew more than she did, and I wasn't about to share the particulars with her. It was enough for her to know that I knew what she knew. She talked quite willingly after that, realizing how futile it would have been to con me. That much was out in the open now, and I wound up hearing more about her relations with Sachs than Sachs ever told me himself. Among other things, that was the day I first saw the photographs she had taken of him, the so-called 'Thursdays with Ben.' Even more importantly, I also learned that Maria had seen Lillian Stern in Berkeley the year before – about six months after Sachs had left. According to what Lillian had told her, Ben had been back to visit twice. That contradicted what he had told me, but when I pointed out the discrepancy to Maria, she only shrugged. 'Lillian's not the only person who lies,' she said. 'You know that as well as I do. After what those two did to each other, all bets are off.'

'I'm not saying that Ben couldn't lie,' I answered. 'I just don't understand why he would.'

'It seems that he made certain threats. Maybe he was too embarrassed to tell you about them.'

'Threats?'

'Lillian said that he threatened to kidnap her daughter.'

'And why on earth would he do that?'

'Apparently, he didn't like the way she was raising Maria. He said that she was a bad influence on her, that the kid deserved a chance to grow up in healthy surroundings. He took the high moral ground, and it turned into a nasty scene.'

'That doesn't sound like Ben.'

'Maybe not, but Lillian was scared enough to do something about it. After Ben's second visit, she put Maria on a plane and sent her to her mother's house back East. The little girl's been living there ever since.'

'Maybe Lillian had her own reasons for wanting to get rid of her.'

'Anything is possible. I'm just telling you what she told me.'

'What about the money he gave her? Did she ever spend it?'

'No. At least not on herself. She told me that she put it in a trust fund for Maria.'

'I wonder if Ben ever told her where it came from. I'm not too clear on that point, and it might have made a difference.'

'I'm not sure. But a more interesting question is to ask where Dimaggio got the money in the first place. It was a phenomenal amount of cash for him to be carrying around.'

'Ben thought it was stolen. At least at first. Then he thought it might have been given to Dimaggio by some political organization. If not the Children of the Planet, then someone else. Terrorists, for example. The PLO, the IRA, any one of a dozen groups. He figured that Dimaggio might have been connected to people like that.'

'Lillian has her own opinion about what Dimaggio was up to.'

'I'm sure she does.'

'Yeah, well, it's kind of interesting once you start to think about it. In her view, Dimaggio was working as an undercover agent for the government. The CIA, the FBI, one of those cloak-and-dagger gangs. She thinks it started when he was a soldier in Vietnam. That they signed him up over there and paid his way through college and graduate school. To give him the right credentials.'

'You mean he was a plant? An *agent provocateur*?'

'That's what Lillian thinks.'

'It sounds pretty farfetched to me.'

'Of course it does. But that doesn't mean it isn't true.'

'Does she have proof, or is she just making a wild guess?'

'I don't know, I didn't ask her. We didn't really talk about it much.'

'Why don't you ask her now?'

'We're not exactly on speaking terms anymore.'

'Oh?'

'It was a pretty rocky visit, and I haven't been in touch with her since last year.'

'You had a falling out.'

'Yeah, something like that.'

'About Ben, I suppose. You're still stuck on him, aren't you? It must have been hard listening to your friend tell you how he'd fallen in love with her.'

Maria suddenly turned her head away from me, and I knew I was right. But she was too proud to admit anything, and a moment later she had composed herself sufficiently to look back in my direction. She flashed me a tough, ironic smile. 'You're the only man I've ever loved, Chiquita,' she said. 'But then you went off and got married on me, didn't you? When a girl's heart is broken, she's gotta do what she's gotta do.'

I managed to talk her into giving me Lillian's address and telephone number. A new book of mine was coming out in October, and my publisher had arranged for me to give readings in a number of cities around the country. San Francisco was the last stop on the tour, and it wouldn't have made sense to go there without trying to meet Lillian. I had no idea if she knew where Sachs was or not (and even if she did, it wasn't certain she would tell me), but I figured we would have a lot to talk about anyway. If nothing else, I wanted to set eyes on her myself, to be able to form my own opinion of who she was. Everything I knew about her had come from either Sachs or Maria, and she was too important a figure for me to rely on their accounts. I called the day after I got her number from Maria. She wasn't in, but I left a message on her machine, and much to my surprise, she called back the next afternoon. It was a brief but friendly conversation. She knew who I was, she said. Ben had talked to her about me, and he had even given her one of my novels, which she confessed she hadn't had time to read. I didn't dare to ask her any questions on the phone. It was enough to have made contact with her, and so I got right to the point, asking her if she would be willing to see me when I was in the Bay Area at the end of October. She hesitated for a moment, but when I told her how much I was counting on it, she gave in. Call me after you check into your hotel, she said, and we'll have a drink together somewhere. It was that simple. She had an interesting voice, I thought, somewhat throaty and deep, and I liked the sound of it. If she had ever made it as an actress, it was the kind of voice that people would have remembered.

The promise of that meeting kept me going for the next month and a half. When the earthquake hit San Francisco in early October, my first thought was to wonder if my visit would have to be canceled. I'm ashamed of my heartlessness now, but at the time I scarcely even noticed it. Collapsed highways, burning buildings, crushed and mangled bodies – these disasters meant nothing to me except insofar as they could prevent me from talking to Lillian Stern. Fortunately, the theater where I had been booked to do the reading escaped without damage, and the trip went off as planned. After checking into the hotel, I went straight to my room and called the house in Berkeley. A woman with an unfamiliar voice answered the phone. When I asked to speak to Lillian Stern, she told me that Lillian was gone, that she'd left for Chicago three days after the earthquake. When was she coming back? I asked. The woman didn't know. You mean to say the earthquake frightened her that much? I said. Oh no, the woman said, Lillian had been planning to leave before it happened. She had run the ad to sublet her house in early September. What about a forwarding address? I asked. She didn't have one, the woman said, she paid her rent directly to the landlord. Well, I said, struggling to overcome my disappointment, if you ever hear from her, I'd appreciate it if you let me know. Before hanging up, I gave her my number in New York. Call me collect, I said, any time day or night.

I understood then how thoroughly Lillian had tricked me. She had known she would be gone before I ever got there – which meant that she had never had any intention of keeping our appointment. I cursed myself for my gullibility, for the time and hope I had squandered. Just to make sure, I checked with Chicago information, but there was no listing for Lillian Stern. When I called Maria Turner in New York and asked her for Lillian's mother's address, she told me she'd been out of touch with Mrs Stern for years and had no idea where she lived. The trail had suddenly gone cold. Lillian was just as lost to me now as Sachs was, and I couldn't even imagine how to begin looking for her. If there was any consolation in her disappearance, it came from the word *Chicago*. There had to have been a reason why she didn't want to talk to me, and I prayed it was because she was trying to protect Sachs. If that were so, then maybe they were on better terms than I had been led to believe. Or maybe the situation had improved after his visit to Vermont. What if he had driven out to California and talked her into running off with him? He had told me that he kept an apartment in Chicago, and Lillian had told her tenant that she was moving to Chicago. Was it a coincidence, or had one or both of them been lying? I couldn't even guess, but for Sachs's sake I hoped they were together now, living some mad outlaw existence as he crisscrossed the country, furtively plotting his next move. The Phantom of Liberty and his moll. If nothing else, he wouldn't have been alone then, and I preferred to imagine him with her than alone, preferred to imagine any life other than the one he had described to me. If Lillian was as fearless as he had said she was, then maybe she was with him, maybe she was wild enough to have done it.

I learned nothing more after that. Eight months passed, and when Iris and I returned to Vermont at the end of June, I had all but given up on the notion of finding him. Of the hundreds of possible outcomes I imagined, the one that seemed most plausible was that he would never surface again. I had no idea how long the bombings would last, no inkling of when the end would come. And even if there was an end, it seemed doubtful that I would ever know about it – which meant that the story would go on and on, secreting its poison inside me forever. The struggle was to accept that, to coexist with the forces of my own uncertainty. Desperate as I was for a resolution, I had to understand that it might never come. You can hold your breath for just so long, after all. Sooner or later, a moment comes when you have to start breathing again – even if the air is tainted, even if you know it will eventually kill you.

The article in the *Times* caught me with my guard down. I had grown so accustomed to my ignorance by then that I no longer expected anything to change. Someone had died on that road in Wisconsin, but even though I knew it could have been Sachs, I wasn't prepared to believe it. It took the arrival of the FBI men to convince me, and even then I clung to my doubts until the last possible moment – when they mentioned the telephone number that had been found in the dead man's pocket. After that, a single image burned itself into my mind, and it has stayed with me ever since: my poor friend bursting into pieces when the bomb went off, my poor friend's body scattering in the wind.

That was two months ago. I sat down and started this book the next morning, and since then I have worked in a state of continual panic – struggling to finish before I ran out of time, never knowing if I would be able to reach the end. Just as I predicted, the men from the FBI have kept themselves busy on my account. They've talked to my mother in Florida, to my sister in Connecticut, to my friends in New York, and all summer long people have been calling to tell me about these visits, worried that I must be in some kind of trouble. I'm not in trouble yet, but I fully expect to be in the near future. Once my friends Worthy and Harris discover how much I've held back from them, they're bound to be irritated. There's nothing I can do about that now. I realize there are penalties for withholding information from the FBI, but under the circumstances I don't see how I could have acted any differently. I owed it to Sachs to keep my mouth shut, and I owed it to him to write this book. He was brave enough to entrust me with his story, and I don't think I could have lived with myself if I had let him down.

I wrote a short, preliminary draft in the first month, sticking only to the barest essentials. When the case was still unsolved at that point, I went back to the beginning and started filling in the gaps, expanding each chapter to more than twice its original length. My plan was to go through the manuscript as many times as necessary, to add new material with each successive draft, and to keep at it until I felt there was nothing left to say. Theoretically, the process could have continued for months, perhaps even for years – but only if I was lucky. As it is, these past eight weeks are all I will ever have. Three-quarters of the way into the second draft (in the middle of the fourth chapter), I was forced to stop writing. That was yesterday, and I'm still trying to come to grips with how suddenly it happened. The book is over now because the case is over. If I put in this final page, it is only to record how they found the answer, to note the last little surprise, the ultimate twist that concludes the story.

Harris was the one who cracked it. He was the older of the two agents, the talkative one who had asked me questions about my books. As it happened, he eventually went to a store and bought some of them, just as he had promised to do when he visited with his partner in July. I don't know whether he was planning to read them or was simply acting on a hunch, but the copies he bought turned out to have been signed with my name. He must have remembered what I told him about the curious autographs that had been cropping up in my books, and so he called here about ten days ago to ask me if I had ever been in that particular store, located in a small town just outside of Albany. I told him no, I hadn't, I'd never even set foot in that town, and then he thanked me for my help and hung up. I told the truth only because I saw no purpose in lying. His question had nothing to do with Sachs, and if he wanted to look for the person who had been forging my signature, what possible harm could come of that? I thought he was doing me a favor, but in point of fact I had just handed him the key to the case. He turned the books over to the FBI lab the next morning, and after a thorough search for fingerprints, they came up with a number of clean sets. One of them belonged to Sachs. Ben's name must have been known to them already, and since Harris was a crafty fellow, he wouldn't have missed the connection. One thing led to another, and by the time he showed up here yesterday, he had already fit the pieces together. Sachs was the man who had blown himself up in Wisconsin. Sachs was the man who had killed Reed Dimaggio. Sachs was the Phantom of Liberty.

He came here alone, unencumbered by the silent, scowling Worthy. Iris and the children were off swimming in the pond, and it was just me again, standing in front of the house as I watched him climb out of his car. Harris was in good spirits, more jovial than the last time, and he greeted me as though we were old familiars, colleagues in the quest to solve life's mysteries. He had news, he said, and he thought it might interest me. They'd identified the person who'd been signing my books, and it turned out to have been a friend of mine. A man named Benjamin Sachs. Now why would a friend want to do a thing like that?

I stared down at the ground, fighting back tears as Harris waited for an answer. 'Because he missed me,' I finally said. 'He went away on a long trip and forgot to buy postcards. It was his way of staying in touch.'

'Ah,' Harris said, 'a real practical joker. Maybe you can tell me something more about him.'

'Yes, there's a lot I can tell you. Now that he's dead, it doesn't matter anymore, does it?'

Then I pointed to the studio, and without saying another word I led Harris across the yard in the hot afternoon sun. We walked up the stairs together, and once we were inside, I handed him the pages of this book.

(1990–1991)

MR VERTIGO

I

I was twelve years old the first time I walked on water. The man in the black clothes taught me how to do it, and I'm not going to pretend I learned that trick overnight. Master Yehudi found me when I was nine, an orphan boy begging nickels on the streets of Saint Louis, and he worked with me steadily for three years before he let me show my stuff in public. That was in 1927, the year of Babe Ruth and Charles Lindbergh, the precise year when night began to fall on the world forever. I kept it up until a few days before the October crash, and what I did was greater than anything those two gents could have dreamed of. I did what no American had done before me, what no one has ever done since.

Master Yehudi chose me because I was the smallest, the dirtiest, the most abject. 'You're no better than an animal,' he said, 'a piece of human nothingness.' That was the first sentence he spoke to me, and even though sixty-eight years have passed since that night, it's as if I can still hear the words coming from the master's mouth. 'You're no better than an animal. If you stay where you are, you'll be dead before winter is out. If you come with me, I'll teach you how to fly.'

'Ain't nobody can fly, mister,' I said. 'That's what birds do, and I sure as hell ain't no bird.'

'You know nothing,' Master Yehudi said. 'You know nothing because you are nothing. If I haven't taught you to fly by your thirteenth birthday, you can chop off my head with an axe. I'll put it in writing if you like. If I fail to deliver on my promise, my fate will be in your hands.'

It was a Saturday night in early November, and we were standing in front of the Paradise Cafe, a slick downtown gin mill with a colored jazz band and cigarette girls in transparent dresses. I used to hang around there on weekends, cadging handouts and running errands and hustling cabs for the swells. At first I thought Master Yehudi was just another drunk, a rich booze hound stumbling through the night in a black tuxedo and a silk top hat. His accent was strange, so I figured him to be from out of town, but that was as far as I took it. Drunks say stupid things, and the business about flying was no stupider than most.

'You get too high in the air,' I said, 'you could break your neck when you come down.'

'We'll talk about technique later,' the master said. 'It's not an easy skill to learn, but if you listen to me and obey my instructions, we'll both wind up millionaires.'

'You're already a millionaire,' I said. 'What do you need me for?'

'Because, my wretched little thug, I barely have two dimes to rub together. I might look like a robber baron to you, but that's only because you have sawdust for brains. Listen to me carefully. I'm offering you the chance of a lifetime, but you only get that chance once. I'm booked on the *Blue Bird Special* at six thirty a.m., and if you don't haul your carcass onto that train, this is the last you'll ever see of me.'

'You still haven't answered my question,' I said.

'Because you're the answer to my prayers, son. That's why I want you. Because you have the gift.'

'Gift? I ain't got no gift. And even if I did, what would you know about it, Mr Monkey Suit? You only started talking to me a minute ago.'

'Wrong again,' said Master Yehudi. 'I've been watching you for a week. And if you think your aunt and uncle would be sorry to see you gone, then you don't know who you've been living with for the past four years.'

'My aunt and uncle,' I said, suddenly realizing that this man was no Saturday-night drunk. He was something worse than that: a truant officer or a cop, and sure as I was standing there, I was up to my knees in shit.

'Your Uncle Slim is a piece of work,' the master continued, taking his time now that he had my attention. 'I never knew an American citizen could be that dumb. Not only does he smell bad, but he's mean and ugly to boot. No wonder you turned into such a weasel-faced guttersnipe. We had a long conversation this morning, your uncle and I, and he's willing to let you go without a penny changing hands. Imagine that, boy. I didn't even have to pay for you. And that dough-fleshed sow he calls his wife just sat there and never said a word in your defense. If that's the best you can do for a family, then you're lucky to be rid of those two. The decision is yours, but even if you turn me down, it might not be such a good idea to go back. They'd be plenty disappointed to see you again, I can tell you that. Just about dumbstruck with sorrow, if you know what I mean.'

I might have been an animal, but even the lowest animal has feelings, and when the master sprang this news on me, I felt as if I'd been punched. Uncle Slim and Aunt Peg were nothing to write home about, but their home was where I lived, and it stopped me in my tracks to learn they didn't want me. I was only nine years old, after all. Tough as I was for that age, I wasn't half as tough as I pretended to be, and if the master hadn't been looking down at me with those dark eyes of his just then, I probably would have started bawling right there on the street.

When I think back to that night now, I'm still not sure if he was telling me the truth or not. He could have talked to my aunt and uncle, but then again, he could have been making the whole thing up. I don't doubt that he'd seen them – he had their descriptions dead on – but knowing my Uncle Slim, it strikes me as next to impossible that he would have let me go without wheedling some cash out of the bargain. I'm not saying that Master Yehudi welshed on him, but given what happened later, there's no question that the bastard felt wronged, whether justice was on his side or not. I'm not going to waste time puzzling over that now. The upshot was that I fell for what the master told me, and in the long run that's the only fact that bears telling. He convinced me that I couldn't go home, and once I accepted that, I didn't give a damn about myself anymore. That must have been how he wanted me to feel – all jangled up and lost inside. If you don't see any reason to go on living, it's hard to care much about what happens to you. You tell yourself you want to be dead, and after that you discover you're ready for anything – even a crazy thing like vanishing into the night with a stranger.

'Okay, mister,' I said, dropping my voice a couple of octaves and giving him my best cutthroat stare, 'you've got yourself a deal. But if you don't come through for me like you say, you can kiss your head goodbye. I might be small, but I never let a man forget a promise.'

It was still dark when we boarded the train. We rode west into the dawn, traveling across the state of Missouri as the dim November light struggled to crack through the clouds. I hadn't been out of Saint Louis since the day they buried my mother, and it was a gloomy world I discovered that morning: gray and barren, with endless fields of withered cornstalks flanking us on both sides. We chugged into Kansas City a little past noon, but in all the hours we spent together I don't think Master Yehudi spoke more than three or four words to me. Most of the time he slept, nodding off with his hat pulled down over his face, but I was too scared to do anything but look out the window, watching the land slip past me as I pondered the mess I'd gotten myself into. My pals in Saint

Louis had warned me about characters like Master Yehudi: solitary drifters with evil designs, perverts on the prowl for young boys to do their bidding. It was bad enough to imagine him taking off my clothes and touching me where I didn't want to be touched, but that was nothing compared to some of the other fears knocking around in my skull. I'd heard about one boy who had gone off with a stranger and was never heard from again. Later on, the man confessed he'd sliced up the lad into little pieces and boiled him for dinner. Another boy had been chained to a wall in a dark cellar and given nothing to eat but bread and water for six months. Another one had had the skin peeled off his bones. Now that I had time to consider what I'd done, I figured I might be in for the same kind of treatment myself. I'd let myself fall into the clutches of a monster, and if he turned out to be half as spooky as he looked, the odds were I'd never see the dawn rise again.

We got off the train and started walking down the platform, wending our way through the crowd. 'I'm hungry,' I said, tugging on Master Yehudi's coat. 'If you don't feed me now, I'm going to turn you in to the first flatfoot I see.'

'What's the matter with the apple I gave you?' he said.

'I chucked it out the window of the train.'

'Oh, not too keen on apples, are we? And what about the ham sandwich? Not to speak of the fried chicken leg and the bag of doughnuts.'

'I chucked it all. You don't expect me to eat the grub you give me, do you?'

'And why not, little man? If you don't eat, you'll shrivel up and die. Everybody knows that.'

'At least you die slow that way. You bite into something filled with poison, and you croak on the spot.'

For the first time since I'd met him, Master Yehudi broke into a smile. If I'm not mistaken, I believe he even went so far as to laugh. 'You're saying you don't trust me, is that it?'

'You're damn straight. I wouldn't trust you as far as I could throw a dead mule.'

'Lighten up, squirt,' the master said, patting me affectionately on the shoulder. 'You're my meal ticket, remember? I wouldn't hurt a hair on your head.'

Those were just words as far as I was concerned, and I wasn't so dumb as to swallow that kind of sugary talk. But then Master Yehudi reached into his pocket, pulled out a stiff new dollar bill, and slapped it into my palm. 'See that restaurant over there?' he said, pointing to a hash house in the middle of the station. 'Go in and order yourself the biggest lunch you can stuff inside that belly of yours. I'll wait for you out here.'

'And what about you? You got something against eating?'

'Don't worry about me,' Master Yehudi replied. 'My stomach can take care of itself.' Then, just as I was turning to go, he added: 'One word of advice, pipsqueak. In case you're planning to run away, this is the time to do it. And don't worry about the dollar. You can keep it for your trouble.'

I walked on into the restaurant by myself, feeling somewhat mollified by those parting words. If he had some sinister purpose, then why would he offer me a chance to escape? I sat down at the counter and asked for the blue-plate special and a bottle of sarsaparilla. Before I could blink, the waiter shoved a mountain of corned beef and cabbage in front of me. It was the largest meal I had ever encountered, a meal as large as Sportsman's Park in Saint Louis, and I wolfed down every morsel of it, along with two slices of bread and a second bottle of sarsaparilla. Nothing can compare to the sense of well-being that washed through me at that filthy lunch counter. Once my belly was full, I felt invincible, as if nothing could harm me again. The crowning touch came when I extracted the dollar bill from my pocket to settle the tab. The whole thing toted tip to just forty-five cents, and even after I threw in a nickel tip for the waiter, that left me with four bits in change. It doesn't sound like much today, but two quarters represented a fortune to me back then. This is my chance to run, I told myself, giving the joint the once-over as I stood up from my stool. I can slip out the side door, and the man in black will never know what hit him. But I didn't do it, and in that choice hung the entire story of my life. I went back to where the master was waiting because he'd promised to turn me into a millionaire. On the strength of those fifty cents, I figured it might be worth it to see if there was any truth to the boast.

We took another train after that, and then a third train near the end of the journey which brought us to the town of Cibola at seven o'clock that night. Silent as he had been all morning, Master Yehudi rarely stopped talking for the rest of the day. I was already learning not to make any assumptions about what he might or might not do. Just when you thought you had him pegged, he would turn around and do the precise contrary of what you were expecting.

'You can call me Master Yehudi,' he said, announcing his name to me for the first time. 'If you like, you can call me Master for short. But never, under any circumstances, are you to call me Yehudi. Is that clear?'

'Is that your God-given name,' I said, 'or did you choose that moniker yourself?'

'There's no need for you to know my real name. Master Yehudi will be sufficient.'

'Well, I'm Walter. Walter Claireborne Rawley. But you can call me Walt.'

'I'll call you anything I like. If I want to call you Worm, I'll call you Worm. If I want to call you Pig, I'll call you Pig. Is that understood?'

'Hell, mister, I don't understand a thing you're talking about.'

'Nor will I tolerate any lying or duplicity. No excuses, no complaints, no back talk. Once you catch on, you're going to be the happiest boy on earth.'

'Sure. And if a legless man had legs, he could piss standing up.'

'I know your story, son. So you don't have to invent any tall tales for me. I know how your pa got gassed over in Belgium in 'seventeen. And I know about your ma, too, and how she used to turn tricks over in East Saint Louis for a buck a tumble, and what happened to her four and a half years ago when that crazy cop turned his revolver on her and blew off her face. Don't think I don't pity you, boy, but you'll never get anywhere if you dodge the truth when you're dealing with me.'

'Okay, Mr Smarty Pants. If you've got all the answers, why waste your breath telling me things you already know?'

'Because you still don't believe a word I've said. You think this stuff about flying is a lot of hot air. You're going to work hard, Walt, harder than you've ever worked before, and you're going to want to quit on me almost every day, but if you stick with it and trust what I tell you, at the end of a few years you'll be able to fly. I swear it. You'll be able to lift yourself off the ground and fly through the air like a bird.'

'I'm from Missouri, remember? They don't call it the Show-Me-State for nothing.'

'Well, we're not in Missouri anymore, my little friend. We're in Kansas. And a flatter, more desolate place you've never seen in your life. When Coronado and his men marched through here in 1540 looking for the Cities of Gold, they got so lost that half of them went insane. There's nothing to tell you where you are. No mountains, no trees, no bumps in the road. It's flat as death out here, and once you've been around for a while, you'll understand there's nowhere to go but up – that the sky is the only friend you have.'

It was dark by the time we pulled into the station, so there was no way to vouch for the master's description of my new home. As far as I could tell, the town was no different from what you'd expect to see in a little town. A trifle colder, perhaps, and more than a trifle darker than what I was used to, but given that I had never been in a little town before, I had no idea what to expect. Everything was new to me: every smell was strange, every star in the sky seemed unfamiliar. If someone had told me I'd just entered the Land of Oz, I don't think I would have known the difference.

We walked through the station house and stood outside the door for a moment scanning the dark village. It was only seven o'clock in the evening, but the whole place was locked up, and except for a few lamps burning in the houses beyond, there was no sign of life anywhere. 'Don't worry,' Master Yehudi said, 'our ride will be along any minute.' He reached out and tried to take hold of my hand, but I yanked my arm away before he could get a firm grip. 'Keep your paws to yourself, Mr Master,' I said. 'You might think you own me now, but you don't own squat.'

About nine seconds after I uttered those words, a big gray horse appeared at the end of the street pulling a buckboard wagon. It looked like something from the Tom Mix western I'd seen that summer at the Picture Palace, but this was 1924, for Christ's sake, and when I caught sight of that antiquated vehicle rumbling down the street, I thought it was an apparition. But lo and behold, Master Yehudi waved when he saw it coming, and then that old gray horse stopped right in front of us, sidling up to the curb as gusts of steam poured from its nostrils. The driver was a round, chunky figure in a wide-brimmed hat whose body was wrapped in blankets, and at first I couldn't tell if it was a man, a woman, or a bear.

'Hello, Mother Sue,' the master said. 'Take a look at what I found.'

The woman gazed at me for a couple of seconds with blank, stone-cold eyes, and then, out of nowhere, flashed one of the warmest, friendliest smiles I've ever had the pleasure to receive. There couldn't have been more than two or three teeth jutting from her gums, and from the way her dark eyes glittered, I concluded that she was a Gypsy. She was Mother Sue, the Queen of the Gypsies, and Master Yehudi was her son, the Prince of Blackness. They were abducting me to the Castle of

No Return, and if they didn't eat me for dinner that night, they were going to turn me into a slavey boy, a groveling eunuch with an earring in my ear and a silk bandana wrapped around my head.

'Hop in, sonny,' Mother Sue said. Her voice was so deep and mannish, I would have been scared to death if I hadn't known she could smile. 'You'll see some blankets in the back. If you know what's good for you, you'll use 'em. We got a long cold ride ahead of us, and you don't want to get there with no frozen fanny.'

'His name is Walt,' the master said as he climbed up beside her. 'A pus-brained ragamuffin from honky-tonk row. If my hunch is correct, he's the one I've been looking for all these years.' Then, turning in my direction, he said brusquely, 'This is Mother Sue, kid. Treat her nice, and she'll give you only goodness in return. Cross her, and you'll regret the day you were born. She might be fat and toothless, but she's the closest thing to a mother you'll ever have.'

I don't know how long it took us to get to the house. It was out in the country somewhere, sixteen or seventeen miles from town, but I didn't learn that until later, for once I climbed in under the blankets and the wagon started down the road, I fell fast asleep. When I opened my eyes again, we were already there, and if the master hadn't roused me with a slap across the face, I probably would have slept until morning.

He led me into the house as Mother Sue unhitched the nag, and the first room we entered was the kitchen: a bare, dimly lit space with a wood stove in one corner and a kerosene lamp flickering in another. A black boy of about fifteen was sitting at the table reading a book. He wasn't brown like most of the colored folks I'd run across back home, he was the color of pitch, a black so black it was almost blue. He was a full-fledged Ethiopian, a pickaninny from the jungles of darkest Africa, and my heart just about stopped beating when I caught sight of him. He was a frail, scrawny fellow with bulging eyes and those enormous lips, and as soon as he stood up from his chair to greet us, I saw that his bones were all twisted and askew, that he had the jagged, hunchbacked body of a cripple.

'This is Aesop,' the master said to me, 'the finest boy who ever lived. Say hello to him, Walt, and shake his hand. He's going to be your new brother.'

'I ain't shaking hands with no nigger,' I said. 'You've got to be crazy if you'd think I'd do a thing like that.'

Master Yehudi let out a loud, prolonged sigh. It wasn't an expression of disgust so much as of sorrow, a monumental shudder from the depths of his soul. Then, with utmost deliberation and calm, he curled the index finger of his right hand into a frozen, beckoning hook and placed the tip of that hook directly under my chin, at the precise spot where the flesh meets the bone. Then he began to press, and all at once a horrific pain shot around the back of my neck and up into my skull. I had never felt pain like that before. I struggled to cry out, but my throat was blocked, and I could do no more than produce a sick gagging noise. The master continued to press with his finger, and presently I felt my feet lift off the ground. I was traveling upward, rising into the air like a feather, and the master seemed to be accomplishing this without the slightest effort, as if I were of no more consequence to him than a ladybug. Eventually, he had me up to where my face was on a level with his and I was looking directly into his eyes.

'We don't talk like that around here, boy,' he said. 'All men are brothers, and in this family everyone gets treated with respect. That's the law. If you don't like it, lump it. The law is the law, and whoever goes against it is turned into a slug and wallows in the earth for the rest of his days.'

They fed me and clothed me and gave me a room of my own. I wasn't spanked or paddled, I wasn't kicked around or punched or boxed on the ears, and yet tolerable as things were for me, I had never been more down at the mouth, more filled with bitterness and pent-up fury. For the first six months, I thought only about running away. I was a city boy who had grown up with jazz in his blood, a street kid with his eye on the main chance, and I loved the hurly-burly of crowds, the screech of trolley cars and the throb of neon, the stink of bootleg whiskey trickling in the gutters. I was a boogie-toed prankster, a midget scatman with a quick tongue and a hundred angles, and there I was stuck in the middle of nowhere, living under a sky that brought only weather – nearly all of it bad.

Master Yehudi's property consisted of thirty-seven acres of dirt, a two-story farmhouse, a chicken coop, a pigpen, and a barn. There were a dozen chickens in the coop, two cows and the gray horse in the barn, and six or seven pigs in the pen. There was no electricity, no plumbing, no telephone, no wireless, no phonograph, no nothing. The only source of entertainment was the piano in the parlor, but Aesop was the only one who could play it, and he made such a botch of even the simplest songs that I always left the room the moment he sat down and touched his fingers to the keys. The joint was a shit hole, the world capital of boredom, and I was already fed up with it after one day. They didn't even know about baseball in that house, and I had no one to talk to about my beloved Cardinals, which was about the only subject that interested me back then. I felt as if I'd fallen through a crack in time and landed in the stone age, a country where dinosaurs still roamed the earth. According to Mother Sue, Master Yehudi had won the farm on a bet with some fellow in Chicago about seven years earlier. That must have been some bet, I said. The loser turns out to be the winner, and the winner's a chump who gets to rot away his future in Bungholeville USA.

I was a fiery little dunce back then, I'll admit it, but I'm not going to make any apologies for myself. I was who I was, a product of the people and places I'd come from, and there's no point in whining about that now. What impresses me most about those early months is how patient they were, how well they seemed to understand me and tolerate my antics. I ran away four times that first winter, once getting as far as Wichita, and each time they took me back, no questions asked. I was scarcely a hair's breadth greater than nothing, a molecule or two above the vanishing point of what constitutes a human being, and since the master reckoned that my soul was no loftier than an animal's, that's where he started me out: in the barn with the animals.

Much as I detested taking care of those chickens and pigs, I preferred their company to the people. It was difficult for me to decide which one I hated most, and every day I would reshuffle the order of my animosities. Mother Sue and Aesop came in for their fair share of inner scorn, but in the end it was the master who provoked my greatest ire and resentment. He was the scoundrel who had tricked me into going there, and if anyone was to blame for the fix I was in, he was the chief culprit. What galled me most was his sarcasm, the cracks and insults he hurled constantly in my direction, the way he would ride me and hound me for no reason but to prove how worthless I was. With the other two he was always polite, a model of decorum, but he rarely wasted an opportunity to say something mean-spirited on my account. It started the very first morning, and after that he never let up. Before long, I realized that he was no better than Uncle Slim. He might not have thrashed me the way Slim did, but the master's words had power, and they hurt just as much as any blow to the head.

'Well, my fine-feathered rascal,' he said to me that first morning, 'give me the lowdown on what you know about the three R's.'

'Three?' I said, going for the quick, wise-guy retort. 'I ain't got but one arse, and I use it every time I sit down. Same as everybody else.'

'I mean school, you twerp. Have you ever set foot in a classroom – and if so, what did you learn there?'

'I don't need no school to teach me things. I've got better ways of spending my time than that.'

'Excellent. Spoken like a true scholar. But be more specific. What about the alphabet? Can you write the letters of the alphabet or not?'

'Some of them. The ones that serve my purpose. The others don't matter. They just give me a pain, so I don't worry about them.'

'And which ones serve your purpose?'

'Well, let's see. There's the *A*, I like that one, and the *W*. Then there's the whatchamacallit, the *L*, and the *E*, and the *R*, and the one that looks like a cross. The *T*. As in T-bone steak. Those letters are my buddies, and the rest can go fry in hell for all I care.'

'So you know how to write your name.'

'That's what I'm telling you, boss. I can write my name, I can count to kingdom come, and I know that the sun is a star in the sky. I also know that books are for girls and sissies, and if you're planning to teach me anything out of books, we can call off our arrangement right now.'

'Don't fret, kid. What you've just told me is music to my ears. The dumber you are, the better it is for both of us. There's less to undo that way, and that's going to save us a lot of time.'

'And what about the flying lessons? When do we start with them?'

'We've already started. From now on, everything we do is connected to your training. That won't always be apparent to you, so try to keep it in mind. If you don't forget, you'll be able to hang in there when the going gets rough. We're embarking on a long journey, son, and the first thing I have to do is break your spirit. I wish it could be some other way, but it can't. Considering the muck you spring from, that shouldn't be too hard a task.'

So I spent my days shoveling manure in the barn, freezing my eyebrows off as the others sat snug and cozy in the house. Mother Sue took care of the cooking and domestic chores, Aesop lounged around on the sofa reading books, and Master Yehudi did nothing at all. His principal occupation seemed to be sitting on a straight-backed wooden chair from sunrise to sundown and looking out the window. Except for his conversations with Aesop, that was the only thing I saw him do until spring. I sometimes listened in when the two of them talked, but I could never make sense of what they were saying. They used so many complicated words, it was as if they were communicating in their own private gibberish. Later on, when I settled into the swing of things a bit more, I learned that they were studying. Master Yehudi had taken it upon himself to educate Aesop in the liberal arts, and the books they read concerned any number of different subjects: history, science, literature, mathematics, Latin, French, and so on. He had his project of teaching me to fly, but he was also engaged in turning Aesop into a scholar, and as far as I could tell that second project meant a lot more to him than mine did. As the master put it to me one morning not long after my arrival: 'He was even worse off than you were, runt. When I found him twelve years ago, he was crawling through a cotton field in Georgia dressed in rags. He hadn't eaten in two days, and his mama, who was no more than a child herself, lay dead from TB in their shack fourteen miles down the road. That's how far the kid had wandered from home. He was delirious with hunger by then, and if I hadn't chanced upon him at that particular moment, there's no telling what would have happened. His body might be contorted into a tragic shape, but his mind is a glorious instrument, and he's already surpassed me in most fields. My plan is to send him to college in three years. He can continue his studies there, and once he graduates and goes out into the world, he'll become a leader of his race, a shining example to all the downtrodden black folks of this violent, hypocritical country.' I couldn't make head or tail of what the master was talking about, but the love in his voice burned through to me and impressed itself on my mind. For all my stupidity, I was able to understand that much. He loved Aesop as if he were his own son, and I was no better than a mutt, a mongrel beast to be spat on and left out in the rain.

Mother Sue was my companion in ignorance, my fellow illiterate and sluggard, and while that might have helped to create a bond between us, it did nothing of the sort. There was no overt hostility in her, but at the same time she gave me the willies, and I think it took me longer to adjust to her oddnesses than it did with the two others – who could hardly be called normal themselves. Even with the blankets removed from her body and the hat gone from her head, I had trouble determining which sex she belonged to. I found that distressing somehow, and even after I glimpsed her naked through the keyhole of her door and saw with my own eyes that she possessed a pair of titties and had no member dangling from her bush, I still wasn't entirely convinced. Her hands were tough like a man's, she had broad shoulders and muscles that bulged in her upper arms, and except when she flashed me one of her rare and beautiful smiles, her face was as remote and ungiving as a block of wood. That's closer to what unsettled me, perhaps: her silence, the way she seemed to look through me as if I wasn't there. In the pecking order of the household, I stood directly below her, which meant that I had more dealings with Mother Sue than with anyone else. She was the one who doled out my chores and checked up on me, who made sure I washed my face and brushed my teeth before going to bed, and yet for all the hours I spent in her company, she made me feel lonelier than if I had been truly alone. A hollowed-out sensation crept into my belly whenever she was around, as if just being near her would start to make me shrink. It didn't matter how I behaved. I could jump up and down or stand still, I could holler my head off or hold my tongue, and the results never varied. Mother Sue was a wall, and every time I approached that wall I was turned into a puff of smoke, a tiny cloud of ashes scattering in the wind.

The only one who showed me any genuine kindness was Aesop, but I was against him from the start, and there was nothing he could say or do that would ever change that. I couldn't help myself. It was in my blood to feel contempt for him, and given that he was the ugliest specimen of his kind I'd ever had the misfortune to see, it struck me as preposterous that we were living under the same roof. It went against the laws of nature, it transgressed everything that was holy and proper, and I wouldn't allow myself to accept it. When you threw in the fact that Aesop talked like no other colored boy on the face of the earth – more like an English lord than an American – and then threw in the additional fact that he was the master's favorite, I couldn't even think about him without succumbing to an onslaught of nerves. To make matters worse, I had to keep my mouth shut whenever he was around. A few choice remarks would have blown off some of my rage, I think, but I remembered the master's finger thrusting under my chin, and I was in no mood to submit to that torture again.

The worst part of it was that Aesop didn't seem to care that I despised him so much. I perfected a whole repertoire of scowls and grimaces to use in his company, but whenever I shot one of those looks in his direction, he would just shake his head and smile to himself. It made me feel like an idiot. No matter how hard I tried to hurt him, he never let me get under his skin, never gave me the satisfaction of scoring a point against him. He wasn't simply winning the war between us, he was winning every damned battle of that war, and I figured that if I couldn't even beat a black devil in a fair exchange of insults, then the whole of that Kansas prairie must have been bewitched. I'd been shanghaied to a land of bad dreams, and the more I struggled to wake up, the scarier the nightmare became.

'You try too hard,' Aesop said to me one afternoon. 'You're so consumed with your own righteousness, it's made you blind to the things around you. And if you can't see what's in front of your nose, you'll never be able to look at yourself and know who you are.'

'I know who I am,' I said. 'There ain't nobody can steal that from me.'

'The master isn't stealing anything from you. He's giving you the gift of greatness.'

'Look, do me a favor, will you? Don't mention that buzzard's name when I'm around. He gives me the creeps, that master of yours, and the less I have to think about him, the better off I'm going to be.'

'He loves you, Walt. He believes in you with every ounce of his soul.'

'The hell he does. That faker don't give a rat's ass about nothing. He's the King of the Gypsies is what he is, and if he's got any soul at all – which I'm not saying he does – then it's packed with evil through and through.'

'King of the Gypsies?' Aesop's eyes bugged out in amazement. 'Is that what you think?' The idea must have bopped him on the funny bone, for a moment later he grabbed his stomach and started shaking in a fit of laughter. 'You sure know how to come up with some good ones,' he said, wiping the tears from his eyes. 'What on earth ever put that notion in your head?'

'Well,' I said, feeling my cheeks blush with embarrassment, 'if he ain't no Gypsy, what the hell is he, then?'

'A Hungarian.'

'A what?' I stammered. It was the first time I'd ever heard anyone use that word, and I was so flummoxed by it that I momentarily lost the power of speech.

'A Hungarian. He was born in Budapest and came to America as a young boy. He grew up in Brooklyn, New York, and both his father and grandfather were rabbis.'

'And what's that, some lesser form of rodent?'

'It's a Jewish teacher. Sort of like a minister or priest, only for Jews.'

'Well now,' I said, 'there you go. That explains everything, don't it? He's worse than a Gypsy, old Doctor Dark Brows – he's a kike. There ain't nothing worse than that on the whole miserable planet.'

'You'd better not let him hear you talking like that,' Aesop said.

'I know my rights,' I said. 'And no Jew man is going to shove me around, I swear it.'

'Easy does it, Walt. You're only asking for trouble.'

'And what about that witch, Mother Sue? Is she another one of them Hebes?'

Aesop shook his head and stared down at the ground. My voice was seething with such anger, he couldn't bring himself to look me in the eyes. 'No,' he said. 'She's an Oglala Sioux. Her grandfather was Sitting Bull's brother, and when she was young, she was the top bareback rider in Buffalo Bill's Wild West Show.'

'You're shitting me.'

'I wouldn't dream of it. What I'm telling you is the pure, unvarnished truth. You're living in the same house with a Jew, a black man, and an Indian, and the sooner you accept the facts, the happier your life is going to be.'

I'd held on for three weeks until then, but after that conversation with Aesop I knew I couldn't stand it anymore. I lit out of there that same night – waiting until everyone was asleep and then crawling out of the covers, sneaking down the stairs, and tiptoeing into the frigid December darkness. There was no moon overhead, not even a star to shine down on me, and the moment I crossed the threshold, I was struck by a wind so fierce that it blew me straight back against the side of the house. My bones were no stronger than cotton in that wind. The night was aroar with clamor, and the air rushed and boomed as if it carried the voice of God, howling down its wrath on any creature foolish enough to rise against it. I became that fool, and time and again I picked myself off the ground and fought my way into the teeth of the maelstrom, spinning around like a pinwheel as I inched my body into the yard. After ten or twelve tries, I was all worn out, a spent and battered hulk. I had made it as far as the pigpen, and just as I was about to scramble to my knees once more, my eyes shut on me and I lost consciousness. Hours passed. I woke at the crack of dawn and found myself encircled by four slumbering pigs. If I hadn't landed among those swine, there's a good chance I would have frozen to death during the night. Thinking about it now, I suppose it was a miracle, but when I opened my eyes that morning and saw where I was, the first thing I did was jump to my feet and spit, cursing my rotten luck.

I had no doubt that Master Yehudi was responsible for what had happened. In that early stage of our history together, I attributed all sorts of supernatural powers to him, and I was fully convinced that he had brought forth that ferocious wind for no other reason than to stop me from running away. For several weeks after that, my head filled with a multitude of wild theories and speculations. The scariest one had to do with Aesop – and my growing certainty that he had been born a white person. It was a terrible thing to contemplate, but all the evidence seemed to support my conclusion. He talked like a white person, didn't he? He acted like a white person, he thought like a white person, he played the piano like a white person, and just because his skin was black, why should I believe my eyes when my gut told me something else? The only answer was that he had been born white. Years ago, the master had chosen him as his first student in the art of flying. He'd told Aesop to jump from the roof of the barn, and Aesop had jumped – but instead of catching the wind currents and soaring through the air, he'd fallen to the ground and broken every bone in his body. That accounted for his pitiful, lopsided frame, but then, to make matters even worse, Master Yehudi had punished him for his failure. Invoking the power of a hundred Jewish demons, he'd pointed his finger at his disciple and turned him into a ghastly nigger. Aesop's life had been destroyed, and I had no doubt that the same fate was in store for me. Not only would I wind up with black skin and a crippled body, but I would be forced to spend the rest of my days studying books.

I absconded for the second time in the middle of the afternoon. The night had thwarted me with its magic, so I countered with a new strategy and stole off in broad daylight, figuring that if I could see where I was going, there wouldn't be any goblins to menace my steps. For the first hour or two, everything went according to plan. I slipped out of the barn just after lunch and headed down the road to Cibola, intent on maintaining a brisk pace and reaching town before dark. From there I was going to hitch a ride on a freight train and wend my way back east. If I didn't mess up, in twenty-four hours I'd be strolling down the boulevards of dear old Saint Louis.

So there I was, jogging along that flat dusty highway with the field mice and the crows, feeling more and more confident with each step I took, when all of a sudden I glanced up and saw a buckboard wagon approaching from the opposite direction. It looked surprisingly like the wagon that belonged to Master Yehudi, but since I'd just seen that one in the barn before I left, I shrugged it off as a coincidence and kept on walking. When I got to within about twelve yards of it, I glanced up again. My tongue froze to the roof of my mouth; my eyeballs dropped from their sockets and clattered at my feet. It was Master Yehudi's wagon all right, and sitting on top of that wagon was none other than the master himself, looking down at me with a big smile on his face. He eased the wagon to a halt and tipped his hat to me in a casual, friendly sort of way.

'Howdy, son. A bit nippy for a stroll this afternoon, don't you think?'

'The weather suits me fine,' I said. 'At least a fellow can breathe out here. You stay in one place too long, you start to choke on your own exhaust.'

'Sure, I know how it is. Every boy needs to stretch his legs. But the outing is over now, and it's time to go home. Hoist yourself aboard, Walt, and we'll see if we can't get there before the others notice we've been gone.'

I didn't have much choice, so I climbed up and sat myself beside him as he flicked the reins and got the horse going again. At least he wasn't treating me with his customary rudeness, and burned as I was that my escape had been foiled, I wasn't about to let him know what I'd been up to. He'd probably guessed that anyway, but rather than reveal how disappointed I was, I pretended to play along with the business about being out for a walk.

'It ain't good for a boy to be cooped up so much,' I said. 'It makes him sad and foul-tempered, and then he don't get down to his chores in the right spirit. If you give a guy a little fresh air, he's that much more willing to do his work.'

'I hear what you're saying, chum,' the master said, 'and I understand every word of it.'

'Well, what's it gonna be, captain? I know Cibola ain't much of a burg, but I'll bet they got a picture show or something. It might be nice to go there one evening. You know, a little jaunt to break the monotony. Or else maybe there's a ball club around here, one of them minor league outfits. When spring comes, why not let's take in a game or two? It don't have to be no big-time stuff like the Cards. I mean Class D is okay with me. Just as long as they use bats and balls, you won't hear a word of complaint from this corner. You never know, sir. If you give it half a chance, you might even take a shine to it yourself.'

'I'm sure I would. But there's a mountain of work still in front of us, and in the meantime the family has to lie low. The more invisible we make ourselves, the safer we're going to be. I don't want to scare you, but things aren't as dull in this neighborhood as they might seem. We have some powerful enemies around here, and they're not too thrilled by our presence in their county. A lot of them wouldn't mind if we suddenly stopped breathing, and we don't want to provoke them by strutting our motley selves in public.'

'As long as we mind our own business, who cares what other folks think?'

'That's just it. Some people think our business is their business, and I aim to keep a wide berth of those meddlers. Do you follow me, Walt?'

I told him I did, but the truth was I didn't follow him at all. The only thing I knew was that there were people who wanted to kill me and that I wasn't allowed to go to any ball games. Not even the sympathetic tone in the master's voice could make me understand that, and all during the ride home I kept telling myself to be strong and never say die. Sooner or later I'd find a way to get out of there, sooner or later I'd leave that Voodoo Man in the dust.

My third attempt failed just as miserably as the other two. I left in the morning that time, and even though I made it to the outskirts of Cibola, Master Yehudi was waiting for me again, perched on the buckboard wagon with that same self-satisfied grin spread across his face. I was utterly disarranged by that episode. Unlike the previous time, I could no longer dismiss his being there as a matter of chance. It was as if he had known I was going to run away before I knew it myself. The bastard was inside my head, sucking out the juices of my brain, and not even my innermost thoughts could be hidden from him.

Still, I didn't give up. I was just going to have to be more clever, more methodical in the way I went about it. After ample reflection, I concluded that the primary cause of my troubles was the farm itself. I couldn't get out of there because the place was so well-organized, so thoroughly self-sufficient. We had milk and butter from the cows, eggs from the chickens, meat from the pigs, vegetables from the root cellar, abundant stores of flour, salt, sugar, and cloth, and it was unnecessary for anyone to go to town to stock up on supplies. But what if we ran out of something, I told myself, what if there was a sudden shortage of some vital something we couldn't live without? The master would have to go off for more, wouldn't he? And as soon as he was gone, I'd sneak out of there and make my escape.

It was all so simple, I nearly gagged for joy when this idea came to me. It must have been February by then, and for the next month or so I thought of little else but sabotage. My mind churned with countless plots and schemes, conjuring up acts of untold terror and devastation. I figured I would start small – slashing a bag of flour or two, maybe pissing into the sugar barrel – but if those things failed to produce the desired result, I wasn't averse to more grandiose forms of vandalism: releasing the chickens from their coop, for example, or slitting the throats of the pigs. There wasn't anything I wasn't willing to do to get out of there, and if push came to shove, I was even prepared to set the straw on fire and burn down the barn.

None of it worked out as I imagined it would. I had my opportunities, but each time I was about to put a plan into operation, my nerve mysteriously failed me. Fear would well up in my lungs, my heart would begin to flutter, and just as my hand was poised to commit the deed, an invisible force would rob me of my strength. Nothing like that had ever happened before. I had always been a mischief-maker through and through, in full command of my impulses and desires. If I wanted to do something, I just went ahead and did it, plunging in with the recklessness of a born outlaw. Now I was stymied, blocked by a strange paralysis of will, and I despised myself for acting like such a coward, could not comprehend how a truant of my caliber could have sunk so low. Master Yehudi had beaten me to the punch again. He'd turned me into a puppet, and the more I struggled to defeat him, the tighter he pulled the strings.

I went through a month of hell before I found the courage to give it another shot. This time, luck seemed to be with me. Not ten minutes after hitting the road, I was picked up by a passing motorist, and he drove me all the way to Wichita. He was about the nicest fellow I'd ever met, a college boy on his way to see his fiancée, and we got along from the word go, regaling each other with stories for the whole two and a half hours. I wish I could remember his name. He was a sandy-haired lummox with freckles around his nose and a nifty little leather cap. For some reason, I remember that his girlfriend's name was Francine, but that must have been because he talked about her so much, going on at length about the rosy nipples on her breasts and the lacy frills attached to her undies. Leather Cap had a shiny new Ford roadster, and he sped down that empty highway as if there was no tomorrow. I got the giggles I felt so free and happy, and the more we yacked about one thing and another, the freer and happier I felt. I'd really done it this time, I told myself. I'd really busted out of there, and from now on there'd be no stopping me.

I can't say precisely what I was expecting from Wichita, but it certainly wasn't the dreary little cow town I discovered that afternoon in 1925. The place was Podunk City, a pimple of yawns on a bare white butt. Where were the saloons and the gunslingers and the professional card sharks? Where was Wyatt Earp? Whatever Wichita had been in the past, its present incarnation was a sober, joyless muddle of shops and houses, a town built so low to the ground that your elbow knocked against the sky whenever you paused to scratch your head. I'd figured I'd get some scam going for myself, hang around for a few days while I built up my nest egg, and then travel back to Saint Louis in style. A quick tour of the streets convinced me to bag that notion, and half an hour after I'd arrived, I was already looking for a train to get me out of there.

I felt so glum and dejected, I didn't even notice that it had started to snow. March was the worst season for storms in that country, but the day had dawned so bright and clear, it hadn't even occurred to me to think the weather might change. It began with a small flurry, a few sprinkles of whiteness slithering through the clouds, but as I continued my walk across town in search of the rail depot, the flakes grew thicker and more intense, and when I stopped to check my bearings five or ten minutes later, I was already up to my ankles in the stuff. Snow was falling by the bucketful. Before I could say the word *blizzard*, the wind kicked up and started whirling the snow around in all directions at once. It was uncanny how fast it happened. One minute, I'd been walking through the streets of downtown Wichita, and the next minute I was lost, stumbling blindly through a white tempest. I had no clue as to where I was anymore. I was shivering under my wet clothes, the wind was in a frenzy, and I was smack in the middle of it, turning around in circles.

I'm not sure how long I blundered through that glop. No less than three hours, I would think, perhaps as many as five or six. I had reached town in the late afternoon, and I was still on my feet after nightfall, pushing my way through the mountainous drifts, hemmed in up to my knees, then up to my waist, then up to my neck, frantically looking for shelter before the snow swallowed my entire body. I had to keep moving. The slightest pause would bury me, and before I could fight my way out, I'd either freeze to death or suffocate. So I kept on struggling forward, even though I knew it was hopeless, even though I knew that each step was carrying me closer to my end. Where are the lights? I kept asking myself. I was wandering farther and farther away from town, out into the countryside where no one lived, and yet every time I shifted course, I found myself in the same darkness, surrounded by unbroken night and cold.

After a while, nothing felt real to me anymore. My mind had stopped working, and if my body was still dragging me along, it was only because it didn't know any better. When I saw the faint glow of light in the distance, it scarcely registered with me. I staggered toward it, no more conscious of what I was doing than a moth is when it zeroes in on a candle. At most I took it for a dream, an illusion cast before me by the shadows of death, and even though I kept it in front of me the whole time, I sensed it would be gone before I got there.

I don't remember crawling up the steps of the house or standing on the front porch, but I can still see my hand reaching out for the white porcelain doorknob, and I recall my surprise when I felt the knob turn and the latch clicked open. I stepped into the hallway, and everything was so bright in there, so intolerably radiant, that I was forced to shut my eyes. When I opened them again, a woman was standing in front of me – a beautiful woman with red hair. She was wearing a long white dress, and her blue eyes were looking at me with such wonder, such an expression of alarm that I almost burst into tears. For a second or two, it crossed my mind that she was my mother, and then, when I remembered that my mother was dead, I realized that I must be dead myself and had just walked through the pearly gates.

'Look at you,' the woman said. 'You poor boy. Just look at you.'

'Forgive the intrusion, ma'am,' I said. 'My name is Walter Rawley, and I'm nine years old. I know this might sound strange, but I'd appreciate it if you told me where I am. I have a feeling this is heaven, and that don't seem right to me. After all the rotten things I done, I always figured I'd wind up in hell.'

'Oh dear,' the woman said. 'Just look at you. You're half frozen to death. Come into the parlor and warm yourself by the fire.'

Before I could repeat my question, she took me by the hand and led me around the staircase to the front room. Just as she opened the door, I heard her say, 'Darling, get this boy's clothes off him and sit him by the fire. I'm going upstairs to fetch some blankets.'

So I crossed the threshold by myself, stepping into the warmth of the parlor as clumps of snow dropped off me and started melting at my feet. A man was sitting at a small table in the corner, drinking coffee from a delicate china cup. He was nattily dressed in a pearl-gray suit, and his hair was slicked back with no part, glistening with brilliantine in the yellow lamplight. I was about to say something to him when he looked up and smiled, and right then and there I knew that I was dead and had gone straight to hell. Of all the shocks I've suffered in my long career, none was greater than the electrocution I received that night.

'Now you know,' the master said. 'Wherever you turn, that's where I'm going to be. However far you run, I'll always be waiting for you at the other end. Master Yehudi is everywhere, Walt, and it isn't possible to escape him.'

'You goddamn son of a bitch,' I said. 'You double-crossing skunk. You shit-faced bag of garbage.'

'Watch your tongue, boy. This is Mrs Witherspoon's house, and she won't countenance any swearing here. If you don't want to get turned out into that storm, you'll strip off those clothes and behave yourself.'

'Make me, you big Jew turd,' I spat back at him. 'Just try and make me.'

But the master didn't have to do anything. A second after I gave him that answer, I felt a flood of hot, salty tears gush down my cheeks. I took a deep breath, gathering as much air into my lungs as I could, and then I let loose with a howl, a scream of pure, unbridled wretchedness. By the time it was halfway out of me, my throat felt all hoarse and choked up, and my head began to spin. I stopped to take another breath, and then, before I knew what was happening, I blacked out and fell to the floor.

I was sick for a long time after that. My body had caught fire, and as the fever burned within me, it looked more and more as though my next mailing address was going to be a wooden box. I spent the first days in Mrs Witherspoon's house, languishing in the upstairs guest room, but I remember none of that. Nor do I remember being taken back home, nor anything else for that matter until several weeks had passed. According to what they told me, I would have been a goner if not for Mother Sue – or Mother Sioux, as I eventually came to think of her. She sat by my bed around the clock, changing compresses and pouring spoonfuls of liquid down my throat, and three times a day she would get up from her chair and do a dance around my bed, beating out a special rhythm on her Oglala drum as she chanted prayers to the Great Spirit, imploring him to look down on me with sympathy and make me well again. I don't suppose it could have hurt the cause, for no professional doctor was ever called in to examine me, and considering that I did come round and make a full recovery, it's possible that her magic was what did the trick.

No one ever gave a medical name to my illness. My own thought was that it had been brought on by the hours I'd spent in the storm, but the master dismissed that explanation as of no account. It was the Ache of Being, he said, and it was bound to strike me down sooner or later. The poisons had to be purged from my system before I could advance to the next plateau of my training, and what might have dragged on for another six or nine months (with countless skirmishes between us) had been cut short by our fortuitous encounter in Wichita. I had been jolted into submission, he said, crushed by the knowledge that I would never triumph against him, and that mental blow had been the spark that triggered off the illness. After that, the rancor was cleansed out of me, and when I woke from the nightmare of my near death, the hatred festering inside me had been transformed into love.

I don't want to contradict the master's opinion, but it seems to me that my turnaround was a good deal simpler than that. It might have started just after my fever went down, when I woke up and saw Mother Sioux sitting beside me with one of those rapturous, beatific smiles on her face. 'Fancy that,' she said. 'My little Walnut's back in the land of the living.' There was such gladness in her voice, such an obvious concern for my well-being, that something inside me started to melt. 'No sweat, Sister Ma,' I said, barely conscious of what I was saying. 'I've just been snoozing is all.' I immediately shut my eyes and sank back into my torpor, but just as I was drifting off, I distinctly felt Mother Sioux's lips brush against my cheek. It was the first kiss anyone had given me since my mother died, and it brought on such a warm and welcoming glow, I realized that I didn't care where it had come from. If that chubby Indian squaw wanted to nuzzle with me like that, then by God let her, I wasn't going to stand in her way.

That was the first step, I think, but there were other incidents as well, not the least of which occurred a few days later, at a moment when my fever had shot back up again. I awoke in the early afternoon to find the room empty. I was about to crawl out of bed to make a stab at using the chamber pot, but once I disentangled my ears from the pillow, I heard whispering outside my door. Master Yehudi and Aesop were standing in the hall, engaged in a hushed conversation, and though I couldn't make out everything they said, I caught enough to determine the gist. Aesop was out there giving it to the master, standing up to the big man and telling him not to be so hard on me. I couldn't believe what I was hearing. After all the trouble and unpleasantness I had caused him, I felt mortally ashamed of myself to know that Aesop was on my side. 'You've crushed the soul out of him,' he whispered, 'and now he's in there lying on his deathbed. It's not fair, master. I know he's a hell-raiser and a scamp, but there's more than just rebellion in his heart. I've felt it, I've seen it with my own eyes. And even if I'm wrong, he still wouldn't deserve the kind of treatment you've given him. No one does.'

It felt extraordinary to have someone speak up for me like that, but even more extraordinary was that Aesop's harangue did not fall on deaf ears. That very night, as I lay tossing and turning in the dark, Master Yehudi himself crept into my room, sat down on the sweat-soaked bed, and took hold of my hand in his. I kept my eyes shut and didn't make a sound, pretending to be asleep the whole time he was there. 'Don't die on me, Walt,' he said softly, as if speaking to himself. 'You're a tough little bugger, and the time hasn't come for you to give up the ghost. We have great things in store for us, wondrous things you can't even imagine. You might think I'm against you, but I'm not. It's just that I know who you are, and I know you can handle the pressure. You've got the gift, son, and I'm going to take you farther than anyone has ever gone before. Do you hear me, Walt? I'm telling you not to die. I'm telling you I need you and that you mustn't die on me yet.'

I heard him all right. He was coming through to me loud and clear, and tempted as I was to say something in response, I beat back the urge and held my tongue. A long silence followed. Master Yehudi sat there in the darkness stroking my hand, and after a while, if I'm not mistaken, if I didn't doze off and dream what happened next, I heard, or at least I thought I heard, a series of broken-off sobs, an almost indiscernible rumbling that spilled out from the large man's chest and pierced the quiet of the room – once, twice, a dozen times.

It would be an exaggeration to say that I abandoned my suspicions all at once, but there's no question that my attitude started to change. I'd learned that escape was pointless, and now that I was stuck there whether I liked it or not, I decided to make the most of what I'd been given. Perhaps my brush with death had something to do with it, I don't know, but once I climbed out of my sickbed and got back on my feet, the chip I'd been carrying around on my shoulder was no longer there. I was so glad to be well again, it no longer bothered me that I was living with the outcasts of the universe. They were a curious, unsavoury lot, but in spite of my constant grumbling and bad behavior, each one of them had developed a certain affection for me, and I would have been a lout to ignore that. Perhaps it all boiled down to the fact that I was finally getting used to them. If you look into someone's face long enough, eventually you're going to feel that you're looking at yourself.

All that said, I don't mean to imply that my life became any easier. In the short run, it proved to be even rougher than before, and just because I'd throttled my resistance somewhat, that didn't make me any less of a wisenheimer, any less of the pugnacious little punk I'd always been. Spring was upon us, and within a week of my recovery I was out in the fields plowing up the ground and planting seeds, breaking my back like some grubby, bird-brained hick. I abhorred manual labor, and given that I had no knack for it whatsoever, I looked upon those days as a penance, an unending trial of blisters, bloody fingers, and stubbed toes. But at least I wasn't out there alone. The four of us worked together for approximately a month, suspending all other business as we hastened to get the crops in on time (corn, wheat, alfalfa, oats) and to prepare the soil for Mother Sioux's vegetable garden, which would keep our stomachs full throughout the summer. The work was too hard for us to stand around and chat, but I had an audience for my complaints now, and whenever I let forth with one of my caustic asides, I always managed to get a laugh out of someone. That was the big difference between the days before and after I fell sick. My mouth never stopped working, but whereas previously my comments had been construed as vicious, ungrateful barbs, they were now looked upon as jokes, the rambunctious patter of a clever little clown.

Master Yehudi toiled like an ox, slogging away at his tasks as if he had been born to the land, and he never failed to accomplish more than the rest of us put together. Mother Sioux was steady, diligent, silent, advancing in a constant crouch as her vast rear end jutted up into the sky. She came from a race of hunters and warriors, and farming was as unnatural to her as it was to me. Inept as I might have been, however, Aesop was even worse, and it comforted me to know that he was not one bit more enthusiastic about wasting his time on that drudgery than I was. He wanted to be indoors reading his books, to be dreaming his dreams and hatching his ideas, and while he never openly confronted the master with his grievances, he was particularly responsive to my cracks, interrupting my jags of whimsy with spontaneous guffaws, and each time he laughed it was as if he were exhaling a loud *amen*, reassuring me that I'd hit the nail on the head. I had always thought of Aesop as a goody-goody, an inoffensive killjoy who never broke the rules, but after listening to his laughter out there in the fields, I began to form a new opinion of him. There was more spice in those crooked bones than I had imagined, and in spite of his earnestness and uppity ways, he was as much on the lookout for fun as any other fifteen-year-old. What I did was to provide him with some comic relief. My sharp tongue tickled him, my sass and pluck buoyed his spirits, and as time went on I understood that he was no longer a nuisance or a rival. He was a friend – the first real friend I'd ever had.

I don't mean to wax sentimental, but this is my childhood I'm talking about, the quiltwork of my earliest memories, and with so few attachments to talk about from later years, my friendship with Aesop deserves to be noted. As much as Master Yehudi himself, he marked me in ways that altered who I was, that changed the course and substance of my life. I'm not just referring to my prejudices, the old witchcraft of never looking past the color of a person's skin, but to the fact of friendship itself, to the bond that grew between us. Aesop became my comrade, my anchor in a sea of undifferentiated sky, and without him there to buck me up, I never would have found the courage to withstand the torments that engulfed me over the next twelve or fourteen months. The master had wept in the darkness of my sickroom, but once I was well again, he turned into a slave driver, subjecting me to agonies that no living soul should have to endure. When I look back on those days now, I'm astonished that I didn't die, that I'm actually still here to talk about them.

Once the planting season was over and our food was in the ground, the real work began. It was just after my tenth birthday, a pretty morning at the end of May. The master pulled me aside after breakfast and whispered into my ear, 'Brace yourself, kid. The fun is about to start.'

'You mean we ain't been having fun?' I said. 'Correct me if I'm wrong, but I thought that Four-H stuff was about the funnest whirl I've had since the last time I played Chinese checkers.'

'Working the land is one thing, a dull but necessary chore. But now we're going to turn our thoughts to the sky.'

'You mean like them birds you told me about?'

'That's it, Walt, just like the birds.'

'You're telling me you're still serious about that plan of yours?'

'Dead serious. We're about to advance to the thirteenth stage. If you do what I tell you, you'll be airborne a year from next Christmas.'

'Thirteenth stage? You mean I've already gone through twelve of them?'

'That's right, twelve. And you've passed each one with flying colors.'

'Well, shave my tonsils. And I never had no inkling. You've been holding out on me, boss.'

'I only tell you what you need to know. The rest is for me to worry about.'

'Twelve stages, huh? And how many more to go?'

'There are thirty-three in all.'

'If I get through the next twelve as fast as the first ones, I'll already be in the home stretch.'

'You won't, I promise you. However much you think you've suffered so far, it's nothing compared to what lies ahead.'

'The birds don't suffer. They just spread their wings and take off. If I got the gift like you say, I don't see why it shouldn't be a breeze.'

'Because, my little pumpkin-head, you're not a bird – you're a man. In order to lift you off the ground, we have to crack the heavens in two. We have to turn the whole bloody universe inside out.'

Once again, I didn't understand the tenth part of what the master was saying, but I nodded when he called me a man, feeling in that word a new tone of appreciation, an acknowledgment of the importance I had assumed in his eyes. He put his hand gently on my shoulder and led me out into the May morning. I felt nothing but trust for him at that moment, and though his face was set in a grim, inward-looking expression, it never crossed my mind that he would do anything to break that trust. That's probably how Isaac felt when Abraham took him up that mountain in Genesis, chapter twenty-two. If a man tells you he's your father, even if you know he's not, you let down your guard and get all stupid inside. You don't imagine that he's been conspiring against you with God, the Lord of Hosts. A boy's brain doesn't work that fast; it's not subtle enough to fathom such chicanery. All you know is that the big guy has placed his hand on your shoulder and given it a friendly squeeze. He tells you, Come with me, and so you turn yourself in that direction and follow him wherever he's going.

We walked out past the barn to the tool shed, a rickety little structure with a sagging roof and walls made of weathered, unpainted planks. Master Yehudi opened the door and stood there in silence for a long moment, gazing at the dark tangle of metal objects inside. At last he reached in and pulled out a shovel, a rusty lug of a thing that must have weighed fifteen or twenty pounds. He put the shovel in my hands, and I felt proud to be carrying it for him once we started walking again. We passed along the edge of the near cornfield, and it was a splendid morning, I remember, filled with darting robins and bluebirds, and my skin was tingling with a strange sense of aliveness, the blessing of the sun's warmth as it poured down upon me. By and by we came to a patch of untilled ground, a bare spot at the juncture of two fields, and the master turned to me and said, 'This is where we're going to put the hole. Do you want to do the digging, or would you rather leave it to me?'

I gave it my best shot, but my arms weren't up to it. I was too small to wield a shovel of that heft, and when the master saw me struggling just to pierce the soil, let alone slide the blade in under it, he told me to sit down and rest, he would finish the job himself. For the next two hours I watched him transform that patch of earth into an immense cavity, a hole as broad and deep as a giant's grave. He worked so fast that it seemed as if the earth was swallowing him up, and after a time he had burrowed down so low that I couldn't see his head anymore. I could hear his grunts, the locomotive huff and puff that accompanied each turn of the spade, and then a volley of loose dirt would come soaring up over the surface, hang for a second in midair, and then drop to the pile that was growing around the hole. He kept at it as if there were ten of him, an army of diggers bent on tunneling to Australia, and when he finally stopped and hoisted himself out of the pit, he was so smudged with filth and sweat that he looked like a man made of coal, a haggard vaudevillian about to die with his blackface on. I had never seen anyone pant so hard, had never witnessed a body so deprived of breath, and when he flung himself to the ground and didn't stir for the next ten minutes, I felt certain that his heart was about to give out on him.

I was too awed to speak. I studied the master's ribcage for signs of collapse, shuttling between joy and sorrow as his chest heaved up and down, up and down, swelling and shrinking against the long blue horizon. Halfway through my vigil, a cloud wandered in front of the sun and the sky turned ominously dark. I thought it was the angel of death passing overhead, but Master Yehudi's lungs kept on pumping as the air slowly brightened again, and a moment later he sat up and smiled, eagerly wiping the dirt from his face.

'Well,' he said, 'what do you think of our hole?'

'It's a grand hole,' I said, 'as deep and lovely a hole as there ever was.'

'I'm glad you like it, because you and that hole are going to be on intimate terms for the next twenty-four hours.'

'I don't mind. It looks like an interesting place to me. As long as it don't rain, it might be fun to sit in there for a while.'

'No need to worry about the rain, Walt.'

'You a weatherman or something? Maybe you haven't noticed, but conditions change around here about every fifteen minutes. When it comes to weather, this Kansas place is as fickle as it gets.'

'True enough. The skies in these parts can't be counted on. But I'm not saying it won't rain. Just that you don't have to worry if it does.'

'Sure, give me a cover, or one of them canvas thingamajigs – a tarp. That's good thinking. You can't go wrong if you plan for the worst.'

'I'm not putting you down there for fun and frolic. You'll have a breath-hole, of course, a long tube to keep in your mouth for purposes of respiration, but otherwise it's going to be fairly dank and uncomfortable. A closed-in, wormy kind of discomfort, if you forgive my saying so. I doubt you'll forget the experience as long as you live.'

'I know I'm dumb, but if you don't stop talking in riddles, we'll be out here all day before I glom onto your drift.'

'I'm going to bury you, son.'

'Say what?'

'I'm going to put you down in that hole, cover you up with dirt, and bury you alive.'

'And you expect me to agree to that?'

'You don't have any choice. Either you go down there of your own volition or I strangle you with my two bare hands. One way, you get to live a long, prosperous life; the other way, your life ends in thirty seconds.'

So I let him bury me alive – an experience I would not recommend to anyone. Distasteful as the idea sounds, the actual incarceration is far worse, and once you've spent some time in the bowels of netherness as I did that day, the world can never look the same to you again. It becomes inexpressibly more beautiful, and yet that beauty is drenched in a light so transient, so unreal, that it never takes on any substance, and even though you can see it and touch it as you always did, a part of you understands that it is no more than a mirage. Feeling the dirt on top of you is one thing, the pressure and coldness of it, the panic of deathlike immobility, but the true terror doesn't begin until later, until after you've been unburied and can stand up and walk again. From then on, everything that happens to you on the surface is connected to those hours you spent underground. A little seed of craziness has been planted in your head, and even though you've won the struggle to survive, nearly everything else has been lost. Death lives inside you, eating away at your innocence and your hope, and in the end you're left with nothing but the dirt, the solidity of the dirt, the everlasting power and triumph of the dirt.

That was how my initiation began. Over the weeks and months that followed, I lived through more of the same, an unremitting avalanche of wrongs. Each test was more terrible than the one before it, and if I managed not to back down, it was only from sheer reptilian stubbornness, a brainless passivity that lurked somewhere in the core of my soul. It had nothing to do with will or determination or courage. I had none of those qualities, and the farther I was pushed, the less pride I felt in my accomplishments. I was flogged with a bullwhip; I was thrown from a galloping horse; I was lashed to the roof of the barn for two days without food or water; I had my skin smeared with honey and then stood naked in the August heat as a thousand flies and wasps swarmed over me; I sat in a circle of fire for one whole night as my body became scorched with blisters; I was dunked repeatedly for six straight hours in a tubfull of vinegar; I was struck by lightning; I drank cow piss and ate horseshit; I took a knife and cut off the upper joint of my left pinky; I dangled for three days and three nights in a cocoon of ropes from the rafters in the attic. I did these things because Master Yehudi told me to do them, and if I could not bring myself to love him, neither did I hate him or resent him for the sufferings I endured. He no longer had to threaten me. I followed his commands with blind obedience, never bothering to question what his purpose might have been. He told me to jump, and I jumped. He told me to stop breathing, and I stopped breathing. This was the man who had promised to make me fly, and even though I never believed him, I let him use me as if I did. We had our bargain, after all, the pact we'd made that first night in Saint Louis, and I never forgot it. If he didn't come through for me by my thirteenth birthday, I was going to lop off his head with an axe. There was nothing personal about that arrangement – it was a simple matter of justice. If the son of a bitch let me down, I was going to kill him, and he knew it as well as I did.

While these ordeals lasted, Aesop and Mother Sioux stuck by me as if I were their flesh and blood, the darling of their hearts. There were lulls between the various stages of my development, sometimes days, sometimes weeks, and more often than not Master Yehudi would vanish, leaving the farm altogether while my wounds mended and I recovered to face the next dumbfounding assault on my person. I had no idea where he went during those pauses, nor did I ask the others about it, since I always felt relieved when he was gone. Not only was I safe from further trials, but I was freed from the burden of the master's presence – his brooding silences and tormented looks, the enormity of the space he occupied – and that alone reassured me, gave me a chance to breathe again. The house was a happier place without him, and the three of us lived together in remarkable harmony. Plump Mother Sioux and her two skinny boys. Those were the days when Aesop and I became pals, and miserable as much of that time was for me, it also contains some good memories, perhaps the best memories of all. He was a great one for telling stories, Aesop was, and I liked nothing better than to listen to that sweet voice of his spinning out the wild tales that were crammed in his head. He knew hundreds of them, and whenever I asked him, lying in bed all bruised and sore from my latest pummeling, he would sit there for hours reciting one story after another. Jack the Giant Killer, Sinbad the Sailor, Ulysses the Wanderer, Billy the Kid, Lancelot and

King Arthur, Paul Bunyan – I heard them all. The best ones, though, the stories he saved for when I was feeling particularly blue, were about my namesake, Sir Walter Raleigh. I remember how shocked I was when he told me I had a famous name, the name of a real-life adventurer and hero. To prove that he wasn't making it up, Aesop went to the book shelf and pulled down a thick volume with Sir Walter's picture in it. I had never seen a more elegant face, and I soon fell into the habit of studying it for ten or fifteen minutes every day. I loved the pointy beard and razor-sharp eyes, the pearl earring fixed in his left lobe. It was the face of a pirate, a genuine swashbuckling knight, and from that day forth I carried Sir Walter inside me as a second self, an invisible brother to stand with me through thick and thin. Aesop recounted the stories of the cloak and the puddle, the search for El Dorado, the lost colony at Roanoke, the thirteen years in the Tower of London, the brave words he uttered at his beheading. He was the best poet of his day; he was a scholar, a scientist, and a freethinker; he was the number-one lover of women in all of England. 'Think of you and me put together,' Aesop said, 'and you begin to get an idea of who he was. A man with my brains and your guts, and tall and handsome as well – that's Sir Walter Raleigh, the most perfect man who ever lived.'

Every night, Mother Sioux would come into my room and tuck me in, sitting on my bed for however long it took me to fall asleep. I came to depend on this ritual, and though I was growing up fast and hard in every other way, I was still just a baby to her. I never let myself cry in front of Master Yehudi or Aesop, but with Mother Sioux I let the ducts give way on countless occasions, blubbering in her arms like some hapless mama's boy. Once, I remember, I even went so far as to touch on the subject of flying, and what she said was so unexpected, so calm in its assurance, that it pacified the turmoil within me for weeks to come – not because I believed it myself, but because she did, and she was the person I trusted most in the world.

'He's a wicked man,' I said, referring to the master, 'and by the time he's through with me, I'll be as hunched and crippled as Aesop.'

'No, sonny, it ain't so. You'll be dancing with the clouds in the sky.'

'With a harp in my hands and wings sprouting from my back.'

'In your own skin. In your own flesh and bones.'

'It's a bluff, Mother Sioux, a disgusting pack of lies. If he aims to teach me what he says, why don't he get down and do it? For one whole year, I've suffered every indignity known to man. I've been buried, I've been burned, I've been mutilated, and I'm still as bound to the earth as I ever was.'

'Those are the steps. It has to be done that way. But the worst is nearly behind you now.'

'So he's suckered you into believing it, too.'

'No one suckers Mother Sioux into anything. I'm too old and too fat to swallow what people say. False words are like chicken bones. They catch in my throat and I spit them out.'

'Men can't fly. It's as simple as that. Men can't fly because God don't want them to.'

'It can be done.'

'In some other world maybe. But not this one.'

'I saw it happen. When I was a little girl. I saw it with my own two eyes. And if it happened before, it can happen again.'

'You dreamed it. You thought you saw it, but it was only in your sleep.'

'My own father, Walt. My own father and my own brother. I saw them moving through the air like spirits. It wasn't flying the way you imagine it. Not like birds or moths, not with wings or anything like that. But they were up in the air, and they were moving. All slow and strange. As if they was swimming. Pushing their way through the air like swimmers, like spirits walking on the bottom of a lake.'

'Why didn't you tell me this before?'

'Because you wouldn't have believed me before. That's why I'm telling you now. Because the time is coming. If you listen to what the master tells you, it's coming sooner than you think.'

When spring rolled around for the second time, the farm work was like a holiday to me, and I threw myself into it with manic good cheer, welcoming the chance to live like a normal person again. Instead of lagging behind and grousing about my aches and pains, I surged along at top speed, daring myself to stick with it, reveling in my own exertions. I was still puny for my age, but I was older and stronger, and even though it was impossible, I did all I could to keep up with Master Yehudi himself. I was out to prove something, I suppose, to stun him into respecting me, to be noticed. This was a new way of fighting back, and every time the master told me to slow down, to ease off and not push so hard ('It's not an Olympic sport,' he would say, 'we're not out here competing for medals, kid'), I felt as if I had won a victory, as if I were gradually regaining possession of my soul.

My pinky joint had healed by then. What had once been a bloody mess of tissue and bone had smoothed over into an odd, nailless stump. I enjoyed looking at it now and running my thumb over the scar, touching that bit of me that was gone forever. I must have done it fifty or a hundred times a day, and every time I did, I would sound out the words *Saint Louis* in my head. I was struggling to hold on to my past, but by then the words had become just words, a ritual exercise in remembrance. They summoned forth no pictures, took me on no journeys back to where I had been. After eighteen months in Cibola, Saint Louis had been turned into a phantom city for me, and a little more of it was vanishing every day.

One afternoon that spring the weather became inordinately hot, boiling up to midsummer levels. The four of us were working out in the fields, and when the master removed his shirt for greater comfort, I saw that he was wearing something around his neck: a leather thong with a small, transparent globe hanging from it like a jewel or an ornament. When I approached him to have a better look – merely curious, with no ulterior motive – I saw that it was my missing pinky joint, encased in the pendant along with some kind of clear liquid. The master must have noticed my surprise, for he glanced down at his chest with an expression of alarm, as if he thought a spider might be crawling there. When he saw what it was, he took hold of the globe in his fingers and held it out to me, smiling with satisfaction. 'A pretty little widget, eh Walt?' he said.

'I don't know about pretty,' I said, 'but it looks awful familiar to me.'

'It should. It used to belong to you. For the first ten years of your life, it was part of who you were.'

'It still is. Just because it's detached from my body, that don't make it any less mine than before.'

'It's pickled in formaldehyde. Preserved like some dead fetus in a jar. It doesn't belong to you now, it belongs to science.'

'Yeah, then what's it doing around your neck? If it belongs to science, why not donate it to the wax museum?'

'Because it has special meaning for me, sport. I wear it to remind myself of the debt I owe you. Like a hangman's noose. This thing is the albatross of my conscience, and I can't let it fall into a stranger's hands.'

'What about my hands, then? Fair is fair, and I want my joint back. If anyone wears that necklace, it's got to be me.'

'I'll make a bargain with you. If you let me hold on to it a little longer, I'll think of it as yours. That's a promise. It's got your name on it, and once I get you off the ground, you can have it back.'

'For keeps?'

'For keeps. Of course for keeps.'

'And how long is this "little longer" going to be?'

'Not long. You're already standing on the brink.'

'The only brink I'm standing on is the brink of perdition. And if that's where I am, that's where you are, too. Ain't that so, master?'

'You catch on fast, son. United we stand, divided we fall. You for me and me for you, and where we stop nobody knows.'

This was the second time I had been given encouraging news about my progress. First from Mother Sioux, and now from the master himself. I won't deny that I felt flattered, but for all their confidence in my abilities, I failed to see that I was one jot closer to success. After that sweltering afternoon in May, we went through a period of epic heat, the hottest summer in living memory. The ground was a caldron, and every time you walked on it, you felt that the soles would melt right off your shoes. We prayed for rain at supper every evening, and for three months not a single drop fell from the sky. The air was so parched, so delirious in its desiccation, you could track the buzzing of a horsefly from a hundred yards away. Everything seemed to itch, to rasp like thistle rubbing against barbed wire, and the smell from the outhouse was so rank it singed the hairs in your nostrils. The corn wilted, drooped, and died; the lettuce bolted to grotesque, gargantuan heights, standing in the garden like mutant towers. By mid-August, you could drop a pebble down the well and count to six before you heard the water plink. No green beans, no corn on the cob, no succulent tomatoes like the year before. We subsisted on eggs and mush and smoked ham, and while there was enough to see us through the summer, our diminishing stores boded ill for the months that lay ahead. 'Tighten your belts, children,' the master would say to us at supper, 'tighten your belts and chew until you can't taste it anymore. If we don't stretch out what we have, it's going to be a long, hungry winter.'

For all the woes that assailed us during the drought, I was happy, much happier than would have seemed possible. I had weathered the most gruesome parts of my initiation, and what stood before me now were the stages of mental struggle, the showdown between myself and myself. Master Yehudi was hardly an obstacle anymore. He would issue his commands and then disappear from my mind, leading me to places of such inwardness that I no longer remembered who I was. The physical stages had been a war, an act of defiance against the master's skull-denting cruelty, and he had never withdrawn from my sight, standing over me as he studied my reactions, watching my face for each microscopic shudder of pain. All that was finished now. He had turned into a gentle, munificent guide, talking in the soft voice of a seducer as he lured me into accepting one bizarre task after another. He had me go into the barn and count every blade of straw in the horse's stall. He had me stand on one leg for an entire night, then stand on the other leg for the whole of the next night. He tied me to a post in the midday sun and ordered me to repeat his name ten thousand times. He imposed a vow of silence on me, and for twenty-four days I did not speak to anyone, did not utter a sound even when I was alone. He had me roll my body across the yard, he had me hop, he had me jump through hoops. He taught me how to cry at will, and then he taught me how to laugh and cry at the same time. He made me teach myself how to juggle, and once I could juggle three stones, he made me juggle four. He blindfolded me for a week, then he plugged my ears for a week, then he bound my arms and legs together for a week and made me crawl on my belly like a worm.

The weather broke in early September. Downpours, lightning and thunder, high winds, a tornado that barely missed carrying away the house. Water levels rose again, but otherwise we were no better off than we'd been. The crops had failed, and with nothing to add to our long-term supplies, prospects for the future were bleak, touch and go at best. The master reported that farmers all over the region had been similarly devastated, and the mood in town was turning ugly. Prices were down, credit was scarce, and talk of bank foreclosures was in the air. When pocketbooks are empty, the master said, brains fill with anger and smut. 'Those peckerwoods can rot for all I care,' he continued, 'but after a while they're going to look for someone to blame their troubles on, and when that happens, the four of us had better duck.' Throughout that strange autumn of storms and drenchings, Master Yehudi seemed distracted with worry, as if he were contemplating some unnameable disaster, a thing so black he dared not say it aloud. After coddling me all summer, urging me on through the rigors of my spiritual exercises, he suddenly seemed to have lost interest in me. His absences became more frequent, once or twice he stumbled in with what smelled like liquor on his breath, and he had all but abandoned his study sessions with Aesop. A new sadness had crept into his eyes, a look of wistfulness and foreboding. Much of this is dim to me now, but I remember that during the brief moments when he graced me with his company, he acted with surprising warmth. One incident stands out from the blur: an evening in early October when he walked into the house with a newspaper under his arm and a big grin on his face. 'I have good news for you,' he said to me, sitting down and spreading out the paper on the kitchen table. 'Your team won. I hope that makes you glad, because it says here it's been thirty-eight years since they came out on top.'

'My team?' I said.

'The Saint Louis Cardinals. That's your team, isn't it?'

'You bet it is. I'm with those Redbirds till the end of time.'

'Well, they've just won the World Series. According to what's printed here, the seventh game was the most breathless, riveting contest ever played.'

That was how I learned my boys had become the 1926 champions. Master Yehudi read me the account of the dramatic seventh inning, when Grover Cleveland Alexander came in to strike out Tony Lazzeri with the bases loaded. For the first few minutes, I thought he was making it up. The last I'd heard, Alexander was top dog on the Philly staff, and Lazzeri was a name that meant nothing to me. It sounded like a pile of foreign noodles smothered in garlic sauce, but then the master informed me that he was a rookie and that Grover had been traded to the Cards in mid-season. He'd hurled nine innings just the day before, shutting down the Yanks to knot the series at three games apiece, and here was Rogers Hornsby calling him in from the bullpen to snuff out a rally with the whole ball of wax on the line. And the old guy sauntered in, drunk as a skunk from last night's bender, and mowed down the young New York hotshot. If not for a couple of inches, it would have been another story. On the pitch before the third strike, Lazzeri drove one into the left field seats, a sure grand slam that hooked foul at the last second. It was enough to give you apoplexy. Alexander hung in there through the eighth and ninth to nail down the win, and to top it off, the game and the series ended when Babe Ruth, the one and only Sultan of Swat, was thrown out trying to steal second base. There had never been anything like it. It was the maddest, most infernal game in history, and my Redbirds were the champs, the best team in the world.

That was a watershed for me, a landmark event in my young life, but otherwise the fall was a somber stretch, a long interlude of boredom and quiet. After a while, I got so antsy that I asked Aesop if he wouldn't mind teaching me how to read. He was more than willing, but he had to clear it with Master Yehudi first, and when the master gave his approval, I confess that I was a little hurt. He'd always said how he wanted to keep me stupid – how it was an advantage as far as my training was concerned – and now he had blithely gone ahead and reversed himself without any explanation. For a time I thought it meant he had given up on me, and disappointment festered in my heart, a hangdog sorrow that dragged down all my bright dreams and turned them to dust. What had I done wrong, I asked myself, and why had he deserted me when I most needed him?

So I learned the letters and numbers with Aesop's help, and once I got started, they came so quickly that I wondered what all the fuss had been about. If I wasn't going to fly, at least I could convince the master that I wasn't a dolt, but so little effort was involved, it soon felt like a hollow victory. Spirits around the house picked up for a while in November when our food shortage was suddenly eliminated. Without telling anyone where he'd found the money to do such a thing, the master had secretly arranged for a delivery of canned goods. It felt like a miracle when it happened, an absolute bolt from the blue. A truck arrived at our door one morning and two burly men began unloading cartons from the back. There were hundreds of boxes, and each box contained two dozen cans of food: vegetables of every variety, meats and broths, puddings, preserved apricots and peaches, an outflow of unimaginable abundance. It took the men over an hour to haul the shipment into the house, and the whole time the master just stood there with his arms folded across his chest, grinning like a crafty old owl. Aesop and I both gawked, and after a while he called us over to him and put a hand on each of our shoulders. 'It can't hold a candle to Mother Sioux's cooking,' he said, 'but it's a damn sight better than mush, eh boys? When the chips are down, just remember who to count on. No matter how dark our troubles might be, I'll always find a way to pull us through.'

However he had managed it, the crisis was over. Our larder was full again, and we no longer stood up from meals craving more, no longer moaned about our gurgling bellies. You'd think this turnaround would have earned our undying gratitude, but the fact was that we quickly learned to take it for granted. Within ten days, it seemed perfectly normal that we should be eating well, and by the end of the month it was hard to remember the days when we hadn't. That's how it is with want. As long as you lack something, you yearn for it without cease. If only I could have that one thing, you tell yourself, all my problems would be solved. But once you get it, once the object of your desires is thrust into your hands, it begins to lose its charm. Other wants assert themselves, other desires make themselves felt, and bit by bit you discover that you're right back where you started. So it was with my reading lessons; so it was with the newfound plenty jammed into the kitchen cupboards. I had thought those things would make a difference, but in the end they were no more than shadows, substitute longings for the one thing I really wanted – which was precisely the thing I couldn't have. I needed the master to love me again. That's what the story of those months came down to. I hungered for the master's affections, and no amount of food was ever going to satisfy me. After two years, I had learned that everything I was flowed directly from him. He had made me in his own image, and now he wasn't there for me anymore. For reasons I couldn't understand, I felt I had lost him forever.

It never occurred to me to think of Mrs Witherspoon. Not even when Mother Sioux dropped a hint one night about the master's 'widow lady' in Wichita did I put six and three together. I was backward in that regard, an eleven-year-old know-it-all who didn't understand the first thing that went on between men and women. I assumed it was all carnal, intermittent spasms of wayward lust, and when Aesop talked to me about planting his boners in a nice warm quim (he had just turned seventeen), I immediately thought of the whores I'd known in Saint Louis, the blowsy, wisecracking dolls who strutted up and down the alleys at two in the morning, peddling their bodies for cold, hard cash. I didn't know dirt about grown-up love or marriage or any of the so-called lofty sentiments. The only married couple I'd seen was Uncle Slim and Aunt Peg, and that was such a brutal combination, such a frenzy of spitting, cursing, and clamor, it probably made sense that I was so ignorant. When the master went away, I figured he was playing poker somewhere or belting back a bottle of rotgut in a Cibola speakeasy. It never dawned on me that he was in Wichita courting a high-class lady like Marion Witherspoon – and gradually getting his heart broken in the process. I had actually laid eyes on her myself, but I had been so sick and feverish at the time that I could scarcely remember her. She was a hallucination, a figment born in the throes of death, and even though her face flashed through me every now and then, I did not credit her as real. If anything, I thought she was my mother – but then I would grow scared, appalled that I couldn't recognize my own mother's ghost.

It took a couple of near disasters to set me straight. In early December, Aesop cut his finger opening a can of cling peaches. It seemed like nothing at first, a simple scratch that would heal in no time, but instead of scabbing over as it should have, it swelled up into a frightful bloat of pus and rawness, and by the third day poor Aesop was languishing in bed with a high fever. It was fortunate that Master Yehudi was home then, for in addition to his other talents, he had a fair knowledge of medicine, and when he went upstairs to Aesop's room the next morning to see how the patient was doing, he walked out two minutes later shaking his head and blinking back a rush of tears. 'There's no time to waste,' he said to me. 'Gangrene has set in, and unless we get rid of that finger now, it's liable to spread through his hand and up into his arm. Run outside and tell Mother Sioux to drop what she's doing and put on two pots of water to boil. I'll go down to the kitchen and sharpen the knives. We have to operate within the hour.'

I did what I was told, and once I'd rounded up Mother Sioux from the barnyard, I dashed back into the house, climbed the stairs to the second floor, and parked myself beside my friend. Aesop looked dreadful. The lustrous black of his skin had turned to a chalky, mottled gray, and I could hear the phlegm rattling in his chest as his head lolled back and forth on the pillow.

'Hang on, buddy,' I said. 'It won't be long now. The master's going to fix you up, and before you know it you'll be downstairs at the ivories again, twiddling out one of your goofy rags.'

'Walt?' he said. 'Is that you, Walt?' He opened his bloodshot eyes and looked in the direction of my voice, but his pupils were so glazed over I wasn't sure he could see me.

'Of course it's me,' I answered. 'Who else do you think would be sitting here at a time like this?'

'He's going to cut off my finger, Walt. I'll be deformed for life, and no girl will ever want me.'

'You're already deformed for life, and that hasn't stopped you from hankering for twat, has it? He ain't going to cut off your dick, Aesop. Only a finger, and a finger on your left hand at that. As long as your willy's still attached, you can bang the broads till kingdom come.'

'I don't want to lose my finger,' he moaned. 'If I lose my finger, it means there's no justice. It means that God has turned his back on me.'

'I ain't got but nine and a half fingers myself, and it don't bother me hardly at all. Once you lose yours, we'll be just like twins. Bonafide members of the Nine Finger Club, brothers till the day we drop – just like the master always said.'

I did what I could to reassure him, but once the operation began, I was shunted aside and forgotten. I stood in the doorway with my hands over my face, peeking through the cracks every now and then as the master and Mother Sioux did their work. There was no ether or anaesthetic, and Aesop howled and howled, belting out a horrific, bloodcurdling noise that never slackened from start to finish. Sorry as I felt for him, those howls nearly undid me. They were inhuman, and the terror they expressed was so deep and so prolonged, it was all I could do not to begin screaming myself. Master Yehudi went about his business with the calm of a trained doctor, but the howls got to Mother Sioux just as badly as they got to me. That was the last thing I was expecting from her. I'd always thought that Indians hid their feelings, that they were braver and more stoical than white folks, but the truth was that Mother S. was unhinged, and as the blood continued to spurt and Aesop's pain continued to mount, she gasped and whimpered as if the knife was tearing into her own flesh. Master Yehudi told her to get a grip on herself. She apologized, but fifteen seconds later she started sobbing again. She was a pitiful nurse, and after a while her tearful interruptions so distracted the master that he had to send her out of the room. 'We need a fresh bucket of boiling water,' he said. 'Snap to it, woman. On the double.' It was just an excuse to get rid of her, and as she rushed past me into the hall, she buried her face in her hands and wept on blindly to the top of the stairs. I had a clear view of everything that happened after that: the way her foot snagged on the first step, the way her knee buckled as she tried to right her balance, and then the headlong fall down the stairs – the thumping, tumbling career of her huge bulk as it crashed to the bottom. She landed with a thud that shook the entire house. An instant later she let out a shriek, then grabbed hold of her left leg and started writhing around on the floor. 'You dumb old bitch,' she said to herself. 'You dumb old floozy bitch, now look what you done. You fell down the stairs and broke your goddamn leg.'

For the next couple of weeks, the house was as gloomy as a hospital. There were two invalids to be taken care of, and the master and I spent our days rushing up and down the stairs, serving them their meals, emptying their potties, and doing everything short of wiping their bedridden asses. Aesop was in a funk of self-pity and dejection, Mother Sioux rained down curses on herself from morning to night, and what with the animals to be looked after in the barn and the rooms to be cleaned and the beds to be made and the dishes to be washed and the stove to be fed, there wasn't so much as a minute left over for the master and me to do our work. Christmas was approaching, the time when I was supposed to be off the ground, and I was still as subject to the laws of gravity as I'd ever been. It was my darkest moment in over a year. I'd been turned into a regular citizen who did his chores and knew how to read and write, and if it went on any longer, I'd probably wind up taking elocution lessons and joining the Boy Scouts.

One morning, I woke up a little earlier than usual. I checked in on Aesop and Mother Sioux, saw that they were both still asleep, and tiptoed down the stairs, intending to surprise the master with my pre-dawn levee. Ordinarily, he would have been down in the kitchen at that hour, cooking breakfast and preparing to start the day. But there were no smells of coffee wafting up from the stove, no sounds of bacon crackling in the pan, and sure enough, when I entered the room it turned out to be empty. He's in the barn, I told myself, gathering eggs or milking one of the cows, but then I realized that the stove had not been lit. Starting the fire was the first order of business on winter mornings, and the temperature downstairs was frigid, cold enough for me to send forth a burst of vapor every time I exhaled. Well, I continued to myself, maybe the old guy is fagged out and wanted to catch up on his beauty sleep. That would certainly put a new twist on things, wouldn't it? For me to be the one to rouse him from bed instead of vice versa. So I went back upstairs and knocked on his bedroom door, and when there was no response after several tries, I opened the door and gingerly stepped across the threshold. Master Yehudi was nowhere to be found. Not only was he not in his bed, but the bed itself was neatly made and bore no signs of having been slept in that night. He's run out on us, I said to myself. He's upped and skedaddled, and that's the last we'll ever see of him.

For the next hour, my mind was a free-for-all of desperate thoughts. I spun from sorrow to anger, from belligerence to laughter, from snarling grief to vile self-mockery. The universe had gone up in smoke, and I was left to dwell among the ashes, alone forever among the smoldering ruins of betrayal.

Mother Sioux and Aesop slept on in their beds, oblivious to my rantings and my tears. Somehow or other (I can't remember how I got there), I was down in the kitchen again, lying on my stomach with my face pressed against the floor, rubbing my nose into the filthy wooden planks. There were no more tears to be gotten out of me – only a dry, choked heaving, an aftermath of hiccups and scorched, airless breaths. Presently I grew still, almost tranquil, and bit by bit a sense of calm spread through me, radiating out among my muscles and oozing toward the tips of my fingers and toes. There were no more thoughts in my head, no more feelings in my heart. I was weightless inside my own body, floating on a placid wave of nothingness, utterly detached and indifferent to the world around me. And that's when I did it for the first time – without warning, without the least notion that it was about to happen. Very slowly, I felt my body rise off the floor. The movement was so natural, so exquisite in its gentleness, it wasn't until I opened my eyes that I understood my limbs were touching only air. I was not far off the ground – no more than an inch or two – but I hung there without effort, suspended like the moon in the night sky, motionless and aloft, conscious only of the air fluttering in and out of my lungs. I can't say how long I hovered like that, but at a certain moment, with the same slowness and gentleness as before, I eased back to the ground. Everything had been drained out of me by then, and my eyes were already shut. Without so much as a single thought about what had just taken place, I fell into a deep, dreamless sleep, sinking like a stone to the bottom of the world.

I woke to the sound of voices, the shuffling of shoes against the bare wood floor. When I opened my eyes, I found myself looking directly into the blackness of Master Yehudi's left trouser leg. 'Greetings, kid,' he said, nudging me with his foot. 'Forty winks on the cold kitchen floor. Not the best place for a nap if you want to stay healthy.'

I tried to sit up, but my body felt so dull and turgid, it took all my strength just to lift myself onto one elbow. My head was a trembling mass of cobwebs, and no matter how hard I rubbed and blinked my eyes, I couldn't get them to focus properly.

'What's the trouble, Walt?' the master continued. 'You haven't been walking in your sleep, have you?'

'No, sir. Nothing like that.'

'Then why so glum? You look like you've been to a funeral.'

An immense sadness swept through me when he said that, and I suddenly felt myself on the verge of tears. 'Oh, master,' I said, grabbing hold of his leg with both arms and pressing my cheek against his shin. 'Oh, master, I thought you'd left me. I thought you'd left me, and were never coming back.'

The moment those words left my lips, I understood that I was wrong. It wasn't the master who had caused this feeling of vulnerability and despair, it was the thing I'd done just prior to falling asleep. It all came back in a vivid, nauseating rush: the moments I'd spent off the ground, the certainty that I had done what most certainly I could not have done. Rather than fill me with ecstasy or gladness, this breakthrough overpowered me with dread. I didn't know myself anymore. I was inhabited by something that wasn't me, and that thing was so terrible, so alien in its newness, I couldn't bring myself to talk about it. I let myself cry instead. I let the tears come pouring out of me, and once I started, I wasn't sure I'd ever be able to stop.

'Dear boy,' the master said, 'my dear, sweet boy.' He lowered himself to the ground and gathered me in his arms, patting my back and hugging me close to him as I went on weeping. Then, after a pause, I heard him speak again – but he was no longer addressing his words to me. For the first time since regaining consciousness, I understood that another person was in the room.

'He's the bravest lad who ever was,' the master said. 'He's worked so hard, he's worn himself out. A body can bear just so much, and I'm afraid the poor little fellow's all done in.'

That was when I finally looked up. I lifted my head off Master Yehudi's lap, cast my eyes about for a moment, and there was Mrs Witherspoon, standing in the light of the doorway. She was wearing a crimson overcoat and a black fur hat, I remember, and her cheeks were still flush from the winter cold. The instant our eyes met, she broke into a smile.

'Hello, Walt,' she said.

'And hello to you, ma'am,' I said, sniffing back the last of my tears.

'Meet your fairy godmother,' the master said. 'Mrs Witherspoon has come to rescue us, and she'll be staying in the house for a little while. Until things get back to normal.'

'You're the lady from Wichita, ain't you?' I said, realizing why her face looked so familiar to me.

'That's right,' she said. 'And you're the little boy who lost his way in the storm.'

'That was a long time ago,' I said, extricating myself from the master's arms and finally standing up. 'I can't say I remember much about it.'

'No,' she said, 'you probably don't. But I do.'

'Not only is Mrs Witherspoon a friend of the family,' the master said, 'she's our number-one champion and business partner. Just so you know the score, Walt. I want you to bear that in mind while she's here with us. The food that feeds you, the clothes that clothe you, the fire that warms you – all that comes courtesy of Mrs Witherspoon, and it would be a sad day if you ever forgot it.'

'Don't worry,' I said, suddenly feeling some spring in my soul again. 'I ain't no slob. When a handsome lady enters my house, I know how a gentleman is supposed to act.'

Without missing a beat, I turned my eyes in Mrs Witherspoon's direction, and with all the poise and bravura I could muster, flashed her the sexiest, most preposterous wink ever beheld by womankind. To her credit, Mrs Witherspoon neither blushed nor stammered. Giving as good as she got, she let out a brief laugh, and then, as cool and collected as an old bawd, tossed back a playful wink at me. It was a moment I still cherish, and the instant it happened, I knew we were going to be friends.

I had no idea what the master's arrangement with her was, and at the time I didn't give the matter much thought. What concerned me was that Mrs Witherspoon was there and that her presence relieved me of my job as nursemaid and bottle-washer. She took things in hand that first morning, and for the next three weeks the household ran as smoothly as a new pair of roller skates. To be honest, I didn't think she'd be capable of it, at least not when I saw her in that fancy coat and those expensive gloves. She looked like a woman who was used to having servants wait on her, and though she was pretty enough in a fragile sort of way, her skin was too pale for my taste and there was too little meat on her bones. It took me some time to adjust to her, since she didn't fit into any of the female categories I was familiar with. She wasn't a flapper or a hussy, she wasn't a meek housewifey blob, she wasn't a schoolmarm or a virgin battle-axe – but somehow a bit of all of them, which meant that you could never quite pin her down or predict what her next move was going to be. The only thing I felt certain about was that the master was in love with her. He always grew very still and softspoken when she entered the room, and more than once I caught him staring at her with a far-off look in his eyes when her head was turned the other way. Since they slept together in the same bed every night, and since I heard the mattress creak and bounce with a certain regularity, I took it for granted that she felt the same way about him. What I didn't know was that she had already turned him down in marriage three times – but even if I had known, I doubt it would have made much difference. I had other things on my mind just then, and they were a hell of a lot more important to me than the ups and downs of the master's love life.

I kept to myself as much as possible during those weeks, hiding out in my room as I explored the mysteries and terrors of my new gift. I did everything I could to tame it, to come to terms with it, to study its exact dimensions and accept it as a fundamental part of myself. That was the struggle: not just to master the skill, but to absorb its gruesome and shattering implications, to plunge into the maw of the beast. It had marked me with a special destiny, and I would be set apart from others for the rest of my life. Imagine waking up one morning to discover that you have a new face, and then imagine the hours you would have to spend in front of the mirror before you got used to it, before you could begin to feel comfortable with yourself again. Day after day, I would lock myself in my room, stretch out on the floor, and wish my body into the air. I practiced so much that it wasn't long before I could levitate at will, lifting myself off the ground in a matter of seconds. After a couple of weeks, I learned that it wasn't necessary to lie down on the floor. If I put myself in the proper trance, I was able to do it standing up, to float a good six inches into the air from a vertical position. Three days after that, I learned that I could begin the ascent with my eyes open. I could actually look down and see my feet rising off the floor, and still the spell would not be broken.

Meanwhile, the life of the others swirled around me. Aesop's bandages came off, Mother Sioux was fitted with a cane and began to hobble around again, the master and Mrs Witherspoon shook the bedsprings every night, filling the house with their groans. With so much hubbub to contend with, it wasn't always easy to come up with an excuse for shutting myself in my room. A couple of times, I felt certain that the master saw straight through me, that he understood my duplicity and was lenient only because he wanted me out of his hair. At any other moment, I would have been consumed with jealousy to be shunned like that, to know that he preferred the company of a woman to my own sterling, inimitable presence. Now that I was airborne, however, Master Yehudi was beginning to lose his godlike properties for me, and I no longer felt under the sway of his influence. I saw him as a man, a man no better or worse than other men, and if he wanted to spend his time cavorting with a skinny wench from Wichita, that was his affair. He had his affairs and I had mine, and that's how it was going to be from now on. I had taught myself how to fly, after all, or at least something that resembled flying, and I assumed that meant I was my own man now, that I was beholden to no one but myself. As it turned out, I had merely advanced to the next stage of my development. Devious and cunning as ever, the master was still far ahead of me, and I had a long road to travel before I became the hotshot I thought I was.

Aesop drooped in his nine-fingered state, a listless shadow of his former self, and though I spent as much time with him as I could, I was too busy with my experiments to give him the kind of attention he needed. He kept asking me why I spent so many hours alone in my room, and one morning (it must have been the fifteenth or sixteenth of December) I let forth with a small lie to help assuage his doubts about me. I didn't want him to think I'd stopped caring about him, and under the circumstances it seemed better to fib than to say nothing.

'It's in the nature of a surprise,' I said. 'If you promise not to breathe a word about it, I'll give you a hint.'

Aesop eyed me with suspicion. 'You're up to another one of your tricks, aren't you?'

'No tricks, I swear. What I'm telling you is on the level, the whole gob straight from the horse's mouth.'

'You don't have to hem and haw. If you have something to say, just come out and say it.'

'I will. But first you've got to promise.'

'This had better be good. I don't like giving my word for no reason, you know.'

'Oh, it's good all right, you can trust me on that.'

'Well,' he said, beginning to lose patience. 'What's the pitch, little brother?'

'Raise your right hand and swear you'll never tell. Swear on your mother's grave. Swear on the whites of your eyeballs. Swear on the pussy of every whore in Niggertown.'

Aesop sighed, grabbed hold of his balls with his left hand – which was how the two of us swore to sacred oaths – and lifted his right hand into the air. 'I promise,' he said, and then he repeated the things I'd told him to say.

'Well,' I said, improvising as I went along, 'it's like this. Christmas is coming up next week, and what with Mrs Witherspoon in the house and all, I've heard talk about a celebration on the twenty-fifth. Turkey and pudding, presents, maybe even a fir tree with baubles and popcorn on it. If this shindig comes off like I think it will, I don't want to be caught with my pants down. You know how it is. It ain't no fun to receive a present if you can't give one in return. So that's what I've been up to in my room all these days. I'm working on a present, concocting the biggest and best surprise my poor little brain can think of. I'll be unveiling it to you in just a few days, big brother, and I hope to hell you aren't disappointed.'

Everything I said about the Christmas party was true. I'd overheard the master and his lady talking about it one night through the walls, but until then it hadn't occurred to me to give anyone a present. Now that I'd planted the idea in my head, I saw it as a golden opportunity, the chance I'd been waiting for all along. If there was a Christmas dinner (and that same night the master announced there would be), I would use the occasion to show off my new talent. That would be my present to them. I would stand up and levitate before their eyes, and at last my secret would be known to the world.

I spent the next week and a half in a cold sweat. It was one thing to perform my stunts in private, but how could I be sure I wouldn't fall on my face when I walked out in front of them? If I didn't come through, I'd be turned into a laughing-stock, the butt of every joke for the next twenty-seven years. So began the longest, most tormented day of my life. From whatever angle you chose to look at it, the Yuletide bash was a triumph, a veritable banquet of laughter and gaiety, but I didn't enjoy myself one bit. I could barely chew the turkey for fear of choking on it, and the mashed turnips tasted like a mixture of library paste and mud. By the time we moved into the parlor to sing songs and exchange presents, I was ready to pass out. Mrs Witherspoon started off by giving me a blue sweater with red reindeer stitched across the front. Mother Sioux followed with a pair of hand-knit argyle socks, and then the master gave me a spanking new white baseball. Finally, Aesop gave me the portrait of Sir Walter Raleigh, which he'd cut out of the book and mounted in a sleek ebony frame. They were all generous gifts, but each time I unwrapped one, I could do no more than mumble a grim, inaudible thanks. Each present meant that I was drawing closer to the moment of truth, and each one sapped a little more of the spirit out of me. I sank down in my chair, and by the time I'd opened the last package, I had all but resolved to cancel the demonstration. I wasn't prepared, I told myself, I still needed more practice, and once I started in with those arguments, I had no trouble talking myself out of it. Then, just when I'd managed to glue my ass to the chair forever, Aesop piped in with his two cents and the ceiling fell on top of me.

'Now it's Walt's turn,' he said in all innocence, thinking I was a man of my word. 'He's got something up his sleeve, and I can't wait for him to spring it on us.'

'That's right,' the master said, turning to me with one of his piercing, all-knowing looks. 'Young Mr Rawley has yet to be heard from.'

I was on the spot. I didn't have another present, and if I stalled any longer, they'd see me for the selfish ingrate I really was. So I stood up from my chair, my knee-bones knocking together, and said in a feeble little church-mouse voice: 'Here goes, ladies and gentlemen. If it don't work, you can't say it's from want of trying.'

The four of them were looking at me with such curiosity, such a raptness of puzzlement and attention, that I shut my eyes to block them out. I took a long slow breath and exhaled, spread my arms in the loose, slack-jointed way I'd worked on for so many hours, and went into my trance. I began to rise almost immediately, lifting off the ground in a smooth and gradual ascent, and when I reached a height of six or seven inches – the maximum I was capable of in those early months – I opened my eyes and looked out at my audience. Aesop and the two women were gaping in wonder, their three mouths formed into identical little o's. The master was smiling, however, smiling as the tears rolled down his cheeks, and even as I hovered before him, I saw that he was already reaching for the leather strap behind his collar. By the time I floated down again, he had slipped the necklace over his head and was holding it out to me in his extended palm. No one said a word. I started walking toward him, crossing the room with my eyes fixed on his eyes, not daring to look anywhere else. When I came to the place where Master Yehudi was sitting, I took my finger joint from him and fell to my knees, burying my face in his lap. I held on like that for close to a minute, and when I finally found the courage to stand up again, I ran from the room, rushing to the kitchen and out into the cold night air – gasping for breath, gasping for life under the immensity of the winter stars.

We said good-bye to Mrs Witherspoon three days after that, waving to her from the kitchen door as she drove off in her emerald green Chrysler sedan. Then it was 1927, and for the first six months of that year I worked with savage concentration, pushing myself a little farther each week. Master Yehudi made it clear that levitation was only the beginning. It was a lovely accomplishment, of course, but nothing to set the world on fire with. Scores of people possessed the ability to lift themselves off the ground, and even after you subtracted the Indian fakirs and Tibetan monks and Congolese witch doctors, there were numerous examples from the so-called civilized nations, the white countries of Europe and North America. In Hungary alone, the master said, there had been five active levitators at the turn of the century, three of them right in his hometown of Budapest. It was a wonderful skill, but the public soon grew tired of it, and unless you could do more than hover just a few inches off the ground, there was no chance of turning it into a profitable career. The art of levitation had been sullied by tricksters and charlatans, the smoke-and-mirror boys out for a quick buck, and even the lamest, most tawdry magician on the vaudeville circuit could pull off the stunt of the floating girl: the bombshell in the scant, glittering costume who hangs in midair as a hoop is placed around her (Look: no strings, no wires) and travels the length of her outstretched body. That was standard procedure now, an established part of the repertoire, and it had put the real levitators out of business. Everyone knew it was a fake, and the fakery was so widespread that even when confronted with an act of genuine levitation, audiences insisted on believing it was a sham.

'There are only two ways of grabbing their attention,' the master said. 'Either one will bring us a good life, but if you manage to combine the two of them into a single routine, there's no telling how far we might go. There isn't a bank in the world that could hold all the money we'd make then.'

'Two ways,' I said. 'Are they part of the thirty-three steps, or are we past that stuff now?'

'We're past it. You've gone as far as I did when I was your age, and beyond this point we're entering new territory, continents no one has ever seen before. I can help you with advice and instruction, I can steer you when you've gone off track, but all the essential things you'll have to discover for yourself. We've come to the crossroads, and from now on everything is up to you.'

'Tell me about the two ways. Give me the lowdown on the whole kaboodle, and we'll see if I've got it in me or not.'

'Loft and locomotion – those are the two ways. By loft I mean getting yourself up into the air. Not just half a foot, but three feet, six feet, twenty feet. The higher you go, the more spectacular the results will be. Three feet is nice, but it won't be enough to stun the crowds into amazement. That puts you just a little above eye-level for most adults, and that can't do the trick over the long haul. At six feet, you're hovering above their heads, and once you force them to look up, you'll be creating the kind of impression we want. At ten feet, the effect will be transcendent. At twenty feet, you'll be up there among the angels, Walt, a wondrous thing to behold, an apparition of light and beauty shining joy into the heart of every man, woman, and child who lifts his face up to you.'

'You're giving me goose bumps, master. When you talk like that, it sets my bones all atremble.'

'Loft is only the half of it, son. Before you get carried away, stop and consider locomotion. By that I mean moving yourself through the air. Forward or backward, as the case may be, but preferably both. Speed is of no consequence, but duration is vital, the very nub of the matter. Imagine the spectacle of gliding through the air for ten seconds. People will gasp. They'll point at you in disbelief, but before they can absorb the reality of what they're witnessing, the miracle will be over. Now stretch the performance to thirty seconds or a minute. It gets better, doesn't it? The soul begins to expand, the blood begins to flow more sweetly in your veins. Now stretch it to five minutes, to ten minutes, and imagine yourself turning figure eights and dancing pirouettes as you move, inexhaustible and free, with fifty thousand pairs of eyes trained on you as you float above the grass of the Polo Grounds in New York City. Try to imagine it, Walt, and you'll see what I've been seeing for all these months and years.'

'In the name of the Lord, Master Yehudi, I don't think I can stand it.'

'But wait, Walt, wait another second. Just suppose, for the sake of argument, just suppose that by some vast stroke of luck you were able to master both those things and perform them at the same time.'

'Loft and locomotion together?'

'That's it, Walt. Loft and locomotion together. What then?'

'I'd be flying, wouldn't I? I'd be flying through the air like a bird.'

'Not like a bird, my little man. Like a god. You'd be the wonder of wonders, Walt, the holy of holies. As long as men walked the earth, they'd worship you as the greatest man among them.'

I spent most of the winter working alone in the barn. The animals were there, but they paid no attention to me, watching my antigravitational feats with dumb indifference. Every now and then, the master would stop in to see how I was doing, but other than a few words of encouragement, he rarely said much. January proved to be the hardest month, and I made no progress at all. Levitation was almost as simple as breathing for me by then, but I was stuck at the same paltry height of six inches, and the idea of moving through the air seemed out of the question. It wasn't that I couldn't get the hang of those things, I couldn't even conceive of them, and work as I did to coax my body to express them, I couldn't find a way to begin. Nor was the master in any position to help. 'Trial and error,' he would say, 'trial and error, that's what it boils down to. You've come to the hard part now, and you can't expect to reach the heavens overnight.'

In early February, Aesop and Master Yehudi left the farm to go on a tour of colleges and universities back East. They wanted to make up their minds about where Aesop should be enrolled in September, and they were planning to be gone for a full month. I don't need to add that I begged to go along with them. They would be visiting cities like Boston and New York, giant metropolises with major league ball clubs and trolley cars and pinball machines, and the idea of being stuck in the boondocks was a bit hard to swallow. If I'd been making some headway on my loft and locomotion, it might not have been so awful to be left behind, but I wasn't getting anywhere, and I told the master that a change of scenery was just what I needed to get the juices flowing again. He laughed in that condescending way of his and said, 'Your time is coming, champ, but it's Aesop's turn now. The poor boy hasn't set eyes on a sidewalk or a traffic light for seven years, and it's my duty as a father to show him a little of the world. Books can only go so far, after all. A moment comes when you have to experience things in the flesh.'

'Talking about flesh,' I said, gulping back my disappointment, 'be sure to take care of Aesop's little pal. If there's one experience he's been craving, it's the chance to put it somewhere other than in his own hand.'

'Rest assured, Walt. It's on the agenda. Mrs Witherspoon gave me some extra cash for precisely that purpose.'

'That was thoughtful of her. Maybe she'll do the same for me one day.'

'I'm sure she would, but I doubt you're going to need her help.'

'We'll see about that. The way things stand now, I ain't interested anyway.'

'All the more reason to stay behind in Kansas and do your work. If you keep at it, there might be a surprise or two for me when I come back.'

So I spent the month of February alone with Mother Sioux, watching the snow fall and listening to the wind blow across the prairie. For the first couple of weeks, the weather was so cold that I couldn't bring myself to go out to the barn. I spent the better part of my time moping around the house, too dejected to think about practicing my stunts. Even with just the two of us, Mother Sioux had to keep up with her chores, and what with the extra effort required because of her bum leg, she tired more easily than she had before. Still, I pestered her to distraction, trying to get her to talk to me as she went about her work. For over two years I hadn't given much thought to anyone but myself, accepting the people around me more or less as they appeared on the surface. I had never bothered to probe into their pasts, had never really cared to know who they'd been before I entered their lives. Now, suddenly, I was gripped by a compulsion to learn everything I could about each one of them. I think it started because I missed them so much – the master and Aesop most of all, but Mrs Witherspoon as well. I'd liked having her around the house, and the place was a lot duller now that she was gone. Asking questions was a way to bring them back, and the more Mother Sioux talked about them, the less lonely I felt.

For all my insistence and nagging, I didn't get much out of her during the daytime. An occasional anecdote, a few dribs and drabs, suggestive hints. The evenings were more conducive to talk, and no matter how hard I pressed her, she rarely got going before we sat down to supper. Mother Sioux was a tight-lipped person, not given to idle chatter or shooting the breeze, but once she settled into the right mood, she wasn't half bad at telling stories. Her delivery was flat, and she didn't throw in many colorful details, but she had a knack for pausing every so often in the middle of a sentence or an idea, and those little breaks in the telling produced rather startling effects. They gave you a chance to think, to carry on with the story yourself, and by the time she started up again, you discovered that your head was filled with all kinds of vivid pictures that hadn't been there before.

One night, for no reason that I could understand, she took me up to her room on the second floor. She told me to sit on the bed, and once I'd made myself comfortable, she opened the lid of a battered old trunk that stood in the corner. I'd always thought it was a storage place for her sheets and blankets, but it turned out to be stuffed with objects from her past: photographs and beads, moccasins and rawhide dresses, arrowheads, newspaper clippings, and pressed flowers. One by one, she carried these mementoes over to the bed, sat down beside me, and explained what they meant. It was all true about her having worked for Buffalo Bill, I discovered, and the thing that got me when I looked through her old pictures was how pretty she'd been back then – pert and slim, with a full set of white teeth and two long, lovely braids. She'd been a regular Indian princess, a dream squaw like the girls in the movies, and it was hard to put that cute little package together with the roly-poly gimp who kept house for us, to accept the fact that they were one and the same person. It started when she was sixteen years old, she said, at the height of the Ghost Dance craze that swept through the Indian lands in the late 1880s. Those were the bad times, the years of the end of the world, and the red people believed that magic was the only thing that could save them from extinction. The cavalry was closing in from all sides, crowding them off the prairies onto small reservations, and the Blue-Coats had too many men to make a counterattack feasible. Dancing the Ghost Dance was the last line of resistance: to jiggle and shake yourself into a frenzy, to bounce and bob like the Holy Rollers and the screwballs who babble in tongues. You could fly out of your body then, and the white man's bullets would no longer touch you, no longer kill you, no longer empty your veins of blood. The Dance caught on everywhere, and eventually Sitting Bull himself threw in his lot with the shakers. The US Army got scared, fearing rebellion was in the works, and ordered Mother Sioux's great-uncle to stop. But the old boy told them to shove it, he could jitterbug in his own tepee if he wanted to, and who were they to meddle in his private business? So General Blue-Coat (I think his name was Miles, or Niles) called in Buffalo Bill to powwow with the chief. They were buddies from back when Sitting Bull had worked in the Wild West Show, and Cody was about the only paleface he trusted. So Bill trekked out to the reservation in South Dakota like a good soldier, but once he got there, the general changed his mind and wouldn't allow him to meet with Sitting Bull. Bill was understandably ticked off. Just as he was about to storm away, however, he caught sight of the young Mother Sioux (whose name back then was She Who Smiles like the Sun) and signed her on as a member of his troupe. At least the journey hadn't gone entirely for nought. For Mother Sioux, it probably meant the difference between life and death. A few days after her departure into the world of show business, Sitting Bull was murdered in a scuffle with some of the soldiers who were holding him prisoner, and not long after that, three hundred women, children, and old men were mowed down by a cavalry regiment at the so-called Battle of Wounded Knee, which wasn't a battle so much as a turkey shoot, a wholesale slaughter of the innocent.

There were tears in Mother Sioux's eyes when she spoke about this. 'Custer's revenge,' she muttered. 'I was two years old when Crazy Horse filled his body with arrows, and by the time I was sixteen, there was nothing left.'

'Aesop once explained it to me,' I said. 'It's a bit fuzzy now, but I recall him describing how there wouldn't have been no black slaves from Africa if the white folks had been given a free hand with the Indians. He said they wanted to turn the redskins into slaves, but the Catholic boss man in the old country put the nix on it. So the pirates went to Africa instead and rounded up a lot of darkies and hauled them off in chains. That's how Aesop told it, and I've never known him to lie about nothing. Indians were supposed to be treated good. Like that live-and-let-live stuff the master is always nattering about.'

'Supposed to,' Mother Sioux answered. 'But supposed to ain't the same as is.'

'You've got a point there, Ma. If you don't put your money where your mouth is, you can make all the promises you want, and it still don't add up to a mound of squash.'

She pulled out more photos after that, and then she started in on the theater programs, poster bills, and newspaper clippings. Mother Sioux had been just about everywhere, not just in America and Canada, but on the other side of the ocean as well. She had performed in front of the king and queen of England, she had signed her autograph for the tsar of Russia, she had drunk champagne with Sarah Bernhardt. After five or six years of touring with Buffalo Bill, she married an Irishman named Ted, a little jockey who rode steeplechase up and down the

British Isles. They had a daughter named Daffodil, a stone cottage with blue morning glories and pink climbing roses in the garden, and for seven years her happiness knew no bounds. Then disaster struck. Ted and Daffodil were killed in a train wreck, and Mother Sioux returned to America with a broken heart. She married a pipe fitter whose name was also Ted, but unlike Ted One, Ted Two was a sot and a roughneck, and by and by Mother Sioux took to drink herself, so great was her sorrow whenever she compared her new life to her old. They wound up living together in a tar-paper shack on the outskirts of Memphis, Tennessee, and if not for the sudden, wholly chance appearance of Master Yehudi on their road one morning in the summer of 1912, Mother Sioux would have been a corpse before her time. He was walking along with the young Aesop in his arms (just two days after he'd rescued him in the cotton field) when he heard shrieks and howls rising from the broken-down hut that Mother Sioux called her home. Ted Two had just commenced pummeling her with his hairy fists, knocking out six or seven teeth with the first blows, and Master Yehudi, who was never one to walk away from trouble, entered the shack, gently placed his crippled child on the floor, and put an end to the donnybrook by sneaking up behind Ted Two, clamping his thumb and middle finger onto the crumbum's neck, and applying enough pressure to dispatch him to the land of dreams. The master then washed the blood from Mother Sioux's gums and lips, helped her to her feet, and glanced about at the squalor of the room. He didn't need more than twelve seconds to come to a decision. 'I have a proposal to make,' he said to the battered woman. 'Leave this louse on the floor and come with me. I have a rickets-plagued boy in want of a mother, and if you agree to take care of him, I'll agree to take care of you. I don't stay anywhere for very long, so you'll have to acquire a taste for travel, but I promise on my father's soul that I'll never let you and the child go hungry.'

The master was twenty-nine years old then, a radiant specimen of manhood sporting a waxed handlebar mustache and an impeccably knotted tie. Mother Sioux joined forces with him that morning, and for the next fifteen years she stuck with him through every twist and turn of his career, raising Aesop as if he were her own. I can't remember all the places she talked about, but the best stories always seemed to be centered around Chicago, a town they visited often. That was where Mrs Witherspoon hailed from, and once Mother Sioux got onto that subject, my head started to spin. She gave me only the sketchiest outline, but the bare facts were so curious, so weirdly theatrical, that it wasn't long before I had embroidered them into a full-blown drama. Marion Witherspoon had married her late husband when she was twenty or twenty-one. He himself had been raised in Kansas, the son of a wealthy family from Wichita who had run off to the big city the moment he came into his inheritance. Mother Sioux described him as a handsome, fun-loving rake, one of those mealy-mouthed charmers who could talk his way into a woman's skirt in less time than it took Jim Thorpe to tie his shoe. The young couple lived high on the hog for three or four years, but Mr Witherspoon had a weakness for the ponies, not to speak of a penchant for dabbling in a friendly game of cards some fifteen or twenty nights a month, and since he demonstrated more enthusiasm than skill at his chosen vices, his once vast fortune shrank to a pittance. Toward the end, the situation became so desperate that it looked as if he and his wife would have to move back to the family home in Wichita and that he, Charlie Witherspoon, the polo-playing gadabout and jokester of the North Side, would actually have to look for nine-to-five employment in some dreary grain-belt insurance company. That was where Master Yehudi entered the picture – in the back room of a Rush Street pool hall at four in the morning with said Mr Witherspoon and two or three anonymous others, all of them sitting around a green felt table holding cards in their hands. As they say in the funny papers, it wasn't Charlie's night, and there he was about to go belly-up, sitting on three jacks and a pair of kings without a dime to throw in the pot. Master Yehudi was the only one left in the game, and since this was clearly the last good chance Charlie would ever have, he decided to go for broke. First he bet his property in Cibola, Kansas (which had once been his grandparents' farm), signing over the house and the land on a scrap of paper, and then, when Master Yehudi hung in there and raised him, the gentleman signed another scrap of paper whereby he relinquished all claims to his own wife. Master Yehudi was holding four sevens, and since four of a kind always beats a full house, no matter how much royalty is crammed into that house, he won the farm and the woman, and poor, defeated Charlie Witherspoon, at last at his wits' end, wobbled home at dawn, entered the room where his wife lay asleep, and extracted a revolver from the bedside table, whereupon he blew his brains out right there on the bed.

That was how Master Yehudi came to pitch his tent in Kansas. After years of wandering, he finally had a place to call his own, and while it wasn't necessarily the place he'd had in mind, he wasn't about to spurn what those four sevens had given him. What puzzled me was how Mrs Witherspoon fit into the setup. If her husband had died broke, from whence had sprung the wherewithal for her to live so comfortably in her Wichita mansion, to pamper herself with fine clothes and emerald-green sedans and still have enough left over to fund Master Yehudi's projects? Mother Sioux had a ready answer for that one. Because she was smart. Once she caught on to the profligate ways of her husband, Mrs Witherspoon had begun fiddling with the books, stashing away bits of their monthly income in high-yield investments, stocks, corporate bonds, and other financial transactions. By the time she was widowed, this hanky-panky had produced some robust profits, multiplying her initial outlay by a factor of four, and with this tidy little fortune tucked into her purse, she was more than able to eat, drink, and make merry. But what about Master Yehudi? I asked. He'd won her fair and square in that poker game, and if Mrs Witherspoon belonged to him, why weren't they married? Why wasn't she here with us darning his socks and cooking his grub and carrying his babies in her womb?

Mother Sioux shook her head slowly back and forth. 'It's a new world we're living in,' she said. 'Ain't nobody can own another's body no more. A woman ain't chattel to be bought and sold by men, least of all one of them new women like the master's lady. They love and hate, they grapple and spoon, they want and don't want, and as time goes on they each sink deeper under the other's skin. It's a real show, patty-cake, the follies and the circus all rolled into one, and dollars to doughnuts it's going to be like that till the day they die.'

These stories gave me a lot to chew on during the hours I spent alone, but the more I pondered what Mother Sioux had told me, the more twisted and confounding it became. My head grew weary from trying to parse the ins and outs of such complex doings, and at a certain point I just stopped, telling myself I'd short my brain wires if I kept up all that cogitation. Grown-ups were impenetrable creatures, and if I ever became one myself, I promised to write a letter back to my old self explaining how they got to be that way – but for now I'd had enough. It was a relief to let go like that, but once I abandoned those thoughts, I fell into a boredom so profound, so taxing in its bland and feathery sameness, that I finally went back to work. It wasn't because I wanted to, it's just that I couldn't think of any other way to fill the time.

I locked myself in my room again, and after three days of fruitless endeavor, I discovered what I had been doing wrong. The whole problem lay in my approach. I had somehow gotten it into my head that loft and locomotion could only be achieved through a two-step process. First levitate as high as I could, then push out and go. I had trained myself to do the one thing, and I figured I could accomplish the second thing by grafting it onto the first. But the truth was that the second thing canceled out what came before it. Again and again, I would lift myself into the air according to the old method, but as soon as I started to think about moving forward, I would flutter back to the ground, landing on my feet again before I had a chance to get going. If I failed once, I failed a thousand times, and after a while I felt so disgusted, so bedeviled by my incompetence, that I took to throwing tantrums and pounding my fists on the floor. At last, in the full flush of anger and defeat, I picked myself up and jumped straight into the wall, hoping to smash myself into unconsciousness. I leapt, and for the briefest eyeblink of a second, just before my shoulder thudded against the plaster, I sensed that I was floating – that even as I rushed forward, I was losing touch with gravity, going up with a familiar buoyant surge as I lunged through the air. Before I could grasp what was happening, I had bounced off the wall and was crumpling onto the floor in pain. My whole left side throbbed from the impact, but I didn't care. I jumped to my feet and did a little dance around the room, laughing my head off for the next twenty minutes. I had cracked the secret. I understood. Forget right angles, I told myself. Think arc, think trajectory. It wasn't a matter of first going up and then going out, it was a matter of going up and out at the same time, of launching myself in one smooth, uninterrupted gesture into the arms of the great ambient nothingness.

I worked like a dog over the next eighteen or twenty days, practicing this new technique until it was embedded in my muscles and bones, a reflex action that no longer required the slightest pause for thought. Locomotion was a perfectible skill, a dreamlike walking through air that was essentially no different from walking on the ground, and just as a baby totters and falls with its first steps, I experienced a goodly dose of stumbles and spills when I began to spread my wings. Duration was the abiding issue for me at that point, the question of how long and how far I could keep myself going. The early results varied widely, ranging anywhere from three to fifteen seconds, and since the speed at which I moved was achingly slow, the best I could manage was seven or eight feet, not even the distance from one wall of my room to another. It wasn't a vigorous, smart-stepping amble, but a kind of shuffling ghost-walk, the way an aerialist advances along a high wire. Still, I kept on working with confidence, no longer subject to swoons of discouragement as I'd been before. I was inching forward now, and nothing was going to stop me. Even if I hadn't risen higher than my standard six or seven inches, I figured it was best to concentrate on locomotion for the time being. Once I'd achieved some mastery in that area, I would turn my attention to loft and tackle that problem as well. It made sense, and even if I had it to do all over again, I wouldn't budge from that plan. How could I have known that time was already running short, that fewer days were left than any of us had imagined?

After Master Yehudi and Aesop returned, spirits in the household percolated as never before. It was the end of an era, and we were all looking ahead to the future now, anticipating the new lives that waited for us beyond the boundaries of the farm. Aesop would be the first to go – off to Yale in September – but if things went according to schedule, the rest of us would be following suit by the turn of the year. Now that I had passed to the next stage of my training, the master calculated that I'd be ready to perform in public in roughly nine months. It was still a long way to go for someone my age, but he talked about it as something real now, and what with his use of words like *bookings, venues,* and *box office net,* he kept me humming in a state of permanent excitement. I wasn't Walt Rawley anymore, the white trash nobody without a pot to piss in, I was Walt the Wonder Boy, the diminutive daredevil who defied the laws of gravity, the one and only ace of the air. Once we hit the road and let the world see what I could do, I was going to be a sensation, the most talked-about personality in America.

As for Aesop, his tour back East had been an unqualified success. They'd given him special exams, they'd interviewed him, they'd picked and probed the contents of his wooly skull, and to hear the master tell it, he'd knocked the socks off the lot of them. Not a single college had turned him down, but Yale was offering a four-year scholarship – along with food and lodging and a small living allowance – and that had tipped the balance in their favor. Boola, boola, bulldogs of the world unite. Recalling these facts now, I understand what an achievement it was for a self-taught black youngster to have scaled the ramparts of those cold-hearted institutions. I knew nothing about books, had no yardstick to measure my friend's abilities against anyone else's, but I took it on blind faith that he was a genius, and the idea that a bunch of sourpusses and stuffed shirts at Yale College should want him as a student struck me as natural, the most fitting thing in the world.

If I was too dumb to grasp the significance of Aesop's triumph, I was more than bowled over by the new clothes he brought back from his trip. He returned in a raccoon coat and a blue-and-white beanie, and he looked so strange in that getup that I couldn't help laughing when he walked through the door. The master had had him fitted for two brown tweed suits in Boston, and now that he was home, he took to wearing them around the house instead of his old farm duds, complete with white shirt, stiff collar, necktie, and a pair of gleaming, dung-hued brogans. It was altogether impressive how he carried himself in those threads – as if they made him more erect, more dignified, more aware of his own importance. Even though he didn't have to, he started shaving every morning, and I would keep him company in the kitchen as he lathered up his mug and dipped his straight-edged razor into the chilly bucket, holding a little mirror for him as he told me about the things he'd seen and done in the big cities along the Atlantic coast. The master had done more than just get him into college, he'd shown him the time of his life, and Aesop remembered every minute of it: the high spots, the low spots, and all the spots in between. He talked about the skyscrapers, the museums, the variety shows, the restaurants, the libraries, the sidewalks thronged with people of every color and description. 'Kansas is an illusion,' he said one morning as he scraped away at his invisible beard, 'a stopping place on the road to reality.'

'You don't have to tell me,' I said. 'This hole is so backward, the state went dry before they even heard of Prohibition in the rest of the country.'

'I drank a beer in New York City, Walt.'

'Well, I figured you must have done.'

'In a speakeasy. An illegal establishment on MacDougal Street, right in the heart of Greenwich Village. I wish you could have been there with me.'

'I can't stand the taste of them suds, Aesop. Give me a good stiff bourbon, though, and I'll drink any man under the table.'

'I'm not saying it tasted good. But it was exciting to be there with all those people, quaffing my drink in a crowded place like that.'

'I'll bet it wasn't the only exciting thing you did.'

'No, not by a long shot. It was just one of many.'

'I'll bet your pecker got some good workouts, too. I'm just making a wild guess, of course, so correct me if I'm wrong.'

Aesop paused with the razor in midair, grew thoughtful for a moment, and then started grinning into the mirror. 'Let's just say it wasn't neglected, little brother, and we'll leave it at that.'

'Can you tell me her name? I don't mean to be pushy, but I'm curious to find out who the lucky girl was.'

'Well, if you must know, her name was Mabel.'

'Mabel. Not bad, all things considered. She sounds like a dolly with some flesh on her bones. Was she old or young?'

'She wasn't old, and she wasn't young. But you hit it right about the flesh. Mabel was the fattest, blackest mama you'd ever hope to sink your teeth into. She was so big, I couldn't tell where she started and where she ended. It was like wrestling with a hippo, Walt. But once you get into the swing of it, the anatomy takes care of itself. You creep into her bed as a boy, and half an hour later you walk out as a man.'

Now that he had graduated to manhood, Aesop decided the moment had come to sit down and write his autobiography. That was how he planned to spend the months before he left home – telling the story of his life so far, from his birth in a rural shack in Georgia to his deflowering in a Harlem bordello, wrapped in the blubbery arms of Mabel the whore. The words began to flow, but the title vexed him, and I remember how he dithered back and forth about it. One day he was going to call the book *Confessions of a Negro Foundling*; the next day he changed it to *Aesop's Adventures: The True History and Unvarnished Opinions of a Lost Boy*; the day after that it was going to be *The Road to Yale: The Life of a Negro Scholar from His Humble Origins to the Present*. Those were just some of them, and for as long as he worked on that book, he kept trying out different ones, shuffling and reshuffling his ideas until he'd built up a stack of title pages every bit as tall as the manuscript itself. He must have toiled eight or ten hours a day on his opus, and I can remember peeking through the door as he sat there hunched over his desk, marveling at how a person could sit still for so long, engaged in no other activity than guiding the nib of a pen across a leaf of white foolscap. It was my first experience with the making of books, and even when Aesop called me into his room to read selected passages of his work aloud, I found it hard to tally all that silence and concentration with the stories that came tumbling from his lips. We were all in the book – Master Yehudi, Mother Sioux, myself – and to my clumsy, untutored ear, the thing had every intention of becoming a masterpiece. I laughed at some parts, I cried at others, and what more can a person want from a book than to feel the prick of such delights and sorrows? Now that I'm writing a book of my own, not a day goes by when I don't think about Aesop up there in his room. That was sixty-five springs ago, and I can still see him sitting at his desk, scribbling away at his youthful memoirs as the light poured through the window, catching the dust particles that danced around him. If I concentrate hard enough, I can still hear the breath going in and out of his lungs, I can still hear the point of his pen scratching across the paper.

While Aesop worked indoors, Master Yehudi and I spent our days in the fields, toiling untold hours on my act. In a fit of optimism after his return, he'd announced to us at dinner that there wouldn't be any planting that year. 'To hell with the crops,' he said. 'There's enough food to last through the winter, and by the time spring comes again, we'll be long gone from this place. The way I look at it, it would be a sin to grow things we'll never need.' There was general rejoicing over this new policy, and for once the early spring was free of drudge work and plowing, the interminable weeks of bent backs and slogging through mud. My locomotion breakthrough had turned the tide, and Master Yehudi was so confident now that he was willing to let the farm go to pot. It was the only sane decision a man could make. We'd all done our time, and why eat dirt when we'd soon be counting our gold?

That doesn't mean we didn't bust our asses out there – particularly myself – but I enjoyed the work, and no matter how hard the master pushed me, I never wanted to quit. Once the weather turned warm, we usually kept going until after dark, working by torchlight in the far meadows as the moon rose into the sky. I was inexhaustible, consumed by a happiness that swept me along from one challenge to the next. By May first, I was able to walk from ten to twelve yards as a matter of routine. By May fifth, I had extended it to twenty yards, and less than a week after that I had pushed it to forty: a hundred and twenty feet of airborne locomotion, nearly ten uninterrupted minutes of pure magic. That was when the master hit upon the idea of having me practice over water. There was a pond in the northeast corner of the property, and from then on we did all our work over there, riding out in the buckboard wagon every morning after breakfast to a point where we could no longer see the house – alone together in the silent fields, barely saying a word to each other for hours on end. The water intimidated me at first, and since I didn't know how to swim, it was no laughing matter to test my prowess over that element. The pond must have been sixty feet across, and the water level in at least half of it was over my head. I fell in sixteen or twenty times the first day, and on four of those occasions the master had to jump in and fish me out. After that, we came equipped with towels and several changes of clothes, but by the end of the week they were no longer necessary. I conquered my fear of the water by pretending it wasn't there. If I didn't look down, I discovered I could propel my body across the surface without getting wet. It was as simple as that, and by the last days of May 1927, I was walking on water with the same skill as Jesus himself.

Somewhere in the middle of that time, Lindbergh made his solo flight across the Atlantic, traveling nonstop from New York City to Paris in thirty-three hours. We heard about it from Mrs Witherspoon, who drove out from Wichita one day with a pile of newspapers in the backseat of her car. The farm was so cut off from the world, even big stories like that one escaped our notice. If it hadn't been for her wanting to come all that way, we never would have heard a peep about it. I've always found it strange that Lindbergh's stunt coincided so exactly with my own efforts, that at the precise moment he was making his way across the ocean, I was traversing my little pond in Kansas – the two of us in the air together, each one accomplishing his feat at the same time. It was as if the sky had suddenly opened itself up to man, and we were the first pioneers, the Columbus and Magellan of human flight. I didn't know the Lone Eagle from a hole in the wall, but I felt linked to him after that, as if we shared some dark fraternal bond. It couldn't have been a coincidence that his plane was called the *Spirit of St Louis*. That was my town, too, the town of champions and twentieth-century heroes, and without even knowing it, Lindbergh had named his plane in my honor.

Mrs Witherspoon hung around for a couple of days and nights. After she left, the master and I got back to business, shifting the focus of our attention from locomotion to loft. I had done what I could do with horizontal travel; now it was time to attempt the vertical. Lindbergh was an inspiration to me, I freely confess it, but I wanted to do him one better: to do with my body what he'd done with a machine. It would be on a smaller scale, perhaps, but it would be infinitely more stupendous, a thing that would dwarf his fame overnight. Try as I did, however, I couldn't make an inch of headway. For a week and a half, the master and I struggled out by the pond, equally daunted by the task we'd set for ourselves, and at the end of that time I was still no higher than I'd been before. Then, on the evening of June fifth, Master Yehudi made a suggestion that began to turn things around.

'I'm just speculating,' he said, 'but it occurs to me that your necklace might have something to do with it. It can't weigh more than an ounce or two, but given the mathematics of what you're attempting, that could be enough. For each millimeter you rise into the air, the weight of the object increases in geometric proportion to the height – meaning that once you're six inches off the ground, you're carrying the equivalent of forty extra pounds. That comes to half your total weight. If my calculations are correct, it's no wonder you've been having such a rough time of it.'

'I've worn that thing since Christmas,' I said. 'It's my lucky charm, and I can't do nothing without it.'

'Yes you can, Walt. The first time you got yourself off the ground, it was slung around my neck, remember? I'm not saying you don't have a sentimental attachment to it, but we're intruding on deep spiritual matters here, and it could be that you can't be whole to do what you have to do, that you have to leave a part of yourself behind before you can attain the full magnitude of your gift.'

'That's just double-talk. I'm wearing clothes, ain't I? I'm wearing shoes and socks, ain't I? If the necklace is bogging me down, then those things are doing it too. And I sure as hell ain't going to flaunt my stuff in public without no clothes on.'

'It can't hurt to try. There's nothing to lose, Walt, and everything to gain. If I'm wrong, so be it. If I'm not, it would be an awful pity if we never had a chance to find out.'

He had me there, so with much skepticism and reluctance I removed the good luck charm and placed it in the master's hand. 'All right,' I said, 'we'll give it a whirl. But if it don't turn out like you say, that's the last we'll ever talk about it.'

Over the course of the next hour, I managed to double my previous record, ascending to heights of twelve to fourteen inches. By nightfall, I had raised myself a good two and a half feet off the ground, demonstrating that Master Yehudi's hunch had been correct, a prophetic insight into the causes and consequences of the levitation arts. The thrill was spectacular – to feel myself hovering at such a distance from the ground, to be literally on the verge of flying – but above two feet it was difficult for me to maintain a vertical position without beginning to totter and grow dizzy. It was all so new to me up there, I wasn't able to find my natural equilibrium. I felt long to myself, as if I were composed of segments and not made of a continuous piece, and my head and shoulders responded in one way while my shins and ankles responded in another. So as not to tip over, I found myself easing into a prone position when I got up there, instinctively knowing it would be safer and more comfortable to have my entire body stretched over the ground than just the soles of my feet. I was still too nervous to think about moving forward in that position, but late that night, just before we knocked off and went home to bed, I tucked my head under my chest and managed to do a slow somersault in the air, completing a full, unbroken circle without once grazing the earth.

The master and I rode back to the house that night drunk with joy. Everything seemed possible to us now: the conquest of both loft and locomotion, the ascension into actual flight, the dream of dreams. That was our greatest moment together, I think, the moment when our whole future fell into place at last. On June sixth, however, just one night after reaching that pinnacle, my training ground to an abrupt and irrevocable halt. The thing that Master Yehudi had been dreading for so long finally came to pass, and when it did, it happened with such violence, caused such havoc and upheaval in our hearts, that neither one of us was ever the same again.

I had worked well all day, and as was our habit throughout that miraculous spring, we decided to linger on into the night. At seven thirty, we ate a supper of sandwiches that Mother Sioux had packed for us that morning and then resumed our labors as darkness gathered in the surrounding fields. It must have been close to ten o'clock when we heard the sound of horses. It was no more than a faint rumbling at first, a disturbance in the ground that made me think of distant thunder, as if a lightning storm were brewing somewhere in the next county. I had just completed a double somersault at the edge of the pond and was waiting for the master's comments, but instead of speaking in his normal calm voice, he grabbed hold of my arm in a sudden, panic-stricken gesture. 'Listen,' he said. And then he said it again: 'Listen to that. They're coming. The bastards are coming.' I pricked up my ears, and sure enough, the sound was getting louder. A couple of seconds passed, and then I understood that it was the sound of horses, a stampeding clatter of hooves charging in our direction.

'Don't move,' the master said. 'Stay where you are and don't move a muscle until I come back.'

Then, without a word of explanation, he started running toward the house, tearing through the fields like a sprinter. I ignored his command and took off after him, racing along as fast as my legs could carry me. We were a good quarter mile from the house, but before we'd traveled a hundred yards, flames were already visible, a glowing surge of red and yellow pulsing against the black sky. We heard whoops and war yodels, a volley of shots rang out, and then we heard the unmistakable sound of human screams. The master kept running, steadily increasing the distance between us, but once he came to the stand of oaks on the far side of the barn, he stopped. I pushed on to the verge of the trees myself, intent on continuing all the way to the house, but the master saw me out of the corner of his eye and wrestled me to the ground before I could go any farther. 'We're too late,' he said. 'If we go in there now, we're only going to get ourselves killed. There's twelve of them and two of us, and they've all got rifles and guns. Pray to God they don't find us, Walt, but there's not a damned thing we can do for the others.'

So we stood there helplessly behind the trees, watching the Ku Klux Klan do its work. A dozen men on a dozen horses pranced about the yard, a mob of yelping murderers with white sheets over their heads, and we were powerless to thwart them. They dragged Aesop and Mother Sioux out of the burning house, put ropes around their necks, and strung them up to the elm tree by the side of the road, each one to a different branch. Aesop howled, Mother Sioux said nothing, and within minutes they were both dead. My two best friends were murdered before my eyes, and all I could do was watch, fighting back tears as Master Yehudi clamped his palm over my mouth. Once the killing was over, a couple of the Klansmen stuck a wooden cross in the ground, doused it with gasoline, and set it on fire. The cross burned as the house burned, the men whooped it up a little more, firing rounds of buckshot into the air, and then they all climbed onto their horses and rode off in the direction of Cibola. The house was incandescent by then, a fireball of heat and roaring timbers, and by the time the last of the men was gone, the roof had already given way, collapsing to the ground in a shower of sparks and meteors. I felt as if I had seen the sun explode. I felt as if I had just witnessed the end of the world.

II

We buried them on the property that night, lowering their bodies into two unmarked graves beside the barn. We should have said some prayers, but our lungs were too full of sobbing for that, so we just covered them up with dirt and said nothing, working in silence as the salt water trickled down our cheeks. Then, without returning to the smoldering house, without even bothering to see if any of our belongings were still intact, we hitched the mare to the wagon and drove off into the darkness, leaving Cibola behind us for good.

It took all night and half the next morning before we made it to Mrs Witherspoon's house in Wichita, and for the rest of that summer the master's grief was so bad I thought he might be in danger of dying himself. He scarcely stirred from his bed, he scarcely ate, he scarcely talked. Except for the tears that dropped from his eyes every three or four hours, there was no way to tell if you were looking at a man or a block of stone. The big fella was all done in, ravaged by sorrow and self-recrimination, and no matter how hard I wished he'd snap out of it, he only got worse as the weeks went by. 'I saw it coming,' he'd sometimes mutter to himself. 'I saw it coming, and I didn't lift a finger to stop it. It's my fault. It's my fault they're dead. I couldn't have done a better job if I'd killed them with my own two hands, and a man who kills deserves no mercy. He doesn't deserve to live.'

I shuddered to see him like that, all useless and inert, and in the long run it scared me every bit as much as what had happened to Aesop and Mother Sioux – maybe even more. I don't mean to sound coldhearted about it, but life is for the living, and shocked as I was by the massacre of my friends, I was still just a kid, a little jumping bean with ants in my pants and rubber in my knees, and I didn't have it in me to walk around mewling and mourning for very long. I shed my tears, I cursed God, I banged my head against the floor, but after carrying on like that for a few days, I was ready to put it behind me and get on to other things. I don't suppose that speaks too well of me as a person, but there's no point in pretending I felt what I didn't feel. I missed Aesop and Mother Sioux, I ached to be with them again – but they were gone, and no amount of begging was going to bring them back. As far as I was concerned, it was time to shake our toes and get cracking. My head was still stuffed with dreams about my new career, and piggish as those dreams might have been, I couldn't wait to get started, to launch myself into the firmament and dazzle the world with my greatness.

Imagine my disappointment, then, as I watched June turn into July and Master Yehudi still languished; imagine how my spirits sank when July became August and he still showed no signs of rebounding from the tragedy. Not only did it put a crimp in my plans, but I felt let down, bollixed, left in the lurch. An essential flaw in the master's character had been revealed to me, and I resented him for his lack of inner toughness, his refusal to face up to the shittiness of life. I had depended on him for so many years, had drawn so much strength from his strength, and now he was acting like any other blithering optimist, another one of those guys who welcomed the good when it came but couldn't accept the bad. It turned my stomach to see him fall apart like that, and as his grief dragged on, I couldn't help but lose some faith in him. If not for Mrs Witherspoon, there's a chance I would have thrown in the towel and split. 'Your master is a big man,' she said to me one morning, 'and big men have big feelings. They feel more than other men – bigger joys, bigger angers, bigger sorrows. He's in pain now, and it's going to last longer for him than it would for someone else. Don't let it frighten you, Walt. He'll get over it eventually. You just have to be patient.'

That's what she said, but deep down I'm not so sure she believed those words herself. As time went on, I sensed that she was growing just as disgusted with him as I was, and I liked it that we saw eye to eye on such an important matter. She was one salty broad, Mrs W., and now that I was living in her house and spending every day in her company, I understood that we had much more in common than I had previously suspected. She'd been on her best behavior when she visited the farm, all prim and fusty so as not to offend Aesop and Mother Sioux, but now that she was on her own turf, she was free to let go and unfurl her true nature. For the first couple of weeks, nearly everything about that nature surprised me, riddled as it was with bad habits and unchecked bouts of self-indulgence. I'm not just talking about her penchant for booze (no less than six or seven gin and tonics per day), nor her passion for cigarettes (puffing on bygone brands like Picayunes and Sweet Caporals from morning to night), but a certain overall laxness, as if lurking behind her ladylike exterior there was a loose, slattern's soul struggling to break free. The tipoff was her mouth, and once she'd imbibed a round or two of her favorite beverage, she'd lapse into some of the coarsest, most vulgar language I've ever heard from the lips of a woman, zinging out the pungent one-liners as fast as a tommy gun burps bullets. After all the clean living I'd done on the farm, I found it refreshing to mingle with someone who wasn't bound by a high moral purpose, whose only aim in life was to enjoy herself and make as much money as she could. So we became friends, leaving Master Yehudi to his anguish as we sweated out the dog days and boredom of the hot Wichita summer.

I knew she was fond of me, but I don't want to exaggerate the depth of her affections, at least not at that early stage. Mrs Witherspoon had a definite reason for keeping me happy, and while I'd like to flatter myself it was because she found me such a sterling companion, such a witty, devil-may-care fellow, the truth was that she was thinking about the future health of her bank account. Why else would a woman of her gumption and sex appeal bother to pal around with a stump-dicked brat like myself? She saw me as a business opportunity, a dollar sign in the shape of a boy, and she knew that if my career was handled with the proper care and acumen, it was going to make her the richest woman in thirteen counties. I'm not saying that we didn't have some fun times together, but it was always in the service of her own interests, and she sucked up to me and won me over as a way to keep me in the fold, to make sure I didn't sneak away before she'd cashed in on my talent.

So be it. I don't blame her for acting like that, and if I'd been in her shoes, I probably would have done the same thing. Still, I won't deny that it sometimes bugged me to see how little an impression my magic made on her. Throughout those dreary weeks and months, I kept my hand in by practicing my routine no less than one or two hours a day. So as not to spook the people who drove past the house, I confined myself to the indoors, working in the upstairs parlor with the shades drawn. Not only did Mrs Witherspoon rarely bother to watch these sessions, but on the few occasions when she did enter the room, she would observe the spectacle of my levitations without twitching a muscle, studying me with the blank-eyed objectivity of a butcher inspecting a slab of beef. No matter how extraordinary the stunts I performed, she accepted them as part of the natural order of things, no more strange or inexplicable than the waxing of the moon or the noise of the wind. Maybe she was too drunk to notice the difference between a miracle and an everyday event, or maybe the mystery of it just left her cold, but when it came to entertainment, she'd have sooner driven through a rainstorm to see some third-rate picture show than watch me float above the goddamn tables and chairs in her living room. My act was no more than a means to an end for her. As long as the end was assured, she couldn't have cared less about the means.

But she was good to me, I won't take that away from her. Whatever her motives might have been, she didn't stint on the amusements, and not once did she hesitate to fork out dough on my behalf. Two days after my arrival, she took me on a shopping spree in downtown Wichita, outfitting me with a whole new set of clothes. After that there was the ice cream parlor, the candy shop, the penny arcade. She was always one step ahead of me, and before I even knew I wanted something, she'd already be offering it to me, thrusting it into my hands with a wink and a little pat on the head. After all the hard times I'd been through, I can't say I objected to whiling away my days in the lap of luxury. I slept in a soft bed with embroidered sheets and down pillows, I ate the gigantic meals cooked for us by Nelly Boggs the colored maid, I never had to put on the same pair of underpants two mornings in a row. Most afternoons, we'd escape the heat by taking a spin through the countryside in the emerald sedan, whizzing down the empty roads with the windows open and the air rushing in on us from all sides. Mrs Witherspoon loved speed, and I don't think I ever saw her happier than when she was pressing her foot on the gas pedal: laughing between snorts from her silver flask, her bobbed red hair fluttering like the legs of an overturned caterpillar. The woman had no fear, no sense that a car traveling at seventy or eighty miles an hour can actually kill someone. I did my best to stay calm when she floored it like that, but once we got to sixty-five or seventy I couldn't help myself. The panic welling up inside me would do something to my stomach, and before long I'd be letting out one fart after another, a whole chain of stink bombs accompanied by loud staccato butt music. I needn't add that I almost died of shame, for Mrs Witherspoon was not someone to let indiscretions like that pass without comment. The first time it happened, she burst out laughing so hard I thought her head was going to fly off her shoulders. Then, without warning, she slammed her foot on the brakes and brought the car to a skidding, heart-pounding stop.

'A few more corkers like those,' she said, 'and we'll have to drive around in gas masks.'

'I don't smell nothing,' I said, giving the only answer that seemed possible.

Mrs Witherspoon sniffed loudly, then screwed up her nose and made a face. 'Smell again, sport. The whole bean brigade's been traveling with us, tooting Dixie from your rear end.'

'Just a little gas,' I said, subtly changing tactics. 'If I'm not mistaken, a car won't run if you don't fill it with gas.'

'Depends on the octane, honey. The kind of chemistry experiment we're discussing here, it's liable to get us both blown up.'

'Yeah, well, at least that's a better way to die than crashing into a tree.'

'Don't worry, snookums,' she said, unexpectedly softening her tone. She reached out and touched my head, gently running her fingertips through my hair. 'I'm a hell of a driver. No matter how fast we're going, you're always safe with Lady Marion at the controls.'

'That sounds good,' I said, enjoying the pressure of her hand against my scalp, 'but I'd feel a lot better if you'd put that in writing.'

She let out a short, throaty guffaw and smiled. 'Here's a tip for the future,' she said. 'If you think I'm going too fast, just close your eyes and yell. The louder you yell, the more fun it's going to be for both of us.'

So that's what I did, or at least what I tried to do. On subsequent outings I always made a point of shutting my eyes when the speedometer reached seventy-five, but a few times the farts came sneaking out at seventy, once even as low as sixty-five (when it looked like we were about to plow into an oncoming truck and veered away at the last second). Those lapses did nothing for my self-respect, but none was worse than the trauma that occurred in early August when my bunghole went for broke and I wound up crapping my pants. It was a brutally hot day. No rain had fallen in over two weeks, and every leaf on every tree in the whole flat countryside was covered with dust. Mrs Witherspoon was a little more plastered than usual, I think, and by the time we left the city limits she'd worked herself into one of those charged-up, fuck-the-world moods. She pushed her buggy past fifty on the first turn, and after that there was no stopping her. Dust flew everywhere. It showered down on the windshield, it danced inside our clothes, it battered our teeth, and all she did was laugh, pressing down on the accelerator as if she meant to break the Mokey Dugway speed record. I shut my eyes and howled for all I was worth, clutching the dashboard as the car shimmied and roared along the dry, divot-scarred turnpike. After twenty or thirty seconds of mounting terror, I knew that my number was up. I was going to die on that stupid road, and these were my last moments on earth. That was when the turd slid out of my crack: a loose and slippery cigar that thudded against my drawers with a warm, sickening wetness, then started sliding down my leg. When I realized what had happened, I couldn't think of any better response than to burst into tears.

Meanwhile, the ride continued, and by the time the car came to a halt some ten or twelve minutes later, I was soaked through and through – with sweat, with shit, with tears. My entire being was awash in body fluids and misery.

'Well, buckaroo,' Mrs Witherspoon announced, lighting up a cigarette to savor her triumph. 'We did it. We broke the century mark. I'll bet you I'm the first woman in this whole tight-assed state who ever did that. What do you think? Pretty good for an old bag like me, no?'

'You ain't no old bag, ma'am,' I said.

'Ah, that's nice. I appreciate that one. You've got a soft touch with the ladies, kid. In a few more years, you'll be knocking them dead with that kind of talk.'

I wanted to go on chatting with her like that, all calm and easy as if nothing had happened, but now that the car had stopped, the smell from my pants was getting more noticeable, and I knew it was only a matter of seconds before my secret came out. Humiliation stung me again, and before I could say another word, I was sobbing into my hands beside her.

'Jesus, Walt,' I heard her say. 'Jesus Christ almighty. You've really done it this time, haven't you?'

'I'm sorry,' I said, not daring to look at her. 'I couldn't help it.'

'It's probably all that candy I've been feeding you. Your belly isn't used to it.'

'Maybe. Or maybe I just don't have no guts.'

'Don't be dumb, boy. You had a little accident is all. It happens to everyone.'

'Sure. As long as you're in diapers it does. I ain't never been so embarrassed in all my life.'

'Forget it. This is no time to feel sorry for yourself. We've got to clean up that little backside of yours before any gunk oozes onto the upholstery. Are you listening to me, Walt? I don't care about your bloody bowel movements, I just don't want my car to bear the brunt. There's a pond behind those trees over there, and that's where I'm taking you now. We'll scrub off the mustard and relish, and then you'll be as good as new.'

I didn't have much choice but to go along with her. It was pretty awful having to stand up and walk, what with all the sloshing and slithering taking place inside my pants, and since I still hadn't quelled my sobs, my chest went on heaving and shuddering, letting forth a whole range of weird, half-stifled sounds. Mrs Witherspoon walked ahead of me, leading the way to the pond. It was about a hundred feet back from the road, set off from its surroundings by a barrier of scrawny trees and shrubs, a little oasis in the middle of the prairie. When we came to the edge of the water, she told me to strip off my clothes, urging me on in a matter-of-fact tone of voice. I didn't want to do it, at least not with her looking at me, but once I realized she wasn't going to turn her back, I fixed my eyes on the ground and submitted to the ordeal. First she undid my shoes and pulled off my socks; then, without the slightest pause, she unbuckled my belt, unbuttoned my fly, and tugged. Pants and undies fell to my ankles in one swoop, and there I was standing with my dick in the breeze before a grown woman, my white legs stained with brown mush and my asshole reeking like yesterday's garbage. It was surely one of the low points of my life, but to Mrs Witherspoon's immense credit (and this is a thing I've never forgotten), she didn't make a sound. Not one groan of disgust, not one gasp. With all the tenderness of a mother washing her newborn baby, she dipped her hands into the water and began cleaning me off, splashing and rubbing my naked skin until every sign of my disgrace had been removed.

'There,' she said, patting me dry with a handkerchief she'd pulled from her red beaded purse. 'Out of sight, out of mind.'

'Fair enough,' I said, 'but what do we do with them fouled-up undies?'

'We leave them for the birds, that's what, and that goes for the pants, too.'

'And you expect me to ride home like that? Without no stitch on my nether bottom?'

'Why not? Your shirttails hang down to your knees, and it's not as though there's much to hide anyway. We're talking microscopes, kid, the crown jewels of Lilliput.'

'Don't cast aspersions on my privates, ma'am. They may be trifles to you, but I'm proud of them just the same.'

'Of course you are. And a cute little dicky-bird it is, Walt, with those bald nuts and smooth, babydoll thighs. You've got everything it takes to be a man' – and here, to my great astonishment, she gathered up the whole package in her palm and gave it a good healthy shake – 'but you're not quite there yet. Besides, no one's going to see you in the car. We'll skip the ice cream parlor today and drive straight home. If it makes you feel any better, I'll smuggle you into the house through the back door. How's that? I'm the only one who's going to know about it, and you can bet your bottom dollar I'll never tell.'

'Not even the master?'

'Least of all the master. What happened out here today is strictly between you and me.'

She could be a good egg, that woman, and whenever it really counted, she was about the best there was. At other times, though, I couldn't make heads or tails of her. Just when you thought she was your bosom buddy, she'd turn around and do something unexpected – tease you, for instance, or snub you, or go silent on you – and the beautiful little world you'd been living in would suddenly go sour. There was a lot I didn't understand, grown-up things that were still over my head, but little by little I began to catch on that she was pining for Master Yehudi. She was bingeing herself into the blues as she waited for him to come round, and if things had gone on much longer, I don't doubt that she would have jumped off the deep end.

The turning point came about two nights after the shit episode. We were sitting on lawn chairs in the backyard, watching the fireflies dart in and out of the bushes and listening to the crickets chirp their tinny songs. That passed for big-time entertainment in those days, even in the so-called Roaring Twenties. I hate to debunk popular legends, but there wasn't a hell of a lot that roared in Wichita, and after two months of scouring that sleepy burg for noise and diversion, we'd more than used up the available resources. We'd seen every motion picture, slurped down every ice cream, played every pinball machine, taken a spin on every merry-go-round. It wasn't worth the effort to go out anymore, and for several nights running we'd just stayed put, letting the torpor spread through our bones like some fatal disease. I was sucking on a glass of tepid lemonade that night, I recall, Mrs W. was off on another bender, and neither one of us had punctured the silence in over forty minutes.

'I used to think,' she finally said, following some secret train of thought, 'I used to think he was the most dashing stud ever to trot out of the fucking stable.'

I took a sip of my drink, looked up at the stars in the night sky, and yawned. 'Who's that?' I said, not bothering to conceal my boredom.

'Who do you think, pisshead?' Her speech was slurred and barely comprehensible. If I hadn't known her better, I would have taken her for a stumblebum with water on the brain.

'Oh,' I said, suddenly realizing where the conversation was headed.

'Yeah, that one, Mr Birdman, that's the one I'm talking about.'

'Well, he's in a bad way, ma'am, you know that, and all we can do is hope his soul mends before it's too late.'

'I'm not talking about his soul, nitwit. I'm talking about his pecker. He's still got one, doesn't he?'

'I guess so. It's not as if I'm in the habit of asking him about it.'

'Well, a man has to do his duty. He can't leave a girl high and dry for two months and expect to get away with it. That's not how it works. A pussy needs love. It needs to be stroked and fed, just like any other animal.'

Even in the darkness with no one looking, I could feel myself blush. 'Are you sure you want to be telling me this, Mrs Witherspoon?'

'There's no one else, sweetheart. And besides, you're old enough to know about these things. You don't want to walk through life like all those other numbskulls, do you?'

'I always figured I'd let nature take care of itself.'

'That's where you're wrong. A man's got to tend his honey pot. He's got to make sure the stopper's in and it doesn't run out of juice. Do you hear what I'm saying?'

'I think so.'

'Think so? What kind of bullshit answer is that?'

'Yeah, I hear you.'

'It's not as if I haven't had other offers, you know. I'm a young, healthy girl, and I'm sick and tired of waiting around like this. I've been diddling my own twat all summer, and it just won't wash anymore. I can't make it any clearer than that, can I?'

'The way I heard it, you've already turned down the master three times.'

'Well, things change, don't they, Mr Know-It-All?'

'Maybe they do, maybe they don't. It's not for me to say.'

It was on the point of turning ugly, and I wanted no part of it – to sit there listening to her blather on about her disappointed cunt. I wasn't equipped to handle that kind of stuff, and peeved as I was at the master myself, I didn't have the heart to join in and attack his manhood. I could have stood up and walked away, I guess, but then she would have started screaming at me, and nine minutes later every cop in Wichita would have been out there in the yard with us, hauling us off to jail for disturbing the peace.

As it was, I needn't have worried. Before she could get in another word, a loud noise suddenly exploded from within the house. It was more of a boom than a crash, I suppose, a kind of long, hollow detonation that immediately gave way to several resounding thuds: *thwack, thwack, thwack*, as if the walls were about to tumble down. For some reason, Mrs Witherspoon found this funny. She threw back her head in a fit of laughter, and for the next fifteen seconds the air rippled out of her windpipe like a swarm of flying grasshoppers. I'd never heard laughter like that before. It sounded like one of the ten plagues, like two-hundred-proof gin, like four hundred hyenas stalking the streets of Crazytown. Then, even as the thuds continued, she started raving at the top of her voice. 'Do you hear that?' she shouted. 'Do you hear that, Walt! That's me! That's the sound of my thoughts, the sound of the thoughts bouncing in my brain! Just like popcorn, Walt! My skull's about to crack in two! Ha, ha! My whole head's going to burst to bits!'

Just then, the thuds were replaced by the noise of shattering glass. First one thing broke, then another: cups, mirrors, bottles, a deafening barrage. It was hard to tell what was what, but each thing shattered differently, and it went on for a long time, more than a minute, I would say, and after the first few seconds the din was everywhere, the whole night was screeching with the sound of splintering glass. Without even thinking, I jumped to my feet and ran toward the house. Mrs Witherspoon made a stab at following me, but she was too drunk to get very far. The last thing I remember is looking back and seeing her slip – flat on her face, just like a sot in the funnies. She let out a yelp. Then, realizing there was no point in trying to get up, she started in on another giggling jag. That was how I left her: rolling around on the ground and laughing, laughing her poor potted guts all over the lawn.

The only idea that flashed through my head was that someone had broken into the house and was attacking Master Yehudi. By the time I got through the back door and started climbing the stairs, however, all was quiet again. That seemed strange, yet even stranger was what happened next. I walked down the hall to the master's room, knocked tentatively on the door, and heard him call out to me in a clear, perfectly normal voice: 'Come in.' So I went in, and there was Master Yehudi himself, standing in his bathrobe and slippers in the middle of the room, hands in his pockets and a curious little smile on his face. Everything was destruction around him. The bed was in a dozen pieces, the walls were gouged, a million white feathers floated in the air. Broken picture frames, broken glasses, broken chairs, broken bits of nameless things – they were all strewn about the floor like so much rubble. He allowed me a couple of seconds to take in what I was seeing, and then he spoke, addressing me with all the calm of a man who's just stepped out of a warm bath. 'Good evening, Walt,' he said. 'And what brings you up here at this late hour?'

'Master Yehudi,' I said. 'Are you all right?'

'All right? Of course I'm all right. Don't I look all right?'

'I don't know. Yes, well, maybe you do. But this,' I said, gesturing to the ruins at my feet, 'what about this? I don't get it. The place is a shambles, it's all in smithereens.'

'An exercise in catharsis, son.'

'An exercise in what?'

'No matter. It's a kind of heart medicine, a balm for ailing spirits.'

'You mean to tell me you done all this yourself?'

'It had to be done. I'm sorry about all the commotion, but sooner or later it had to be done.'

From the way he was looking at me, I sensed he was back to his old snappy self. His voice had regained its haughty timbre, and he seemed to be mixing kindness and sarcasm with the old familiar cunning. 'Does that mean,' I said, still not daring to hope, 'does that mean things are going to be different around here now?'

'We have an obligation to remember the dead. That's the fundamental law. If we didn't remember them, we'd lose the right to call ourselves human. Do you follow me, Walt?'

'Yes, sir, I follow. There ain't a day that goes by when I don't think about our dear darlings and what was done to them. It's just . . .'

'Just what, Walt?'

'It's just that time is wasting, and we'd be doing the world an injustice if we didn't think about ourselves, too.'

'You have a quick mind, son. Maybe there's hope for you yet.'

'It's not just me, you understand. There's Mrs Witherspoon, too. These last couple of weeks, she's worked herself into quite a conniption. If my eyes didn't fool me just now, I believe she's passed out on the lawn, snoring in a puddle of her own barf.'

'I'm not going to apologize for things that need no apology. I did what I had to do, and it took as long as it had to take. Now a new chapter begins. The demons have fled, and the dark night of the soul is over.' He took a deep breath, removed his hands from his pockets, and clasped me firmly on the shoulder. 'What do you say, little man? Are you ready to show them your stuff?'

'I'm ready, boss. You bet your boots I'm ready. Just rig up a place for me to do it, and I'm your boy till death do us part.'

I gave my first public performance on August 25, 1927, appearing as Walt the Wonder Boy for a one-show booking at the Pawnee County Fair in Larned, Kansas. It would be hard to imagine a more modest debut, but as things turned out, it came within an inch of being my swan song. It wasn't that I flubbed up the act, but the crowd was so raucous and mean-spirited, so filled with drunks and hooters, that if not for some quick thinking on the master's part, I might not have lived to see another day.

They'd roped off a field on the other side of the horticultural exhibits, out past the stalls with the prize-winning ears of corn and the two-headed cow and the six-hundred pound pig, and I remember traveling for what seemed like half a mile before coming to a little pond with murky green water and white scum floating on top. It struck me as a woeful site for such a historic occasion, but the master wanted me to start small, with as little fuss and fanfare as possible. 'Even Ty Cobb played in the bush leagues,' he said, as we climbed out of Mrs Witherspoon's car. 'You have to get some performances under your belt. Do well here, and we'll start talking about the big time in a few months.'

Unfortunately, there was no grandstand for the spectators, which made for a lot of tired legs and surly complaints, and with tickets going at ten cents a pop, the crowd was already feeling chiseled before I made my entrance. There couldn't have been more than sixty or seventy of them, a bunch of thick-necked hayseeds milling around in their overalls and flannel shirts – delegates from the First International Congress of Bumpkins. Half of them were guzzling bathtub hootch from little brown cough-syrup bottles and the other half had just finished theirs and were itching for more. When Master Yehudi stepped forward in his black tuxedo and silk hat to announce the world premiere of Walt the Wonder Boy, the wisecracks and heckling began. Maybe they didn't like his clothes, or maybe they objected to his Brooklyn-Budapest accent, but I'm certain it didn't help that I was wearing the worst costume in the annals of show business: a long white robe that made me look like some midget John the Baptist, complete with leather sandals and a hemp sash tied around my waist. The master had insisted on what he called an 'otherworldly look,' but I felt like a twit in that getup, and when I heard some clown yell at the top of his voice – 'Walt the Wonder Girl' – I realized I wasn't alone in my sentiments.

If I found the courage to begin, it was only because of Aesop. I knew he was looking down on me from wherever he was, and I wasn't going to let myself fail him. He was counting on me to shine, and whatever that soused-up mob of fools might have thought of me, I owed it to my brother to give it the best shot I could. So I walked to the edge of the pond and went into my spread-arms-and-trance routine, struggling to shut out the catcalls and insults. I heard some oohs and ahs when my body rose off the ground – but dimly, only dimly, for I was already in a separate world by then, walled off from friend and foe alike in the glory of my ascent. It was the first performance I had ever given, but I already had the makings of a trouper, and I'm certain I would have won over the crowd if not for some birdbrain who took it upon himself to hurl a bottle in my direction. Nineteen times out of twenty, the projectile sails past me and no harm is done, but this was a day for flukes and long-shots, and the damned thing clunked me square in the noggin. The blow addled my concentration (not to speak of rendering me unconscious), and before I knew which end was up, I was sinking like a bag of pennies to the bottom of the water. If the master hadn't been on his toes, diving in after me without bothering to shed his coat and tails, I probably would have drowned in that crummy mudhole, and that would have been the first and last bow I ever took.

So we left Larned in disgrace, hightailing it out of there as those bloodthirsty hicks pelted us with eggs and stones and watermelons. No one seemed to care that I'd almost died from that blow on the head, and they went on laughing as the good master rescued me from the drink and carried me to the safety of Mrs W.'s car. I was still semidelirious from my visit to Davy Jones's locker, and I coughed and puked all over the master's shirt as he ran across the field with my wet body bouncing in his arms. I couldn't hear everything that was said, but enough reached my ears for me to gather that opinions about us were sharply divided. Some people took the religious view, boldly asserting that we were in league with the devil. Others called us fakes and charlatans, and still others had no opinion at all. They yelled for the pure pleasure of yelling, just glad to be part of the mayhem as they let forth with angry, wordless howls. Fortunately, the car was waiting for us on the other side of the roped-off area, and we managed to get inside before the rowdies caught up with us. A few eggs thudded against the rear window as we drove off, but no glass shattered, no shots rang out, and all in all I suppose we were lucky to escape with our hides intact.

We must have traveled two miles before either one of us found the courage to speak. We were out among the farms and pastures by then, tooling along a bumpy byway in our drenched and sopping clothes. With each jolt of the car, another spurt of pond water gushed from us and sank into Mrs Witherspoon's deluxe suede upholstery. It sounds funny as I tell it now, but I wasn't the least bit tempted to laugh at the time. I just sat there stewing in the front seat, trying to control my temper and figure out what had gone wrong. In spite of his errors and miscalculations, it didn't seem fair to blame the master. He'd been through a lot, and I knew his judgment wasn't all it should have been, but it was my fault for going along with him. I never should have allowed myself to get sucked into such a half-assed, poorly planned operation. It was my butt on the line out there, and when all was said and done, it was my job to protect it.

'Well, partner,' the master said, doing his best to crack a smile, 'welcome to show biz.'

'That wasn't no show biz,' I said. 'What happened back there was assault and battery. It was like walking into an ambush and getting scalped.'

'That's the rough and tumble, kid, the give and take of crowds. Once the curtain goes up, you never know what's going to happen.'

'I don't mean to be disrespectful, sir, but that kind of talk ain't nothing but wind.'

'Oh, ho,' he said, amused by my plucky rejoinder. 'The little lad's in a huff. And what kind of talk do you propose we engage in, Mr Rawley?'

'Practical talk, sir. The kind of talk that'll stop us from repeating our mistakes.'

'We didn't make any mistakes. We just drew a bum audience, that's all. Sometimes you get lucky, sometimes you don't.'

'Luck's got nothing to do with it. We did a lot of dumb things today, and we wound up paying the price.'

'I thought you were brilliant. If not for that flying bottle, it would have been a four-star success.'

'Well, for one thing, I'd sincerely like to ditch this costume. It's about the awfulest piece of hokum I ever saw. We don't need no otherworldy trappings. The act's got enough of that already, and we don't want to confuse folks by dressing me up like some nancy-boy angel. It puts them off. It makes me look like I'm supposed to be better than they are.'

'You *are* better, Walt. Don't ever forget that.'

'Maybe so. But once we let them know that, we're sunk. They were against me before I even started.'

'The costume had nothing to do with it. That crowd was stoned, pickled to the toe jam in their socks. They were so crosseyed, not one of them even saw what you had on.'

'You're the best teacher there is, master, and I'm truly grateful to you for saving my life today, but on this particular point, you're as wrong as any mortal man can be. The costume stinks. I'm sorry to be so blunt, but no matter how hard you yell at me, I ain't never wearing it again.'

'Why would I yell at you? We're in this together, son, and you're free to express your opinions. If you want to dress another way, all you have to do is tell me.'

'On the level?'

'It's a long trip back to Wichita, and there's no reason why we shouldn't discuss these things now.'

'I don't mean to grumble,' I said, jumping through the door he'd just opened for me, 'but the way I see it, we ain't got a prayer unless we win them over from the get-go. These rubes don't like no fancy stuff. They didn't take to your penguin suit, and they didn't take to my sissy robes. And all that high-flown talk you pitched them at the start – it went right over their heads.'

'It was nothing but gibberish. Just to get them in the mood.'

'Whatever you say. But how's about we skip it in the future? Just keep it simple and folksy. You know, something like "Ladies and gentlemen, I'm proud to present," and then back off and let me come on. If you wear a plain old seersucker suit and a nice straw hat, no one will take offense. They'll think you're a friendly, good-hearted Joe out to make an honest buck. That's the key, the whole sack of onions. I stroll out before them like a little know-nothing, a wide-eyed farm boy dressed in denim overalls and a plaid shirt. No shoes, no socks, a barefoot nobody with the same geek mug as their own sons and nephews. They take one look at me and relax. It's like I'm a member of the family. And then, the moment I start rising into the air, their hearts fail them. It's that simple. Soften them up, then hit them with the whammy.

It's bound to be good. Two minutes into the act, they'll be eating out of our hands like squirrels.'

It took almost three hours to get home, and all during the ride I talked, speaking my mind to the master in a way I'd never done before. I covered everything I could think of – from costumes to venues, from ticket-taking to music, from show times to publicity – and he let me have my say. There's no question that he was impressed, maybe even a little startled by my thoroughness and strong opinions, but I was fighting for my life that afternoon, and it wouldn't have helped the cause to hold back and mince words. Master Yehudi had launched a ship that was full of holes, and rather than try to plug those holes as the water rushed in and sank us, I wanted to drag the thing back to port and rebuild it from the bottom up. The master listened to my ideas without interrupting or making fun of me, and in the end he gave in on most of the points I raised. It couldn't have been easy for him to accept his failure as a showman, but Master Yehudi wanted things to work as much as I did, and he was big enough to admit that he'd gotten us off on the wrong track. It wasn't that he didn't have a method, but that method was out of date, more suited to the corny prewar style he'd grown up with than to the jump and jangle of the new age. I was after something modern, something sleek and savvy and direct, and little by little I managed to talk him into it, to bring him around to a different approach.

Still, on certain issues he refused to fall in line. I was keen on taking the act to Saint Louis and showing off in front of my old hometown, but he nipped that proposition in the bud. 'That's the most dangerous spot on earth for you,' he said, 'and the minute you go back there, you'll be signing your own death warrant. Mark my words. Saint Louis is bad medicine. It's a poison place, and you'll never get out of there alive.' I couldn't understand his vehemence, but he talked like someone whose mind was set, and there was no way I could go against him. As it turned out, his words proved to be dead on the mark. Just one month after he spoke them to me, Saint Louis was hit by the worst tornado of the century. The twister shot through town like a cannonball from hell, and by the time it left five minutes later, a thousand buildings had been flattened, a hundred people were dead, and two thousand others lay writhing in the wreckage with broken bones and blood pouring from their wounds. We were on our way to Vernon, Oklahoma, by then, on the fifth leg of a fourteen-stop tour, and when I picked up the morning edition of the local rag and saw the pictures on the front page, I almost regurgitated my breakfast. I'd thought the master had lost his touch, but once again I'd sold him short. He knew things I would never know, he heard things no one else could hear, and not a man in the world could match him. If I ever doubt his words again, I told myself, may the Lord strike me down and scatter my corpse to the pigs.

But I'm going too fast. The tornado didn't come until late September, and for the time being it's still August twenty-fifth. Master Yehudi and I are still sitting in our clammy clothes, and we're still driving back to Mrs Witherspoon's house in Wichita. After our long conversation about revamping the act, I was beginning to feel a little better about our prospects, but I wouldn't go so far as to say that my mind was totally at ease. Putting the lid on Saint Louis was one thing, a minor difference of opinion, but there were other matters that troubled me more deeply. Essential flaws in the arrangement, you might call them, and now that I had bared my soul about so much, I figured I should go for the brass ring. So I plunged in and brought up the subject of Mrs Witherspoon. I had never dared to speak about her before, and I hoped the master wasn't going to haul off and belt me in the snout.

'Maybe it's none of my business,' I said, stepping as gingerly as I could, 'but I still don't see why Mrs Witherspoon didn't come with us.'

'She didn't want to be in the way,' the master said. 'She thought she might jinx us.'

'But she's our backer, ain't she? She's the one who's footing the bill. You'd think she'd want to stick around and keep a close eye on her investment.'

'She's what they call a silent partner.'

'Silent? You're funning me, boss. That missus is about the unsilentest frail this side of a car factory. Why, she'll chew off your ear and spit out the pieces before you can get a word in.'

'In life, yes. But I'm talking about business. In life, there's no question she's got a tongue on her. I'm not going to argue with you about that.'

'I don't know what her problem is, but all those days when you were out of commission there, she did some awfully strange things. I'm not saying she ain't a good sport and all that, but there were times, let me tell you, there were times when it gave me the creeps to see her carry on the way she did.'

'She's been distraught. You can't blame her, Walt. She's had some rough things to swallow these past months, and she's a lot more fragile than you think she is. You just have to be patient with her.'

'That's pretty much the same thing she said about you.'

'She's a smart woman. A little high-strung, perhaps, but she's got a good head on her shoulders, and her heart's in the right place.'

'Mother Sioux, may her soul rest in peace, once told me you were fixing to marry her.'

'I was. Then I wasn't anymore. Then I was. Then I wasn't. Now who knows. If the years have taught me anything, kid, it's that anything can happen. When it comes to men and women, all bets are off.'

'Yeah, she's a frisky one, I'll grant you that. Just when you think you've roped her in, she slips the knot and bolts to the next pasture.'

'Exactly. Which explains why it's sometimes best to do nothing. If you just stand there and wait, there's a chance the thing you're hoping for will come right to you.'

'It's all too deep for me, sir.'

'You're not the only one, Walt.'

'But if and ever you do get hitched, I'll lay odds it won't be a very smooth ride.'

'Don't worry yourself about that. Just concentrate on your work and leave the love business to me. I don't need any advice from the peanut gallery. It's my song, and I'll sing it in my own way.'

I didn't have the balls to push it any farther than that. Master Yehudi was a genius and a wizard, but it was growing abundantly clear to me that he didn't understand the first thing about women. I'd been privy to Mrs Witherspoon's innermost thoughts, I'd listened to her drunken, bawdy confidences on many an occasion, and I knew the master was never going to get anywhere with her unless he took the bull by the horns. She didn't want to be deferred to, she wanted to be stormed and conquered, and the longer he shilly-shallied around, the worse his chances would be. But how to tell him that? I couldn't do it. Not if I valued my own skin I couldn't, so I kept my mouth shut and let the matter ride. It was his damned goose, I told myself, and if he was so bent on cooking it, who was I to stand in his way?

So we returned to Wichita and got busy making plans for a fresh start. Mrs W. said nary a word about the water stains on the seats, but I suppose she thought of them as a business expense, part of the risk you take when you set your sights on making big money. It took about three weeks to wrap up the preparations – scheduling performances, printing handbills and posters, rehearsing the new routine – and during that time the master and Mrs Witherspoon were pretty cozy with each other, a lot more lovey-dovey than I'd expected them to be. Maybe I was all wrong, I thought, and the master knew exactly what he was doing. But then, on the day of our departure, he committed an error, a tactical blunder that showed up the weakness of his overall strategy. I saw it with my own eyes, standing on the porch as the master and the missus said their farewells, and it was a painful thing to behold, a sad little chapter in the history of heartbreak.

He said: 'So long, sister. We'll see you in a month and three days.' And she said: 'Off you go, boys – into the wild blue yonder.' There was an awkward silence after that, and since it made me feel uncomfortable, I opened my big mouth and said: 'What do you say, ma'am? Why not hop in the car and come with us?'

I could see her eyes light up when I said that, and sure as *dog* and *god* are the same word spelled backwards and forwards, she would have given six years off her life to chuck everything and climb aboard. She turned to the master and said: 'Well, what do you think? Should I go with you or not?' And he, pompous oaf that he was, patted her on the shoulder and said: 'It's up to you, my dear.' Her eyes clouded over for a second, but even then all was not lost. Still hopeful of hearing the right words from him, she gave it another shot and said: 'No, you decide. I wouldn't want to be in the way.' And he said: 'You're a free agent, Marion. It's not for me to tell you what to do.' And that was that. I saw the light go out in her eyes; her face closed up into a taut, quizzical expression; and then she shrugged. 'Never mind,' she said. 'There's too much to do here anyway.' Then, forcing a brave little smile to her lips, she added: 'Drop me a postcard when you get a chance. The last I heard, they still go for a penny apiece.'

And there it was, folks. The opportunity of a lifetime – lost forever. The master let it slip right through his fingers, and the worst part of it was, I don't even think he realized what he'd done.

We traveled in a different car this time – a black, secondhand Ford that Mrs Witherspoon had picked out for us after our return from Larned. She'd dubbed it the Wondermobile, and though it couldn't match the size and smoothness of the Chrysler, it did everything it was asked to do. We set off on a rainy morning in mid-September, and one hour out of Wichita I'd already forgotten about the hearts-and-flowers fumble I'd witnessed on the porch. My mental beams were fixed on Oklahoma, the first state booked for the tour, and when we pulled into Redbird two days later, I was as keyed up as a jack-in-the-box and crazier than a monkey. It's going to work this time, I told myself. Yes sir, this is where it all begins. Even the name of the town struck me as a good omen, and since I was nothing if not superstitious in those days, it had a powerful effect on my spirits. Redbird. Just like my ball club in Saint Louis, my dear old chums the Cardinals.

It was the same act in a new set of clothes, but everything felt different somehow, and the audience took a shine to me the moment I came on – which was half the battle right there. Master Yehudi did his cornpone spiel to the hilt, my Huck Finn costume was the last word in understatement, and all in all we knocked them dead. Six or seven women fainted, children screamed, grown men gasped in awe and disbelief. For thirty minutes I kept them spellbound, prancing and tumbling in midair, gliding my little body over the surface of a broad and sparkling lake, and then, at the end, pushing myself to a record height of four and a half feet before floating back to the ground and taking my bow. The applause was thunderous, ecstatic. They whooped and cried, they banged pots and pans, they tossed confetti into the air. This was my first taste of success, and I loved it, I loved it in a way I've never loved anything before or since.

Dunbar and Battiest. Jumbo and Plunketsville. Pickens, Muse, and Bethel. Wapanucka. Boggy Depot and Kingfisher. Gerty, Ringling, and Marble City. If this were a movie, here's where the calendar pages would start flying off the wall. We'd see them fluttering against a background of country roads and tumbleweed, and then the names of those towns would flash by as we followed the progress of the black Ford across a map of eastern Oklahoma. The music would be jaunty and full of bounce, a syncopated chug-chug to ape the noise of ringing cash registers. Shot would follow shot, each one melting into the other. Bushel baskets brimming with coins, roadside bungalows, clapping hands and stomping feet, open mouths, bug-eyed faces turned to the sky. The whole sequence would take about ten seconds, and by the time it was over, the story of that month would be known to every person in the theater. Ah, the old Hollywood razzmatazz. There's nothing like it for hustling things along. It may not be subtle, but it gets the job done.

So much for the quirks of memory. If I'm suddenly thinking about movies now, it's probably because I saw so many of them in the months that followed. After the Oklahoma triumph, bookings ceased to be a problem, and the master and I spent most of our time on the road, moving around from one backwater to another. We played Texas, Arkansas, and Louisiana, dipping farther and farther south as winter came on, and I tended to fill in the dead time between performances by visiting the local Bijou for a peek at the latest flick. The master generally had business to take care of – talking to fair managers and ticket sellers, distributing handbills and posters around town, adjusting nuts and bolts for the upcoming performance – which meant he seldom had time to go with me. More often than not, I'd come back to find him alone in the room, sitting in a chair reading his book. It was always the same book – a battered little green volume that he carried with him on all our travels – and it became as familiar to me as the lines and contours of his face. It was written in Latin, of all things, and the author's name was Spinoza, a detail I've never forgotten, even after so many years. When I asked the master why he kept studying that one book over and over again, he told me it was because you could never get to the bottom of it. The deeper you go, he said, the more there is, and the more there is, the longer it takes to read it.

'A magic book,' I said. 'It can't never use itself up.'

'That's it, squirt. It's inexhaustible. You drink down the wine, put the glass back on the table, and lo and behold, you reach for the glass again and discover it's still full.'

'And there you are, drunk as a skunk for the price of one drink.'

'I couldn't have put it better myself,' he said, suddenly turning from me and gazing out the window. 'You get drunk on the world, boy. Drunk on the mystery of the world.'

Christ but I was happy out there on the road with him. Just moving from place to place was enough to keep my spirits up, but when you added in all the other ingredients – the crowds, the performances, the money we made – those first months were hands down the best months I'd ever lived. Even after the initial excitement wore off and I grew accustomed to the routine, I still didn't want it to stop. Lumpy beds, flat tires, bad food, all the rainouts and lulls and boring stretches were as nothing to me, mere pebbles bouncing off the skin of a rhinoceros. We'd climb into the Ford and blow out of town, another seventy or hundred bucks stashed away in the trunk, and then mosey on to the next whistle-stop, watching the landscape roll by as we chewed over the finer points of the last performance. The master was a prince to me, always encouraging and counseling and listening to what I said, and he never made me feel that I was one bit less important than he was. So many things had changed between us since the summer, it was as if we were on a new footing now, as if we'd reached some kind of permanent equilibrium. He did his job and I did mine, and together we made the thing work.

The stock market didn't crash until two years later, but the Depression had already started in the hinterlands, and farmers and rural folks throughout the region were feeling the pinch. We came across a lot of desperate people on our travels, and Master Yehudi taught me never to look down on them. They needed Walt the Wonder Boy, he said, and I must never forget the responsibility that need entailed. To watch a twelve-year-old do what only saints and prophets had done before him was like a jolt from heaven, and my performances could bring spiritual uplift to thousands of suffering souls. That didn't mean I shouldn't make a bundle doing it, but unless I understood that I had to touch people's hearts, I'd never gain the following I deserved. I think that's why the master started my career in such out-of-the-way places, such a rinky-dink collection of forgotten corners and crevices on the map. He wanted the word about me to spread slowly, for support to begin from the ground up. It wasn't just a matter of breaking me in, it was a way of controlling things, of making sure I didn't turn out to be a flash in the pan.

Who was I to object? The bookings were organized in a systematic way, the turnouts were good, and we always had a roof over our heads when we went to sleep at night. I was doing what I wanted to do, and the feeling it gave me was so good, so exhilarating, I couldn't have cared less if the people who saw me perform were from Paris, France, or Paris, Texas. Every now and then, of course, we encountered a bump in the road, but Master Yehudi seemed to be prepared for any and all situations. Once, for example, a truant officer came knocking on the door of our rooming house in Dublin, Mississippi. Why isn't this lad in school? he said to the master, pointing his long bony finger at me. There are laws against this, you know, statutes, regulations, and so on and so forth. I figured we were sunk, but the master only smiled, asked the gentleman to step in, and then pulled a piece of paper from the breast pocket of his coat. It was covered with official-looking stamps and seals, and once the truant officer read it through, he tipped his hat in an embarrassed sort of way, apologized for the mixup, and left. God knows what was written on that paper, but it did the trick in one fast hurry. Before I could make out any of the words, the master had already folded up the letter and slipped it back into his coat pocket. 'What does it say?' I asked, but even though I asked again, he never answered me. He just patted his pocket and grinned, looking awfully smug and pleased with himself. He reminded me of a cat who'd just polished off the family bird, and he wasn't about to tell me how he'd opened the cage.

From the latter part of 1927 through the first half of 1928, I lived in a cocoon of total concentration. I never thought about the past, I never thought about the future – only about what was happening now, the thing I was doing at this or that moment. On the average, we didn't spend more than three or four days a month in Wichita, and the rest of the time we were on the road, bee-lining hither and yon in the black Wondermobile. The first real pause didn't come until the middle of May. My thirteenth birthday was approaching, and the master thought it might be a good idea to take a couple of weeks off. We'd go back to Mrs Witherspoon's, he said, and eat some home cooking for a change. We'd relax and celebrate and count our money, and then, after we were done playing pasha, we'd pack up our bags and take off again. That sounded fine with me, but once we got there and settled in for our holiday, I sensed that something was wrong. It wasn't the master or Mrs Witherspoon. They were both lovely to me, and relations between them were particularly harmonious just then. Nor was it anything connected to the house. Nelly Boggs's cooking was in top form, the bed was still comfortable, the spring weather was superb. Yet the moment we walked through the door, an inexplicable heaviness invaded my heart, a murky sort of sadness and disquiet. I assumed I'd feel better after a night's sleep, but the feeling didn't go away; it just sat inside me like a lump of undigested stew, and no matter what I said to myself, I couldn't get rid of it. If anything, it seemed to be growing, to be taking on a life of its own, and to such an extent that by the third night, just after I put on my pajamas and crawled into bed, I was overcome by an irresistible urge to cry. It seemed crazy, and yet half a minute later I was sobbing into the pillow, weeping my blinkers out in an onrush of misery and remorse.

When I sat down to breakfast with Master Yehudi early the next morning, I couldn't hold myself back, the words came out before I even knew I was going to say them. Mrs Witherspoon was still upstairs in bed, and it was just the two of us at the table, waiting for Nelly Boggs to come out of the kitchen and serve us our sausages and scrambled eggs.

'Remember that law you told me about?' I said.

The master, whose nose was buried in the paper, glanced up from the headlines and gave me a long blank stare. 'Law?' he said. 'What law is that?'

'You remember. The one about duties and such. How we wouldn't be human no more if we forgot the dead.'

'Of course I remember.'

'Well, it seems to me we've been breaking that law left and right.'

'How so, Walt? Aesop and Mother Sioux are inside us. We carry them in our hearts wherever we go. Nothing's ever going to change that.'

'But we just walked away, didn't we? They was murdered by a pack of devils and demons, and we never did nothing about it.'

'We couldn't. If we'd gone after them, they would have killed us, too.'

'That night, maybe. But what about now? If we're supposed to remember the dead, then we don't have no choice but to hunt down the bastards and see they get what's coming to them. I mean, hell, we're having a fine old time, ain't we? Barnstorming around the country in our motor car, raking in the dough, strutting before the world like a pair of hotshots. But what about my pal Aesop? What about funny old Mother Sioux? They're moldering in their graves is what, and the trash that hung them's still running free.'

'Get a grip on yourself,' the master said, studying me closely as the tears sprang forth again and started running down my cheeks. His voice was stern, almost on the point of anger. 'Sure, we could go after them,' he said. 'We could track them down and bring them to justice, but that's the only job we'd have for the rest of our lives. The cops won't help us,

I'll guarantee you that, and if you think a jury would convict them, think again. The Klan is everywhere, Walt, they own the whole rotten charade. They're the same nice smiling folks you used to see on the streets of Cibola – Tom Skinner, Judd McNally, Harold Dowd – they're all part of it, every last one of them. The butcher, the baker, the candlestick maker. We'd have to kill them ourselves, and once we went after them, they'd go after us. A lot of blood would be shed, Walt, and most of it would be ours.'

'It ain't fair,' I said, sniffling through another rush of tears. 'It ain't fair, and it ain't right.'

'You know that, and I know that, and as long as we both know it, Aesop and Mother Sioux are taken care of.'

'They're writhing in torment, master, and their souls won't never be at peace until we do what we've got to do.'

'No, Walt, you're wrong. They're both at peace already.'

'Yeah? And what makes you such an expert on what the dead are doing in their graves?'

'Because I've been with them. I've been with them and spoken to them, and they're not suffering anymore. They want us to go on with our work. That's what they told me. They want us to remember them by keeping up with the work we've started.'

'What?' I said, suddenly feeling my skin crawl. 'What the hell are you talking about?'

'They come to me, Walt. Almost every night for the past six months. They come to me and sit down on my bed, singing songs and stroking my face. They're happier than they were in this world, believe me. Aesop and Mother Sioux are angels now, and nothing can hurt them anymore.'

It was about the strangest, most fantastical thing I'd ever heard, and yet Master Yehudi told it with such conviction, such straightforward sincerity and calm, I never doubted that he was telling the truth. Even if it wasn't true in an absolute sense, there was no question that he believed it – and even if he didn't believe it, then he'd just turned in one of the most powerful acting performances of all time. I sat there in a kind of feverish immobility, letting the vision linger in my head, trying to hold on to the picture of Aesop and Mother Sioux singing to the master in the middle of the night. It doesn't really matter if it happened or not, for the fact was that it changed everything for me. The pain began to subside, the black clouds began to disperse, and by the time I stood up from the table that morning, the worst of the grief was gone. In the end, that's the only thing that matters. If the master lied, then he did it for a reason. And if he didn't lie, then the story stands as told, and there's no cause to defend him. One way or the other, he saved me. One way or the other, he rescued my soul from the jaws of the beast.

Ten days later, we picked up where we had left off, driving away from Wichita in yet another new car. Our earnings were such that we could afford something better now, so we traded in the Ford for Wondermobile II, a silver-gray Pierce Arrow with leather seats and running boards the size of sofas. We'd been in the black since early spring, which meant that Mrs Witherspoon had been reimbursed for her initial expenditures, there was money in the bank for the master and myself, and we no longer had to pinch pennies as we had before. The whole operation had moved up a notch or two: larger towns for the performances, small hotels instead of rooming houses and guest cottages to flop our bones in, more stylish transportation. I was back on the beam by the time we left, all charged up and ready to roll, and for the next few months I pulled out one stop after another, adding new wrinkles and flourishes to the act almost every week. I had grown so accustomed to the crowds by then, felt so at ease during my performances, that I was able to improvise as I went along, actually to invent and discover new turns in the middle of a show. In the beginning I had always stuck to the routine, rigidly following the steps the master and I had worked out in advance, but I was past that now, I had hit my stride, and I was no longer afraid to experiment. Locomotion had always been my strength. It was the heart of my act, the thing that separated me from every levitator who had come before me, but my loft was no better than average, a fair to middling five feet. I wanted to improve on that, to double or even triple that mark if I could, but I no longer had the luxury of all-day practice sessions, the old freedom of working under Master Yehudi's supervision for ten or twelve hours at a stretch. I was a pro now, with all the burdens and scheduling constraints of a pro, and the only place I could practice was in front of a live audience.

So that's what I did, especially after that little holiday in Wichita, and to my immense wonderment I found that the pressure inspired me. Some of my finest tricks date from that period, and without the eyes of the crowd to spur me on, I doubt that I would have mustered the courage to try half the things I did. It all started with the staircase number, which was the first time I ever made use of an 'invisible prop' – the term I later coined for my invention. We were in upper Michigan then, and smack in the middle of the performance, just as I rose to begin my crossing of the lake, I caught sight of a building in the distance. It was a large brick structure, probably a warehouse or an old factory, and it had a fire escape running down one of the walls. I couldn't help but notice those metal stairs. The sunlight was bouncing off of them at just that moment, and they were gleaming with a frantic kind of brightness in the late afternoon sun. Without giving the matter any thought, I lifted one foot into the air, as if I were about to climb a real staircase, and put it down on an invisible step; then I lifted the other foot and put it down on the next step. It wasn't that I felt anything solid in the air, but I was nevertheless going up, gradually ascending a staircase that stretched from one end of the lake to the other. Even though I couldn't see it, I had a definite picture of it in my mind. To the best of my recollection, it looked something like this:

LAKE

At its highest point – the platform in the middle – it was roughly nine and a half feet above the surface of the water – a good four feet higher than I'd ever been before. The eerie thing was that I didn't hesitate. Once I had that picture clearly in my mind, I knew I could depend on it to get me across. All I had to do was follow the shape of the imaginary bridge, and it would support me as if it were real. A few moments later, I was gliding across the lake with nary a hitch or a stumble. Twelve steps up, fifty-two steps across, and then twelve steps down. The results were nothing less than perfect.

After that breakthrough, I discovered that I could use other props just as effectively. As long as I could imagine the thing I wanted, as long as I could visualize it with a high degree of clarity and definition, it would be available to me for the performance. That was how I developed some of the most memorable portions of my act: the rope-ladder routine, the slide routine, the seesaw routine, the high-wire routine, the countless innovations I was heralded for. Not only did these turns enhance the audience's pleasure, but they thrust me into an entirely new relationship with my work. I wasn't just a robot anymore, a wind-up baboon who did the same set of tricks for every show – I was evolving into an artist, a true creator who performed as much for his own sake as for the sake of others. It was the unpredictability that excited me, the adventure of never knowing what was going to happen from one show to the next. If your only motive is to be loved, to ingratiate yourself with the crowd, you're bound to fall into bad habits, and eventually the public will grow tired of you. You have to keep testing yourself, pushing your talent as hard as you can. You do it for yourself, but in the end it's this struggle to do better that most endears you to your fans. That's the paradox. People begin to sense that you're out there taking risks for them. They're allowed to share in the mystery, to participate in whatever nameless thing is driving you to do it, and once that happens, you're no longer just a performer, you're on the way to becoming a star. In the fall of 1928, that's exactly where I was: on the brink of becoming a star.

By mid-October we found ourselves in central Illinois, playing out a last few gigs before we headed back to Wichita for a well-earned breather. If I remember correctly, we'd just finished up a show in Gibson City, one of those lost little towns with a Buck Rogers skyline of water towers and grain elevators. From a distance you think you're approaching a hefty burg, and then you get there and discover those grain elevators are all they've got. We'd already checked out of the hotel and were sitting in a diner on the main drag, slurping down some liquid refreshments before we jumped into the car and took off. It was a dead hour of the day, somewhere between breakfast and lunch, and Master Yehudi and I were the only customers. I had just downed the last bits of foam from my hot chocolate, I remember, when the bell on the door jangled and a third customer walked in. Out of idle curiosity, I glanced up to take a gander at the new arrival, and who should it turn out to be but my Uncle Slim, the old chinless wonder himself? It couldn't have been warmer than thirty-five degrees that day, but he was dressed in a threadbare summer suit. The collar was turned up against his neck, and he was clutching the two halves of the jacket in his right hand. He shivered as he crossed the threshold, looking like a chihuahua blown in by the north wind, and if I hadn't been so stunned, I probably would have laughed at the sight.

Master Yehudi's back was turned to the door. When he saw the expression on my face (I must have gone white), he wheeled around to have a look at what had so discombobulated me. Slim was still standing in the entrance, rubbing his hands together and surveying the joint with his squinty eyes, and the moment he zoomed in on us, he broke into one of those snaggletoothed grins I'd always dreaded as a boy. This meeting was no accident. He'd come to Gibson City because he wanted to talk, and sure as six and seven made thirteen, the unluckiest number there was, we were staring at a mess of trouble.

'Well, well,' he said, oozing false amiability as he sauntered over to our table. 'Fancy that. I come to the back of beyond on personal business, drop in at the local beanery for a cup of java, and who should I run into but my long-lost nephew? Little Walt, the apple of my eye, the freckle-faced boy wonder. It's like destiny is what it is. Like finding a needle in a haystack.' Without a word from either the master or myself, he parked himself in the empty chair beside me. 'You don't mind if I sit down, do you?' he said. 'I'm just so bowled over by this joyful occasion, I have to get off my pins before I pass out.' Then he banged me on the back and tousled my hair, still pretending how happy he was to see me – which maybe he was, but not for any of the reasons a normal person would be. It gave me the chills to be touched by him like that. I squirmed away from his hand, but he paid no attention to the rebuff, chattering on in that slimy way of his and baring his crooked brown teeth at every opportunity. 'Well, old bean,' he continued, 'it looks like the world's been treating you pretty good these days, don't it? From what the papers tell me, you're the cat's pajamas, the greatest thing since rye bread. Your mentor here must be flush with pride – not to speak of just plain flush, since his wallet can't have suffered none in the process. I can't tell you the good it does me, Walt, seeing my kin make a name for himself in the big world.'

'State your business, friend,' the master said, finally breaking in on Slim's monologue. 'The kid and I were just on our way out, and we don't have time to sit around shooting the breeze.'

'Hell,' Slim said, doing his best to look offended, 'can't a guy catch up on the news with his own sister's son? What's the rush? From the looks of that machine you got parked at the curb, you'll get where you're going in no time.'

'Walt's got nothing to say to you,' the master said, 'and as far as I'm concerned, you've got nothing to say to him.'

'I wouldn't be so sure about that,' Slim said, reaching for the crumpled cheroot in his pocket and lighting up. 'He's got a right to know about his poor Aunt Peg, and I've got the right to tell him.'

'What about her?' I said, barely getting my voice above a whisper.

'Hey, the kid can talk!' Slim said, pinching my cheek with mock enthusiasm. 'For a moment there, I thought he'd cut out your tongue, Walt.'

'What about her?' I repeated.

'She's dead, son, that's what. She got took by that tornado that demolished Saint Louis last year. The whole house fell on top of her, and that was the end of sweet old Peg. It happened just like that.'

'And you escaped,' I said.

'It was the Lord's will,' Slim said. 'As chance would have it, I was on the other side of town, doing an honest day's work.'

'Too bad it wasn't the other way around,' I said. 'Aunt Peg was no great shakes, but at least she didn't sock me around like you did.'

'Hey, now,' Slim said, 'that's no way to talk to your uncle. I'm your own flesh and blood, Walt, and you don't have to tell no fibs about me. Not when I'm here on such a vital errand. Mr Yehudi and me got things to talk about, and I don't need no cracks from you gumming up the works.'

'I believe you're mistaken,' the master said. 'You and I have nothing to talk about. Walt and I are running late now, and I'm afraid you'll have to excuse us.'

'Not so fast, mister,' Slim said, suddenly forgetting his fake charm. His voice was seething with petulance and anger, just as I'd always remembered it. 'You and I made a deal, and you're not going to worm out on me now.'

'Deal?' the master said. 'What deal was that?'

'The one we made in Saint Louis four years ago. Did you think I'd forget or something? I'm not stupid, you know. You promised me a cut of the profits, and I'm here to claim my fair share. Twenty-five percent. That's what you promised, and that's what I want.'

'As I recall, Mr Sparks,' the master said, trying to control his temper, 'you just about kissed my feet when I told you I'd take the boy off your hands. You were slobbering all over me, telling me how glad you were to be rid of him. That was the deal, Mr Sparks. I asked for the boy, and you gave him to me.'

'I had my conditions. I spelled them out for you, and you agreed. Twenty-five percent. You're not going to tell me there's no deal. You promised me, and I took you at your word.'

'Dream on, laddie. If you think there's a deal, then show me the contract. Show me the piece of paper where it says you have one dime coming to you.'

'We shook hands on it. It was a gentlemen's agreement, all on the up and up.'

'You have a splendid imagination, Mr Sparks, but you're a liar and a crook. If you have a complaint against me, take it to a lawyer, and we'll see how well your case stands up in court. But until that happens, kindly have the decency to remove your ugly face from my sight.' Then the master turned to me and said, 'Come on, Walt, let's go. They're waiting for us in Urbana, and we don't have a minute to lose.'

The master threw a dollar on the table and stood up, and I stood up with him. But Slim wasn't finished having his say, and he managed to get in the last word, delivering a few parting shots as we left the diner. 'You think you're smart, mister,' he said, 'but you ain't done with me yet. Nobody calls Edward J. Sparks a liar and gets away with it, you hear? That's right, keep on walking out the door – it don't matter. But that's the last time you'll ever turn your back on me. Be warned, pal. I'm coming after you. I'm coming after you and that scummy kid, and once I get to you, you'll be sorry you ever talked to me like that. You'll be sorry till the day you die.'

He pursued us to the door of the restaurant, showering us with his deranged threats as we climbed into the Pierce Arrow and the master started up the engine. The noise drowned out my uncle's words, but his lips were still moving, and I could see the veins bulging in his scrawny neck. That was how we left him: beside himself with fury as he watched us pull away, shaking his fist at us and mouthing his inaudible vengeance. My uncle had been wandering in the desert for forty years, and all he had to show for it was a history of stumbles and wrong turns, an endless string of failures. Watching his face through the rear window of the car, I understood that he had a purpose now, that the fucker had finally found a mission in life.

Once we were out of town, the master turned to me and said, 'That bigmouth doesn't have a leg to stand on. It's all a bluff, jive and nonsense from start to finish. The guy's a born loser, and if he ever so much as lays a hand on you, Walt, I'll kill him. I swear it. I'll chop that grifter into so many pieces, they'll still be finding bits of him in Canada twenty years from now.'

I was proud of the way the master had handled himself in the diner, but that didn't mean I wasn't worried. My mother's older brother was a slippery customer, and now that he'd set his mind on something, he wasn't likely to be distracted from his goal. Personally speaking, I had no wish to consider his side of the dispute. Maybe the master had promised him twenty-five percent and maybe he hadn't, but that was all water down the toilet now, and the only thing I wanted was to have that son of a bitch out of my life for good. He'd bounced me off the walls too many times for me to feel anything but hatred for him, and whether he had a rightful claim to the money or not, the truth was he didn't deserve a penny. But alas, what I felt didn't count for a damn. Nor what the master felt. It was all up to Slim, and I knew in my bones that he was coming, that he'd keep on coming until his hands were pressed around my throat.

These fears and premonitions didn't leave me. They cast a pall over everything that happened in the days and months that followed, affecting my mood to the point where even the joy of my growing success was contaminated. It was particularly bad in the beginning. Everywhere we went, every town we traveled to, I kept expecting Slim to pop up again. Sitting in a restaurant, walking into a hotel lobby, stepping out of the car: my uncle was liable to appear at any humdrum moment, bursting through the fabric of my life with no warning. That was what made the situation so hard to bear. It was the uncertainty, the thought that all my happiness could be smashed in the blink of an eye. The only spot that felt safe to me anymore was standing before a crowd and doing my act. Slim wouldn't dare to make a move in public, at least not when I was the center of attention like that, and given all the anxiety I carried around with me the rest of the time, performing became a kind of mental repose, a respite from the terror that stalked my heart. I threw myself into my work as never before, exulting in the freedom and protection it gave me. Something had shifted inside my soul, and I understood that this was who I was now: not Walter Rawley, the kid who turned into Walt the Wonder Boy for one hour a day, but Walt the Wonder Boy through and through, a person who did not exist except when he was in the air. The ground was an illusion, a no-man's land mined with traps and shadows, and everything that happened down there was false. Only the air was real now, and for twenty-three hours a day I lived as a stranger to myself, cut off from my old pleasures and habits, a cowering bundle of desperation and fright.

The work kept me going, and fortunately there was lots of it, an endless parade of winter bookings. After our return to Wichita, the master worked out an elaborate tour, with a record number of weekly performances. Of all the smart moves he made, his cleverest stroke was getting us to Florida for the worst of the cold weather. We were there from mid-January to the end of March, covering the peninsula from top to bottom, and for this one extended trip – the first and only time it ever happened – Mrs Witherspoon tagged along with us. Contrary to all that garbage about being a jinx, she brought me nothing but good luck. Luck not only as far as Slim was concerned (we saw neither hide nor tail of him), but luck in terms of packed audiences, large box-office receipts, and good companionship (she liked going to the movies as much as I did). Those were the days of the Florida land boom, and rich people had begun flocking down there in their white suits and diamond necklaces to dance away the winter under the palm trees. It was my first experience going out in front of swells. I did my act at country clubs, golf courses, and dude ranches, and for all their polish and sophistication, those blue-bloods took to me with the same gusto as the wretched of the earth. It made no difference. My act was universal, and it floored everyone in the same way, rich and poor alike.

By the time we returned to Kansas, I was beginning to feel more like myself again. Slim hadn't shown his face in over five months, and I figured that if he was planning any surprises, he would have sprung them on us by now. When we took off again for the upper Midwest at the end of April, I had more or less stopped thinking about him. That scary scene in Gibson City was so far in the past, it sometimes felt as if it had never happened. I was relaxed and confident, and if there was anything on my mind beside the act, it was the hair that had started growing in my armpits and around my crotch, all that late-sprouting stuff that announced my entrance into the land of wet dreams and dirty thoughts. My guard was down, and just as I'd always known it would, just as I'd feared when the whole business started, the blade fell at the very moment I was least expecting it. The master and I were in Northfield, Minnesota, a little town about forty miles south of Saint Paul, and as was my custom prior to evening performances, I went to the local movie house to fritter away a couple of hours. The talkies were in full swing by then, and I couldn't get enough of them, I went every chance I had, sometimes seeing the same picture three or four times. On that particular day, the feature show was *Cocoanuts*, the new Marx Brothers comedy set in Florida. I'd already seen it before, but I was crazy about those clowns, especially Harpo, the mute one with the nutty wig and the loud honker, and I hopped to when I heard it was playing that afternoon. The theater was a fair-size establishment, with seats for two or three hundred people, but owing to the good spring weather, there couldn't have been more than half a dozen folks in attendance with me. Not that I cared, of course. I settled in with a bag of popcorn and proceeded to laugh my head off, oblivious to the other bodies scattered in the dark. About twenty or thirty minutes into it, I sniffed something strange, a curiously sweet medicinal odor wafting up from behind me. It was a strong smell, and it was getting stronger by the second. Before I could turn around to see what it was, a rag drenched in that pungent concoction was clamped over my face. I bucked and struggled to break free of it, but a hand pushed me back, and then, before I could gather my strength for a second effort, the fight suddenly went out of me. My muscles went limp; my skin melted into a buttery ooze; my head detached itself from my body. Wherever I was from then on, it wasn't any place I'd been to before.

I had imagined all kinds of battles and confrontations with Slim – fistfights, holdups, guns going off in dark alleys – but not once did it enter my mind that he'd kidnap me. It wasn't in my uncle's M.O. to do something that required such long-term planning. He was a hothead, a banjo-brain who jumped into things on the spur of the moment, and if he broke the mold on my account, it only shows how bitter he was, how deeply my success had rankled him. I was the one big chance he'd ever have, and he wasn't going to blow it by flying off the handle. Not this time. He was going to act like a proper gangster, a slick professional who thought of all the angles, and he'd end up putting the screws to us but good. He wasn't in it just for the money, and he wasn't in it just for revenge – he wanted both, and snatching me for ransom was the magic combination, the way to kill those two birds with one stone.

He had a partner this time, a corpulent yegg by the name of Fritz, and considering what mental lightweights they were, they did a pretty thorough job of keeping me hidden. First they stashed me in a cave on the outskirts of Northfield, a dank, filthy hole where I spent three days and nights, my legs bound in thick ropes and a gag tied around my mouth; then they gave me a second dose of ether and took me somewhere else, a basement in what must have been an apartment building in Minneapolis or Saint Paul. That lasted only a day, and from there we drove to the country again, settling into an abandoned prospector's house in what I later learned was South Dakota. It looked more like the moon than the earth out there, all treeless and desolate and still, and we were so far back from any road that even if I'd managed to run away from them, it would have taken me hours to find help. They'd stocked the place with a couple of months' worth of canned food, and all signs pointed to a long, nerve-racking siege. That was how Slim had chosen to play it: as slowly as he could. He wanted to make the master squirm, and if that meant dragging things out a little bit, so much the better. He wasn't in any rush. It was all so delicious for him, why put a stop to it before he'd had his fun?

I had never seen him so cocky, so buoyed up and satisfied with himself.

He strutted around that cabin like a four-star general, barking out orders and laughing at his own jokes, a whirlwind of lunatic bravado. It disgusted me to see him like that, but at the same time it spared me from the full impact of his cruelty. With everything coming up aces for him, Slim could afford to be generous, and he never went at me with quite the savagery I was expecting. That isn't to say he didn't slap me around from time to time, zinging me across the mouth or twisting my ears when it struck his fancy, but most of his abuse came in the form of taunts and verbal digs. He never wearied of telling me how he'd 'turned the tables on that lousy Jew', or of making fun of the acne eruptions that mottled my face ('Look, boy, another pus-gusher'; 'Whoa there, pal, get a load of them volcanoes stitched across your brow'), or of reminding me how my fate now rested in his hands. To emphasize this last point, he'd sometimes saunter over to me twirling a gun on his finger and press the tip of the barrel against my skull. 'See what I mean, fella?' he'd say, and then burst out laughing. 'A little squeeze on this trigger here, and your brains go splat against the wall.' Once or twice, he went ahead and pulled the trigger, but that was only to scare me. As long as he hadn't pocketed the ransom money, I knew he wouldn't have the guts to load that gun with live ammunition.

It was no picnic, but I found I could handle that stuff. Sticks and stones, as they say, and I realized it was a lot better to listen to his yammering than get my bones broken in two. As long as I kept my mouth shut and didn't provoke him, he usually ran out of steam after fifteen or twenty minutes. Since they kept the gag on me most of the time, I didn't have much choice in the matter anyway. But even when my lips were free, I did everything I could to ignore his cracks. I came up with scores of juicy rebuttals and insults, but I generally kept them to myself, knowing full well that the less I wrangled with the bastard, the less he would get under my skin. Beyond that, I didn't have much to cling to. Slim was too crazy to be trusted, and there was nothing to guarantee he wouldn't find a way to kill me once he collected the money. I couldn't know what he had in mind, and that not knowing was the thing that tortured me most. I could endure the hardships of incarceration, but my head was never free of visions of what was to come: having my throat cut, having a bullet fired through my heart, having the skin peeled off my bones.

Fritz did nothing to assuage these torments. He was little more than a yes-man, a blundering fatso who wheezed and shuffled his way through the various minor tasks that Slim doled out to him. He cooked the beans on the wood stove, he swept the floors, he emptied the shit buckets, he adjusted and tightened the ropes around my arms and legs. God knows where Slim had dug up that bovine gumball, but I don't suppose he could have asked for a more willing henchman. Fritz was maid, butler, and errand boy, the stalwart ninny who never spoke a word of complaint. He sat through those long days and nights as if the Badlands were the finest vacation spot in America, perfectly content to bide his time and do nothing, to stare out the window, to breathe. For ten or twelve days he didn't say much of anything to me, but then, after the first ransom note was sent to Master Yehudi, Slim started driving off to town every morning, presumably to post letters or make telephone calls or communicate his demands by some other means, and Fritz and I started spending a portion of every day alone together. I wouldn't go so far as to say that we developed an understanding, but at least he didn't scare me the way Slim did. Fritz had nothing personal against me. He was just doing his job, and it wasn't long before I realized that he was as much in the dark about the future as I was.

'He's going to kill me, ain't he?' I said to him once, sitting in a chair as he fed me my midday meal of baked beans and crackers. Slim was so intimidated by the thought that I'd fly away, he never let the ropes come off, not even when I was eating or sleeping or taking a shit. So Fritz spoon-fed me my grub, shoveling it into my mouth as if I were a baby.

'Huh?' Fritz said, responding in that bright, rapid-fire way of his. His eyes looked blank, as if his brain had stalled in traffic somewhere between Pittsburgh and the Allegheny Mountains. 'You just say somethin'?'

'He's going to bump me off, ain't he?' I repeated. 'I mean, there ain't a chance in hell I'll ever walk out of here alive.'

'Dunno about that, bub. Your uncle don't tell me nothin' about what he's going to do. He just goes and does it.'

'And you don't mind that he doesn't let you in on things?'

'Nope, I don't mind. As long as I get my cut, why should I mind? What he does with you is none of my beeswax.'

'And what makes you so sure he'll pay up what he owes you?'

'Nothin'. But if he don't do what he's supposed to do, I'll bust his ass.'

'It's never going to work, Fritz. All those letters Slim's been mailing from the post office in town – why, they'll trace you turtles to this shack in no time, no time at all.'

'Ha, that's a good one. You think we're stupid, don't you?'

'Yeah, that's what I think. Pretty stupid.'

'Ha. And what if I told you we got another partner? And what if that partner happens to be the guy those letters was goin' to?'

'Well, what if you did?'

'Yeah, as if I just didn't. See what I'm drivin' at, bub? This other party passes on the notes and such to the folks with the cash. There ain't no way they'll find us here.'

'And what about him, the guy you're in cahoots with? He invisible or something?'

'Yeah, that's right. He took one of them vanishin' powders and went up in a puff of smoke.'

That was about the longest conversation I ever had with him: Fritz at his most eloquent and long-winded. It wasn't that he was mean to me, but he had ice in his veins and crackerjacks wadded in his skull, and I could never get through to him. I couldn't turn him against Uncle Slim, I couldn't persuade him to untie the ropes ('Sorry, bub, no can do'), I couldn't shake his loyalty and steadfastness by one jot. Any other person would have answered my question in one of two ways: by telling me it was true or telling me it was false. Yes, he would have said, Slim was planning to cut my throat, or else he would have patted me on the head and assured me that my fears were groundless. Even if the person lied when he said those things (for any number of reasons, both good and bad), I would have been given a straight answer. But not with Fritz. Fritz was honest to a fault, and since he couldn't answer my question, he said he didn't know, forgetting that normal human decency requires a person to give a firm answer to a question as monumental as that one. But Fritz hadn't learned the rules of human behavior. He was a nobodaddy and a clod, and any pimple-faced boy could see that talking to him was a waste of breath.

Oh, I had a jolly time in South Dakota, all right, a regular laughathon of nonstop fun and entertainment. Bound and gagged for more than a month, left alone in a locked room with twelve rusty shovels and pitchforks to keep me company, certain that I would die a brutal, pulverizing death. My only hope was that the master would rescue me, and again and again I dreamed of how he and a posse of men would swoop down on the hut, plug Fritz and Slim full of lead, and carry me back to the land of the living. But the weeks passed, and nothing ever changed. And then, when things did change, it was only for the worse. Once the ransom notes and negotiations started, I thought I detected a gradual hardening of Slim's mood, an ever-so-slight ebbing of his confidence. The game had turned serious now. The first rush of enthusiasm had subsided, and little by little his jocularity was losing out to his old snappish, foul-tempered self. He nagged at Fritz, he groused about the dull food, he broke some plates against the wall. Those were the earliest signs, and eventually they were followed by others: kicking me off my chair, poking fun at Fritz's blimpy torso, tightening the ropes around my limbs. It seemed clear that the pressure was getting to him, but why this should have been so I couldn't say. I wasn't privy to the discussions that went on in the other room, I didn't read the ransom notes or see the newspaper articles that were written about me, and the little I heard through the door was so muffled and fragmented, I could never fit the pieces together. All I knew was that Slim was acting more and more like Slim. The trend was unmistakable, and once he got back to being who he was, I knew that everything that had happened so far would feel like a holiday, a cruise to the Lesser Antilles on a goddamn luxury yacht.

By early June, he'd pushed himself close to the snapping point. Even Fritz, the ever placid and unbudgeable Fritz, was beginning to show symptoms of wear and tear, and I could see in his eyes that Slim's razzing could only go so far before his fellow dunderhead took offense. That became the most fervent object of my prayers – an out-and-out brawl – but even if it didn't come to that, it gave me no small comfort to see how often their conversations were erupting into minor squabbles, which mostly consisted of Slim needling Fritz and Fritz sulking in the corner, staring down at the floor and muttering curses under his breath. If nothing else, it took some of the burden off me, and with so many dangers lurking in the air, to be forgotten for even five or ten minutes was a blessing, an unimaginable boon.

Each day, the weather grew a little hotter, bore down a little more heavily on my skin. The sun never seemed to set anymore, and I itched almost constantly from the ropes. With the coming of the heat, spiders had infested the back room where I spent most of my time. They ran up and down my legs, covered my face, hatched their eggs in my hair. No sooner would I shake one off than another would find me. Mosquitoes dive-bombed into my ears, flies wriggled and buzzed in sixteen different webs, I excreted a never-ending flow of sweat. If it wasn't the creepy-crawlies that got me, it was the dryness in my throat. And if it wasn't thirst, it was sadness, a relentless crumbling of my will and resolve. I was turning into porridge, a moondog boiling in a pot of spit and ragged fur, and no matter how hard I struggled to be brave and strong, there were moments when I couldn't help myself anymore, when the tears just fell from my eyes and wouldn't stop.

One afternoon, Slim burst into my little hideaway and caught me in the middle of one of these crying fits. 'Why so glum, pal?' he said. 'Don't you know that tomorrow is your big day?'

It mortified me for him to see me like that, so I turned away my head without responding. I didn't have any idea what he was talking about, and since I could only speak with my eyes, there was no way I could find out. By then, it hardly seemed to matter anymore.

'Pay day, chum. Tomorrow we get the dough, and a pretty little bundle it's going to be. Fifty thousand dancing girls lying cheek to jowl in a battered straw suitcase. Just what the doctor ordered, eh kid? It's a hell of a retirement plan, let me tell you, and when you throw in the fact that them bills is unmarked, I can spend them all the way to Mexico and the feds won't be none the wiser.'

I didn't have any reason to doubt him. He was talking so fast, and his nerves were so jangled, it seemed clear that something was up. Still, I didn't respond. I didn't want to give him the satisfaction, so I continued looking away. After a moment, Slim sat down on the bed opposite my chair. When I still didn't respond, he leaned forward, untied the gag, and pulled it away from my mouth.

'Look at me when I'm talking to you,' he said.

But still, I kept my eyes fixed on the floor, refusing to return his gaze. Without any warning, he sprang forward and slapped me across the cheek – once, very hard. I looked up.

'That's better,' he said. Normally, he would have smiled over his little victory, but he was beyond such petty antics today. His expression turned grim, and for the next few seconds he stared at me so hard, I thought I'd shrivel up in my clothes. 'You're a lucky boy,' he continued. 'Fifty thousand bucks, nephew. Do you think you're worth that kind of dough? I never thought they'd go that high, but the price just kept climbing, and they never even flinched. Shit, boy, there ain't nobody in the world who'd cough up them apples for me. On the open market I wouldn't fetch no more than a nickel or two – and that's on a good day, when I'm at my sweetest and most lovable. And here you got that Jew crud willing to fork over fifty grand to get you back. I suppose that makes you kind of special, don't it? Or do you think he's just bluffing? Is that what he's up to, nephew? Making more promises he don't intend to keep?'

I was looking at him now, but that didn't mean I had any intention of answering his questions. Uncle Slim was nearly on top of me, coiled like an infielder on the edge of the bed, thrusting his face right against mine. He was so close, I could see every bloodshot vein in his eyes, every craterlike pore of his skin. His pupils were dilated, he was short of breath, and any second now it looked as if he was going to lunge forward and bite off my nose.

'Walt the Wonder Boy,' he said, lowering his voice to a whisper. 'It's got a nice ring to it, don't it? Walt . . . the . . . Wonder . . . Boy. Everybody's heard about you, kid, you're the talk of the whole fucking country. I've seen you perform myself, you know. Not once, but several times – six or seven times in the past year. There ain't nothing like it, is there? A runt who walks on water. It's the damnedest trick I ever saw, the slickest bit of hocus-pocus since the radio. No wires, no mirrors, no trapdoors. What's the gimmick, Walt? How in hell do you get yourself off the ground like that?'

I wasn't going to talk, I wasn't going to say a word to him, but after staring him down through the silence for ten or fifteen seconds, he jumped up and whacked me in the temple with the heel of his hand, then slapped me across the jaw with the other hand.

'There's no gimmick,' I said.

'Ho, ho,' he said. 'Ho, ho, ho.'

'The act's on the level. What you see is what there is.'

'And you expect me to believe that?'

'I don't care what you believe. I'm telling you there's no trick.'

'Lying's a sin, Walt, you know that. Especially to your elders. Liars burn in hell, and if you don't stop feeding me this bullshit, that's exactly where you're going. Into the fires of hell. Count on it, boy. I want the truth, and I want it now.'

'And that's what I'm giving you. The whole truth and nothing but the truth, so help me God.'

'All right,' he said, slapping his knees in frustration. 'If that's how you want to play it, that's how we'll play it.' He bounced up from the bed and grabbed me by the collar, yanking me out of my chair with one swift jerk of his arm. 'If you're so goddamn sure of yourself, then show me. We'll step outside and have a little demonstration. But you better deliver the goods, wise guy. I don't truck with no fibbers. You hear me, Walt? It's put up or shut up. You get yourself off the ground, or your ass is fucking grass.'

He dragged me into the other room, yelling and haranguing as my head thumped against the floor and splinters jabbed into my scalp. There was nothing I could do to fight back. The ropes were still fastened around my arms and legs, and the best I could do was writhe and scream, begging for mercy as the blood trickled through my hair.

'Untie him,' he ordered Fritz. 'The squirt says he can fly, and we're going to hold him to his word. No ifs, ands, or buts. It's show time, gents. Little Walt's going to spread his wings and dance in the air for us.'

I could see Fritz's face from my position on the floor, and he was looking at Slim with a mixture of horror and confusion. The fat man was so stunned, he didn't even try to speak.

'Well?' Slim said. 'What are you waiting for? Untie him!'

'But Slim,' Fritz stammered. 'It don't make no sense. We let him fly into the air, and he'll fly clear away from us. Just like you always said.'

'Forget what I said. Just undo the ropes, and we'll see what kind of bullshitter he really is. I'm betting he don't get a foot off the ground. Not one measly inch. And even if he does, who the fuck cares? I've got my gun, don't I? One shot in the leg, and he'll fall down faster than a goddamn duck.'

This cockeyed argument seemed to persuade Fritz. He shrugged, walked to the center of the room where Slim had deposited me, and bent down to do what he'd been told. The moment he loosened the first knot, however, I felt a surge of fear and revulsion wash through me.

'I ain't going to do it,' I said.

'Oh, you'll do it,' Slim said. My hands were free by then, and Fritz had turned his attention to the ropes around my legs. 'You'll do it all day if I tell you to.'

'You can shoot me dead,' I blubbered. 'You can slit my throat or burn me to ashes, but there ain't no way I'm going to do it.'

Slim chuckled briefly, then sent the point of his shoe flying into my back. The breath burst out of me like a rocket, and I hit the floor in pain.

'Aw, lay off him, Slim,' Fritz said, working on the last knot around my ankles. 'He ain't in the mood. Any dope can see that.'

'And who asked your opinion, tubby?' Slim said, turning his anger on a man who weighed twice what he did and was three times as strong.

'Cut it out,' Fritz said, grunting from the effort as he raised himself off the floor. 'You know I don't like it when you call me them names.'

'Names?' Slim shouted. 'What names are you talking about, fatso?'

'You know. All that tubby and fatso stuff. It ain't nice to mock a fella like that.'

'Getting sensitive, are we? And what am I supposed to call you, then? Just take a look in the mirror and tell me what you see. A mountain of flesh, that's what. I calls 'em as I sees 'em, fatso. You want another name, then start shedding a few pounds.'

Fritz had about the longest, slowest fuse of any man I'd ever met, but this time Slim had pushed him too far. I could feel it, I could taste it, and even as I lay there gasping for air and trying to recover from the blow to my back, I understood that this was the one opening I'd ever have. My arms and legs were free, a hostile hubbub was brewing above me, and all I had to do was pick my moment. It came when Fritz took a step toward Slim and poked him in the chest. 'You got no call to go on like that,' he said. 'Not when I asked you to stop.'

Without making a sound, I began crawling in the direction of the door, inching forward as smoothly and unhurriedly as I could. I heard a thud behind me. Then there was another thud, followed by the noise of scuffling shoes on the bare wood floor. Shouts and grunts and foul words punctuated the sandpaper tango, but by then I was pushing my hand against the screen door, which luckily was too warped to fit into the jam. I opened it with one shove, crept forward another half foot or so, and then tumbled out into the sunlight, landing shoulder-first on the hard South Dakota dirt.

My muscles felt all strange and spongy. When I tried to stand up, I scarcely recognized them anymore. They'd gone stupid on me, and I couldn't get them to work. After so much confinement and inactivity, I'd been turned into a spastic clown. I battled my way to my feet, but no sooner did I take a step than I began to stumble. I fell, picked myself up, lurched forward another yard or two, then fell again. I didn't have a second to waste, and there I was wobbling around like a wino, belly-flopping between every third and fourth step. By sheer persistence, I finally made it to Slim's car, a dented old jalopy parked around the side of the house. The sun had turned the thing into an oven, and when I touched the door handle, the metal was so hot I almost let out a scream. Fortunately, I knew my way around cars. The master had taught me how to drive, and I had no trouble releasing the hand brake, pulling out the choke, and turning the key in the ignition. There was no time to adjust the seat, however. My legs were too short, and the only way I could get my foot on the gas pedal was to slide down, hanging onto the steering wheel for dear life. The first cough of the motor halted the fight inside the cabin, and by the time I got the car in gear, Slim was already bolting out the door and racing toward me with his gun in his hand. I spun out in an arc, trying to keep as much distance between us as I could, but the bastard was gaining on me and I couldn't take my hand off the wheel to shift into second. I saw Slim lift the gun and take aim. Instead of swerving right, I swerved left, barreling straight into him with the fender. It caught him just above the knee, and he bounced off and fell to the ground. That gave me a few seconds to work with. Before Slim could stand up, I'd straightened out the wheel and pointed myself in the right direction. I threw the car into second and pressed the pedal to the floor. A bullet went crashing through the rear window, shattering the glass behind me. Another bullet thumped into the dashboard, opening up a hole in the glove-compartment door. I groped for the clutch with my left foot, shifted into third, and then I was off. I pushed the car up to thirty, forty miles an hour, bouncing over the rough terrain like a bronco buster as I waited for the next bullet to come tearing through my back. But there were no more bullets. I'd left that shitbag in the dust, and when I came upon the road a few minutes later, I was home free.

Was I happy to see the master again? You bet your life I was. Did my heart pound with joy when he opened his arms and smothered me in a long embrace? Yes, my heart pounded with joy. Did we weep over our good fortune? Of course we did. Did we laugh and celebrate and dance a hundred jigs? We did all that and more.

Master Yehudi said: 'I'll never let you out of my sight again.'

And I said: 'I'll never go nowhere without you, not for the rest of my days.'

There's an old adage about not appreciating what you have until you've lost it. Accurate as that wisdom is, I can't say it ever applied to me. I knew what I'd lost all along: from the moment I was carried out of that movie theater in Northfield, Minnesota, to the moment I laid eyes on the master again in Rapid City, South Dakota. For five and a half weeks I mourned the loss of everything that was good and precious to me, and I stand before the world now to testify that nothing can compare to the sweetness of getting back what was taken from you. Of all the triumphs I ever notched in my belt, none thrilled me more than the simple fact of having my life returned to me.

The reunion was held in Rapid City because that's where I wound up after my escape. Penny-pincher that he was, Slim had neglected the health of his car, and the heap ran out of gas before I'd driven twenty miles. If not for a traveling salesman who picked me up just before dark, I might still be wandering around those Badlands now, vainly searching for help. I asked him to drop me at the nearest police station, and once those cops found out who I was, they treated me like the crown prince of Ballyball. They fed me soup and Coney Island hotdogs, they gave me new clothes and a warm bath, they taught me how to play pinochle. By the time the master arrived the next afternoon, I had already talked to two dozen reporters and posed for four hundred pictures. My kidnapping had been front-page news for more than a month, and when a stringer from the local press came snooping around the station house for some late-breaking crumbs, he recognized me from my photos and put out the word. The bloodhounds and ambulance chasers poured in after that. Flashbulbs popped like firecrackers all around me, and I bragged my head off into the wee hours of the morning, telling wild stories about how I'd outwitted my captors and stolen off before they could swap me for the loot. I suppose the bare facts would have done just as well, but I couldn't resist the urge to exaggerate. I reveled in my newfound celebrity, and after a while I grew giddy from the way those reporters looked at me, hanging on my every word. I was a showman, after all, and blessed with an audience like that one, I didn't have the heart to let them down.

The master put a stop to the nonsense the moment he walked in. For the next hour our hugs and tears occupied all my attention – but none of that was seen by the public. We sat alone in a back room of the constabulary, sobbing into each other's arms as two police officers guarded the door. After that, statements were made, papers were signed, and then he whisked me out of there, elbowing past a throng of gawkers and well-wishers in the street. Cheers went up, huzzahs rang out, but the master only paused long enough to smile and wave once to the rubberneckers before hustling me into a chauffeur-driven car parked at the curb. An hour and a half later, we were sitting in a private compartment on an eastbound train, headed for New England and the sandy shores of Cape Cod.

It wasn't until nightfall that I realized we weren't going to be stopping off in Kansas. With so much catching up to do with the master, so many things to describe and explain and recount, my head had been churning like a milkshake machine, and it was only after the lights were out and we were tucked into our berths that I thought to ask about Mrs Witherspoon. The master and I had been together for six hours by then, and her name hadn't come up once.

'What's the matter with Wichita?' I said. 'Ain't that just as good a place for us as Cape Cod?'

'It's a fine place,' the master said, 'but it's too hot this time of year. The ocean will be good for you, Walt. You'll recuperate faster.'

'And what about Mrs W.? When's she planning to join us?'

'She won't be along this time, kid.'

'Why not? You remember Florida, don't you? She loved it down there so much, we just about had to drag her out of the water. I never seen a body happier than she was sloshing around in them waves.'

'That might be so, but she won't be doing any swimming this summer. At least not with us.'

Master Yehudi sighed, filling the darkness with a soft, plaintive flutter of sound, and even though I was dead tired, just on the brink of dozing off, my heart began to speed up, pumping inside me like an alarm.

'Oh,' I said, trying not to betray my worry. 'And why's that?'

'I wasn't going to tell you tonight. But now that you've brought it up, I don't suppose there's any point in keeping it from you.'

'Tell me what?'

'Lady Marion is about to take the plunge.'

'Plunge? What plunge?'

'She's engaged to be married. If all goes according to plan, she'll be joined in holy wedlock before Thanksgiving.'

'You mean hitched? You mean coupled in matrimony for the rest of her natural life?'

'That's it. With a ring on her finger and a husband in her bed.'

'And that husband ain't you?'

'Perish the thought. I'm here with you, aren't I? How can I be back there with her if I'm here with you?'

'But you're her main squeeze. She don't have no right to ditch you like that. Not without your say-so.'

'She had to do it, and I didn't stand in her way. That woman's one in a million, Walt, and I don't want you breathing a word against her.'

'I'll breathe all the words I want. Somebody does you a bad turn, and I breathe fire.'

'She didn't do me a bad turn. Her hands were tied, and she made a promise that couldn't be broken. If I were you, boy, I'd thank her for making that promise every hour on the hour for the next fifty years.'

'Thank her? I spit on that trollop, master. I spit and curse on that two-faced bitch for doing you wrong.'

'Not when you find out why she did it, you won't. It's all because of you, little man. She put herself on the line for a pipsqueak named Walter Claireborne Rawley, and it was about the bravest, most selfless thing I've ever seen a person do.'

'Bullroar. I don't have nothing to do with it. I wasn't even there.'

'Fifty thousand dollars, sport. You think that kind of money grows on bushes? When the ransom notes started coming in, we had to act fast.'

'It's a lot of dough, sure, but we must have earned twice that much by now.'

'Not even close. Marion and I couldn't even raise half that amount between us. We've done nicely for ourselves, Walt, but nowhere what you'd think. The overhead is enormous. Hotel bills, transportation, advertising – it all adds up, and we've just barely kept our heads above water.'

'Oh,' I said, doing some quick mental calculations on how much money we must have spent – and growing dizzy in the process.

'Oh is right. So what to do – that's the question. Whither goest us before it's too late? Old Judge Witherspoon turns us down. He hasn't talked to Marion since Charlie killed himself, and he's not about to interrupt his silence now. The banks laugh, the loan sharks won't touch us, and even if we sell the house, we're still going to fall short. So what to do – that's the question burning a hole in our stomachs. The clock's ticking, and every day we lose, the price is only going to go up.'

'Fifty thousand bucks to save my ass.'

'And a cheap price it was, too, considering your box-office potential in the years ahead. A cheap price, but we just didn't have it.'

'So where'd you go?'

'As I'm sure you understand by now, Mrs Witherspoon is a woman of manifold charms and allurements. I might have won a special place in her heart, but I wasn't the only man who carried the torch for her. Wichita teems with them, her suitors lurk behind every fencepost and fire hydrant. One of them, a young grain tycoon by the name of Orville Cox, has proposed to her five times in the past year. When you and I were out touring the sticks, young Orville was back in town, pressing his case pretty hard. Marion rebuffed him, of course, but not without a certain wistfulness and regret, and each time she said no, I think that wistfulness and regret grew a little stronger. Need I say more? She turned to Cox for the fifty thousand, a sum he was all too willing to part with, but only on the condition that she cast me aside and join him at the altar.'

'That's blackmail.'

'More or less. But this Orville really isn't such a bad character. A little on the dull side, maybe, but Marion's going into it with her eyes open.'

'Well,' I sputtered, not knowing what to make of all this, 'I guess I owe her an apology. She came through for me like a real trouper.'

'That she did. Like an honest-to-goodness heroine.'

'But,' I continued, still not willing to give up, 'but that's all done with now. I mean, all bets is off. I got away from Slim on my own, and nobody had to fork out no fifty thousand. Orville's still got his rotten dough, and by rights that means old Mrs Witherspoon's still free.'

'Maybe so. But she's still planning to marry him. I talked to her just yesterday, and that was how things stood. She intends to go ahead with it.'

'We should break it up, master, that's what we should do. Storm right into the wedding and snatch her away.'

'Just like the movies, eh Walt?' For the first time since we'd started this dreadful conversation, Master Yehudi let out a laugh.

'You're damn straight. Just like a two-reeler punch-'em-up.'

'Let her go, Walt. Her mind's set on it, and there's nothing we can do to stop her.'

'But it's my fault. If it wasn't for that lousy kidnapping, none of this would have happened.'

'It's your uncle's fault, son, not yours, and you mustn't blame yourself – not now, not ever. Put it to rest. Mrs Witherspoon is doing what she wants to do, and we're not going to gripe about it. Understood? We're going to act like gentlemen, and not only are we not going to hold it against her, we're going to send her the prettiest wedding present any bride ever saw. Now get some sleep. We have a ton of work ahead of us, and I don't want you fretting about this business a second longer. It's done. The curtain is down, and the next act is about to begin.'

Master Yehudi talked a good game, but when we sat down to breakfast in the dining car the next morning, his face looked wan and troubled – as if he'd been up all night, staring into the darkness and contemplating the end of the world. It occurred to me that he seemed thinner than he had in the past, and I wondered how this could have escaped my notice the day before. Had happiness made me that blind? I looked more closely, studying his face with as much detachment as I could. There was no question that something had changed in him. His skin was pinched and sallow, a certain haggardness had crept into the creases around his eyes, and all in all he looked somewhat diminished, less imposing than I'd remembered him. He'd been under duress, after all – first the ordeal of my kidnapping, then the blow of losing his woman – but I hoped that was all there was to it. Every now and then, I thought I detected a slight wince as he chewed his food, and once, toward the end of the meal, I unmistakably saw his hand dart under the table and clutch his belly. Was he unwell, or was it simply a passing attack of indigestion? And if he wasn't well, how bad was it?

He didn't say a word, of course, and since I was looking none too healthy myself, he managed to keep the spotlight on me throughout the breakfast.

'Eat up,' he said. 'You've dwindled down to a stick. Chomp down the waffles, son, and then I'll order you some more. We've got to put some meat on your bones, get you back to full strength.'

'I'm doing my best,' I said. 'It's not as though I got put up in some ritzy hotel. I lived on a steady diet of dog food with those bums, and my stomach's shrunken to the size of a pea.'

'And then there's the matter of your skin,' the master added, watching me struggle to get down another rasher of bacon. 'We'll have to do something about that, too. All those blotches. It looks like you've broken out with a case of the chicken pox.'

'No, sir, what I've got is the zits, and sometimes they're so sore, it hurts me just to smile.'

'Of course it does. Your poor body's gone haywire from all that captivity. Cooped up without any sunshine, sweating bullets day and night – it's no wonder you're a mess. The beach is going to do you a world of good, Walt, and if those pimples don't clear up, I'll show you how to take care of them and keep the new ones at bay. My grandmother had a secret remedy, and it hasn't failed yet.'

'You mean I don't have to grow another face?'

'This one will do. If you didn't have so many freckles, it wouldn't look so bad. Combine those with the acne, and it creates quite an effect. But don't brood, kid. Before long, the only thing you'll have to worry about is whiskers – and that's permanent, they stay with you until the bitter end.'

We spent more than a month in a little beach house on the Cape Cod shore, one day for every day I'd been locked up by Uncle Slim. The master rented it under a false name to protect me from the press, and for purposes of simplicity and convenience we posed as father and son. Buck was the alias he'd chosen: Timothy Buck for himself and Timothy Buck II for me, or Tim Buck One and Tim Buck Two. We got some good laughs out of that, and the funny thing was, it wasn't a whole lot different from Timbuktu where we were, at least as far as remoteness was concerned: high up on a promontory overlooking the ocean, with no neighbors for miles around. A woman named Mrs Hawthorne drove out from Truro every day to cook and clean for us, but other than kibbitzing with her, we pretty much kept to ourselves. We soaked up the sun, took long walks on the beach, ate clam chowder, slept ten or twelve hours every night. After a week of that loafer's regimen, I was feeling fit enough to try my hand at levitation again. The master started me off slowly with some routine ground exercises. Push-ups, jumping jacks, jogs on the beach, and when the time came to test the air again, we worked out behind the cliff, where Mrs Hawthorne couldn't spy on us. I was a little rusty at first, and I took some flops and spills, but after five or six days I was back in my old form, as limber and bouncy as I'd ever been. The fresh air was a great healer, and even if the master's remedy didn't do all he promised (a warm towel soaked in brine, vinegar, and drugstore astringents, applied to my face every four hours), half my zits began to fade on their own, no doubt from the sunshine and the good food I was eating again.

My strength would have returned even more quickly, I think, if not for a nasty habit I developed during that holiday among the dunes and foghorns. Now that my hands were free to move again, they began to show a remarkable independence. They were filled with wanderlust, fidgety with urges to roam and explore, and no matter how many times I told them to stay put, they traveled wherever they damn pleased. I had only to crawl under the covers at night, and they would insist on flying to their favorite hot spot, a forest kingdom just south of the equator. There they would visit their friend, the great finger of fingers, the all-powerful one who ruled the universe by mental telepathy. When he called, no subject could resist. My hands were in his thrall, and short of tying them up in ropes again, I had no choice but to give them their freedom. So it was that Aesop's madness became my madness, and so it was that my pecker rose up to take control of my life. It no longer resembled the little squirt gun that Mrs Witherspoon had once cupped in her palm. It had gained in both size and stature since then, and its word was law. It begged to be touched, and I touched it. It cried out to be fondled, yanked, and squeezed, and I bowed to its whims with a willing heart. Who cared if I went blind? Who cared if my hair fell out? Nature was calling, and every night I ran to it as breathlessly and hungrily as Adam himself.

As for the master, I didn't know what to think. He seemed to be enjoying himself, and while his complexion and color undoubtedly improved, I witnessed three or four stomach-clutching episodes, and the facial twinges occurred almost regularly now, at every second or third meal. But his spirits couldn't have been brighter, and when he wasn't reading his Spinoza or working with me on the act, he kept himself busy on the telephone, haggling over arrangements for my upcoming tour. I was big stuff now. The kidnapping had seen to that, and

Master Yehudi was more than ready to take full advantage of the situation. Hastily revising his plans for my career, he settled us into our Cape Cod retreat and went on the offensive. He was holding the chips now and could afford to play hard-to-get. He could dictate terms, press for new and unheard-of percentages from the booking agents, demand guarantees matched by only the biggest draws. I'd reached the top a lot sooner than either of us had expected, and before the master's wheelings and dealings were done, he'd booked me into scores of theaters up and down the East Coast, a string of one- and two-night stands that would keep us going until the end of the year. And not just in puny towns and villages – in real cities, the front-line places I'd always dreamed of going to. Providence and Newark; New Haven and Baltimore; Philadelphia, Boston, New York. The act had moved indoors, and from now on we'd be playing for high stakes. 'No more walking on water,' the master said, 'no more farm-boy costume, no more county fairs and chamber of commerce picnics. You're an aerial artist now, Walt, the one and only of your kind, and folks are going to pay top dollar for the privilege of seeing you perform. They'll dress up in their Sunday finery and sit in plush velvet seats, and once the theater goes dark and the spotlight turns on you, their eyes will fall out of their head. They'll die a thousand deaths, Walt. You'll prance and spin before them, and one by one they'll follow you up the stairs of heaven. By the time it's over, they'll be sitting in the presence of God.'

Such are the twists of fortune. The kidnapping was the worst thing that had ever happened to me, and yet it turned out to be my big break, the fuel that finally launched me into orbit. I'd been given a month's worth of free publicity, and by the time I wriggled out of Slim's grasp, I was already a household name, the number-one cause célèbre in the land. The news of my escape created a stir, a second sensation on top of the first, and after that I could do no wrong. Not only was I a victim, I was a hero, a mighty-mite of spunk and derring-do, and beyond just being pitied, I was loved. How to figure such a business? I'd been thrown into hell. I'd been bound and gagged and given up for dead, and one month later I was everybody's darling. It was enough to fry your brain, to sizzle the boogers in your snout. America was at my feet, and with a man like Master Yehudi pulling the strings, the odds were it would stay there for a long time to come.

I'd outfoxed Uncle Slim, all right, but that didn't change the fact that he was still at large. The cops raided the shack in South Dakota, but other than a mess of fingerprints and a pile of dirty laundry, they found no trace of the culprits. I suppose I should have been scared, on the alert for more trouble, but curiously enough I didn't spend much time worrying. It was too peaceful on Cape Cod for any of that, and now that I'd bested my uncle once, I felt confident I could do it again – quickly forgetting how close a shave I'd just had. But Master Yehudi had promised to protect me, and I believed him. I wasn't going to stroll into any movie theaters on my own anymore, and as long as he was with me wherever I went, what could possibly happen? I thought about the kidnapping less and less as the days wore on. When I did think about it, it was mostly to relive my getaway and to wonder how badly I'd hurt Slim's leg with the car. I hoped it was real bad – that the fender had clipped him in the kneecap, maybe hard enough to shatter the bone. I wanted to have done some serious damage, to know that he'd be walking with a limp for the rest of his life.

But I was too busy with other things to feel much desire to look back. The days were full, crammed with preparations and rehearsals for my new show, and there weren't any blanks on my nighttime dance card either, considering how ready my dick was for dalliance and diversion. Between these nocturnal escapades and my afternoon exertions, I didn't have a spare moment to sulk or feel frightened. I wasn't haunted by Slim, I wasn't bogged down by Mrs Witherspoon's impending marriage. My thoughts were turned to a more immediate problem, and that was enough to keep my hands full: how to remake Walt the Wonder Boy into a theatrical performer, a creature fit for the confines of the indoor stage.

Master Yehudi and I had some mammoth conversations on this subject, but mostly we worked out the new routines by trial and error. Hour after hour, day after day, we'd stand on the windy beach making changes and corrections, struggling to get it right as flocks of seagulls honked and wheeled overhead. We wanted to make every minute count. That was our guiding principle, the object of all our efforts and furious calculations. Out in the boondocks I'd had every show to myself, a good hour's worth of performing time, even more if I'd felt in the mood. But vaudeville was a different brand of beer. I'd be sharing the bill with other acts, and the program had to be boiled down to twenty minutes. We'd lost the lake, we'd lost the impact of the natural sky, we'd lost the grandeur of my hundred-yard sallies and locomotion-struts. Everything had to be squeezed into a smaller space, but once we began to explore the ins and outs of it, we saw that smaller didn't necessarily mean worse. We had some new tools at our disposal, and the trick was to turn them to our advantage. For one thing, we had lights. The master and I both drooled at the thought of them, imagining all the effects they made possible. We could go from pitch black to brightness in the blink of an eye – and vice versa. We could dim the hall to squinty obscurity, throw spots from place to place, manipulate colors, make me appear and disappear at will. And then there was the music, which would sound far more ample and sonorous when played indoors. It wouldn't get lost in the background, it wouldn't be drowned out by traffic and merry-go-round noises. The instruments would become an integral part of the show, and they'd navigate the audience through a sea of shifting emotions, subtly cueing the crowd on how it should react. Strings, horns, woodwinds, drums: we'd have pros down in the pit with us every night, and when we told them what to play, they'd know how to put it across. But best of all, the crowd was going to be more comfortable. Undistracted by the buzzing of flies and the glare of the sun, people would be less prone to talk and lose their concentration. A hush would greet me the moment the curtain went up, and from beginning to end the performance would be controlled, advancing like clockwork from a few simple stunts to the wildest, most heart-stopping finale ever seen on a modern stage.

So we hashed out our ideas, batting it back and forth for a couple of weeks, and eventually we came up with a blueprint. 'Shape and coherence,' the master said. 'Structure, rhythm, and surprise.' We weren't going to give them a random collection of tricks. The act was going to unfold like a story, and little by little we'd build up the tension, leading the audience into bigger and better thrills as we went along, saving the best and most spectacular stunts for last.

The costume couldn't have been more basic: a white shirt open at the collar, loose black trousers, and a pair of white dance slippers on my feet. The white shoes were essential. They had to jump out at you, to create the greatest possible contrast with the brown floor of the stage. With only twenty minutes to work with, there was no time for costume changes or extra entrances and exits. We made the act continuous, to be performed without pause or interruption, but in our minds we broke it down into four parts, and we worked on each part separately, as if each was an act in a play:

Part the First Solo clarinet, trilling a few bars of pastoral fluff. The melody suggests innocence, butterflies, dandelions bobbing in the breeze. The curtain goes up on a bare, brightly lit stage. I come on, and for the first two minutes I act like a know-nothing, a boob with a stick up my ass and pudding for brains. I bump into invisible objects strewn about me, encountering one obstacle after another as the clarinet is joined by a rumbling bassoon. I trip over a stone, I bang my nose against a wall, I catch my finger in a door. I'm the picture of human incompetence, a stumbling nincompoop who can barely stand on the ground – let alone rise above it. At last, after several near misses, I fall flat on my face. The trombone does a dipping glissando, I get some laughs. Reprise. But even clutzier than the first time. Again the sliding trombone, followed by a thumpity-thump on the snare drum, a boom on the kettle drum. This is slapstick heaven, and I'm on a collision course with thin ice. No sooner do I pick myself up and take a step than my foot snags on a roller skate and I fall again. Howls of laughter. I struggle to my feet, tottering about as I shake the cobwebs from my head, and then, just when the audience is beginning to get puzzled, just when it looks like I'm every bit as inept as I seem, I pull the first stunt.

Part the Second It has to look like an accident. I've just tripped again, and as I stagger forward, desperately trying to regain my balance, I reach out my hand and catch hold of something. It's the rung of an invisible ladder, and suddenly I'm hanging in midair – but only for a split second. It all happens so fast, it's hard to tell if I've left my feet or not. Before the audience can figure it out, I release my grip and tumble to the ground. The lights dim, then go off, plunging the hall into darkness. Music plays: mysterious strings, tremulous with wonder and expectation. A moment later, a spotlight is turned on. It wanders left and right, then stops at the place occupied by the ladder. I stand up and begin to look for the invisible rung. When my hands make contact with the ladder again, I pat it gingerly, gaping in astonishment. A thing that isn't there is there. I pat it again, testing to make sure it's steady, and then begin to climb – very cautiously, one agonizing rung at a time. There's no doubt about it now. I'm off the ground, and the tips of my bright white shoes are dangling in the air to prove it. During my ascent, the spotlight expands, dissolving into a soft glow that eventually engulfs the entire stage. I reach the top, look down, and begin to grow frightened. I'm five feet off the ground now, and what the hell am I doing there? The strings vibrate again, underscoring my panic. I begin to climb down, but halfway to the floor I reach out with my hand and come against something solid – a plank jutting into the middle of the air. I'm flabbergasted. I run my fingers over this invisible object, and little by little curiosity gets the better of me. I slide my body around the ladder and crawl onto the plank. It's strong enough to hold my weight. I stand up and begin to walk, slowly crossing the stage at an altitude of three feet. After that, one prop leads to another. The plank becomes a staircase, the staircase becomes a rope, the rope becomes a swing, the swing becomes a slide. For seven minutes I explore these objects, creeping and tiptoeing upon them, gradually gaining confidence as the music swells. It looks as if I'll be able to cavort like this forever. Then, suddenly, I step off a ledge and begin to fall.

Part the Third I'm floating down to the ground with my arms spread, descending as slowly as someone in a dream. Just as I'm about to touch the stage, I stop. Gravity has ceased to count, and there I am, hovering six inches off the ground with no prop to support me. The theater darkens, and a second later I'm enclosed in the beam of a single spotlight. I look down, I look up, I look down again. I wiggle my toes. I turn my left foot this way and that. I turn my right foot this way and that. It's really happened. It's really true that I'm standing on air. A drumroll breaks the silence: loud, insistent, nerve-shattering. It seems to announce terrible risks, an assault on the impossible. I shut my eyes, extend my arms to their fullest, and take a deep breath. This is the exact midpoint of the performance, the moment of moments. With the spotlight still fixed on me, I begin to rise into the air, slowly and inexorably taking myself upward, climbing to a height of seven feet in one smooth heaven-bound soar. I pause at the top, count three long beats in my head, and then open my eyes. Everything turns to magic after that. With the music playing at full throttle, I go through an eight-minute routine of aerial acrobatics, darting in and out of the spotlight as I turn twists and somersaults and full gainers. One contortion flows into another, each stunt is more beautiful than the last. There is no sense of danger anymore. Everything has been turned into pleasure, euphoria, the ecstasy of seeing the laws of nature crumble before your eyes.

Part the Fourth After the final somersault, I glide back to my position at the center of the stage, seven feet off the ground. The music stops. A triple spotlight is thrown on me: one red, one white, one blue. The music starts up again: a stirring of cellos and French horns, loveliness beyond measure. The orchestra is playing 'America the Beautiful', the most cherished, most familiar song of all. When the fourth bar begins, I start to move forward, walking on the air above the heads of the musicians and out into the audience. I keep on walking as the music plays, traveling to the very back of the theater, eyes set before me as necks crane and people stand up from their seats. I reach the wall, turn, and begin to head back, walking in the same slow and stately manner as before. By the time I reach the stage again, the audience is one with me. I have touched them with my grace, let them share in the mystery of my godlike powers. I turn in midair, pause briefly once again, and then float down to the ground as the last notes of the song are played. I spread my arms and smile. And then I bow – just once – and the curtain comes down.

It wasn't too shabby. A trifle bloated at the end, perhaps, but the master wanted 'America the Beautiful' come hell or high water, and I couldn't talk him out of it. The opening pantomime sketch came straight from yours truly, and the master felt so keen about those pratfalls that he got a little carried away. A clown suit would make them even funnier, he said, but I told him no, it was just the opposite. If people expect a joke, you have to work a lot harder to make them laugh. You can't go whole hog from the start; you have to sneak up and goose them. It took me half a day of arguing to win that point, but on other matters I wasn't nearly so persuasive. The bit I worried about most was the end – the part where I had to leave the stage and go off on an aerial tour of the audience. I knew it was a good idea, but I still didn't have total confidence in my loft abilities. If I didn't maintain a height of eight and a half or nine feet, all sorts of problems could arise. People could jump up and swat at my legs, and even a weak, glancing blow would be enough to knock me off course. And what if someone actually grabbed hold of my ankle and wrestled me to the ground? A riot would break out in the theater, I'd wind up getting myself killed. This felt like a definite danger to me, but the master pooh-poohed my nervousness. 'You can do it,' he said. 'You got to twelve feet in Florida last winter, and I can't even remember the last time you dipped under ten. Alabama maybe, but you had a cold that day and your heart wasn't in it. You've gotten better, Walt. Little by little, you've shown improvement in every area. It's going to take some concentration, but nine feet isn't a stretch anymore. It's just another day at the office, a walk around the block and then home. No sweat. One time and you'll be over it. Believe me, son, it's going to go like gangbusters.'

The hardest trick was the ladder jump, and I must have spent as much time on that one as all the others put together. Most of the act was a recombination of turns I already felt comfortable with. The invisible props, the skyward rushes, the midair acrobatics – all those things were old hat to me by then. But the ladder jump was new, and the entire program hinged on my being able to pull it off. It might not sound like a big deal compared to those dramatic flourishes – just three inches off the ground for one tick of the clock – but the difficulty was in the transition, the lightning-fast two-step required to get me from one state to another. From flopping and careening madly about the stage, I had to go straight into liftoff, and it had to be done in one seamless movement, which meant tripping forward, grabbing the rung, and going up at the same time. Six months earlier, I never would have attempted such a thing, but I had made progress on reducing the length of my prelevitation trances. From six or seven seconds at the beginning of my career, I had brought them down to less than one, a nearly simultaneous fusion of thought and deed. But the fact remained that I still lifted off from a standing position. I had always done it that way; it was one of the fundamental tenets of my art, and just to conceive of such a radical change meant rethinking the whole process from top to bottom. But I did it. I did it, by gum, and of all the feats I accomplished as a levitator, this is the one I'm proudest of. Master Yehudi dubbed it the Scattershot Fling, and that's roughly what it felt like: a sensation of being in more than one place at the same time. Falling forward, I'd plant my feet on the ground for a fraction of a second, and then blink. The blink was crucial. It brought back the memory of the trance, and even the smallest vestige of that fibrillating blankness was enough to produce the necessary shift in me. I'd blink and raise my arm, latching my hand onto the unseen rung, and then I'd start going up. It wouldn't have been possible to sustain such a convoluted stunt for very long. Three quarters of a second was the limit, but that was all I needed, and once I perfected the move, it became the turning point of the show, the axis on which everything else revolved.

Three days before we left Cape Cod, the Pierce Arrow was delivered to our door by a man in a white suit. The driver had brought the thing all the way from Wichita, and when he stepped out and pumped the master's hand, grinning and gushing his hearty hellos, I assumed I was looking at the infamous Orville Cox. My first thought was to kick the four-flusher in the shins, but before I could deliver my scout's welcome, Master Yehudi saved me by addressing him as Mr Bigelow. It didn't take long to figure out that he was another one of Mrs Witherspoon's lunkhead admirers. He was a youngish guy of about twenty-four with a round face and a gee-whiz booster's laugh, and every other word that came from his mouth was 'Marion'. She must have done a hell of a snow job to conscript him into running such a long-distance errand for her, but he seemed pleased with himself and oh-so-proud to have done it. It made me want to puke. By the time the master suggested going into the house for a cool drink, I had already turned my back on him and was clomping up the wooden stairs.

I headed straight for the kitchen. Mrs Hawthorne was in there washing the dishes from lunch, her small bony figure perched on a stool beside the sink. 'Hi, Mrs H.,' I said, still churning inside, feeling as if the devil himself were doing handsprings in my head. 'What's for dinner tonight?'

'Flounder, mashed potatoes, and pickled beets,' she said, answering in her curt New England twang.

'Yum. I can't wait to sink my chompers into them beets. Make me a double portion, okay?'

That got a little smile from her. 'No problem, Master Buck,' she said, swiveling around on the stool to look at me. I took three or four steps in her direction, then went in for the kill.

'Good as your cooking is, ma'am,' I said, 'I'll bet you ain't never rustled up a dish half so tasty as this one.'

And then, before she could say another word, I flashed her a big smile, spread my arms, and lifted myself off the ground. I went up slowly, taking myself as high as I could without bumping my head against the ceiling. Once I'd reached the top, I hung there looking down at Mrs Hawthorne, and the shock and consternation that spread across her face were everything I'd hoped for. A choked howl died in her throat; her eyes rolled back into her head; and then she toppled off the stool, fainting onto the floor with a tiny thud.

As it happened, Bigelow and the master were just entering the house at that point, and the thud brought them running into the kitchen. Master Yehudi got there first, bursting through the door in the middle of my descent, but when Bigelow arrived a couple of seconds later, my feet were already touching the ground.

'What's this!' the master said, sizing up the situation in a single glance. He pushed me aside and bent down over Mrs Hawthorne's comatose body. 'What the hell is this!'

'Just a little accident,' I said.

'Accident my foot,' he said, sounding angrier than I'd heard him in months, perhaps years. I suddenly regretted the whole stupid prank. 'Go to your room, you idiot, and don't come out until I tell you. We have company now, and I'll deal with you later.'

I never did get to eat those beets, nor any other of Mrs Hawthorne's dishes for that matter. Once she recovered from her swoon, she promptly picked herself up and marched out the door, vowing never to set foot in our house again. I wasn't around to witness her departure, but that's what the master told me the next morning. At first I thought he was pulling my leg, but when she didn't show up by the middle of the day, I realized I'd scared the poor woman half to death. That's exactly what I'd wanted to do, but now that I'd done it, it didn't seem so funny to me anymore. She never even returned to collect her wages, and though we stayed on for another seventy-two hours ourselves, that was the last we ever saw of her.

Not only did the meals deteriorate, but I suffered a final indignity when Master Yehudi made me clean the house on the morning we packed up and left. I hated to be punished like that – sent off to bed without any supper, consigned to KP duty and household chores – but fume and bitch as I did about it, he was well within his rights. It didn't matter that I was the hottest child star since David loaded up his slingshot and let 'er rip. I had stepped out of line, and before my head swelled to the size of a medicine ball, the master had no choice but to crack down and let me have it.

As for Bigelow, the cause of my temperamental outburst, there isn't much to be said. He hung around for only a few hours, and by late afternoon a taxi came to fetch him – presumably to drive him to the nearest railroad station, where he would begin his long trip back to Kansas. I watched him leave from my second-floor window, despising him for his moronic cheerfulness and the fact that he was a buddy of Orville Cox, the man Mrs Witherspoon had chosen over me and the master. To make matters worse, Master Yehudi was on his best behavior, and it addled my spleen to see how politely he treated that twit of a bank clerk. Not only did he shake his hand, but he entrusted him with delivering his wedding present to the bride-to-be. Just as the cab door was about to close, he placed a large, beautifully wrapped package into the scoundrel's hands. I had no idea what was hidden in the box. The master hadn't told me, and though I fully intended to ask him about it at the first opportunity, so many hours passed before he released me from my prison, I clean forgot to when the moment arrived. As it turned out, seven years went by before I discovered what the gift was.

From Cape Cod we went to Worcester, half a day's drive to the west. It felt good to be traveling in the Pierce Arrow again, ensconced in our leather seats as of yore, and once we headed inland, whatever conflicts we'd been having were left behind like so many discarded candy wrappers, blowing out into the dune grass and the surf. Still, I didn't want to take anything for granted, and just to make sure there was no bad blood between us, I apologized to the master again. 'I done wrong,' I said, 'and I'm sorry,' and just like that the whole business was as stale as yesterday's news.

We holed up in the Cherry Valley Hotel, a dingy hooker's nest two doors down from the Luxor Theatre. That's where I'd been slotted for my first performance, and we rehearsed in that music hall every morning and afternoon for the next four days. The Luxor was a far cry from the grand entertainment palace I'd been hoping for, but it had a stage and curtains and a setup for lights, and the master assured me that the theaters would get better once we hit some of the larger stops on the tour. Worcester was a good quiet place to begin, he said, to familiarize myself with the feel of the stage. I caught on fast, learning my marks and cues without much trouble, but even so there were all sorts of kinks and glitches to be worked on: perfecting the spotlight sequences, coordinating the music with the stunts, choreographing the finale to avoid the balcony that jutted out over half the seats in the orchestra. The master was consumed by a thousand and one details. He tested the curtains with the curtain man, he adjusted the lights with the lighting men, he talked endlessly about music with the musicians. At no small expense, he hired seven of them to join us for the last two days of rehearsals, and he kept scribbling changes and corrections onto their scores until the last minute, desperate to get everything just right. I got a kick out of working with those guys myself. They were a bunch of hacks and has-beens, old-timers who'd started out before I was born, and when you added it up, they must have spent twenty thousand nights in variety theaters and played for a hundred thousand different acts. Those geezers had seen everything, and yet the first time I came out and did my stuff for them, all hell broke loose. The drummer passed out, the bassoonist dropped his bassoon, the trombonist sputtered and went sour. It felt like a good sign to me. If I could impress those hard-boiled cynics, just think what I'd do when I got in front of a regular audience.

The hotel was conveniently located, but the nights in that fleabag almost did me in. With all the whores walking up and down the stairs and sauntering through the halls, my dick throbbed like a broken bone and gave me no rest. The master and I shared a double room, and I'd have to wait until I heard him snoring in the next bed before I dared to beat my meat. The buildup could be interminable. He liked to talk in the dark, discussing small points about that day's rehearsal, and rather than attend to the matter at hand (which was also in my hand), I'd have to think of polite answers to his questions. With every minute that passed, the agony became that much more crushing, that much more painful to bear. When he finally drifted off, I'd reach down and remove one of my dirty socks. That was my cum-catcher, and I'd hold it in my left hand while I got to work with my right, squirting jism into the bunched-up folds of cotton. After so much delay, it never took more than one or two tugs. I'd moan forth a quiet hymn of thanks and try to fall asleep, but once was rarely enough for me in those days. A hooker would burst out laughing in the hall, a bedspring would creak in an upstairs room, and my head would fill with every kind of fleshy obscenity. Before I knew it, my cock would stiffen, and I'd be at it again.

One night, I must have made too much noise. It was the eve of the Worcester performance, and I was winging my way toward another sockful of bliss when the master suddenly woke up. Talk about a jolt to the nerves. When his voice broke through the darkness, it felt like the chandelier had landed on my head.

'What's the trouble, Walt?'

I dropped my unit as if it had sprouted thorns. 'Trouble?' I said. 'What do you mean trouble?'

'I mean that noise. That jostling and shaking and squeaking. That ruckus coming from your bed.'

'I got an itch. It's a doozy of an itch, master, and if I don't scratch hard, it'll never go away.'

'It's an itch, all right. An itch that starts in the loins and ends up all over the sheets. Give it a rest, kid. You'll tire yourself out, and a tuckered showman is a sloppy showman.'

'I ain't tuckered. I'm fit as a fiddle and raring to go.'

'For the time being maybe. But wanking takes its toll, and before long you'll start to feel the strain. I don't need to tell you what a precious thing a pecker is. You get too fond of it, though, and it's liable to turn into a stick of dynamite. Preserve the bindu, Walt. Save it for when it really counts.'

'Preserve the what?'

'The bindu. An Indian term for the stuff of life.'

'You mean the stickum?'

'That's right, the stickum. Or whatever else you want to call it. There must be a hundred names, but they all mean the same thing.'

'I like bindu. It beats them others hands down.'

'Just so long as you don't beat yourself down, little man. We have some big days and nights ahead of us, and you're going to need every ounce of strength you've got.'

None of it mattered. Tired or not tired, preserving the bindu or producing it in buckets, I broke from the gate like a bat out of hell. We stunned them in Worcester. We wowed them in Springfield. They dropped their drawers in Bridgeport. Even the mishap in New Haven proved to be a blessing in disguise, since it buttoned the lips of the doubters once and for all. With so much talk about me circulating in the air, I suppose it was natural that some people should begin to suspect fraud. They believed the world was set up in a certain way, and there was no place in it for a person of my talents. To do what I could do upset all the rules. It contradicted science, overturned logic and common sense, made mincemeat of a hundred theories, and rather than change the rules to accommodate my act, the big shots and professors decided I was cheating. The newspapers were full of that stuff in every town we went to: debates and arguments, charges and countercharges, all the pros and cons you could count. The master took no part in it. He stood outside the fray, grinning happily as the box-office receipts rolled in, and when reporters pressed him to give a comment, his answer was always the same: 'Come to the theater and judge for yourself.'

After two or three weeks of mounting controversy, things finally came to a head in New Haven. I hadn't forgotten that this was the home of Yale College – and that if not for the villainies and outrages committed in Kansas two years before, it also would have been my brother Aesop's home. It saddened me to be there, and all day prior to the performance I sat in the hotel room with a heavy heart, remembering the crazy times we'd lived through together and thinking about what a great man he would have become. When we finally left for the theater at six o'clock, I was an emotional wreck, and try as I did to get my bearings, I turned in the flattest performance of my career. My timing was off, I wobbled during my spins, and my loft was a disgrace. When the moment came to crank it up and fly out over the heads of the audience, the dreaded bomb finally went off. I couldn't maintain altitude. By sheer will-power I'd managed to lift myself to seven and a half feet, but that was the best I could do, and I started the finale with grave misgivings, knowing that a tall person with only moderate reach could nab me without bothering to jump. After that, things went from bad to worse. Halfway out over the orchestra seats, I decided to make a last gallant effort to see if I couldn't get myself a little higher. I wasn't hoping for miracles – just a little breathing room, maybe six or eight more inches. I paused for a moment to regroup, hovering in place as I shut my eyes and concentrated on my task, but once I started moving again, my altitude was just as dismal as before. Not only was I not going up, but after a few seconds I realized that I was actually beginning to sink. It happened slowly, ever so slowly, an inch or two for every yard I went forward, and yet the decline was irreversible – like air leaking out of a balloon. By the time I reached the back rows, I was down to six feet, a sitting duck for even the shortest dwarf. And then the fun began. A bald-headed goon in a red blazer shot out of his seat and whacked me on the heel of my left foot. I spun out from the blow, tilting like a lopsided parade float, and before I could right my balance, someone else batted my other foot. That second bump clinched it. I tumbled out of the air like a dead sparrow and landed forehead-first on the rim of a metal chair back. The impact was so sudden and so fierce, it knocked me out cold.

I missed the bedlam that followed, but by all accounts it was a honey of a rumble: nine hundred people shouting and jumping every which way, an outbreak of mass hysterics that spread through the hall like a brushfire. Unconscious though I might have been, my fall had proved one thing, and it had proved it beyond a shadow of a doubt for all time. The act was real. There were no invisible wires attached to my limbs, no helium bubbles hidden under my clothes, no silent engines strapped around my waist. One by one, members of the audience passed my dormant body around the theater, groping and pinching me with their curious fingers as if I were some kind of medical specimen. They stripped off my costume, they looked inside my mouth, they spread my cheeks and peered into my bunghole, and not one of them found a damned thing that God himself hadn't put there. Meanwhile, the master had sprung from his position backstage and was fighting his way toward me. By the time he'd leapfrogged over nineteen rows of customers and wrested me from the last pair of arms, the verdict was unanimous. Walt the Wonder Boy was the real goods. The act was on the up-and-up, and what you saw was what you got, amen.

The first of the headaches came that night. Considering how I'd crashlanded on the chair back, it was no surprise that I should have felt some twinges and aftereffects. But this pain was monstrous – a horrific jackhammer assault, an endless volley of hailstones pounding against the inner walls of my skull – and it woke me from a deep sleep in the middle of the night. The master and I had connecting rooms with a bathroom in between, and once I'd found the courage to pry myself out of bed, I staggered toward the bathroom, praying I'd find some aspirins in the medicine cabinet. I was so woozy and distracted by the pain, I didn't notice that the bathroom light was already on. Or, if I did notice, I didn't pause to think about why that light should be burning at three o'clock in the morning. As I soon found out, I wasn't the only person who had left his bed at that ungodly hour. When I opened the door and stepped into the dazzling white-tiled room, I nearly stumbled into Master Yehudi. Dressed in his lavender silk pajamas, he was clutching the sink with his two hands and doubled over in pain, gasping and retching as if his insides had caught fire. The siege lasted for another twenty or thirty seconds, and it was such a terrible thing to witness, I almost forgot I was in pain myself.

Once he saw that I was there, he did everything he could to cover up what had just happened. He turned his grimaces into forced, histrionic smiles; he straightened up and threw back his shoulders; he slicked down his hair with his palms. I wanted to tell him that he should stop pretending, that I was on to his secret now, but my own pain was so bad that I couldn't summon the words to do it. He asked me why I wasn't asleep, and when he learned about my headache, he took charge of the situation by rushing about and playing doctor: shaking aspirins out of the bottle, filling up a glass with water, examining the bump on my forehead. He talked so much during these ministrations, I couldn't get a word in edgewise.

'We're quite a pair, aren't we?' he said, as he carried me to my room and tucked me into bed. 'First you take a nosedive and clunk your bean, and then I gorge myself on rancid cherrystones. I should learn to lay off those buggers. Every time I eat them, I come down with the goddamn bends.'

It wasn't a bad story, especially for one he'd made up on the spur of the moment, but it didn't fool me. No matter how much I wanted to believe him, I wasn't fooled for a second.

By the middle of the next afternoon, the worst of the headache was gone. A dull throbbing persisted near my left temple, but it wasn't enough to keep me off my feet. Since the bump was on the right side of my forehead, it would have made more sense for the tender spot to be there, but I was no expert on these matters and didn't dwell on the discrepancy. All I cared about was that I was feeling better, that the pain was subsiding, and that I would be ready for the next performance.

What worries I did have were centered around the master's condition – or whatever it was that had caused the gruesome attack I'd seen in the bathroom. The truth couldn't be hidden anymore. His sham had been exposed, and yet because he seemed so much better the next morning, I didn't dare to mention it. My nerve simply failed me, and I couldn't bring myself to open my mouth. I'm not proud of how I acted, but the thought that the master had been struck by some terrible disease was too frightening even to consider. Rather than jump to morbid conclusions, I let him cow me into accepting his version of the incident. Cherrystone clams my eye. He'd clammed up on me all right, and now that I'd seen what I shouldn't have seen, he'd make sure I'd never see it again. I could count on him for that kind of performance. He'd gut it out, he'd put up a tough front, and little by little I'd begin to think I hadn't seen it after all. Not because I would believe such a lie – but because I'd be too afraid not to.

From New Haven we went to Providence; from Providence to Boston; from Boston to Albany; from Albany to Syracuse; from Syracuse to Buffalo. I remember all those stops, all those theaters and hotels, all the performances I gave, everything about everything. It was late summer, early fall. Little by little, the trees lost their greenness. The world turned red and yellow and orange and brown, and everywhere we went the roads were lined with the strange spectacle of mutating color. The master and I were on a roll now, and it seemed that nothing could stop us anymore. I played to packed houses in every city. Not only did the shows sell out, but hundreds more were turned away at the box office every night. Scalpers did a bang-up business, peddling tickets for three, four, even five times their face value, and every time we pulled up in front of a new hotel, there would be a crowd of people waiting at the entrance, desperate fans who'd stood for hours in the rain and frost just to get a glimpse of me.

My fellow performers were a little envious, I think, but the truth was they'd never had it so good. When the mobs poured in to see my act, they saw the other acts, too, and that meant money in all our pockets. Over the course of those weeks and months, I topped bills that included every kind of wigged-out entertainment. Comics, jugglers, falsetto singers, birdcallers, midget jazz bands, dancing monkeys – they all took their spills and did their turns before I came on. I liked watching that loopy stuff, and I did my best to make pals backstage with anyone who seemed friendly, but the master wasn't too keen on having me mix with my cohorts. He was standoffish with most of them and urged me to follow his example. 'You're the star,' he'd whisper. 'Act like it. You don't have to give those chumps the time of day.' It was a small bone of contention between us, but I figured I'd be on the vaudeville circuit for years to come, and I saw no point in making enemies when I didn't have to. Unbeknownst to me, however, the master had been hatching his own plans for our future, and by the end of September he was already talking out loud about a one-man spring tour. That was how it was with Master Yehudi: the better things went for us, the higher he set his sights. The current tour wouldn't be over until Christmas, and yet he couldn't resist looking beyond it to something even more spectacular. The first time he mentioned it to me, I gulped at the pure ballsiness of the proposition. The idea was to work our way east from San Francisco to New York, playing the ten or twelve biggest cities for special command performances. We'd book the shows in indoor arenas and football stadiums like Madison Square Garden and Soldier's Field, and no crowd would ever be smaller than fifteen thousand. 'A triumphal march across America' was how he described it, and by the time he finished his sales pitch, my heart was pounding four times faster than normal. Christ, could that man talk. His mouth was one of the great huckster machines of all time, and once he got it going full tilt, the dreams poured out of it like smoke rushing through a chimney.

'Shit, boss,' I said. 'If you can swing a tour like that, we'll rake in millions.'

'I'll swing it all right,' he said. 'Just keep up the good work, and it's in the bag. That's all it takes, Walt. You keep on doing what you've been doing, and Rawley's March is a sure thing.'

Meanwhile, we were gearing up for my first theatrical performance in New York. We wouldn't be there until Thanksgiving weekend, still a long way down the road, but we both knew it was going to be the highlight of the season, the pinnacle of my career so far. Just thinking about it was enough to make me dizzy. Add ten Bostons to ten Philadelphias, and they wouldn't equal one New York. Put eighty-six performances in Buffalo together with ninety-three in Trenton, and the sum wouldn't amount to a minute's worth of stage time in the Big Apple. New York was top banana, ground zero on the show business map, and no matter how many raves I got in other cities, I wouldn't be anything until I took my act to Broadway and let them see what I could do. That's why the master had booked New York for so late in the tour. He wanted me to be an old hand by the time we got there, a seasoned, battle-tested soldier who knew what bullets tasted like and could roll with any punch. I became that vet with time to spare. By October twelfth, I'd done forty-four variety theater gigs, and I felt ready, as lean and mean as I'd ever be, and yet we still had more than a month to go. I had never endured such suspense. New York ate at me day and night, and after a while I didn't think I could stand it anymore.

We played Richmond on the thirteenth and fourteenth, Baltimore on the fifteenth and sixteenth, and then headed for Scranton, Pennsylvania. I turned in a good performance there, certainly up to snuff and no worse than any of the others, but immediately upon finishing the show, just as I took my bow and the curtain came down, I passed out and fell to the floor. I had felt perfectly fine until that moment, going through my aerial turns with all the ease and aplomb I was accustomed to, but as soon as my feet touched the stage for the last time, I felt as if I weighed ten thousand pounds. I held my position just long enough for the smile, the bow, and the closing of the curtain, and then my knees buckled, my back gave way, and my body was thrust to the ground. When I opened my eyes in the dressing room five minutes later, I felt a little light-headed, but it seemed that the crisis had passed. But then I stood up, and it was precisely then that the headache returned, ripping through me with a blast of savage, blinding pain. I tried to take a step, but the world was swimming, undulating like a belly dancer in a funhouse mirror, and I couldn't see where I was going. By the time I took a second step, I had already lost my balance.

If the master hadn't been there to catch me, I would have fallen flat on my face again.

Neither one of us was ready to panic at that point. The headache and dizziness could have been caused by any number of things – fatigue, a touch of the flu, an ear infection – but just to play it safe, the master called Wilkes-Barre and canceled my performance for the following night. I slept soundly in the Scranton hotel, and by the next morning I was well again, utterly free of pain and discomfort. My recovery defied all logic, but we both accepted it as one of those things, a fluke that didn't deserve to be second-guessed. We set off for Pittsburgh in good spirits, glad of the day off, and once we got there and checked into the hotel, we actually took in a movie together to celebrate my return to form. The next night, however, when I did my show at the Fosberg Theatre, it was Scranton all over again. I turned in a jewel of a performance, and just as the curtain came down and the act was done, I collapsed. The headache started up again immediately after I opened my eyes, and this time it didn't go away in one night. When I woke up the next morning, the daggers were still lodged in my skull, and they didn't leave until four o'clock in the afternoon – several hours after Master Yehudi had been forced to cancel that night's performance.

Everything pointed to the knock on the head I'd received in New Haven. That was the most likely cause of my problem, and yet if I'd been walking around with a concussion for the past few weeks, it must have been the mildest concussion in medical history. How else to account for the odd and unsettling fact that as long as I kept my feet on the ground, I remained in good health? The headaches and dizzy spells came only after I performed, and if the link between levitating and my new condition was as definite as it seemed, then the master wondered if my brain hadn't been jarred in such a way as to put undue pressure on my cranial arteries every time I went up into the air, which in turn caused the excruciating attacks when I came down. He wanted to put me in the hospital and have some X-rays taken of my skull. 'Why chance it?' he said. 'We've hit the flat part of the tour, and a week or ten days off might be just what you need. They'll do some tests, probe around in your neurological gearbox, and maybe they'll figure out what this cursed thing is.'

'No way,' I said. 'I ain't going into no hospital.'

'The only cure for a concussion is rest. If that's what it is, then you don't have any choice.'

'Forget it. I'd sooner work on a chain gang than park my butt in one of them joints.'

'Think of the nurses, Walt. All those sweet little gals in white uniforms. You'll have a dozen honeybuns doting on you night and day. If you play it smart, you might even see some action.'

'You can't tempt me. Nobody's going to turn me into a sucker. We're signed up to do some shows, and I aim to do them – even if it kills me.'

'Reading and Altoona aren't where the action is, son. We can skip Elmira and Binghampton, and it won't make a pea-shooter's worth of difference. I'm thinking about New York, and I know you are, too. That's the one you've got to be in shape for.'

'My head don't hurt when I do the act. That's the bottom line, chief. As long as I can go on, I gotta go on. Who cares if I smart some afterwards? I can live with pain. Life's a pain anyway, and the only good thing about it is when I'm up on stage doing my act.'

'Problem is, the act is wiping you out. You keep coming down with those headaches, and you won't be Walt the Wonder Boy much longer. I'll have to change your name to Mr Vertigo.'

'Mr Who?'

'Mr Dizzy-in-the-Head. Mr Fear-of-Heights.'

'I ain't afraid of nothing. You know that.'

'You're all guts, kid, and I love you for it. But there comes a time in every levitator's career when the air is fraught with peril, and I'm afraid we've come to that time now.'

We kept on jawing about these things for the next hour, and in the end I wore him down enough to give me one last chance. That was the bargain. I'd play Reading the next night, and headache or no headache, if I was well enough to go on in Altoona the night after that, I would perform as scheduled. It was a crazy thing to push for, but that second attack had scared me stiff, and I was afraid it meant I was losing my touch. What if the headaches were only the first step? I figured my only hope was to fight my way through it, to go on performing until I got better or couldn't take it anymore – and then see what happened. I was so unhinged, I really didn't care if my brain burst into a thousand pieces. Better to be dead than to lose my powers, I told myself. If I couldn't be Walt the Wonder Boy, I didn't want to be anyone.

Reading turned out badly, much worse than I had feared. Not only did my gamble not pay off, but the results were even more catastrophic than before. I did the show and collapsed, just as I'd known I would, but this time I didn't wake up in the dressing room. Two stagehands had to carry me across the street to the hotel, and when I opened my eyes fifteen or twenty minutes later, I didn't even have to stand up to feel the pain. The instant the light hit my pupils, the agony began. A hundred trolley cars jumped the rails and converged on a spot behind my left temple; airplanes crashed there; trucks collided there; and then two little green gremlins picked up hammers and started driving stakes through my eyeballs. I writhed about on the bed, howling for someone to put me out of my misery, and by the time the master summoned the hotel quack to come upstairs and administer a hypo, I was fit to be tied, a toboggan of flames twisting and plunging through the valley of the shadow of death.

I woke up in a Philadelphia hospital ten hours later, and for the next twelve days I didn't budge. The headache continued for another forty-eight hours, and they kept me under such heavy sedation that I can't remember anything until the third day, when I finally woke up again and discovered that the pain was gone. After that, they subjected me to all kinds of examinations and procedures. Their curiosity was inexhaustible, and once they got started they didn't leave me alone. Every hour on the hour a different doctor would walk into the room and put me through my paces. My knees were tapped with hammers, cookie-cutters were rolled over my skin, flashlights were shone in my eyes; I gave them piss and blood and shit; they listened to my heart and looked into my ears; they X-rayed me from conk to toe. There was nothing to live for anymore except science, and those boys in the white coats did a thorough job of it. Within a day or two they turned me into a quivering naked germ, a microbe trapped in a maze of needles, stethoscopes, and tongue depressors. If the nurses had been good to look at, there might have been some relief, but the ones I got were all old and ugly, with fat behinds and hair on their chins. I'd never come across such a crew of dog-show contestants, and whenever one of them came in to take my temperature or read my chart, I'd shut my eyes and pretend I was asleep.

Master Yehudi sat by my side throughout this ordeal. The press had got wind of my whereabouts, and for the first week or so the papers were full of updates about my condition. The master read these articles out loud to me every day. I found some comfort in the hullaballoo while I was listening, but the moment he stopped reading, boredom and cussedness would close in on me again. Then the New York stock market crashed, and I got pushed off the front pages. I wasn't paying much attention, but I figured the crisis was only temporary, and once that Black Tuesday business was over I'd be back in the headlines where I belonged. All those stories about people jumping out of windows and shooting themselves in the head struck me as tabloid flimflam, and I shrugged them off like so many fairy tales. The only thing I cared about was getting the show back on the road. My headache was gone and I felt terrific, one-hundred-percent normal. When I opened my eyes in the morning and saw Master Yehudi sitting by my bed, I would begin the day by asking the same question I'd asked the day before: When do I get out of here? And every day he would give me the same answer: As soon as the test results are in.

When they did come in, I couldn't have been more pleased. After all that rigmarole of pricking and poking, all those tubes and suction cups and rubber gloves, the doctors couldn't find a thing wrong with me. No concussion, no brain tumor, no blood disease, no inner-ear imbalance, no lumps, no mumps, no bumps. They gave me a clean bill of health and declared me the fittest specimen of fourteen-year-old manhood they'd ever seen. As far as the headaches and dizziness went, they couldn't determine the precise cause. It might have been a bug that had already passed through my system. It might have been something I'd eaten. Whatever it was, it wasn't there anymore, and if by chance it *was* there, it was too small to be detected – not even by the strongest microscope on the planet.

'Hot diggity,' I said, when the master broke the news to me. 'Hot diggity dog.'

We were alone in my room on the fourth floor, sitting side by side on the edge of the bed. It was early morning, and the light was pouring in on us through the slats of the venetian blinds. For three or four seconds, I felt as happy as I've ever been in my life. I felt so happy I wanted to scream.

'Not so fast, son,' the master said. 'I haven't finished yet.'

'Fast? Fast's the name of the game, boss. The faster the better. We've already missed eight shows, and the sooner we pack up and get me out of here, the sooner we get to where we're going. Which city we booked in next? If it ain't too far, we might even make it by curtain time.'

The master took hold of one of my hands and squeezed. 'Calm down, Walt. Take a deep breath, close your eyes, and listen to what I have to say.'

It didn't sound like a joke, so I did what he asked and tried to sit still.

'Good.' He spoke that one word and stopped. There was a long pause before he spoke again, and in that interval of darkness and silence, I knew that something awful was about to happen. 'There aren't going to be any more shows,' he said at last. 'We're all washed up, kid. Walt the Wonder Boy is kaput.'

'Don't josh me, master,' I said, opening my eyes and looking at his glum, determined face. I kept waiting for him to throw me a wink and burst out laughing, but he just sat there gazing at me with those dark eyes of his. If anything, his expression grew even sadder.

'I wouldn't tease at a moment like this,' he said. 'We've come to the end of the line, and there's not a fucking thing we can do about it.'

'But the docs just gave me the thumbs up. I'm healthy as a horse.'

'That's the trouble. There's nothing wrong with you – which means there's nothing to be cured. Not with rest, not with medicine, not with exercise. You're perfectly well, and because you're well, your career is over.'

'That's crazy talk, master. It don't make a bit of sense.'

'I've heard about cases like yours before. They're very rare. The literature speaks of only two of them, and they're separated in time by hundreds of years. A Czech levitator in the early nineteenth century had what you have, and before that there was Antoine Dubois, a Frenchman who was active during the reign of Louis the Fourteenth. As far as I know, those are the only two recorded cases. You're the third, Walt. In all the annals of levitation, you're just the third one to confront this problem.'

'I still don't know what you're talking about.'

'Puberty, Walt, that's what. Adolescence. The bodily changes that turn a boy into a man.'

'You mean my boners and such? My curly hairs and the crack in my voice?'

'Just so. All the natural transformations.'

'Maybe I've been whacking off too much. What if I stopped that tomfoolery? You know, preserved the bindu a little more. Do you think that would help?'

'I doubt it. There's only one cure for your condition, but I wouldn't dream of inflicting it on you. I've already put you through enough.'

'I don't care. If there's a way to fix it, then that's what we've got to do.'

'I'm talking about castration, Walt. You cut off your balls, and then maybe there's a chance.'

'Did you say *maybe*?'

'Nothing's guaranteed. The Frenchman did it, and he went on levitating until he was sixty-four. The Czech did it, and it didn't do an ounce of good. The mutilation went for naught, and two months later he jumped off the Charles Bridge and killed himself.'

'I don't know what to say.'

'Of course you don't. If I were in your shoes, I wouldn't know what to say either. That's why I'm suggesting we pack it in. I don't expect you to do a thing like that. No man could ask that of another man. It wouldn't be human.'

'Well, seeing that the verdict is sort of fuzzy, it wouldn't be too smart to risk it, would it? I mean, if I give up being Walt the Wonder Boy, at least I've got my balls to keep me company. I wouldn't want to be in a position where I wound up losing both.'

'Exactly. Which is why the subject is closed. There's no point in talking about it anymore. We've had a good run, and now it's over. At least you get to quit while you're still on top.'

'But what if the headaches go away?'

'They won't. Believe me they won't.'

'How can you know? Maybe those other guys still got them, but what if I'm different?'

'You're not. It's a permanent condition, and there's no cure for it. Short of taking the risk we've already rejected, the headaches will be with you for the rest of your life. For every minute you spend in the air, you'll be racked with pain for three hours on the ground. And the older you are, the worse that pain will be. It's gravity's revenge, son. We thought we had it licked, but it turns out to be stronger than we are. That's the way it goes. We won for a while, and now we've lost. So be it. If that's what God wants, then we have to bow to his will.'

It was all so sad, so depressing, so futile. I'd struggled to make a success of myself for so long, and now, just when I was about to become one of the immortals of history, I had to turn my back on it and walk away. Master Yehudi swallowed this poison without flinching a muscle. He accepted our fate like a stoic and refused to make a fuss. It was a noble stance, I suppose, but it wasn't in my repertoire to take bad news lying down. Once we'd run out of things to say, I stood up and started kicking the furniture and punching the walls, storming about the room like some nutso shadowboxer. I knocked over a chair, sent the night table clattering to the floor, and cursed my bad luck with vocal chords going at full blast. Wise old man that he was, Master Yehudi did nothing to stop me. Even when a couple of nurses rushed into the room to see what the trouble was, he calmly shooed them out, explaining he would cover any damages in full. He knew how I was built, and he knew that my fury needed a chance to express itself. No bottling up for me; no turning the other cheek for Walt. If the world hit me, I had to hit back.

Fair enough. Master Yehudi was smart to let me carry on like that, and I'm not going to blame him if I acted like a dumbbell and carried it too far. Right in the middle of my outburst, I came up with what had to be my all-time stupidest idea, the howler to end all howlers. Oh, it seemed pretty clever at the time, but that was only because I still couldn't face up to what had happened – and once you deny the facts, you're only asking for trouble. But I was desperate to prove the master wrong, to show him that his theories about my condition were so much flat fizzy water. So, right there in that Philadelphia hospital room, on the third day of November 1929, I made a sudden, last-ditch attempt to resurrect my career. I stopped punching the wall, turned around and faced the master, and then spread my arms and lifted myself off the ground.

'Look!' I shouted at him. 'Take a good look and tell me what you see!'

The master studied me with a dark, mournful expression. 'I see the past,' he said. 'I see Walt the Wonder Boy for the last time. I see someone who's about to be sorry for what he just did.'

'I'm as good as I ever was!' I yelled back at him. 'And that's the goddamned best in the world!'

The master glanced down at his watch. 'Ten seconds,' he said. 'For every second you stay up there, you'll have three minutes of pain. I guarantee it.'

I figured I'd put my point across, so rather than risk another long bout of agony, I decided to come down. And then it happened – just as the master had promised it would. The instant my toes touched the ground, my head cracked open again, exploding with a violence that sucked the daylights out of me and made me see stars. Vomit burst through my windpipe and landed on the wall six feet away. Switchblades opened in my skull, tunneling deep into the center of my brain. I shook, I howled, I fell to the floor, and this time I didn't have the luxury of fainting. I thrashed about like a flounder with a hook in his eye, and when I pleaded for help, imploring the master to call in a doctor to give me a shot, he just shook his head and walked away. 'You'll get over it,' he said. 'In less than an hour, you'll be as good as new.' Then, without offering me a single word of comfort, he quietly straightened up the mess in the room and started packing my bag.

That was the only treatment I deserved. His words had fallen on deaf ears, and that left him with no choice but to back off and let my actions speak for themselves. So the pain spoke to me, and this time I listened. I listened for forty-seven minutes, and by the time class was out, I'd learned everything I needed to know. Talk about a crash course in the ways of the world. Talk about boning up on sorrow. The pain fixed me but good, and when I walked out of the hospital later that morning, my head was more or less screwed on straight again. I knew the facts of life. I knew them in every crevice of my soul and every pore of my skin, and I wasn't about to forget them. The glory days were over. Walt the Wonder Boy was dead, and there wasn't a chance in hell he'd ever show his face again.

We walked back to the master's hotel in silence, wending our way through the city streets like a pair of ghosts. It took ten or fifteen minutes to get there, and when we reached the entrance I couldn't think of anything better to do than stick out my hand and try to say good-bye.

'Well,' I said. 'I guess this is where we part company.'

'Oh?' the master said. 'And why is that?'

'You'll be looking for a new boy now, and there ain't much point in hanging around if I'm just going to be in the way.'

'And why would I look for a new boy?' He seemed genuinely astonished by the suggestion.

'Because I'm a dud, that's why. Because the act is finished, and I ain't no good to you no more.'

'You think I'd drop you like that?'

'Why not? Fair is fair, and if I can't deliver the goods, it's only right for you to start making other plans.'

'I have made plans. I've made a hundred of them, a thousand of them. I've got plans up my sleeves and plans in my socks. My whole body's crawling with plans, and before the itch works me into a frenzy, I want to pluck them out and put them on the table for you.'

'For me?'

'Who else, squirt? But we can't have a serious discussion standing in the doorway, can we? Come on up to the room. We'll order some lunch and get down to brass tacks.'

'I still don't get it.'

'What's to get? We might be out of the levitation business, but that doesn't mean we've closed up shop.'

'You mean we're still partners?'

'Five years is a long time, son. After all we've been through together, I've sort of grown attached. I'm not getting any younger, you know. It wouldn't make sense to start looking for someone else. Not now, not at my age. It took me half a life to find you, and I'm not going to kiss you off because we've had a few setbacks. Like I said, I've got some plans to discuss with you. If you like those plans and want in, you're in. If not, we divide up the money and part ways.'

'The money. Jesus God, I clean forgot about the money.'

'You've had other things on your mind.'

'I've been so low in the dumps, my noodle's been on holiday. So how much we got? What's it tote up to in round figures, boss?'

'Twenty-seven thousand dollars. It's sitting in the hotel safe, and it's all ours free and clear.'

'And here I thought I was down-and-out broke again. It kind of puts things in a different light, don't it? I mean, twenty-seven grand's a nice little booty.'

'Not bad. We could have done worse.'

'So the ship ain't sunk after all.'

'Not by a long shot. We did okay for ourselves. And with hard times coming, we'll be pretty snug. Dry and warm in our little boat, we'll sail the seas of adversity a lot better than most.'

'Aye aye, sir.'

'That's it, mate. All aboard. As soon as the wind is up, we'll lift anchor – and with a heave and a ho we'll be off!'

I would have traveled to the ends of the earth with him. By boat, by bicycle, by crawling on my belly – it didn't matter what means of transportation we used. I just wanted to be where he was and to go where he went. Until that conversation in front of the hotel, I thought I'd lost everything. Not only my career, not only my life, but my master as well. I assumed he was finished with me, that he'd kick me out and never give it a second thought, but now I knew different. I wasn't just a paycheck to him. I wasn't just a flying machine with a rusty engine and damaged wings. For better or worse, we were booked for the duration, and that counted more to me than all the seats in all the theaters and football stadiums put together. I'm not saying that things weren't black, but they weren't half as black as they could have been. Master Yehudi was still with me, and not only was he with me, he was carrying a pocketful of matches to light the way.

So we went upstairs and ate our lunch. I don't know about a thousand plans, but he certainly had three or four of them, and he'd thought each one through pretty carefully. The guy just wouldn't quit. Five years of hard work had flown out of the window, decades of scheming and preparation had turned to dust overnight, and there he was bubbling over with new ideas, plotting our next move as if everything still lay before us. They don't make them like that anymore. Master Yehudi was the last of a breed, and I've never run across the likes of him since: a man who felt perfectly at home in the jungle. He might not have been the king, but he understood its laws better than anyone else. Bash him in the gut, spit in his face, break his heart, and he'd bounce right back, ready to take on all comers. Never say die. He didn't just live by that motto, he was the man who invented it.

The first plan was the simplest. We'd move to New York and live like regular people. I'd go to school and get a good education, he'd start up a business and make money, and we'd both live happily ever after. I didn't say a word when he finished, so he passed on to the next one. We'd go out on tour, he said, giving lectures at colleges, churches, and ladies' garden clubs on the art of levitation. There'd be a big demand for us, at least for the next six months or so, and why not continue to cash in on Walt the Wonder Boy until the last lingering bits of my fame had dried up? I didn't like that one either, so he shrugged and moved on to the next. We'd pack up our belongings, he said, get into the car, and drive out to Hollywood. I'd start a new career as a movie actor, and he'd be my agent and manager. What with all the notices I'd had from the act, it wouldn't be hard to swing me a tryout. I was already a big name, and given my flair for slapstick, I'd probably land on my feet in no time.

'Ah,' I said. 'Now you're talking.'

'I figured you'd go for it,' the master said, leaning back in his chair and lighting up a fat Cuban cigar. 'That's why I saved it for last.'

And just like that, we were off to the races again.

We checked out of the hotel early the next morning, and by eight o'clock we were on the road, heading west to a new life in the sunny hills of Tinseltown. It was a long, grueling drive back in those days. There were no superhighways or Howard Johnsons, no six-lane bowling alleys stretching back and forth between coasts, and you had to twist your way through every little town and hamlet, following whatever road would take you in the right direction. If you got stuck behind a farmer hauling a load of hay with a Model-T tractor, that was your tough luck. If they were digging up a road somewhere, you'd have to turn around and find another road, and more often than not that meant going hours out of your way. Those were the rules of the game back then, but I can't say I was perturbed by the slow going. I was just a passenger, and if I felt like dozing off for an hour or two in the backseat, there was nothing to stop me. A few times, when we hit a particularly deserted stretch of road, the master let me take over at the wheel, but that didn't happen often, and he wound up doing ninety-eight percent of the driving. It was a hypnotic sort of experience for him, and after five or six days he fell into a wistful, ruminating state of mind, more and more lost in his own thoughts as we pushed toward the middle of the country. We were back in the land of big skies and flat, dreary expanses, and the all-enveloping air seemed to drain some of the enthusiasm out of him. Maybe he was thinking about Mrs Witherspoon, or maybe some other person from his past had come back to haunt him, but more than likely he was pondering questions about life and death, the big scary stuff that worms its way into your head when there's nothing to distract you. Why am I here? Where am I going? What happens to me after I've drawn my last breath? These are weighty subjects, I know, but after mulling over the master's actions on that trip for more than half a century, I believe I know whereof I speak. One conversation stands out in memory, and if I'm not wrong in how I interpreted what he said, it shows the sorts of things that were beginning to prey on his spirit. We were somewhere in Texas, a little past Fort Worth, I think, and I was jabbering on to him in that breezy, boastful way of mine, talking for no other reason than to hear myself talk.

'California,' I said. 'It never snows there, and you can swim in the ocean all year round. From what folks say, it's the next best thing to paradise. Makes Florida look like a muggy swamp by comparison.'

'No place is perfect, kid,' the master said. 'Don't forget the earthquakes and the mudslides and the droughts. They can go for years without rain there, and when that happens, the whole state turns into a tinderbox. Your house can burn down in less time than it takes to flip an egg.'

'Don't worry about that. Six months from now, we'll be living in a stone castle. That stuff can't burn – but just to play it safe, we'll have our own fire department on the premises. I'm telling you, boss, the flicks and me was made for each other. I'm going to rake in so much dough, we'll have to open a new bank. The Rawley Savings and Loan, with national headquarters on Sunset Boulevard. You watch and see. In no time at all, I'm going to be a star.'

'If everything goes well, you'll be able to earn your crust of bread. That's the important thing. It's not as if I'm going to be around forever, and I want to make sure you can fend for yourself. It doesn't matter how you do it. Actor, cameraman, messenger boy – one trade's as good as another. I just need to know there'll be a future for you after I'm gone.'

'That's old man talk, master. You ain't even fifty yet.'

'Forty-six. Where I come from, that's pretty long in the tooth.'

'Swizzle sticks. You get out in that California sun, it'll add ten years to your life the first day.'

'Maybe so. But even if it does, I still have more years behind me than in front of me. It's simple mathematics, Walt, and it can't do us any harm to prepare for what's ahead.'

We switched onto another subject after that, or maybe we just stopped talking altogether, but those dark little comments of his loomed larger and larger to me as the days dragged on. For a man who worked so hard at hiding his feelings, the master's words were tantamount to a confession. I'd never heard him open up like that before, and even though he couched it in a language of *what ifs* and *what thens*, I wasn't so stupid as to ignore the message buried between the lines. My thoughts went back to the stomach-clutching scene in the New Haven hotel. If I hadn't been so bogged down with my own troubles since then, I would have been more vigilant. Now, with nothing better to do than stare out the window and count the days until we got to California, I resolved to watch his every move. I wasn't going to be a coward this time. If I caught him grimacing or grabbing his stomach again, I was going to speak up and call his bluff – and hustle him to the first doctor I could find.

He must have noticed my worry, for not long after that conversation, he clamped down on the gloom-and-doom talk and started whistling a different song. By the time we left Texas and crossed into New Mexico, he seemed to perk up considerably, and alert as I was for signs of trouble, I couldn't detect a single one – not even the smallest hint. Little by little, he managed to pull the wool over my eyes again, and if not for what happened seven or eight hundred miles down the road, it would have been months before I suspected the truth, perhaps even years. Such was the master's power. No one could match him in a battle of wits, and every time I tried, I wound up feeling like a horse's ass. He was so much quicker than I was, so much defter and more experienced, he could fake me out of my pants before I even put them on. There was never any contest. Master Yehudi always won, and he went on winning to the bitter end.

The most tedious part of the trip began. We spent days riding through New Mexico and Arizona, and after a while it felt like we were the only people left in the world. The master was fond of the desert, however, and once we entered that barren landscape of rocks and cacti, he kept pointing out curious geological formations and delivering little lectures on the incalculable age of the earth. To be perfectly honest, it left me pretty cold. I didn't want to spoil the master's fun, so I kept my mouth shut and pretended to listen, but after four thousand buttes and six hundred canyons, I'd had enough of the scenic tour to last me a lifetime.

'If this is God's country,' I finally said, 'then God can have it.'

'Don't let it get you down,' the master said. 'It goes on forever out here, and counting the miles won't shorten the trip. If you want to get to California, this is the road we have to take.'

'I know that. But just because I put up with it don't mean I have to like it.'

'You might as well try. The time will go faster that way.'

'I hate to be a party pooper, sir, but this beauty stuff's a great big ho-hum. I mean, who cares if a place looks crummy or not? As long as it's got some people in it, it's bound to be interesting. Subtract the people, and what's left? Emptiness, that's what. And emptiness don't do a thing for me but lower my blood pressure and make my eyelids droop.'

'Then close your eyes and get some sleep, and I'll commune with nature myself. Don't fret, little man. It won't be long now. Before you know it, you'll have all the people you want.'

The darkest day of my life dawned in western Arizona on November sixteenth. It was a bone-dry morning like all the others, and by ten o'clock we were crossing the California border to begin our glide through the Mojave toward the coast. I let out a little whoop of celebration when we passed that milestone and then settled in for the last leg of the journey. The master was clipping along at a nice speed, and we figured we'd make it to Los Angeles in time for dinner. I remember arguing in favor of a swank restaurant for our first night in town. Maybe we'd run into Buster Keaton or Harold Lloyd, I said, and wouldn't that be a thrill, huh? Imagine shaking hands with those guys over a mound of baked Alaska in some posh supper club. If they were in the mood for it, maybe we could get into a pie fight and tear the joint apart. The master was just beginning to laugh at my description of this screwy scene when I looked up and saw something on the road in front of us. 'What's that?' I said. 'What's what?' the master said. And a couple of moments later, we were running for our lives.

The *what* was a gang of four men spread out across the narrow turnpike. They were standing in a row – two, three hundred yards up ahead – and at first it was tough to make them out. What with the glare from the sun and the heat rising off the ground, they looked like specters from another planet, shimmering bodies made of light and thin air. Fifty yards closer, and I could see that their hands were raised over their heads, as if they were signaling us to stop. At that point I took them for a crew of road workers, and even when we got still closer and I saw that they had handkerchiefs over their faces, I didn't think twice about it. It's dusty out here, I said to myself, and when the wind blows a man needs some protection. But then we were sixty or seventy yards away, and suddenly I could see that all four of them were holding shiny metal objects in their upraised hands. Just when I realized they were guns, the master slammed on the brakes, skidded to a stop, and threw the car into reverse. Neither one of us said a word. Gas pedal to the floor, we backed up with the engine whining and the chassis shaking. The four desperadoes took off after us, running up the road as their gun barrels glinted in the light. Master Yehudi had turned his head in the other direction to look through the rear window, and he couldn't see what I saw, but as I watched the men gaining ground on us, I noticed that one of them ran with a limp. He was a scrawny, chicken-necked sack of bones, but in spite of his handicap he moved faster than the others. Before long, he was out in the lead by himself, and that was when the handkerchief slipped off his face and I got my first real look at him. Dust was flying in all directions, but I would have known that mug anywhere. Edward J. Sparks. The one and only was back, and the moment I laid eyes on Uncle Slim, I knew my life was ruined forever.

I shouted through the noise of the straining engine: 'They're catching up to us! Turn around and go forward! They're close enough to shoot!'

It was a rough call. We couldn't go fast enough in reverse to get away, and yet the time it took to turn around would slow us down even more. But we had to risk it. If we didn't increase our speed in about four seconds, we wouldn't have a chance.

Master Yehudi swung out sharply to the right, angling into a frantic, backwards U-turn as he shifted into first. The gears made a hideous grinding noise, the back wheels jumped off the edge of the road and hit some stray rocks, and then we were spinning, flailing without traction as the car groaned and shook. It took a second or two before the tires caught hold again, and by the time we shot out of there with our nose pointed in the right direction, the guns were coughing behind us. One shell snagged a back tire, and the instant the rubber blew out, the Pierce Arrow lurched wildly to the left. The master rolled with it and never lifted his foot from the floor. Steering like a madman to keep us on the road, he was already shifting into third when another bullet came blasting through the back window. He let out a howl, and his hands flew off the steering wheel. The car bucked off the road, bounced onto the rock-strewn desert floor, and a moment later blood started gushing out of his right shoulder. God knows where he found the strength, but he managed to grab hold of the wheel again and give it another try. It wasn't his fault that it didn't work. The car was careening out of control by then, and before he could get us turned back toward the road, the left front tire skidded up the ramp of a large protruding stone and the whole machine tipped over.

The next hour was a blank. The jolt flung me out of my seat, and the last thing I remember is flying through the air in the master's direction. Somewhere between takeoff and landing, I must have clunked my head against the dashboard or steering wheel, for by the time the car stopped moving, I was already out cold. Dozens of things happened after that, but I missed them all. I missed seeing Slim and his men swoop down on the car and rob us of the strongbox in the trunk. I missed seeing them slash the other three tires. I missed seeing them open our suitcases and scatter our clothes on the ground. Why they didn't shoot us after that is still something of a mystery to me. They must have talked about whether to kill us or not, but I heard nothing of what they said and can't begin to speculate on why we were spared. Maybe we looked dead already, or maybe they just didn't give a damn. They had the strongbox with all our money in it, and even if we were still breathing when they left, they probably figured we'd die from our injuries anyway. If there was any comfort in being robbed of every cent we had, it came from the smallness of the sum they walked off with. Slim must have thought we had millions. He must have been counting on a once-in-a-lifetime jackpot, but all he got from his efforts was a paltry twenty-seven thousand dollars. Split that into four, and the shares didn't add up to much. No more than a pittance, really, and it made me glad to think about his disappointment. For years and years, it warmed my soul to imagine how crushed he must have been.

I think I was out for an hour – but it could have been more than that, it could have been less. However long it was, when I woke up I found myself lying on top of the master. He was still unconscious, and the two of us were wedged against the door on the driver's side, limbs tangled together and our clothes soaked in blood. The first thing I saw when my eyes blinked into focus was an ant marching over a small stone. My mouth was filled with crumbled bits of dirt, and my face was jammed flat against the ground. That was because the window had been open at the time of the crash, and I suppose that was a piece of luck, if *luck* is a word that can be used in describing such things. At least my head hadn't gone through the glass. There was that to be thankful for, I suppose. At least my face hadn't been cut to shreds.

My forehead hurt like hell and my body was bruised all over, but no bones were broken. I found that out when I stood up and tried to open the door above me. If any real damage had been done, I wouldn't have been able to move. Still, it wasn't easy to push that thing out on its hinges. It weighed half a ton, and what with the strange tilt of the car and the difficulty of getting any leverage on it, I must have struggled for five minutes before clambering through the hatch. Warm air hit my face, but it felt cool after the sweatbox confines of the Pierce Arrow. I sat on my perch for a couple of seconds, spitting out dirt and sucking in the languid breeze, but then my hands slipped, and the moment I touched the red-hot surface of the car, I had to jump off. I crashed to the ground, picked myself up, and began staggering around the car to the other side. On the way, I caught sight of the open trunk and noticed that the money box was missing, but since that was already a foregone conclusion, I didn't pause to think about it. The left side of the car had landed on a stone outcrop, and there was a small space between the ground and the door – about six or eight inches. It wasn't wide enough to stick my head through, but by lying flat on the ground I could see far enough inside to get a glimpse of the master's head dangling out the window. I can't explain how it happened, but the moment I spotted him through that narrow crack, his eyes opened. He saw me looking at him, and a moment later he twisted his face into something that resembled a smile. 'Get me out of here, Walt,' he said. 'My arm's all busted up, and I can't move on my own.'

I ran around to the other side of the car again, took off my shirt, and bunched it up in my hands, improvising a pair of makeshift mittens to protect my palms against the burning metal. Then I scrambled to the top, braced myself along the edge of the open door, and reached in to pull the master out. Unfortunately, his right shoulder was the bad one, and he couldn't extend that arm. He made an effort to turn his body around and give me his other arm, but that took work, real work, and I could see how excruciating the pain was for him. I told him to stay still, removed the belt from my pants, and then tried again by lowering the leather strap into the car. That seemed to do the trick. Master Yehudi grabbed hold of it with his left hand, and I began to pull. I don't want to remember how many times he bumped himself, how many times he slipped, but we both fought on, and after twenty or thirty minutes we finally got him out.

And there we were, marooned in the Mojave Desert. The car was wrecked, we had no water, and the closest town was forty miles away. That was bad enough, but the worst part of our predicament was the master's wound. He'd lost an awful lot of blood in the past two hours. Bones were shattered inside him, muscles were torn, and the last bits of his strength had been spent on crawling out of the car. I sat him down in the shade of the Pierce Arrow and then ran off to collect some of the clothing scattered about on the ground. One by one, I picked up his fine white shirts and custom-made silk ties, and when my arms were too full to hold anymore, I carried them back to use as bandages. It was the best idea I could think of, but it didn't do much good. I linked the ties together, tore the shirts into long strips, and wrapped him as tightly as I could – but the blood came seeping through before I was finished.

'We'll rest here for a while,' I said. 'Once the sun starts going down, we'll see if we can't stand you on your feet and get moving.'

'It's no good, Walt,' he said. 'I'm never going to make it.'

'Sure you will. We'll start walking down the road, and before you know it, a car will come along and pick us up.'

'There hasn't been a car by here all day.'

'That don't matter. Someone's bound to turn up. It's the law of averages.'

'And what if no one comes?'

'Then I'll carry you on my back. One way or another, we're going to get you to a sawbones and see that he patches you up.'

Master Yehudi closed his eyes and whispered through the pain. 'They took the money, didn't they?'

'You got that one right. It's all gone, every last penny of it.'

'Oh well,' he said, doing his best to crack a smile. 'Easy come, easy go, eh Walt?'

'That's about the size of it.'

Master Yehudi started to laugh, but the jostling hurt too much for him to continue. He paused to get a grip on himself, and then, apropos of nothing, he looked into my eyes and announced: 'Three days from now, we would have been in New York.'

'That's ancient history, boss. One day from now, we're going to be in Hollywood.'

The master looked at me for a long time without saying anything. Then, unexpectedly, he reached out and took hold of my arm with his left hand. 'Whatever you are,' he finally said, 'it's because of me. Isn't that so, Walt?'

'Of course it is. I was a no-good bum before you found me.'

'I just want you to know that it works both ways. Whatever I am, it's because of you.'

I didn't know how to answer that one, so I didn't try. Something strange was in the air, and all of a sudden I couldn't tell where we were going anymore. I wouldn't say that I was scared – at least not yet – but my stomach was beginning to twitch and flutter, and that was always a sure sign of atmospheric disturbance. Whenever one of those fandangos started up inside me, I knew the weather was about to change.

'Don't worry, Walt,' the master continued. 'Everything's going to be all right.'

'I hope so. The way you're looking at me now, it's enough to give a guy the heebie-jeebies.'

'I'm thinking, that's all. Thinking things through as carefully as I can. You shouldn't let that upset you.'

'I ain't upset. As long as you don't pull a fast one on me, I won't be upset at all.'

'You trust me, don't you, Walt?'

'Sure I trust you.'

'You'd do anything for me, wouldn't you?'

'Sure, you know that.'

'Well, what I want you to do for me now is climb back into the car and fetch the pistol from the glove compartment.'

'The gun? What do you want that for? There's no robbers to shoot now. It's just us and the wind out here – and whatever wind there is, it ain't much to speak of.'

'Don't ask questions. Just do as I say and bring me the gun.'

Did I have any choice? Yes, I probably did. I probably could have refused, and that would have ended the matter right then and there. But the master had given me an order, and I wasn't about to give him any lip – not then, not at a time like that. He wanted the gun, and as far as I was concerned, it was my job to get it for him. So, without another word, I scrambled into the car and got it.

'Bless you, Walt,' he said when I handed it to him a minute later. 'You're a boy after my own heart.'

'Just be careful,' I said. 'That weapon's loaded, and the last thing we need is another accident.'

'Come here, son,' he said, patting the ground next to him. 'Sit down beside me and listen to what I have to say.'

I'd already begun to regret everything. The sweet tone in his voice was the giveaway, and by the time I sat down, my stomach was turning cartwheels, pole-vaulting straight into my esophagus. The master's skin was chalk-white. Little dots of sweat clung to his mustache, and his limbs were trembling with fever. But his gaze was steady. Whatever force he still had was locked inside his eyes, and he kept those eyes fixed on me the whole time he talked.

'Here's how it is, Walt. We're in a nasty spot, and we have to get ourselves out of it. If we don't do it pretty soon, we're both going to croak.'

'That could be. But it don't make sense to leave until the temperature cools off a bit.'

'Don't interrupt. Hear me out first, and then you'll have your say.' He stopped for a moment to wet his lips with his tongue, but he was too low on saliva for the gesture to do him any good. 'We have to stand up and walk away from here. That's definite, and the longer we wait, the worse it's going to be. Problem is, I can't stand up and I can't walk. Nothing's going to change that. By the time the sun goes down, I'll only be weaker than I am now.'

'Maybe yes, maybe no.'

'No maybes about it, sport. So instead of sitting around and losing precious time, I have a proposition for you.'

'Yeah, and what's that?'

'I stay here, and you go off on your own.'

'Forget it. I ain't budging from your side, master. I made that promise a long time ago, and I intend to stick by it.'

'Those are fine sentiments, boy, but they're only going to cause you trouble. You've got to get out of here, and you can't do that with me dragging you down. Face the facts. This is the last day we're ever going to spend together. You know that, and I know that, and the faster we get it into the open, the better off we're going to be.'

'Nothing doing. I don't buy that for a second.'

'You don't want to leave me. It's not that you think you shouldn't go, but it pains you to think of me lying here in this condition. You don't want me to suffer, and I'm grateful to you for that. It shows you've learned your lessons well. But I'm offering you a way out, and once you think about it a little bit, you'll realize it's the best solution for both of us.'

'What's the way out?'

'It's very simple. You take this gun and shoot me through the head.'

'Come on, master. This is no time for jokes.'

'It's no joke, Walt. First you kill me, and then you go on your way.'

'The sun's got to your head, and it's turned you bonkers. You caught a bullet in the shoulder, that's all. Sure it hurts, but it's not as though it's going to kill you. The docs can mend those things one, two, three.'

'I'm not talking about the bullet. I'm talking about the cancer in my belly. We don't have to fool each other about that anymore. My gut's all mangled and destroyed, and I don't have more than six months to live. Even if I could get out of here, I'm done for anyway. So why not take matters into our own hands? Six months of pain and agony – that's what I've got to look forward to. I was hoping to get you started on something new before I kicked the bucket, but that wasn't meant to be. Too bad. Too bad about a lot of things, but you'll be doing me a big favor if you pull the trigger now, Walt. I'm depending on you, and I know you won't let me down.'

'Cut it out. Stop this talk, master. You don't know what you're saying.'

'Death isn't so terrible, Walt. When a man comes to the end of the line, it's the only thing he really wants.'

'I won't do it. Not in a thousand years I won't. You can ask me till kingdom come, but I'll never raise a hand against you.'

'If you won't do it, I'll have to do it myself. It's a lot harder that way, and I was hoping you'd spare me the trouble.'

'Jesus God, master, put the gun down.'

'Sorry, Walt. If you don't want to see it, then say your goodbyes now.'

'I ain't saying nothing. You won't get a word out of me until you put that gun down.'

But he wasn't listening anymore. Still looking into my eyes, he raised the pistol against his head and cocked the hammer. It was as if he was daring me to stop him, daring me to reach out and grab the gun, but I couldn't move. I just sat there and watched, and I didn't do a thing.

His hand was shaking and sweat was pouring off his forehead, but his eyes were still steady and clear. 'Remember the good times,' he said. 'Remember the things I taught you.' Then, swallowing once, he shut his eyes and squeezed the trigger.

III

It took me three years to track down Uncle Slim. For more than a thousand days I roamed the country, hunting the bastard in every city from San Francisco to New York. I lived from hand to mouth, scrounging and hustling as best I could, and little by little I turned back into the beggar I was born to be. I hitchhiked, I traveled on foot, I rode the rails. I slept in doorways, in hobo jungles, in flophouses, in open pastures. In some cities, I threw my hat on the sidewalk and juggled oranges for the passersby. In other cities, I swept floors and emptied garbage cans. In still other cities, I stole. I pilfered food from restaurant kitchens, money from cash registers, socks and underwear from the bins at Woolworth's – whatever I could lay my hands on. I stood in breadlines and snored through sermons at the Salvation Army. I tap-danced on street corners. I sang for my supper. Once, in a movie theater in Seattle, I earned ten dollars from an old man who wanted to suck my cock. Another time, on Hennepin Avenue in Minneapolis, I found a hundred-dollar bill lying in the gutter. In the course of those three years, a dozen people walked up to me in a dozen different places and asked if I was Walt the Wonder Boy. The first one took me by surprise, but after that I had my answer ready. 'Sorry, pal,' I'd say. 'Never heard of him. You must be confusing me with someone else.' And before they could insist, I'd tip my cap and vanish into the crowd.

I was pushing eighteen by the time I caught up with him. I'd grown to my full height of five feet five and a half inches, and Roosevelt's inauguration was just two months away. Bootleggers were still in business, but with Prohibition about to give up the ghost, they were selling off their last bits of stock and exploring new lines of crooked investment. That's how I found my uncle. Once I realized that Hoover was going to be thrown out, I started knocking on the door of every rum-runner I could find. Slim was just the sort to latch onto a dead-end operation like illegal booze, and the odds were that if he'd begged someone for a job, he would have done it close to home. That eliminated the east and west coasts. I'd already lost enough time in those places, so I began zeroing in on all his old haunts. When nothing happened in Saint Louis, Kansas

City, or Omaha, I fanned out through wider and wider swatches of the Midwest. Milwaukee, Cincinnati, Minneapolis, Chicago, Detroit. From Detroit I went back to Chicago, and even though I hadn't turned up any leads on three previous visits there, the fourth one changed my luck. Forget about lucky three. Three strikes and you're out, but four balls and you walk, and when I returned to Chicago in January of 1933, I finally got to first base. The trail led to Rockford, Illinois – just eighty miles down the road – and that's where I found him: sitting in a warehouse at three o'clock in the morning, guarding two hundred smuggled cases of bonded Canadian rye.

It would have been easy to shoot him right then and there. I had a loaded gun in my pocket, and seeing that it was the same gun the master had used on himself three years before, there would have been a certain justice in turning that gun on Slim now. But I had different plans, and I'd been nurturing them for so long, I wasn't about to let myself get carried away. It wasn't enough just to kill Slim. He had to know who his executioner was, and before I allowed him to die, I wanted him to live with his death for a good little moment. Fair was fair, after all, and if revenge couldn't be sweet, why bother with it in the first place? Now that I'd entered the pastry shop, I aimed to gorge myself on a whole platterful of goodies.

The plan was nothing if not complicated. It was all mixed up with memories from the past, and I never would have thought of it without the books that Aesop read to me back on the farm in Cibola. One of them, a large tome with a ragged blue cover, was about King Arthur and the knights of the Round Table. Except for my namesake, Sir Walter, those boys in the metal suits were my top heroes, and I asked for that collection more than any other. Whenever I was most in need of company (nursing my wounds, say, or just feeling low from my struggles with the master), Aesop would break off from his studies and come upstairs to sit with me, and I never forgot how comforting it was to listen to those tales of black magic and adventure. Now that I was alone in the world, they came back to me often. I was on a quest of my own, after all. I was looking for my own Holy Grail, and a year or so into my search, a curious thing started to happen: the cup in the story started turning into a real cup. Drink from the cup and it will give you life. But the life I was looking for could only begin with my uncle's death. That was my Holy Grail, and there could be no real life for me until I found it. Drink from the cup and it will give you death. Little by little, the one cup turned into the other cup, and as I went on moving from place to place, it gradually dawned on me how I was going to kill him. I was in Lincoln, Nebraska, when the plan finally crystallized – hunched over a bowl of soup at the Saint Olaf Lutheran Mission – and after that there were no more doubts. I was going to fill a cup with strychnine and make the bastard drink it. That was the picture I saw, and from that day on it never left me. I'd hold a gun to his head and make him drink down his own death.

So there I was, sneaking up behind him in that cold, empty warehouse in Rockford, Illinois. I'd spent the past three hours crouched behind a stack of wooden boxes, waiting for Slim to get drowsy enough to nod off, and now the moment was upon me. Considering how many years had gone into planning for this moment, it was remarkable how calm I felt.

'Howdy there, unc,' I said, whispering into his ear. 'Long time no see.'

The gun was pressed into the back of his head, but just to make sure he got the point, I cocked the hammer with my thumb. A bare, forty-watt bulb hung above the table where Slim was sitting, and all the tools of his night watchman's trade were spread out before him: a thermos of coffee, a bottle of rye, a shot glass, the Sunday funnies, and a thirty-eight revolver.

'Walt?' he said. 'Is that you, Walt?'

'In the flesh, buddy. Your number-one favorite nephew.'

'I didn't hear a thing. How the hell'd you sneak up on me like that?'

'Put your hands on the table and don't turn around. If you try to reach for the gun, you're a dead man. Got it?'

He let out a nervous little laugh. 'Yeah, I got it.'

'Sort of like old times, huh? One of us sits in a chair, and the other one holds a gun on him. I thought you'd appreciate my sticking to family tradition.'

'You got no call to be doing this, Walt.'

'Shut up. You start to plead with me, and I plug you on the spot.'

'Jesus, kid. Give a guy a break.'

I sniffed the air behind his head. 'What's that smell, unc? You haven't shit your pants already, have you? I thought you were supposed to be tough. All these years, I've been walking around remembering what a tough guy you were.'

'You're nuts. I ain't done nothing.'

'Sure smells like a turd to me. Or is that just fear? Is that what fear smells like on you, Eddie boy?'

The gun was in my left hand, and in my right I was holding a satchel. Before he could continue the conversation – which was already grating on my nerves – I swung the bag around past his head and plunked it on the table before him. 'Open it,' I said. As he was unzipping the satchel, I moved around to the side of the table and pocketed his gun. Then, slowly pulling my own gun away from his head, I continued walking until I was directly opposite him. I kept the gun pointed at his face as he reached in and dug out the contents of the bag: first the screw-top jar filled with the poisoned milk, then the silver chalice. I'd pinched that thing from a Cleveland pawnshop two years before and had been carrying it with me ever since. The metal wasn't pure – just silver plate – but it was embossed with little figures on horseback, and I'd polished it up that evening until it glowed. Once it was sitting on the table with the jar, I backed up a couple of feet to give myself a broader view. The show was about to start, and I didn't want to miss a thing.

Slim looked old to me, as old as the hills. He'd aged twenty years since I'd last seen him, and the expression in his eyes was so hurt, so filled with pain and confusion, a lesser man than myself might have felt some pity for him. But I felt nothing. I wanted him to be dead, and even as I looked into his face, searching it for the smallest sign of humanity or goodness, I thrilled at the idea of killing him.

'What's all this?' he said.

'Cocktail hour. You're going to pour yourself a good stiff drink, amigo, and then you're going to drink to my health.'

'It looks like milk.'

'One hundred percent – and then some. Straight from Bessie the cow.'

'Milk's for kids. I can't stand the taste of that shit.'

'It's good for you. Makes for strong bones and a sunny disposition. Old as you look now, unc, it might not be such a bad idea to sip from the fountain of youth. It'll work wonders, believe me. A few sips of that liquid there, and you'll never look a day older than you do now.'

'You want me to pour the milk into the cup. Is that what you're saying?'

'Pour the milk into the cup, lift it in the air and say "Long life to you, Walt," and then start drinking. Drink the whole thing down. Drink it to the last drop.'

'And then what?'

'Then nothing. You'll be doing the world a great service, Slim, and God will reward you.'

'There's poison in this milk, ain't there?'

'Maybe there is, maybe there isn't. There's only one way to find out.'

'Shit. You gotta be crazy if you think I'm going to drink that stuff.'

'You don't drink it, a bullet goes into your head. You drink it, and maybe you've got a chance.'

'Sure. Just like that Chinaman in hell.'

'You never know. Maybe I'm doing this just to scare you. Maybe I want to drink a little toast with you before we get down to business.'

'Business? What kind of business?'

'Past business, present business. Maybe even future business. I'm broke, Slim, and I need a job. Maybe I'm here to ask your help.'

'Sure, I'll help you get a job. But I don't have to drink no milk to do that. If you want me to, I'll talk to Bingo first thing tomorrow morning.'

'Good. I'll hold you to that. But first we're going to drink our vitamin D.' I stepped forward to the edge of the table, reached out with the gun, and jabbed it under his chin – hard enough to make his head snap back. 'And we're going to drink it now.'

Slim's hands were trembling by then, but he went ahead and unscrewed the top of the jar. 'Don't spill it,' I said, as he started pouring the milk into the chalice. 'You spill one drop and I squeeze the trigger.' The white liquid flowed from one container into the other, and none of it landed on the table. 'Good,' I said, 'very good. Now lift the cup and say the toast.'

'Long life to you, Walt.'

The skunk was sweating bullets. I breathed in the whole foul stench of him as he brought the goblet to his lips, and I was glad, glad that he knew what was coming. I watched the terror mount in his eyes, and suddenly I was trembling along with him. Not from shame or regret – but from joy.

'Snark it down, you old fuck,' I said. 'Open your gullet and make with the glug-glug-glug.'

He shut his eyes, held his nose like a kid about to take his medicine, and started to drink. He was damned if he did and damned if he didn't, but at least I'd held out a little scrap of hope to him. Better that than the gun. Guns killed you for sure, but maybe I was only teasing him about the milk. And even if I wasn't, maybe he'd get lucky and survive the poison. When a man has only one chance, he's going to take it, even if it's the longest long shot on the board. So he plugged up his nose and went for it, and in spite of how I felt about him, I'll say this for the creep:

he took his medicine like a good boy. He downed his death as if it were a dose of castor oil, and even though he shed some tears along the way, gasping and whimpering after each swallow, he gulped on bravely until it was gone.

I waited for the poison to kick in, standing there like a dummy as I watched Slim's face for signs of distress. The seconds ticked by, and still the bastard didn't keel over. I'd been expecting immediate results – death after one or two swallows – but the milk must have buffered the sting, and by the time my uncle slammed the empty cup down on the table, I was already wondering what had gone wrong.

'Fuck you,' he said. 'Fuck you, you bluffing son of a bitch.'

He must have seen the astonishment in my face. He'd drunk enough strychnine to kill an elephant, and yet there he was standing up and shoving his chair to the floor, grinning like a leprechaun who'd just won at Russian roulette. 'Stay where you are,' I said, gesturing at him with the gun. 'You'll be sorry if you don't.'

For all response, Slim burst out laughing. 'You don't have the guts, asshole.'

And he was right. He turned around and started walking away, and I couldn't bring myself to fire the gun. He was giving me his back as a target, and I just stood there watching him, too shaken to pull the trigger. He took one step, then another step, and began disappearing into the shadows of the warehouse. I listened to his mocking, lunatic laughter bounce off the walls, and just when I couldn't stand it anymore, just when I thought he'd licked me for good, the poison caught up with him. He'd managed to take twenty or thirty steps by then, but that was as far as he got, which meant that I had the last laugh after all. I heard the sudden, choked-off gurgling in his throat, I heard the thud of his body hitting the floor, and when I finally stumbled my way through the dark and found him, he was flat-out stone dead.

Still, I didn't want to take anything for granted, so I dragged his corpse back toward the light to have a better look, pulling him face-down by the collar across the cement floor. I stopped a few feet from the table, but just when I was about to crouch down and put a bullet through Slim's head, a voice interrupted me from behind.

'Okay, buster,' the voice said. 'Drop the gat and put your hands in the air.'

I let go of the gun, I raised my hands, and then, very slowly, I turned around to face the stranger. He didn't strike me as anything special: a nondescript sort of guy in his late thirties or early forties. He was dressed in spiffy blue pinstripes and expensive black shoes and sported a peach-colored hanky in his front pocket. At first I thought he was older, but that was only because his hair had turned white on him. Once you looked into his face, you realized he wasn't old at all.

'You just knocked off one of my men,' he said. 'That's a no-no, kid. I don't care how young you are. You do something like that, you gotta pay the penalty.'

'Yeah, that's right,' I said, 'I killed the son of a bitch. He had it coming, and I did him in. That's the way you treat vermin, mister. They crawl into your house, you get rid of them. You can shoot me if you want, I don't care. I done what I came to do, and that's all that matters. If I die now, at least I'm going to die happy.'

The man's eyebrows went up about a sixteenth of an inch, then fluttered there for a moment in surprise. My little speech had thrown him, and he wasn't sure how to react. After thinking it over for a couple of seconds, it looked as if he decided to be amused. 'So you want to die now,' he said. 'Is that it?'

'I didn't say that. You're the one holding the gun, not me. If you want to pull the trigger, there's not a hell of a lot I can do about it.'

'And what if I don't shoot? What am I supposed to do with you then?'

'Well, seeing as how you just lost one of your men, you might think about hiring someone to replace him. I don't know how long Slim was on the payroll, but it must have been long enough for you to figure out what a crud-brained bucket of slime he was. If you didn't know that, I wouldn't be standing here now, would I? I'd be stretched out on the floor with a bullet in my heart.'

'Slim had his faults. I'm not going to argue with you about that.'

'You didn't lose much of anything, mister. You look at the plus and minus, and you'll see you're better off without him. Why pretend to feel sorry for a no-good nobody like Slim? Whatever he did for you, I'll do better. That's a promise.'

'You got some mouth on you, shorty.'

'After what I've been through these past three years, it's about the only thing I got left.'

'And what about a name? You still got one of those?'

'Walt.'

'Walt what?'

'Walt Rawley, sir.'

'Do you know who I am, Walt?'

'No, sir. I don't have a clue.'

'The name's Bingo Walsh. You ever hear of me?'

'Sure, I've heard of you. You're Mr Chicago. Right-hand man to Boss O'Malley. You're King of the Loop, Bingo, the shaker and mover who cranks the wheel and makes things spin.'

He couldn't help smiling at the buildup. You tell a number-two guy he's number one, and he's bound to appreciate the compliment. Considering that he still hadn't lowered the gun, I was in no mood to spread unkind words about him. As long as it kept me alive, I'd stand there scratching his back until the cows came home.

'Okay, Walt,' he said. 'We'll give it a shot. Two, three months, and then we'll see where we stand. Sort of a trial period to get acquainted. But if you don't pan out by then, I dump you. I send you off on a long trip.'

'To the same place where Slim just went, I suppose.'

'That's the deal I'm offering. Take it or leave it, kid.'

'It sounds fair to me. If I can't do the job, you cut off my head with an axe. Yeah, I can live with that. Why the hell not? If I can't catch on with you, Bingo, what's the use of living anyway?'

That was how my new career began. Bingo broke me in and taught me the ropes, and little by little I became his boy. The two-month trial period was hard on my nerves, but my head was still attached to my body by the time it ended, and after that I found myself warming to the business. O'Malley had one of the largest setups in Cook County, and Bingo was responsible for running the show. Gambling parlors, numbers operations, whorehouses, protection squads, slot machines – he managed all these enterprises with a firm hand, accountable to no one but the boss himself. I met up with him at a tumultuous moment, a period of transition and new opportunities, and by the time the year was out he'd solidified his position as one of the cleverest talents in the Midwest. I was lucky to have him as my mentor. Bingo took me under his wing, I kept my eyes open and listened to what he said, and my whole life turned around. After three years of desperation and hunger, I now had food in my stomach, money in my pocket, and decent clothes on my back. I was suddenly on my way again, and because I was Bingo's boy, doors opened whenever I knocked.

I started out as a gofer, running errands for him and doing odd little jobs. I lit his cigarettes and took his suits to the cleaners; I bought flowers for his girlfriends and polished the hubcaps on his car; I hopped to his commands like an eager pup. It sounds humiliating, but the fact was I didn't mind being a lackey. I knew my chance would come, and in the meantime I was just thankful he'd taken me on. It was the Depression, after all, and where else was someone like me going to get a better deal? I had no education, no skills, no training for anything except a career that was already finished, so I swallowed my pride and did what I was told. If I had to lick boots to earn my living, then so be it, I'd turn myself into the best bootlicker around. Who cared if I had to listen to Bingo's stories and laugh at his jokes? The guy wasn't a bad storyteller, and the truth was, he could be pretty funny when he wanted to be.

Once I proved my loyalty to him, he didn't hold me back. By early spring I was already climbing the ladder, and from then on the only question was how fast it would take me to get to the next rung. Bingo paired me with an ex-pug named Stutters Grogan, and Stutters and I began going the rounds of bars, restaurants, and candy stores to collect O'Malley's weekly protection money. As his name suggests, Stutters wasn't much on speechmaking, but I had a vivid way with words, and whenever we came across a slacker or deadbeat, I would paint such colorful pictures of what happened to clients who reneged on their payments that my partner rarely had to employ his fists. He was a useful prop, and it was good to have him for purposes of either-or demonstrations, but I prided myself on being able to settle conflicts without having to call on his services. Eventually, word got back to Bingo about my good track record, and he moved me up to a position on the South Side running numbers. Stutters and I had worked well together, but I preferred being on my own, and for the next six months I pounded the sidewalks in a dozen different colored neighborhoods, chatting up my regulars as they parted with their nickels and dimes for a shot at winning a few extra bucks. Everyone had a system, from the corner newsboy to the sexton in the church, and I liked listening to people tell me how they picked their combinations. The numbers came from everywhere. From birthdays and dreams, from batting averages and the price of potatoes, from cracks in the pavement, license plates, laundry lists, and the attendance at last Sunday's prayer meeting. The chances of winning were almost nil, so no one held it against me when they lost, but on those rare occasions when somebody hit the mark, I got turned into a messenger of good tidings. I was the Count of Lucky Dough, the fat-wadded Duke of Largesse, and I loved watching people's faces light up when I forked over the money. All in all, it wasn't an unpleasant job, and when Bingo finally promoted me again, I was almost sorry to leave.

From numbers I was shifted over to gambling, and by 1936 I was chief operating boss of a betting parlor on Locust Street, a snug, smoke-filled joint hidden away in the back room of a dry-cleaning establishment. The customers would arrive with their rumpled shirts and pants, drop them off at the front counter, and then push their way past the racks of hanging clothes to the secret room in the rear. Almost everyone who stepped into that place made some crack about getting taken to the cleaners. It was a standing joke with the men who worked under me, and after a while we began making bets on how many people would come out with it on a given day. As my bookkeeper Waldo McNair once put it: 'This is the only place in the world where they empty your pockets and press your pants at the same time. Blow your wad on the ponies, and you still can't lose your shirt.'

I ran a good little business in that room behind Benny's Cleaners. Traffic was heavy, but I hired a kid to keep it spic-and-span for me, and I always saw to it that butts were put out in ashtrays and not on the floor. My ticker-tape machines were the last word in modern equipment, with hookups to every major hippodrome around the country, and I kept the law off my back with regular donations to the private pension funds of half a dozen cops. I was twenty-one years old, and any way you looked at it I was sitting pretty. I lived in a classy room at the Featherstone Hotel, I had a closetful of suits that a wop tailor had cut for me at half price, I could trot out to Wrigley and take in a Cubs game any afternoon I pleased. That was already good, but on top of that there were women, lots of women, and I made sure my crotch saw all the action it could handle. After facing that terrible decision in Philadelphia seven years before, my balls had become exceedingly precious to me. I'd given up my shot at fame and fortune for their sake, and now that Walt the Wonder Boy was no more, I figured the best way to justify my choice was to use them as often as I could. I was no longer a virgin when I reached Chicago, but my career as a cocksman didn't get fully off the ground until I joined up with Bingo and had the cash to buy my way into any bloomers I fancied. My cherry had been lost to a farm girl named Velma Childe somewhere in western Pennsylvania, but that had been fairly rudimentary stuff: fumbling around with our clothes on out in a cold barn, our faces raw with saliva as we groped and grappled our way into position, not exactly certain what went where. A few months later, on the strength of the hundred-dollar bill I found in Minneapolis, I'd had two or three experiences with whores, but for all intents and purposes I was still a rank novice when I hit the streets of Hogtown. Once I settled into my new life, I did everything I could to make up for lost time.

So it went. I made a home for myself in the organization, and I never felt the smallest pang about throwing in my lot with the bad guys. I saw myself as one of them, I stood for what they stood for, and I never breathed a word to anyone about my past: not to Bingo, not to the girls I slept with, not to anyone. As long as I didn't dwell on the old days, I could deceive myself into thinking I had a future. It hurt too much to look back, so I kept my eyes fixed in front of me, and every time I took another step forward, I drifted farther away from the person I'd been with Master Yehudi. The best part of me was lying under the ground with him in the California desert. I'd buried him there along with his Spinoza, his scrapbook of Walt the Wonder Boy clippings, and the necklace with my severed finger joint, but even though I went back there every night in my dreams, it drove me crazy to think about it during the day. Killing Slim was supposed to have squared the account, but in the long run it didn't do a bit of good. I wasn't sorry for what I'd done, but Master Yehudi was still dead, and all the Bingos in the world couldn't begin to make up for him. I strutted around Chicago as if I were going places, as if I were a regular Mr Somebody, but underneath it all I was no one. Without the master I was no one, and I wasn't going anywhere.

I had one chance to pull out before it was too late, a single opportunity to cut my losses and run, but I was too blind to go for it when the offer fell in my lap. That was in October of 1936, and I was so puffed up with my own importance by then, I thought the bubble would never burst. I'd ducked out of the cleaner's one afternoon to attend to some personal business: a shave and a haircut at Brower's barbershop, lunch at Lemmele's on Wabash Avenue, and then on to the Royal Park Hotel for some hanky-panky with a dancer named Dixie Sinclair. The rendezvous was set for two thirty in suite 409, and my pants were already bulging at the prospect. Six or seven yards before I reached Lemmele's door, however, just as I rounded the corner and was about to go in for my lunch, I looked up and saw the last person in the world I was expecting to see. It stopped me dead in my tracks. There was Mrs Witherspoon with her arms full of bundles, looking as pretty and smartly turned out as ever, rushing toward a taxi at a hundred and ten miles an hour. I stood there with a lump forming in my throat, and before I could say anything, she glanced up, flicked her eyes in my direction, and froze. I smiled. I smiled from one ear to the other, and then followed one of the most astonishing double-takes I've ever seen. Her jaw literally dropped open, the packages slipped out of her hands and scattered on the sidewalk, and a second later she was flinging her arms around me and planting lipstick all over my newly shaven mug.

'There you are, you rascal,' she said, squeezing me for all she was worth. 'Now I've got you, you goddamn slippery son of a bitch. Where the hell have you been, kiddo?'

'Here and there,' I said. 'Around and about. Up and down, down and up, the usual story. You look swell, Mrs Witherspoon. Really grand. Or should I be calling you Mrs Cox? That's your name now, isn't it? Mrs Orville Cox.'

She backed off to get a better look at me, holding me at arms' length as a big smile spread across her face. 'I'm still Witherspoon, honey. I got all the way to the altar, but when the time came to say "I do", the words got stuck in my throat. The dos turned into don'ts, and here I am seven years later, still a single girl and proud of it.'

'Good for you. I always knew that Cox guy was a mistake.'

'If it hadn't been for the present, I probably would have gone through with it. When Billy Bigelow brought back that package from Cape Cod, I couldn't resist taking a peek. A bride's not supposed to open her presents before the wedding, but this one was special, and once I unwrapped it, I knew the marriage wasn't meant to be.'

'What was in the box?'

'I thought you knew.'

'I never got around to asking him.'

'He gave me a globe. A globe of the world.'

'A globe? What's so special about that?'

'It wasn't the present, Walt. It was the note he sent along with it.'

'I never saw that either.'

'One sentence, that's all it was. *Wherever you are, I'll be with you.* I read those words, and then I fell apart. There was only one man for me, sweetie-pie. If I couldn't have him, I wasn't going to fool around with substitutes and cheap imitations.'

She stood there remembering the note as the downtown crowds swirled past us. The wind fluttered against the brim of her green felt hat, and after a moment her eyes started filling with tears. Before she could let go in earnest, I bent down and gathered up her packages. 'Come on inside, Mrs W.,' I said. 'I'll buy you some lunch, and then we'll order a tub of Chianti and get good and crocked.'

I slipped a ten-spot to the maître d' at the door and told him we wanted privacy. He shrugged, explaining that all the private tables were booked, so I peeled off another ten from my wad. That was good enough to cause an unexpected cancellation, and less than a minute later one of his minions was leading us through the restaurant to the back, where he installed us in a snug, candlelit alcove furnished with a set of red velvet curtains to shield us from the other customers. I would have done anything to impress Mrs Witherspoon that day, and I don't think she was disappointed. I saw the flash of amusement in her eyes as we settled into our chairs, and when I whipped out my monogrammed gold lighter to get her Chesterfield going, it suddenly seemed to hit her that little Walt wasn't so little anymore.

'We're doing all right for ourselves, aren't we?' she said.

'Not bad,' I said. 'I've been running pretty hard since you last saw me.'

We talked about this and that, circling around each other for the first few minutes, but it didn't take long for us to start feeling comfortable again, and by the time the waiter came in with the menus, we were already talking about the old days. As it turned out, Mrs Witherspoon knew a lot more about my last months with the master than I thought she did. A week before he died, he'd written her a long letter from the road, and everything had been spelled out to her: the headaches, the end of Walt the Wonder Boy, the plan to go to Hollywood and turn me into a movie star.

'I don't get it,' I said. 'If you and the master were quits, what was he doing writing you a letter?'

'We weren't quits. We just weren't going to get married, that's all.'

'I still don't get it.'

'He was dying, Walt. You know that. You must have known it by then. He found out about the cancer not long after you were kidnapped. A fine little mess, no? Talk about hell. Talk about your rough patches. There we were, scrambling around Wichita trying to scrape up the money to free you, and he comes down with a goddamn fatal disease. That's how all the marriage talk got started in the first place. I was gung-ho to marry him, you see. I didn't care how long he had to live, I just wanted to be his wife. But he wouldn't go for it. "You hitch up with me," he said, "and you'll be marrying a corpse. Think of the future, Marion" – he must have said those words to me a thousand times – "think of the future, Marion. This Cox fellow isn't too bad. He'll give us the money to spring Walt, and then you'll be set up in style for the rest of your days. It's a sweet deal, sister, and you'd be a fool not to jump at it."'

'Sweet fucking Christ. He really loved you, didn't he? I mean, he really fucking loved you.'

'He loved us both, Walt. After what happened to Aesop and Mother Sioux, you and I were the whole world to him.'

I had no intention of telling her how he'd died. I wanted to spare her the gory details, and all through drinks I managed to hold her off – but she kept pressing me to talk about the last part of the trip, to explain what happened to us after we got to California. Why hadn't I gone into the movies? How long had he lived? Why was I looking at her like that? I started to tell her how he'd slipped off gently in his sleep one night, but she knew me too well to buy it. She saw through me in about four seconds, and once she understood that I was covering up something, it was no use pretending anymore. So I told her. I told her the whole ugly story, and step by step I crawled down into the horror of it again. I didn't leave anything out. Mrs Witherspoon had a right to know, and once I got started, I couldn't stop. I just talked on through her tears, watching her makeup smudge and the powder run off her cheeks as the words tumbled out of me.

When I got to the end, I opened my jacket and pulled the gun from the holster strapped around my shoulder. I held it in the air for a moment or two and then set it down on the table between us. 'Here it is,' I said. 'The master's gun. Just so you know what it looks like.'

'Poor Walt,' she said.

'Poor nobody. It's the only thing of his I've got left.'

Mrs Witherspoon stared at the small, oak-handled revolver for ten or twelve seconds. Then, very tentatively, she reached out and put her hand on top of it. I thought she was going to pick it up, but she didn't. She just sat there looking at her fingers as they closed around the gun, as if touching what the master had touched allowed her to touch him again.

'You did the only thing you could,' she finally said.

'I let him down is what I did. He begged me to pull the trigger, and I couldn't do it. His last wish – and I turned my back on him and made him do it himself.'

'Remember the good times, that's what he told you.'

'I can't. Before I get to the good times, I remember what it was like when he told me to remember them. I can't get around that last day. I can't go back far enough to remember anything before it.'

'Forget the gun, Walt. Get rid of the damn thing and wipe the slate clean.'

'I can't. If I do that, he'll be gone forever.'

That was when she stood up from her chair and left the table. She didn't say where she was going, and I didn't ask. The conversation had turned so heavy, so awful for both of us, we couldn't say another word and not go crazy. I put the gun back in the holster and looked at my watch. One o'clock. I had plenty of time until my appointment with

Dixie. Maybe Mrs Witherspoon would be back, and maybe she wouldn't. One way or the other, I was going to sit there and eat my lunch, and afterward I was going to prance over to the Royal Park Hotel and spend an hour with my new flame, bouncing on the bed with her silky gams wrapped around my waist.

But Mrs W. hadn't flown the coop. She'd merely gone to the ladies' to dry her tears and freshen up, and when she returned about ten minutes later, she was wearing a new coat of lipstick and had redone her lashes. Her eyes were still red around the rims, but she shot me a little smile when she sat down, and I could see that she was determined to push the conversation onto a different subject.

'So, my friend,' she said, taking a bite of her shrimp cocktail, 'how's the flying business these days?'

'Packed away in mothballs,' I said. 'The fleet's been grounded, and one by one I've been selling off the wings for scrap.'

'And you don't feel tempted to give it another whirl?'

'Not for all the crackers in Kalamazoo.'

'The headaches were that bad, huh?'

'You don't know the meaning of bad, toots. We're talking high-voltage trauma here, life-threatening toaster burns.'

'It's funny. I sometimes hear conversations. You know, sitting in a train or walking down the street, little snatches of things. People remember, Walt. The Wonder Boy made quite a stir, and a lot of people still think about you.'

'Yeah, I know. I'm a fucking legend. The problem is, nobody believes it anymore. They stopped believing when the act folded, and by now there's nobody left. I know the kind of talk you mean. I used to hear it, too. It always ended up in an argument. One guy would say it was a fake, the other guy would say maybe it wasn't, and pretty soon they'd be so pissed off at each other they'd stop talking. But that was a while ago. You don't hear so much of it anymore. It's like the whole thing never happened.'

'About two years ago they ran an article about you somewhere, I forget which paper. Walt the Wonder Boy, the little lad who fired the imagination of millions. Whatever happened to him, and where is he now? That kind of article.'

'He fell off the face of the earth, that's what happened to him. The angels carried him back to where he came from, and no one's ever going to see him again.'

'Except me.'

'Except you. But that's our little secret, isn't it?'

'Mum's the word, Walt. What kind of person do you take me for anyway?'

Things loosened up quite a bit after that. The busboy came in to haul off the appetizer plates, and by the time the waiter returned with the main course, we'd drunk enough to be ready for a second bottle.

'I see you haven't lost your taste for the stuff,' I said.

'Booze, money, and sex. Those are the eternal verities.'

'In that order?'

'In any order you like. Without them the world would be a sad and dismal place.'

'Speaking of sad places, what's new in Wichita?'

'Wichita?' She put down her glass and gave me a gorgeous shit-eating grin. 'Where's that?'

'I don't know. You tell me.'

'I can't remember. I packed my bags five years ago and haven't set foot in that town since.'

'Who bought the house?'

'I didn't sell it. Billy Bigelow lives there with his chatterbox wife and two little girls. I thought the rent would give me some nice pin money, but the poor sap lost his job at the bank a month after they moved in, and I've been letting him have it for a dollar a year.'

'You must be doing okay if you can afford that.'

'I pulled out of the market the summer before the crash. Something to do with ransom notes, cash deliveries, drop-off points – it's all a bit blurry now. It turned out to be the best thing that ever happened to me. Your little misadventure saved my life, Walt. Whatever I was worth then, I'm worth ten times that now.'

'Why stay in Wichita with that kind of dough, right? How long since you moved to Chicago?'

'I'm just here on business. I go back to New York tomorrow morning.'

'Fifth Avenue, I'll bet.'

'You bet right, Mr Rawley.'

'I knew it the second I saw you. You look like big money now. It gives off a special smell, and I like sitting here breathing in the vapors.'

'Most of it comes from oil. That stuff stinks in the ground, but once you convert it into cash, it does release a lovely perfume, doesn't it?'

She was the same old Mrs Witherspoon. She still liked to drink, and she still liked to talk about money, and once you uncorked a bottle and steered her onto her favorite subject, she could hold her own with any cigar-chomping capitalist this side of Daddy Warbucks. She spent the rest of the main course telling me about her deals and investments, and when the plates were carted off again and the waiter slid back in with the dessert menus, something went click, and I could see the lightbulb go on in her head. It was a quarter to two by my watch. Come fire or flood, I aimed to be out of there in half an hour.

'If you want in, Walt,' she said, 'I'll be happy to make a place for you.'

'Place? What kind of place?'

'Texas. I've got some new wildcat rigs down there, and I need someone to watch over the drilling for me.'

'I don't know the first thing about oil.'

'You're smart. You'll catch on fast. Look at the progress you've made already. Nice clothes, fancy restaurants, money in your pocket. You've come a long way, sport. And don't think I haven't noticed how you've cleaned up your grammar. Not one "ain't" the whole time we've been together.'

'Yeah, I worked hard on that. I didn't want to sound like an ignoramus anymore, so I read some books and retooled my word-box. I figured it was time to step out of the gutter.'

'That's my point. You can do anything you want to do. As long as you put your mind to it, there's no telling where you might go. You watch, Walt. Come in with me, and two or three years from now we'll be partners.'

It was a hell of an endorsement, but once I'd soaked up her praise I snubbed out my Camel and shook my head. 'I like what I'm doing now. Why go to Texas when I've got everything I want in Chicago?'

'Because you're in the wrong business, that's why. There's no future in this cops-and-robbers stuff. You keep it up, and you'll either be dead or serving time before your twenty-fifth birthday.'

'What cops-and-robbers stuff? I'm clean as a surgeon's fingernails.'

'Sure. And the pope's a Hindu snake charmer in disguise.'

Dessert was wheeled in after that, and we nibbled at our eclairs in silence. It was a bad way to end the meal, but we were both too stubborn to back down. Eventually, we made small talk about the weather, threw out some inconsequential remarks about the upcoming election, but the juice was gone and there was no getting it back. Mrs Witherspoon wasn't just peeved at me for turning down her offer. Chance had thrown us together again, and only a bungler would pass up the call of fate as blithely as I had. She wasn't wrong to feel disgusted with me, but I had my own path to follow, and I was too full of myself to understand that my path was the same as hers. If I hadn't been so hot to run off and plant my pecker in Dixie Sinclair, I might have listened to her more carefully, but I was in a rush, and I couldn't be bothered with any soul-searching that day. So it goes. Once your groin gets the upper hand, you lose the ability to reason.

We skipped coffee, and when the waiter delivered the check to the table at ten past two, I snatched it out of his fingers before Mrs Witherspoon could grab hold of it.

'My treat,' I said.

'Okay, Mr Big Time. Show off if it makes you happy. But if you ever wise up, don't forget where I am. Maybe you'll come to your senses before it's too late.' And with that she reached into her purse, pulled out her business card, and laid it gently in my palm. 'Don't worry about the cost,' she added. 'If you're belly-up by the time you remember me, just tell the operator to reverse the charges.'

But I never called. I stuck the card in my pocket, fully intending to save it, but when I looked for it before going to bed that night, it was nowhere to be found. Given the tusseling and tugging those trousers were subjected to immediately following lunch, it wasn't hard to guess what had happened. The card had fallen out, and if it hadn't already been tossed into the trash by a chambermaid, it was lying on the floor in suite 409 of the Royal Park Hotel.

I was an unstoppable force in those days, a comer to beat all comers, and I was riding the express train with a one-way ticket to Fat City. Less than a year after my lunch with Mrs Witherspoon, I landed my next big break when I went out to Arlington one sultry August afternoon and put a thousand dollars on a long shot to win the third race. If I add that the horse was dubbed Wonder Boy, and if I further add that I was still in the thrall of my old superstitions, it won't take a mind reader to understand why I bit on such a hopeless gamble. I did crazy things as a matter of routine back then, and when the colt came in by half a length at forty to one, I knew there was a God in heaven and that he was smiling down on my craziness.

The winnings provided me with the clout to do the thing I most wanted to do, and I promptly set about to turn my dream into reality. I requested a private counsel with Bingo in his penthouse apartment overlooking Lake Michigan, and once I laid out the plan to him and he got over his initial shock, he grudgingly gave me the green light. It wasn't that he thought the proposition was unworthy, but I think he was disappointed in me for setting my sights so low. He was grooming me for a place in the inner circle, and here I was telling him that I wanted to go my own way and open a nightclub that would occupy my energies to the exclusion of all else. I could see how he might interpret it as an act of betrayal, and I had to tread carefully around that trap with some fancy footwork. Luckily, my mouth was in good form that evening, and by showing how many advantages would accrue to him in terms of both profit and pleasure, I eventually brought him around.

'My forty grand can cover the whole deal,' I said. 'Another guy in my shoes would tip his hat and say so long, but that's not how I conduct business. You're my pal, Bingo, and I want you to have a piece of the action. No money down, no work to fuss with, no liabilities, but for every dollar I earn, I'll give you twenty-five cents. Fair is fair, right? You gave me my chance, and now I'm in a position to return the favor. Loyalty has to count for something in this world, and I'm not about to forget where my luck came from. This won't be any two-bit cheese joint for the hoi polloi. I'm talking Gold Coast with all the trimmings. A full-scale restaurant with a Frog chef, top-notch floor shows, beautiful girls slithering out of the woodwork in skin-tight gowns. It'll give you a hard-on just to walk in there, Bingo. You'll have the best seat in the house, and on nights when you don't show up, your table will sit there empty – no matter how many people are waiting outside the door.'

He haggled me up to fifty percent, but I was expecting some give-and-take and didn't make an issue of it. The important thing was to win his blessing, and I did that by jollying him along, steadily wearing down his defenses with my friendly, accommodating attitude, and in the end, just to show how classy he was, he offered to kick in an extra ten thousand to see that I did up the place right. I didn't care. All I wanted was my nightclub, and with Bingo's fifty percent subtracted from the take, I was still going to come out ahead. There were numerous benefits in having him as a partner, and I would have been kidding myself to think I could get along without him. His half would guarantee me protection from O'Malley (who ipso facto became the third partner) and help keep the cops from breaking down the door. When you threw in his connections with the Chicago liquor board, the commercial laundry companies, and the local talent agents, losing that fifty percent didn't seem like such a shabby compromise after all.

I called the place Mr Vertigo's. It was smack in the heart of the city at West Division and North LaSalle, and its flashing neon sign went from pink to blue to pink as a dancing girl took turns with a cocktail shaker against the night sky. The rhumba rhythm of those lights made your heart beat faster and your blood grow warm, and once you caught the little stutter-step syncopation in your pulse, you didn't want to be anywhere except where the music was. Inside, the decor was a blend of high and low, a swank sort of big town comfort mixed with naughty innuendos and an easy, roadhouse charm. I worked hard on creating that atmosphere, and every nuance and effect was planned to the smallest detail: from the lip rouge on the hat-check girl to the color of the dinner plates, from the design of the menus to the socks on the bartender's feet. There was room for fifty tables, a good-size dance floor, an elevated stage, and a long mahogany bar along a side wall. It cost me every cent of the fifty thousand to do it up the way I wanted, but when the place finally opened on December 31, 1937, it was a thing of sumptuous perfection. I launched it with one of the great New Year's Eve parties in Chicago history, and by the following morning Mr Vertigo's was on the map. For the next three and a half years I was there every night, strolling among the customers in my white dinner jacket and patent leather shoes, spreading good cheer with my cocky smiles and quick-tongued patter. It was a terrific spot for me, and I loved every minute I spent in that raucous emporium. If I hadn't messed up and blown my life apart, I'd probably still be there today. As it was, I only got to have those three and a half years. I was one-hundred-percent responsible for my own downfall, but knowing that doesn't make it any less painful to remember. I was all the way at the top when I stumbled, and it ended in a real Humpty Dumpty for me, a spectacular swan-dive into oblivion.

But no regrets. I had a good dance for my money, and I'm not going to say I didn't. The club turned into the number-one hot spot in Chicago, and in my own small way I was just as much a celebrity as any of the bigwigs who came in there. I hobnobbed with judges and city councilmen and ball players, and what with all the showgirls and chorines to audition for the flesh parades I presented at eleven and one every night, there was no lack of opportunity to indulge in bedroom sports. Dixie and I were still an item when Mr Vertigo's opened, but my carryings-on wore her patience thin, and within six months she'd moved to another address. Then came Sally, then came Jewel, then came a dozen others: leggy brunettes, chain-smoking redheads, big-butted blondes. At one point I was shacked up with two girls at the same time, a pair of out-of-work actresses named Cora and Billie. I liked them both the same, they liked each other as much as they liked me, and by pulling together we managed to produce some interesting variations on the old tune. Every now and then, my habits led to medical inconveniences (a dose of the clap, a case of crabs), but nothing that put me out of commission for very long. It might have been a putrid way to live, but I was happy with the hand I'd been dealt, and my only ambition was to keep things exactly as they were. Then, in September 1939, just three days after the German Army invaded Poland, Dizzy Dean walked into Mr Vertigo's and it all started to come undone.

I have to go back to explain it, all the way back to my tykehood in Saint Louis. That's where I fell in love with baseball, and before I was out of diapers I was a dyed-in-the-wool Cardinals fan, a Redbird rooter for life. I've already mentioned how thrilled I was when they took the 'twenty-six series, but that was only one instance of my devotion, and after Aesop taught me how to read and write, I was able to follow my boys in the paper every morning. From April to October I never missed a box score, and I could recite the batting average of every player on the squad, from hot dogs like Frankie Frisch and Pepper Martin to the lowest journeyman scrub gathering splinters on the bench. This went on during the good years with Master Yehudi, and it continued during the bad years that followed. I lived like a shadow, prowling the country in search of Uncle Slim, but no matter how dark things got for me, I still kept up with my team. They won the pennant in 'thirty and 'thirty-one, and those victories did a lot to buck up my spirits, to keep me going through all the trouble and adversity of that time. As long as the Cards were winning, something was right with the world, and it wasn't possible to fall into total despair.

That's where Dizzy Dean enters the story. The team dropped to seventh place in 'thirty-two, but it almost didn't matter. Dean was the hottest, flashiest, loudest-mouthed rookie ever to hit the majors, and he turned a crummy ball club into a loosey-goosey hillbilly circus. Brag and cavort as he did, that cornpone rube backed up his boasts with some of the sweetest pitching this side of heaven. His rubber arm threw smoke; his control was uncanny; his windup was a wondrous machine of arms and legs and power, a beautiful thing to behold. By the time I got to Chicago and settled in as Bingo's protégé, Dizzy was an established star, a big-time force on the American scene. People loved him for his brashness and talent, his crazy manglings of the English language, his brawling, boyish antics and fuck-you pizzazz, and I loved him, too, I loved him as much as anyone in the world. With life growing more comfortable for me all the time, I was in a position to catch the Cards in action whenever they came to town. In 'thirty-three, the year Dean broke the record by striking out seventeen batters in a game, they looked like a first-division outfit again. They'd added some new players to the roster, and with thugs like Joe Medwick, Leo Durocher, and Rip Collins around to quicken the pace, the Gas House Gang was beginning to jell. 'Thirty-four turned out to be their glory year, and I don't think I've ever enjoyed a baseball season as much as that one. Dizzy's kid brother Paul won nineteen games, Dizzy won thirty, and the team fought from ten games back to overtake the Giants and win the pennant. That was the first year the World Series was broadcast on the radio, and I got to listen to all seven games sitting at home in Chicago. Dizzy beat the Tigers in the first game, and when Frisch sent him in as a pinch runner in the fourth, the lummox promptly got beaned with a wild throw and was knocked unconscious. The next day's headlines announced: *X-Rays of Dean's Head Reveal Nothing.* He came back to pitch the following afternoon but lost, and then, just two days later, he shut out Detroit 11–0 in the final game, laughing at the Tiger hitters each time they swung and missed at his fastballs. The press cooked up all kinds of names for that team: the Galloping Gangsters, River Rowdies from the Mississippi, the Clattering Cardinals. Those Gas Housers loved to rub it in, and when the score of the final game got out of hand in the late innings, the Tiger fans responded by pelting Medwick with a ten-minute barrage of fruits and vegetables in left field. The only way they could finish the series was for Judge Landis, the commissioner of baseball, to step in and pull Medwick off the field for the last three outs.

Six months later, I was sitting in a box with Bingo and the boys when Dean opened the new season against the Cubs in Chicago. In the first inning, with two down and a man on base, the Cubs' cleanup hitter Freddie Lindstrom sent a wicked line drive up the middle that caught Dizzy in the leg and knocked him down. My heart skipped a beat or two when I saw the stretcher gang run out and carry him off the field, but no permanent damage was done, and five days later he was back on the mound in Pittsburgh, where he hurled a five-hit shutout for his first win of the season. He went on to have another bang-up year, but the Cubs were the team of destiny in 1935, and by knocking off a string of twenty-one straight wins at the end of the season, they pushed past the Cards and stole the flag. I can't say I minded too much. The town went gaga for the Cubbies, and what was good for Chicago was good for business, and what was good for business was good for me. I cut my teeth on the gambling rackets in that series, and once the dust had settled, I'd maneuvered myself into such a strong position that Bingo rewarded me with a den of my own.

On the other hand, that was the year when Dizzy's ups and downs began to affect me in a far too personal way. I wouldn't call it an obsession at that point, but after watching him go down in the first inning of the opener at Wrigley – so soon after the skull-clunking in the 'thirty-four series – I began to sense that a cloud was gathering around him. It didn't help matters when his brother's arm went dead in 'thirty-six, but even worse was what happened in a game against the Giants that summer when Burgess Whitehead scorched a liner that hit him just above the right ear. The ball was hit so hard that it caromed into left field on a fly. Dean went down again, and though he regained consciousness in the locker room seven or eight minutes later, the initial diagnosis was a fractured skull. It turned out to be a bad concussion, which left him woozy for a couple of weeks, but an inch or so the other way and the big guy would have been pushing up daisies instead of going on to win twenty-four games for the season.

The following spring, my man continued to curse and scuffle and raise hell, but that was only because he didn't know any better. He triggered brawls with his brushback pitches, was called for balks two games in a row and decided to stage a sit-down strike on the mound, and when he stood up at a banquet and called the new league president a crook, the resulting fracas led to some fine cowboy theater, especially after Diz refused to put his signature on a self-incriminating formal retraction. 'I ain't signin' nothin'' was what he said, and without that signature Ford Frick had no choice but to back down and rescind Dean's suspension. I was proud of him for behaving like such a two-fisted asshole, but the truth was that the suspension would have kept him out of the All-Star Game, and if he hadn't pitched in that meaningless exhibition, he might have been able to hold off the hour of doom a little longer.

They played in Washington, D.C., that year, and Dizzy started for the National League. He breezed through the first two innings in workmanlike fashion, and then, after two were gone in the third, he gave up a single to DiMaggio and a long home run to Gehrig. Earl Averill was next, and when the Cleveland outfielder lined Dean's first pitch back to the mound, the curtain suddenly dropped on the greatest righthander of the century. It didn't look like much to worry about at the time. The ball hit him on the left foot, bounced over to Billy Herman at second, and Herman threw to first for the out. When Dizzy went limping off the field, no one thought twice about it, not even Dizzy himself.

That was the famous broken toe. If he hadn't rushed back into action before he was ready, it probably would have mended in due time. But the Cardinals were slipping out of the pennant race and needed him on the mound, and the dumb-cluck yokel fool assured them he was okay. He was hobbling around on a crutch, the toe was so swollen he couldn't get his shoe on, and yet he donned his uniform and went out and pitched. Like all giants among men, Dizzy Dean thought he was immortal, and even though the toe was too tender for him to pivot on his left foot, he gutted it out for the whole nine innings. The pain caused him to alter his natural delivery, and the result was that he put too much pressure on his arm. He developed a sore wing after that first game, and then, to compound the mischief, he went on throwing for another month. After six or seven times around, it got so bad that he had to be yanked just three pitches into one of his starts. Diz was lobbing canteloupes by then, and there was nothing for it but to hang up his spikes and sit out the rest of the season.

Even so, there wasn't a fan in the country who thought he was finished. The common wisdom was that a winter of idle repose would fix what ailed him and come April he'd be his old unbeatable self again. But he struggled through spring training, and then, in one of the great bombshells in sports history, Saint Louis dealt him to the Cubs for $185,000 in cash and two or three warm bodies. I knew there was no love lost between Dean and Branch Rickey, the Cards' general manager, but I also knew that Rickey wouldn't have unloaded him if he thought there was some spit left in the appleknocker's arm. I couldn't have been happier that Dizzy was coming to Chicago, but at the same time I knew his coming meant that he was at the end of the road. My worst fears had been borne out, and at the ripe old age of twenty-seven or twenty-eight, the world's top pitcher was a has-been.

Still, he provided some good moments that first year with the Cubs. Mr Vertigo's was only four months old when the season started, but I managed to sneak off to the park three or four times to watch the Dizmeister crank out a few more innings from his battered arm. There was an early game against the Cards that I remember well, a classic grudge match pitting old teammates against each other, and he won that showdown on guile and junk, keeping the hitters off-stride with an assortment of dipsy-doodle floaters and change-ups. Then, late in the season, with the Cubs pushing hard for another pennant, Chicago manager Gabby Hartnett stunned everyone by giving Dizzy the nod for a do-or-die start against the Pirates. The game was a genuine knuckle-biter, joy and despair riding on every pitch, and Dean, with less than nothing to offer, eked out a win for his new hometown. He almost repeated the miracle in the second game of the World Series, but the Yanks finally got to him in the eighth, and when the assault continued in the ninth and Hartnett took him out for a reliever, Dizzy left the mound to some of the wildest, most thunderous applause I've ever heard. The whole joint was on its feet, clapping and cheering and whistling for the big lug, and it went on for so long and was so loud, some of us were blinking away tears by the time it was over.

That should have been the end of him. The gallant warrior takes his last bow and shuffles off into the sunset. I would have accepted that and given him his due, but Dean was too thick to get it, and the farewell clamor fell on deaf ears. That's what galled me: the son of a bitch didn't know when to stop. Casting all dignity aside, he came back and played for the Cubs again, and if the 'thirty-eight season had been pathetic – with a few bright spots sprinkled in – 'thirty-nine was pure, unadulterated darkness. His arm hurt so much he could barely throw. Game after game he warmed the bench, and the brief moments he spent on the mound were an embarrassment. He was lousy, lousier than a hobo's mutt, not even the palest facsimile of what he'd once been. I suffered for him, I grieved for him, but at the same time I thought he was the dumbest yahoo clod on the face of the earth.

That was pretty much how things stood when he walked into Mr Vertigo's in September. The season was winding down, and with the Cubs well out of the pennant race, it didn't cause much of a stir when Dean showed up one crowded Friday night with his missus and a gang of two or three other couples. It certainly wasn't the moment for a heart-to-heart talk about his future, but I made a point of going over to his table and welcoming him to the club. 'Pleased you could make it, Diz,' I said, offering him my hand. 'I'm a Saint Louis boy myself, and I've been following you since the day you broke in. I've always been your number-one backer.'

'The pleasure's all mine, pal,' he said, engulfing my little hand in his enormous mitt and giving a cordial shake. He started to flash one of those quick, brush-off smiles when his expression suddenly grew puzzled. He frowned for a second, searching his memory for some lost thing, and when it didn't come to him, he looked deep into my eyes as if he thought he could find it there. 'I know you, don't I?' he said. 'I mean, this ain't the first time we've met. I just can't place where it was. Way back somewhere, ain't I right?'

'I don't think so, Diz. Maybe you caught a glimpse of me one day in the stands, but we've never talked before.'

'Shit. I could swear you ain't no stranger to me. Damnedest feeling in the world it is. Oh well,' he shrugged, beaming me one of his big yap grins, 'it don't matter none, I guess. You sure got a swell joint here, mac.'

'Thanks, champ. The first round's on me. I hope you and your friends have a good time.'

'That's why we're here, kid.'

'Enjoy the show. If you need anything, just holler.'

I'd played it as cool as I could, and I walked away feeling I'd handled the situation fairly well. I hadn't sucked up to him, and at the same time I hadn't insulted him for going to the dogs. I was Mr Vertigo, the downtown sharpie with the smooth tongue and elegant manners, and I wasn't about to let Dean know how much his plight concerned me. Seeing him in the flesh had broken the spell somewhat, and in the natural course of things I probably would have written him off as just another nice guy down on his luck. Why should I care about him? Whizzy Dizzy was on his way out, and pretty soon I wouldn't have to think about him anymore. But that's not the way it happened. It was Dean himself who kept the thing alive, and while I'm not going to pretend we became bosom buddies, he stayed in close enough contact to make it impossible for me to forget him. If he'd just drifted off the way he was supposed to, none of it would have turned out as badly as it did.

I didn't see him again until the start of the next season. It was April 1940 by then, the war in Europe was going full tilt, and Dizzy was back – back for yet another stab at reviving his tumbledown career. When I picked up the paper and read that he'd signed another contract with the Cubs, I nearly choked on my salami sandwich. Who was he kidding? 'The ol' soup bone ain't the buggy whip it used to be,' he said, but Christ, he just loved the game too damned much not to give it another try. All right, dumbbell, I said to myself, see if I care. If you want to humiliate yourself in front of the world, that's your business, but don't count on me to feel sorry for you.

Then, out of the blue, he wandered back into the club one night and greeted me like a long-lost brother. Dean wasn't someone who drank, so it couldn't have been booze that made him act like that, but his face lit up when he saw me, and for the next five minutes he gave me an all-out dose of herkimer-jerkimer bonhomie. Maybe he was still stuck on the idea that we knew each other, or maybe he thought I was somebody important, I don't know, but the upshot was that he couldn't have been more delighted to see me. How to resist a guy like that? I'd done everything I could to harden my heart against him, and yet he came on in such a friendly way that I couldn't help but succumb to the attention. He was still the great Dean, after all, my benighted soulmate and alter ego, and once he opened up to me like that, I fell right back into the snare of my old bedevilment.

I wouldn't say that he became a regular at the club, but he stopped by often enough over the next six weeks for us to strike up more than just a passing acquaintance. He came in alone a few times to eat an early supper (dowsing every dish with gobs of Lea & Perrins steak sauce), and I'd sit with him shooting the breeze while he chomped down his food. We skirted baseball talk and mostly stuck to the horses, and since I gave him a couple of excellent tips on where to put his money, he began listening to my advice. I should have spoken up then and told him what I thought about his comeback, but even after he muddled through his first starts of the season, disgracing himself every time he stepped onto the field, I didn't say a word. I'd grown too fond of him by then, and with the sad sack trying so hard to make good, I couldn't bring myself to tell him the truth.

After a couple of months, his wife Pat persuaded him to go down to the minors to work on a new delivery. The idea was that he'd make better progress out of the spotlight – a frantic ploy if there ever was one, since all it did was support the delusion that there was still some hope for him. That's when I finally got up the nerve to say something, but I didn't have the guts to push hard enough.

'Maybe it's time, Diz,' I said. 'Maybe it's time to pack it in and head home to the farm.'

'Yeah,' he said, looking about as dejected as a man can look. 'You're probably right. Problem is, I ain't fit for nothin' but throwin' baseballs. I flunk out this time, and I'm up shit's creek, Walt. I mean, what else can a bum like me do with hisself?'

Plenty of things, I thought, but I didn't say it, and later that week he left for Tulsa. Never had a great one fallen so far so fast. He spent a long, miserable summer in the Texas League, traveling the same dusty circuit he'd demolished with fastballs ten years before. This time he could barely hold his own, and the rinky-dinks and Mickey Mousers sprayed his pitches all over the lot. Old delivery or new, the verdict was clear, but Dizzy went on busting his chops and didn't let the rough treatment get him down. Once he'd showered and dressed and left the park, he'd go back to his hotel room with a stack of racing forms and start phoning his bookies. I handled a number of bets for him that summer, and every time he called we'd jaw for five or ten minutes and catch up on each other's news. The incredible thing to me was how calmly he accepted his disgrace. The guy had turned himself into a laughingstock, and yet he seemed to be in good spirits, as gabby and full of jokes as ever. What was the use of arguing? I figured it was only a matter of time now, so I played along with him and kept my thoughts to myself. Sooner or later, he was bound to see the light.

The Cubs recalled him in September. They wanted to see if the bush-league experiment had paid off, and while his performance was hardly encouraging, it wasn't as dreadful as it might have been. Mediocre was the word for it – a couple of close wins, a couple of shellackings – and therein hung the final chapter of the story. By some ditsy, screwball logic, the Cubs decided that Dean had shown enough of his old flair to warrant another season, and so they went ahead and asked him back. I didn't find out about the new contract until after he left town for the winter, but when I did, something inside me finally snapped. I stewed about it for months. I fretted and worried and sulked, and by the time spring came around again, I understood what had to be done. It wasn't as if I felt there was a choice. Destiny had chosen me as its instrument, and gruesome as the task might have been, saving Dizzy was the only thing that mattered. If he couldn't do it himself, then I'd have to step in and do it for him.

Even now, I'm hard-pressed to explain how such a twisted, evil notion could have wormed its way into my head. I actually thought it was my duty to persuade Dizzy Dean that he didn't want to live anymore. Stated in such bald terms, the whole thing smacks of insanity, but that was precisely how I planned to rescue him: by talking him into his own murder. If nothing else, it proves how sick my soul had become in the years since Master Yehudi's death. I'd latched onto Dizzy because he reminded me of myself, and as long as his career flourished, I could relive my past glory through him. Maybe it wouldn't have happened if he'd pitched for some town other than Saint Louis. Maybe it wouldn't have happened if our nicknames hadn't been so similar. I don't know. I don't know anything, but the fact was that a moment came when I couldn't tell the difference between us anymore. His triumphs were my triumphs, and when bad luck finally caught up with him and his career fell apart, his disgrace was my disgrace. I couldn't stand to live through it again, and little by little I began to lose my grip. For his own good, Dizzy had to die, and I was just the man to urge him into making the right decision. Not only for his sake, but for my sake as well. I had the weapon, I had the arguments, I had the power of madness on my side. I would destroy Dizzy Dean, and in so doing I would finally destroy myself.

The Cubs hit Chicago for the home opener on April tenth. I got Diz on the horn that same afternoon and asked him to stop by my office, explaining that something important had come up. He tried to get me to come out with it, but I told him it was too big to discuss on the phone. If you're interested in a proposition that will turn your life around, I said, you'll come. He was tied up until after dinner, so we set the appointment for eleven o'clock the next morning. He showed up only fifteen minutes late, sauntering in with that loose-jointed stride of his and rolling a toothpick around on his tongue. He was wearing a worsted blue suit and a tan cowboy hat, and while he'd put on a few pounds since I'd seen him last, his complexion had a healthy tint after six weeks in the Cactus League sun. As usual, he was all smiles when he walked in, and he spent the first couple of minutes talking about how different the club looked in the daytime without any customers in it. 'Reminds me of an empty ballpark,' he said. 'Kinda creepy like. Still as a tomb, and a helluva lot bigger.'

I told him to take a seat and fixed him up with a root beer from the ice box behind my desk. 'This will take a few minutes,' I said, 'and I don't want you getting thirsty while we talk.' I could feel my hands starting to shake, so I poured myself a shot of Jim Beam and took a couple of sips. 'How's the wing, old timer?' I said, settling back into my leather chair and doing my best to look calm.

'Same as it was. Feels like there's a bone stickin' out of my elbow.'

'You got knocked around pretty hard in spring training, I heard.'

'Them's just practice games. They don't mean nothin'.'

'Sure. Wait till it really counts, right?'

He caught the cynicism in my voice and gave a defensive shrug, then reached for the cigarettes in his shirt pocket. 'Well, little guy,' he said, 'what's the scoop?' He shook out a Lucky from his pack and lit up, blowing a big gust of smoke in my direction. 'From the way you talked on the phone, it sounded like life and death.'

'It is. That's exactly what it is.'

'How so? You got a patent on a new bromide or somethin'? Christ, you come up with a medicine to cure sick arms, Walt, and I'll give you half my pay for the next ten years.'

'I've got something better than that, Diz. And it won't cost you a cent.'

'Everything costs, fella. It's the law of the land.'

'I don't want your money. I want to save you, Diz. Let me help you, and the torment you've been living in these past four years will be gone.'

'Yeah?' he said, smiling as if I'd just told a moderately amusing joke. 'And how you aimin' to do that?'

'Any way you like. The method's not important. The only thing that counts is that you go along with it – and that you understand why it has to be done.'

'You've lost me, kid. I don't know what you're talkin' about.'

'A great person once said to me: "When a man comes to the end of the line, the only thing he really wants is death." Does that make it any clearer? I heard those words a long time ago, but I was too dumb to figure out what they meant. Now I know, and I'll tell you something, Diz – they're true. They're the truest words any man ever spoke.'

Dean burst out laughing. 'You're some kidder, Walt. You got that wacko sense of humor, and it don't never let up. That's why I like you so much. There ain't no one else in this town that comes out with the ballsy things you do.'

I sighed at the man's stupidity. Dealing with a clown like that was hard work, and the last thing I wanted was to lose my patience. I took another sip of my drink, sloshing the spicy liquid around in my mouth for a couple of seconds, and swallowed. 'Listen, Diz,' I said. 'I've been where you are. Twelve, thirteen years ago, I was sitting on top of the world. I was the best at what I did, in a class by myself. And let me tell you, what you've accomplished on the ball field is nothing compared to what I could do. Next to me, you're no taller than a pygmy, an insect, a fucking bug in the rug. Do you hear what I'm saying? Then, just like that, something happened, and I couldn't go on. But I didn't hang around and make people feel sorry for me, I didn't turn myself into a joke. I called it quits, and then I went on and made another life for myself. That's what I've been hoping and praying would happen to you. But you just don't get it, do you? Your fat hick brain's too clogged with cornbread and molasses to get it.'

'Wait a second,' Dizzy said, wagging his finger at me as a sudden, unexpected glow of delight spread across his face. 'Wait just a second. Now I know who you are. Shit, I knowed it all along. You're that kid, ain't you? You're that goddamned kid. Walt . . . Walt the Wonder Boy. Christ almighty. My daddy took me and Paul and Elmer out to the fair one day in Arkansas, and we seen you do your stuff. Fuckin' out of this world it was. I always wondered what happened to you. And here you are, sittin' right across from me. I can't fuckin' believe it.'

'Believe it, friend. When I told you I was great, I meant great like nobody else. Like a comet streaking across the sky.'

'You were great, all right, I'll vouch for that. The greatest thing I ever saw.'

'And so were you, big man. As great as they come. But you're over the hill now, and it breaks my heart to see what you're doing to yourself. Let me help you, Diz. Death isn't so terrible. Everybody has to die sometime, and once you get used to the idea, you'll see that now is better than later. If you give me the chance, I can spare you the shame. I can give you back your dignity.'

'You're really serious, ain't you?'

'You bet I am. As serious as I've ever been in my life.'

'You're off your trolley, Walt. You're fuckin' looped outa your gourd.'

'Let me kill you, and the last four years will be forgotten. You'll be great again, champ. You'll be great again forever.'

I was going too fast. He'd thrown me off balance with that Wonder Boy talk, and instead of circling back and modifying my approach, I was charging ahead at breakneck speed. I'd wanted to build up the pressure slowly, to lull him with such elaborate, airtight arguments that he'd eventually come round on his own. That was the point: not to force him into it, but to make him see the wisdom of the plan for himself. I wanted him to want what I wanted, to feel so convinced by my proposal that he would actually beg me to do it, and all I'd done was leave him behind, scaring him off with my threats and half-baked platitudes. No wonder he thought I was crazy. I'd let the whole thing get out of hand, and now, just when we should have been getting started, he was already standing up and making his way for the exit.

I wasn't worried about that. I'd locked the door from the inside, and it couldn't be opened without the key – which happened to be in my pocket. Still, I didn't want him pulling on the knob and rattling the frame. He might have started shouting at me then to let him out, and with half a dozen people working in the kitchen at that hour, the ruckus surely would have brought them running. So, thinking only about that small point and ignoring the larger consequences, I opened the drawer of my desk and removed the master's gun. That was the mistake that finally did me in. By pointing that gun at Dizzy, I crossed the boundary that separates idle talk from punishable crimes, and the nightmare I'd set in motion could no longer be stopped. But the gun was crucial, wasn't it? It was the linchpin of the whole business, and at one moment or another it was bound to come out of that drawer. Pull the trigger on Dizzy – and thus go back to the desert and do the job that was never done. Make him beg for death in the same way Master Yehudi had begged, and then undo the wrong by summoning the courage to act.

None of that matters now. I'd already botched it by the time Dizzy stood up, and pulling out the gun was no more than a desperate attempt to save face. I talked him back into the chair, and for the next fifteen minutes I made him sweat a lot more than I'd ever intended to. For all his swagger and size, Dean was a physical coward, and whenever a brawl broke out he'd duck behind the nearest piece of furniture. I already knew his reputation, but the gun terrorized him even more than I thought it would. It actually made him cry, and as he sat there moaning and blubbering in his seat, I almost pulled the trigger just to shut him up. He was begging me for his life – not to kill him, but to let him live – and it was all so upside-down, so different from how I'd imagined it would be, I didn't know what to do. The standoff could have gone on all day, but then, just around noon, someone knocked on the door. I'd left clear instructions that I wasn't to be disturbed, but someone was knocking just the same.

'Diz?' a woman's voice said. 'Is that you in there, Diz?'

It was his wife, Pat: a bossy, no-nonsense piece of work if there ever was one. She'd come by to pick up her husband for a lunch date at Lemmele's, and of course Dizzy had told her where she could find him, which was yet another potential snag I'd neglected to think of. She'd barged into my club looking for her henpecked better half, and once she collared the sous-chef in the kitchen (who was busy chopping spuds and slicing carrots), she made such a nuisance of herself that the poor sap finally spilled the beans. He led her up the stairs and down the hall, and that was how she happened to be standing in front of my office door, pounding on the white veneer with her angry bitch knuckles.

Short of planting a bullet in Dizzy's head, there was nothing I could do but put away the revolver and open the door. The shit was sure to hit the fan at that point – unless the big guy came through for me and decided to play mum. For ten seconds my life dangled from that gossamer thread: if he was too embarrassed to tell her how scared he'd been, he'd keep the imbroglio to himself. I put on my warmest, most debonair smile as Mrs Dean stepped into the room, but her sniveling husband gave the whole thing away the instant he set eyes on her. 'The little fucker was gonna kill me!' he said, blurting out the goods in a high-pitched, incredulous voice. 'He was holdin' a gun to my head, and the little fucker was gonna shoot!'

Those were the words that knocked me out of the nightclub business.

Instead of keeping their reservation at Lemmele's, Pat and Dizzy tramped out of my office and headed straight for the local precinct to swear out a complaint against me. Pat told me they were going to do as much when she slammed the door in my face, but I didn't stir a muscle. I just sat behind my desk and marveled at how stupid I was, trying to collect my thoughts before the bulls showed up to cart me away. It took them less than an hour, and I went off without a peep, smiling and cracking jokes when they put the cuffs around my wrists. If not for Bingo, I might have done some serious time for my little stab at playing God, but he had all the right connections, and a deal was struck before the case ever came to court. It was just as well that way. Not only for me, but for Dizzy too. A trial wouldn't have been good for him – not with all the flak and scandal-mongering that would have gone with it – and he was perfectly happy to accept the compromise. The judge gave me a choice. Plead guilty to a lesser charge and do six to nine months at Joliet, or else leave Chicago and enlist in the army. I opted to walk through the second door. It wasn't that I had any great desire to wear a uniform, but I figured I'd outstayed my welcome in Chicago and that it was time to move on.

Bingo had pulled strings and paid bribes to keep me out of the can, but that didn't mean he had any sympathy for what I'd done. He thought I was nuts, ninety-nine-point-nine-percent nuts. Bumping off a guy for money was one thing, but what kind of dimwit would go after a national treasure like Dizzy Dean? You had to be stark raving mad to cook up a thing like that. That's what I probably was, I said, and didn't try to explain myself. Let him think what he wanted to think and leave it at that. There was a price to pay, of course, but I wasn't in any position to argue. In lieu of cash for services rendered, I agreed to compensate Bingo for his legal help by signing over my share of the club to him. Losing Mr Vertigo's was hard on me, but not half as hard as giving up the act had been, not a tenth as hard as losing the master. I was nobody special now. Just my old ordinary self again: Walter Claireborne Rawley, a twenty-six-year-old GI with a short haircut and a pair of empty pockets. Welcome to the real world, pal. I gave my suits to the busboys, I kissed my girlfriends good-bye, and then climbed aboard the milk train and headed for boot camp. Considering what I was about to leave behind me, I suppose I was lucky.

By then, Dizzy was gone, too. His season had consisted of one game, and after Pittsburgh shelled him for three runs in the first inning of his first start, he'd finally called it quits. I don't know if my scare tactics had knocked some sense into him, but I felt glad when I read about his decision. The Cubs gave him a job as their first-base coach, but a month later he got a better offer from the Falstaff Brewing Company in Saint Louis, and he went back to the old town to work as a radio announcer for the Browns and Cardinals games. 'This job ain't gonna change me none,' he said. 'I'm just gonna speak plain ol' pinto-bean English.' You had to hand it to the big clodhopper. The public went for the folksy garbage he spewed out over the airwaves, and he was such a success at it that they kept him on for twenty-five years. But that's another story, and I can't say that I paid much attention to him. Once I left Chicago, it had nothing to do with me anymore.

IV

My eyes were too weak for flight school, so I spent the next four years crawling through the mud. I became an expert in the habits of worms and other creatures who slither along the ground and prey on human skin for nourishment. The judge had said the army would make a man of me, and if eating dirt and watching limbs fly off soldiers' bodies is proof of manhood, then I suppose the Honorable Charles P. McGuffin called it right. As far as I'm concerned, the less said about those four years the better. At first, I thought seriously about swinging a medical discharge for myself, but I could never find the courage to go through with it. My plan was to start levitating again in secret – and bring on such violent, crippling attacks of pain that they'd be forced to send me home. The problem was, I had no home to go to anymore, and once I'd mulled over the situation for a little while, I realized that I preferred the uncertainty of combat to the certain torture of those headaches.

I didn't distinguish myself as a soldier, but I didn't disgrace myself either. I did my job, I avoided trouble, I hung in there and didn't get killed. When they finally shipped me back in November 1945, I was burned out, incapable of thinking ahead or making plans. I drifted around for three or four years, mostly up and down the east coast. The longest stretch was in Boston. I worked as a bartender there, supplementing my income by playing the horses and sitting in on a weekly poker game at Spiro's pool hall in the North End. It was only medium-stakes action, but if you keep on winning those ones and fives, it begins to add up. I was just on the point of putting together a deal to open a place of my own when my luck turned sour. My nest egg dribbled away, I went into debt, and before many moons had passed, I had to sneak out of town to slough off the loan sharks I was in hock to. From there I went to Long Island and found a job in construction. Those were the years when suburbs were sprouting up around the cities, and I went where the money was, doing my bit to change the landscape and turn the world into what it looks like today. All those ranch houses and tidy lawns and spindly little trees wrapped in burlap – I was the guy who put them there. It was dreary work, but I stuck with it for eighteen months. At one point, for reasons I can't explain, I let myself get talked into marriage. It didn't last more than half a year, and the whole experience is so foggy to me now, I have trouble remembering what my wife looked like. If I don't think hard about it, I can't even remember her name.

I had no idea what was wrong with me. I had always been so fast, so quick to pounce on opportunities and turn them to my advantage, but now I felt sluggish, out of sync, unable to keep up with the flow. The world was passing me by, and the oddest thing about it was that I didn't care. I had no ambitions. I wasn't on the make or looking for an edge. I just wanted to be left in peace, to scrape along as best I could and go where the world took me. I'd already dreamed my big dreams. They hadn't gotten me anywhere, and now I was too exhausted to think of any new ones. Let someone else carry the ball for a change. I'd dropped it a long time ago, and it wasn't worth the effort to bend down and pick it up.

In 1950, I moved across the river to a low-rent apartment in Newark, New Jersey, and started my ninth or tenth job since the war. The Meyerhoff Baking Company employed over two hundred people, and in three eight-hour shifts we churned out every baked good imaginable. There were seven different varieties of bread alone: white, rye, whole wheat, pumpernickel, raisin, cinnamon raisin, and Bavarian black. Add in twelve kinds of cookies, ten kinds of cakes, six kinds of doughnuts, along with breadsticks, breadcrumbs, and dinner rolls, and you begin to understand why the factory was in operation twenty-four hours a day. I started out on the assembly line, adjusting and preparing the cellophane wrappers that went around the pre-sliced loaves of bread. I figured I'd stick around for a few months at most, but once I caught the hang of it, it turned out to be a decent place to earn a living. The smells in that factory were so pleasant, and with the aroma of fresh bread and sugar wafting continually through the air, the hours didn't drag as heavily as they had on my other jobs. That was part of it in any case, but even more important was the little redhead who started making eyes at me about a week after I got there. She wasn't much to look at, at least not compared to the showgirls I'd horsed around with in Chicago, but there was a bemused flicker in those green eyes that struck a chord with me, and I didn't waste much time in getting to know her. I've made only two good decisions in my life. The first one was following Master Yehudi onto that train when I was nine years old. The second one was marrying Molly Fitzsimmons. Molly put me together again, and considering the kind of shape I was in when I landed in Newark, that was no small job.

Her maiden name was Quinn, and she was this side of thirty when we met. She'd married her first husband straight out of high school, and five years later he was drafted into the army. By all accounts, Fitzsimmons was a friendly, hardworking mick, but his war had been less lucky than mine. He took a bullet at Messina in 'forty-three, and since then Molly had been on her own, a young widow without any kids looking after herself and waiting for something to happen. God knows what she saw in me, but I fell for her because she made me feel comfortable, because she brought out my old wise-cracking self and knew a good joke when she heard one. There was nothing flashy about her, nothing to make her stand out in a crowd. Pass her on the street, and she was just another working stiff's wife: one of those women with pudgy hips and a broad bottom who didn't bother to put on makeup unless she was going out to a restaurant. But she had spirit, Molly did, and in her own quiet, watchful way, she was as sharp as any person I've ever known. She was kind; she didn't bear grudges; she stood up for me and never tried to turn me into someone I wasn't. If she was a bit of a slob as a housekeeper and something less than a good cook, that didn't matter. She wasn't my servant, after all, she was my wife. She was also the one true friend I'd had since my days in Kansas with Aesop and Mother Sioux, the first woman I'd ever loved.

We lived in a second-floor walkup apartment in the Ironbound section of Newark, and since Molly wasn't able to bear children, it was always just the two of us. I made her quit her job after the wedding, but I stuck with mine, and over the years I rose through the ranks at Meyerhoff's. A couple could get by on one salary back then, and after they promoted me to foreman of the night shift, we had no money worries to speak of. It was a modest life by the standards I'd once set for myself, but I'd changed enough not to care about that anymore. We went to the movies twice a week, we ate out on Saturday night, we read books and watched the tube. In the summer, we drove down to the shore at Asbury Park, and nearly every Sunday we got together with one of Molly's relatives. The Quinns were a large family, and her brothers and sisters had all married and begotten children. That gave me four brothers-in-law, four sisters-in-law, and thirteen nieces and nephews. For a man with no kids of his own, I was up to my elbows in youngsters, but I can't say I objected to my role as Uncle Walt. Molly was the good fairy godmother, and I was the court jester: the chunky little guy with all those quips and slapstick gags, Rootie Kazootie rolling down the steps of the back porch.

I spent twenty-three years with Molly – a good long run, I suppose, but not long enough. My plan was to grow old with her and die in her arms, but cancer came along and took her from me before I was ready to let go. First one breast went, then the other breast, and by the time she was fifty-five, she wasn't there anymore. The family did what it could to help, but it was an awful period for me, and I spent the next six or seven months in an alcoholic stupor. It got so bad that I eventually lost my job at the factory, and if two of my brothers-in-law hadn't hauled me off to a drying-out clinic, there's no telling what might have happened to me. I stayed for a full sixty-day cure at Saint Barnabas Hospital in Livingston, and that's where I finally started dreaming again. I don't mean daydreams and thoughts about the future, I mean actual sleep dreams: vivid, movie-show extravaganzas almost every night for a month. Maybe it had something to do with the drugs and tranquilizers I was taking, I don't know, but forty-four years after my last performance as Walt the Wonder Boy, it all came rushing back to me. I was back on the circuit with Master Yehudi, traveling from town to town in the Pierce Arrow, doing my act again every night. It made me incredibly happy, and it brought back pleasures I'd long since forgotten I could feel. I was walking on water again, strutting my stuff before gigantic, overflowing crowds, and I could move through the air without pain, floating and spinning and prancing with all of my old virtuosity and assurance. I'd worked so hard to bury those memories, had struggled for so many years to hug to the ground and be like everyone else, and now it was all surging up again, blasting forth in a nightly display of Technicolor fireworks. Those dreams turned everything around for me. They gave me back my pride, and after that I was no longer ashamed to look at the past. I don't know how else to put it. The master had forgiven me. He'd canceled out my debt to him because of Molly, because of how I'd loved her and mourned her, and now he was calling out to me and asking me to remember him. There's no way to prove any of this, but the effect was undeniable. Something had been lifted inside me, and I walked out of that drunk tank as sober as I am now. I was fifty-eight years old, my life was in ruins, and yet I didn't feel too bad about it. When all was said and done, I actually felt pretty good.

Molly's medical bills had wiped out whatever cash we'd managed to save. I was four months behind on the rent, the landlord was threatening to evict me, and the only thing I owned was my car – a seven-year-old Ford Fairlane with a dented grille and a faulty carburetor. About three days after I left the hospital, my favorite nephew called me from Denver about a job. Dan was the bright one in the family – the first college professor they'd ever had – and he'd been living out there with his wife and son for the past few years. Since his father had already told him how hard-up I was, I didn't waste my breath telling fibs about my big bank account. The job wasn't much, he said, but maybe a change of scenery would do me good. What sort of job? I asked. Maintenance engineer, he replied, trying not to make it sound too funny. You mean a janitor? I said. That's it, he said, a mop jockey. A position had opened up in the building where he taught his classes, and if I felt like moving to Denver, he'd put in a word for me and swing the deal. Sure, I said, why the hell not, and two days later I packed some things into the Ford and set off for the Rocky Mountains.

    I never did make it to Denver. It wasn't because the car broke down, and it wasn't because I had second thoughts about becoming a janitor, but things happened along the way, and instead of winding up in one place, I wound up in another. It's really not hard to explain. Coming so soon after all those dreams in the hospital, the trip brought back a flood of memories, and by the time I crossed the Kansas border, I couldn't resist making a short, sentimental detour to the south. It wasn't so far out of the way, I told myself, and Dan wouldn't mind if I was a little slow in getting there. I just wanted to spend a few hours in Wichita – and go back to Mrs Witherspoon's house to see what the old place looked like. Once, not long after the war, I'd tried to look her up in New York, but there was no listing for her in the phone book, and I'd forgotten the name of her company. For all I knew she was dead now, just like everyone else I'd ever cared about.

    The city had grown a lot since the 1920s, but it still wasn't my idea of a good time. There were more people, more buildings, and more streets, but once I adjusted to the changes, it turned out to be the same backwater pancake I remembered. They called it the 'Air Capital of the World' now, and it gave me a good laugh when I saw that slogan plastered on billboards around town. The chamber of commerce was referring to all the aircraft companies that had set up factories there, but I couldn't help thinking about myself, the original birdboy who'd once called Wichita his home. I had some trouble finding the house, which made my tour a bit more thorough than I'd planned. Way back when, it had been located on the outskirts of town, sitting by itself on a dirt road that led to open country, but now it was part of the residential hub, and other houses had been built around it. The street was called Coronado Avenue, and it came with all the modern accoutrements: sidewalks, street lamps, and a blacktop surface with a white stripe running down the middle. But the house looked good, there was no question about that: the shingles gleamed white under the gray November sky, and the little trees that Master Yehudi had planted in the front yard towered over the roof like giants. Whoever owned the place had been treating it well, and now that it was so old, it had taken on the air of something historic, a venerable mansion from a bygone age.

I parked the car and walked up the steps of the front porch. It was late afternoon, but a light was on in a first-floor window, and now that I was there, I figured I had to go through with it and ring the bell. If the people weren't ogres, they might even let me in and show me around for old time's sake. That was all I was hoping for: just a glimpse. It was cold out on the porch, and as I stood there waiting for someone to appear, I couldn't help thinking back to the first time I'd come to this house, half-dead from losing my way in that infernal blizzard. I had to ring twice before I heard footsteps stirring within, and when the door finally opened, I was so wrapped up in remembering my first encounter with Mrs Witherspoon, it took a couple of seconds before I realized that the woman standing in front of me was none other than Mrs Witherspoon herself: an older, frailer, more wrinkled version to be sure, but the same Mrs Witherspoon for all that. I would have known her anywhere. She hadn't gained a pound since 1936; her hair was dyed the same snazzy shade of red; and her bright blue eyes were as blue and bright as ever. She was seventy-four or seventy-five by then, but she didn't look a day over sixty – sixty-three tops. Still dressed in fashionable clothes, still holding herself erect, she came to the door with a burning cigarette wedged between her lips and a glass of Scotch in her left hand. You had to love a woman like that. The world had gone through untold changes and catastrophes since I'd last set eyes on her, but Mrs Witherspoon was the same tough broad she'd always been.

I recognized her before she recognized me. That was understandable, since time had taken a more drastic toll on my looks than on hers. My freckles had all but vanished now, and I'd turned into a squat, dumpy sort of guy with thinning gray hair and a set of Coke-bottle lenses perched on my nose. Hardly the dashing smoothy she'd dined with at Lemmele's thirty-eight years before. I was dressed in dull workaday clothes – lumber jacket, khaki pants, cordovan shoes, white socks – and my collar was turned up to ward off the chill. She probably couldn't see much of my face, and what she could see was so haggard, so worn out from my struggle with the booze, there wasn't anything to be done but to tell her who I was.

The rest goes without saying, doesn't it? Tears were shed, stories were told, we gabbed and carried on until the wee small hours. It was auld lang syne on Coronado Avenue, and I doubt there could have been a better reunion than the one we had that night. I've already given the gist of what happened to me, but her story was no less strange, no less unexpected than mine. Instead of parlaying her millions into more millions during the Texas wildcat boom, she'd sunk her drills into dry ground and gone bust. The oil game was largely guesswork back then, and she made one too many bad guesses. By 1938, she'd lost nine-tenths of her fortune. That still didn't qualify her as a pauper, but she was no longer in the Fifth Avenue league, and after floating a few more ventures that didn't pan out, she finally packed it in and returned to Wichita. She thought it would be only temporary: a few months in the old house to take stock and then on to the next bright idea. But one thing led to another, and by the time the war came she was still there. In what can only be called a startling about-face, she got caught up in the patriotic fervor of the time and spent the next four years working as a volunteer nurse at the Wichita VA Hospital. I was hard-pressed to imagine her doing that Florence Nightingale bit, but Mrs W. was a woman of many surprises, and if money was her strong point, it was by no means the only thing she thought about. After the war she went into business again, but this time she stayed in Wichita, and little by little she built it into a nice profitable concern. With Laundromats of all things. It sounds funny after all that high-stakes speculation in stocks and oil – but why not? She was one of the first to see the commercial possibilities of the washing machine, and she got a jump on her competitors by entering the field early. By the time I showed up in 1974, she had twenty Laundromats scattered around the city and another twelve in neighboring towns. The House of Clean, she called them, and all those dimes and quarters had turned her into a wealthy woman again.

And what about men? I asked. Oh, lots of men, she answered, more men than you could shake a stick at. And Orville Cox – what about him?

Dead and gone, she said. And Billy Bigelow? Still among the living. As a matter of fact, his house was just around the corner. She'd brought him into the Laundromat business after the war, and he'd worked as her manager and right-hand man until his retirement six months ago. Young Billy was pushing seventy now, and with two heart attacks already behind him, the doctor had told him to go easy on the pump. His wife had died seven or eight years back, and with his kids all grown and gone, Billy and Mrs Witherspoon were still in close touch. She described him as the best friend she'd ever had, and from the way her voice softened when she said it, I gathered that relations between them went beyond simple shop talk about washers and dryers. Ah ha, I said, so patience finally won out, and sweet little Billy got what he wanted. She threw me one of her devilish winks. Sometimes, she said, but not always. It depends on my mood.

It didn't take much arm-twisting to get me to stay. The janitor thing was only a stopgap measure, and now that something better had turned up, I didn't have to think twice about changing my plans. The salary was only a small part of it, of course. I was back where I belonged, and when Mrs Witherspoon invited me to step in and take over Billy's old job, I told her I'd start first thing in the morning. It didn't matter what the work was. If she'd invited me to stay on to scrub the pots in her kitchen, I would have said yes to that, too.

I slept in the same top-floor room I'd occupied as a boy, and once I learned the business, I did all right for her. I kept the washing machines humming, I jacked profits up, I persuaded her to expand in different directions: a bowling alley, a pizza joint, a pinball arcade. With all the college kids pouring into town every fall, there was a demand for quick food and cheap entertainment, and I was just the man to provide those things. I put in long hours and worked my buns off, but I liked being in charge of something again, and most of my schemes turned out pretty well. Mrs Witherspoon called me a cowboy, which from her mouth was a compliment, and for the first three or four years we galloped along at a sprightly clip. Then, very suddenly, Billy died. It was another heart attack, but this one took place on the twelfth fairway of the Cherokee Acres Country Club, and by the time the medics got to him, he had already breathed his last. Mrs W. went into a tailspin after that. She stopped going to the office with me in the morning, and little by little she seemed to lose interest in the company, leaving most of the decisions in my hands. I'd been through something like that with Molly, but it wasn't much good telling her that time would take care of it. The one thing she didn't have was time. The man had worshiped her for fifty years, and now that he was gone, no one was ever going to replace him.

One night in the midst of all this, I heard her sobbing through the walls as I lay upstairs reading in bed. I went down to her room, we talked for a while, and then I took her in my arms and held her until she drifted off to sleep. Somehow or other, I wound up falling asleep, too, and when I woke in the morning I found myself lying under the covers with her in the large double bed. It was the same bed she'd shared with Master Yehudi in the old days, and now it was my turn to sleep beside her, to be the man she couldn't live without. It was mostly a matter of comfort, of companionship, of preferring to sleep in one bed rather than two, but that isn't to say the sheets didn't catch fire every now and then. Just because you get old, that doesn't mean you stop getting the urge, and whatever qualms I had about it in the beginning soon went away. For the next eleven years we lived together like husband and wife. I don't feel I have to make any apologies for that. Once upon a time I'd been young enough to be her son, but now I was older than most grandfathers, and when you get to be that age, you don't have to play by the rules anymore. You go where you have to go, and whatever it takes to keep on breathing, that's what you do.

She stayed in good health for most of the time we were together. In her mid-eighties she was still drinking a couple of Scotches before dinner and smoking the occasional cigarette, and most days saw her with enough spunk to doll herself up and go out for a spin in her giant blue Cadillac. She lived to be ninety or ninety-one (it was never clear which century she'd been born in), and things didn't get too rough for her until the last eighteen months or so. Towards the end she was mostly blind, mostly deaf, mostly unable to get out of bed, but she remained herself for all that, and rather than put her into a home or hire a nurse to take care of her, I sold off the business and did the dirty work myself. I owed her that much, didn't I? I bathed her and combed her hair; I carried her around the house in my arms; I wiped the shit from her ass after every accident, just as she had once wiped mine.

The funeral was a bang-up affair. I made sure of that and didn't stint on the extras. Everything belonged to me now – the house, the cars, the money she'd made for herself, the money I'd made for her – and since there was enough in the cookie jar to keep me going for another seventy-five or hundred years, I decided to throw her a big send-off, the biggest bash Wichita had ever seen. A hundred and fifty cars joined in the motorcade to the cemetery. Traffic was tangled up for miles around, and once the burial was over, mobs tramped through the house until three o'clock in the morning, swilling liquor and stuffing their maws with turkey legs and cakes. I'm not going to say I was a respectable member of the community, but I'd earned some respect for myself over the years, and people around town knew who I was. When I asked them to come for Marion, they turned out in droves.

That was a year and a half ago. For the first couple of months I moped around the house, not quite sure what to do with myself. I'd never been fond of gardening, golf had bored me the two or three times I'd played it, and at seventy-six I didn't have any hankering to go into business again. Business had been fun because of Marion, but without her around to liven things up, there wouldn't have been any point. I thought about getting away from Kansas for a few months and seeing the world, but before I could make any definite plans, I was rescued by the idea of writing this book. I can't really say how it happened. It just hit me one morning as I climbed out of bed, and less than an hour later I was sitting at a desk in the upstairs parlor with a pen in my hand, scratching away at the first sentence. I had no doubt that I was doing something that had to be done, and the conviction I felt was so strong, I realize now that the book must have come to me in a dream – but one of those dreams you can't remember, that vanish the instant you wake up and open your eyes on the world.

I've worked on it every day since last August, pushing along from word to word in my clumsy old man's script. I started out with a school composition book from the five-and-ten, one of those hardbound things with a black-and-white marble cover and wide blue lines, and by now I've filled nearly thirteen of them, about one a month for every month I've been working. I haven't shown a single word to anyone, and now that I'm at the end, I'm beginning to think it should stay that way – at least while I'm still kicking. Every word in these thirteen books is true, but I'd bet both my elbows there aren't a hell of a lot of people who'd swallow that. It's not that I'm afraid of being called a liar, but I'm too old now to waste my time defending myself against idiots. I ran into enough doubting Thomases when Master Yehudi and I were on the road, and I have other fish to fry now, other things to keep me busy after this book is done. First thing tomorrow morning, I'll go downtown to the bank and put all thirteen volumes in my safe-deposit box. Then I'll go around the corner and see my lawyer, John Fusco, and have him add a clause to my will stating that the contents of that box should be left to my nephew, Daniel Quinn. Dan will know what to do with the book I've written. He'll correct the spelling mistakes and get someone to type up a clean copy, and once *Mr Vertigo* is published, I won't have to be around to watch the mugwumps and morons try to kill me. I'll already be dead, and you can be sure I'll be laughing at them – from above or below, whichever the case may be.

For the past four years a cleaning woman has been coming to the house several times a week. Her name is Yolanda Abraham, and she's from one of the warm-weather islands – Jamaica or Trinidad, I forget which. I wouldn't call her a talkative person, but we've known each other long enough to be on fairly cozy terms, and she was a great help to me during Marion's last months. She's somewhere between thirty and thirty-five, a round black woman with a slow, graceful walk and a beautiful voice. As far as I know, Yolanda doesn't have a husband, but she does have a child, an eight-year-old named Yusef. Every Saturday for the past four years, she's parked her offspring in the house with me while she does her work, and having watched this kid in action for more than half his life, I can say in all fairness that he's one monumental pain in the ass, a junior hooligan and wise-talking brat whose sole mission on earth is to spread mayhem and bad will. To top it off, Yusef is one of the ugliest children I've ever set eyes on. He has one of those jagged, scrawny, asymmetrical little faces, and the body that comes with it is a pathetic, sticklike bundle of bones – even if pound for pound it happens to be stronger and more supple than the bodies of most fullbacks in the NFL. I hate the kid for what he's done to my shins, my thumbs, and my toes, but I also see myself in him when I was that age, and since his face resembles Aesop's to an almost appalling degree – so much so that Marion and I both gasped the first time he walked into the house – I continue to forgive him everything. I can't help myself. The boy has the devil in him. He's brash and rude and incorrigible, but he's lit up with the fire of life, and it does me good to watch him as he flings himself headlong into a maelstrom of trouble. Watching Yusef, I now know what the master saw in me, and I know what he meant when he told me I had the gift. This boy has the gift, too. If I could ever pluck up my courage to speak to his mother, I'd take him under my wing in a second. In three years, I'd turn him into the next Wonder Boy. He'd start where I left off, and before long he'd go farther than anyone else has ever gone.

Christ, that would be something to live for, wouldn't it? It would make the whole fucking world sing again.

The problem is the thirty-three steps. It's one thing to tell Yolanda I can teach her son to fly, but once we got past that hurdle, what about the rest? Even I'm sickened by the thought of it. Having gone through all that cruelty and torture myself, how could I bear to inflict it on someone else? They don't make men like Master Yehudi anymore, and they don't make boys like me either: stupid, susceptible, stubborn. We lived in a different world back then, and the things the master and I did together wouldn't be possible today. People wouldn't stand for it. They'd call in the cops, they'd write their congressman, they'd consult their family physician. We're not as tough as we used to be, and maybe the world's a better place because of it, I don't know. But I do know that you can't get something for nothing, and the bigger the thing you want, the more you're going to have to pay for it.

Still, when I think back to my dreadful initiation in Cibola, I can't help wondering if Master Yehudi's methods weren't too harsh. When I finally got off the ground for the first time, it wasn't because of anything he'd taught me. I did it by myself on the cold kitchen floor, and it came after a long siege of sobbing and despair, when my soul began to rush out of my body and I was no longer conscious of who I was. Maybe the despair was the only thing that really mattered. In that case, the physical ordeals he put me through were no more than a sham, a diversion to trick me into thinking I was getting somewhere – when in fact I was never anywhere until I found myself lying face-down on that kitchen floor. What if there were no steps in the process? What if it all came down to one moment – one leap – one lightning instant of transformation? Master Yehudi had been trained in the old school, and he was a wizard at getting me to believe in his hocus-pocus and high-flown talk. But what if his way wasn't the only way? What if there was a simpler, more direct method, an approach that began from the inside and bypassed the body altogether? What then?

Deep down, I don't believe it takes any special talent for a person to lift himself off the ground and hover in the air. We all have it in us – every man, woman, and child – and with enough hard work and concentration, every human being is capable of duplicating the feats I accomplished as Walt the Wonder Boy. You must learn to stop being yourself. That's where it begins, and everything else follows from that. You must let yourself evaporate. Let your muscles go limp, breathe until you feel your soul pouring out of you, and then shut your eyes. That's how it's done. The emptiness inside your body grows lighter than the air around you. Little by little, you begin to weigh less than nothing. You shut your eyes; you spread your arms; you let yourself evaporate. And then, little by little, you lift yourself off the ground.

Like so.

(1992–1993)